THE LOCALS BOXED SET

THE LOCALS SERIES #1-4

LOCALS SERIES 1234

HALEY RHOADES

HR
Haley Rhoades
Author

TO ENHANCE YOUR READING

To Enhance Your Reading of The Local Series
read the Trivia Page near the end of the book
prior to opening chapter #1.

No Spoilers—I promise.

Check out my Pinterest Boards for
The Locals Series & its characters.

DEDICATION

To all my high school classmates that remain in our hometown.
Years and parenthood led me to see what you always knew.

Special thanks to my family for letting me live my dream even if it means I am
writing all night.
If you were a book you'd be a BEST SELLER.

TAILGATES & TRUCK DATES

The Locals #1

1

Athens has only two stoplights, one of the 4,724 reasons I want to leave this town.

I glance at the dashboard clock. I'm twenty minutes earlier than usual. Although I'm sitting at a red light now, I know stoplights won't help me pass the time.

Athens is a quintessential small, rural town. My mother was born and raised here. My father was born and raised here. As were their parents and most of the town's population. 'The Locals', as I like to refer to them, love everything about Athens. They plan to always stay in Athens—this is not my goal.

When the light turns green, I decide to treat myself to breakfast as I don't have anything else to do. I pull into the busy parking lot of our one and only grocery store. I prefer the store's bakery department donuts over gas station pastries. My stomach growls as I exit the car. Maybe I will allow myself two donuts this morning.

Breakfast is not a meal I usually consume. I enjoy my lunch, dinner, and snacks in between. I'm not a morning person, and usually don't allow myself time for breakfast. I pay for my donuts and milk to wash them down, then I return to my car. I enjoy one sweet pastry ring before exiting the grocery parking lot.

2

The grocery selection is limited to the tiny grocery store and two gas station/convenience stores. This is one of the 4,724 reasons I want to escape this town.

I park beside Adrian in the high school parking lot.

"Madison, you're early," Adrian greets. When she lowers her squeaking tailgate, we hop up to await the arrival of the rest of our group of friends. The metal is cool against my thighs at the hem of my shorts. I'm glad I didn't wear the sundress I had laid out for today. Kicking my legs forward and back, I glance at Adrian's cell phone as she sets a reminder for after school. Her calendar for the day is cluttered from 3:30 on. I smile, loving that her dream of owning her own business is coming to fruition.

"I had a craving for donuts." I explain my early arrival.

She's no fool. She knows about my mom and home life. She knows I needed to escape. I attempt to put the focus back on her. "Why are you so early?"

"I'm having trouble sleeping. All I can think about is opening my shop." She can't subdue her wide smile. "I'm constantly making notes and jotting

3

down ideas. Would you like to go with me to garage sales in the morning before school? I need to start gathering inventory."

For three months she's focused on paperwork, city and state forms for licenses, opening bank accounts, and securing a storefront for her resale shop. She recently set her tentative opening date, and now she's afraid she won't have the inventory she needs to open.

"Before school?"

"I've mapped out a few garage sales that open tonight at 5:00. Troy and Bethany plan to go to them with me. I've found four that open between 6 and 7:30 in the morning." My interest grows as she explains. "We'll just look for anything I can turn a profit on and leave my name and number for anything they have left over when they close their sale."

"If you provide the donuts and caffeine, I'll join you."

Adrian wraps me in an embrace while thanking me. I've already helped quite a bit in the planning stages, and I will continue to assist as she opens. Adrian opens her Notes App, then lists her upcoming tasks with me. All eight of us assist her as best as we can. Winston, and I are the most involved. Winston through his involvement in his family's theater, knows more about the business side of things. I'm a planner and creative helper. Adrian chose one of my ideas to name her shop.

"Next Thursday and Friday are free trash pick-up days in Athens," I mention. "We should pair up in teams of two with the trucks, divide the town, and pillage each morning and afternoon. I've seen everything from furniture to clothes sitting on the curb in years past."

"That's a fabulous idea."

I offer to plan our attack and direct the group for Adrian. A knowing smirk graces her face. She's very aware I will plan the outing as if I'm preparing an army at war.

"So, how was the rest of your night with Canton? I can't believe the two of you ducked out of the movie before the halfway point." I elbow her.

Adrian sighs deep before reliving an encounter she seems to have forgotten in less than twelve hours. "He may be eye-candy, but Canton is lacking, if you know what I mean."

"Seriously Adrian, you are so hard on guys. Nobody is perfect, even you."

"Please." She begins to explain her rating system. "When he kisses, his lips and mouth are too soft. They are like wet spaghetti noodles. He likes to lick and not in a hot, turn-me-on way. He's like a cow at the salt block. He doesn't believe in foreplay; he just gets naked and attempts to mount." A shiver of revulsion quakes through her. She holds up her thumb, inspecting it. "Yep, not much bigger than my thumb. It was all I could do to pretend it was fun when we parted ways."

I shake my head at her. "You probably scared the poor guy. You know not all men want a dominant woman."

"I wasn't even worked up enough to need my vibrator when I got home. I wish I would have stayed for the whole movie and parted ways alone when you did."

We joke about the night a bit more. Adrian notices my eyes focus on the far corner of the lot. She turns her head to find Hamilton and Troy approaching in their trucks. Within minutes, all nine of us will be here, visiting, joking, and dreaming of our graduation only a week away.

Adrian asks, "Mind if I share a few things with you to see what you think?" When I nod, she begins. She scrolls through her cell phone for her Notes app to share with me. "I thought I would open the store 11 to 6 on Wednesday through Saturday. I'd be available 4 to 6pm on Saturday, Monday, and Tuesday for the community to drop off items they no longer want. Then, I could use Mondays and Tuesdays to prep the items, display them in the store, or work on updates to social media and advertising." Adrian anxiously looks to me for input.

"I like it. I'm glad you planned times the store is closed for you to get stuff ready. I worried you might try to help customers while you worked on new items, stretching yourself too thin." I nod decisively. "I think this schedule will work."

I hope my words are exactly what she needs to keep her motivated. Adrian squeezes my hand in thanks. My friend is a strong, competent woman. I know she will rock at running her own business. She knows she can do it. With opening day drawing near, she's faltering a bit in her confidence of her abilities. I attempt to provide her with affirmation that she can do this.

3

There are only three chain restaurants in town: Pizza Hut, McDonald's, and Hardee's. Yet another of the 4,724 reasons I want to escape Athens.

As Troy and Bethany pull next to Adrian in the small parking lot behind her future resale shop, I wave. She's surprised to see me in the cab of the truck with them. I said nothing about helping her tonight. She thought we only had plans for the morning.

"Surprise!" I shout as I exit from the cab.

"Madison, what are you doing here?" she asks, thrilled I tagged along. "Are you really so bored that you want to visit garage sales on a Thursday evening?"

"Not bored. I come bearing gifts." I extend my hand, which contains a little, rectangular box, towards Adrian.

Her fingers fumble a bit trying to open the packing tape, causing Troy to offer his pocket knife. When she lifts the lid, she finds business cards. A gasp of excitement escapes her lips as she pulls out the first card. A large, bold font greets her near the top. "Gingham Frog Repurposed Treasures." Her business

6

is typed in black to share with everyone. Her shop's address, her cell phone number, and a website domain are present.

"I don't have a website." Adrian's brow furrows, and she chews on her lower lip. She feels bad for pointing out the error.

"I'm currently creating it for you. Winston and I have been working on it for a few weeks already. Turn it over."

She flips the business card over in her hand. On the back it reads, "Please feel free to drop off or call for a pickup of any items that remain at the end of your sale."

I explain, "Tonight, and in the morning, you can leave these at each garage sale. I thought maybe you'd get inventory this way."

I planned ahead and secured business cards; I'm sure Adrian is mentally kicking herself for not thinking of it.

"Okay," Troy interrupts. "Let's get going. Inventory won't magically appear on your shelves." We pile into the crew cab of Troy's old Ford truck, and Adrian directs him towards the first garage sale address.

4

No need to call for references when an applicant applies for a job; everyone knows everyone. This is one of the 4,724 reasons I want to escape this town.

In my hand, I clutch the letter I've been anxiously awaiting since mid-April. It seems so long ago that Hamilton drove with me to Columbia, Missouri. visiting with the baseball coach and team while I sat through a few exams. I'm nervous now as the contents of this envelope might speed up my studies at college.

I choose to open the letter in my favorite place. I tuck it into my short's pocket, then grab a bottle of water for my walk. From the front yard, I cross the gravel road, and walk through the cow pasture on the gentle path among the green ground cover. I'm the only one to venture this way; my many trips have created this narrow path.

It only takes ten minutes to find my secluded spot. Large trees surround the fenced area. I easily climb over the chain-link fence that protects the forty-two weathered headstones. I find this old, forgotten cemetery peaceful. Those that lie here intrigue me. I've often imagined the lives they've led and families they left behind.

In summers past, I took photos of each headstone then used the internet to see if I could uncover any information on them. In my research, I found some relatives on ancestry sites. They were grateful for the photos I shared and the address of the final resting place of those they desperately searched to connect with.

I choose to sit near my favorite headstone belonging to W. Taul with dates of 1840-1899. Slowly, I slide my finger under the edge and tear the envelope open. I pull the letter out. As I unfold it, I browse the information one time then read it more thoroughly the second. The scores are high enough to test out of 12 college hours. I tip my head to the sky and whisper a prayer of thanks to Heaven.

My excitement is not that my tuition will be greatly lowered but that my time spent obtaining my diploma shrinks. With the 48 hours I completed while in high school and during summer classes, these 12 CLEP hours allow me to start as a junior this fall. I will only need two years to become a teacher. It's not that I plan to hurry back to Athens. I am not sure where I will decide to teach—I am anxious to start earning money that will allow me to start my new life away from this small town.

5

You can't try to sneak into a bar or buy alcohol while underage—they know your age, they know your parents, or they know your family. This is one of the 4,724 reasons I want to leave Athens.

Friday morning, after visiting three garage sales, Adrian drives me back to the high school lot. I smile noting we are the last to arrive. Hamilton and Latham have lowered their tailgates, Salem, Savannah, Winston, Troy, and Bethany sit beside them or stand nearby. I'm barely out of the truck when Bethany calls for us to hurry.

"We found a house to rent," Troy's masculine voice greets as he squeezes Bethany, who is tucked at his side. Perpetually touching, she has her right hand tucked in his back pocket and her left on his chest.

I'm not shocked. They've been planning on finding a place to live together since junior year. Their parents support it, and they already act like a married couple. In our group of nine, they are the only two that dated each other through high school. I love my group of eight friends standing here with me, and can't wait to see what the years following graduation hold for us.

Recently, Senior Prom added a second couple to our group as Latham asked to escort Salem as friends. That night and the days that followed surprised them as much as the rest of us. They claim sparks flew, and they tried to deny them while holding each other. Considering they were kissing on the dance floor by the last song of the evening, they didn't struggle long against the pull they claim to have suddenly felt. I assume they had feelings for each other prior to the dance, but they emphatically deny it. I just find it hard to accept they'd been around each other for the past four years in our group then suddenly one night while dressed to the nines, surrounded by balloons and streamers, in the dim lighting of the high school gym, with music playing that BAM something ignited between them. I call BS.

I'm reminded of a recent conversation with Adrian. She stated our little clan seems to be infatuated with pairing up. When she claimed Salem and Latham were twitterpated with one another while batting her eyelashes, I claimed it's the circle of life in this small town; residents are born, grow up, graduate, marry, work, start a family, and die here. It's just another of the reasons I need to leave Athens, and the sooner the better. I smile know as I realize we quoted from *Bambi* and *The Lion King*.

My thoughts return to the present. Bethany's sweet smile conveys her love and utter happiness to begin life after graduation with the man of her dreams. "The living room is big enough to have you all over. You're welcome anytime to drop by and hang out."

"Well..." Troy draws out the word before whispering in Bethany's ear. She giggles and swats at his chest while a blush creeps upon her face.

"We all promise to text or call prior to showing up," I promise, hoping to avoid Troy announcing what they might be doing sometimes if we just drop in. Everyone nods in agreement.

"We'll throw a big housewarming bash when we get moved in the Monday after graduation," Troy announces. "And our house will be party central. No need to worry about getting caught in public with alcohol." He beams proudly.

6

Everyone drives pick-up trucks in Athens, another of the 4,724 reasons I want to escape this town.

Today is the day. Adrian gets to meet the realtor at 11:00 a.m. She gets the keys and will officially be leasing her store space. Weeks of paperwork and filing forms with the city and state led to this. I guess she's already a business owner on paper, but with keys in hand she can begin working on the physical space.

"Good morning," she greets me immediately, cheer clear in her voice. "Today's the big day."

"How are you feeling?" I ask, knowing her excitement must be at an all-time high.

"Eleven o'clock can't get here fast enough. I'm running out of things to keep me busy. I've cleaned my room, folded a load of laundry, eaten breakfast, walked our dog, showered, dried and styled my hair, but it's only 9:15."

"I'm on my way to town," I state. "Want to meet somewhere? I could distract you for a bit."

"Okay. Where?"

"The Blue Jays are practicing. We could sit and watch."

We agree to meet at the park; I need to be with her. I want to share in her excitement.

Adrian backs into a shaded spot beside my car. We meet at the rear and simultaneously hop to sit on her tailgate.

"I always feel like a stalker, a wanna-be girlfriend, and a pervert sitting in my car watching them practice." I smile at Adrian before scanning the action on the baseball field.

"After four years, I'm sure everyone in town knows what a devoted fan you are of the Blue Jays." She squeezes my forearm. "I'm sure the newbies see the older players wave and call to you. They'll figure it out soon enough."

"I won't be able to get away with this at college this fall." I don't pull my eyes from the field and players. "I'll have class, and they have closed practices. I'm gonna have withdrawals." I wave at Hamilton as he runs a lap around the outside of the field. He's not surprised we are here. In fact, I'm sure the team would worry if I didn't pop in on practices. They'd probably text or call to check on me.

I hop off the tailgate, retrieve bottles of water from my backseat. Adrian holds my water bottle as I lift myself up onto the truck.

"Question," Adrian attempts to pull my attention her way for a moment. "Would you possibly want to work with me at the resale shop?" She quickly explains, "I know your many scholarships will cover books and courses, along with room and board. Everyone could use a little cash, right?"

I look at her with a big grin on my face. "Of course, I will. Just know I planned to do it for free until I need to leave for college in the fall. But since you are offering to pay me, I'll take your money."

7

You can't purchase any major label clothing without over an hour drive. This is one of the 4,724 reasons I want to escape Athens.

Today, Adrian and I are command central at her store while the troops comb neighborhoods for treasures on the curb during free-pickup-days. I gave each team a route to run this morning and again this evening. Adrian knew my planning would be thorough. We plan to organize the store into sections and begin setting out products as we price them.

"Wow! The cleaning crew did an awesome job," I announce.

"Yeah, mom and her friends are a force to be reckoned with while in cleaning mode. They had steam cleaners and wet-vacs running all day."

"It's great that your entire family helps out." I smile as she moves a metal clothes rack to the right side of the store while I stream our local radio station through a Bluetooth speaker.

Being the only child of parents that were only children, the concept of a family supporting each other is foreign to me. I've been alone with my mother since the age of thirteen. I spend most of my time with my friends to avoid the troubles at home.

"While you perfectly arrange the clothes racks where you want them, I'm going to jazz up your front window a bit." I walk through the backroom to my car for the surprise I created for her windows.

Adrian busies herself arranging the clothing section of the store into a children's, teens', women's and men's area as she envisioned. I strategically cover the windows and doors by taping newsprint over them. The thin paper blocks out some but not all of the sunlight. This is good; it will help make the large letters that I've painted on the front of the newspaper pop just a little bit more. I realize Adrian may see letters painted on the paper, but she can't make out the words from the back.

Soon, I approach, waving a blue bandana at her. "Cover your eyes, please."

She shakes her head at me. "I can see the paper. I know there are words on it. Why do I have to cover my eyes?"

"Fine. Let's go out and take a look at my hours of hard work." I tease smiling brightly as I tug her arm towards the backdoor.

Once we make our way around the entire strip mall and down to the front of her store, she seems amazed at my work. She reads out loud, "Coming Soon! Gingham Frog Repurposed Treasures." The words "Gingham" and "Frog" are green and white gingham squares. "Coming Soon" is crimson while "Repurposed Treasure" looks like old boards are nailed together to make the letters. It's not just a sign; it's a work of art.

"I..." She fans her face as she gulps in air. "It's absolutely perfect! Madison, this must have taken you forever to make."

I smile proudly, eyes on the covered storefront. "I had a little help. Winston supplied the newsprint and suggested what to write on it. I mentioned it to Mrs. Foster in art class. She helped me come up with the design to make it pop." I turn to face her, smile still wide. "I didn't want black letters on paper. It needed to be special, like you."

Adrian wraps me in a tight hug as tears fall from her eyes. "Thank you."

My buzzing phone interrupts our moment. "Better get back inside," I announce. "Troy's group has a full load, and they are almost here."

My stomach growls loudly, demanding I give it attention. I look at my cell phone to find it is nearly seven. "We should think about dinner soon," I tell Adrian. She nods and tells me she will take care of it. I barely blink before she places her cell phone at her ear, on her way to the backroom. I rearrange the rack we are currently working on by size as she retrieves more clothing from the back.

"I texted everyone that pizza will be here in twenty minutes," Adrian informs me, emerging from the backroom with her arms full of children's clothes on hangers. We quickly place them on the front rack.

I step back, admiring the progress we made today. Nearly all of the clothing stock fills several metal racks on the right half of the sales floor. She placed Troy's repurposed furniture on the left side near the large windows for future customers to see. Adrian hopes seeing them in the windows will pull customers inside. Then, she has shelves full of household items and the electronics plugged in at the wall. I love the fact that her customers can ensure they work before purchasing them.

The muted green back wall pops against the stark white side walls. The green adds color to the large, fluorescent-lighted store space.

Adrian opens her Notes App and reads through her pre-opening checklist. She still needs interior and exterior signs, changing rooms, check-out counter, and advertising. She crosses off inventory as we filled much of the space today. She's happy with our progress.

"Pizza guy is out back!" Winston announces from the backroom.

I scurry to meet him, waving at Winston as I pass. He informs Adrian his truck is full of more furniture, some good quality coats, and books.

"Crap!" Adrian shouts. "I forgot to put up shelves for books and vinyl records." She slowly browses the non-clothing side of her store for a space to add shelving.

Placing his hands upon her shoulders, Winston soothes, "Calm down. Let's enjoy our pizza with the gang, and let Latham share an idea he thought of today." Winston smirks. "He's got you covered." With Winston's help, she sets up a folding card table and enough chairs for all of us.

"We're back!" Troy yells.

Adrian smiles widely while Troy, Salem, Latham, Savannah, and Bethany emerge from the backroom as I bring up the rear carrying the pizzas. Our friends have helped Adrian immensely today. She admitted she was a bit worried about filling her sales floor prior to her grand opening but after today, it's full.

"Latham," Winston speaks through his current bite of pizza. "Tell Adrian your idea." He winks at her before she turns her attention to Latham.

"Why don't you let us guys build you a horseshoe shaped countertop to use as a check-out area? We can make it two-tiered and even include cabinets below it for storage." Sensing Adrian not following his description, he sketches it out on his napkin. "We also found a large shelving unit we can paint or stain and anchor to the wall for you to display products on."

Latham constantly surprises me. At first glance, he's a farm boy or a cowboy. He's all tall and lanky, wearing western shirts, worn Levi's, dusty boots, and his cowboy hat. Occasionally, he'll wear a solid-colored t-shirt and a John Deere or Dekalb cap. Only close friends know underneath he's really long, lean muscles with a wicked farmers tan. I nearly died of laughter the first time he joined us at the lake. It was as if his legs and chest hadn't seen sunlight his entire life.

The man can fix about anything—it must be from tinkering around his parents' farm on equipment and buildings for years. He's fixed many of our cars, and now he's planning to construct counters and cabinets for her store.

Salem has herself quite a hottie. His jawline usually sports two days of dark stubble. His dark hair, that peeks from under his hat, with dark eyes on his tanned face are like catnip to all the girls. When he smiles, his face and eyes light up all sexy-like, melting the panties off any females in the area. When Adrian states she loves his idea, said sex-smoldering smile shines like a hundred-watt bulb. I may need to remind Adrian he belongs to Salem.

"We could varnish it if you prefer a wood finish or paint it any color you desire," Troy chips in. "I have most of the wood we need, so the cost would be minimal."

"When could you build it?" Adrian inquires, wondering if they can finish it before she opens.

"We can start this weekend," Latham says.

"If we work Friday night and Saturday, we should have it done by Sunday," Troy promises.

Troy is all bulk to Latham's long and lean. Clothes cannot conceal his massive arms and chest. His jeans hug his huge, muscular thighs. If he wasn't nearly six-feet tall, he'd look too heavy. He enjoys working with his hands. Lucky for Adrian, he loves working on furniture and hopes to sell it in her store.

"Really?" She can't believe her ears. "You'd give up your weekend to do this for me?"

"It will cost you meals and drinks," Latham states.

"You've got a deal. I'll give Winston my spare key, so you can get in and out if I'm not around. Will it make much of a mess?"

I sense that Adrian worries her mother's hard day of cleaning might be ruined as well as all the inventory we've already displayed.

"We'll throw sheets over nearby stuff, keep the saws out back, and the mess will be minimized." Adrian smiles at Troy's statement.

Quick and not too messy; I love these guys even more for being Adrian's heroes.

8

There are no Chinese, Italian, or barbeque places in Athens. This is one of the 4,724 reasons I want to escape this town.

I start my morning in the cemetery, letting the sound of nearby birds fill my excited soul. When I can't hang with friends, I escape to my favorite place. It's a short walk across my neighbor's pasture and the chain link fence keeping livestock from disturbing this area, never stops me from entering. The cemetery where my dad rests requires a drive and is frequented by the citizens of Athens paying their respects. In this long-forgotten cemetery, I often think of my dad, talk to him, and contemplate my future. It also allows me a break from my mother, her drinking, and often hurtful words.

Now, I think about the importance of this day for the families of Athens. For me, it's just a ceremony I must attend. My mother went out until 3:00 a.m. last night—she is in no condition to watch me graduate, not that she planned to.

I'm sure Adrian will be sad that our graduation day has arrived. I need to remember to text her to place tissues in her pockets. She still wants to deny the fact that I will leave Athens for college this fall. Of our tight group of nine, only two aspire to ever leave. Hamilton and I have planned our post-graduation exit for the past four years. College is our excuse, our catalyst to our life beyond Athens. In a twist of fate, we will be attending the same college in the fall.

I chose the education department at The University of Missouri-Columbia fall my junior year after extensively researching available scholarships and work-study programs. I planned to keep my grades up and earn a full-tuition scholarship. Here we are, a year and a half later, my mission accomplished.

Although he excelled in all sports and toyed with the idea of participating in both track and baseball post-high school, Hamilton chose to allow the college baseball scouts choose his launching site. He was heavily scouted for the past two years by Division-1 universities in Texas, Florida, Arizona, Nebraska, Iowa, and Missouri. He narrowed it down to Nebraska, Missouri, and Texas by fall his senior year. After college visits and awards package discussions, he committed to Mizzou with me.

To say I'm excited we will both be Mizzou Tigers is an understatement. One of my best friends will be attending college with me in the fall. I'll already have one friend on campus and someone to hang with. I'll get to attend his games instead of following him online from a distance.

In my new life this fall, I will attend class, go to the store, or go out to eat and not know everything about everyone there. The people I interact with daily will be diverse in the lives they led before college, and their future goals for work and family will vary, unlike those of my friends in Athens. With the exception of Hamilton, no one will know of my alcoholic mother. I won't be judged by her actions or thought to be destined to follow in her footsteps. In Athens, I'm haunted by horrible memories created by my mother in the years since my dad passed. I feel like there's nothing to keep me here. Sure, I will miss my friends, but I want more. I want diversity, culture, adventure, and variety. I want to go out and not know 90% of the people I see. At college this fall, my life will begin.

9

Forget six degrees of separation, most locals are only three people away from sharing relatives. I crave variety. Another of the 4,724 reasons I need to leave this town.

Adrian smiles as she walks up to join Hamilton and me on the grass just outside the school. As our group of nine friends arrive, preparing to graduate today, Adrian hasn't hidden her sadness that two of us plan to leave Athens behind. I haven't shared with her that I imagine once I'm in Columbia I will try to avoid visiting Athens like the plague.

Although I often knock the small-town life they crave, I've hidden most of my excitement to leave and my true plans for a life after college. I desire new friends, a new community, and a future far from my mother. This means I also look forward to a new life free of Adrian, Salem, Bethany, and Savannah. I know we will remain in touch for a while via texts and email, but as I don't plan to drive back to Athens, we will drift apart

Hamilton's talent on the baseball diamond will ensure he never moves back to town. I'm his biggest fan and plan never to lose touch with him. He is close to his mom and sister, so he will visit when he can, but he will live and play in a city much larger than Athens, Missouri.

I don't fault Adrian for loving everything about Athens. Unlike me, she is close to both her parents. She's always felt safe and looks forward to raising her future children here. Major crimes and tragedies are rare in this little farm community. I cringe at the small pool of candidates for a future husband that awaits Adrian in this town, but she states they will have known each other most of their lives. She's only minutes away from her family for any support she might need. Unlike me, she can't wait to open her business and raise her family in the town she loves.

My eyes follow Adrian as she approaches a flailing Winston. I smile as he attempts to place his cap on his sandy-blonde hair. After graduation, he will run the family's three-plex movie theater in Athens. Taking over his family's business this summer is all he has talked about recently. Next to him, Troy looks so happy with Bethany in his bulky arms. They will be moving in together in two days. They'll soon start classes at the local community college. Troy plans to become an Athens' Police Officer, and Bethany hopes to teach elementary kids.

At Adrian's side, Latham is very uncomfortable in his black cap and gown. I've never seen him in public without his jeans, boots, or a hat.

"I'm wearing a black dress," Latham pouts. "I'd rather go barefoot than wear these old-man shoes." He lifts one foot in our direction.

"Hey," Winston chides. "They look just like mine."

Latham motions that Winston just proved his point.

Salem attempts to calm him by telling him that he looks very handsome. The sparkle in her eyes for him gives me hope that someday I might find the man of my dreams, too. Latham plans to work his family farm, and Salem will attend community college this summer with dreams of nursing in her future.

Last, but not least, Savannah approaches our group, running a bit late as usual. She mumbles curse words as she fights to put on her cap and gown in the gusty May breeze. No one is really sure what the future holds for Savannah, not even herself. For now, she works at the local grocery store part-time.

"Bring it in," Adrian prompts our friends. With arms over each other's shoulders, we make a circle and lower our heads. In what might look like a rugby scrum to outsiders, she speaks to our tight-knit group. "We've made it! Today we graduate. It's the last step before adulthood. As we walk across the stage today, I want you all to know I couldn't have made it through high school without you. I vow to keep us together as we attempt to spread our wings and move on to bigger and better things in the next couple of months. I love each and every one of you. I will always be here to bail you out of jail, laugh at your stupid mistakes, and kick your ass when you need it." I can hear the lump forming in her throat as she speaks, and I can imagine her eyes beginning to fill up with tears. "I love you. Now let's go get a diploma!"

Cheers erupt as we break apart only to take turns with high-fives and one-armed guy-hugs. Our administrator calls for us to take our places in the line. The ceremony is about to start, and forty-five of us have to be in alphabetical order. We rush off to find our spots.

Bored in the single file line, I dread the impending graduation party. It's just another reminder of how messed up my life is. I feel a bit guilty at my desire to leave such good friends behind. Adrian talked the parents of my eight friends into planning one large joint party for the nine of us. She claims it is to allow us to spend the entire day together, but I know it's really because my mother would not be throwing me a graduation party and Adrian didn't want me to feel left out. Our large party will be at Winston's parents' house. Each of us decorated an individual table reflecting on our school years. Hamilton insisted his table sit next to mine, so his mother could stand near both of us. Memphis took me under her wing shortly after Hamilton and I grew close in eighth grade. I know I only survived these last five years because she acted as my surrogate mother. I imagine I will spend the party counting down the hours until we can change into comfortable clothes and party at the bonfire on the sandbar tonight.

10

There is a blue-law in Athens, only gas stations, restaurants, and grocery stores may be open on Sunday's. This is one of the 4,724 reasons I want to leave this town.

"I come bearing gifts," Salem sings as she enters from the backroom.

Adrian and I look up from the laptop. Salem carries a large paper grocery bag in each hand. We already ate lunch and Adrian didn't assign any tasks for her to assist the store with. "What ya got?" Adrian asks, our curiosity peaked.

Salem places the bags on the floor, then bends over out of our view behind the counter the guys made. She emerges, placing a white picture frame glued on a candle holder upon the counter. Our brows furrow as we try to understand her gift. She slowly spins the frame around. "Ta-da!"

The white five-by-seven frame on its stand proudly displays a gingham green paper with very large, bold, black words. The first line reads "Tadpoles" and below it reads, "Children's Clothing". Before I can express my love of this sign, Salem explains they can sit atop the round metal clothing racks on the sales floor.

"They are perfect!" I'm sure Adrian loves that she played with the word "frog" from her store name.

"I have three 'Tadpoles' for the kids' racks, two 'Froglets' signs for the teen's racks, three 'Female Frogs' signs for the women's racks, and two 'Male Frogs' signs for the men's racks." Salem stands tall, pride for her work evident.

"Will you help me put them out?" Adrian allows Salem to place each sign, making them visible from the front of the store. We notice she even alternated the colors from white to green as the frogs grow bigger.

Tears pool as Adrian attempts not to cry. "Thank you," her quivering voice squeaks.

Winston's voice from the back door breaks the moment. "I have a surprise for you," he calls. Taking in the two of them wiping tears and red-faced, he pauses. "I'm sorry. I can come back later…"

"No!" Adrian blurts. "Salem brought me these signs she crafted, and it just brought me to tears."

"We've cried enough," Salem vows. "What's the surprise?"

Winston approaches in his collared shirt and golf shorts. As always, his outfit matches his shoes. I swear he owns more shoes than I do. His sandy-blonde hair, styled with product, is perfect. My fingers always ache to rumple it a bit. No man should ever be so put together. I like guys a bit rougher around the edges. I'm not looking for a bad boy—Winston's golfer style does nothing for me.

He places the heavy box he carries on the front counter. As he fumbles to open the lid to reveal the gifts inside, I can't help wondering why Adrian is receiving so many gifts today.

Winston raises a pale green paper for us to see. It's a flyer. It announces the opening of a new business in Athens, the name of her store, and the items it will include. Details for selling and donating to the store are also printed on the bottom.

"Winston," Adrian searches for the words to express her gratefulness.

"Troy and I plan to run them to businesses all over Athens, hopes they will display them for you." Winston explains his plan. "We will post them on community bulletin boards anywhere we can. We will talk to businesses to ask if they will allow us to leave a stack for customers to take one. Of course, we will display them at my theater."

"I have a few other ideas for you." Winston places a few flyers in a stack on her counter before closing the box. "I'd like to text you when Troy and I are about done so we can eat, and I can share them with you."

Salem elbows Adrian's ribcage. She startles from her thoughts. "I could do dinner tonight." A blush grows on her cheeks.

"It should be about six or so," he informs her as he secures the box of flyers in his arm and strides to the backroom to leave.

"Winston," she calls to him. When he pauses, turning to face Adrian, he smiles. "Thank you." He simply nods, smiling, and leaves.

Late that night, I'm on the phone with Adrian. She called me, frustrated with all she still needs to do.

"I may never get to sleep tonight. Although I took notes on my phone as Winston and I ate dinner, everything still swirls around, adding questions and items for me to place on my to do list. Don't get me wrong, I'm grateful Winston shares everything he has learned from his parents' business with me. It's just that I've been working so hard doing everything to start my new store, and he just added many more items."

Adrian talks a mile a minute. I try but I can't speak while she continues.

"With his help, I plan to join the Athens Chamber of Commerce, the Athens Jaycees, advertise in the Athens Gazette, and on our local radio station." Adrian quickly lists these items, further demonstrating the stress she's under. "He pointed out how each will help my business. I hope it will not be too overwhelming. He promises he will attend the meetings and events with me. He's been attending with his parents, so he can introduce me to community members that can help my business, too. I don't understand why he is taking such an interest in helping me with my business, but I am glad he is."

Finally finding a break in her words, I begin. "Friends help friends. Winston enjoys helping you. I can see it on his face. I think he's glad he's not the only one of our group choosing business over college. The two of you have that in common."

Adrian tilts her head to the side, contemplating my words for a moment, before we finally say goodnight. I smile. Hamilton once told me, a drunk Winston confessed to him Adrian was hot. Winston hasn't acted on it, but I can see he still likes her.

11

Athens doesn't even have a Walmart—it's another of the 4,724 reasons I want to escape this town.

I've needed to pee for two hours now. I refuse to leave Adrian alone on her first day open. Her parents are here now, so I finally have a chance to excuse myself to the backroom.

My feet ache from standing all day. I should have thought better of my flip-flops on the concrete floor. I will know for tomorrow. I take a few sips of a diet-cola from the fridge before stepping back on the sales floor. I'm exhausted but love every minute of it.

I position myself at the pay station for the remainder of the day as Adrian and her parents work the floor. I begin making a list of items we need to restock from the backroom before we open tomorrow. We have a few furniture pieces in back but will need Troy to bring more as soon as possible.

Adrian's mother locks the front door at six, her father begins moving furniture for us, Adrian stocks the clothes, and I run the end of day sales receipts and count the cash. I leave start up cash in the drawer and prepare the rest for deposit.

"Your attention please," I call to the room. "Our opening day total is $479.54."

"Nearly $500," Winston cheers entering from the back, startling all of us. "What a busy day you've had." His big, blue eyes are clearly locked on Adrian as he approaches. "Congratulations, Adrian." He places a chaste kiss on her cheek.

Adrian nervously thanks him, stating that she never could have done this without his help.

"Well, I really couldn't have done it without all of her help." She corrects sweeping her hand around the room.

Winston and Adrian's father return to moving furniture, and Adrian finds a spot at the clothing racks next to me, pretending to look busy.

I catch her sideways glances in Winston's direction. I witness the small smile she tries to hide while I assume, she's thinking of him. She has it bad, and she's doing everything she can to deny it, which is odd. Adrian rarely holds back—when she wants something she goes for it. She's interested in Winston, but she's hesitating. The cat-and-mouse game they are playing is very entertaining.

I elbow her. "Are you okay? It's been a big day. You should take the deposit and go home. I'll lock up for you." I know there is no way she will leave before me.

We make quick work of closing up. Winston insists on escorting Adrian to the bank with the deposit. Since I did the end of day receipts, I know most of her income today is credit cards—I don't believe $100 requires an escort for safety. It's cute how Winston is weaving himself into her life.

Today is game day. Baseball season is my favorite time of the year. I love the smell of fresh cut grass, the heat of the sun, and the taste of sunflower seeds. Nothing beats the view from the top of the bleachers during the National Anthem as the two teams stand near the fresh chalk lines to address the Stars and Stripes.

I love the rituals each team and player believe in. Hamilton is one of the most superstitious players I've ever known. His mom delivers a cold Snickers bar to him in the dugout before each game. He has rules for hanging his uniform, each one specific. First on the hanger, his socks and his belt. Next, his pants. His sleeves go on next, then the jersey. Lastly, his hat slips over the bend of the hook. He always loads his bat-bag and sleeps with his glove under his pillow the night before a game. Each year, he writes The Lord's Prayer on the underside of the bill of his cap with an ink pen so it's visible to his eyes only during the game. He winks at his mom and me in the on-deck circle before each at bat. In the event of a team loss he refuses to wash his socks until they win again. Fortunately, the Blue Jays win most of the time.

I hardly slept a wink last night. I fear I am more anxious about today's home opener than Hamilton is. I attempt to busy myself cleaning my room, doing laundry, and washing my car to pass the time this morning. I still have two hours before the first pitch. I decide to head into Athens. Maybe I will find someone to visit with until it's time to show up at the field.

Upon entering town, I need to stop at the grocery store to procure snacks for the double-header today. I grab a hand-held basket to carry as I shop. I choose one box of Milk Duds to consume before they melt, a Mike & Ike box, Dakota Sunflower Seeds, and Tootsie Pops. Every game, I bring the same four items. I always bring my own—I can't take the risk the concession stand is out or doesn't carry them.

I'm as superstitious as Hamilton is. He has his game day routines, and I have mine. I don't have to consume all four items, but they must be in my possession at the game. It's a team effort, and I do my part.

I wear my replica jersey, although I have created two new shirts to wear to games this season. I refuse to break them in at a game in which Hamilton will be the starting pitcher. I can't risk bad luck on behalf of my new shirt.

Before I pull out from the grocery parking lot, I text Adrian, Savannah, Bethany, and Salem.

ME

I'm early, anyone ready for the game?

ADRIAN

pick me up

> I'm ready.

ME
heading your way now

SALEM
I'll be there soon

Savannah gets off at game time

ME
see ya soon

With my snacks and cooler of water in hand, Adrian and I head across the parking lot toward the ball park. Adrian carries her homemade, blue, white, and red colors, fleece blanket for us to sit on in the wooden bleachers. As we approach, the team is warming up in the outfield, Hamilton is throwing in the bullpen, and a few parents from both teams sit in lawn chairs scattered around the infield fence. Adrian and I sit on the top row of the bleachers in our usual corner.

As game time draws near, I don't see Hamilton's mother here yet—this concerns me. From the height of our seats, I search the parking lot, but her truck is not there. I purchase a Snickers bar at the concession stand before making my way to the home team dugout. Through the gaps between wooden boards, I spot Hamilton on the end of the bench. Without a word, I pass the candy bar through a crack. Hamilton grabs it with a smile. In his mother's absence, I couldn't let this pregame ritual go undone. I only hope he doesn't worry why his mother is not here. As his head coach doesn't allow girls near the players on gameday, I quietly slip back to my seat in the stands. My cell phone vibrates in my pocket.

HAMILTON
TY (thank you)

mom told me she'd be here @ game time today

. . .

Shocked that he is using his cell phone as they are prohibited in the dugout, I look toward the field and note both coaches are speaking to the umpires near home plate. With no coach in the dugout, Hamilton took a second to message me. I hurry to reply so he doesn't get caught.

ME

no worries

good Luck

12

Everyone waves at everyone while driving. Yet another of the 4,724 reasons I want to escape Athens.

The Saturday after Adrian's store opens, Troy and Bethany wed in a private ceremony at the courthouse before their parents host a reception party. Our group of friends volunteered to assist the parents with decorating the stone building on the fairgrounds for the reception. Salem gathered props and is currently setting up a photo booth area near the front door. Savannah and Adrian string fairy lights from the rafters.

Troy's parents place centerpieces on each table. Troy's mother crafted a simple floral piece, then added handcuffs and ABC chalkboards along with other cop and teacher paraphernalia.

Bethany's mother harasses the caterer as she sets up the wedding cake table. Her father conveniently is nowhere to be found. I assist Latham and Hamilton as they set up the DJ table. The guys will play music from our playlists, saving the parents money. As Savannah and Adrian climb down the ladders to plug in the last strand, I approach.

"Wow, this looks amazing." After several moments, we pull our eyes from the twinkle lights. "Wanna help me request a few songs to start the evening?" I wave an ink pen and clipboard towards them. We giggle as we jot down a couple of our favorite songs.

Salem's raised voice interrupts our brainstorming session. "Ladies, I can't find Bethany's father anywhere. Someone needs to pull her mom away to rescue the poor caterer." We follow Salem's extended arm pointing toward the cake table. "I'm worried the caterer might burst into tears soon."

Adrian accepts the challenge and distracts Mrs. Lamar by asking her to let us know if we need to adjust any light strings. While they walk the entire space, analyzing light spacing, I notice the caterer dash away from the barn.

"Special delivery!" Mr. Lamar shouts as he rolls a cart of beverages toward the refreshment tables.

The four of us assist him in displaying the various drinks, cups, and ice along with the snack mix, nuts, and popcorn.

"Perfect," Troy's mother announces. "It's time we all go cleanup. Remember to be back here by 6 p.m."

Walking on the fairgrounds, I marvel at how this large, stone barn, built in 1938, transforms into a charming venue. The rustic stone facade loses its golden hues for a shaded gray as the summer sun begins to set. The warm stones embody strength to stand many storms in years to come just as I believe Troy and Bethany's union will stand the test of time.

Adrian wraps her arms around Savannah and me. "Can you believe we are adults? I mean, we are 18, and our friends are now married. I know adulting will not be easy, but with friends like you, I will survive." She places a kiss on both our cheeks before throwing open the heavy doors. Turning to face us, she asks, "Who's ready to party?"

The three of us freeze just inside the front doors. Bethany and Troy's parents occupy a table at the far side of the barn. The fairy lights shine from above, and the large space is completely silent.

"This will not do." Adrian strides to the music table.

I quickly turn on the five Bluetooth speakers strategically placed around the dance area and near the doors. Adrian selects Latham's country music playlist to entertain us. Keith Urban's lyrics fill the space as two of Troy's relatives enter. Savannah places their gift on the gift table before Salem whisks them into the photo booth.

Adrian and I greet a steady influx of guests while Savannah and Salem continue to man their stations over the next hour. Promptly at 7 p.m., Troy escorts our beautiful Bethany into the party amidst cheers. Fair-complected Bethany flushes red head to toe while both hands cover her mouth.

I love her reaction to our decorations, her family, and friends.

"Ladies and gentlemen, Mr. and Mrs. Troy Sullivan," Latham's voice announces into the microphone.

Troy attacks Bethany's mouth with a hot, somewhat inappropriate kiss for such a public venue. Loud cheers fill the space. The couple slowly greets each guest, working their way through the room.

I join the rest of our gang at the music table where Salem attempts to persuade the group toward the photo booth. Adrian quickly joins in her persuasive endeavor. I fetch the dry erase props and a marker.

On one large arrow I write "most likely to wear plaid at his wedding" and points, it at Latham. While we laugh, I write "most likely to marry a Barbie Doll", pointing it at Hamilton.

I erase both signs. "What would you write on mine?" I taunt the guys as I slowly back up towards the photo area. The guys accept my challenge and follow.

Adrian suggests Hamilton and I go first. The rest of the group giggle as they conspire to write on our dry erase arrows. They don't allow us to see the words as we hold the signs and a picture is snapped. Hamilton's sign states "most likely to earn millions". My sign reads "most likely to become famous". After the photo and reading each sign, we argue their choice of words. As a future teacher, I claim fame seems like a huge stretch. I remind them that Hamilton will be famous for his baseball career. Hamilton begins to argue, but I shut him up with the raising of one hand in front of his face".

We continue taking turns with groups of two, four, and all seven of us. Bethany and Troy join us for two photos of our group of nine. Troy writes "most likely to share a jail cell together" for one of our pictures.

I excuse myself to answer my cell phone when it vibrates. I can't imagine who might be calling as our group of friends are all at this party. As I walk away, Latham informs the group the display showed unknown caller.

13

I'll never escape the judgement that I am just like my mother; yet another of the 4,724 reasons I want to escape this town.

"Hello. This is Madison." I greet the unknown caller interrupting Troy and Bethany's reception.

"Ms. Crocker, I'm Officer Campbell at the Athens Police Station. Your mother was brought in for driving under the influence and resisting arrest..."

As his voice continues in my ear, I don't hear a word he says. She's done it again. This is her second DUI. I cringe at the possibility she might have hurt others with her decision to drive impaired. I've attempted to help her attend Alcoholics Anonymous. I've urged her to speak to our minister and others. I've pleaded with her to call me for a ride. My words fell on deaf ears. I thank the officer for calling then hang-up.

Turning around, I find Troy standing in my path to return to the party. He heard me thanking Officer Campbell. Troy's very close to the officers as he hopes to become one.

"Your mom at the station?"

I can only nod while attempting to hold back my anger and tears.

"Let's go."

I blink up at Troy attempting to understand his words. Shaking my head, I find my voice. "Troy, you can't leave your reception. You need to get back inside to Bethany." I gently push his chest. "I'll join you in a few more minutes."

I lean against a wooden pole in the livestock barn. During the fair this area is alive with animals, farmers, and youth. Now it's quiet and free of the smells associated with livestock. I don't know what to do to help my mom. I can't make her second DUI go away. Maybe this time she will wake up to the risky behavior she's engaging in.

A large, warm hand connects with my lower back. "Troy asked me to accompany you to the police station." Hamilton positions himself in front of me. "My truck is over here."

Without thinking my body moves alongside his. He opens the passenger door then holds my hand as I carefully climb into the cab in my dress. I look his way when he turns the key in the ignition and the engine roars to life.

"She'll be okay." His words mean to comfort me. I simply nod, though I'm not feeling confident.

At the station, Hamilton maintains constant contact with me to show his support. I do feel stronger with his hand in mine, on my lower back, and on my shoulder. We learn my mother will be kept overnight to sleep off her bender. They divulge the location of her car, hand me the keys, and encourage me to return after 10 a.m. to pick mom up.

Hamilton and I slip back into the reception. While he fetches beverages, I join our friends at the table. Adrian embraces me before I can sit. No words are spoken.

Hamilton places our two drinks on the table. "Why aren't people dancing?"

All heads turn to the dance floor. It seems my friends were too worried about me to keep the party atmosphere lively. To ensure Troy and Bethany's reception remains magical, we rise and start dancing as I attempt to ignore my mother's mess.

Bethany grasps my hand and proceeds to tug me from the dance floor. She is a woman on a mission as she leads me outside. As the door closes the music fades and we find ourselves surrounded by the dark summer night.

"Troy shared about your mother." I avert my eyes unable to witness the pity on her face. "I must confess I've wanted to share something with you but worried you might think I was overstepping." She takes both my hands in hers. "My father is in AA." She watches my face as her words sink in. "He's now sober seven years. It wasn't pretty when he hit rock-bottom. I want to share this because I know what you are going through. I could speak to my dad and see if he might talk to your mom. By sharing his journey, it might help her."

"I don't know. I've mentioned Alcoholics Anonymous several times. It seems to upset her causing her to drink more."

"Why don't you think about it. I'm not going anywhere—my offer still stands." She releases my hands, placing them on my shoulders while looking me straight in the eyes. "I found virtual Al-Anon and Alateen meetings. Since Athens doesn't have a group here, I used the internet to connect with others in similar situations. I found it helped chatting with others." She pauses deepening her stare. "Go to Al-Anon's website and join a virtual meeting. It helps. You've endured this too long on your own, it's time to reach out."

I nod. Bethany hugs me before announcing it's time we return to the party. No longer in the party mood, I will fake it for my friends on their special day.

14

When a house catches on fire, the adults all call each other to gossip about it. This is one of the 4,724 reasons I want to escape this town.

Adrian totally ignores my insistence that I can handle picking my mother up at the police station by myself. She hid my car keys last night for fear I might attempt to leave while she slept. Shaking the keys in front of me, she states she is accompanying me to the police station and taking my mother home.

Pulling into the lot at the police station, Adrian growls, "I can't believe they texted Troy."

"You've got to be shitting me." Adrian scowls, "Boys can be so dumb. I can't believe they texted Troy while he was on his honeymoon."

"Adrian." My tone conveying that I'm upset the entire gang is here, "I don't need an audience today. It's embarrassing enough without the entire town of Athens talking about it."

Trying to lighten the mood, she reminds me the gossips of Athens heard about the DUI on their police scanners last night. I sigh. Adrian reminds me they are here for me, I can't drive both cars home, and I might need them to assist with my mother. She explains she didn't know if my mother would be mean to me and couldn't bear the thought of me physically attempting to get my mother home. That's why she texted for the muscles to join us. Resigning to the current situation, I open my car door.

Troy approaches, stopping us in our tracks. "Madison, she's pissed off. I spoke to the desk clerk. You need to sign a form, then they will release her to you." Troy looks to Adrian for support before continuing. "I could hear her ranting while I was at the front desk. She's already mad at you and not using flattering words when referring to you. I want you to be ready for it. This will not be fun. But we are all here to help. Please understand we know she doesn't mean anything she is about to say to you."

I nod, sigh deeply, then with head high and shoulders back I stride into the station. Minutes later, I open the door and peek my head out. I ask Troy and Hamilton to help. The two men carry my mother from the station to the backseat of the car with her shrieking the entire way.

"You fucking whore." I no longer flinch when the drunken words pierce my heart. "Had to beg your fuck buddies to drag your mom home today, didn't you?" The guys struggle against her attempts to slap as they close the car door. Only slightly muffled she continues her screaming through the car window. "She misses her daddy, I bet she gives you every dirty thing you ask for just to keep you from leaving her." I mouth the words I am sorry to Troy and Hamilton while I attempt to fight the sting of tears threatening the back of my eyes. "Pathetic slut. She'll do anything to prevent being alone with me."

My mother is only partially right. It's not my daddy issues, but her drunken stupors that cause me to seek the company of my friends. I miss my dad, but I am not sexually active due to daddy issues. She's projecting. She's the one seeking men to erase the pain of losing my dad.

My mother's words are hard for me to ignore. I'm not sure how my friends can ignore the hateful taunts. I've shared how mean my drunk mother was with Adrian. She isn't drunk now. She pretends she can't even find the strength to walk, yet she can belittle me, her only living relative, publicly. This is why I'm counting the days until I can escape to college.

Luckily, my mother falls asleep as we drive through Athens. Thankful for the silent passenger in the backseat, I don't dare whisper to wake her. I grasp Adrian's hand in mine, giving her a tight squeeze of thanks.

Hamilton's red truck sits in the driveway when Adrian places the car in park. Troy and Latham pull up behind us in my mother's car. The guys gather outside the backseat door and plan. Adrian and I hold the doors open while the men carry my still sleeping mother into the house. I cringe as they near her bedroom.

My friends attempt to control their reactions to their surroundings. I've allowed Adrian inside our house once many years ago. Hamilton entered a time or two, also long ago. Mother's bedroom is decorated in recycled chic; empty vodka and whiskey bottles adorn every surface and the floor. I cringe at the large wastebasket full of bottles near the door. We must tread carefully during our exit to refrain from kicking a bottle. The last thing we want is to wake her.

Back outside, I assure everyone my mother will sleep all day. I encourage them to leave, promising I'll come to dinner and the movies with them tonight. Hamilton clearly wishes to remain with me, but Troy, Latham, and Adrian need him to give them a lift to town. They say their goodbyes while making me promise to call if I need them or want to talk.

I'm sure they discuss my situation on the fifteen-minute drive to Athens. My mother wasn't always like this. We were the perfect family while my dad was alive. We camped, cooked, and were in public together. I was close to both parents. It's hard to see my mother now and remember how normal she was years ago.

I believe my mother's heart broke with my father's death. I think she drinks to forget the love she lost and believes she'll never find again. She's the only family I've got and she doesn't make it easy to be around her.

15

Everyone knows everything about everyone—this is another of the 4,724 reasons I want to escape Athens.

Late in the afternoon, I quickly grab my vibrating phone. I am walking on eggshells trying not to wake my mother.

BETHANY

ready for dinner & movie?

ME

yes

BETHANY

good

I'm in your driveway

What? She's here? Why would she drive all the way out to my house? I grab my cash and quietly slip from the house.

Bethany waves through her open car window. She wears her usual smile, but I know she is up to something.

"I'm driving. Hop in."

I slide into her passenger seat and buckle my safety belt.

After she pulls from my driveway, she dives right in. "I don't like to talk about friends when they aren't present. I need to let you know Adrian and Hamilton shared with Troy their memories of your family story before and after your dad's death. Of course, Troy then mentioned it to me and I had an epiphany." Bethany's eyes remain on the road.

I open my mouth to stop her.

"Just hear me out," she continues. "You don't go on many dates. You try to plan group outings instead of alone time with interested guys. You never go out with a guy more than a couple of times. I think you are avoiding the possibility of finding love."

I'm sure my eyes bug out. Is she really going to force a therapy session upon me for the fifteen minutes she has me held captive in her moving car?

"Whether you are aware of it or not, you are afraid. You are trying to prevent the heartache your mother endures."

"You're hurting yourself. Madison, you need to allow yourself the possibility to find love. You can't let your fear of heartache prevent you from experiencing the magic. It breaks my heart."

I argue. "There's no one for me in Athens. I'm waiting for college."

Bethany doesn't believe my lame excuse. "I don't want you to live your entire life never feeling what I have with Troy. You're a terrific friend. You're so caring and genuine. You need to open yourself up to the possibility and let a guy in. Trust me, the joy of love far outweighs the difficult times when you break up with a guy."

I can only smile at Bethany. Her words hit their mark. She's given me much to think about.

16

There are only three movies to choose from with only two showtimes. Reason number 4,724 that I want to escape Athens.

A week later, my day starts as any other summer day. I wake, removing my eye mask at about nine. As I tiptoe down the hallway, I peek into her room to find my mother and a couple of empty bottles sprawled on her bed. I hurry to get myself around and leave before she might stir and force me to have to interact with her.

Yesterday, I felt an anxious pit building in my stomach. I thought the big event might happen; of course, Hamilton denies he stands any chance of being drafted at all. Yesterday came and went without a word. I know in my heart it will be today; he deserves to be drafted before the final day.

I climb into the driver's seat at 10:30 a.m. I shoot a quick text to Hamilton's mother prior to starting my car.

ME

I hope you are ready for this

today will be the day!

MEMPHIS

I love your faith sweetheart

but it might not happen at all

ME

I'm headed to your house now

it will be today

trust me

My engine grinds to life, and I pull from my driveway. It is a quick drive to Hamilton's family farm. I am proud of the fact I stayed away yesterday, although every part of me wanted to be present when he got a call. I can't stay away anymore. I've been crabby and jumpy since the start of the draft. Today, I can't sit still. I need to be with Hamilton, so I might calm down.

I wave to Hamilton who's working on the tractor near the barn as I walk into his house. Memphis is busy cutting homemade noodles on the kitchen table when I enter.

"Good morning," I sing as I squeeze her from the side quickly and pour myself a glass of iced tea. "Who are all those noodles for?"

She makes quick work of cutting row after row of noodles as flour dusts the air. "Tonight's the Bible study potluck. You know how they love my beef and noodles," she brags, shrugging her shoulders.

"Potluck means everyone brings food. Won't that be way too much?"

"Four of us signed up for the main dish. Everyone else brings salads, sides, or desserts." She wipes her flour-covered hands on her navy apron, leaving white powder everywhere. "There are eighteen of us plus spouses and kids."

"Wow, that will be a large group then." I now understand the need for several batches of noodles. It amazes me she insists on making them from scratch instead of buying them at the store. But, having enjoyed her beef and noodles in the past, I know they taste divine the way she makes them. They are full of love from this magnificent woman.

"Ham is at the barn, tinkering around." Memphis moves from the noodles to the broth simmering in two large roasters on the counter. As she stirs, I notice the beef is already in the broth.

"I waved at him. Anything I can do to help you?" I know I am not a great cook, but with her watching over me, I can't ruin anything.

"You can scoop up handfuls of noodles, and I'll stir as you drop them in." She smiles gratefully. I quickly wash my hands at the sink before I assist moving noodles from the table to the roaster at her prompting.

I love helping Memphis in the kitchen. It reminds me of helping my mom bake before dad arrived home from work each night. In those days, I loved spending time with my mother. She would turn on the radio, and we would sing or dance around the kitchen. Dad liked to make a big production when eating the meals he knew I assisted with.

"Look at you," Memphis' words draw me from my happy memories. "You've got flour in your hair, on your nose, and all the way up to your elbows." We laugh at my mess. I have no idea how it happened.

"What's going on in here?" Hamilton's deep voice booms from the back-door. When he enters the kitchen, a smile glides upon his face. It reaches up to the crinkles at the corners of his twinkling brown eyes. "Are we having a flour fight?" he asks, preparing to grab a glob from the table.

"No," his mother warns in that tone that means she is serious. "Madison is just a messy chef." I'm not insulted by her explanation. I know Memphis means it as a compliment.

"I've got the tractor up and runnin' again." Hamilton takes a long drink of my iced tea. "I need to load a few bales of hay and drop 'em off at the Ag building. I promised him I'd be there before lunch. I'm runnin' late. Need anything from town while I am out?" He looks from me to his mother.

"Memphis, why don't we ride along with him and keep him company?" I suggest. I'm not sure how long his trip to town might take, and I want Memphis present when this important phone call comes today.

Memphis smiles a knowing smile at me. I might be fooling Hamilton today since he is in denial, but nothing gets by her. "Let's stop somewhere for lunch before we head back."

Hamilton excuses himself to clean up. Memphis hands me a wet dishcloth to do the same. She pats the flour from my hair while I take care of my nose and arms.

17

The radio station airs local high school sporting events and live radar reports during storms, interrupting music for hours. This is one of the 4,724 reasons I want to leave this town.

I quickly glance at my phone and note it is nearly two o'clock as we finish up our meal. In my mind, I know it is day two of the draft. It started at noon today, our time with round three. My nerves kick into high gear as I realize his call might come at any moment.

"Can I drive us back?" I ask Hamilton as I follow him to the driver's door.

He tilts his head to the side and furrows his brow. "Why?"

"My stomach feels a little off from eating lunch so late. I don't want to get carsick," I lie. It's a half-truth. My stomach is in all kinds of knots but not for the reason I gave him. I climb behind the wheel as Hamilton climbs in the passenger side after his mother.

Memphis grins at Hamilton "If you don't have plans this evening you should bring Madison to the potluck dinner."

Being the nice boy, he is, Hamilton promises his mother. "I'll think about it." He throws a smile my way.

When Hamilton's cell phone ringtone blares in the cab, I squeal while attempting to keep the large truck on the road. This is it—I know it. Goosebumps appear over my entire body as the hairs on the back of my neck stand on end. I slow a bit, turn on my blinker and take the next gravel road off the main highway, while Hamilton answers the unknown number.

He looks to me, questioning my actions as he responds to the caller. "Yes, this is Hamilton Armstrong."

I keep the truck running and air conditioner on low but turn off the stereo. My mouth is as dry as a desert. My stomach is full of massive butterflies. I am so excited for my best friend.

"Yes, sir," Hamilton says into his cell. "I'm honored, sir. Might I have a minute to speak with my mother?" He places his phone on mute holding it out from his body.

"Hamilton, what's wrong?" Memphis places her hand on his tanned forearm.

He motions for us to exit the truck. When the three of us stand in front of his truck, he speaks. "Nothing is wrong, Mom." He pauses to look at me then back to Memphis. "It's a member of the Chicago Cubs. Seems they just picked me in the draft today."

Tears and audible sobs escape from a smiling Memphis. Hamilton wraps his long, masculine arms around her. He looks my way while cuddling her. "Get over here, you." I join in this family hug. "What should I tell them?" he teases.

I swat his chest at the same time as Memphis. "You tell them yes," she states, wiping away her tears and fanning her face.

Hamilton takes his phone off mute and continues to talk with the representative. He doesn't speak much, just replies "yes" every now and then.

I pull up a contact on my phone and show it to Hamilton while he listens on his phone.

"Yes, sir, I have his information right here." He rattles off the name of his agent and the digits in his number from my phone screen.

This causes me to beam even more. I insisted he find an agent for when he was drafted. Hamilton stated that would be a few years away. So, I found him an agent that agreed to step in immediately should he be drafted this year.

When I close the contact information, I wish I had a better phone so I could open the draft information on the internet.

I quietly ask Memphis if I might borrow her smartphone. Standing next to her with her arm squeezing me, I pull up Draft Tracker. I enlarge it a bit then share it with her. Hamilton was the first pick in the eighth round. Officially, he was pick number two-hundred twenty-five in the draft, selected by the Chicago Cubs as a left-handed pitcher from Athens High School in Athens, Missouri."

Pride swells in my chest. My cheeks begin to ache from smiling so big.

Memphis asks me how I knew. How did I know to encourage him to enter this draft and not wait three years? How did I know today would be the day? And how did I know to drive so he could take the call on our way home?

I shrug before answering. "He's very talented. I've known this for years. I listened in the stands as the college scouts looked at him last summer. That's why I pushed him to enter the draft. He's a left-handed pitcher that throws in the high ninety-two to ninety-five miles per hour range, can play outfield, and can hit. He's a unicorn. He's just what the National League dreams of. Because we are from a small town in Missouri, and he's considered a high school senior in the draft, I figured he'd go somewhere between the fifth and tenth rounds. His stats are enough to make them drool, even if no one in an organization has seen him in action."

I smile proudly. Finally, others see the talent I've marveled at for years.

"It started at noon today, so I figured they were in round five or later by now. I had faith in his talent and faith that a team would see what I see in him." It's hard to explain. It was a feeling based on years of stats, watching him play, watching Major League Baseball on television, and listening to the scouts at his games. He throws very hard for a lefty, and he is only eighteen. With knowledgeable coaching and trainers, he might hit one-hundred miles per hour. I just knew he couldn't be ignored.

Memphis wraps me in a tight hug. "His dream and his father's dream just came true." She kisses my forehead. "He'll leave soon; are we ready for this?" she whispers.

"We've got each other," I remind her. "We will get through this together." Until this moment, the gravity of the situation hadn't fully hit me. Hamilton's plans may change. Our plans may change.

"They are calling my agent right now. We need to hurry home, so I am ready when he calls me. So, let's head that way while I share what I know so far."

I pull back onto the highway as Hamilton shares he has been drafted by the Chicago Cubs Organization. They will now contact his agent to negotiate the terms before they can share the details of when and where this will take him.

That's it. Until he hears from the agent, that's all he knows. Memphis talks excitedly about how proud she is, how proud his father would be, and how much his life might change because he was drafted. I focus only on the road. I can't freak out about a change in our plans until I know for sure.

Hamilton's phone rings the minute we enter the house. He answers while pulling out a kitchen chair. I pour three tall glasses of tea before joining the two of them at the table.

"I'm putting you on speaker phone," Hamilton announces then presses a button on his iPhone screen. "I'm here with my mother, Memphis, and my best friend, Madison."

"Hello. My name is Nelson Sheridan. Madison, I believe we spoke on the phone previously." His deep voice is pleasant yet professional.

"Yes, it's a pleasure to speak to you again," I reply as I busy myself opening a nearby notepad and grabbing a pen to take notes for Hamilton.

"I've spoken with the general manager of The Chicago Cubs. I believe we have negotiated terms you will be pleased with, Hamilton." Nelson pauses before continuing. "They are offering a signing bonus of $175,000. This figure is on the high end of those available in the eighth round of the draft this year. The terms of the contract are for you to report to triple-A ball for the remainder of the season in Des Moines, Iowa."

I continue jotting notes as he lists the amount Hamilton will earn for the rest of this year and in subsequent years in the AAA league. I list the figures if he drops to AA or A teams as my head spins. The signing bonus alone has me feeling nauseous. As a future teacher, it is much more than I will make in many years of teaching.

"The terms of the contract lay out contingencies if you are called up to the Majors, but I got them to agree to insert a clause for us to renegotiate prior to that occurring." Nelson sounds proud of this fact. "Our hopes are for you to move up this season or the next. I want to renegotiate after they personally see what a value you will be for their club. I'm confident we will agree on a much larger figure when this occurs, thus the reason for the clause."

Hamilton thanks Nelson for taking care of that.

"Is there anything you want to see in the contract before we verbally agree upon it? Anything you want changed?"

Hamilton finishes a sip of iced tea. "I would like to see the contract state that the club will furnish an apartment or condo for me while I am in the AAA and Major Leagues. Should I drop lower, it will be my responsibility. This will take the burden of searching on my own off my plate, so I may focus solely on the game. I'd also like them to pay for a bachelor's degree either online or in the off-season. Are these possibilities?"

Nelson responds these are very good stipulations and we should further add they supply accommodations in the spring-training city for the off-season also. The two discuss further and end the call with a promise that Nelson will call back after he discusses this with the Cubs.

The three of us sit a moment in silence, staring at each other and sipping our tea.

Memphis is the first to break the silence. "In my wildest dreams, I had no idea the figures were so large."

"What have I been saying forever?" I break in. "Hamilton is a rare unicorn in the MLB. He's a hard throwing lefty that can hit and play the field. He is versatile. He deserves big figures. He will earn even bigger ones."

Hamilton smiles while shaking his head at me. "My number one fan. You've had this figured out for years, haven't you?"

Agreeing, Memphis shares. "I must admit, your texts this morning made me a little nervous, but I still denied it would happen."

Hamilton's brows pinch at Memphis' words. "What text this morning?" He turns to face me.

I explain the texts I sent his mother before I drove over here today. Hamilton's face goes blank.

"You knew it would happen today? You texted my mom that today was the day? That's why you came over, isn't it?" I see the disbelief as he works it all out in his mind. "That's the real reason you wanted to drive my truck home?" He smirks.

I nod. "It was a hunch, a gut feeling. I've believed it for so long, I just knew it would happen."

Hamilton shakes his head, unable to believe I saw this coming. He's still in denial of the magnitude of his abilities. If he ever grasps the enormity of it all, I will pity anyone at the plate to face him.

His cell phone rings. "I've got you on speaker again." Hamilton greets.

"Hello everyone," Nelson greets. "They agreed to all of our terms. Congratulations, Hamilton, you have a verbal agreement with the Chicago Cubs."

We cheer loudly on our end as Nelson can be heard laughing on the other end of the phone. When our celebration tapers off, Nelson continues. "Someone from the Cubs organization will contact you later today with arrangements for your arrival in Des Moines in two days. Until then, celebrate. You deserve it. And Hamilton, remember to call me if you have any questions anytime day or night."

While Memphis and Hamilton celebrate, I contemplate the fact he will leave us in two days. Hamilton and I are not going to college together this fall. He will leave in two days, and I will finish the summer without him. I end my train of thought right there. Today, I celebrate with my friend and his mom. Tonight, I can allow myself to mourn the plans we shared.

18

The young cops party with high school kids while off-duty on the weekends, another one of the 4,724 reasons I want to escape this town.

ME

I'm bored

are you coming to town?

HAMILTON

about ready to leave

meet you in 20

ME

C Ya Soon

I exit my car to sit on the hood. I watch my fellow teenagers of this small burg cruise the strip. August can't arrive soon enough. The only entertainment for the under-twenty-one crowd is Winston's three-plex Theater, to cruise the strip for hours, or to party in remote locations. I choose to busy myself on my cell phone instead of wave at the cruisers.

It's already 8:30 p.m. Hamilton leaves at noon tomorrow for Des Moines. We planned to attend college together for the next four years; instead, I now have hours before I lose my friend. I'm proud of him, excited he received this opportunity, but I am not ready for hundreds of miles to separate us. Our plan has always been to escape this town together before he played professional baseball. Now we will be leaving Athens in two different directions.

Adrian backs her old truck next to me, lays down the tailgate, and invites me over to sit with her.

"Town's dead tonight," I state.

Adrian offers me a sip of her cup from the local gas station. I shake my head. I don't consume alcohol if I will be driving. "There's a huge party under the bridge tonight. Rumor has it they have two kegs." She grins.

I'm not privy to the party invites. It's not that I am not welcome; it's that I have an alcoholic mother and tend not to drink at such parties. I usually tag along with my friends, attempt to keep everyone safe, and chauffeur several home later. I have fun mingling and watching everyone.

"Want to ride out with us?" Adrian offers, still sipping on her vodka-laced fountain drink.

"Hamilton's on his way in. I'll ride with him." I plan to be stuck to him like glue until noon tomorrow. I have plans for our last night together.

"Speak of the devil…" Adrian laughs as Hamilton pulls his large red truck into the lot.

Finally! It felt like he might never get here! I've thought of nothing all day but my time tonight with Hamilton. He joins us on the tailgate.

"Your last night in Athens," Adrian greets. "I figured you would be out with the guys."

"We hung out last night and today." Hamilton looks to me. "I promised to spend tonight with Madison." Wearing a smirk, I see sparks in his eyes. I guess being drafted by the Chicago Cubs can do that to an eighteen-year-old.

It's a normal sandbar party by the river bridge. A large bonfire blazes near the center of the sand. There are several trucks backed in, circling the fire. As we approach, Hamilton is greeted with fist-bumps, high-fives, and words of congratulations. Most offer him beer and shots, but he doesn't partake. He is polite to everyone, and I follow slowly behind him.

I break away when I spot Adrian, Bethany, Salem, and Savannah on the tailgate of Troy's truck. Adrian hands me a water bottle from her cooler after I hop onto the tailgate beside her.

"He looks like a politician," Salem states, nodding towards Hamilton in the crowd two trucks away.

"Yeah," I agree. "Everyone wants a moment with him before he leaves." A heavy weight settles in my chest. I'm not in the mood for this large crowd. I'd prefer my last evening with Hamilton to be just the nine of us somewhere we could chat and hear each other easily. "Where are the guys?" Savannah points them out on the other side of the bonfire.

A round of cheers erupts as country music begins to blare through large speakers in the bed of nearby truck, making it harder to hear each other. Hamilton finally arrives our tailgate. Adrian attempts to pass him a beer—he grabs a water bottle instead. I don't draw attention to it but wonder why he isn't drinking tonight. He always enjoys a couple of beers at parties.

Troy, Winston, and Latham return to our group. Ever the hostess, Adrian passes out cups of beer from the keg. Bethany pulls Troy between her legs and tugs his lips toward hers. Salem points to her lips, and Latham obediently kisses her, too.

"I'm going for a walk," I inform the group. "Hamilton, will you join me?"

We slip between the trucks to avoid the large crowd around the fire. As we walk away, the light of the fire grows faint, and the music fades. In the moonlight, we easily stroll near the water's edge.

"I'm going to miss this," Hamilton confesses, tossing sticks into the river.

Far enough we can no longer see the fire, I take a seat on a large log. I remove my flip-flops and dig my toes into the cool sand. Hamilton sits beside me. I need to confess the true reason I suggested a walk.

"I want you to promise me something," Hamilton states, eyes locked on mine. "I want you to put down the books and go out in Columbia. I want you to remember to have fun and enjoy the college experience. I'll never forgive myself if my being drafted ruins college for you." He places his hands on my shoulders, his arms fully extended, eyes still peering deep into mine. "Promise me you will make friends, go to games, leave the dorm and live. Yeah?"

I nod, knowing his fear is warranted. I planned to hang with him, and now he won't be attending MU. I've already vowed to take heavy class loads, buckle down, and graduate as fast as possible.

"Mady." He tugs my chin back up so our eyes meet. "I need you to promise me. I need to hear your voice."

He knows me too well. If I speak the words, I will keep my promise. "I promise I will attempt to make friends and attend a game or two." Even now, fear fills my stomach at the thought of putting myself out there with strangers. My words appease him; he smiles at me.

Now it's my turn to ask something of Hamilton. I don't want a promise—I want a favor. "I planned to ask a favor of you in August but need to ask you tonight instead." I wring my hands in my lap, struggling, to find the words. I thought I would have another two months before I needed to know the perfect words to urge him to assist me. I decide to just go for it. "Um, I want you to take my virginity." I witness the shock on his face. I'm a little relieved I don't see disgust and revulsion. This will be a true test of our friendship.

Hamilton leaps from the log. His eyes look anywhere but at me as he kicks at sand with the toe of his boot.

"I don't want some stupid college guy at a frat party to be the one." This is awkward. I growl in frustration. "You wouldn't want that for me, would you?"

I pause for a moment hoping for his agreement. He runs his hands through his hair then replaces his hat. He looks toward me as his lips part, then he quickly looks away. It's clear he's struggling for a reply.

"I want it to mean something. I don't want to be ashamed of it. I need it to be you."

Hamilton rubs his hands over his face, before pacing from one end of the log to the other. He clasps his hands together behind his neck, growling he looks up to the stars.

"How can you ask this of me? Seriously? Darn it, I mean, Madison, you are my best friend. If I granted your request," His eyes lock on mine. "We wouldn't be best friends anymore. I can't lose you." His hands on my jaws, his bold,/ brown eyes bore into mine. "I *WON'T* lose you. Although our plans have changed, I will still need you. We'll just use our phones more. Please don't ask this of me. I can't refuse you—I don't want to lose you."

"Just hear me out," I plead. "I'm not asking you to fall in love with me, I am just asking you to share a very important moment with me. It will mean more with you than some random guy I haven't met yet. I just can't go to college a virgin. I will be far from all of my friends, far from you. I won't have someone close to talk to. I didn't plan to be a virgin at eighteen. Hell, I haven't gone past over the shirt second base. I can't go to college like this. I worry that I might never…"

"You'll make new friends. You'll meet nice guys, guys worthy of you." Hamilton kneels in front of me, taking my hands in his. "You'll want to share this with one of them. It won't be some random guy at a frat party. I know you; frat parties won't be a common event for you."

"Please," I beg. "I want it to be you." I place my hand upon his cheek. His stubble prickles my palm. "Do this for me, please."

"It's time to go." Hamilton roughly pulls me up from the log and escorts me back toward the bonfire.

We say our goodbyes. Adrian raises a brow my way. I shake my head and she mouths "okay". Silently, following him, I return to Hamilton's truck. Without a word, we head down a dirt road, then a gravel road, before the blacktop, and then the highway. The silence allows my mind to worry. Did we leave because he plans to honor my wish? Did we leave because he is tired and has a long drive tomorrow? Or did we leave because he is angry with me?

"Madison…"

"Hamilton…" We speak at the same time causing us to chuckle.

He changes the radio from the local country station to a rock station for me. *Mötley Crüe* fills the cab. I refrain from speaking as he returns me to my car in the grocery lot.

I timidly wave goodbye as he pulls away. It's not like him to leave prior to ensuring my old car starts for me. As my car sputters to life, I kick myself for not speaking up during the drive. I need to know if he's mad at me. I need to know I didn't just ruin the best thing in my life. I need to know if I just lost my best friend for asking a favor of him. I pound my palms against my steering wheel in frustration.

19

If you attempt to purchase condoms, you went to school with the checker, are related to the checker, or they are friends of your parents. It's just one of the 4,724 reasons I want to leave Athens.

My thoughts consuming all of my attention, I don't remember the drive home. I really need to be more careful. As I pull myself from my car, I barely notice my mother's car is not in the driveway. Instead of cursing her as I begin to worry, I trudge up the sidewalk, in the unlocked front door, and down to my room. Huffing, I dramatically throw myself onto my bed. I stare at my ceiling for a couple of minutes.

I can't be here. It feels like the walls close in and the ceiling drops to crush me. I snag a bottle of water from the refrigerator, a quilt from the back of the sofa, and escape the house with all of its formerly happy memories now erased by my mother's addiction. As my feet follow the path I've taken hundreds of times, I allow myself to breath in the humid night air. Although it cooled twenty degrees from today's high, it's still nearly 80 degrees. I love summer nights. The bullfrogs croak loudly in the nearby pond. Crickets sing from the grass below my feet. Lightning bugs twinkle like the millions of stars in the midnight blue sky. On the way to my favorite spot, my mood lightens fractionally.

I scale the chain-link fence to enjoy my safe-haven. I spread my quilt near the base of the large oak tree in the center of the cemetery. I lay on my blanket, my eyes taking in the stars visible just outside the canopy of my tree, desperately wishing I wasn't alone in this moment. Only one person knows of my special spot and considering the excruciatingly quiet ride from the river to my car, I doubt he'll venture here tonight.

I believe everything happens for a reason. I feel if something is meant to be, opportunities will continue to present themselves until it occurs. People enter and exit our lives not by chance but by fate. It was fate that caused me to bump into Hamilton in the hallway in middle school. Fate threw us into several classes together. Then, fate sealed our friendship by revealing we share the same special spot at the cemetery where we found we lived on farms on opposite sides of it.

I try to convince myself that I am glad Hamilton will not be sharing this space with me tonight. I realize I need time to figure out how to undo the damage that I caused by asking a favor of my best friend. I only have eleven hours to undo the mess I made. Lying alone under my tree, surrounded by the headstones, is all I need while I search for remedies. I text Adrian. When she doesn't reply, I assume she's still at the party. I resign myself to the fact that I am alone in finding my solution to my request of Hamilton.

Saying goodbye to him tomorrow scares me in ways I never thought it would. He was to be my nearest and dearest until we were real adults with real jobs out in the real world. He entered my life for a reason. I would not have survived losing my dad and my mother's subsequent downward spiral without him by my side. I've leaned on him so much that the thought of my upcoming life changes without him causes panic.

Focus. How can I fix this? How can I fix us? I can't claim I consumed alcohol, and it was the alcohol talking. I can't play it off as a joke gone wrong since I didn't try to laugh it off in his presence. I could claim it was a dare, Adrian dared me to approach him on his last night in Athens. I'm not convinced he'd buy that. Think. Think. Think!

I sit up to sip from my water bottle, tilting my head to the side. I hear it, my favorite sound in the world, the only thing missing from this beautiful summer's night graces my ears. *Whip-poor-will, Whip-poor-will.* Usually only heard at dusk, I am thrilled this bird chose the middle of the night to sing. *Whip-poor-will, Whip-poor-will.* It's music to my ears. I lay back on my elbows, enjoying the entire setting. The warmth, the humidity, the sounds, the smells, the location, I allow it all to caress my soul.

Crack. Snap. I dart up at the sounds of something approaching. I turn my head, trying to decipher the direction of its approach. I'm somewhat safe within the chain-link fence. Fear prickles the hair on the back of my neck as I realize it is not an animal approaching.

Fuck a duck! It's Hamilton. As much as I want to undo the mess I created, I hoped I had a bit more time to come up with a strategy. As he approaches the fence to enter our safe place, I scramble to find words to greet him.

"Hey," he greets, placing his blanket next to mine.

"Hey."

Several long, quiet moments pass as we lie staring at the night sky.

"I'm gonna miss this." Hamilton's words are a punch to my gut. I pull my eyes from the heavens as I hear the rustling of Hamilton turning on his side to face me. "I'm gonna miss you."

"In a year, you'll be wearing a suit, riding in a car service, jetting all over the states and around the world." I turn on my side to face him. "You'll be so citified, you'll laugh at your redneck youth, your redneck friends, and the country life you once led. You'll enjoy blonde arm-candy everywhere you go. You'll be well on your way to a million-dollar house with a million-dollar family." *And you'll forget all about me,* I think to myself. My words leave an acrid taste in my mouth.

Hamilton's laughter pierces the night. I love his laugh. It's a full belly laugh. I'm gonna miss it.

"I may live in the big city. I may travel by jet, but I will never be citified." In the moonlight, I see traces of his smile. "I will always drive a truck. I will never enjoy arm-candy; if I make millions I will invest for my future rather than spend it quickly, and I will never go a week without speaking to you." He presses the tip of my nose with his index finger.

I want to believe him, but I know friends drift apart after high school. Long distances between us will probably cause us to lose touch. His busy ball season and my course load will tug us in different directions.

"When my father died, and things were tough on the farm," his words and eyes hold me captive, "you refused to let me quit baseball to help Mom with the work. You're my number one fan." He chuckles. "You're the one that pushed me to put my name into the draft. I am who I am because of you. No matter what changes come in the upcoming year, I will not let you slip away."

I want to believe him. I want to keep him in my life forever. I need his friendship even at a distance.

"Come here," he prompts, pulling me tight to his chest.

With my face pressed to him, my nostrils fill with his masculine scent. Taking a deep inhale, I save it to memory.

"Did you just sniff me?" He laughs.

"Maybe."

I feel his laughter vibrate through his chest. I extricate myself from his hug, placing several inches between us. I need to see his face. I want to see his dark brown eyes.

Hamilton sighs. "I was serious about the promise you made me tonight."

Oh crap! Are we going to discuss his promise and my favor now? Fuck a duck! "I promised. I will make an effort and even send you proof."

"I don't need proof," he states. "You promised; that's all I need. I might remind you every now and then, but proof isn't necessary. Your word is all I need." He places his right hand on my forearm. "I need to ask something else from you. Tomorrow, at my house, with my mom, I need you to promise not to cry."

Judging by his reaction, I know my eyes bug out.

"My mom is really struggling with my leaving so soon. She's going to be a mess. I need you to be the strong one. I need you to help me. I'm going to attempt to make a quick exit. I think the longer I draw it out, the harder it will be for her."

I nod as words are caught behind the tears burning the back of my eyes and throat. I can do this for him. I can keep it together until the dust from his truck billows on the lane. I cannot promise to hold them off after that. I roll to my back, needing our surroundings to calm me. Hamilton mimics my movements.

"Hear my whippoorwill?" I ask, moving on to lighter topics. "You won't hear those in Des Moines or Chicago."

"I hear your annoying little friend," he teases. "He's probably warning you it's too late to be out and to go home."

"I can't go home." I confess what he already knows to be true.

"Not any better, huh?"

"She's staying out later and later," I admit. "She's out much later than the bars stay open. I don't want to even think of what that means."

"It's harsh, but you can't help her if she refuses the help." Hamilton's words ring true but do nothing to dissuade my guilt. "I can't help but think your life will start when you leave that house. You'll be free of her tirades and binges, no longer spending every minute at home worrying for her safety."

"True," I agree. "I worry that without me around, she'll hurt herself or others while under the influence. I'd like to think knowing I'm at home, a tiny part of her brain worries about me. With me gone, she will have nothing to guilt her into sober moments."

I don't know how long he's been doing it, but I notice Hamilton's fingers playing with my loose tendrils. We've shared emotional discussions in the past. This touch, his actions, seem much more intimate.

Turning my head towards him and into his hand, I look up through my lashes to find him gazing at me. He doesn't withdraw his hand. Instead, it cups my jaw while his thumb caresses my cheek.

"Are you nervous?" I ask, trying to make the moment less awkward.

"I'm excited, not so much nervous," Hamilton admits. "They've scouted me for more than a year. They have faith in me, so I just need to keep doing what I'm doing and see where it leads." He shrugs his shoulders.

His thumb pauses at the corner of my mouth. All the air evaporates around us. I can't breathe. I can't think. This touch is more intimate. My eyes are locked on his and my mind is focused on his thumb on my lips. I can't blink. I can't move. I should react, but I have no idea what to do.

"Breathe,'., Madison," his deep voice murmurs.

I gulp in air like a fish out of water, still frozen in place. He gently brushes the pad of his thumb over my lower lip from one corner to the other. A gasp escapes. It's the clue he waited for. His lips collide with mine. In his kiss, I feel his need, his hunger. His plump lower lip is heavy and hot on mine.

When he pulls away, I'm left needing more, wanting more, desiring more. My eyes lock on his. His pupils dilate while watching my tongue slowly moisten my lip from one side to the other. Breath catches in my throat. His eyes on mine, he slowly brings his mouth to mine, pausing at the last moment to ensure my consent. I lean towards him.

His firm lips press to mine. His familiar scent surrounds me. My hands move from his upper arms into his hair. I clutch at his curly strands while removing his cap. His hot tongue lingers upon my lower lip, seeking entrance. My lips part, allowing the joining of our mouths. It's unlike anything I've ever imagined.

It's as if my body knows what to do although I have no experience in a situation like this. My hormones control my brain—pleasure is all I care about. As Hamilton's hand on the back of my neck secures my mouth to his, my hands abandon his hair, feather down his neck, and begin their descent over his hard chest. I fist my hands in his T-shirt at his abdomen. My need to hold on to him is fierce.

He pulls his mouth from mine. I groan its loss. Tenderly, he licks and nips along my jaw, past my ear, to my neck. I tilt my head away, opening up to him. Moans escape as I revel in the pleasure he bestows upon me.

Hamilton's hands slowly raise the hem of my shirt. His fingers graze over my skin ever so lightly. My already pebbled nipples turn rock hard with his touch. Desire overwhelms me. My body wiggles and writhes with need. I feel a strong need to squeeze my thighs together.

His thumbs caress the skin just below my breasts. He traces the line where my bra and ribs meet. Unable to wait any longer, I tug my shirt over my head in one swift movement. Hamilton traps my wrists above my head, his strong hands holding me in place. My breasts arch into his hard chest as I bite my lower lip.

"Impatient much?" he smirks. "I need you to trust me. We are in no rush tonight."

I nod because I trust him wholeheartedly. My trust in him is the reason I asked this favor of him. Only I didn't know I'd react to his every touch and kiss. I'd thought it would be awkward and quick. I've turned to putty in his hands, and I've wilted to a puddle of need. My body aches for him. After tonight, I am sure I will be forever ruined.

Hamilton peppers kisses on my brow, my nose, my cheeks, and down my neck to my breastbone. His fingers deftly unhook my bra. As I slip it off my arms, he pinches, before his hot tongue laves each breast gently to soothe. He suckles one nipple as his hands clutch my ribs then slide to my waist. I'm equal parts nervous and anxious for our union. I tug his T-shirt up, but he denies my attempt.

"Patience," he croons. "Trust me to take care of you."

I replace my hands upon his chest. I attempt to restrain myself and allow him to lead. With hands on my shoulders, he playfully pushes me backwards. While I lie bare from my waist up, Hamilton's eyes slowly appraise me. I desperately try not to cover myself. As he continues to stare, my feverish skin begs for his contact.

I slowly extend one arm toward his, hoping to encourage his hands upon me once more. He playfully swats my hand away then rewards me by raising two hands behind his head to tug his shirt off in that way guys like to do. I want to see everything. I internally curse the leaves of my favorite tree for blocking so much moonlight. In this lighting with his back to the moon, each contour of his muscles creates a dark shadow. My fingers flex, wanting to explore. I feel a strong need to rub my thighs together as dampness pooling there contrasts the heat at my center. Hamilton's powerful thighs have mine pinned between his knees, planted on either side of my hips.

He bends at the waist. His warm breath caresses my abdomen before he places kisses at my navel then from hip to hip. As amazing as the sensations are, they fail to distract me from his fingers unbuttoning then unzipping my shorts. I tamp down my panic as the reality of our actions sets in. I want *this*, I remind myself as I steady my racing thoughts.

While pulling my shorts down my thighs, he peppers kisses along my panties at my hips. When I whimper, I feel a smile on his hot lips, then his wet tongue darts out and slips beneath the fabric.

A tsunami of heat flows to my core, my breath hitches, and Hamilton chuckles, proud of himself.

"You are very responsive."

Crap! What does that mean? Am I doing this wrong?

Knowing me better than anyone else, Hamilton assures me it's a good thing when he tosses my shorts into the grass. He positions his long body beside mine. His fingertips trace my panties at my thigh as his lips cover mine.

He prevents my turning into him. Pulling his lips from mine, he moves into the plank position over me. On his elbows, he looks into my eyes. My cheeks heat as his gaze seems to penetrate my soul. I lie nearly naked below him, my every cell acutely aware of his touch. A slow smile slides upon my face as I feel his erection through his jeans pressed into my thigh.

"You like that?" I can't play naïve when he grinds his pelvis even closer.

I bite my lower lip. His pupils swell, and suddenly, the warm night air feels electric. In a moment of boldness, I lift my hips, causing friction at the apex of my thighs. My back arches and eyes close as Hamilton sucks, nips, and licks down my breast bone and abdomen and blows hot breath on my panties. His thumbs hook at my hips then achingly slowly slip the silk down my thighs before tossing them over his shoulder. I open my eyes in anticipation. A sly grin graces his face. His eyes move to the area I need him the most.

His hand rests upon my mound then presses up slightly. His eyes lock on mine. He purses his lips, blowing warm air on my sex. Unable to control my reaction, I writhe beneath him. Eyes still looking at mine he darts his tongue out. I mewl, as he licks slowly. My wetness burns hotter still.

I'm unable to keep my eyes open, my lips part, and my breath quickens. My body hums, no longer in my control. I feel every beat of my racing heart pumping through every vein. Every muscle flexes, and my abdomen tightens.

Hamilton alternates between licking then gently sucking. My core coils tighter and tighter. He introduces one long finger then a second. When he curls his fingers against my inner wall while he continues to suckle, I shatter into a million glorious pieces. I pulse from head to toe. Hamilton slows his movements as I ride my very first orgasm.

"Breathe," his gruff voice urges.

I pant as I slowly come back down. I lazily stretch my arms above my head. Never has a stretch felt so good. Gaining control of my senses once again, I feel Hamilton's low chuckle against my arm.

I raise one eyebrow in question, causing his chuckles to continue.

"Very, very responsive."

I hide my face in his chest, suddenly embarrassed. He kisses the top of my head before pulling me back. With his dark eyes on mine, he smiles. "How was that?"

As if he doesn't know. He's very aware he pushed my every button. He played me like I was a rookie at the plate and he deftly painted the corners with his curveballs before striking me out looking at his fastball. The man has skills.

"You are very aware of just how good that was." I'm not very well versed on sex. I hope my orgasm proved my enjoyment.

With a sexy smirk upon his lips, he informs me he loves how I react to him. He takes pride in his success.

Although my orgasm was more than I ever dreamed it would be, my body craves even more from him. I trace my fingers down his abdomen to his jeans. I nervously fumble a bit with the button. I breathe a sigh as I slowly lower his zipper. My breath hitches when I find no undergarments hinder my trek toward him. Commando. Wow. I've seen boxers in his bedroom a couple of times but have no complaint in their absence at this moment.

My enjoyment of young adult, new adult, and romance books did not prepare me for holding him in my hand. Although the size and weight of it are surprising, I marvel at the contrast of the silky skin covering hard steel. It's both delicate and strong, inviting and scary.

His shallow breaths stall when I begin exploring every inch of him. I tighten my grip and pump a few times. Hamilton's guttural groan encourages my novice attempts to pleasure him.

Placing his hand on mine, he begs me to stop, claiming he won't last long if I continue. I pull my hand back while he removes his boots, socks, and jeans. I glide my hand up his muscular back.

I release a nervous sigh as he returns to my side. As much as I want this favor from him, I worry it might harm our friendship, and I need him too much to lose him. But, I need this favor before I attack life on my own.

Sensing his hesitation, I place my hands on his head and pull his lips to mine. Our kiss begins soft but immediately turns urgent. My fingers curl in his hair, desperate to hold him to me.

The calluses on his pitching hand rub over my flesh. Years of his fingers rubbing against the seams of a baseball, gift me with a delicious friction. Relaxing my grip on him, he suckles my nipple. The harsh friction followed by his warm soft tongue are sweet torture. When he blows warm air across each, I can take no more.

"Please," I beg.

He places his forehead to mine, his eyes searching me for what I don't know. In his eyes, I see the war within him. I lift my pelvis to meet his, grinding slightly to signal I am still ready.

His hand parts my thighs before a finger plunges inside. Yes, like a brazen hussy, I meet each thrust, grinding into his palm. A second long, strong finger enters then a third.

Hamilton withdraws his fingers but continues circling my bud. Once again, our foreheads meet.

"I think you are ready."

"Very ready."

"I don't want to hurt you," he whisper-growls while we stare.

"You won't hurt me. Please," I beg.

Rising up on one forearm, he sheaths himself in a condom that seems to appear out of nowhere, then nudges my slick entrance. He slowly presses himself inside.

"Relax and breathe," he whispers into my ear.

When I comply, he plunges in another inch. I revel in the full sensation as I stretch to accommodate him inch by inch. He pauses—his arm muscles straining. For a long moment, he kisses me then places one last kiss on the corner of my lips.

"When I move again, it's gonna hurt a bit." His worried eyes seek my understanding.

I smile up at him then nod. With a bit more force, he pushes through the resistance within. I tense at the pinch and slight burn. Prompting me to breathe again, he slowly pulls back before pressing back into me.

With each stroke, my body relaxes more and more. Moving on their own, my legs wrap around his waist. My heels dig into his glutes as his thrusts are deeper in this position. I alternate kisses with licks on his neck and collarbone. I feel the tightness forming again, low in my belly. Hamilton pulls his torso from mine. Sitting on his haunches, he lifts my calves over his shoulders while maintaining his rhythm.

In the pale moonlight, I take in his hooded eyes and slightly parted lips. He slows his hips. Not wanting my approaching orgasm to wane, I shyly slide my hand between us. I slowly circle my fingers against my clit in unison with his thrusts.

When my inner muscles clinch, signaling my rapidly approaching release, Hamilton's eyes open wide. My impending orgasm gives him the greenlight to stop fighting his own release.

His hands tighten on my hips as he pistons at a punishing pace. I don't just reach the edge of a cliff but plummet down from it. My orgasm ripples through me, clenching his cock, causing his own release. He pulses within me then collapses. His heated skin on mine, my arms wrap around him. I smile into his neck while we catch our breath and fall back down to Earth. His warmth encompasses me. I revel in the knowledge that "little ol' me" could cause this reaction in such a strong guy. I expected the wham-bam-thank-you-ma'am experience while Hamilton helped me lose my virginity. I wasn't prepared to experience my first orgasm, let alone my second. I didn't plan to feel so aroused by his touch or so at home in his embrace.

"Please don't cry." Hamilton's words make me aware of the warm streams of tears on each cheek. I frantically wipe them.

"I'm not sure why I'm crying," I chuckle in an attempt to make light of the tears. "I haven't cried since..."

"Since your dad's funeral." Hamilton finishes my sentence before wiping away a stray tear. He kisses the tip of my nose.

"I think they are happy tears."

Hamilton searches my face to access my honesty. "Did I hurt you?"

I pinch the tender flesh beneath his upper right arm.

Hamilton wails before asking, "Why the hell did you do that?"

"It felt like that. A pinch. Then," I pause to lick and kiss his earlobe and neck. "Then the pain was replaced by overwhelming desire and a second orgasm."

"You never cease to amaze me with your words and actions. You'd think after five years I would be ready for it all."

His words are music to my ears. He likes my honesty, my descriptions, and the way I live life. Warmth swells within me. I snuggle closer to Hamilton's chest with my back as he holds me in his arms. Do I feel different as a woman? Not really. It is silly of me to think I'd feel changed by losing my V-card. I won't dress or walk differently tomorrow. It's similar to my eighteenth birthday. Suddenly I was legally an adult but didn't feel any different. I still went to high school each day and worried about college in the fall, just as I won't change after tonight.

I'm so close to sleep. Lying wrapped in Hamilton's arms, snug to his chest, listening and feeling his steady breaths, this is bliss. Just as I begin to drift off, Hamilton's whisper tugs me back.

"It was better than I fantasized." Hamilton's sleepy masculine voice murmurs.

Wait what? He thought of this? Of me? When? "Better than I fantasized". Did my best friend Hamilton fantasize about sex with me? Did he think about this before I asked a favor of him tonight? Fuck a duck! How do we go back to a friendship now? This wasn't a quickie to lose my virginity. I felt things for Hamilton. They were the type of feelings best friends don't have. I craved him in a primal way. Hamilton tightens his arms around me as he shifts positions. I try to lie still. I'm a bit uncomfortable with my confused thoughts.

Hamilton's breathing is even as his limbs are heavy around me. After a few moments, I realize he's asleep. Asleep? Was he talking in his sleep? His confession about his fantasies for me remain an even bigger mystery.

"I'm sorry," Hamilton whispers, stirring from sleep prior to kissing my shoulder. "I guess you wore me out." I turn in his arms. He smiles, pulling me to his chest.

"And I'm sorry I fucked up our plans." Hamilton states. "But really it is your fault. You pushed me to enter the draft this year instead of three to four years from now when I planned to. I honestly didn't believe I would be drafted. I hoped but never dreamed."

Hamilton always underestimates his true worth. He knows he is talented. He knows he can play college baseball. His dream of playing Major League Baseball is one he only shared with his parents and me. I encouraged him to enter the draft. It is my fault he will leave me tomorrow. His gift needs to be shared—I pushed him to enter, knowing others would recognize it, too.

Hamilton's fingers trace my smug smile. "You're proud of yourself, aren't you?" His thumb caresses my cheekbone. "You were relentless about the draft. I gave in just to shut you up. And now, I'm playing minor league baseball for the Chicago Cubs." He rolls to his back.

I place my hand upon his arm. "God blessed you with a rare gift in your left arm. He gave you the strength and love for the game to endure your greatness." I feel his muscles tighten as he makes a fist. "You've entertained Athens long enough. Soon you will entertain baseball fans everywhere."

Hamilton rolls to face me. He pulls me to his chest in a tight embrace. "You've always been my biggest fan."

"I still will be. I plan to follow you online, drive to Des Moines for a game or two, and I will even call to ride your ass if you slack off."

Hamilton places a chaste kiss on my forehead. Then his lips linger but a hair's breadth away from mine. I lift my eyes to meet his while my tongue peeks out to wet my lower lip. I blink. He lowers his head.

I draw in a sharp breath as Hamilton's stubbled jaw grates against my nipple. The roughness brings the perfect amount of friction to contrast his soft, warm tongue. He alternates chin whiskers and mouth on each of my breasts. It's the perfect torment to tighten the coil in my core yet again. Hamilton's ministrations wind me tighter and tighter. I feel I will explode any minute. One minute he's touching me, then next he's gone.

He struggles to find his discarded jeans, looking for a condom. I giggle as he crawls on all fours around me desperately. Looking toward me, stone-faced, with a foil packet in hand, I cover my mouth to stifle my giggles. Visible in the pale moonlight, I gawk, open-mouthed, at the magnificent male specimen as he slowly slides the condom on. The sight of his hands holding his shaft stirs everything within me. My fingers itch to touch him.

"Ham," I moan in a drawn-out whisper. "Please." My body writhes as my need becomes too much for me to bear. "I need you, now." The heat pooling in my belly and the wetness coating my thighs needs his attention.

Hamilton quickly lies beside me. I roll towards him and squeal when he rolls me atop him. I plant my hands over each of his shoulders and press myself over him. His huge hands squeeze each of my butt cheeks. In this position, we align perfectly. His erection extends under my abdomen. I fight the urge to grind myself this way and that upon his impressive length.

Not quite sure how to proceed in our current position, I tilt my head to the side. Hamilton moves to a sitting position. With hands on my hips, he lifts me then one hand positions himself at my entrance. Oh, now I see how this will work. Ever up for a challenge, I quickly slide myself upon him.

"Easy!" He warns too late.

"Ahh!"

"It's deeper in this position." Hamilton caresses my ribcage. My skin prickles beneath his touch. He licks his lips as he cups my breasts.

Enjoying the sensations, I forget about Hamilton's cock buried deep within me until he nudges his pelvis upwards. Oh yeah, I should probably move. As I raise and lower myself, I quickly realize this is my favorite sexual position. I know I've only experienced two positions, but this one is so g-o-o-d.

On my next downward thrust, Hamilton's hands at my hips grind me against him. Sparks shoot through my core. Enjoying it immensely, I now rise up, glide down, and swivel my hips before repeating. My head falls back— my long hair against my heated back adds yet another sensation to the mix. I lift my hands from his chest to mine.

Hamilton's fingertips softly pinch and pull then rub my clit, and I'm a goner. I grind myself against his fingers mere moments before I collapse on his chest riding out my orgasm. As my every muscle clenches, my body pulses, and lightning flashes behind my eyelids, Hamilton's hands continue to move my hips, seeking his release while extending mine. Finally, his pulsing orgasm ceases his movements, and my long orgasm begins to wane.

His hands, sluggish from the exertion, rub up and down my back. I am bouncing up and down. Wait! Is he laughing?

"What's so funny?"

He instructs me to listen. Listen? What? He's laughing. Oh… In the distance, I hear the howls of coyotes. They sound like a litter of little ones calling for their mother. An owl above us hoots and a dog barks in the distance.

"What has them all worked up?"

Hamilton's laughter deepens. With great difficulty, I rise to glare at him.

Through his laughter he states. "You're not exactly quiet." He taps a finger on the tip of my nose.

"Me?" My mind replays our most recent sex session. My eyes grow wide as I realize I growled. I cried out. I even chanted, "yes, yes, yes". Embarrassment floods my cheeks and neck. I fan myself in an attempt to counter the heat. I'm in so much trouble. This is way more than the favor I asked of him.

Tugging on a strand of my hair, Hamilton assures me. "I found it very hot. It's very late so no one heard you but the animals."

I swat him playfully while ordering him. "Don't tease me."

Hamilton squeezes me tightly while releasing a deep sigh.

"As much as I hate for this to end, it is late, and we should head home." Hamilton continues to hug me.

We use our cell phone lights to gather our clothes. Once dressed, I hand Hamilton his hat.

"Uh, thanks." Hamilton's voice hesitates.

"Um, yeah." Words clog my throat while I dart my eyes over our surroundings. This is the awkwardness I expected. I stand hands on my hips not sure how to stand or what to say. I'm not sure what my body language expresses to him at this moment. I am so out of my element here.

Fortunately, Hamilton ends my discomfort. He says goodnight, I nod, and we walk in opposite directions. Tears fill my eyes as I realize this is probably the last time Hamilton and I will share our favorite place. Tomorrow, our lives venture down opposite forks in the road.

20

The newspaper comes out once a week — it's one of the 4,724 reasons I want to leave Athens.

"No tears." Hamilton's words from last night play on a loop in my head. I need to focus on the positives, while I show my support and excitement for the ball games in his future. I exit my car, parked beside his large red truck in his driveway. Making my way onto the deck, I enter through the screen door, and into his home for the last time. I paint a smile upon my face.

"Good morning, Madison," Memphis greets. "Can I get you something to drink?" She looks tired. I doubt she slept last night. The redness ringing her eyes leads me to believe she's cried already today.

"I'll get it." I pull a cup from the cabinet and pour a glass of unsweetened iced tea. I scan the nearby family room for evidence of Hamilton. "Is he ready?" I hope she understands the many meanings of this question.

"He's all packed, and the truck is loaded." She scoots closer to my side, leans in, and whispers, "He's excited. We need to put on a brave face for his sake." She motions her head toward the stairs. "Why don't you run up and light a fire under his butt."

I nod, place my iced tea on the table, then climb the stairs to Hamilton's room as I have a million times before, reminding myself to smile with every step.

"You better get a move on if you plan to blow this pop stand by noon," I tease with all the faux excitement I can.

With duffle bag in hand he scans his bedroom one more time before motioning me to exit as he follows. I descend the steps, feeling the heaviness of his stare on my back. Thoughts of last night creep into the forefront of my mind. Thoughts of his hands, his lips, his tongue, his breath, and his body upon mine heat my every cell. His nearness heightens my senses. Although I promised nothing would change, I fear it has for me. I wonder if it has for him, too.

"There you are," his mother calls upon our reaching the kitchen. Her proud smile lights up her entire face.

Hamilton passes me to wrap his mother in a tight hug. He murmurs words, near her ear, I cannot make out. When he pulls away, she nods in agreement. Hamilton encourages the two of us to lead the way to his truck. I hope the smile I fake doesn't allow my fear and sadness to show. It feels as though I am walking the green mile to my death. Concrete hardens in my stomach. I want to change colleges and follow him to Des Moines. Hamilton happiness is the only thing keeping me from begging him not to leave me alone. I don't want to return to life without Hamilton by my side. How will I ever adjust to college this fall without him? A big part of my life will end with his pickup truck driving away from us.

I tuck my thumbs in the front pockets of my shorts. My eyes stare at my red Converse and the gravel around them. The toes of Hamilton's worn work boots enter my line of sight. I feel his stare. I sense his reluctance.

"Remember our promise?" he whispers.

"No tears," I murmur while raising my eyes to meet his. I don't feel like crying at this moment. I feel an open chasm in my chest. I struggle to breathe as the empty hole hurts more with each passing second.

Hamilton shakes his head. "The other promise," he prompts.

I'm unable to prevent the squinting of my eyes. The promise that I will struggle to keep. The promise to overcome my greatest fears, to make myself available to new friendships and activities. I purse my lips and nod.

Hamilton's long arms pull me tight to his chest. Turning my head to the side, I lay it upon his chest. I inhale his masculine scent. Tipping his head down, he whispers in my ear, "I'm still here for you. I'm only one text or call away. I hope you will be the same for me. I'm going to need my biggest fan now more than ever."

"I'm here for you." My voice is barely a whisper.

I smile as he breaks our embrace. I see the sparkle in his eyes as his smile lights his entire face. He cannot mask his excitement to play minor league baseball. I am excited for him, too.

As he opens his truck door and climbs in the cab, the aching hole in my chest burns. I jump when the truck door slams. The engine roars to life as Hamilton lowers his window. Memphis stands beside me, her arm over my shoulders. He waves goodbye before backing out of the driveway and disappearing down the lane.

Memphis' arm tightens, pulling me closer. "We'll get through this." Her words sound resolute. "I'll be here for you anytime, and I'm gonna need you to keep me company from time to time." She turns to face me. "I hope we can continue our Sunday trips to church and dinner together."

I nod, afraid of the sobs that might escape if I open my mouth. My heart feels made of stone; surrounding it is only emptiness, a large void. I ache.

21

The driver's license exam is only given one day a week. It's another of the 4,724 reasons I want to escape this town.

Hamilton's mother leads me back into the kitchen, encouraging me to sit and enjoy my tea. She fixes a glass and joins me at the table. My eyes squint as they follow the slow movement of her hand pushing a blue envelope toward me.

"What's this?"

"All I know is Hamilton asked me to pass this to you after he left today." Her warm smile and brown eyes remind me of her son. I fear everything will remind me of him in the months to come.

I cannot contain my excitement as I open the flap and pull a card from the envelope. Bright flowers shine on the front as I read, "Roses are red. Violets are blue." I open the card, anxiously awaiting Hamilton's parting words of wisdom for me. Inside, I find a black sharpie has crossed out the printed words, and I spot his handwriting underneath. "I have planned a scavenger hunt for you." My brow furrows as I attempt to understand the words I read.

"Well?" his mother prompts. "What does it say?"

"I guess he planned a scavenger hunt for me."

As she laughs out loud, she points to a royal blue gift bag on top of the refrigerator. My name graces the gift tag in large black letters. I hop from my chair and bring the bag back to the table. I look to Memphis questioningly before I peek in the top of the bag. I pull out the notecard. I smile at Hamilton's messy print decorating both sides.

"Read it out loud," Memphis demands.

"I've prepared a series of clues to remind you how we came to be. A blue gift bag waits for you in every location. Clue #1: One day in September a nerd and a jock collided, I remember."

In my mind, I recreate the day we officially bumped into each other over and over which led to us talking which led to our friendship. In the busy middle school hallway, we collided on the way to our third period classes. My armful of books toppled to the floor and he scrambled to help me pick them all up. I thanked him, and we went our separate ways—or so we thought. Moments later he took the empty seat next to mine in math class. We found ourselves in three more classes together.

"The answer to the first clue is the middle school," I inform Memphis. "Would you like to come with me?"

"This is his gift to you," she states, shaking her head. "I'll want all the details when you are done."

I spring up from my seat, pat her on the shoulder, and hurry to my car. I am both nervous and excited to see what memories Hamilton found important enough to use as clues to entertain me this afternoon.

My eyes scan the middle school parking lot as I exit the car. I'm looking for a blue bag. I'm not sure how big or small it might be. There are so many places around the school he might have hidden the next clue that I worry I might not find it. As I slowly walk and scan the area, I contemplate inviting Adrian to assist me on the scavenger hunt. I decide to try it on my own first and call for help if I need it later.

I pass the main entrance then one side of the building before I stop to think. Hamilton and I found a squirrel's nest outside the language arts windows. We often watched the baby squirrels in the nest instead of reading as instructed in class. I jog to the opposite side of the building. At the base of the squirrel tree, I find the royal blue gift bag with my name on the tag.

Inside is a five-by-seven inch wooden frame with pictures of Hamilton in his little league uniform and me in my softball uniform from the summer after eighth grade. I giggle at how goofy we were. Hamilton's smile reveals the space between his front teeth that braces later fixed. My thumb nail between my teeth as I smile, reminds me of the large zit I sported that day, that my hand covers.

The distressed, white-washed frame perfectly surrounds this photo. I pull out the notecard with my next clue.

"Clue #2: I begged my mother to take me to your softball game to cheer for you—the next week you returned the favor. Go to the place that sold more than one bubble gum flavor."

I return to my car with my gift in tow to drive to the concession stand near the city league ball fields. I loved sour apple gum. Hamilton preferred grape or original flavor. In the concession stand, they carried all three flavors. The nights his parents worked the concession stand, we conducted a test to see which flavor was more popular. I guessed it would be grape while Hamilton thought it was original. We counted every piece prior to opening the windows and then again after closing the stand. While the two of us watched ball games, his parents pulled half the tub of sour apple gum and hid it. When we finished counting, we were shocked that neither one of us was correct. His parents waited over a year before confessing they rigged our experiment.

On the ledge by the closed concession window, I spy the royal blue gift bag. Inside, I find a framed picture of the two of us. These photos are only a year old now, and I can see so many differences in the two of us. I clutch the frame to my chest as I pull out the next clue.

"Clue #3: On the day I passed my driver's test, I took you to the place with the drink you liked best."

The day Hamilton got his license, he drove me to Sonic Drive-In after school. I lived for their vanilla cola. He treated me to a large one before he drove me home.

I turn the card over. "Ask for today's special." This concerns me. They don't have daily specials. I don't ponder his rationale. I drive to Sonic, looking forward to ordering myself a vanilla cola to accompany today's special.

When I push the large red button to order, I nervously order "today's special". I hope the disembodied voice inside knows what my order means. Moments pass before a carhop delivers a large vanilla cola to my car. I attempt to pass my cash to her, but she informs me the drink has already been paid for. Then, she hands me a royal blue gift bag. Inside, I find a $25 Sonic gift card and my next clue.

"Clue #4: We started each day the same if practice didn't interfere. With our diploma we earned our way out of here."

I exit my parking stall, pull from Sonic back onto the main drag, and point my car to Athens High School. Although the district didn't assign parking spots, our group parked in the same slots every day and arrived early enough to hang out prior to the first bell.

I quickly see the royal blue gift bag in my parking spot for the last three years. Inside, I find a framed photo of the two of us that graced the back cover of our yearbook. Hamilton and I sit on his tailgate. I face Hamilton, a smile on my profile, as he faces the camera, laughing.

In this moment, captured by a yearbook staff member, I had just shared the story of slipping in the hog pen and ripping out my jeans doing chores that morning, early in our senior year. Our friend, Savannah, claimed I should have showered again as I still smelled of the hog lot. Hamilton found this super funny.

I am not sure how long I lean on the hood of my car, staring at the two of us. My heart aches. I thought college would continue where high school left off, Hamilton and I sharing moments along the way in Columbia. The last 48 hours changed all of that. Our paths officially split today. I'm glad I now have these photos to remind me, but they are no replacement for him. I underestimated his importance in my life. How will I ever make it on my own?

"Clue #5: In eighth grade for each other we started to care. For we found we had more than classes to share."

My head tilts to the side as I reread this clue several times. *We ran into each other in the hallway eighth grade year. We shared four classes together. We both liked sports. What else did we SHARE?*

It's the cemetery Hamilton stumbled upon only the week before we met there. I accused him of stalking me. He found my accusation hilarious. We learned that we lived on opposite sides of the cemetery from each other. I used it to escape—he used it to dream. We kept our cemetery between the two of us.

Approaching the cemetery, under the large acorn tree I find the royal blue gift bag. My body tingles as I recall our actions last night. I shake off those thoughts as I focus on my scavenger hunt. I pull out a wrapped box and Hamilton's handwritten note. I read the words out loud.

"This is your final stop. Our shared favorite place sealed our friendship. Here I learned we were destined to be together." A sob escapes. We are no longer together. He follows his dream and I wonder what I should do now. "Although our journeys are hundreds of miles apart, as my best friend, you hold a special place in my heart. As you open my final gift, I know you'll be angry with me. I couldn't leave you today without a plan in place to ensure constant contact between the two of us. Now, open the gift and don't rant until you read the note inside."

Tears fall from my lashes to my cheeks and my hands tremble as I turn the rectangular box. It's heavy. I peel a corner of the paper away to reveal a white box. As I tear more, I find it's an iPhone box. *No way! He better not have.* I slide the lid from its base, unfold the paper, and read.

"We now share an unlimited plan. I expect you to use the hell out of the unlimited texts, calls, and data. Your number is the same. Transfer your contacts from your antiquated flip-phone before you toss it in the trash where it belonged years ago." I follow the arrow to flip the note over. "Cuss all you want, but you better call and text me from this gift tonight. Your BFF, Hamilton"

Damn him! As upset as I am that he spent so much money on me, I am beyond grateful. I can't afford to upgrade my plan or my cell phone, and my mother uses her money on liquids rather than me. I want to stay in our special place but scurry home to move my contacts into the new phone.

22

You run into your general practitioner, who is also your gynecologist, at church, at the store, and at restaurants. This is a very important reason I want to escape Athens.

After setting up my new cell phone, I shoot a quick text to Hamilton.

ME

my what a busy boy you've been the last 48 hrs

(smiling emoji)

I'm not sure of his schedule upon arriving in Des Moines. I imagine he would see the stadium, meet with the coach, and maybe practice with the team. I busy myself placing my new photo frames around my bedroom.

Hours later, my new iPhone plays *Centerfield* by John Fogerty, alerting me to Hamilton's text.

. . .

> **HAMILTON**
> The emoji = new phone
>
> (smiling emoji)

ME
I (heart emoji) my gifts!

can't believe you had time

> **HAMILTON**
> Adrian did photos & frames
>
> Savannah bags & wrapped
>
> rest I did on my own

ME
you're going to make some girl (smiling emoji)
some day

I cringe. Why did I send that? It's bad enough he's a state away. If he gets a serious girlfriend…My vibrating phone rescues me from that train of thought.

> **HAMILTON**
> no time for chicks
>
> they mess with my game

ME
good boy

> **HAMILTON**
> boy?
>
> (sad emoji)

ME
good man

HAMILTON

that's more like it

time for practice

text or call you after

ME

sounds good

A few days later, I select Nelson Sheridan from my contacts and dial.

"Mr. Sheridan's office, how may I help you?" a receptionist greets.

"May I speak with Nelson Sheridan please?"

"May I ask who is calling?"

"Tell him Hamilton Armstrong's number one fan is calling." She hedges a moment before placing me on hold. Maybe I should email instead of call. He might not take my phone call—I'm sure he is a busy guy.

"Madison, what can I do for you?" Nelson answers.

"I would like to help Hamilton's mother attend tomorrow night's game to see him pitch for the first time. I can drive her to Des Moines and back but need help securing tickets."

"I'll have my assistant secure two tickets for tomorrow night's game and leave them for you at the Will Call window in your name." I'm amazed how easy this was. I assume it's because Hamilton's an elite pitcher—with his talent comes the perks.

I quickly thank him. I cross tickets off my to do list. Up next is hotel room. I open Safari and search for hotels near the ballfield. Where would I be without this new phone Hamilton gave me? Lost, that's where. I reserve a room with two double beds. I cross hotel room off the list. All I need to do now is tell Memphis and pack.

I take a chance and drive over to the Armstrong farm. Memphis is watering her flower beds as I emerge from my car.

"Madison." She stands to greet me. "This is a surprise."

"No, the surprise is I have secured us two tickets to tomorrow night's I-Cubs game to watch Hamilton make his debut."

"Oh, Madison." I see the tears fill her eyes as her hand covers her mouth. "How? Where?"

"Let's sit on the porch swing." I prompt. As a gentle motion rocks us, Memphis is all ears. "I've arranged a room for us half a mile from the stadium. Nelson was happy to arrange tickets for us to pick up at will call."

The shock of my surprise wears off, and Memphis begins to plan. "Let's take my car. Can we leave early enough to arrive during pre-game warm-ups?"

"Sounds good." I agree. "Let's keep it a surprise for Hamilton."

I stroll up to the will call window, more nervous to watch this game than any before. I state my name and the staff member pulls an envelope from a nearby tub. But, before returning to the window, she makes a phone call. I can't hear her conversation from where I stand outside. I start to worry there might be an issue with our tickets. I fear we drove over three hours and now will not even see the game.

"Miss Crocker," a male voice calls from behind me. I turn. An older gentleman wearing a gold "Event Staff" shirt waits. I nod. "I'll escort you to your seats," he states before taking the envelope from the staff behind the window. "Please follow me."

Memphis and I grin at each other before following behind the large man. He walks us into the stadium then down closer to the field with every step. When I asked for tickets, I didn't plan on seats this close to the field. He pauses at the end of the first row of seats, at the far end of the home-team dugout. He hands me the two tickets and motions us to sit.

"The I-Cubs will be in this dugout. Pitchers warm up over here on this mound." He points to our left. The bullpen is just over the wall from the first row of seats. From our seats, we will have a perfect view of Hamilton warming up. "This is my section. I will be nearby. Please let me know if you need anything."

Memphis and I thank him for his help. When he walks away, we giggle and discuss how perfect our seats are. I am even more glad that we planned to arrive early to watch warm-ups. We head to the restroom then purchase beverages and snacks before returning to our seats.

When Memphis purchases a Snickers bar to keep Hamilton's pre-game ritual alive, I confess that I have a plastic bag in my pocket with a couple sunflower seeds, a sucker, a Milk-Dud, and a Mike & Ike. Laughing, we decide we are true baseball fans.

The teams are on the field warming up. Some run, some throw, and others stretch. Our eyes focus on the door in the outfield wall each time it opens. We've seen several team members emerge from it and are eager to catch our first glimpse of Hamilton.

I nudge Memphis when I witness a catcher appear, wearing his gear, followed by two players. As we watch, they spread out more, and we have our first sight of Hamilton. He looks tall and strong in his new uniform. Blue is definitely his color. He smiles as he walks and talks to the other players. It warms my heart to see him happy.

On the foul line, the three stretch and sprint a few times before playing catch. With each throw, Hamilton moves farther and farther away from his catcher on the line. It seems the third man is not a player but a coach. Perhaps he's the pitching coach. He walks by us into the dugout for a moment then returns to the catcher.

When Hamilton jogs over to his catcher, we watch as the three talk. The coach turns and points towards the dugout. Hamilton and the catcher crane their necks, looking where the coach points. In the moment Hamilton's smile turns megawatt, I realize the coach was pointing at us, not the dugout. Hamilton pats the catcher on the back before jogging towards us.

"He's coming." Memphis excitedly grasps my arm.

"This is a surprise," Hamilton states as he reaches over the wall to hug Memphis when she bends down.

"Surprise," I fake cheer.

"Did I miss a voicemail or a text?" he asks.

"No," Memphis replies. "Is it okay we came? We don't want to make you nervous."

"Mom," Hamilton's deep voice soothes. "I love you at my games. I want you at my games. If I had my way, the two of you would attend every game." His words are perfect. They are everything Memphis and I hope for.

Memphis slides the Snickers bar from her purse and hands it to Hamilton. He chuckles as the catcher and coach walk up behind him.

"What's this?" the coach asks, pointing to the candy bar.

"Just a pre-game ritual," Hamilton replies.

"Armstrong, where are your manners?" the catcher teases. "Introduce us."

Hamilton shakes his head. "This is my mother Memphis, and this is my number one fan, Madison." He tugs on the hem of my new I-Cubs jersey.

The coach greets us. The catcher nudges Hamilton. "I thought you said you didn't have a girl back home."

I snort. Yes. Making a great impression, I snort at his words. "I'm Hamilton's best friend, Madison. And although he left many broken hearts in Athens, I am not among them." I hope my words sound believable.

I don't hear the catcher's next words but laugh when the coach swats him on the back of the head and quickly maneuvers between the two players. Hamilton looks ready to kill him. I assume he made a comment about dating me or hooking up. After a few calming words, the catcher apologizes and ducks into the dugout. The coach asks if there are any other pre-game rituals he needs to be aware of before excusing himself.

"I'm so glad the two of you are here." Hamilton's brown eyes twinkle. He loves this game, and he loves his momma. "I need to go warm up, but hang around after the game. I'd like to see you." When we agree, he heads over to the bullpen area.

Memphis and I watch with rapt attention every pitch that Hamilton throws. Having watched him pitch for years, I can make out his slider, his curve, and his fastball. He looks a little tight. His pitches are on target; it's his stance that seems off.

The pitching coach heads back to the dugout while Hamilton tosses a few more to his catcher. Stopping in front of us, he asks, "How's he look?"

This catches me off guard. Is he just making small talk, or does he really want to know? I decide I need to do what is best for Hamilton. "You really want to know?"

At his nod, I share, "Pitches look good, but he is tight." I now have the coach's full attention. "It's his upper back--in his stance." I pause before continuing. "He probably needs to stretch his back more."

"If anyone can spot a difference in his stance, it would be Madison." Memphis states.

It's why I'm known as his biggest fan. My chest warms with Memphis' praise. It's as if she's a proud mom, and I am her daughter.

Coach hollers into the dugout. A trainer appears at his side before jogging to Hamilton. I hesitantly wave when Hamilton looks my way. I hope I didn't over step. He is now in the minor leagues—he probably doesn't want a friend telling his coach what he needs. Hamilton smiles and shakes his head at me before following the trainer back into the locker room. He's inside about ten minutes. I fret and stew the entire time.

When they emerge, Hamilton takes the bullpen mound again to throw a few more pitches. I smirk as it's now fixed. Maybe it's me, but it seems there is more pop when the ball hits the catcher's mitt. The catcher slings his arm around Hamilton's back. The two laugh as they walk and talk.

"I need to get me a number one fan," the catcher states when the two stand before our seats. He waves to us, pats Hamilton on the back, and disappears into the dugout.

"I needed an adjustment," Hamilton confesses, a smirk upon his face. "Thank you for pointing it out. I thought it was just nerves. But it's all better now."

I can only smile. We wish him good luck before he joins his teammates in the dugout.

23

The only books sold in town are textbooks at the community college and book orders through the elementary school—it's one of the 4,724 reasons I need to leave Athens.

We stand as the teams are announced. When Hamilton's name is called, he hops from the dugout onto the field. The crowd roars a welcome for their new pitcher. He turns to wave at his new fans, a wide smile upon his face. He's the luckiest man alive—he gets paid to play the game he loves. He winks our way before turning his back and assuming his place near the mound.

Goosebumps cover my entire body during the National Anthem. I squeeze Memphis' hand—she pulls me into a side-hug. My nerves ratchet higher as He takes his warm-up pitches upon the mound. He looks like the same man that took the mound in Athens less than a week ago. I would be a blubbering mess in his shoes. The pressures of a new league and level of play would be too much for me. Add to that coaches that are also his boss, large stadiums, bigger crowds, and tougher opponents. How he looks as he always does on the mound, I have no idea.

The umpire signals to Hamilton to start the game. Hamilton scans his fielders before assuming his throne on the white rubber. He studies the signs his catcher signals between his legs. With a slight nod, Hamilton agrees with his catcher. I grin as my favorite player delivers his first minor league pitch across the plate. The umpire calls strike. I glance to the scoreboard. His first minor league pitch a ninety-three mile per hour fastball for a strike, a perfect start to this part of his baseball career.

Memphis and I cheer along with the I-Cubs fans surrounding us. I notice a difference in this crowd compared to the games I've attended. It seems the entire crowd supports the home team. These are now Hamilton's fans in Hamilton's new city. I hope they treat him well.

In his first inning, Hamilton throws ten pitches for two strike-outs and a ground-out. His new fans cheer loudly. Many on our side of the field call to Hamilton by name with congratulations. Hamilton smiles towards the stands before ducking into the dugout.

In the bottom of the sixth, the coach pulls Hamilton after two-thirds of an inning. I mentally tally his stats while I watch him wave to the crowd and disappear below. He earned fourteen strike outs, gave up one hit, and walked one. The I-Cubs hold a two to nothing lead as a right-handed closer assumes the mound. I am so proud of Hamilton's strong performance. I see good things in his future.

Memphis and I stand at the wall, cheering with the other I-Cubs fans for the two to one victory. Hamilton gets the win, adding more icing on the cake of his first outing for the Cubs franchise. Hamilton asks us to meet him at the players' entrance, and our Event Staff member returns to escort us to meet him. As we walk, he comments on Hamilton's pitching and stats. I hope all the fans are this impressed with Hamilton on their team.

Our guide remains with us for the twenty minutes it takes Hamilton to join us. He shakes Hamilton's hand and says goodbye to us. Teammates invite Hamilton to join them at a local bar to celebrate. I know it's important for him to bond with the team, but I want to spend some time with him, too.

Hamilton states he will join them in half an hour. He throws an arm over

Memphis' and my shoulder. "Let's go somewhere we can visit, someplace quiet." When we agree, he asks us to follow him back to his condo nearby.

Our time at Hamilton's condo passes quickly. He animatedly shares stories of practices then the locker room and dugout of tonight's game. It's easy to see he is exactly where he is meant to be. The butterflies fluttering in my abdomen during the game and in his presence morph heavily into the pit of my stomach as the end of our visit draws near. Goodbye's don't get any easier, do they? I want to instruct Memphis to leave me here. I long to remain in Des Moines sneaking time with Hamilton while he's away from the ball park. I ponder giving up my goal of teaching to find a job nearby and attend all of Hamilton's games. The idea of being his groupie suddenly appeals to me. All I need to be happy is to be in his presence. Nothing else matters.

24

The biggest employer in Athens is the school district followed by the grocery store. This is one of the 4,724 reasons I want to escape this town.

I'm excited for my friends today as they start summer classes at Athens Community College. I decide to send them a text.

ME

1st day of college-Go For It!

I wish I was starting class

I'm jealous

ADRIAN

have a great 1st day at ACC

BETHANY

thanks

TROY

stop bragging you don't have school

SALEM

thank you

Hours later, as I drive to Adrian's store, my phone vibrates with a group text from Adrian.

ADRIAN

regret not going college?

WINSTON

No

we have businesses to run

WINSTON

no time for classes

you regret it?

I realize Adrian didn't mean to include me in the text, so I refrain from responding. I feel like a spy reading their conversation.

ADRIAN

no!

hate school

you know that

just miss time with the gang

WINSTON

they're not in same classes

we're together nights & weekends

ADRIAN

not the same without Hamilton

Madison leaves soon

WINSTON

change is hard

our friendships won't change

ADRIAN

I know

just sentimental today

WINSTON

I'm on my way to you

bringing lunch

ADRIAN

(heart emoji)

Crap! I already purchased lunch for Adrian and me.

"I come with lunch," I declare, walking towards the counter.

"I have lunch, too." Winston chuckles before claiming we'll have a buffet to choose from.

Adrian assists in arranging Winston's deli sandwiches, chips, and slice of pie with my pizza, plates, and utensils. I remind them cold pizza will make a good snack later or for breakfast tomorrow.

Adrian enjoys lunch with the two of us. I don't look forward to leaving her for college. I know I need to spend as much time with her now while I can.

I'm not sure how he does it, but Winston weasels himself closer and closer to Adrian every day. It seems Adrian enjoys and looks forward to his company. She depends on him and seeks his input.

25

Adults contact each other to compare the amount of rain in their rain gauges. Another of the 4,724 reasons I want to leave this town.

Weeks pass. Hamilton and I text or call each other daily. I'm about a month away from move-in day at college. I can't sleep. Tired of tossing and turning, I climb the stairs from the basement hoping not to see my mother. Walking through the living room, I spot a stranger sleeping on the sofa. Two empty bottles lie on the floor. Seems my mother didn't return home alone. I lock the bathroom door for privacy while I relieve myself. It's not bad enough I hide from my mother in my own home, now I have another to avoid. I tiptoe to the kitchen for water before returning to the safety of my bedroom. I don't dare make any noise—I don't want to deal with two drunks tonight.

As I sip from my water glass at the sink, a naked man opens the refrigerator door. I freeze and quickly realize this is not the man from the sofa. I shield my eyes as I excuse myself. I nearly stumble twice as I scramble down the stairs. Earlier tonight, I felt relieved when GPS showed she made it home safely. Now I stand panic-stricken in my own room behind a locked door. So many times, I've felt like a prisoner in this house. I'm a prisoner of her alcoholism. I spend my evenings and nights worrying over her, looking up her location, and praying she makes it home without any harm. She's spent many nights in town. I realize she's stayed with men, tonight she flaunted it right in front of me. She's brought even more danger and stress into my life.

I can no longer deny her recklessness with her drinking and the giving of her body to others. Rage boils inside my belly at her thoughtlessness. Her years of neglect and destructive behaviors have hardened my heart. I still need my mother but can no longer be a part of her toxic life. I throw items into a backpack. I throw it over my shoulder, snag my phone and charger, then dart to my car.

The winds are picking up and I see lightning approaching from the west as I back from my driveway. While I drive the two gravel roads between my home and Hamilton's, I make a plan. I will tape a note to Memphis' bedroom door and her refrigerator letting her know I am sleeping in Hamilton's room. If I text she might wake up and I don't want her to be afraid if she hears me upstairs. I'll need to share everything with her tomorrow. For tonight, I will be safe. I just hope I can fall asleep.

My vibrating phone wakes me. "Hello," I mumble, not even looking at the caller ID.

"Why are you sleeping in my bed?" Hamilton's deep voice greets.

"How…"

"My mother texted me when she found your notes this morning. Now, stop stalling and tell me what is wrong."

"I didn't feel safe, and your house was the only one I felt I could run to in the middle of the night. I knew the doors would be unlocked, and Memphis wouldn't mind my intrusion," I confess.

"Did they…?" Hamilton's voice breaks at the thought of what drunk men might have done to me.

"No, I made sure to go straight to my room and lock the door." It kills me that he might have such a horrible thought. "I'm a big girl; I can take care of myself."

"I know that," he quickly replies. "I just…it enrages me that your mother put you in such a dangerous position. They could have done anything while she was passed out in her bedroom."

"Hamilton, please stop thinking about that." I can't have him upset over something that didn't happen. He has games to worry about. "I'm going to talk with your mother in hopes that I might be able to stay here for a while."

"You can stay until you leave for college," Hamilton firmly states. "My mother and I have talked about your mother in the past. I know she will have no problem with you staying. In fact, she's a bit lonely in my absence and will enjoy your company."

"I should probably head downstairs to chat with her. I am sure she is very worried." I don't want to let him go, but know he has things to tend to on his end, too. "Good luck tonight."

I attempt to call my mother around 2:00 p.m. Of course, she refuses to answer. I use my GPS app to ensure she is still at home before I shoot her a text.

ME

I'll be staying at the Armstrong's for a while

your 2 guests scared me last night

1 was naked in kitchen with me

I didn't feel safe, so escaped

text or call me please

"Everything okay, dear?" Memphis queries from outside my car window.

"Just trying to contact Mom." I pop my trunk before exiting the car. "I have a few groceries. Do you mind helping me carry them in?"

Memphis is not happy I thought I needed to chip in on food while I stayed with her. As we put the groceries away, I ask if I might prepare supper for us before Hamilton's game this evening. I'm glad to have someone to understand my constant refreshing of my browser for updates during the I-Cubs game.

While I cook, Memphis answers her cell phone. "Good afternoon," she greets. I listen to her side of the conversation as I fix myself a bowl of cereal. "My rain gauge had an inch and three-quarters in it when I woke this morning." Another pause then she parrots the callers words, "Only a half inch, really? Well, it is better than nothing at all." I busy myself looking out the kitchen window for the rest of the conversation.

I smile, knowing I'll move to college soon. A new life awaits me in Columbia. I want to live in a world where daily life doesn't revolve around the moisture in the ground for crops.

Before I turn in for the night, I text Hamilton.

ME

great game tonight!

ate popcorn & followed score online with your mom

we had fun

HAMILTON

how are you doing?

ME

tried to reach mom, no luck

so left her a message

plan to stay here indefinitely

HAMILTON

if I was there I'd confront her

ME

that never works with her

HAMILTON

are you sure you're ok?

ME

better than I was at home

very cozy here.

enjoy your mom's company

I made street tacos for us for dinner

HAMILTON

never made me dinner

ME

never asked

HAMILTON

you didn't give her food poisoning?

ME

nice one

group of us will be at game next time on the mound in Des Moines

will send details in next day or 2

HAMILTON

can't wait to see everyone

got to go I need to load the bus

ME

safe travels, get some sleep

26

A stranger driving through or visiting town quickly becomes hot gossip. This is one of the 4,724 reasons I want to escape this town.

Adrian video calls me late the next afternoon.

"My nerves are kicking into high gear the closer to the time for Winston to arrive draws near. I'm not sure why I agreed to attend dinner with him tonight at his parents' house. I mean, I've enjoyed our time spent together getting my store ready. I enjoy that we share similar goals for the next year and beyond. While all my friends go to college classes, we chose to work full-time on our businesses. There's something about dining with his parents that seems more like a couple than just friends. He claims this is not a date, just a casual dinner to discuss business. What do you think?"

"What should I wear? I think my definition of casual and Winston's family's might be very different. Should I wear my simple yellow sundress that has pale green flowers with my ballet flats?"

"That's perfect." It's funny that I am giving fashion advice for a dinner with a guy. I've never dated, let alone attended a dinner with a guy's parents. She's usually the clothing advice queen for our group.

Adrian actually squeals, causing me to jump, as her doorbell rings, signaling Winston has arrived.

"Adrian," her mother calls from the front door.

"Take a breath, you've got this." I marvel as my always confident friend is nervous about a guy for the first time. "Just be the Adrian we all love and have fun."

She quickly ends the video call.

27

It is common for a tractor or combine to drive down main street in the middle of the day. Just another one of the 4,724 reasons I want to wave goodbye to Athens.

The next morning, as I piddle around my bedroom, a text alert pings my phone.

ADRIAN

need to talk

can you swing by the store today

Not even bothering to reply, I throw on some jeans and head into town. At her store I find Adrian is all out of sorts. Her appearance is disheveled, and her body language displays signs of stress. It could be the daily stress of running her store, but I fear it is something else. My friend is in need, and I'm going to get the bottom of this.

"Spill it," I demand, placing my hand on her shoulder.

"I may have done something very stupid." Adrian fiddles with a pile of paperclips on the counter in front of us. "I broke a rule, and you're going to be so mad at me."

The sound of the bell above the front door of the store interrupts her confession. "Delivery for Adrian Slater," a young man calls as he approaches with a dozen red roses and baby's breath in a large glass vase.

I take the roses and slip a tip in his hand. I bite my lip in an attempt to hide the rather large, knowing smile upon my face. I place the vase in front of Adrian on the counter, spinning it so the card is right in front of her. She pulls the card from the tiny envelope.

"You slept with Winston, didn't you?" I state more than ask.

She clutches the card to her chest as her eyes dart to me from the opposite side of the counter. The look on her face asks me how I know without her telling me.

"There are only three possibilities with which you might have broken a rule and made me mad at you." I signal air-quotes with the word mad. "Hamilton is in Des Moines, played a game last night, then according to the texts we shared until 2 a.m. was on a bus with his team headed to Tennessee for tonight's game." I hold up my fingers. "So that leaves two options. Although I would be very happy for you to have hooked-up with Savannah last night, neither of you swing that way, and she would *not* have sent you roses today." I hold up my index finger. "That leaves one possibility. The two of you have spent a lot of time together setting up your business. You've made it no secret in the past that you find him hot. Therefore, I know you hooked-up with Winston last night. So, spill it. How? Where? How good was he? And where do you go from here?"

"Crap, woman! Enough of the third degree!" Adrian places the card back in the roses before she signals me to sit with her behind the counter.

"We had dinner with his parents last night. It wasn't just the four of us. So, we snuck out; then we went to the park to walk and ended up on the swings."

I nod my head, encouraging her to continue.

"Winston pulled me in for a kiss, things got heated, we drove, we parked, and I attacked him." Adrian attempts to summarize the evening in a brief synopsis.

I know her too well. She's having second thoughts about last night. "Nice try," I chuckle. "Let's start over, and if I'm to help you, I'll need *most* of the details." My friend tends to overshare of her sexual encounters. I don't need to hear about my friend Winston.

Adrian's eyes fog over as she settles in to share the entire evening with me. "When we hang up from our call, I descended the stairs happy to find Winston in gray plaid golf shorts with a solid Heather gray shirt and matching Sperrys. I smiled, knowing my sundress was a wise choice for the evening. Winston met me at the bottom step, commenting on my beauty. I remind myself 'he claimed this was not a date'. My mother told us to have fun as we walked to Winston's truck. In the safety of the truck cab, my nerves grew knowing a short drive then we would be at his parents' place."

"I asked him what was for dinner to break the awkward silence. He stated he wasn't sure. His mother asked that he invite me to dinner, so the two of us could share all we've accomplished for the store."

When we turned onto Winston's street, I noticed several vehicles parked on both sides of the little road. Winston commented that someone must be having a barbeque in the neighborhood. In the driveway, he turned to face me after he turned off his truck. He placed his hand on my forearm, smiled my way, and urged me to just be myself. He reminded me I'd met his parents before, and they loved me. Then, he stated it's just a simple dinner with some talk about my new store." Adrian smiles at me. "He was very sweet."

"I figured there's no time like the present to start the awkward evening, so I opened my truck door. Winston jogged to meet me at the front of the truck and took my hand in his. I had no time to contemplate the meaning of such a gesture, as his mother popped her head out the front door." Adrian's eyebrows rise, while she looks for my reaction to Winston's hand holding. I prompt her to continue, as I need more details before I can assume Winston's motives.

"She acted excited we were there with a smile on her face as she invited us to follow her. Imagine my horror when a large group yelled, surprise. A simple, casual dinner with his parents-my ass. What the hell? At the time I was sure Winston knew all about this dinner party and knew I would never agree to accompany him if he told me."

"Winston's voice immediately caught my attention, as he approached his mom seeking an explanation. His mother merely pulled Winston further into the family room toward the guests, claiming It's just a little surprise party to celebrate him taking over the theater. He quickly turned to me, swearing he didn't know." Adrian sighs dramatically. "His expression matched his words and he apologized to me. I barely had time to believe him before the crowd engulfed him, and I was pushed away from his side. When I scanned the crowd, I noticed many people I knew but have never socialized with."

"Winston's father rescued me by handing me a bottle of chilled water as I took a seat beside him on the sofa. He explained his wife got carried away. He told her Winston would hate this but claimed there was no stopping her when she had an idea. He told her she should contact me, so I was in on the secret, but he could tell by my shock that she neglected to do it.

"He ushered me out back. Large banners and balloons hung on the wooden privacy fence. The tablecloths, balloons, napkins, and cups all matched. I took a seat in a comfortable lounge chair on the outside of the patio seating area. While the crowd funneled into the backyard, Winston smiled my way attempting to walk over. Of course, he was stopped by several adults to congratulate him for taking over the family business. I felt out of place. If I had driven my own car, I would have left."

"When his father announced it was time to eat at the large grill, Winston directed me to join him at a table with his mother. He filled a plate for me." She pauses, scanning my reaction. "Can you believe that? Who does that? No *friend* of mine would ever do that." I nod and Adrian continues.

"I noticed several guests filter out the side gate during the meal. Winston's mother commented on my dress and about all the details he had shared with her about my store. I invited her to stop by and take a peek. I asked Winston to bring his parents by sometime." She shrugs. "I felt like they thought I was his girlfriend. It was kind of awkward."

"After dinner the crowd thinned. Winston decided we'd been there long enough and pushed me towards the door. I stated we should say goodbye to his parents before we left, he didn't agree. He stated they were enjoying time with their friends and he'd see them later."

"When he pulled from the drive he headed the opposite direction from my house. He stated he was embarrassed and sorry his mother sprung this upon us. He even claimed he was really looking forward to it just being the four of us. My stomach began to flutter at his actions. He wasn't the same Winston we've hung around with during high school. I couldn't tell, at first, if I liked the change or not." Adrian absentmindedly fiddled with a stack of papers on the sales counter.

"When Winston turned off the truck, we were at the city park. He exited the truck, jogged to my side, opened my door, and helped me step down. Hand-in-hand again we walked through the grass and trees towards the playground."

"You know me, I like to control situations. I felt anything but in control last night. The more he touched me and the sweeter he became, I felt more and more awkward. So, I let go of his hand and took a seat on the swing. I motioned my head to the empty seat beside me for Winston to join me and pushed off the ground. I love swings. I pumped my legs back and forth climbing higher and higher. Slowly I felt my control returning. I tucked my dress tight around my thighs to prevent any unwanted wardrobe malfunctions. Winston kept his feet on the ground, barely moving forward and back. When our eyes met—he was smiling."

"I taunted him to join me as I swung past him." A smile slips onto Adrian's face at the memory. "His serious face prompted me to still my pumping legs and drag my toes to slow down. As I halted my swing and spun it sideways to face Winston, he extended his arms, grasped onto the metal chains of my swing, and pulled me towards him."

Adrian's voice lowers to near a whisper. "His intense stare caught me off guard. Before I could decipher it, his lips latched onto mine in a slow, simmering kiss. The heat and strength of his lips upon mine drew a low moan from me. He took advantage of my parted lips, slipping his tongue next to mine. As the kiss heated, my body grew hotter and hotter." Her eyes search mine.

"So, you liked Winston kissing you?" I smile approvingly.

"I released the chain of my swing allowing my hands to rest on his shoulders. My body leaned into his, seeking more of a connection. Winston's hand on the back of my neck pulled me tight against his mouth. We couldn't seem to get close enough. I tangled my fingers in his thick blonde hair. I clung to him as if I might fall into a crevice without him."

"Winston lowered his hands to my hips and pulled me forward. As if my body spoke a silent language with his, my legs slipped past his hips in the swing and I found myself on his lap. I loved the long groan that escaped him when I eased my pelvis forward and back a tiny bit. I sought this friction to sate the aching need between my own legs."

Now begins the portion of Adrian's story that I dread hearing. In order to help my friend, decipher her interactions with Winston last night, I need to know what happened. I hate hearing intimate details since Winston is my friend, it's awkward. How will I ever look him in the eye after Adrian reveals these details? There are some things I don't need to know about him. Leave it to Adrian to share every tiny detail while enjoying my embarrassment.

"Winston begged me through gritted teeth, to go easy or he'd explode right there on the playground." Adrian's eyes return to mine. In them I see a hint of vulnerability. *This is new. My brave, strong, empowered friend for the first time has met her match.* Silently I nod for her to continue her story.

"Winston is a controlling alpha male yet in the moment, I seemed to affect him. He let me set the pace. I connected my mouth with his. My hands grasped at his hair, clawed at his back, and clutched his biceps. He paused our kiss, placing his forehead to mine. My eyes were greeted by his blue ones. He took several minutes attempting to control his labored breathing, then suggested we get out of there."

"Those are my favorite five words or at least they are now my favorite. I have no idea if anyone witnessed our little swing make-out session. At that moment I didn't care." Adrian giggles. "We scurried to the pickup truck needing the privacy its cab could provide. Winston opened the passenger door, placed his hands on my hips, and he lifted me up to the seat. I longed to melt in my seat as I watched him eagerly round the truck to the driver's door. Instead, I slid across the bench seat needing to close the distance between us as he drove." She shakes her head. "I vowed I would never be *that girl*. I can't stand when needy girls cling to their man as he drives his truck. My body betrayed me. It sought what it desired instead of waiting on me to control it. I had no idea where we drove. As you know, we both live with our parents. I trusted he had a plan."

"I must confess I love, love, love the fire Winston has ignited within me. Why haven't I encouraged him before last night? Winston has always been a hottie. His commanding presence exudes sexuality. Until now, I've never found an alpha appealing. I tend to be the dominate one, I make the first move, and I control every aspect of my relationships." Adrian shrugs, pretending to be embarrassed. "I know Winston well enough to know he's always in control. I've enjoyed our work together on the business but worry we might not fit together as well sexually. What if I can't submit to him? What if he won't submit to me?"

I offer no answers or insight to my friend. I need to know the rest of the last night's events. "Adrian, I need more information about last night. Continue telling me, and I will try to help you when you finish."

"We parked in an unkept gravel driveway of a worn-down old farm house. The overgrown trees and bushes hid Winston's truck from view of the nearby gravel road. After he exited, I slid toward the driver's door and he lowered me from his truck seat. His hands tightened possessively on my hips, I darted my tongue out to lick my lips in anticipation of what was to come. Winston didn't kiss me. Instead his eyes seemed to search mine. I stood frozen in his gaze. He broke the moment by grabbing a quilt from behind the truck seat."

"He lowered his tailgate, tossed the blanket into the truck bed, then lifted me up. I sat frozen until he joined me. He spread the quilt out and motioned for me to join him on top it. Lying side-by-side, we looked up into the clear night sky. I needed his touch, so I took his hand in mine. I wanted him to stoke the embers he started within me. I didn't long for words, I wanted actions.

I rolled towards him, placing my hands upon his hard chest. Let me assure you although he's not a jock, Winston takes care of his body." Adrian fans her heated face. "Remind me to thank Hamilton for inviting Winston to run and lift weights with him. He's damn fine."

I motion for her to focus on continuing her story.

"I placed a kiss on the corner of Winston's lips. It's all the invitation he needed. He rolled me on top him. Our mouths and tongues danced while our bodies touched chest to toes. I was acutely aware of his erection pressing hard against my waist. The goddess in me fed on such a reaction in him."

"My hands played in his sandy blonde hair, lightly I scratched his scalp and tugged on the strands. I needed more, so much more. I sat up strattling his hips. The position caused wondrous pressure from his erection to the apex of my thighs. I paused, distracted for a moment before I placed my hands on the hem of his shirt and slid it up. I slowly dragged my fingers over his abdomen, ribs, and chest on my mission to remove the it. Winston successfully ab-curled to lift the shirt over his shoulders and head. His movement ground his erection causing friction where I needed it most. I allowed my fingertips to explore on their descent from his pectorals, over his ribcage, to the defined lines of his abdominals."

I continue to listen but resist visualizing my two friends together.

"Winston distracted my explorations as his hands slid up my bare thighs. Climbing higher and higher my anticipation built as he neared where I wanted them most. I pouted when I realized his goal was the removal of my sundress and not to play in my panties. He continued his slow torture caressing my hips. I squirmed when he slid over my ribcage. Unable to continue his slow torture, he quickly extricated me from the dress and tossed it aside."

"In the moonlight, I felt Winston's blue eyes admiring my breasts. With my hands on his shoulders, I pulled him to me. My nipples grazed his hard and heated chest. I longed to brush them side to side seeking more friction from his nearness. He pulled my mouth to his as his large hands cupped my swollen breasts. He was tender at first, then pinched and plucked each nipple drawing a guttural groan from me."

"Needing more, wanting more, I threw my head back enjoying his touch. He trailed kisses across one shoulder before he licked one rock hard nipple. I wanted to scream, my desire so overwhelming, so hot, so unexpected. He continued his assault. He plucked, pinched, and sucked from one needy globe to the other."

While I've heard Adrian share her sex-capades in the past, this time is different. I've had my own experience with Hamilton now. Her descriptions bring back memories, feelings, and my body reacts. I struggle to focus on her to help her. I mentally gather my willpower to listen instead of daydream of Hamilton.

"My body acted on its own. It started grinding against the zipper of his shorts over his erection. I was so hot and so wet I knew he could feel it, too. My fingers fumbled on his belt then button of his shorts. Winston took pity on me. He leaned back, deftly unfastened his shorts, then placed my hand on him."

"Of course, I moaned approvingly at the contact while I brought my other hand to join the first. He was rock hard under the silky soft skin of his shaft. As my fingertips feathered lightly over the mushroom shaped head, I heard his intake of breath through gritted teeth. I enjoyed the power I wielded at that moment. His most prized possession was literally in the palm of my hand. My every touch drew a response as it lengthened, it swelled, and he moaned beneath me. I had the power to melt this strong man to a puddle in my hands as I stroked up and down his growing length."

Listen, don't visualize. Listen, don't visualize. I chant to myself.

Adrian seems to enjoy her retelling. Her cheeks flush and her eyes are half-mast. "I slid myself down to his thighs while I bent down to wrap my lips around him. Winston ab-curled to a sitting position, quickly reversed our positions, and tucked his fingers under the lace of my panties. In my shock, I panted as if I ran a marathon. I silently urged him to rip my panties from me and plunge inside. I've never wanted to be taken but it felt sublime."

"Winston slowly slid my panties from my hips while he placed feath-erlight kisses in their wake. I whimpered at his torment. Once at my thighs, he quickly removed and tossed them aside. His warm lips climbed. As much as I would enjoy the oral pleasure he hinted to, I couldn't wait for him any longer. I sat up, I clutched my hands to the sides of his head and tugged his lips to mine. With my lips and tongue, I attempted to convey my level of need for him to connect with me. I pulled him, but a hairsbreadth away and huskily whispered, 'I need you inside, now.'"

A proud smile upon her face, Adrian continues. "I rolled him to his back, kissed the head of his cock on my way by, and straddled his hips with my thighs. I informed him I'm clean and protected, before I asked to skip the condom? In the faint light of the moon, I saw his furrowed brow as he processed my words. Winston stated he never goes without a condom. He asked if I was sure I wouldn't get pregnant."

Adrian never ceases to amaze me how comfortable she is with her sexuality or her private life. I never share such private matters with her or any of my friends.

Her story progresses. "I explained to him, I get my shot every three months like clockwork. I slid my slick folds along his shaft while I waited for his answer. Winston nodded. I lifted his heavy cock to my entrance and slowly slid down him. I moaned at the exquisite sensation as he filled and stretched me. 'Y – E – S -!' I drawled out as I impaled myself balls deep on his massive erection. I paused as he was seated to the root, enjoying the fullness."

My cheeks heat. I'm sure she enjoys my discomfort as she shares her porno-esque retelling.

"Winston's hands were on my hips, his fingertips bit into my flesh. I slowly ground myself against his pubis before I rose ever so slowly to repeat it all over again and again. Through gritted teeth Winston claimed he wouldn't last much longer. I never want to be stranded. I removed one of his hands from my hip and positioned the pad of his thumb on my clit. As I rose and fell upon his shaft, I demonstrated the friction I desired from Winston's thumb. To my delight, he was a quick learner. I placed my hands upon his chest. I switched from my up and down motion, to one of grinding. I balanced myself with one hand upon his chest, ground forward and back upon him, while his thumb circled on my clit, and I tugged on my nipple with my free hand. I felt the warm heat from my core slide outward. My thighs squeezed tighter and my toes curled. I ground forward in one more deep movement. Every muscle tightened. Sparks of white light erupted behind my eyelids; my fingers dug into his chest. I attempted to hold myself to earth as my body shattered into a million red-hot shards."

Surely, she is almost done. There cannot be much more to their evening.

Adrian resumes. "Winston's hands guided me forward and back, forward and back. He prolonged the delicious orgasm. My muscles spasmed. My walls contracted around his cock and he pumped up into me one last time with a deep guttural growl. I sat statue still as I began to float down from my high."

Adrian chuckles as she recalls the next part. "I whimpered as the pain of a cramp in my right butt cheek hit me. I swatted at Winston's chest as I attempted to form the words to beg for assistance. 'butt...cramp' I got out between shuttering breaths. Winston's palms connected with my two cheeks and fingers attempted to massage. He felt the tightness in my right side, then focused all his attention there. When the massage didn't work, he clasped my ankle and carefully straightened my leg. Like a key in a padlock, he unlocked the cramp. His hand returned to massage. I slowly melted upon his chest as my body softened and my breath evened out. We were still connected for several silent moments under the warm, clear night sky." Her dreamy voice pauses.

I place my hand lightly on her shoulder. This draws Adrian's attention from her daydream.

"I was almost asleep when Winston gently rolled us to our sides and withdrew from me. I didn't like the immediate emptiness. I longed once again for our connection. I rolled to my other side and I wiggled my backside snug to his front. Winston secured his arms around my shoulders and my waist. With his warm breath near my ear, he whispered, 'Are you okay? Did I hurt you?' His words caught me off guard. I've never had a guy ask about me after sex. I guess I've never spooned with a guy after sex for that matter. I thought I should be the one to ask if I hurt him. I took control, took what I wanted, moved upon him with only regard for how I felt."

"I pulled his arm tighter around my belly. Smiling to myself, I asked him how he liked going bareback for the first time? I felt the rumble as he chuckled against my back. He claimed he liked it so much he didn't last very long then continued to explain how good I felt around him. I asked him where this left us. Voices of reason flooded back to me. I'm not one to regret sexual encounters, I need Winston's friendship, he's part of our group of nine, and feared I might lose it all."

"His warm breath still warmed my neck. He struggled for words as he tried to whisper near my ear. He said I'm hot. He has thought I was hot for years. He claimed he even told me that I was hot. He needed me as a friend and he couldn't lose me. I turned in his arms to face him. In a moment of temporary insanity, I told him the sex we just had was by far the best sex I'd ever had. I reminded him he knew me, when I wanted something I took it, and when I liked something I admitted it. I confessed I liked him, and I *really* liked sex with him."

Adrian shakes her head. "His grin was barely visible in the light of the night when he mentioned we could try to be friends with benefits. I pressed my index finger into his chest for emphasis. 'Fuck buddies!' Can you believe he wanted me as a fuck buddy? When I didn't answer his grin was gone. He asked what I had in mind"

"I tried to quickly decide what I wanted. "I confessed I didn't know, I needed time to think. I cuddled a little closer to his chest. I admitted that I liked that I didn't scare him when I came on a bit strong. He informed me, I do scare the shit out of him. His laugh was contagious as we lay in each other's arms."

Adrian sighs heavily running a hand through her messy hair. "Madison, I have never, and I mean *never*, been kissed like that before. It was slow, it was smooth, it was hot, and it reached to every cell in my body."

I smirk. Before June, I would not have understood that such a kiss could exist. After Hamilton's kisses, I know exactly what she means. I tuck my memories of Hamilton away, I focus on her at this moment. "So, this magic kiss swept you off your feet."

My best friend enjoyed her share of hook-ups during high school. But not once did she describe an encounter with these oohey-goohey emotions tied to it. Last night meant something to her. "Please tell me you didn't get R-rated on the playground of the city park."

"We kept it PG-13 while at the park." She traces an X over her heart with her index finger. She sighs a dreamy sigh at the memory. "The man gets an A+ for foreplay." We giggle. "It was sweet, slow torture. I tried to relax and enjoy it, but he had me so worked up, I pounced on him." Adrian rises from her chair to stare out the front window nearby. "Madison, I was a woman possessed. I stripped him, I rolled him over, I sucked him, and I impaled myself on him. I even suggested he forego using a condom. I've never done that before. I was out of control."

"The poor guy didn't stand a chance," I tease. Adrian is the type of woman that just goes for what she wants. I'm a little worried for Winston's condition after last night. He doesn't strike me as they type of guy that likes to be topped.

"Honestly, I was so wrapped up in how I felt and what I wanted that I didn't consider his needs at all." She turns to face me, leaning her arms on the counter. "I was so excited that I had an orgasm. I've never had an orgasm from penetration. And what an orgasm it was. My muscles actually cramped so bad we had to rub them to loosen them. I've never…I mean all of it was an out of body experience. We even spooned. You know, like old people. I didn't know it could feel so good. While he clutched me to his chest, we asked where we go from here, and we didn't have an answer." She shrugs as if it is no big deal.

"It might be hard on the two of you and all your joint friends if it was a one-night stand. Dating is good, I think. So, when is he taking you out?"

"He's not."

I'm confused. My brow furrows, and I tilt my head. "You're not going out with him?"

She explains she told him she needed time to think about it. He knows she likes control and is impulsive—he's letting her lead.

I challenge her. "What's with all the uncertainty?"

"I've never allowed myself to feel this much before. He woke something in me, and now my world is all kinds of mixed up."

"Adrian, I think that's a good thing. I know this scares you, but it also makes you feel alive. You're over-thinking everything. It's like you're a junkie, and you constantly need a fix." My words of understanding describe my feelings towards Hamilton after our one night together. Unfortunately, unlike Adrian's situation, I won't have the opportunity to see Hamilton every day. "You should go for it. Just enjoy the ride."

"How do you know so much about this?"

I understand her question. She knows I barely went on any dates in high school. She believes I have never had sex. "I've read my share of romance novels. I've even read a few erotic romance titles." None of it's really a lie. Just an omission of truth. I'm just not ready to tell her about my night with Hamilton. "I'm not mad at you. I'm actually excited for you. If I knew Winston would be this good for you, I would have set the two of you up a year ago."

"So, you think I should date him?" When I nod, Adrian continues. "What if it doesn't work out? Right now, we might just have the awkwardness of a night together. If we date, it could come between Winston and me while it effects all nine of us."

"Stop being a wimp." I blurt. "Go on dates. Have wild sex. Make public displays of affection. Adrian, you have to give it a shot. Feelings like last night don't happen every day. You know this. You've shared details in the past. You can't let the potential for happiness slide through your fingers."

"Okay, Mom. Geez." she expresses her annoyance at my mini-lecture. "I'll think about giving it a chance."

I fight the urge to share my recent fear with Adrian. She'd be very supportive and help me find out for sure. There's just no way to keep Hamilton's name out of it. If I randomly hooked-up with any other guy, I would confide in my friend. Of course, she would poke and pry trying to get every little sexy detail out of me. Unlike her, I believe intimate details should remain between two people. I can't tell her the desperate favor I asked of our friend. She wouldn't be able to keep a Madison and Hamilton hook-up secret from the rest of our group. Since I can't tell her I slept with Hamilton, I can't tell her how my fear grows exponentially with every passing day. I attempted to remain positive the past eight days, but I can't not know any longer.

28

Reasons for visits to the doctor or small local hospital are topics of gossip. HIPPA doesn't prevent sharing of this confidential information in a place like Athens. It's just one of the 4,724 reasons I want to escape this town.

ADRIAN

what are you doing today?

ME

chores around the house

ADRIAN

text me when you're done

we'll plan something

ME

(thumbs up emoji)

I want nothing more than to hang with my friends today. Almost anything is preferred to what I must do. I pray I'm wrong. I hope I miscalculated or the stress of college this fall is the cause. I am not the type of person that can wait and see. I need to know. I must know, and the sooner the better.

I leave a note on the refrigerator, letting Memphis know I am running errands and to text me if she needs anything from town. It's not a lie. I just didn't say which town I would be in. I found online that the next town west of Athens has a family-owned pharmacy. I plan to make my purchase there, hoping no one from Athens is around or works inside. It's far enough away they shouldn't know my mom, so that is good.

I blare my playlist through my car stereo the entire drive. I attempt to let the heavy beats and lyrics rescue my thoughts from my worries. I find that even Slipknot, Nine Inch Nails, Hailstorm, and Seether can't distract me today.

The outcome of this test will affect so many things. College this fall, my part-time job in Columbia, as well as the plans for the rest of my life. My future may change, but I will not let it affect Hamilton. If it isn't to affect him, that means I can't stay in Athens where his family and friends reside. How can so much ride on the outcome of this little test? My favor of Hamilton may change the trajectory of my entire life. I try to remind myself to not jump to any conclusions, but it is hard not to think of the worst possible outcome.

My heart rate speeds up when I park in the tiny parking lot. I take a moment in an attempt to work up the nerve to walk inside. I mentally tell myself to pull up my big girl panties and make my purchase.

Only two other vehicles populate the small lot. When inside, I realize they most likely belong to the pharmacist and the clerk at the register. The neat-as-a-pin pharmacy is void of customers. I am greeted by the clerk, informing me to be sure to ask if I have any questions. Nope. There won't be any questions. I pick up the major brand pregnancy test in its slim box and quickly approach the register in hopes of completing my transaction before any customers arrive.

"Will this be all for you?" the middle-aged woman at the register inquires. I simply nod, pay with my debit card, then graciously accept the white paper bag concealing the test. "Thank you and come again."

I breathe a sigh of relief when safely sitting behind the wheel of my car. My next step is a stop at the McDonald's on the edge of town. My bladder is anxiously awaiting its first visit to the restroom today. I found online that first morning urine is the best to test with early in a pregnancy. I slide the test from its box and slip it into my purse.

Safely tucked in a locked stall, I prepare to perform the test. I've never given much thought to peeing on a stick before. Turns out it isn't an easy task for a woman. Certainly not a graceful task to say the least. I recap the test, wrap it in tissue, and place it in my purse. I avoid looking in the mirror while I wash my hands. With little sleep last night and the fear of my test results, I am sure I look affright.

I set my cell phone alarm for two more minutes, assume the driver's seat in my car, and begin my journey back towards Athens. At the end of the longest minutes of my life, I peek at the result window. A pink plus sign ensures I am indeed pregnant with Hamilton's baby. Tears well in my eyes, and my hands tremble on the steering wheel. I swerve dangerously at the last minute onto a gravel road. When I throw my car into park, my chest tightens, and I struggle to pull in a breath. I should have known not to read the test while driving sixty miles per hour down the highway.

I allow myself several minutes to cry, to feel sorry for myself, and to overreact. Then, I wipe away my tears, take several deep breaths, and shake my hands out. I pull out my cell phone and start to plan, making a list.

First, I should contact my college advisor, Odessa, to see what options I still have for the year. Next, I should buy a pregnancy book to ensure I do everything I can to have a healthy baby. I should research towns to relocate to in case I cannot attend college this fall. The last note I type on my digital list is to schedule an obstetrics appointment far away from Athens.

Calmer now with a plan in place and certainty to my status, I continue my drive home. I opt to listen to the local radio station, turned low, as my mind needs no further distractions. Although my thoughts should be one-hundred percent on the road, I realize my summer plans will change now, too. I'll need to pack meals when I am working away from the house, I'll need to limit my time in the hot sun, and I should give up caffeine immediately. This seals my duty as the designated driver, not that I ever really drank alcohol.

I wish I had a close friend to share my secret with. Hamilton would be that person, but this is one secret I can't share with him. He would quit baseball and take over his mother's farm the very day I told him. He'd abandon his lifelong dream, the dream his father talked so proudly of. It was never assumed he would take over the farm. They hoped he would attend college and play baseball as long as he could. I can't let the favor I asked of Hamilton change his life and the hopes of his parents.

Still driving, I silently hope I don't start to show before I leave for college or am able to move from Athens. Perhaps I should attempt to move up my departure.

Back in Athens, I stop at the grocery store to pick up the items I know I need to purchase. I say hi to a few people in the store, my secret weighing heavy in my thoughts.

"You need more cereal," Savannah's voice informs as my cart rolls by her stocking the grocery shelves.

"Not that kind of cereal," I state as she attempts to place two boxes in my cart. We chat for a few minutes before I excuse myself to let her get back to work.

I feel guilty that I can't share with her or any of my girlfriends. They won't understand my not wanting Hamilton to give up everything to take care of me. They would fill my thoughts with the idea of moving to Des Moines to be with him. But I know him better than they do. He wouldn't be able to give one-hundred percent to baseball if we were there, and he wouldn't be able to give one-hundred percent to me and the baby while playing baseball. That would not sit well with him. He would drop everything and move back to Athens where he knew he would be able to support us easily. One of us may have to give up our dream of escaping Athens, but I won't allow both of us.

29

Back-to-school supplies are only available at the grocery store and the farm supply store — that's another of the 4,724 reasons I want to escape this town.

I nervously flip through a random magazine as I wait to meet with my advisor. I desperately still wanted to attend college this year, so I reached out to her via email, explaining the change in my situation. I pleaded with her to discuss options that might allow me to still attend classes while pregnant and later with a newborn. She scheduled this meeting without explaining if options existed. Thus, I nervously wait to hear if I can indeed leave Athens for college, or if I will have to move somewhere else.

"Your advisor will see you now." The receptionist informs.

I rise and enter her office.

"Hello, Madison, I'm Odessa." She motions to the two chairs facing her desk. "Please make yourself comfortable."

She moves several papers and file folders from in front of her to the credenza at her back. Placing her elbows on the cleared desktop, she leans towards me, a smile upon her face.

"I am glad you emailed me about the change in your situation," Odessa begins. "How have you been feeling?"

I don't want idle chit-chat. I want to know if the life I planned is still an option. I want to demand answers but know I must be courteous. "I feel good; nervous, anxious, scared, but no morning sickness yet."

She nods, selects a paper from the stack in her wire basket, and places it before her on the desk. "Let's see what we can do to ease your mind. Pregnant students are permitted to live in the dormitories. Those who marry choose to reside in married housing or off campus. The university will still honor all scholarships and dorm assignments for you this fall and spring until you deliver the baby. Children are not allowed in the dorms. You will need to find other accommodations at that time. Your academic scholarships will still be available for your studies."

I nod my understanding as a wave flows over me. I can still attend college. I still have a place to live this fall. I haven't messed my entire future up.

"Madison, I don't see you as the typical MU student. You arrive as a junior, not a freshman. Your previous coursework, grades, and CLEP testing demonstrate you will be an asset in our student body. In our two previous meetings, I feel I learned much about you, so I have another possibility for your housing." Odessa takes a sip of her coffee.

"An acquaintance of mine recently shared information about her family. I think we may be able to assist her, and she may be able to help us. My friend's father recently passed; her mother lives alone in the large family home, and all of the children reside out of state. She is contemplating placing her mother in a retirement community or moving her out of state. Her mother's name is Alma, and she's still active in the church and community. She is mobile, still drives, takes walks, and takes care of herself. The children are concerned she will be lonely and has no one nearby to keep an eye on her. I wonder if you might consider living in one of the four bedrooms, visit with her from time to time, and give the family peace of mind. She doesn't need a nurse, just someone near to check in with her occasionally."

My thoughts churn. I am not sure about this arrangement. Living off campus in a house beats a dorm room. There are many logistics to think of. I cannot afford to pay for my own meals, and my scholarships cover those on campus. I prepare to share my concerns when Odessa continues.

"I have arranged for us to have lunch with Alma today. I would like the two of you to meet prior to either of you agreeing to this arrangement. We should be going so we arrive prior to her."

On the ride, I recall all that Odessa shared in her office. I am not sure if I hope to live with Alma or in the dorm. I'm anxious to meet her to see if we are a good match.

As we make our way inside Murray's, we pass two teenage girls chatting with an older woman near the front door. They are discussing books they enjoyed reading this summer. One book they mention is the erotic romance I finished recently.

At our table, Odessa leans towards me. "Alma is in the group standing at the door."

I follow her pointing finger, to find the group discussing books. I now hope, since Alma and I enjoy the same types of books, maybe living together could work out. She can't be a stuffy, elderly woman if she openly speaks of erotic romance in public.

As we begin to nibble on our meal, Alma shares the story of how she met her husband on campus decades ago. I nearly spit my water across the table as she shares in detail the hot chemistry between them at the dance. It's as if I'm sitting across from an older version of Adrian. My fears lesson with her every word. I think this will be a good match.

"Odessa shared very little with me," Alma leans towards me from her side of the table and lowers her voice a bit. "Are you excited about your pregnancy? Do you plan to raise the baby?"

Just like Adrian, Alma holds nothing back. I sip my water as I search for the difficult answers. I decide honesty is important if I am to live with this stranger. "I didn't plan to become pregnant. Excited isn't the first word that comes to mind. Overwhelmed, scared, and stressed are a few of the feelings constantly swarming in my head." I take a deep breath in an attempt to open the tightness in my throat. "I didn't want to become pregnant at eighteen but finding myself in my current situation I *want* to keep our baby."

I scan surrounding tables to ensure other patrons are not listening to our conversation. "The father is my best friend. I plan to tell him about our baby later. He's chasing a dream, and I can't rip that away from him. I have no doubt he would drop everything and support us. One day in the future, I will give him that opportunity. For now, I plan to do the best I can on my own."

"What about your family? Memphis mentioned you are an only child, but what of your parents?" Instead of Adrian, Alma now resembles Memphis.

"I am an only child and my parents are only children." I fight the urge to rant negatively about my mother. Sometimes my rage outweighs my rational mind. "My dad passed when I was thirteen. My mother hasn't coped well since then. She struggles with depression and will not be helping me with the baby." If I live with Alma, I know I will need to share more about my relationship with my mother. In this moment it doesn't seem appropriate.

Alma places her wrinkled hand upon mine on the table. "From what I know of your academic ability and in meeting you today, I have no doubt you can handle this on your own until you are ready to let your friend in. I sense your fortitude. Although you haven't shared in detail, your eyes divulge you've experienced hardship. You have prevailed for eighteen years, you are a survivor."

Her words comfort. I desperately fight the tears pricking the back of my eyes and my sinuses. It's too early to blame them on pregnancy hormones. I deflect the topic from me. "Have you discussed a tenant with your family?" Please take the bait. No more about my situation. It's too new and I haven't come to terms with every facet of it. I need time to adjust before I open my chest and share all of my secrets and fears.

"My son, Trenton, attempts to assume the role as head of our family in these few months since my husband passed." Alma sighs while fiddling with her butter knife. "He doesn't like the idea of me remaining in my home alone. He coerces my daughters to urge me to move into an assisted living community." She chuckles. "That's just a fancy word for a nursing home. I don't need that. I'm healthy, active, and in control of all of my faculties. I know they worry about my living alone. My involvement in the church and community should be enough to ease their worries, but they are persistent."

Odessa excuses herself to the restroom. Alma slides closer to me. "I miss my husband. I love my home. It's full of memories of my babies and now my grandchildren. I can't box those up and take them with me. Every dent in the woodwork and scratch on the hardwood is a precious memory to me. I'll admit the house it much too large for one person. Heck, it's too big for two."

She genuinely smiles at me. "I'm sure my oldest daughter, Taylor, reached out to Odessa. They went to high school together. When Odessa mentioned the opportunity for me to help a promising scholar attain her degree, I saw it as a solution to continue living the life I love while sharing my love with another."

"My children may not like a stranger living in my home. Trenton will blow a gasket." She smiles fondly thinking of the son. "He only means to protect me, but I'm about to remind him of his place in our family. I am his mother and he is my child. I'm sure the time will come when he will need to control my life, but I am not ready to give up just yet."

Her smirk is that of a defiant teenager. I fear Trenton is in for a long battle with his mother. I'm glad she continues to battle after the loss of her husband. I wish my mother had half of the strength I've witnessed in Alma today.

Before I know it, the check has been paid and Odessa announces she needs to return to campus. I love Alma. I can see myself living with her, spending time with her, and being happy.

"I would like to propose the two of you spend a couple of hours together at Alma's home today." Odessa's eyes dart between Alma and me. "Then, take a day or two to think it over before you let me know your decision." She flashes an encouraging smile our way.

Alma's eyes look to mine. "Madison, I would love to show you my home and visit this afternoon." I nod.

Odessa suggests Alma ride back to the office with us. Then, I can drive Alma home and leave from her house later this afternoon. I'm nervous for Alma to see my old car but realize I'm a college student; she expects me to drive an old car.

Alma's house is absolutely adorable. The two-story exterior is neat as a pin. I can tell it's been re-sided recently with fresh paint to the trim and shutters. The wrap around porch, complete with pillars and a porch swing, perfectly finish its curb appeal.

The interior is decorated with comfortable furnishings, family photos, and thriving house plants. Alma explains her bedroom moved into the back dining room a few years ago as the kids worried about their parents climbing the stairs each day. The kitchen is updated with stainless steel appliances and marble countertops. She seems to climb the stairs with ease. I understand why her children might worry but am glad to see Alma is indeed active.

She states that I would have my choice of the four bedrooms and three bathrooms if I choose to move in. The rooms are completely furnished with queen-size beds, dressers, bedside tables, lamps, and armoires. The color schemes are neutral, modern, and match the quilts that adorn the beds. One bathroom contains a glass-enclosed shower, the other a clawfoot tub with a tile shower stall in the corner. I know which bed and bathroom I will choose.

"Any questions about the house?" Alma asks as we return to the first floor.

"Alma, I want to be honest with you," I begin. "I enjoy your company, and I love the house." I like the soft smile my words bring to her face. "I only found out about the pregnancy last week. As I mentioned earlier, it's all new to me, and I'm scrambling to see if attending college is still an option for me."

Alma interrupts my confession. "Would you like a drink, maybe some water?"

"I'd love a water."

I join her in the kitchen. With water in hand, I continue at the kitchen island. "If I told the father about the baby, he would throw away his dreams and take care of me. I can't allow him to do that. I won't let him give up everything for me." I sip my water. "I already have enough credits, so I will be a junior this fall. I need only complete my final two years to graduate." I search my brain for anything else I should share.

She pats my hand upon the marble countertop. "Let's find a comfy chair, dear." I follow her back to the living room with water in my shaking hand. I really want this to work out. "I've shared my children's fears of my living alone so many miles away from them. I'm fortunate to be in excellent health. My husband left me financially secure. I enjoy shopping, dining out, going to movies, and attending church." She sighs. "By allowing a college student to move in, my children will gain peace of mind, I can continue living the life I love, and I receive a new friend. I've enjoyed our time together today. I want to offer you the opportunity to live with me while you attend college. I will not ask you to do chores or nurse me—I don't need that." She chuckles. "I have a cleaning lady visit twice a week. In exchange for room and board, I only need you to ease my children's worries. During our weekly calls, from time to time, you could say hello, and let them know all is good."

"Alma, I can't live here for free, and I can't let you buy my groceries."

"Madison, I am a mother and a grandmother. I love being a mother and as you will soon learn, you can't turn it off. Your living here will give me a purpose again. My late husband was a very successful surgeon. Trust that supplying meals for two instead of one will not inconvenience me." She smiles, morphing her voice from stern to calm. "We can cook together if you would like. The cost of remaining in my home is so much lower than the exorbitant amounts they charge to live in a retirement village."

I am grateful for the offer. With a baby on the way, not paying for meals would be helpful. A bubble of excitement swells in my belly. I really want to live here. I really want to help Alma by keeping her company. I know she will be helping me much more than I help her.

"If the offer still stands, I would love to live with you."

30

The fair parade is over an hour long, with more tractors and horse clubs than other floats—it's one of the 4,724 reasons I want to leave.

Memphis and Adrian join me at our spot along the fair parade route at 3:45. It's a humid, ninety-five-degree day. It will be a great night for the fair when the hot sun sets. We fan ourselves with a magazine while we wait, seated in our lawn chairs, in the outer part of the grocery store parking lot. Even this early, as we drove through town, most of the streets were lined, lawn chair to lawn chair, along the route. Kids sit, anxiously clutching plastic bags to fill with the candy that will be tossed from the floats.

Sometime after five, we hear the approach of police sirens signaling the parade is drawing near us. Adrian quickly connects FaceTime with Hamilton, like I promised we would, to include him in this tradition. He can't stay on long but gets a kick out of sharing it with his teammates.

Later the three of us walk around the midway for over an hour, often stopping to talk with people. The fair is a major event in Athens. Many people attend all six nights as well as an afternoon or two for the livestock competitions and other displays.

When we run into Salem, Latham, and Winston, Adrian joins their group for the rest of the evening. I'm sure Memphis and I will leave hours before she is ready to. The fair is not my thing. The carnival workers scare me, and it's like walking through a redneck convention. I smirk as Winston switches spots with Latham to walk beside Adrian. Their hands bump into each other a couple of times before the crowd envelops them.

It's my last evening in Athens. I am glad the fair distracts my friends as I slip away for the night.

31

The local radio station reads obituaries on the news daily—it's one of the 4,724 reasons I want to escape this town.

This drive to Columbia isn't, as exciting as first planned. It was to be Hamilton and I in his truck. Today, it's just me in my old car with a few boxes of clothes and things. The excitement I planned is replaced by fear. I planned to be on my own with one friend on campus; instead, I am responsible for a mini-human growing inside me. I planned to arrive the end of August—instead I'm starting my new life in late July.

I'm excited to live with Alma; we really hit it off, and I believe our arrangement will be mutually beneficial. I look forward to learning more about her family and the history of her house. She mentioned teaching me to cook, and I offered to help her with new technologies her children and grand-children purchase for her. She'll teach me about my new town and help me not hide in my room. I'll ensure she stays active and safe for her family. She's nowhere near my age, but she assures me there are many students my age that attend her church and participate in activities there throughout the week.

I find, during my three hour drive, that my mind is free to contemplate many things. The guilt I feel for keeping my pregnancy a secret from Hamilton comes to mind. I regret not telling Memphis about our situation. She is an awesome mother and a great friend to me. I think she might have understood my desire not to share the pregnancy with Hamilton, but I didn't want to put her in a position to keep it from him. Then, the guilt for not opening up with Adrian floods my thoughts. Of my group of friends, she's the one that would have my back and hold my hair while I bent over the toilet with morning sickness. I only hope each of them will understand why I am keeping my pregnancy a secret for now. I realize I take the risk of losing them with my actions in this situation.

The cell phone Hamilton gave me is a blessing today as I use the Maps app for driving directions to Alma's home. When the voice alerts me that my destination is on the right, I find Alma sitting in her porch swing, smiling and waving as I pull in the driveway. As I exit my car, Alma makes her way to me.

"Welcome to your home away from home," she greets, pulling me into a hug. "Would you like to unload now or relax a bit?" She stands with her hands upon my shoulders.

"I could really use a restroom," I answer.

"Then we will unload after dinner," Alma states, guiding me up the steps into her home. "The restroom is second door on the left."

I nod and take my leave to relieve myself. While washing my hands, I look in the large mirror. I look the same as I did before I took the pregnancy test, met with my advisor, and plotted this new course. It hits me that I am officially in Columbia. I am officially starting my new life. I am equal parts scared and excited.

Upon joining Alma in the front room, I find she's prepared a tray with iced tea, cheese, and crackers. I join her on the sofa, gladly sipping the tea. Just as I prepare to start a conversation, the front door bell rings.

"Who could that be?" Alma looks to me before making her way across the room to peek through the curtain at the door. "What are you...?" She opens the heavy wooden door.

"Surprise!" What looks like a family of four shout.

Two little people wrap their arms around Alma while commenting on how they surprised grandma. She hugs the boys before greeting the man and woman, each holding a puppy.

"Who are these two adorable guys?" Alma asks while petting them both.

"Mom, may we come in?"

"Where are my manners?" she chides herself. "Madison, this is my son, Trenton, his wife Ava, and my grandchildren, Hale and Grant. Everyone, this is Madison." Alma explains I arrived only minutes before they did.

I exchange pleasantries with Alma's family. I feel I'm an intruder. My desire to move before August is interfering with her family plans. Trenton and his wife place the curly puppies down on the hardwood floor. Exploring the space, the two are so excited it appears their short little tails wag their entire back end. I join them on the floor. Immediately, two puppies take residency in my lap, lick my neck or face, and with paws on my shoulders, knock me backwards. As I lay on the floor, they continue to lavish licks as I laugh.

"Rescue her," Ava instructs Trenton.

He tucks one puppy under each arm while I return to my seat upon the sofa. Trenton explains they decided to take a family vacation to surprise Alma and meet me. I wonder if he really means to vet me. Alma seems surprised they are here. I'm sure her three children decided someone needed to meet me in person to ensure Alma's safety.

With our added guests, unloading my car takes little time at all.

I enjoy Trenton's short two-day visit. Although I know he's here to check me out, I find him easy to talk to. His boys are absolutely adorable. As they play, I find myself imagining my little one as a boy playing games and talking baseball with his father, Hamilton.

As we eat dinner, I have to bite my lip not to giggle at them.

"You ask him," Grant whispers.

"No, you ask him," Hale whispers.

How the two boys think the four adults also seated at the table don't hear their whispers amazes me. Trenton tells his sons it's not polite to whisper at the table.

His oldest son, Hale, finds the nerve to speak up. "Dad, when can we tell Grandma?" Hale's eyes dart from his father to mother anxiously.

Trenton ruffles his son's hair. "Mom," he turns the conversation to Alma's side of the table. "One of the puppies is a gift from Hale and Grant for you." The boys preen. "When we visited the breeder, they couldn't choose between these two puppies. Hale, ever the negotiator, suggested we purchase both and let Grandma choose one, and we keep the other."

All eyes turn to Alma for her reaction. I pity the pressure her family just placed upon her. Not only would it be difficult to choose between the two adorable puppies, but her decision also decides which puppy her grandchildren get to keep. As Hale prefers one and Grant prefers another, it's like choosing one child over the other.

The visit passes quickly. As they pack up their gear, I assist Alma in preparing breakfast. We eat, say our goodbyes with promises to call soon, and they back out of the driveway on their way back home. Alma and I wave from her porch while Alma's new chocolate mini Labradoodle gnaws on his new leash in my hand. Of the two puppies, I am glad she chose the chocolate over the golden—he was my favorite, too.

Trenton's gift of a puppy is genius. A pet provides comfort and companionship while keeping Alma active. I smile to myself. Alma's son killed two birds with one stone this weekend. He vetted the strange college girl living with his mother, and he gifted Alma with another purpose to enjoy her life.

32

The grocery and farm store are the only places to purchase children's Halloween costumes. For variety or larger sizes, one must drive forty-minutes or shop online. This is one of the 4,724 reasons I want to escape this town.

While enjoying a meal with Alma after church, my phone vibrates. It's a group text from Adrian.

ADRIAN

video call 7pm tonight

ME

yes, call my phone

SAVANNAH

see you tonight

SALEM

I can't wait

BETHANY

will be there

Promptly at seven, a video call from the girls rings my phone. The girls ask a million questions about my new room and the city of Columbia. I pull Alma into the video call for a bit to meet all of them. Later, I share about Trenton's visit, brag about Alma's adorable grandsons, and show them Alma's new puppy named McGee.

The girls chat about the latest gossip in Athens, the weather and crops, Adrian shares about her business, Savannah about the busy grocery store, then Salem and Bethany complain about their classes.

I miss my friends, and Columbia seems so far away. I know I wanted to get settled in before classes started, but I hate that I needed to leave weeks earlier than I originally planned. All too soon, we must end our call.

After much discussion, I relent and allow Alma to contact the obstetrics physician she and her late husband were close friends with. She assures me he is one of the best in the state. I worry about affording him, but she insists on taking care of that for me. I will not allow this. When I arrive at my first appointment, I will inform the doctor and his staff that I refuse to allow her to cover my medical expenses.

I find, in Alma's world of connections, things happen quickly at Alma's request. I'm anxious to learn if others quickly do her bidding out of fear or out of love for this caring woman. She called Dr. Anderson's office, and I have an appointment the next day. In a city as large as Columbia, this has to be unheard of. Even in Athens, we were lucky to get an appointment in two to three days' time. So, now I have little time to prepare myself for my first pregnancy appointment.

I've read the first few chapters in the pregnancy book Alma gave to me. It seems very comprehensive. Although it tells me what to expect on my first physician visit, I am still very nervous.

My nerves stem from my desire to be a great mom from the start. I worry that the changes I saw in my own mother after my father's passing might be genetic, affecting my ability to protect my baby. I want to be the mother I had in my childhood, but I worry things weren't the way I remember them. I'm nervous that my limited funds might not allow me to provide the best care possible. I also worry my bouts with depression may hinder my parenting.

As I am a single-mother, I am prepared for some to be unsupportive of my situation. I don't have to like it, but I've vowed to be strong. I fear that guilt will be the thorn in my side during my pregnancy. Although I know I am keeping my secret for the right reasons, I struggle with the guilt of not sharing with those I love.

Finally, thoughts of tomorrow's appointment fade and sleep finds me. As is my new routine, I wake twice to go to the bathroom and drink a glass of water. I find I am often very thirsty which, of course, leads to frequent trips to the restroom. It's a vicious cycle that I am sure I will endure the entire pregnancy.

The next morning, I wake after nine. I hear Alma's television on in the kitchen as I descend the stairs. The aroma of fresh-brewed coffee pulls me towards the kitchen. I've always loved the smell of coffee; I just haven't fallen in love with the taste. I'm lucky, because I would need to avoid it for the next several months if I did like it.

"I didn't start breakfast," Alma states as I enter. "Morning sickness can be harsh. Smells and tastes can set it off. I wanted to see how you felt first."

"Alma, you are so kind." Not only is she giving up a part of her house, but now she pauses her breakfast on my account. "So far, no signs of morning sickness. In fact, I'm starving." I look around the counters. "I think I'll fix some toast with peanut butter."

Alma enjoys her toast with jam. When she insists I didn't eat enough for breakfast, I promise to eat cereal in a couple of hours. She chuckles at my love of cereal. Apparently, she thought I was exaggerating when I told her I eat a bowl or two every day. It's actually my favorite snack.

An hour later, I am sitting beside Alma in the waiting room of the physician's office. Women in varying stages of pregnancy surround us. Some have a doting man with them, others have children in tow. I pat Alma's hand, glad I am not alone.

When my name is called, and I follow the petite nurse into the hall. She records my weight, takes my temperature, then escorts me to the exam room. I find the room much bigger than any room I've been in before. I'm instructed to fill a cup for my urine sample, remove all my clothes, and put on the gown with openings in the front. My situation just became very real to me.

As I sit on the crisp, crackling paper upon the exam table, I busy myself looking around the room. The posters on the wall share information on stages of pregnancy, location of the fetus moving through the birth canal, and even possible sleep positions for comfort. I ignore the metal utensils and tube of cream on the counter beside the sink. I notice many flyers filed on the side of a counter set at desk height.

A light rap at the door signals the doctor's entry. "Good morning, Madison, I'm Dr. Anderson and this is my nurse, Dawn." He makes his way to the stool at the desk and opens my chart on his tablet. Instead of reading my vitals or examining me, he sets the tablet down and rolls towards me. "You're a friend of Alma's. I'm so very glad she sent you my way. How do you like Columbia so far?"

This is not how I envisioned my appointment beginning. I explain Alma has taken me many places to shop, to walk, and to eat. I admit, I am looking forward to classes starting in about a month. He admits that Alma told him about my major and that I am starting as a junior instead of a freshman. He comments that I should consider medicine if learning comes easy to me, but admits teaching is a noble profession that is the backbone of all other careers.

Finally, he directs his attention to the reason for my visit. "So, you've taken a pregnancy test or two with a positive result. Let's get started." He sticks a strip in my urine that quickly gives him a positive pregnancy result. "Yep, very pregnant," he chuckles. "Can you tell me when you had your last period?"

"I can do better than that," I state. "I know the exact night I conceived."

He furrows his brow and explains it is very difficult to pinpoint the moment of conception. We usually count from the last day of the last period and use that as our base.

"I've only had sex once. It was the night of June Eighth. Well, I guess I had sex more than once that night, but that is the only date I've been with anyone." I shrug. "We used condoms, but since then I've read they are not one-hundred percent effective."

Dr. Anderson studies me for a minute to judge my honesty. "Alma shared some of your situation with me." He looks a bit embarrassed of his admission. "The father is not in the picture?"

"Oh, he would be if I told him. He got drafted by the Chicago Cubs. We were supposed to attend MU together this fall. He was to play baseball for the Tigers. Anyway, he got drafted, had 48 hours before he reported to their triple-A team in Des Moines, and I refuse to tell him about the pregnancy, because he will give up his dream of baseball to farm and care for me and the baby." I quickly swallow and continue rambling. "He's a good guy. The best. In fact, he's the perfect guy to have a family with. But I know how important his dream is. It was a dream he shared with his father before he died. I can't be the reason he gives up on his dream. So, I will attend school, have the baby, and a year or two down the road, when he is settled in Major League Baseball, I will tell him about our baby." Talk about diarrhea of the mouth—I'm out of breath.

Dr. Anderson looks to his nurse then back at me. "Not an easy situation to be in at the age of eighteen. Alma stated you have no family support either. I'm glad you have Alma with you during your pregnancy, but I am worried that you might need to tell others for additional help."

I know he only wants what is best for his patient and the baby, but I know my life situation better than anyone. I am doing the right thing for now. I can do this. With Alma's help, I will cope with the changes and stress of pregnancy and college and come out strong in the end.

Dr. Anderson, with the help of his nurse, complete my first patient exam. We discuss prenatal vitamins, eating healthy, exercise, and other information I need to know about the upcoming appointment schedule. He tells me to call his office with any questions or if any unusual symptoms arise. He says his nurse will give me a print out of important numbers to call in case of emergency. Then, he says goodbye.

"Um, Dr. Anderson," I call. His nurse has already exited the room. "One more thing." I wring my hands in my lap. "I want to pay for my appointments myself. I don't want Alma to cover my medical bills. She is already doing me a big favor by sharing her house; it wouldn't be right for her to pay for my medical bills, too." *Not that I know how I will be able to pay for the bills,* I think to myself.

"I agree," he states, resuming his seat on the rolling stool. "But Alma isn't paying for your treatment. I am taking on your case pro-bono."

"I can't ask you to do that. Please, let me make payment arrangements," I attempt to argue.

"You didn't ask—I offered. I do research with the university. As an alumnus, I like to assist students when I can. From what I hear, you are an exceptional student. You will be one that MU can be proud of. I only want to help ensure you complete your education. For most appointments, I am only out my time. Occasionally, we will run a test that I will cover. All I ask in return is that you take care of yourself and your little one while you earn your degree."

I stare at him. Is this guy for real? Who does this? I shake my head. I am finding many people around Alma do these types of things. The blessing I thought I found in a place to live off campus is turning out to be a mega-blessing in disguise. I only hope I am able to repay the favors I am being given.

I set my Mac on the dresser, open the webcam, and begin recording. I walk to the edge of the bed and take a seat. I ensure I see myself on the screen and begin.

"Today is August Eighth; I had my first obstetrics appointment with Dr. Anderson today. He assures me I am nine weeks pregnant. Both the baby and I are in good health. Thus far, we have no cause for concern. Well, he was a bit worried that I don't have a large support system, but I believe Alma and I will be able to handle this. I haven't gained any weight yet. I don't have any signs of morning sickness. I am tired all the time. I've learned I like naps, and if I didn't have to pee, I would sleep through the night." I pause, trying to think of anything else I wanted to share.

"Hamilton, you have a game tonight in Des Moines versus the New Orleans Baby Cakes. You're slated to be the starting pitcher." I lift the laptop to show the large schedule I have on the wall, the whiteboards with Hamilton's ERA and pitching rotation. "Alma joins the baby and I as we comb the internet for stats, pictures, and videos of you and the I-Cubs. I not only have ESPN app alert me and the baby of my favorite team, the Cardinals, but also the Cubs now, too. I hope I don't lose my Cardinals fan club membership for doing so. I've even set up Google alerts on the phone you gave me for the 'I-

Cubs', 'Hamilton Armstrong+baseball', and 'Chicago Cubs+pitch.'" I return the laptop to the dresser. "That way, the three of us will know any news as soon as it goes public. It turns out your three biggest fans all live in Columbia, MO under one roof." I turn sideways in front of the webcam. "So, you can watch our little bundle grow…" I lift my T-shirt over my head. My abdomen is visible in my sports bra and low-waist shorts. "We are nine weeks pregnant. Our little baby is right in here." I point to my belly. "We love you and will post again soon." I walk over and stop the recording as tears well up in my eyes.

I want to create this visual journal for Hamilton. I want him to be able to see everything. I know my recording is no replacement for him helping me during the pregnancy, but he will be able to watch these videos and know we were thinking of him always. I hope in some small way, it will allow him to sort of experience our baby from the start.

33

The local radio station airs live interviews from the county fair. I don't need to hear how a fifteen-year-old boy raised his bull then won grand champion. Yet another of the 4,724 reasons I want to escape Athens.

I sign for a letter while Alma is fixing lunch. I see Taylor's name, Alma's oldest daughter, in the return address area. I assume it's our itinerary for the upcoming Chicago trip Alma's oldest daughter mentioned on our last call. Alma quickly opens the cardboard envelope to reveal our airline tickets for Thursday's flight. I quickly help Alma text Taylor to let her know we received the tickets before we enjoy our grilled cheese and chips. I'm actually looking forward to the trip. I've never been to Chicago. I know Taylor said we wouldn't do too much to wear out Alma, but I might try to slip away to do a bit of sight-seeing. During our light lunch, we plot our time to leave for St. Louis to ensure we have time for TSA before our flight. In my weather app, I share the Chicago forecast during our stay, so Alma and I will be prepared when we pack tonight and tomorrow. As I wash our lunch dishes my phone vibrates on the counter. It's a quick vibration, so I know it is an alert, not a text; I keep cleaning the dishes.

Later, I dry my hands then check for the alert that pinged my phone. The words cause me to drop my phone like it's on fire. I can't take a breath. I'm trying and trying; nothing is working. I bend over, lowering my head towards my legs. It takes everything I have to pull in short little puffs of air. I lean my hands on the counter, letting my head drop to the cold granite. The sensation calms me and helps me focus.

"Alma!" I scream. McGee runs toward me, barking.

She quickly comes to my side. "Madison, honey, what is it? Is it the baby?"

I can only shake my head and point to the ESPN alert on my phone screen. She reads it out loud. "The Chicago Cubs call up left-handed pitcher, Hamilton Armstrong, from their AAA team."

I witness the light bulb moment when the words compute for Alma. Her eyebrows rise sharply, eyes open wide, and jaw drops straight down. I nod my head in agreement. Although we speak no words, we agree this is freaking awesome. Alma breaks from the shock before me. She calms McGee with a dog treat before fetching a bottle of water. She removes the cap and urges me to sip while she rubs my back in a circular motion. McGee, still concerned, lies on my feet.

"He did it," I whisper. "In two months, he moved from the triple-A ball team to the Major League." I shake my head. "I knew he would, but now that he did, I can't believe it."

"This means we can watch his games live on television instead of constantly refreshing the computer browser to update the games stats."

This is why I've grown to love Alma. She quickly shared in my excitement of all things baseball and following Hamilton's stats. "We'll get the MLB package, so we can see all of his games."

I pick up my phone to shoot a text to the man himself.

ME

just read the ESPN alert

had mini heart attack

I am so proud of you

Congrats!

you're in the big leagues

I'm sure you're swamped today

just know we are celebrating down here in Columbia

Next, I call Memphis. "Are you sitting down?" I ask immediately. When she confirms, I share the news. "I'm not sure if Hamilton will have time to call you today, so I wanted to tell you. I just saw on ESPN that the Cubs called Hamilton up to Chicago today!" After my squeal, I give her time to have a mini-panic attack like I did.

"Madison!" I know she is struggling for words just like me. "I'm so proud of him. I guess you were right all along. You said he'd play in the Major Leagues. I never had the conviction you did. Thank you for being such a big fan and friend to him all these years." We chat for a bit before she lets me go to call her daughter.

I don't hear back from Hamilton until after ten p.m.

HAMILTON

are you awake?

ME

yes!

I answer my ringing phone.

"Can you believe this?" Hamilton begins. "You would not believe everything I had to do today."

"I want to hear everything!" I feel disconnected from him at this distance. I long to experience everything with him—I am his number one fan after all.

Hamilton shares the details of his exciting day.

"Did they tell you when you might get your debut?" I can't believe I am seriously asking my best friend when he will pitch for the Chicago Cubs.

"I take the mound Sunday against the Brewers. I can't believe I get to say that. I will be pitching against the Milwaukee Brewers at Wrigley Field."

"That is so cool." I know my words sound lame. There are no words grand enough for this.

We talk for over an hour before I let him go, stating he needs to rest before practice tomorrow. We promise to talk again before his big day Sunday. I fall asleep with a happy heart for my friend and all he has accomplished. I can't wait for the world to see how great he is.

34

In Athens, most students are related to several of their teachers, one of the 4,724 reasons I want to leave this town.

Our first evening in Chicago flies by. I enjoy meeting Taylor's husband and two pre-teen daughters. Their apartment is a huge, two floor home. Alma and I stay in a guest room on the lower level with the girls' rooms next door.

Taylor's daughters ask if they can 'do it now'. I can't wait to see what the 'it' is they have for Alma. They jog into the kitchen and return with an envelope for Alma and one for me. We are urged to open them at the same time. As we pull the ticket from inside, they shout "Surprise!" in unison while hopping up and down.

I can't believe my eyes. In my hand, I hold a ticket to Sunday's Chicago Cubs game versus the Brewers. It's a ticket to Hamilton's MLB debut. Taylor's husband explains they are season ticket holders at Wrigley. They sweet-talked the couple with season tickets next to theirs for the extra two Sunday game tickets. All four adults will attend Sunday's afternoon game at Wrigley Field. I get to see Hamilton's debut live in person. I can't believe my luck. Alma appears as excited as I am.

Before Alma and I shut the light off for bed, I shoot an email to Hamilton's agent.

Dear Mr. Sheridan,
I have a surprise for Hamilton Armstrong and was wondering if I might ask for your help.
I will be attending Sunday's Cubs vs. Brewers game. Below, I have attached a copy of my ticket for the game. I wonder if there might be any way for me and the three attending with me to see Hamilton after the game. I realize his MLB debut will come with a lot of press and other obligations. We would just like a brief moment to surprise him and say hello.
Thank you for all you do for Hamilton.
Sincerely,
Madison Crocker

I swim in the atmosphere that is Wrigley Field. Our seats are three rows behind the Cubs dugout. Taylor's husband must pay a fortune for them each year. I enjoy every stress-filled moment of Hamilton's big debut. I marvel at his fire-bolt of a left arm, the precision with which he paints the corners of the plate at will, his instincts and knowledge of the game, and watching a few MLB players buckle at the knees with his curveball. It takes everything in me not to wave like a fan-girl as he returns to the dugout each inning. In the bottom of the sixth inning, the pitching coach approaches the mound and makes a change. I nudge Alma, standing to wave frantically at Hamilton. I call his name as he returns to the dugout. He wears a huge smile as he waves to the excited fans, cheering the end of his debut.

"Hamilton!" I hop up and down as I yell at him over and over, waving both my arms above my head.

His eyes scan in our direction. In the exact moment he recognizes me, I freeze with my hand still in the air, mid-wave. His smile grows warmer for me. He gives a tip of the bill of his ballcap to me as he disappears into the dugout below.

"I can't believe you really know him," Taylor's husband leans forward to address me. "He had a huge game today."

I nod. In the top of the eighth, Alma nudges my shoulder then points to the aisle. My eyes follow her finger to find an event staff member asking for Madison Crocker. I carefully make my way to the aisle. I smile at his words.

I ask Alma to get Taylor's attention. "Want to go with me to see Hamilton?"

Alma and her family excitedly follow me.

We are escorted from the stands to an under the stadium hallway where Nelson Sheridan waits for us. I introduce Alma and her family. Mr. Sheridan ushers us to a small conference room where he asks us to wait for Hamilton after the game. Taylor and her spouse quickly take a selfie to brag about seeing private parts of Wrigley today. As the game plays on a mounted TV, we watch the Cubs claim the victory.

Waiting sucks. The anticipation of seeing Hamilton in person seems more than I can bear. This will be the first time I've been in his presence since learning I'm carrying his child. As our door is barely cracked open, we hear the press fill the hallway outside the locker room. It is announced that the pressroom doors are open. The excited throng exits the hallway, and the noise level greatly decreases. Mr. Sheridan pops his head in to state that Hamilton will be here in a moment.

I feel my belly flip-flop when Hamilton enters our room. His agent quickly closes the door, allowing us privacy for a moment. I am scooped into a tight embrace. Hamilton buries his head in my neck and hair.

"I can't believe you're really here," he murmurs. His hot breath on my ear prickles my skin and brings back memories of our night together. As he pulls away, we grin like fools. "Alma, it's nice to meet you in person."

"I'm glad to meet the man behind the stats we've reverently followed online." Alma shakes his hand. She introduces Hamilton to her family. He signs the back of all of our tickets, claiming they are his first four autographs as a Chicago Cub.

We congratulate him on his great outing today. He tries to put into words the moment his name was announced and when he first took the mound. He confesses he is nervous for the post-game press conference he will be leaving us for in a moment. Our time in his presence is brief, and I wouldn't trade it for all the gold in the world.

Once back at Taylor's home, I excuse myself for a bit. I record today's video journal entry by proudly displaying my ticket with Hamilton's signature from the game. I state that today was our baby's first time attending one of Daddy's games. I share Hamilton's comments about the crowd, the atmosphere, and his stats for today's game. I apologize on camera for keeping my secret, share that his talent for the game is the reason, and vow in the future, I will tell him everything.

35

There is only one small shoe store in Athens, and it doesn't carry sports shoes. To get sports gear and shoes, you must order online or drive over forty minutes to the closest store. This is one of the 4,724 reasons I want to escape this town.

Back from Chicago, Adrian asks me, via text, to call her as soon as I get unpacked. When I call, she excitedly shares how my seven friends in Athens watched Hamilton's Cubs debut.

"Two part-time employees volunteered to run the concession stand. Troy and Latham planned to start the projectors in all three theaters during the pre-game show to ensure all attending viewed the entire game. Bethany and Savannah offered to take tickets outside the outer door to help with the flow of the crowd. With all this help, Winston and I were free to float as needed and to welcome everyone."

"Wow!" If I wasn't in Chicago, I would have joined you."

Adrian beams. "I wish you could have seen Winston and his parents' surprise when I announced tickets sold out in less than twenty-four hours. We raised $750 from ticket sales for the Athens Ball Association. Our community support for Hamilton's Major League debut was overwhelming. The entire $5 ticket price for the viewing was all donated to youth baseball and softball programs in Athens. The concession stand offered drinks and popcorn. All funds collected from food were also donated."

"Winston's family loved my idea to share Hamilton's debut as a local fundraising opportunity. I was so happy that I was able to help Winston in return for his assisting with my store."

"Before we began the viewing in each theater, Winston welcomed and thanked each group and reminded them the concession stand was open the entire game and all money would be donated. As each theater applauded, Troy and Latham started their projector."

"Winston invited Troy, Latham, Bethany, and Savannah to watch the game with us in his office. We took turns checking on all areas while the Cubs were at bat."

"In addition to the $750 we raised in ticket sales, we made $1250 in concessions and the free-will donation tubs. Athens truly came through on Hamilton's big day. They supported Hamilton in his debut and our local ball programs. Winston posted the total raised on the theater's Facebook page that night, and the community's comments were awesome. You should pull them up to read."

Sensing the end of her story, I can finally speak. "Adrian, that is awesome. You need to text Hamilton to call you when he can and share this with him. He will love this. Not only that Athens watched his debut, but donated money to help baseball and softball to do it." I am so proud of her.

"It's surreal that our friend is pitching in the Major Leagues. I am so happy you were able to be at Wrigley."

"I hope Winston rewarded you for all the planning you did on this. I'm sure it doubled as positive publicity for his theaters."

"I have no complaints," she giggles.

I'm so glad she's found Winston. I worried for so long that her need to be in control would prevent her from finding love in the small town of Athens. Although I am shocked that Winston allows her to lead at times, I am happy he does. My friend deserves happiness and he provides that for her.

36

There is only one dentist in Athens. For an orthodontist, you must drive twenty minutes, and he's only available two days a month. This is one of the 4,724 reasons I want to escape this town.

The next week, Adrian calls me. I love that she still reaches out to me for advice or to brag about her encounters with Winston.

"Hi Adrian," I greet. "I hope you have a juicy sex story to share with your lonely, much-too-busy-to-date friend in Columbia."

"I did it again," Adrian confesses.

"Don't you mean, 'Oops I did it again'?"

"Nice one," she responds. "Madison, be serious. In my post two-orgasm haze, I even suggested we start dating like a real couple." She waits nervously for my reaction.

"Oh, Adrian, I am so proud of you. You should date him. Winston likes you a lot. And I could see while working at the store with you that you are smitten by him."

"Smitten? What the heck? I am not smitten. I don't lose control to be smitten. This isn't the 1960s. People don't get smitten. I don't know what to do. Help me please." She sounds frantic.

"Adrian, dating Winston is a good thing. It's okay to be nervous and scared. That means your feelings are new and genuine. Tell me what happened the last night, so I can help you."

"Winston texted me to come help him cover at the theater last night when I closed the store."

He ties her up in knots, and while Adrian fights her inability to control her reaction to him. She refuses to follow my advice to give the poor guy a chance and start dating.

"I recently realized I love the theater. The popcorn smell, the excited ticket purchasers, the red velvet seats, and curtains feel like home to me."

I desperately want to mention to her that it feels like home because Winston is there. She's not ready to hear that—she's getting closer but isn't quite there yet.

"I sold tickets while Winston covered the concession stand. I'm glad I don't hire part-time teenagers. They seem to be very unreliable."

"Adrian." I interject. Technically, we're still teenagers." We are only eighteen; we have two more teen years left. "I do understand what you mean, though."

"Winston asked me to keep him company until he closed. I nodded and asked what I could do to help. He simply flashed his sexy smirk, causing my body to hum, and walked me towards the office where we spent most of the next hour."

When Adrian pauses, I assume she means to signal they had sex in his office. "Tell me you didn't. Adrian, in his office?"

"No!" Adrian admonishes me. "Please, even I can restrain myself while at his work. Winston entered the ticket sales information into the computer, counted my sales drawer, and placed the cash in the safe. We talked about my day at the store and his visit with Troy. He described three pieces of furniture Troy has ready for me."

"I'm glad Troy is able to sell his work in your store. He has a great eye. Where I see a beat up old dresser missing a drawer, he sees a piece to repurpose." Although I pin many of these projects on Pinterest, I could never tackle such a project. "When I get my own place, I plan to buy several of his pieces."

"Cool. Now, stop distracting me. I'm getting to the important part, so listen up."

Adrian needs to get the entire story off her chest so I can help her. I attempt to bite my tongue until she spills the detail-laden story.

"Winston informed me we were going for a ride after he locked up. I paused at the passenger door of his truck to let him know I'm not the type of girl he can order around. Before I could speak, Winston leaned close and whispered he'd wanted to do *this* all night. I had no time to ask what he meant. His lips connected with mine. His kiss was needy, as our lips melded together. He turned my body into a swirling mess of need, then he pulled away too soon. I mean, I was left a panting, leaning on his truck."

"He unlocked the passenger door and reached behind me to open it. Then, he had the nerve to take advantage of my position, climbing into his truck, and swatted my ass."

"He didn't."

"Not only that, but he closed my door and slowly strode to his side, wearing his sexy smirk. Then, with a shrug, he said he wanted to bite or swat my ass, and I was just lucky that swatting won out. I mean, who does that?"

I don't answer but want to tell her it sounds like something she would do.

"As he drove, I found I didn't care where we were going. I liked the last time he took me for a ride in his pickup. We returned to the same old farmhouse we visited before. We exited the truck, Winston lowered his tailgate, and I hopped upon it. Winston's strong hands parted my thighs, then he moved to stand between them. His eyes locked on mine as he slowly leaned towards me." Adrian's words are thick with emotion as she recalls last night.

"As we kissed, he didn't let me take control. He fought me every step of the way. He positioned me where he wanted. He pulled away if I tried to speed things up. It was frustrating at first, then Winston's hands grasped my hips to assist in repeating my tiny thrust over his erection and I didn't care anymore. My flames grew higher and higher as I grew needier and needier. I needed to touch him to undress him, but he wouldn't allow it. He positioned me on the very edge of the tailgate and went down on me. The warm night air on my exposed skin while Winston's tongue worked magic on me was an assault on my senses. When I could take no more, I begged him. Seriously, me, Adrian, begged a man to give me an orgasm. I can't handle what he does to me. Of course, being all macho-like, he simply wiggled a finger inside me, and I exploded on the tailgate of his pick-up truck. You would think he would take mercy on me, but oh no, Winston continued to stroke and suck. My head fell forward, and I think I bit his shoulder in an attempt to ground myself."

"Finally, he moved faster. He tore his clothes off. I wasted no time grasping his shaft and gently tugging toward me. I pressed my hands against the tailgate, raising my hips as he lined up at my entrance. He thrust in, balls deep. He remained still while my body stretched to accommodate his length and girth. Madison, words don't even exist to tell you how good it felt. One of these days, you will experience this, and, trust me, you will absolutely love it."

I remember the feeling. My night with Hamilton opened me up to feelings and pleasures I didn't understand in Adrian's previous stories. Now, when she briefs me on her escapades, I am very aware of the sensations and reactions she speaks of.

"This was the hottest sex I've ever had. As he found a rhythm, I braced my hands on the tailgate. With each thrust, he pounded my thighs against the truck. The slight pain combined with the marvelous friction within was heavenly. When Winston's fingertip gently circled then pressed into my clit while he continued pistoning into me, my orgasm surprised me."

"I love that I bring him to release. I marvel at the way he plays my body with precision. I love the feelings only he can give me. Our first time wasn't a fluke. I'll never look at his tailgate again without thinking of last night."

Adrian shakes her head as she continues. "Then, I experienced diarrhea of the mouth. I blurted I'd be up for seeing where this thing goes."

"What was Winston's reaction?"

"I think his words were, 'Seriously? You mean if I had asked you out on a date you would have considered saying yes?' To which I asked if he wanted to ask me out before. Winston admitted a couple of times in the last year or so, he entertained the idea of asking me out."

"When I asked why he didn't, he said, and I quote, 'Adrian, you've got to know you kinda do what you want and say what you want anytime you want. I figured if I interested you, you'd have let me know.' I informed him I did tell him I thought he was hot before."

"He then had the balls to respond, 'You did, but I'm not sure if you are aware of it or not; you tend to state a lot of guys are hot. I wasn't sure if you meant anything by it.' Can you believe this guy?"

I don't dare answer her. She's on a roll. She has a story to finish.

"So, I informed him we're trying it now. No reason to discuss any time we wasted. I asked when he would take me on our first date."

"Placing his index finger on my chest, he said I needed to plan to take him on a first date. I mean the guy gave me bruises on the backs of my thighs then tells me I will take him on our first date. Madison, how do I react to this?"

I choose my words carefully. I need to coax Adrian in to doing what she wants but fears. "First, Winston is a sex god. You need to claim him before someone else reaps the double orgasms he provides." My words make her laugh. "Seriously, Adrian, you state you feel very different, and you lose control with him. Your body and your mind want Winston. I know it scares you, but you feel more alive when he's near, right?"

"Yes." Her voice sounds small. "I feel weak, and I don't like that."

"Do you feel weak, or do you lose control?"

She ponders my question. "I lose control. The things he does, the way he makes me feel, I just…"

"It's primal," I explain. "Your body takes over, your mind shuts down, and you just feel. That's not weak. It's actually the opposite. You're letting your body and his body give you pleasure. You're still in control. You know what feels good, you know what you like, and you know what to do. You are still in control. He's not taking your control away. He's opening you up to feel, to love. I love this. Winston is *good*. He knows you well enough to know you like to be in control. I think he'll have staying power." I smile. loving Winston's effect on my friend.

"Easy. We've only agreed to one date to see how it goes. Don't start talking about staying power. We're not planning to marry."

"So, when and where are you taking him on your first date?"

"That's where I need your help."

"You don't need my help. You know what he likes. You know what you like. Just plan something simple."

"You're no help."

"You should cook for him. You could putt with him on the practice green at his golf course. Allow him to teach you proper putting techniques. Guys like to teach girls. Watch the sunset from the dock at the lake or park on top of a hill." I pause to think. "Oh, I know. After dark, park somewhere quiet. Spread thick blankets and pillows in the bed of his truck. Then, watch a movie on a laptop or iPad. It would be your own private drive-in movie."

"I like that one," Adrian admits. "I knew you were the girl to ask for advice. Thank you. I need to let you go now so I can start planning it all."

"Eager much? You could wait to take him on a date tomorrow night."

"Duh," she quips. "I need to give him notice so his parents can cover at the theaters. Now that I know what I want to do, I'm going to call him, so we can plan when to do it."

"Text me the details. Then text me after the date."

"Got to go! Bye!"

37

The nearest furniture store is forty minutes away. Only used furniture is available in Athens. This is one of the 4,724 reasons I want to escape this town.

"Hey Madison," Adrian greets when our FaceTime connects near the end of September. "How's college life treating you?"

"I love my methods classes. The professors are cool. How's everything in Athens?" I wonder if the camera angle shows I've put on a little weight. It might only be five pounds, but I see changes in my face and stomach already.

Adrian jumps right in. "I get to go first; my news is juicy." She wiggles her eyebrows up and down. "I am officially dating Winston."

I puff up like a peacock. I'm proud that Adrian listened to me during our phone calls and recent texting sessions. I encouraged her to take a chance. She never would have without my encouragement.

"Hey, where is Savannah?"

Salem answers before Adrian can. "It's deer season, silly," she giggles. "You know how much Savannah enjoys bow hunting this time of year."

"Before you groan, we know. Deer season in Athens seems like a holiday,

157

and it's one of the reasons you couldn't wait to leave Athens." Adrian attempts to sound like me when I complain about their little town. They've heard my complaints a million times.

"You forgot to complain about the disgusting deer carcasses hanging from trees in peoples' front yards during deer season," Bethany adds, and I groan loudly.

"And last but not least, she hates how half the grocery store parking lot doubles as the deer check-in station where people hang out and compare racks in the back of their trucks." Salem adds.

"Nice guys, real nice," I admonish. "Let's just say, I am not missing any part of deer season this year."

"So, you aren't curious to see if the guys have a deer yet?" Adrian asks.

I remind them Savannah's the only one that participates in archery season. Since she's missing the call, she must not have one yet. Since the guys only go during gun season, they don't have theirs yet either.

Our call tonight is shorter than usual. I claim I need to read chapters for tomorrow's classes, but I'm exhausted. The first trimester of pregnancy is taking its toll on me.

Several days later, Adrian calls as soon as I am home from classes. She shares that they've developed a new couples habit. Winston tends to bring her lunch at the store, and she takes him dinner at the theater.

"So, last night, I grabbed a pizza and spent the evening keeping him company in his office. I enjoy the nights all the part-timers show up for their shifts, letting us chill in the office instead of covering their shifts."

"I announced I had an idea after we enjoyed a few bites of our meal. I told Winston he should hire an assistant manager to allow him a couple of nights off each week. He didn't respond while he pondered my words. Then, he smiled and motioned for me to join him on the other side of his desk. He pulled me onto his lap."

"We discussed hiring an assistant means we could enjoy evenings together, go on real dates, and attend parties. I was relieved he liked the idea immediately. I had planned to convince him, so I decided to push my luck and share my other idea."

"I rose from his lap and closed his office door. When I turned back, Winston's blue eyes were liquid, and his lips quirked up on one corner in a devilish smirk. I licked my lips while I stepped closer to him, explaining I had an even better idea I wanted to share with him."

Winston got the wrong idea. He said, 'While I want nothing more than to bury myself deep inside you, we really should act responsibly while I am at work.'"

"I stated while I loved where his mind went, that was not what I wanted to share. I mentioned one of us should get an apartment. I explained it would be nice to spend an evening together that isn't in our parents' house."

"He added we wouldn't need to use his truck to park in the country either. He could ravish me in a bed, and we could even spend nights together."

"We spent the rest of the night discussing rentals: where we could find one, who to call, and how nice it would be to have alone time there. We pulled a few listings up on the internet. Of the five we found, two were cute little houses."

"So, I think we will be looking at rentals later today and tomorrow. Winston liked the idea so much, he's eager to move forward as soon as possible."

I share in Adrian's excitement as we discuss all the good points of a place of his or her own. I'm glad she is enjoying her time with Winston instead of fighting her feelings. I share a bit about my classes, assignments, and the Bible study I enjoy each week at Alma's church before we say goodbye.

The next Monday night, Adrian texts me a photo of a house. Her text claims Winston decided to buy this house instead of rent. This news is much too big to be texting about.

I dial her phone. Adrian shares how he surprised her by blindfolding her as he drove her to the house. She explains as he gave her a tour, he mentioned how each room reminded him of her and that it had plenty of room for their future children.

Of course, I have to calm her worries that he is moving too fast. We discuss that he bought the house; they didn't buy it together. He plans to move in and didn't mention the two of them living together yet. I'm sure it's the mention of their future children that causes her concern. I know she is eager to run her business, marry, and start a family, but she is scared of the feelings Winston gives her.

We chat for more than an hour. Before I feel she is in a good place, and I can let her go.

Two months later, I'm counting down the minutes until my call with the girls. Adrian claims to have good news to share with all of us.

"Hello girls," I greet when the video call connects with my phone. I take great care to only frame my face in the camera view. At five months pregnant, my body is beginning to show my added weight.

Adrian is not visible on my screen. She's usually up front in the center.

"We have been dying to call you for three hours now," Salem states.

She explains. "Adrian texted us this afternoon that she had a juicy secret to share on the video call tonight," Savannah informs.

"She wouldn't give us hints or let us call you early either," Bethany fake pouts.

"So, where is Miss Adrian with this juicy secret?"

At my question, Adrian appears behind the three girls. She doesn't speak; she simply slips her left arm through the girls and wiggles her ring finger.

"No way!" I scream.

Savannah, Salem, and Bethany swarm the diamond then wrap Adrian in a tight group hug. As the celebration calms, Adrian assume her usual position in front of the webcam.

She shares in great detail how Winston proposed last night while recreating the drive-in movie date we concocted for their first real date months ago. A permanent smile graces her face.

"We're planning a May wedding. Oh, and Madison, will you be my maid-of-honor?"

I'm sure my eyes are the size of saucers. I quickly calculate the time from my due date to a May wedding. I might have lost most of my pregnancy weight by then.

"I will be honored to be your maid-of-honor," I inform my friend.

"Madison gets to plan the bachelorette party!" Bethany squeals.

"Adrian, you'll need to call me, so we can start planning," I state.

Later, as we say goodbye, I'm sad I'm not there to celebrate with them. I wish I could have driven up to share news in person. I must continue to hide my secret, so I pretend my schedule doesn't match theirs anytime they invite me up. This is my sacrifice. For my little one and for Hamilton, I can hide here in Columbia. My classes and homework keep me very busy. The visits each week with the girls keep them in my life. Although I regret my slow withdrawal from them, I must think of my future and of my baby.

38

Clothing must be purchased at a Walmart a few towns away, in a city an hour away, or online. Just another of the 4,724 reasons I want to escape this town.

It's March, and I'm gigantic. I spend most of the day horizontal on the sofa before turning in early to bed. I slide from the sofa with the grace of an elephant. Slowly, I waddle towards the restroom. The urge to pee grows with each step.

"Alma!" I call. When she peeks into the hallway from the kitchen where she is fixing dinner, I inform her I just peed myself.

As she nears, Alma states it's not urine—my water broke. She turns me towards the front door. "Go! I'll meet you in the van."

As I waddle, she quickly grabs our purses and my overnight bag. I make my way to the porch, down the steps, toward her car. As I open the passenger door, I remember the dog. McGee! I mention to Alma he is still in the backyard. She quickly places him in his kennel before joining me in her car.

I don't hear anything she says during the drive. I'm sure she is attempting to calm my nerves. I can only worry about the upcoming pain and the fact that Alma is the only one with me for the delivery.

Once at the hospital, I'm whisked to the obstetrics ward with Alma by my side. Alma's phone vibrates often, and she replies to each text. I know she is letting her children know we are at the hospital. They've called and texted me every day for the past two weeks to offer words of encouragement or distract me from my constant need to rest.

Nurses scurry around; I'm in a gown, on a bed, with monitors upon my belly within minutes. I'm told Dr. Anderson will arrive in moments, and I should rest as much as I can before the labor progresses and the baby arrives. How am I supposed to rest with the loud fetal monitor? The baby's rapid heartbeat drums from the speaker. It calms my nerves. My baby is safe, and soon, I will hold him or her in my arms.

Dr. Anderson informs me that my water did indeed break, and, although I don't feel any labor pains yet, they will be arriving soon. Again, I am encouraged to rest while I can.

The next knock at the door brings Alma's daughter Taylor into my room. "Surprise!" She places a kiss on my cheek and squeezes my hand. "You didn't think I would miss the big day, did you?"

In my confusion, I cannot reply.

"I made plans to visit after your last appointment. Imagine my surprise when mom texted that your water broke, and you were on your way to the hospital; I was already driving to Columbia when I got the message." She chuckles. "We timed it perfectly. Now, do you mind if I am in the room while you are in labor? Or would you prefer I wait in the other room?"

"Stay," I beg as I clutch her forearm. "Please stay." my voice quivers, advertising my fear to both of them.

"I need to ask a favor." She purses her lips. "The girls would like a picture of you before and after the baby arrives." She quickly continues before I refuse. "Trust me, I told them no one wants a picture while they are in labor. But, you know my girls; they are the selfie queens."

"Let's take a selfie before I start screaming and sweating."

Alma and Taylor lean in while Taylor snaps the picture. She shows it to me for my approval prior to sending it to the girls. She tells me how the girls begged to be taken out of school and be here for the birth. I smile at their antics.

I quickly record a video for Hamilton, explaining where and when my water broke, that Alma drove me to the hospital, and Taylor met us here to surprise me. I include Alma and Taylor in the video. They smile, wave, and promise to take good care of me.

Soon, my labor pains begin. Although the nurses claim these are mild contractions, I find them unpleasant. If these are mild, I am not sure I will survive natural childbirth. Suddenly, a C-section sounds like a good idea to me.

I find I slide in and out of sleep between contractions. When Alma excuses herself to find some coffee and breakfast, I realize morning has arrived.

"Taylor." She hops from the chair in the corner to my bedside. "Will you record me for a minute?" She gladly takes my phone and tells me to begin.

"Hi Hamilton," I greet. "Hours have passed. As you can tell by my appearance, the labor pains are taking their toll on me. On his last check, Dr. Anderson claimed I am progressing nicely. He predicts our baby will arrive later today. I hope he is right. Delivering on March Tenth sounds much better to me than labor continuing until March Eleventh. Although I wish you could be here, I'm glad you aren't. I can't control myself when a contraction occurs. I'm verbally abusing Alma and Taylor. I'll never be able to make this up to them."

I pause as a contraction begins. "Keep recording," I instruct through gritted teeth.

"Remember to breathe," Taylor prompts.

"I am fucking breathing. I'd be dead if I didn't...UHH!"

Alma returns. She quickly places a cold cloth upon my brow and whispers calming words into my ear. She talks of baseball, Hamilton pitching, and watching the games this season with a little baby on our laps. She promises to buy tiny Cubs attire for Hamilton's newest fan. Her words help me through the pain.

I take a couple deep breaths before looking back at the camera. "As you can see, you are missing all the fun here. This will probably be my last post until our little one makes its way into the world. I am looking forward to finding out if we have a son or a daughter very soon. We love you." I signal for Taylor to end the recording as the next contraction hits me.

"I can't believe you allowed Taylor to record the birth," Cameron, Alma's youngest daughter, states. I laugh at the FaceTime screen as Alma holds her phone. "Trust me, I don't want to see it. EVER."

"I made her stay above my waistline. It just shows me in my supermodel delivery room face, the doctor announcing it's a baby girl, and me holding her for the first time." I kiss the top of my daughter's tiny, dark-hair-covered head and pink cap. "But, I won't force anyone to watch it. I recorded it for Hamilton."

Taylor extends her FaceTime call with her daughters toward me. "The girls want to know if you have chosen a name yet?"

I signal for Alma and Taylor to bring the cameras closer to my little one. "I'd like for you to meet Liberty Armstrong. Libby, this is your new family." I tickle her cheek with my index finger. Liberty yawns before placing her little fist in her mouth and sucking.

The loud reactions to her little movements through the phone startle her from her nap. Her eyes peek open over her chubby cheeks framed by her dark lashes moments before she begins to cry. Instant fear that I might not know how to calm my daughter floods over me. I tramp down my fear. I don't have time for doubt. I am her mother and I can do this. I tuck her tighter to my chest. I soothe her while Alma and Taylor end their calls across the room.

Once calm, I ask Taylor to record a message for me before we attempt to nap. "Hamilton, I would like to introduce you to your daughter, Liberty 'Libby' Armstrong. I opted for no middle name, so she may keep her maiden name when she marries. Stop. Breath." I imagine overprotective new dad Hamilton freaking out at the thought of his daughter dating, let alone getting married. I laugh into the camera.

"I know it will be two or three decades before she needs to worry about that. She weighs nine pounds and three ounces, is twenty-three inches long, and very healthy." I remove her little pink cap and brush her curly dark hair down. "She has her daddy's curls, brown hair, and appetite. She makes little piglet sounds as she nurses. We're both exhausted but wanted to say hi to you before we attempt to nap. We'll record more later tonight and tomorrow."

Alma places Libby in her bassinet then coaxes me to sleep while Taylor and she eat dinner. Food sounds good, but I'm too tired to eat right now. They shut off the light as they leave the room, and I quickly slide into slumber.

39

Athens has one small hardware store. For home improvements, you must drive over an hour away. This is one of the 4,724 reasons I want to escape this town.

Three weeks pass as if only a day. Alma expertly assisted in creating a schedule at home. She insists I sleep when Liberty sleeps and takes care of everything around the house. Between nursing every three hours and completing my classes online, I don't have much time for anything else. Occasionally, Alma asks me to help her in the kitchen while Liberty swings nearby.

Tonight, is my weekly call with the girls. I still avoid video calls. As my hands are a doughy mess, Alma connects the call while holding a sleeping Liberty in her arms.

"Hello," Alma's voice greets. "I'm putting you on speaker as Madison is currently rolling cookie dough into balls for me."

"Good. I'm glad you are on the phone, Alma," Adrian begins. "I have a big announcement for all of you to hear at the same time. I'm pregnant!"

You could hear a pin drop for moments before Savannah laughs, Salem coughs, and I can only imagine Bethany's wide-eyed reaction.

"How did Winston react?" I ask. "Will you two get married right away?"

My questions catch Adrian off guard. She expected shock and comments about safe sex. Instead, I am calm and start to plan for her future. I know how pregnancy and the birth of a baby can change many things in their life, but she doesn't know about my own pregnancy experience.

"He was shocked and scared but supportive. We only found out yesterday, so we want to wait a day or two before we plan the future," Adrian states before seeking more of a reaction from the group. "C'mon you guys, where is my support? Say something."

She allows the conversation to continue for about five minutes before she jumps back in. "April Fools!"

Curse words and playful swats attack Adrian. Apparently, as her friends, we could see her being irresponsible in her relations with Winston. We inform her this is an April Fool's Day prank in very poor taste.

The next Tuesday, Adrian calls me yet again for advice. She calls promptly at 1:00 p.m. as she knows I will be home from classes. I let the phone ring four times while I lay Libby in her bassinet before I answer.

"Hi," I greet, not pulling my eyes off the television.

"What's up?" Adrian nonchalantly asks.

"Seriously?" I ask in disbelief. "I'm watching Hamilton pitch—it's opening day. Please tell me you knew that."

"Sorry, I forgot. How's he doing?"

I share in great detail the changes in his stance and the increased strength in his arm this season. I tell her how many miles per hour each of his pitches gained during the off-season. Finally, I inform her he struck out all three batters he faced in the first inning, and they have two outs so far in the second inning.

"Can I just hang on until he gets another out, then we can chat while the Cubs bat?" She must really want to talk to me today. She waits patiently as I give her the pitch-by-pitch commentary to finish the half inning.

"Okay, I can focus now," I prompt.

"I need some advice. I know we talked about holding my bachelorette party the night before the wedding, but I want to really party and not be in bad shape on my wedding day. I mean, it is the first time you're coming back since August. We need to really celebrate. What do you think?"

I don't immediately answer. "I'm opening my calendar, so I'm putting you on speaker," I say as I move into the kitchen so as not to disturb my sleeping daughter. "The weekend before is Mother's Day, and I don't want to be in the same county with my mom then. So, it needs to be the first weekend in May." I pause, and she waits. "We could do it May Fifth. Salem graduates from her LPN program that day, and it's Cinco de Mayo, so it would be a great night to party. I had contemplated driving up for Salem's pinning; this would allow me to do it."

This is why she needed to call me today. I'm organized. I'm a planner. She knew her freaking out about moving the bachelorette party wouldn't be necessary if she asked me for advice. "You are AWESOME! This is why I love you. You can figure out and plan things so much easier than I can. Thank you. Thank you. Thank you." She makes kissing sounds in the phone for me.

"No problem," I reply. "Everything else falling into place? No 'bridezilla' moments or fights with the mother-of-the-bride?"

"No, all is calm here. Winston keeps worrying I will have a breakdown at any moment. I tease that he has seen too many movies. We're planning a casual wedding and reception. Easy-peasy."

I wish I were closer to help her with the plans, but Bethany and Salem have stepped up to help with items we discuss frequently over the phone.

"I'll send out the online e-vites for the bachelorette party after the game today. I'll probably just drive up the morning of the fifth. I'll ask Memphis if I can crash with her Saturday night, and I'll need to be back in Columbia before dinner on Sunday."

"Sounds great." She knows I want her to let me go so I can get back to Hamilton's game. "I'll let you get back to the game. Cheer loud for Hamilton for me. Bye."

40

There are two mechanics in Athens. Yet another one of the 4,724 reasons I want to escape this town.

Adrian is the first to arrive in the auditorium for Salem's pinning ceremony. So, she texts all of us where she is saving seats.

Though they attempt to keep their excitement and celebrating to a minimum, we get many stares as they welcome me when I arrive in the auditorium. They even fight a tear or two when I hug each friend. I've been away too long. It seems surreal that I will be in Athens twice this month.

My girls attempt to pry details of tonight's party from me. "All I'll say," I begin as all ears lean toward me eagerly, "is that we are meeting at Adrian's house at four this afternoon. You need to bring cash, debit cards, your ID, dress to impress, and bring a full change of comfy clothes for later." I only share what I've already put in the e-vite for the event.

We quiet as the ceremony begins. When Salem is announced, we whoop and cheer loudly to show we are proud of our friend. They keep the ceremony less than an hour long, and we congratulate She with her family afterwards. Salem asks us to wait for her while she says goodbye to them.

When she returns, she actually skips toward us. Her excitement with finishing her classes shines on her sun-kissed face.

"Bring it in ladies," she greets while motioning us to make a tight huddle. "Closer." We squeeze in even tighter. She raises her left hand to display a tiny new diamond on her ring finger.

"Engaged!" All eyes turn our way, but we don't hide the celebration this time. I see another bachelorette party and wedding in our future.

41

You have to know your family tree extensively before dating in a small town. Be sure to look out for second and third cousins. Another of the 4,724 reasons I want to escape Athens.

I knock loudly on the door to Latham's barn. It seems silly to knock on a barn door, but I don't want to see anything I shouldn't. When they yell "come in," I only stick my head in. "Everyone decent?" Of course, Latham claims he's naked, Troy states he is never decent, and Winston laughs at their antics.

"I'm doing my maid-of-honor duties and ensuring we are all ready to begin in ten minutes." I take in their appearance. They seem to be dressed and ready.

A stall door opens. "How do I look? I tried to match as best I could."

I stand frozen. I cannot breathe. I cannot speak. It's Hamilton. He's here at the wedding. He told me he couldn't make it. I didn't prepare for seeing my friend, the father of my child. I'm just frozen numb, I squeeze my eyes closed tightly.

"Breathe." Hamilton's hot breath prickles my neck.

My eyes fly open as I jump back. Unable to stop myself, I continue taking steps back until I collide with the barn door. I'm trapped. I can't leave. I can't ruin Adrian's wedding. I have a job to do. I'm the maid-of-honor. I have to be front and center. I can't avoid him.

"Hey, I'm not going to hurt you." Hamilton holds his hands palm-out in front of him. He doesn't approach.

I see hurt in his eyes. My reaction to his surprise is unexpected, and I've hurt him. The last thing I want to do is hurt Hamilton. Drawing on an inner strength I didn't know I had, I run to him.

Hamilton wraps me in his arms while whispering in my ear. "I missed you too much."

His warm breath on my neck, sends a chill down my spine.

He chuckles at my shiver. "I'm sorry I didn't visit you this winter." He clasps his hands over jaws; eyes staring through mine into my soul. "I'm sorry for hurting you and for scaring you just now." His lips place a soft kiss on the tip of my nose.

Wiping my tears, I pull back. I swat his chest several times. "You lied to me. You said you couldn't make the wedding. Why?"

Hamilton grasps my wrists tightly. "My plans changed at the last minute. Coach made a change to our pitching rotation, so I asked if I might take one day to attend the wedding. I barely had time to arrange a flight to Kansas City and a rental car." He releases my wrists, then wipes stray tears from my cheeks. "By the time I made it to I-35 you were already with Adrian; I thought it best to surprise everyone." He looks to the guys. "At least, they were happy to see me."

I scramble to gather myself. I need to be normal, or, at least, the Madison he remembers. "I'm happy to see you. I've dreamt of you visiting me so many times. I feared I was imagining you here. I thought I lost my mind, because you told me more than once you couldn't come today." It's not a lie.

"Madison," Latham calls for my attention. "Rumor has it five females were found skinny dipping at a lake in Livingston County after midnight a couple of weeks ago. You wouldn't happen to know who they were, would you?" He folds his arms over his chest, tilts his head, and wears a knowing smile.

"I heard the Livingston County Sheriff's Department received a call and forced the girls from the lake then transported them to the county jail." Troy's love for law enforcement ensures he knows everyone in the field in a five-county area. I don't doubt he heard every little detail. "I can't wait to go on calls like that."

I stand stone-faced, letting nothing show. "Guys, I live in Columbia not Livingston County." I walk confidently in a circle around them. "If Bethany and I were picked up and booked for skinny dipping, we would never be able to attain our teaching licenses. And, you know Adrian has a big mouth. There is no way she would be able to keep such a juicy secret." I waggle my index finger at all of them. "What happens at the bachelorette party remains at the bachelorette party, and a public-nudity-with-trespassing arrest would not remain at the bachelorette party." I shrug and smirk.

"A friend of mine told me that some women crashed a bachelor party the same night in Daviess County." Troy claims. "They did a striptease and gave lap dances at a bar hosting a private party." His eyes scrutinize my face for any sign of guilt. "The women wore Zorro-like masks. Apparently, they were very hot and put on quite a show."

"C'mon! Sweet Salem crashing a party, stripping, and giving lap dances?" I scoff. "That I would pay good money to witness. As for the rest of us, those men only wish we would crash their party. There wouldn't be a dry fly in the place when we left." A maniacal laugh escapes me. "Are you really so desperate to know what we were up to that you would believe such wild stories?" I glance from man to man.

"Now, if you are done grasping at straws, we have a wedding to attend." I use my teacher voice to inflict guilt upon them. When they nod, I continue. "I'll let Adrian know you are ready and will meet us at the altar. Bye, gentlemen."

I walk from the barn, a cocky smirk upon my face and confidence in my shoulders and steps. Rumors about our activities have spread far and wide. The guys only wish they knew how ornery we were for ten hours that Saturday night.

Fuck a duck! Adrian is going to freak if I don't hurry back. I sprint back inside the house. I've been gone too long. I can't take the time I need to cope with Hamilton's arrival. I bury it deep for the moment. Hurrying inside the master bedroom, I lean against the door when I shut it.

"What's wrong?" Adrian's eyes bore into me.

I rescue my friend from her worst fears on her wedding day. "Nothing's wrong. The guys are ready," I proclaim. "Oh, and they have heard rumors of two of our activities from the bachelorette party. Wanna guess which two?"

Adrian, ever dominant, guesses first. "Soaping all the car windows at the dealership?"

I shake my head.

Savannah guesses next. "Placing the blow-up sex dolls in all the golf carts at the club?"

I chuckle.

"TP-ing the trees at the park?" Bethany asks, and I shake my head.

"Just tell us already," Adrian demands. "We don't have time to keep guessing. We have a wedding to attend."

As I touch up my eye make-up, I share what the guys asked, how I acted, and how I answered. We enjoy a long laugh. I remind the girls that we agreed not to share our adventures until after the reception tonight. We plan to keep the guys wondering for a bit longer. At the end of the reception, when the slideshow is viewed, our mugshots, along with several selfies from the bachelorette party, will be shared. While the guys remained on Latham's farm to play poker and party, we ventured to four counties, pulling many pranks and having loads of fun.

"Okay ladies," Adrian says. "It's time I get married so I can finally sleep with Winston tonight on our honeymoon." We laugh so hard our sides ache. I actually have tears. I've missed these friends.

42

Deer season is like a holiday in Athens. This is one of the 4,724 reasons I want to escape this town.

One by one, our friends step onto the porch, down the steps, and make their way to the barn. The faint strains of guitar drift from the front. I places a kiss upon Adrian's cheek before I follow the path of those before me.

As I descend the farmhouse steps, I realize I am walking toward the makeshift altar where Hamilton will be standing with Winston and the guys. I try my best to mask my fear. I knew someday I would be face to face with Hamilton. I was not prepared for it to be today.

I round the barn, taking in the first sight of Adrian and Winston's family and friends. They sit upon the quilts we cushioned the top of hay bales with to make the rows of seats. As the sun begins to fade in the evening sky, it shoots rays of light from behind the barn. Slowly, I walk down the makeshift aisle between the rows of hay bales; my eyes find Hamilton, standing tall in his jeans, shirt, and vest. Sans hat, his hair is a bit longer than I've ever seen. I long to run my fingers through his dark waves, blowing in the breeze. His warm, brown eyes are locked on me. His sexy smile melts my insides to pudding. I mentally slap myself. He's not here for me. As much as I desire another night in his arms, it won't happen. He did me a favor, nothing more. I had my one night with Hamilton—it's the only one I'll ever have. At least a little part of him will be near me always in Libby. I concentrate on my steps and assuming my place of honor.

Try as I might, I can't prevent my eyes from glancing towards Hamilton during the service or my mind from imagining this is our wedding. Hamilton's presence stirs up every memory of our night together, every fantasy I've had since that night and my hopes that maybe, someday, we might have a chance.

I pull myself together for Adrian. I listen to the minister. I focus on our place in the ceremony and the rest of my duties as her maid-of-honor. When Adrian doesn't repeat her vows for the minister, I realize she must be daydreaming, like I was. I nudge her side with my elbow. Adrian blinks from her thoughts, desperately trying to find where we are in our ceremony. They repeat their vows and exchange rings. When the minister says he may now kiss the bride, Winston bends her over backwards as his tongue invades her mouth. They enjoy a long, smoldering kiss amidst whistles, laughter, and cat-calls.

When they turn to face our guests as they are introduced as Mr. and Mrs. Hale, I hand Adrian her bouquet. With Winston's hand in hers, they run down the aisle. The crowd laughs at their escape.

Winston steals a kiss, full of promises for their time later tonight, before the entire wedding party catches up. As we join Adrian and Winston under the large tree and twinkle lights, our group of nine pull in tight. Adrian expresses her excitement that Hamilton made it to her wedding. I remind our group that guests are headed our way. After taking turns hugging the bride, we make the receiving line.

Hamilton stands next to me. I smile up at him. He places his hand on the back of my neck, pulling me in to whisper in my ear. "I can't keep my eyes off of you. Promise me we will find a moment alone tonight." His lips kiss my ear before he pulls away.

My attempt at control just evaporated. His hands, his touch, his lips, his kiss, I can't control my body's reaction to him. A moment for what? To talk? To touch? To...

Get a grip, Madison! I'm a grown ass woman. I'm a mother. I can't let my hormones control me. My heart can't handle another magical moment with Hamilton. I barely survived the first time. I need to think about Liberty. I need to get through tonight and head back to my new life in Columbia. I can't spend time alone with Hamilton, or I might tell him everything. I can't be the reason his dream, his career, ends. I need to leave Athens. In Columbia, I'm strong, and it's easier to remember why I'm keeping my secret from everyone. I must avoid him the rest of the night. I'll glue myself to the bride—it's my duty after all.

As we greet and thank each of the guests, the lights inside the barn rafters and stalls come to life. I love the simplicity of Adrian's special day. They are relaxed and stress free as they enjoy the time with others.

We delight in an evening of laughter, photos, dancing, and toasts. Adrian poses for pictures with us girls. The five of us stand in identical dresses with fluffy tutu skirts. We wear a denim vest over ours and the matching boots finish off our ensemble. Next, the guys join us in their new jeans, matching plaid shirts, grey vests, and boots. Winston wears a white shirt with the same vest, jeans, and boots as the guys. We pose for a few pictures in the beautiful red barn with twinkling lights.

Crap! Hamilton is walking my way. I've successfully eluded him for the past two hours. I frantically scan the area for a maid-of-honor task.

"Let's dance." Once again, Hamilton's warm hand is on my wrist as he pulls me to the dance floor.

Focus, Madison. It's a slow song. Prepare to be in his arms. No swooning. We are just good friends. We are just good friends.

I place my left hand on his right shoulder as he places my right hand in his. He wraps a long arm around my waist to my back and pulls me tight. Friends don't dance this close. What is the meaning of this?

"I'm sorry I've neglected you while I focused on my career."

Hamilton's word causes me to lift my chin to make eye contact.

"It's no excuse. I know I've hurt you."

I shake my head, unable to reply.

"Seeing you, touching you, I can't believe I led myself to believe our texts and phone calls were enough."

He releases my hand to run his fingers through his dark brown waves. The same hair his daughter has. I style hers to keep the curl—he fights the curl to make waves. She has his eyes, his hair, his height, and his smile.

This line of thought is nothing but trouble. I attempt to gather myself and blurt the first thing that comes to mind. "Your hair is long. Are you striving for a manbun?"

Hamilton's head falls back in laughter. "It's your fault. You've denied me video calls for several months now. As my number one fan, it's your job to keep me presentable for the rest of my fans."

"I figure you have a new number one fan, and she urges you to grow your hair out." I've missed our banter.

"How many times must I tell you? If I don't have time to visit you in person, then I definitely don't have time for anyone else. There can only be one number one fan and that is you forever."

The song ends. I lead Hamilton to the bridal party table to join the rest of our gang. I look to Adrian. She signals it is indeed time for the video presentation. I know she longs to jump Winston as soon as possible. I've already made her wait thirty minutes after her requested time to end the reception.

The guests react to the baby pictures, school photos, and casual pictures of our group of friends. A slide reading "The Bachelorette Party" causes gasps and groans.

Winston whispers in Adrian's ear that finally he will know the truth while wrapping his arms tightly around her waist. The wedding party surrounds them. The comments from the guys are exactly the reaction we hoped for. First, our mug shots are shared. I smile, recalling the deputies' agreement to treat us like criminals for a while. We were caught trespassing and skinny-dipping, but no charges were filed. When we shared we were a bachelorette party, they offered to help us make memories to last a lifetime.

One thing is for sure; I can plan a perfect bachelorette party. We've always partied and had fun. However, that night, we did things we will brag about well into our golden years.

With the final slide reading, "And they lived happily ever after," the guests cheer. Winston and Adrian promptly make their way to the loft of the barn as it is announced all single men and women should gather just outside the barn doors. Winston removes Adrian's garter with his teeth. He shoots it from the loft to the gentlemen below. It lands in Latham's hands. Next,

Adrian turns her back and throws the bouquet to the single ladies. Bethany pushes and shoves to catch it as the crowd laughs at her antics.

They climb down, exiting the barn through a tunnel of extended arms and sparklers. It feels like they are running through a field of lightning bugs as they make their way to Winston's truck and pull away.

Their wedding day was perfect. Winston is everything Adrian desires in a husband. It's funny how he's always been in her life. One day, it changed. Suddenly, Winston was more than her friend. He stirred desires within her and made her dream of a future together. Now that they are married, and their businesses are strong, they will start a family in their beloved small town of Athens.

The evening has ended. I nervously say goodbye to many of the guests as they exit the barn. I am acutely aware of Hamilton, standing by Latham, near the barn doors. As he chats with Latham, his eyes remain on me. How can I elude him on my way to my car?

Adrian's mother and father wrap me in hugs and thank me for all my help with the wedding. They invite me to brunch in the morning, but I confess I must return to Columbia tonight, claiming I have a project I need to spend all of tomorrow on for class. I bid them goodbye, noticing that Hamilton vacated his post at the barn door.

"Driving in the dark?" Hamilton's deep voice asks from behind me. "You should stay at my mom's and leave early in the morning. I don't like the thought of you driving three hours this late at night." He tucks a stray tendril behind my right ear.

"I'm much too excited to sleep. It's a group project, and my partner is meeting me at nine in the morning at Alma's; so I need to pick up the house in the morning." I lie more and more each day. It started with me keeping my pregnancy a secret and developed into multiple lies to continue my charade. "What time is your flight?"

"My flight to Philadelphia leaves at 2:30 a.m." He runs his hands through his hair and over his face. "I really should be heading out now to ensure I get the rental returned, and I get through airport security."

I nod. I attempted to avoid him all evening, and now I don't want him to go.

"Come here, you." His open arms invite me for a hug. "I promise I'll arrange a visit after the season ends. I can't take another winter without spending time with you." He kisses the top of my head.

It takes all I have to keep it together.

He holds me at arm's length. "Goodbyes never get easier, do they?"

I shake my head.

Hamilton insists on escorting me to my car. We happen to be parked near each other in the front yard of the house. We quickly say our goodbyes, and he follows me down the gravel road and on the blacktop. When we meet the highway, he flashes his lights at me while we are at the stop sign. In my rearview mirror, I see him exit his rental.

Outside my door, he prompts me to roll down my window. In the blink of an eye, his large shoulders enter my car. His lips smother mine. In his kiss, I feel all the emotions I hid inside for him.

Pulling away he smirks. "Eleven months seemed like an eternity away from you. Drive careful. I love you."

I watch in my mirror as he trots back to his car. Unsure what to do, I slowly pull onto the highway headed east. In my mirror, I watch his taillights as he drives west.

During my three hour drive to Columbia, my thoughts attempt to process the current state of my life. I'm nowhere near where I planned to be. My life looks nothing like I planned my senior year of high school.

The year following my high school graduation was nothing like I planned. Although I am seeking my teaching degree, Hamilton is not attending college with me. After asking my favor of him, I'm not sure if we are still friends or if we are more. With the birth of Liberty, my future goals seem to be morphing more and more by the day. I miss my friends in Athens and the life we all once shared.

Caring for Liberty helps distract me from the guilt of keeping the secret from Hamilton, his family, and our friends. Motherhood is more magnificent than words could ever describe. I can't regret the night with Hamilton as it gave me the greatest gift. A piece of him lives with me in our daughter.

Alma, Liberty, and I continue to watch every game of Hamilton's.

During my pregnancy, I recorded fifty-two videos in the digital journal for Hamilton and continued after Libby's arrival. I realize it will never make up for the time I kept from him.

Later this summer, I have tickets for Alma, Liberty, and me to see Hamilton pitch against my favorite team in St. Louis. We will enjoy a mini-vacation while I record many moments for him.

It's not time to share my monumental secret. I will continue to ask for Alma's help in caring for Libby when my friends call. I need her to care for Libby when I attend celebrations back in Athens. I'm beginning to accept that I am not free from the pull of the small town of Athens. As my friends will always call it home, I will return from time to time.

With Alma's help, I can continue living one life in Columbia while pretending I live a different life for those in Athens. It's not easy, but Hamilton's career in Major League Baseball is worth it. I dream of the day I reveal Liberty to Hamilton and my friends, but, at least for the remainder of this baseball season, we need to remain in our own little bubble of secrets.

I'm glad Hamilton attended Adrian and Winston's wedding. I've missed him. Our continued calls and texts, while keeping us in touch aren't the same as seeing each other. I anticipated awkwardness the first couple of times I was in his presence after giving birth to Libby. I was not prepared for his actions today. He misses me, he misses touching me, he misses kissing me, and he loves me. I have no idea where this might lead, but a spark of hope lies within me that we will become more than friends.

When my enlightening drive ends as I pull into Alma's driveway, I smile. I'm happy with my life as I complete my degree. I have many blessings. I enjoy my classes. I belong to a caring and active church family. I am grateful for the time I spend with Alma, her family, and McGee. My biggest blessing of all is a healthy daughter and a renewed hope that in the next year I may unite her with her father. My life is truly blessed.

TAILGATES & HEARTACHES

The Locals #2

43

MADISON

I turn off my playlist opting instead for random radio stations as background noise. The three-hour drive seems longer tonight. My thoughts fly all over the place—I contemplate my past, my present, and my future. I haven't heard a lyric of any songs since they started over an hour ago when I left Athens.

I struggle to process every interaction with Hamilton earlier this evening. My best friend since eighth grade seemed to be much more tonight. I wonder if our friends noticed, and what did he really mean when he said goodbye and I love you?

Did he mean 'I love you best friend'? Or like his extra touches and closeness all evening was he sending me a message? Were we still best friends or are we becoming more?

Once the shock of Hamilton attending the wedding wore off, I expected to be on pins and needles around him—I was not prepared for his actions. He was the same old Hamilton with new touches. When in my proximity, his hands were constantly on me. In the past, he did touch me to offer his support in a friendly manner. Tonight, he played with my loose tendrils, his lips grazed my ear, and he kissed me goodbye telling me he loved me. He didn't hide any of this from our friends at the reception. To further cloud my thoughts, at moments he was friendly while at others he was *more*. I don't know where we stand—to say I am confused by his actions is an understatement.

More. Do I want more? Of course, I do. I need him—*we* need him. He's in Chicago or on the road while we're in Columbia. Where do we go from here?

That kiss. Oh my gosh what a goodbye kiss and to me it felt like so much more than a friendly goodbye.

I quickly swat my cheeks to snap out of the lust-filled, hopeful thoughts of Hamilton before returning my hands to the steering wheel. I attempt to focus as I sing along with Imagine Dragons on the radio. The lyrics speak to me. They explain we have no tomorrow without having what we did yesterday. Our past AKA yesterday affects our future AKA our tomorrow. The song is a message, a sign. My past affects every part of my future.

My mind drifts as I remember playing with magnets as a child. When I placed the north-pole of one magnet near the south-pole of another magnet, they attracted each other. But, when I placed two north-poles or two south-poles near each other the magnets repelled one another. It's the whole opposites attract saying come to life. I'm a south-pole magnet while many of my friends are north-pole magnets. We grew up in the small rural town of Athens, Missouri. My friends (north-poles) and the town of Athens (south-pole) attract each other. They are happy to be born, raised, attend school, marry, start a family, and live their entire lives in Athens. Since Athens and I are south-pole magnets we repel one another. In high school, my one goal was to leave town after graduation and never return.

One year has now passed since my high school graduation. I remain in contact with my girlfriends during our Sunday evening phone and video calls. They keep me up-to-date on their lives as well as some of the gossip in Athens. I share about my college classes at the University of Missouri, Alma, and her family. She opened her home to me while I attend classes and is much more than a roommate.

I made only one trip to Athens in the eleven months since I left town—now I hope to visit more often. I miss my friends and find phone calls aren't enough. I long to see them more often and to share everything I've kept from them. The weight of my secret grows heavier with each passing day. I made a promise to myself to meet with Hamilton at the end of this Chicago Cubs season—it's time to tell him *everything*. As it's nearly June now, I have four months to figure out how to explain my actions to the second most important person in my life.

As my car enters the city limits of Columbia, I know my three-hour drive comes to an end. Relief washes over me as I pull in Alma's driveway at just after 2:00 a.m. This drive from Adrian's wedding to her hunky man Winston allowed me to contemplate the past twelve months and plan for the next twelve. My mind seems clearer than it has been in a long time, except for one thing that still haunts me.

Stepping from my car, my tender foot makes contact with a rock on the concrete reminding me I removed my boots an hour into the drive. I grab my cowboy boots from the passenger seat and my small suitcase from the back. Barefoot I carefully tiptoe up the porch steps into our house.

Alma kindly left a lamp on in the front sitting room for my middle of the night return. I take my boots and bag up to my room and change into pajamas before making my way to the kitchen. With Alma's bedroom just off the back and Liberty sleeping soundly in her portable crib in one corner of the kitchen, I quietly place a water and two of Alma's homemade oatmeal raisin cookies on the corner of the counter. I flip off the lights, carefully lift Libby to my chest, and grab my snack. Juggling water, cookies, and my daughter prove a challenge as I head back upstairs. I drop my treats on the hall table before entering the nursery.

Attending the wedding today is my first trip away from Liberty. Although I didn't spend the night, eighteen hours away seems like forever. I slip into the rocker to enjoy a few more moments cuddling her in my arms. I pepper her forehead with kisses and tug on a couple of her springy chestnut curls.

"I saw daddy today," I whisper. "You look so much like him. His hair, his eyes, and his smile made me miss you even more." I attempt to swallow the lump forming in my throat. "He looked so handsome in his western attire. We even danced together. Your daddy is a great dancer."

My long, exciting, and emotional day settles in. Tears well in my eyes, I kiss my daughter one more time before I lay her in the crib, turn on the baby monitor, and head to my bedroom. I want nothing more than to cuddle Libby in my bed tonight—I feel raw. Seeing all eight of my high school friends in Athens today, celebrating Adrian and Winston's wedding, and the mixed signals from Hamilton wore me out emotionally and physically. I long for her sweet baby cuddles to comfort me tonight. I've been up since 5:00 a.m.—it's almost 3:00 a.m. now. Liberty usually wakes around 7:00, so I need to grab sleep while I can. After breakfast, Alma will help me process everything from my long confusing day. With no more strength, sleep engulfs me.

44

MADISON

Shortly after 7:00 a.m., Liberty's soft coos filter through the monitor on my beside table. Although I am exhausted, I need to see her little face. I peek into the crib loving the instant excitement on her face at seeing her mommy. I bid her good morning as I lift her. While I change her diaper, she mumbles around the chubby fist in her mouth. I like to think she is filling me in on her day alone with Alma. I place a kiss on her chubby cheek as we make our way to the kitchen.

Alma sips coffee while reading the Sunday paper in the breakfast nook enjoying the late-May sunlight through the bay window. She smiles at the sight of us then asks what time I got in last night claiming she didn't hear me.

I grab a bottle of formula from the refrigerator, place it in hot water to warm, and grab a diet cola before joining Alma at the table. Liberty continues sucking on her little fist and cooing as I answer Alma. As I take long drinks from my cola, I internally wish the caffeine to rapid-fire into my blood stream. I'm going to need more than one caffeinated beverage this morning.

"I loved the photos you texted me. Adrian was a lovely bride."

"It was..." I search for the perfect word that comes close to describing Adrian's special day. "It was a stress-free, magical day. Simple plans carried out by her large family and friends allowed everyone to enjoy the day.

I enjoy another drink of my diet cola, test Libby's bottle on my wrist, then offer it to her. She sucks the bottle as if she's gone days without eating. Even after two and a half months, I still giggle at the little piglet sounds she makes while eating. I blame her unladylike appetite her father. I lovingly gaze at her while I continue my conversation with Alma.

"The sun's rays were like a halo behind the barn during the ceremony and just as the vows ended twilight began. The fairy lights inside the barn illuminated perfectly. I'm not sure I want bridesmaids in cowboy boots and a country wedding someday, but I hope it can run as smoothly and everyone enjoy themselves just like Adrian's wedding."

"And Hamilton?" Alma doesn't allow me to ignore the elephant in the room. I'm certain she spotted him in the group photos I texted her.

I share my shock in finding him in the barn before the ceremony. I explain my attempts to busy myself with maid-of-honor duties to avoid him all evening and I share in detail his every word and touch at the reception. Then as Alma furrows her brow, I tell her everything that happened at the stop sign before we drove away from each other into the pitch-black night.

I take a gulp from my beverage waiting for Alma's words of wisdom. In the past twelve months I've benefited from her wealth of knowledge and lessons learned in her sixty-five years of life. She's raised two daughters and a son while active in her church and community, it seems she's experienced it all.

I remove the bottle from Libby's lips with her immediately protesting. "Patience sweetie, patience," I croon as I pat her back in search of a burb from her little belly. Alma and I laugh when the loud belch sounds and I kiss Libby on the cheek before returning the bottle. Alma uses Libby's distraction to ponder all I've shared.

"I don't know Hamilton, except from what you have shared, so I am just spit-balling here." Alma begins. "He's alone and far from home in Chicago. He spends endless hours on busses, on airplanes, and in hotel rooms. He's in the public-eye and commentators are hyper-critical of his performance on the mound. He's a small-town farm boy very far from his element. I'm sure he misses Athens and you." Alma pauses to sip from her coffee mug with its words 'grandma's go-go juice'.

"In an unexpected twist of fate, his schedule changed at the last minute, and he was permitted to spend mere hours surrounded by everyone important to him. I bet he didn't plan to constantly touch you, to kiss you, or to confess his love for you. I think the sight of you rekindled his feelings and the brevity of your time together spawned him into action." She fiddles with the corners of her newspaper. "If his feelings for you are like your feelings for him, he may have found himself powerless to fight them. Perhaps the thought of going eleven more months without physically being in your presence drove him to act."

Reaching across the table, Alma squeezes my free hand. "I agree they don't seem the actions of a best friend. I think he has feelings for you. Now what he plans to do going forward, I don't dare speculate. You have two options. You can discuss this with him the next time you speak over the phone, or you can sit back and wait for him to make the next move."

Her words help. I worried I had read more into Hamilton's actions exaggerating them in my mind. Alma interprets the same as I. Where I go from here, I don't know but I have time to contemplate it for a day or two before I speak to him next. For now, my insides are toasty warm with a flicker hope.

45

MADISON

Alma offers to take Liberty for a walk in her stroller with McGee on his leash, while I am on my weekly video call with my girls in Athens. I love that Alma's puppy calmly walks near Libby's stroller. On our first few walks in April, it took both of us to handle the stroller and Alma's ten-month-old, male, mini-chocolate Labradoodle. Among the hundreds of things, she's taught me this year is how to successfully train her puppy McGee.

Promptly at 7:00 p.m. Salem's FaceTime rings and Alma slips with our two little ones out the front door. "Long time no see," She greets in Adrian's absence. I greet my three friends. We animatedly relive yesterday evening's wedding and reception. Savannah asks what we think Adrian and Winston are doing right at this moment—we all agree we don't want to even think about it.

"Speaking of couples doing the nasty, Bethany, I didn't plan to see you on tonight's video call. Shouldn't you be celebrating your first anniversary with Troy right now?" I assumed she'd be on some romantic dinner date with her man spoiling her. The two are very affectionate when in public. Even in high school, I marveled at their constant contact with hands in each other's pockets, arms around each other, and kissing regardless who might see.

A blush quickly creeps up Bethany's neck and face. With her fair-complexion it borders between bright pink and red. "We celebrated before breakfast, in the shower, before our afternoon nap, and just before I drove to Salem's," she confesses proudly. "I wanted to share last night but didn't want to rob Adrian of her moment. She'll be pissed I shared without her here, but I can't keep the secret another minute." She bites her lower lip, smiles, then announces, "We are officially trying to get pregnant!"

Although it's no surprise, we celebrate with our friend. During our junior year of high school, the couple planned to move-in together immediately after graduation, marry, and start a family within a year. Excited to share her news, Bethany fills us in on ovulation calendars, fertility windows, and many other facts that as single women we aren't interested in.

"Bethany, honey," ever-sweet Salem interrupts. "The only thing we need to know from you is the three-day window during which we don't want to visit or even drive by your love shack." Loud laughter fills the air.

"Oh, laugh now Salem," Bethany quips. "your day will come. Your wedding is on the calendar sweetie, so little Latham's won't be far from that." More laughter erupts from all four of us.

When we regain our breath, Salem proceeds to inform me Bethany will be her maid-of-honor for the December wedding. Behind Salem, I notice Savannah and Bethany whispering while glancing at me before whispering some more.

"What are you two rudely whispering about?" I interrupt causing Savannah to elbow Bethany.

"Was last night *really* the first time you've seen Hamilton since he was drafted?" Bethany blurts. "I mean except for saying hi to him after his Major League debut at Wrigley Field?"

My three friends stare at me through my laptop screen. "Yes. I said goodbye to him from his mother's driveway the day he left for Des Moines. Memphis and I spent an hour with him after his first game pitching for the I-Cubs. You were all with me when we attended another I-Cubs game. Then Alma and her family joined me for fifteen minutes after his Wrigley debut. Why?"

"Seriously?" Bethany taunts. "Did you think we were blind last night at Adrian's reception?" She crosses her arms in front of her chest. I imagine she is also tapping her toe annoyed at me.

Salem jumps in, "Hamilton couldn't keep his eyes off you the entire night. Something is up—I think you have been holding out on us."

I play dumb in hopes they will describe what they witnessed and what they believe it meant. I can use all the help I can get on this topic.

"Madison, you know I tend not to weigh in on relationship crap," Savannah chimes in. "I personally witnessed two incidents that his lips brushed your ear and temple. He's never done that in public before that I know of. In fact, with all of his high school dating, I've never witnessed public displays of affection from him. He didn't hold their hands, put his arm around them, whisper in their ear, or kiss them in public. He held your hand last night, he placed his hand at the small of your back, he kissed your temple, whispered in your ear, and held you tight against him while the two of you danced." She shrugs. "It caught me off guard. When these two mentioned it, I knew it wasn't just my imagination."

"So, you can see why we might think the two of you have met sometime in the off-season. There was a new chemistry between you that wasn't your normal best friend interactions." Bethany urges. "I'll only ask once and then I'll let it go. Did the two of you get together this past winter?"

Here I go again. In keeping my pregnancy from Hamilton, I've needed to creatively avoid some topics and tell little white lies several times to keep my secret. I didn't see him this past winter—it's not a lie, but it is a lie by omission. I did spend the night with him last June before he left for minor league baseball. We haven't been alone together since his last night in Athens, but I do share a daughter with Hamilton. Here goes another avoidance of the truth that I hope they don't hate me for in the years to come.

"We did not have a secret rendezvous during the off-season. I must confess I was caught off-guard by his actions last night, too." I nervously shrug. "I've got a tropical storm swirling inside my head. I'm mega confused." I swirl my index finger in a circle above my head.

"Did he call you today?" Salem asks.

I answer that he probably spent the day trying to catch up with the team on East Coast while catching up on his sleep for tomorrow's game where he takes the mound, they attempt to make me feel better by stating they are sure he will call tomorrow.

"What should I do when he calls?" I know they don't know the major details that led up to last night, but I still need some advice.

Bethany tells me to play it cool and let him explain when he is ready. Salem seems stumped and Savannah says I should demand answers. So, no help from these three. Adrian might be better help, but she would also poke and pry until I cracked revealing our night together last June and that we have a daughter. She'd see right through my lie that I have no idea what might have prompted his actions.

Lucky for me, Bethany states she really must get back to Troy and their baby-making. I'm made to promise I will keep them posted on Hamilton's explanations when we do finally talk before we end this week's call.

The weight of the secrets I am keeping from Hamilton, his family, and my friends grows heavier tonight. Part of me wonders if Hamilton is settled enough in his career that revealing we have a daughter might not lead him to leave the Cubs and move back to Athens. But another stronger part of me wants to give him until the end of this season. Not wanting to wallow any longer, I decide to slip on my flip-flops and join Alma, Liberty, and McGee on the rest of their walk.

46

HAMILTON

Not even the cold post-practice ice strapped to my left shoulder and elbow can pull my thoughts from Madison. My bullpen catcher and pitching coach reprimanded me for not keeping my head on my job today.

Although she's filled most of my thoughts over the past year, everything changed yesterday. A switch flipped inside of me, I can't fight my feelings and now I can't get Madison off my mind.

The moment I walked out from changing into my wedding attire to match the guys, I felt my world shift. All of the air in the barn left—I felt like I took a punch to the gut. I couldn't breathe. Madison stood hands on hips in cowboy boots, a tutu, and denim vest. Although she dressed just as all of Adrian's friends for the ceremony, on her it worked. My tumultuous thoughts clicked into place like a puzzle piece. My body hummed to life in a way that did not say she was my best friend. It became clear that I wanted more than friend-ship—I wanted *every* part of her. I needed Madison.

In the hours that followed I found myself constantly touching her—she called to me. I played with her hair and leaned closer than usual to whisper in her ear as I reveled in her scent. My lips found their way to her cheeks and temples many times during the evening, but I longed for more.

The favor she asked of me my last night in Athens plunged her into the starring role of every one of my fantasies. That one night with Madison has played on my spank bank reel ever since.

Yeah, I know it sounds bad. I had a one-night-stand with my virginal best friend on my last night in town. Instead of putting myself on the market in Des Moines and Chicago, I relive that night while in the shower and in my bed. I sound like a creep.

She almost slipped away last night. At the stop sign where we would drive in opposite directions, I had to make my move. I darted from my car to hers. When she lowered her window, my brain failed me, and my heart took over. I leaned in, covered her lips with mine, and poured all of my feelings into our kiss. Madison's lips shared the feelings she'd been hiding from me, too. When I pulled back to catch my breath, her wide eyes, flushed face, and swollen lips parted as they gasped for breath. The vision is now burned in my mind. She wanted me, and my kiss affected her.

Luckily, my brain kicked in and knew I needed to drive, or I'd miss my flight and today's practice. My parting words haunt me, 'Eleven months seemed like an eternity away from you. Drive careful. I love you.' After my confession, I jogged to my car and drove away from my best friend, the girl who owns my heart.

I wince as I adjust the icepack on my shoulder. I attempted to share my true feelings for her during every phone conversation for eleven months. Many times, I opened my mouth, the words on the tip of my tongue, then froze. I promised her our one night together, her 'virginity favor' wouldn't change our friendship. I really did try for months to erase that one night from my mind to allow me to just be friends again. But during our phone calls, I felt her through the receiver. She shared her new college-life, her hectic schedule, about her new friend Alma, and her fears. With each conversation, my heart grew, and I fell deeper in love with my best friend Madison.

Last night I shared my feelings—I admitted I love her. Of course, I quickly ran to my car to hide as soon as I spoke the words, but I meant them. I hope she knows how much I meant my kiss and words. I hope she wants me like I want her. I need her to love me and not just as best friends loves each other.

Coach's gruff voice cuts into my silent reflections. "Armstrong, we need your mind on throwing and not back in Podunk Missouri. Don't make me regret letting you take an unscheduled day off. Lock. It. Down." Watching coach's back as he walks from the training room, I vow to keep my thoughts on baseball when at work and save my confusing thoughts of Madison for my private time.

47

MADISON

As May fades into June, my texts and calls with Hamilton remain as they were prior to Adrian's wedding. I don't allude to our good bye. I allow him time to focus on his pitching and to work out his feelings. I'm sure he is as confused as I am.

This week I began my senior year of college by taking summer classes. My goal to fast track my education came to fruition. I begin student teaching this fall, have my college graduation in December, and hopefully I will secure a teaching position for the spring semester. My summer classes move at a rapid pace providing me with many hours of homework each day. So, this morning Liberty is enjoying tummy time on her quilt in the center of the floor while I finish up my lesson plan assignment for Monday's class.

I find my eyes constantly drift to my daughter when I should be working. She's currently holding her head up and babbling at her nearby toys. I slide my laptop to the side of the sofa and crawl down to join her. We babble, she drools, and we smile. She's growing too fast. Everyday there is something new—Hamilton is missing too much. My ringing phone interrupts our playtime.

"I love you baby girl," I whisper to my sleepy daughter. "One day, you will meet your daddy. You will meet Bethany and Troy, Adrian and Winston,

Salem and Latham, and my friend Savannah." I kiss her cheek. "For now, it's time for a bottle and little girls to nap."

48

HAMILTON

Sitting on the air-conditioned charter bus waiting for my teammates to arrive, I turn my iPhone to entertain myself. The post-game interviews and showers droned on today. I'm irritable. Our long road trip is taking its toll on me.

Finally, the bus pulls from the stadium, escorting us back to our nearby Minneapolis hotel. My life is a blur of hotels, shuttles, airplanes, and restaurant food. While I enjoy every minute at our country's ballparks, the rest of the traveling is torture. My life depends upon my teammates to pack, load, and unload the airplanes and shuttle busses. A handful of players are perpetually late, slower than the rest, and inconsiderate of everyone's time.

It's nearly 7:00 p.m., we're hungry, we're tired, we're sore, and we need time away from each other. We're not even halfway through our 162-game season. We are on our final leg of a fourteen-game road trip, and most of us need time away from the other twenty-four men in the traveling circus that is our Chicago Cubs team.

As a boy dreaming of playing Major League Baseball, I looked forward to traveling. Now, I detest away games and all that they entail. I crave a home-cooked meal. Phone conversations with Madison and my mom stir my homesick feelings even more. I miss my mom and the farm, I miss hanging with Madison, and I'm tired of eating alone.

We won today's game after eleven innings, thus we're later than usually returning to the hotel. As I take the mound tomorrow, I'll stay in this evening. I have a pregame meal and routine I never stray from. I'll have chicken breast and steamed vegetables delivered to my room. I'll study my opponents for tomorrow's game, then shoot a text to Madison before I turn in for the night. I never imagined how lonely and exhausting being a professional ball player could be.

49

MADISON

I've asked Alma to care for Liberty while I drive to Athens and back today. My heartaches at the thought of time away from my baby, but I've never missed a Father's Day with my dad. Although this year it requires careful planning, I find a way to make it possible. I've reached out to Hamilton's mother, Memphis, asking if I might drop by her place this morning and enjoy lunch with her. Of course, she is thrilled with the promise of my long overdue visit. The Cubs play today, so I will not run into Hamilton during this visit to our hometown—a fact that is both a relief and a disappointment.

It's days like this when the double-life I lead haunts me. I need to talk to Hamilton. My world is over-complicated. Talking to him will allow my two worlds to combine. I'll no longer hide my daughter while visiting Athens. I'll no longer dread such trips. Alma and Liberty would be able to travel with me. My three-hour drive wouldn't be as lonely. As this weekend drew closer, I debated my need to visit my father and I pondered remaining in Columbia this year.

I arrive at The Armstrong Farm just before ten to find Memphis chatting with three farm-hands as they sit on a truck tailgate near the barn. I make my way to her before she can end their conversation. I squeeze her from the side unable to restrain myself—visiting her excites me. Memphis introduces me to the men that help her keep the farm running. In our many phone conversations she's shared that many boys and men from surrounding farms and the Athens community offer to help her with crops, harvests, and livestock year-round.

I marvel at her fortitude in running this large farm without her husband and son. She's one of the two very strong women as mentors I'm blessed with in my life and I hope to be this strong in the eyes of my daughter.

Memphis wraps her arm around my shoulders as she escorts me toward the house. Everything seems just as it was last summer. Hamilton had just left for Des Moines to play minor league baseball and I spent much of my time with his mother. With iced tea in hand we take a seat in the shade on her porch swing.

She asks questions about my summer classes and placement for student teaching this fall. We discuss Hamilton and the exciting season the Cubs are having. I teasingly remind her I am a Cardinals fan, so we need to end our affections for the Cubs right there. Memphis fills me in on her daughter, the crops she has in, the new calves, and how much Troy has been assisting her.

As our conversation wanes a bit, thoughts of my gigantic secret creep into my mind. It would be easy to share my burden with her at this moment. I'd first explain my reason for not visiting last winter was due to my pregnancy. I could tell her I had a daughter on March 10th and explain it was a one-night stand. I know she would discuss my situation in great detail and support me from today on. She'd visit Columbia and insist I visit her more often with my daughter. It would feel so good to have her support.

But I can't tell her the father is her son—I can't ask her to keep my secret from her son. Upon laying eyes on Liberty, Memphis would instantly know Hamilton is her father. I've marveled at the many photos Memphis decorates her home with—Liberty is the spitting image of Hamilton's big sister. Earlier while Memphis excused herself to the bathroom and our poured our tea, I held a pic of Liberty on my phone next to a photo of Hamilton's sister at approximately the same age. Her brown curls, chocolate eyes, long lashes, even her Cupid's Bow lips are a mirror image of her aunt. Thus, there is no way I can confide in Memphis until I reveal to Hamilton. I don't regret my night with him or my daughter—I do regret keeping my secret. For now, this must be my burden and my burden alone. I clear my thoughts and return to my conversation with Memphis.

We snap a selfie on the porch swing and I Snapchat to Hamilton. We know he has an afternoon game today, so we don't expect him to reply. I've missed this. I spent much of my high school life with Hamilton and his mother, being near Memphis today demonstrates how much she means to me. While in Columbia, Alma fills the void formerly owned by Memphis. Alma's not her replacement, just another strong woman to guide me in the absence of my own mother.

From time-to-time I still dream my mother is in recovery, that slowly we mend fences, and I eventually share Liberty with her. I don't delude myself— it is only a silly dream. Liberty *will not* be exposed to her alcoholism. I want her nowhere near the constant hurt my mother inflicts on those around her. Alma fills the role of grandmother until I tell Hamilton and Memphis. Then, Liberty's family will grow in people and in love.

Out of the blue, Memphis asks me if Hamilton shares his personal life with me in texts or calls. My face scrunches not sure what she means. She explains he doesn't speak of dating or girls in any of his visits or calls to her. I let her know he claims girls mess with his game as I speak of blonde arm-candy or his dating.

"I'm not old-fashioned," Memphis begins. "I know he's no angel. I just hope he remembers our talks from high school about preventing pregnancy scares."

She searches my face for any knowledge I might have on her son's dating. I hope the fact he has a daughter with me doesn't show on my face. I try not to look guilty. I can't let her know that although we used condoms, I still became pregnant. I explain to Memphis that although I bring it up and tease him about women, he emphatically denies spending time with anyone.

She turns the tables to ask if I have dated in Columbia. I explain I am far too busy to waste time anywhere that men hang out. I confess a guy from Bible study asked me out and I opted instead for a group of us going out. I am focusing on me and my education right now—I don't need a boyfriend to add to my busy schedule. She encourages me to put myself out there to start the hunt for my future boyfriend.

I pretend to go along with it. I'm a single mom on a fast track to graduation, I have no time to spare. I don't share that anytime I'm not studying or sitting in class I'm focusing on Liberty. I sense Memphis has something she wants to ask me. Can she tell I'm keeping a secret? Although I wait she keeps it to herself.

50

MADISON

I say my goodbye to Memphis after lunch. The reason for this trip is to visit my dad and it's time that I head that way. During the ten-minute drive from the Armstrong farm to the cemetery, I contemplate how far I live now from my dad and how visiting once a year is not enough.

"Hey dad," I say out loud. "I'm here like I promised." I kneel next to his headstone. I brush the grass shavings and dust from the top and the engraved lettering of his light-gray granite stone. My mind floods with all I need to say. I wonder with him in heaven does he already know everything that happened to me in the last twelve months. "I love you." My words fail to tell him how much I miss and need him. I continue as if he isn't on my shoulder each and every day. I talk of Hamilton and Liberty, my classes, and Alma. I express my constant worry about my mother and how far she fell without him around. I share my plans for the upcoming year for my career, for Liberty, and for Hamilton. After several quiet moments, I promise I'll bring Liberty with me next time and say goodbye.

My phone buzzes as I walk from his headstone to my car at the edge of the cemetery.

MOTHER

I hope you miss your father today as much as I do

I freeze at her texted words. Is she guilting me? Is she sober enough to remember I visit his grave every year on Father's Day? She was rarely sober when I lived at home, so I doubt she is ever sober now that I am gone.

ME

I visit his grave EVERY Father's Day

Hope you find 1 hour a year to visit him

without alcohol in your system

MOTHER

I see a year at college didn't soften your heart

ME

I've texted you & left voicemail for you every week for 52 weeks

Not a word from you

Until you are sober DON'T text me

MOTHER

after everything I have done for you

ME

I hope you are referring to the time before dad's death

because the last 6 years I've been without a dad & a mom

I set my phone on Do Not Disturb mode. Now I can ignore her texts. I'm fuming—she has some nerve. The fact that she texted me at all shocks me. I assume she has at least half a bottle in her by now at home since the bars can't open on Sunday in Athens. For that matter, I'm surprised she even knows it is Father's Day.

I want to text her that she has a granddaughter and if she sobers up she can visit me, or I will visit her, but I've not the energy to hope anymore. I've been burned too many times. In the past I hoped, and I prayed, then I waited for her to be the mom I needed. She's perpetually on my prayer list. I've shared information and resources to help yet it is always me without her.

In my virtual Al-anon and Al-Ateen meetings, I've learned I can't help her until she is ready to accept help. I've learned her actions don't reflect upon me and others don't hold me accountable for her actions. I've met so many others online in my same situation. We share our stories, our hopes, our prayers, and our reality that our own life is all that we may control.

With my phone no longer alerting me to her texts or calls, I sit in my car for a moment. I don't want to leave this way. I can't allow her to taint this visit, so I return to my dad's grave. Sitting in the green grass, I rest my right hand on his name.

"Dad, I miss you. I wish you were here. I know it's not your fault mother has fallen so far, but if you were here she might still be the mom I need. I have so many things in my life that I wish you were here to help me with. Liberty grows so fast. I know you would spoil her rotten. She would love visits to papa's farm—you would have a little helper at the hog lot and on your tractors." I wipe my tears from my chin. "She'd wrap you around her little finger."

I continue to wipe tears from my cheeks as I sit quietly for several long minutes. When my phone rings interrupting the silence, I realize it's one of the ten people I have on my favorites list, otherwise it wouldn't ring while on Do Not Disturb mode. A sad smile slides on my face when I see Hamilton's name and picture for this FaceTime call.

"Hello."

"Are you still in..." his words trail off. "Hey."

"Hey."

"Visiting your dad, I wish I was there with you right now." I'm not sure if it is the tears and my red puffy eyes, or the cemetery in the background that tipped him off. "We have a rain out and I was attempting to call you before you left Athens."

"Sorry about your game and yes you caught me just in time." I wipe my face on my sleeve trying to look less pathetic. "Did you need something?"

Hamilton's face falls a bit. "I thought if I caught you, I could ask you to do a favor for me."

"I can try." I begin walking back towards my car as we chat.

"Do you need to hurry back to Columbia?"

"Nope. Come on it's me just tell me what you need already." The more he avoids asking the favor, the more worried I become. Thoughts of him coming to Athens to see me, asking me to come to Chicago to visit him, plus many others swirl in my mind.

"Could you walk me over to my dad's headstone? I'd like to spend a moment with him for Father's Day, too."

I freeze. It's at this moment that I realize this is actually Hamilton's first Father's Day and he doesn't even know it. Liberty should be spending the day with her daddy. We could have bought him a gift or two and a sweet card. My heart weighs a ton in my chest. This is yet another milestone I deprive them of.

"Mady..." Hamilton's voice draws me back.

"Yeah, sure, no problem." I change my direction walking towards Mr. Armstrong's final resting place on the opposite end of the cemetery from my dad's. "I'm glad you called when you did. A few more minutes and I would have already been speeding down the highway."

At the graveside, I turn the camera view from me to the headstone. I remove my shoes and prop my cell phone between them angled up with a full view of his father's stone. I peek into the camera's line of sight. "I propped the camera up. I'll take a walk for a few minutes so the two of you can have some time alone. I'll announce myself when I walk back." I smile into the camera hoping Hamilton knows I'll still be with him in my thoughts as I take my walk.

"Thank you."

I look at my Fitbit on my wrist noting it is 2:15 p.m. I wander down and back through several rows of headstones. I recognize many common last names of Athens as I read each monument. I keep track of the birthdates trying to see what the oldest date I might find is. The stones here are not as old as the ones in the little cemetery near our farm that Hamilton and I spent many hours in during high school.

As I return to my phone fifteen minutes later, I announce here I come a few times as I approach. I'm caught off guard to find Hamilton is no longer connected. I wonder why he hung up or if he was disconnected. As I slip my shoes back on, I notice he texted me.

HAMILTON

TY(thank you)

Call when you are on highway

I'll keep you company for part of your drive

ME

Ok, call in about 10 minutes

Before leaving Athens, I stop for gas and a few snacks then pull onto the highway pointed back towards Liberty, Alma, and my other life in Columbia.

"Libby," Alma plays. "Look at my tractor." Alma pushes the large toy with soft edges, resembling a tractor forward on the blanket.

My mind drifts to my times helping my dad on the farm. Liberty would enjoy riding on my dad's lap as he drove the tractors. I envision her sitting alone in the seat while he climbed down to open the gates to the pasture. Dad would help her ride a goat and I'm sure he would buy her a pony when she was old enough. My mind easily flips through the many farm activities my dad would enjoy sharing with his granddaughter.

I fight back my tears at the interactions Liberty will never have with my dad. Come to think of it, Libby will never have a grandfather as Hamilton's father also passed away. I lost all four of my grandparents before I turned five. With the current situation with my mother, Alma and someday soon Memphis will be the only grandparents she will know.

Of course, now thoughts of my mother are all I can think of. Although I think of her from time-to-time, I don't worry about her every day. I love my new life free of a daily reminder of the danger my mother carries with her. I have a routine. It's smooth. I do not miss the perpetual out-of-control feeling I once carried around while living with my alcoholic mother. I've resigned to the fact she is who she is and lives the life she chooses. I have removed myself, moved on as best I can, and have Troy to inform me when anything goes wrong. It's all I can handle and enjoy my life as I deserve to.

51

HAMILTON

The tiny red two alerts me I have Snapchats to view. As is my habit, I quickly snap a screenshot of each allowing me more time to view them. The first pic is a selfie of Madison on the porch swing with my mother. They are the two most important people in my life and it warms my heart they still get together in my absence. I trace my finger over Madison's giant smile. Her golden-tanned face glows and bright blue eyes twinkle in the summer sun. She's happy—they both seem happy. It reads 'wish you were here'. The second picture displays a view of the barn from the driver's seat of the tractor. Madison typed 'Must feed the cows'. If only they knew how I longed for my former farm life.

Although Madison stated she'd go for a walk and alert me of her return, I hope she will stand nearby and listen.

"I love you, dad and I'm sorry I can't be there in person." I clear my throat, my mouth suddenly very dry. "I'm still in Minneapolis. They called the game after five innings and an hour rain and lightning delay. I'm still living our dream and feel your presence every time I take the mound." A chuckle escapes as I prepare to share about the game. "I took a chance in the third inning. The guys shared that coach's face turned beet-red and he cursed twice before he changed to cheering for me. It kills me to bunt at each of my at-bats. I decided today to show coach what I've been telling him all season. The count was 2-0. Ever cocky Mosby gift-wrapped a fastball right down the middle. I wish you could have seen his face when I took a full swing knocking his gift in the upper section of the left-center bleachers. I was just so tired of American League pitchers assumed to be an easy out via bunt. I now have one homerun and two RBI's on my stats. In a long conversation with the manager and batting coach, they've decided to let me officially bat instead of bunt for the rest of the season."

I run my fingers through my hair. "They'll soon be knocking on my hotel room door signaling it's time to head to the airport." I sigh as I organize all I wish to share with dad today.

"I'm in love with Madison." I blurt then quietly listen to see if I hear a reaction from Madison if she remained within earshot. Hearing nothing, I continue. "It kills me to be in Chicago with her in Columbia. I long to share my life with her. It's lonely in my condo and on the road as much as the Cubs are. I try to share everything with her via our texts and calls. Hearing her voice helps some. I miss her every day. I need her more now than ever before, both mentally and physically." Again, I chuckle. "I showed her and told her I loved her the end of May. Then we each returned to our lives."

"Dad, I'm lost and need you now more than ever. How do I allow her to chase her dream while I chase mine, yet show her how much I love her? I need you to guide me. I need you to help me. She's too close to mom. If I ask for mom's help, you know her, she would get her hopes up. If something were to happen and we don't become a couple both Madison and mom would be devastated. I can't risk their friendship with each other until I figure out how to make us work. You know what I mean? I'm sure you do. I need one of your deep philosophical conversations we shared while mending fences or sitting at the livestock barn. I desperately need your guidance. So, I'll be looking for your signs. Just remember I'm a novice at love and might need more than a gentle prod in the right direction."

Knock. Knock. Knock.

"Well, I've gotta go. I love and miss you so much, dad. I hope I make you proud."

52

MADISON

As the heat of July in the Midwest takes a firm grip on the exposed throat of the Midwest, Alma and I begin walking Liberty and McGee early in the morning or after seven in the evening. My summer classes require me to leave late morning and return midafternoon when the sun is the hottest. I'm thankful my old car's air conditioner still works.

The three of us take a mini-weekend-vacation to St. Louis. It will be a weekend of firsts for Liberty. I'm excited to share my love for the St. Louis Cardinals while she sees her daddy pitch for the first time. We plan to attend the Saturday evening and Sunday afternoon games. We settle into our hotel room to relax a bit after our long drive. Liberty slept as I drove. Now she is awake and hungry. Alma offers to feed her while I unpack then set up the portable crib.

Due to the heat, we arrive only thirty minutes before the first pitch. Alma assists as I record Liberty with eyes open entering the ballpark and in our lower level seats for the video journal I keep to share with Hamilton in the future. I smile to myself as she and I wear our Cardinals jerseys. Libby has a red headband in her dark brown curls. By the first pitch, her yawns grow more frequent. Alma pulls a bottle from the diaper bag. Liberty's eyes lock on it immediately while her legs and arms begin to animate with excitement.

Fans sitting in the seats around us laugh at her reaction. One kind Cardinals fan offers to take a picture of the three of us with the field in the background while her husband holds the baby bottle. She claims we need a photo while Libby is awake of all of us at her first game. Fortunately, Libby cooperates. I'm surprised she didn't start to cry as her bottle moved farther away instead of closer. When my little girl is hungry she doesn't like to wait for her food.

When her tummy is full she falls sound asleep. I place her in the baby sling swaddled to my chest for the remainder of the game. Alma snaps photos occasionally of Libby and I, the game, and beautiful Busch Stadium all lit up after dark. Between the fifth and sixth inning a camera zooms in on the sleeping Libby still wearing her red Cardinals headband and me. We are projected on the jumbotron. A loud 'ahh' erupts from the stadium. Luckily a fan nearby snaps a picture of us on the big screen and asks to text it to me.

I stare at the perfect photo on my phone screen for many minutes. Suddenly fear envelops me. What if Hamilton heard the 'ah' and glanced at the jumbotron? He would no doubt recognize me. He might have seen Liberty. My heartbeat quickens. Please, please, please don't let him have seen us.

"Madison," Alma's concerned voice calls. "What's wrong?" She places her hand on my forearm.

I quietly share my concern that Hamilton might have seen me on the jumbotron with Liberty. Alma calmly asks to see the photo on my phone. She studies it for a moment. She points out with my Cardinals hat and Libby at my chest, Hamilton might simply think it was someone that resembles me. Most of my face is shaded by the hat, Alma isn't in the shot, and he has no reason to think I would bring a baby girl to a ballgame. Her words calm most of my fears. I'll need to wait until I hear from him next to see if he brings it up to know for sure.

The next day, Libby wakes from her nap as we enter the stadium. I selected seats in the shade for this sultry day to ensure she remains as cool as possible. Alma records me helping Libby clap when her daddy is announced as the starting pitcher for the Chicago Cubs. Today, I wear my Cardinals attire while

Libby wears her daddy's jersey, a Cubs diaper cover, and a blue Cubs headband in her damp ringlets. Alma and I keep our voices low when we refer to Hamilton as Libby's daddy. We don't want anyone to hear us and start rumors on social media about Hamilton having a daughter. I am acutely aware he is in the public eye.

Hamilton's pitches vex my Cardinals. The Cards trail by two when he leaves the game in the seventh. Alma and I decide due to the heat we should leave, too. At Alma's van, we remove the plastic bags she insisted we keep in the cooler. In each of the three bags Alma placed a washcloth for after the game. Yet another trick I've learned in our time together. I wipe Liberty down from head to toe, change her diaper, then secure her in her car seat for the drive home. Alma and I use our washcloths on the back of our neck and face to cool down as I drive.

53

HAMILTON

It's one-hundred five degrees on the turf at game time. With the hot July sun bearing down and all eyes on me, I deliver the first pitch in the bottom of the first inning. It's a ninety-eight-mph fastball for a strike. Cardinal fans boo loudly from all directions as I play with the rosin bag in my left hand. A smirk graces my face as I realize Madison both cheers for me and groans for her team. I mentally chide myself. Not at work. I must not let thoughts of Madison affect my work. With my head back in the game and a strike under my belt the oppressive heat melts away and I find my rhythm.

During the top of the third inning I mentally prepare myself to face the bottom of the St. Louis line-up as well as hit this inning. As I stand at the edge of the dugout I pray Stan gets on, so I can bat this inning.

While securing my batting gloves, Humphreys leans close. "Your girl's a huge Cardinal's fan, isn't she?" He chuckles while his elbow prods my ribcage. "Don't hold anything back to make her happy. Our team comes first."

Is this guy for real? Have my six strikeouts and one walk not demonstrated my loyalty to the Cubs? I try to remind myself Humphreys is angry I get to hit as a pitcher. My homerun and RBI total are quickly approaching his stats. It wouldn't look good for a pitcher to put up better stats than a fielder with many more at bats. I smile knowing Madison wants me to succeed, even against her Cardinals. I wish she were in the stands today as I approach the batter's box.

With a 2-1 count, I connect with the next pitch and send it soaring over the centerfield wall. I begin my homerun trot amidst St. Louis boos and knowledge my homerun and 2 RBI's pissed Humphreys off even more.

The pitching coach pulls me from the mound in the bottom of the seventh inning. The Cubs lead six to three, I leave with a double, a homerun, and three RBI's along with my many strikeouts from the mound. Although I struggled keeping my fingertips dry in the sweltering July heat, I had a great showing today.

As I sit, icing my shoulder and elbow on the bench. I lose my battle to keep my thoughts off Madison at work. I look forward to chatting with her tonight. I wanted to arrange a visit with her while I was in St. Louis, but this long road trip kept me too busy. With the All-Star break later this month, perhaps I can arrange some time for the two of us. I mentally flip through my upcoming schedule. Home games this week for the Fourth of July, photo shoot and endorsement meetings between games, and three days off for the All-Star break on the Fifteenth. Not much time to work with. I'll need to confirm a few things tomorrow, then I can schedule time with Madison during the three-day break.

I long for the day we live in the same city, are a real couple, and we can relive the entire game together as we did in high school. I dream of a relationship with Madison more with each passing week. In the upcoming off-season I plan to move us forward—I plan to make her mine.

54

MADISON

My phone signals a text from Adrian shortly after we leave St. Louis. Alma reads each text while I remain focused on the road.

ADRIAN

Can't call tonight

Dinner with Winston's parents

Sorry

I ask Alma to text her back for me.

ME

I understand

ADRIAN

Twice as much gossip for next Sunday

ME

(winking emoji)

I'm surprised that I'm not more upset by her texts. Over the past year, we've only missed three Sunday evening calls. Lately, each call leaves me sad. I'm no longer a constant in the lives of my friends. Perhaps the decision to keep my daughter a secret pulls me farther from my friends.

I fill the kitchen sink with warm water, gather bath items from the nursery, then announce to Liberty it's time for a bath. She loves the water as much as I enjoy watching her in it.

Barely sitting in the sink, Liberty begins slapping her palms against the water while cheering and spraying me with warm droplets. As I pretend to protest, she laughs her adorable deep-belly laugh. Alma joins our fun time.

When my cell vibrates on the counter, Alma offers to play with Liberty while I check it.

HAMILTON

Busy?

ME

Never too busy for u

Immediately my cell phone signals and incoming FaceTime call. I step from the kitchen after Alma takes over bath duty, briskly seeking my quiet bedroom as I answer.

"Is it raining there?" Hamilton's voice greets.

"No, why?"

His laughter causes my belly to flip-flop. Liberty laughs just like her daddy. I quickly lie claiming I was cleaning my shower.

I take in his dress clothes and use of his Bluetooth ear piece. He's not on an airplane. "Where are you?"

Hamilton explains he's on the shuttle from O'Hare back to Wrigley. "I wanted to call you before it got too late." His hushed tone calls to every cell in me. I recall this whispered voice while cuddling in his arms, his lips near my ear.

"Madison," he calls to me. "Where'd you go just now?" His chocolate eyes squint as his brow furrows.

I shake it off. "You had a great game today." I mentally scold myself for my lustful thoughts as I change the subject.

"Tell me you didn't hear your Cardinal fans boo me through your TV."

"Actually, Alma and I were at the game today." I witness shock slide over his face. "I cheered for you on the inside while Alma jumped up and down in her Armstrong jersey beside me."

"Crap!" Hamilton turns to his right informing his teammate everything is okay. Looking back into his phone, he rejoins our call. "I wanted to plan dinner or something while in St. Louis. I got so busy with the long road trip that I couldn't get the logistics straightened out." He runs his hands from his scalp slowly down his face. This draws my attention to his dark brown tired eyes. "I can't believe you were in Busch Stadium today and I didn't get to see you. You were so close…"

"With my summer classes and your schedule, I'm not sure it would've worked out." I can't take the sad eyes he now stares back at me with. "Alma and I had to make a quick day trip to squeeze the game in. We left when they made the pitching change."

"I need to check on a few things tomorrow." A small smile slips upon his perfect lips. "What does your schedule look like the 15th though the 17th?"

My eyes look to the ceiling as I attempt to recall my calendar. "That's dead week. I'll have projects to work on, papers to write, and finals to study for." His smile fades and the twinkle in his eye disappears. "But, I can shift things to squeeze you in."

"That's my number one fan," he teases. "Give me a day or two then we'll make our plans."

"I hate to seem like I don't want to see you, but what happens when you make the All-Star roster?" I *know* Hamilton doesn't believe he stands a chance his first full season with the Cubs, but I know he will be playing in this season's All-Star Game. Which means he will be much too busy to visit me. As much as I want to see him, it's easier than arranging a visit and asking Alma to keep Liberty for me.

Hamilton rises from his charter-bus seat, he promises to call me in a day or two, then ends our call with an 'I love you'. His teammates within earshot catcall and tease him as he disconnects.

My mind reels. Hamilton stated he loves me in earshot of his team. He pretty much just outed our long-distance relationship to his closest friends. Relationship. Is it really a relationship? We haven't been on a first date. We only share conversations via text and phone calls a couple of times a week. He did step things up a notch at Adrian's wedding over a month ago, but he hasn't really made it clear where we stand since then.

The remainder of the night I spend reliving every word, touch, and kiss from May until now. Even though I give up finding there's no way I can figure out what's in his head, sleep evades me for many hours.

55

MADISON

Mid-week I receive a call from Adrian as I am driving to my class. "Hi," I answer leery why she calls at a time she knows I am headed to class for the day.

"Can you talk for a couple of minutes?" she asks instead of a greeting. When I let her know I have ten minutes before class begins she continues. "Bethany lost the baby early this morning. We are just leaving the hospital to get her settled back at home."

Bile rises up my throat as my stomach burns. I have no words for this news. My heart aches for my dear friend.

"I know." Adrian assures me—she understands my current inability to process this horrible news. "Call me this afternoon. I will give you more details and let you know how she is doing at home. I'm sorry I dropped this on you before class, but I couldn't slip away earlier at the hospital and couldn't wait until three this afternoon to tell you. I didn't want someone to text you about it, and you not knowing what they were referring to."

"Thank you." My voice is hoarse,

"Try to focus during class. I realize it will be hard, but there is nothing anyone can do but pray for Bethany and Troy." Adrian's attempts do nothing to comfort me as we disconnect.

Walking into the classroom, I turn on the voice recorder app in my phone to keep track of items covered today. When I walk out hours later, I can't recall a thing the professor covered. I'm glad I thought to use the recorder—my mind was on Bethany, how much she longed for a family, the miscarriage, and Troy. Even now as I unlock my car I fight tears. I crave Alma's help processing Bethany's tragedy.

When I arrive home, Alma attempts to comfort me as she shares a wealth of information. She admits she had two miscarriages—one before her oldest child was born and one before her second child. She explains that is how she met Dr. Anderson the first time. Of course, he was much younger back then than last March when he delivered Liberty for me. Alma shares both of her experiences in great detail.

After dinner, with tissues in hand for my leaking eyes, I continue my online research. I visit health sites covering the clinical side of miscarriages and recovery. I find several sites focused on successfully conceiving that explain the causes and likelihood of miscarriages. Then they positively paint the months following a miscarriage and steps toward conceiving again.

Having struggled with my own bouts of depression, I understand the loneliness, despair, and the feeling of being lost lying ahead of Bethany and Troy. Although I will continue to hope the couple successfully mourns, heals, and tries again—I know they will struggle. It's hard to accept help and open up to others when one falls into the dark pit. It's a journey comparable to climbing up Mt. Everest to find your way back out.

I startle when Alma slaps my laptop closed. I look up through my wet lashes at her expressionless face.

"That's enough. There are too many horror stories on the web and no amount of research will help Bethany." She forces a smile. "Be there when she calls. Be the daily phone call that makes her day. Listen when she needs an ear. That's all you can do for her." Alma wraps her arms around me from behind while I remain seated. I absorb her words and her warmth.

Liberty doesn't enjoy floor time this evening. I keep my daughter on my lap in my arms. I've always believed her to be my little miracle—now I better understand the blessing I have with my healthy daughter.

I memorize once more every little finger, toe, and dimple. I marvel at her dark curly hair like Hamilton's. I take in the changes of the four months since I first held her in my arms at the hospital.

With Liberty tucked in for the night, I turn in early. I continue to struggle.

Athens feels like it's on the other side of the planet from me. Three hours is too far to drive with my schedule to spend some time with Bethany. I feel the deep need to be with her, to help her, and to hug her tightly as she cries. My friend is hurting—my phone calls don't seem enough. Bethany and Troy's large families and their Athens friends will surround them. I have no doubt she will be well taken care of—I wish I could be there, too.

The next day, Bethany calls me at 5:00 p.m. I excuse myself to my room silently pointing to ask Alma to watch Libby while she grabs the toys on her blanket. I say a quick prayer to be strong enough to carry on a conversation with Bethany without too much crying. She needs me to listen and comfort her, not to cry like a baby.

"Hey honey."

"Madison," Bethany's quivering voice weakly whispers. "Is this a good time?"

I assure her I am here anytime she wants to call and chat. I ask how she is today because I know *how she is doing*. My friend will not be good for quite a while. She shares the entire heartbreaking story. She woke up around 2:00 a.m. spotting on her sheets. Having read that can sometimes happen she wasn't worried until she went to the restroom where cramping and a gush of bright red blood occurred. She screamed to wake up Troy and they hurried to the emergency room. She claims Troy remained calm and tried to calm her as well. It seems he was strong in this situation just as my friend needed.

As she shares the rest of the story, my heart breaks for her all over again.

Silently I think maybe it's a good thing I've kept my secret. It might be hard for Bethany to talk to me if she knew I am already a mother she desires to be. With her fluctuating hormones and recent loss, I might more like an enemy than a friend. I focus on Bethany once again.

"Adrian spent the morning with me, today then Salem came for the afternoon. She left minutes ago as Troy should be home anytime now." Bethany's words cause red flags to pop up.

"Did he go to work today?" It's a stupid question—she just alluded to him being gone all day. I cannot believe he didn't stay home at least one day at home with her. She wanted a baby and to start their family—it's all she could talk about. She needs him today. They lost a baby, both of them need to grieve and comfort each other. "Bethany, if you need him to stay with you, you may have to tell him. I'm sure he will stay if he knows you need him."

"He spent yesterday afternoon and evening with me. Once he tucked me into bed, he slept on the sofa. I didn't even hear him get ready this morning before he left." A tearful hiccup escapes. Bethany attempts to gather herself to continue. "I'm sure he thought I would just sleep all day today."

"Did you want him to stay with you today?" My voice is gruffer than it should be. Bethany needs my support not my anger.

"Yeah, I think so. I mean it never occurred to me he might not be there when I woke up this morning. He did text me to tell me he arranged for Adrian to visit this morning."

"Bethany, promise me you will talk to him about this tonight. Just mention how sad you were that you didn't see him when you woke up. Tell him you missed him today. Honey, he's a guy—you have to spell it out for him. Okay?"

"Yeah." She pauses to blow her nose.

"So how are you physically? Any pain?"

"I'm just tired and still spotting a tiny bit." Bethany sighs deeply. "Now I have to wait six weeks to have a period and maybe a month or two after that before we may be able try again." Her sobs grow louder in my ear. I allow her several minutes to let it all out.

"Honey, you have to allow your body time to repair itself. I'm sure your doctor wants to make sure everything is okay before you get pregnant again. I know you want a baby right now, but even with waiting you could have a baby by this time next year." I hope my words provide comfort.

"When I got home from class yesterday, I shared your news with Alma. Honey, she had two miscarriages and has three healthy children. Taylor was born within a year of her first miscarriage. She wanted me to let you know she is here if you ever want to talk to her about it. She's helped me with so much already, so talking to her might be a good thing when you are ready. I'll text you her number later tonight, okay?"

I hope Bethany reaches out. Hearing from others might renew her hope of a family in the future, while also helping her cope with this painful loss.

"Troy's home."

"Bethany," I call wanting to remind her one more time. "Please talk to Troy tonight. Tell him what you want, what you need from him, and how you feel. He's hurting, too. He may try to keep it all inside to protect you and that won't be a good thing. You need each other right now."

"I promise," her quiet voice answers. She quickly lets me go before Troy enters the house.

I worry for my friend. She's hurting, and Troy is avoiding her. Although she has a large family, lots of close friends, and is active in her church, I fear she may need a different kind of help in the upcoming months. I set a reminder in my calendar app every afternoon at four to check on Bethany. I'm aware there is only so much I can do from here, so I need to do what I can even if it's only a phone call to let her know I care.

Returning to the living room, I spot Alma holding on to Libby's hands as she toddles across the floor. Libby jabbers excitedly the entire way. When they turn my daughter's eyes and smile lighten my mood.

"Come here." I make 'gimme-gimme' gestures. "Come to mama. You can do it. Come on Libby." With Alma's support she tiptoes toward me.

Less than a step away, I scoop up my daughter placing a raspberry on her neck. Giggles erupt from my tiny human. I squeeze her tight against my chest needing her to comfort my worries for Bethany. Alma pats my shoulder as she heads to the kitchen for drinks.

56

MADISON

On the Eighth, I search Twitter a few times during class anxiously awaiting the release of the All-Star rosters. I know in my heart he'll make it—I just need official confirmation.

Finally, my phone vibrates in my pocket. I click the link in the tweet, scroll past the American League Roster for now, and there it is. He did it. His fans voted. Hamilton made the All-Star Team his first full season in the Majors.

I fidget in my chair. An hour of class remains. How will I ever sit still? After a couple more minutes, I gather my items and slip out the door. My mind is not on today's class—I decide it won't hurt anything for me to leave early.

On the way to my car, I didn't notice the hot July sun as I shoot a text.

ME

congrats!

I told you

why do you ever doubt me?

I excitedly drive home to celebrate with Liberty and Alma. Hamilton should already be at the ballpark for tonight's game as they host San Francisco. I will celebrate with them, until he calls me after the game and I can celebrate with him.

HAMILTON

don't gloat

I glance up from my laptop noting it's nearly 11:00 pm. I clear my college work from my thoughts.

ME

how excited are you?

I don't wait for him to call me before I FaceTime him. He's standing outside his condo-elevator when he answers.

"If I lose you on the elevator, I'll call you right back." It's not the greeting I expect.

"Oh, sorry. I just wanted to see you. It's the next best thing to congratulating you in person."

"I'm glad you called. I needed to see you. Things never seem real until I can share them with you."

My heart melts with his words. He's in the elevator now and I'm thankful we didn't lose our connection.

"Can I entice you to spend a few days in Cincinnati with me?"

I bite my lower lip while gazing into his pleading puppy dog eyes. I'm going to make him sadder. A large hand squeezes tight around my heart. It always comes to this. Our schedules never quite sync up. It's a tiny part of the reason I keep putting off letting him meet Liberty.

"Hey," his voice attempts to soothe. "It's okay—I know you are busy that week." He runs his hand through his thick waves, now seated in his living room. His masculine tongue licks his lips before he continues. "It's been a long two months and I'm ready to see you in person. Don't get me wrong, I live for the chats and calls. It's just not the same. I long to hold you in my arms."

He's killing me. At the sight of his tongue, I fantasize it upon mine. My blood loudly pulses in my ears, my girly bits spark to attention, I wiggle in my bed praying he doesn't notice my need to rub my thighs together.

"Ham," my voice quivers divulging just how much his words have affected me. "I can't travel that week, I'll have too many things to complete for my classes. I'd love to experience your first All-Star Week…"

"I understand. My schedule is busier than yours. It's just frustrating."

57

HAMILTON

My schedule continues to prevent my spending time with Madison. My plans to make her mine can't happen if I can't be with her. I long to take her on our first date. I want to demonstrate how important she is to me in every way. I dream of holding her close in public to let the world know she's mine. While at dinner I want to show her off, then I plan to enjoy her privately at home.

While I've masturbated to the memory of our one night together more times than I care to admit, I need to reconnect with her intimately. I long to hear her pants, her moans, and the sound of my name on her lips when she finds her release. I hope our calls leave her as hot and bothered as I find myself. I've imagined her pleasuring herself in bed after we disconnect. Perhaps she relives our night together as I do—I'm sure it's not as often as I do though.

58

MADISON

HAMILTON

hopping on jet to Cincinnati

Me

fly safe

call if you get a chance

HAMILTON

we're attending Homerun Derby

U should watch

ME

always do

HAMILTON

gotta go

I read into each text. He's as excited as a little boy. It's got to be pretty exciting for him to watch his friends in the Homerun Derby then play in the All-Star Game. I wish I were there with him instead of working on my two papers tonight and studying tomorrow.

McGee whines tapping my arm with his paw as he lays on the floor alongside me. He's pouting that we won't let him into the backyard while it's raining. Poor puppy. It was too hot to walk earlier and now it's raining. I stop typing my paper to pet him. Alma invites him over to the sofa for loves—she claims I need to focus on my paper and not McGee. I'm almost done with my second draft of my second paper. She's right, if I focus I can take a break when the derby begins.

My fingertips continue to click clack away for twenty minutes more. I close my laptop with a flourish announcing I am done for the night. Alma carries in our snacks for the evening and we find a comfortable seat in time for the broadcast to begin.

The announcers welcome us to the All-Star festivities then introduce the finalists for tonight's competition. Liberty fusses loudly for a moment, then the sounds of her soiling her diaper fill the room. Leave it to my daughter to expertly choose a quiet transition to commercial to make such unladylike noises. McGee darts to the backdoor and Alma follows to let him out for only a minute. I wish I could run with them from the task at hand. I lay the changing mat on the carpet and proceed to change Liberty's diaper.

The announcers return as I place Liberty back on her blanket surrounded by her favorite toys. "This year's Homerun Derby holds two new twists. First, all pitches will be delivered at ninety-eight mph by a pitching machine. This has led to much discussion on social media leading up to tonight's broadcast. Second, starting off our first round and now standing at Homeplate is our 'Mystery Contestant'.

"For our viewers at home, I would like to explain what we at the stadium witnessed during the commercial break. The large four-sided white screen contraption on wheels you now see around Homeplate slowly rolled from the outfield bullpen, down the foul line to its current location. The entire time we observed the dark shadow of this 'Mystery Contestant' walking inside it. Notice how he stands swinging his bat at Homeplate."

The second announcer continues, "Every precaution has been taken to conceal his true identity. Neither of us in the broadcast booth know his identity. No cameras are inside the four-sided contraption ensuring the crowd knows not who we have before us. They're telling us now only three camera angles will be available to record his homerun attempts. There will be no camera angles from the field toward Homeplate."

The other announcer jumps in. "Should our 'Mystery Contestant' continue to another round, the identity will continue to be concealed during the entire competition. I cannot fathom the amount of planning that goes into planning and carrying out this 'Mystery Contestant' in this year's Homerun Derby.

"Fans are encouraged to use #HRDerbyMystery to post guesses regarding this player's identity."

"And the MLB Twitter account will tweet polls for fan voting and the results at the end of each round tonight."

"Follow along on Twitter @MLB."

"Cameras are ready, the entire front panel is removed, we can only see a shadow, and it's time for the first pitch."

My eyes are glued on the silhouette-outline as the player swings and sends the ball soaring over the centerfield fence for homerun number one.

"It's Hamilton!" I turn to Alma while hopping up and down. "Hamilton's the mystery contestant." I frantically open Twitter on my phone and tweet.

Alma states there's no way I should know in one swing. I inform her, he's left-handed, and hips and left elbow positions during the swing and follow through are Hamilton's. She smiles still not convinced.

"You are my witness when he calls later tonight, I knew after his first homerun."

We continue to watch as the 'Mystery Contestant' racks up twelve homeruns in the first round before the fourth white screen is repositioned and slowly walks down the foul line to the secure location behind the outfield bullpen.

Repeating the twelve homeruns in the second round the 'Mystery Contestant' qualifies for the finals. He will be representing the National League. I only look at Alma knowing this further proves my case that it's Hamilton.

Hamilton's FaceTime call arrives at 10:30 pm. Liberty long tucked into bed, I answer the phone as I walk toward Alma in the kitchen.

"Seriously?" I greet. "You kept that a secret from me? Your number one fan?" I position Alma in the camera with me. "I told Alma it was you after your first swing."

Alma assures Hamilton I did immediately claim it was him. She chats for a bit before turning in for the night. I continue the rest of our conversation while sitting propped against the head of my bed.

Hamilton claims if he took batting practice as often as other position players he would not have run out of steam during the finals. I assure him his ten homeruns in the final round were awesome. He only lost by five. I encourage him to read the social media posts following the big reveal of his identity.

Hamilton confesses he's been shown a few already. I hear someone talking loudly near him.

"Hey Mady, I need to let you go. I'll text you later. If you're still up, then I'll call you."

59

HAMILTON

I scowl at my agent for interrupting my call with Madison. I've jumped through his hoops all day—I need my personal time now. We walk towards our waiting transportation while he prattles on and on regarding my rising star-power, the new endorsement contacts tonight, and all of the appointments he will need to set up in the next two weeks.

When the outer stadium door opens, I'm not prepared for the number of fans still standing behind the barricades over two hours after the event. I've been spotted by those standing nearest the exit. I estimate one-hundred fans now yell my name in hopes of directing my attention towards them for autographs and selfies. Of course, they aren't yelling in unison—the noise is unnerving. Seems with 'rising star-power' comes new fans and thus less personal space and time.

I smile and wave but refuse to approach them. With the size of this crowd I'd be here several more hours if I began shaking hands, signing autographs, and posing for pictures. I respect fans—I know without them the league would not be what it is today. I'm exhausted and need to focus on tomorrow's game.

We follow the two bulky event staff t-shirt wearing men to our waiting SUV.

My agent waxes poetically at my skyrocketing star-power and all of the money it will bring our way. All I see is my current struggles with personal time, friends, and personal space growing smaller and smaller. I only trust a few in my inner-circle. Too many want to exploit me for their own personal gain. I learned in my first months in Chicago how cruel fame can be. Quick photos with female fans in public were leaked by the woman to the press claiming to be my current girlfriend or even my new fiancé. Complete strangers seek attention my fame can spark for them.

After only three months in the majors, during my first off-season a female fan with a picture at my side claimed to be carrying my baby. My agent found me a publicist and after days of emphatically stating I hadn't hooked-up with a girl since I left Athens, they went to work proving her allegations false. From that event on, I trusted only my agent, publicist, and a few teammates.

Any thoughts of dating I might have had evaporated that day. I witness my teammates and other players cheat on wives, enjoy random hook-ups, and constantly fight battles with pregnancy scares. They claim great sex is worth the hassle. I blame it on my rural Missouri small-town values. I believe in love and trust. I need to trust someone before I can share sex with them.

As we pull up to the hotel, swarms of press and paparazzi poise themselves near the entrance awaiting our arrival. I strap on my public persona, step from the SUV, and share my smile as I briskly enter the hotel.

The hotel lobby is busy for after eleven on a weeknight. While waiting for our elevator I notice several impeccably dressed women. No doubt they hope to snag more than just my eye tonight. I breathe an audible sigh of relief once the elevator sweeps us toward my room.

"Better get used to it, you've earned nationwide notoriety tonight."

My agent's words trigger bile to rise in my throat. I love playing ball. I leave everything on the field each game. I pour my heart and soul into my pitching. I love the game but hate all that comes with it. I text Madison as I lock my hotel room door. I promised to reach out to her when I could—I need to hear her voice tonight.

After an hour with no text reply from Madison, I make my peace with not performing my pregame rituals tonight, I give in to my need for sleep, and dream about the girl that holds all of my trust and owns my heart.

60

MADISON

After dinner Alma, Liberty, McGee, and I head out for our evening walk through our neighborhood. The late-August evenings are cooler now, so we no longer need to wait until later to walk. We chat with some neighbors and McGee barks when dogs bark at him. We are gone about forty minutes when we turn the corner and our house comes into view.

Alma's elbow gently bumps my arm. I look away from McGee and follow her eyes. Bethany is sitting in our porch swing.

Bethany is here in Columbia. She didn't call me, instead she drove all the way here. Fear fills me. My legs weigh a ton as I approach. Her red eyes and blotchy face alert me the reason Bethany's here is not a pleasant one.

Alma takes the stroller from my hands while still leading McGee. They say hi as they pass Bethany and continue into the house. I slowly take a seat in the swing before saying hello to my friend. I don't ask if everything is alright. I know it isn't—Bethany would not be here without Troy if it were. I lay my hand on her forearm.

"I just hopped in my car needing to take a drive." She sniffles. "I didn't have a plan." She gulps in a breath. "Next thing I knew, I was halfway here." Bethany wipes tears from her puffy red eyes and dabs her running nose on her sleeve.

"What happened honey? Does Troy know where you are?" Several scenarios stream through my mind.

"I made a special dinner last night for the two of us. I waited for quite a while before I told Troy my period started. I wanted to tell him as soon as he walked in the door. But did my best to wait until halfway through the meal." Again, she wipes her tears and gasps for breath. "He tried to be nice about it, he really did. He told me he isn't ready to try again. Can you believe that? I'm the one that suffered the pain, the trauma and I am ready. How can he not be ready?"

I don't answer. I don't know enough to answer yet. I'm not sure how to proceed here. I'm thankful Alma is inside if I need more help.

"The doctor told both of us we could have sex two weeks after the miscarriage. I've tried to sleep with my husband every week since. It's clear Troy is avoiding sex. What kind of husband won't have sex with his wife?" Again, her sleeve wipes her face. Her lower lip now quivers, and she blubbers.

"Bethany, I think he is still scared. He may just need a little more time. It had to be scary seeing someone he loves so much bleeding and in pain." I need her to know I am on her side, but support Troy here, too. "You really need to be with Troy talking this out right now. Running away just puts it off, you need to talk honestly with each other. Maybe you should call Troy right now and let him know where you are and that you are safe."

"I can't," her voice quakes. "I need some time before I talk to him. I just can't." She runs her fingers through her hair while staring at the top of the porch.

"May I call him and let him know you made it here safely and that you will talk to him tomorrow?" Please agree I chant to myself. Although loyal to Bethany, I feel caught in the middle right now.

"I just need a distraction that's why I went for a drive. I just wanted to think about something else for a while. I didn't plan on driving all the way to Columbia." A loud, frustrated groan rises from her chest. "Can I stay here tonight, just hang out, relax, and let you distract me? I don't want Troy to worry about me, but I think I need some time away."

I pull my phone from my back pocket, search for Troy's name in my contacts, and call. I squeeze Bethany's hand before I stand from the porch swing walking out into the front yard. I can understand Bethany needing to forget about the current situation in her life for a bit. When Troy answers, I immediately state that Bethany is here in Columbia and safe. He states he's been calling and texting for the past two hours. I'm farther away from Bethany, now.

"She's upset, hurt, asked to spend the night, and for me to distract her from her reality for an evening. I think she just needs some time away to cope. We'll take good care of her and I'll be sure she calls you tomorrow afternoon." I murmur quietly.

"Take care of her for me. I can't believe she left me," his voice breaks.

"Troy, she didn't leave you. She said she went for a quiet drive and didn't plan to end up driving all the way here. She hasn't left you, she's just trying to process everything. I think she just needs a bit to catch her breath."

Troy thanks me again and ends the call. I pause a moment before I remove the phone from my ear to return to Bethany. She is no longer crying and has no tears, just blotchy face, and red puffy eyes.

"Troy knows you are safe and sound. He asked me to take good care of you. Would you like to come inside?"

Fuck a duck! Like a punch to the gut, all air vacates my lungs. It is not until this very moment that it hits me Bethany is here and saw my daughter. My extreme worry for Bethany prevented me from thinking of this before now. Bethany saw Liberty. My secret is no more. When she comes inside, when she spends the night, she will meet Liberty. She will know.

61

MADISON

Bethany rises from the porch swing with a small smile upon her face. My heart rapidly pounds inside my chest, I am light-headed, and my palms are sweaty as I open the door. Alma sits near the front door in her reading chair book in hand. Libby is on her blanket, arms fully extended, chest and head held up, looking my way a huge drooling smile on her face.

Alma doesn't rise from her chair. "Bethany it is so nice to see you in person. I hope your drive was good."

"Thank you," Bethany responds a large smile upon her face. "It feels like I've been here many times before. I love our video calls." She leans to her left peeking around me. "Who is this precious baby girl?"

Alma looks to me. I only have a moment to decide to share the truth or lie stating we are babysitting. "This is Liberty." I scoop her into my arms. "Libby this is mommy's friend, Bethany." I turn her back against my chest to face our guest. Libby's arms extend toward Bethany.

"May I?" Bethany asks extending her arms and I pass Liberty to her. "Aren't you just the most precious baby girl ever? Yes, you are. Yes, you are." Bethany's sadness quickly morphs to happy baby talk. The two sit on the blanket where Bethany offers a plastic teething ring decorated with Teddy bears to Libby.

Unsure what to do, I awkwardly choose a seat near Alma. After long, nervous moments Bethany turns her attention to me. "She looks like her father." That's all she says. She wears no smile, no sign on being mad. It's a statement. My face wears my confusion.

"She has Hamilton's dark curly hair and his beautiful brown eyes." She smiles at me. "I'm right aren't I?" I nod. "You really fooled us when we talked about his actions at the reception."

I prepare to explain, but Alma jumps in. "Bethany do you like grilled hamburgers?" When she nods, Alma excuses herself to the kitchen to fix dinner. I know she is giving me time to confess everything to my friend.

"You've been keeping your daughter from all of us. Why?" With Libby in her lap facing me, Bethany moves a bit closer.

"No one knows, not even Hamilton." I pause for a shocked reaction but see none. "On Hamilton's last night in Athens we were together—it was only the one night. Then he went to Des Moines and I didn't see him again until Adrian's wedding. I wasn't lying when I told you I didn't see him in the off-season." The tilt of Bethany's head and her smirk let me know she still thinks it is a lie if even by omission.

"I freaked the end of July when I took the pregnancy test. I knew Hamilton would drop everything, return to the farm, and take care of me and our baby. Bethany, I couldn't be the reason he gave up on his dream. He is talented. He deserves to play Major League Baseball—I couldn't ruin that."

"He wouldn't have seen you as ruining anything. Hamilton loves you, he'd love a baby the two of you created even more, it wouldn't have been your fault."

I shake my head. "I met with my college advisor, she suggested I meet Alma, and so here we are. I plan to tell Hamilton everything the end of this season. I just wanted to allow him enough time to settle in baseball in hopes he might continue even after I introduce the two of them." I hope Bethany understands.

"She's gorgeous and you gave her such a pretty name. Liberty Armstrong." Bethany looks to me for confirmation I gave our daughter Hamilton's last name before she picks Libby up pecking her on each cheek. Baby talk returns. "So, you are the reason your mommy didn't allow video calls for several months. She's so sneaky. Yes, she is."

I love the happiness Libby brings out in my friend. Bethany's struggles this past month banish as the light that I now see returns to her eyes.

"When is your birthday?" Bethany asks my daughter.

"March 10th," I answer.

"Five months old, Libby you're a big girl like your daddy aren't you. You're gonna be tall just like your daddy." Bethany stops baby-talk and looks my way. "Adrian is going to kick your butt for this. You know that, right?" she laughs. Yes, my friend laughs for the first time since the miscarriage and it's because I'm going to be in big, big, BIG trouble with our blunt and bossy friend, Adrian. When her laughter fades she states Libby seems like a happy baby.

"She really is very easy going. Our only major issue was really for me more than her. When I returned to my spring classes, I struggled with her three-hour nursing schedule. I attempted to pump twice between my morning and then my afternoon classes on campus. It was difficult. Add to that the constant interruption to my attempts to sleep," I still have a pit in my stomach when I think of my dilemma. "I felt like a bad mother for having to change to baby formula and stop nursing. It felt selfish. I felt like I was already letting her down in the second month of her life."

"You did the right thing. You made a decision that caused less stress on you, so you could be the best mom you could be. You're not the first woman to choose formula over breast milk." She holds Liberty up in front of us. "She's happy, she's healthy, and she has a mommy that loves her. You, my friend, are a terrific mom. I have no doubts about it."

I love her faith in me. I strive to be the best mom possible. I refuse to let her down as my mother did me. Even with money tight and my being a single parent, I spend every moment I can reading, learning, and practicing parenting for her.

"Hey, Bethany," I need to make one thing crystal clear and the sooner the better. "I need you to keep my secret until I talk to Hamilton after September. You can't tell Troy, you can't tell the girls, and you can't tell your family."

Bethany turns her attention back to the prettiest girl in the room. "Liberty please assure your mommy I can and will keep this secret. But it will cost her. I require a video call with you every week and the open invitation to come visit anytime."

"Deal," I give my friend a side-hug. "Let's go help Alma with dinner."

Bethany's overnight stay passes quickly. Liberty is only away from Bethany while sleeping. I think my baby girl has proven to be the cure for

Bethany's blues. We've talked about her upcoming conversation with Troy, and how the two of them should decide mutually when to try again. She's shared her fears and how she now has hope again. She claims Liberty reminded her how much she wants a baby. She can't do it alone. She understands she needs Troy's help and support to have a family.

After lunch she excuses herself to phone Troy. In the front room I can hear her happy voice and even a giggle. When she returns, she tells me Troy is cooking for her tonight. He's planned a romantic evening for the two to talk and share everything. She's excited to return home, so I am happy for them.

On the porch, Bethany says goodbye to Alma, to Libby, and to me. She snaps a picture of the three of us to hide on her cell phone before she walks to her car. She pauses with her door in hand, turns, then she returns to kiss, hug, and say goodbye one more time to my daughter before climbing into her car and heading for Athens. I can only hope that Bethany remains strong, so she may keep my secret.

Late that evening I've tucked Libby into her crib, have the monitor next to me, and am enjoying a glass of wine with Alma as we watch the end of the Cubs game. My phone vibrates next to the baby monitor.

"Who could that be?" Alma wonders out loud.

TROY

> I can never thank you enough for what you did for Bethany

> I know she's not completely healed

> but she seems like herself again

ME

> I think she was ready and I think some time away did the trick

TROY

> whatever your conversations were

> know I can never thank you enough

ME

> I know she asked to visit me more often

she is always welcome

TROY

thank you, thank you, thank you

ME

please take care of her

she is still very fragile

Alma asks why I am smiling. I read Troy's texts to her. We both agree our little Libby had an effect on Bethany. We are so happy she did. We believe a higher power guided her to drive to us in Columbia.

Horrible nightmares haunt me for several days following Bethany's visit. The topics of the dreams range from another miscarriage for Bethany, me having a miscarriage instead of a healthy Liberty, and Bethany telling everyone in Athens about Liberty. I struggle to fall asleep and wake up often when I do sleep. Lack of sleep begins to disrupt my days.

62

MADISON

Bethany continues to call once a week as September draws to an end. Her mood continues to improve as she and Troy begin conversations of attempting to get pregnant in the approaching fall. McGee hints at wanting another walk, however with Hamilton on the mound tonight, it won't happen. While the Cubs bat, I let him out in the backyard. Our routine changed a bit with my being at school from 7:30 a.m.-4:00 p.m. each weekday while student-teaching. I usually spend an hour each evening reviewing my lessons for the next day. I spend most of Sunday afternoon and evening extensively planning for the week. On game nights when Hamilton is pitching, we take a shorter walk with Liberty and McGee at 4:30 p.m. then I bathe Libby, while Alma fixes dinner. We position ourselves in front of the television for a 6 or 7 o'clock ballgame unless they are on West Coast. We watch all of Hamilton's games, which the way the Cubs are playing this season is a joy. If Hamilton isn't pitching, we no longer glue ourselves in front of the TV.

As I re-enter the living room, Libby's eyes move from the toy she holds to me. She sits on her blanket with pillows propping her up. The smile she awards me warms my heart. I wave my fingers at her.

"Da-da-da," she babbles, arms flapping.

"Yes, daddy is on TV." I grab my cell phone and begin filming. "Libby, where's daddy?"

Libby smiles. "Da-da-da-da-da." Drool spills from the corner of her mouth. Her hands holding the toy animatedly fly up and down. "Da-da-da." She loves the smiles and attention she receives thus repeats her babbles. I'm still recording.

"Her first word is da-da." Alma announces for the video.

With our excitement, we miss the next three outs Hamilton pitches.

I wait until bedtime to document her first word and the date in her baby book. I replay the video on my phone several times prior to falling asleep for the night.

63

MADISON

Tonight, I anxiously await Hamilton's promised phone call. I cut Liberty's bath time in half in hopes of laying her down before he calls. Of course, tonight would be first night, that she fusses at bedtime. Alma and I each take turns rocking her while standing and sitting. Finally, we lay her in the crib and walk away. Through the monitor we listen as she babbles until she fades to sleep only minutes before her normal bedtime.

I attempt to prepare myself for Hamilton's teasing that the Cubs are going to knock my St. Louis Cardinals out of the post-season tomorrow night. As a life-long Cardinals fan, it hurts me to say that I really want the Cubs to advance. I want Hamilton to pitch in The World Series. I'm sure any other true-blue Cardinals fan would also want this opportunity for their best friend —it just sucks that it must play out this way. The Cubs and Cardinals rivalry began long before I was born.

Hamilton's video call comes through after nine. I answer on my laptop at my desk.

"I thought you might not answer," he teases.

"Are you kidding? It's a win-win for me tomorrow night." I laugh. "Either my best friend will pitch in The World Series or my favorite team will play in it."

"Wow, I wish it was that easy for me." I can't imagine the stress he's under as the starting pitcher in tomorrow night's matchup. This game extends or ends the season for the entire team. Although baseball is a team sport, pitchers often catch the blame, thus the reason they are awarded a wins and losses stat.

"You certainly make it look easy when you are on the mound. Alma and I are nervous especially when it's a full-count." I smile knowing he does stress about his pitching before, during, and after games.

"I've completed my entire pre-game routine for the night."

I know this means he eats his usual night before a game meal, he ensures his uniform hangs in his locker exactly as he likes it, and his ball glove will be tucked under his pillow for the night. This is his ritual that started in middle school that he still is superstitious about today.

"You've got this." I know he will have a great outing tomorrow. He's much more confident this season and his arm strength is stronger than ever. With each outing his confidence grows with the best defense behind him, and Cubs' comradery on and off the field.

"It's the biggest game I've ever taken the mound in. I've never faced a game in which a win means we move on and a loss means our season ends. There's a lot riding on this game. Every pitch will be vital." He runs his hands over his exhausted face. "It's a lot of pressure for everyone. Your Cardinals will not make it easy for us."

"Ham, you've wanted this game and The World Series your entire life. You've dreamt of bottom of the ninth inning, two outs, and a full-count with you on the mound. This is your moment. Trust yourself, trust your team, trust your coach, and trust your fans. You have homefield advantage. The odds are stacked in the Cubs' favor."

He chuckles while shaking his head. "Still my biggest fan, aren't you?"

"Yes, and you know if I weren't student-teaching in Columbia tomorrow, I would have found a way to be at the game." I struggle with the guilt for not taking a day off for him. I want to be there, but my future career depends on my success during student-teaching. I hope he understands my reason for missing the game. And I hope he will understand my reasons when I introduce him to Liberty in the off-season that draws nearer with every passing day.

"When you win, I'm not sure I'll ever be able to fall asleep."

"One game at a time please. It will be a long nine innings—we must win these nine innings before we think about The World Series games." His large left hand runs through his wavy, brown hair.

I remember how soft his waves felt in my fingers when his hair was much shorter over a year ago. I long to run my fingers through these even longer waves. I long for the day, after a shower with wet curly hair, I can see him and Liberty side by side. When wet, his hair forms ringlets like our daughter's— they are alike in many ways.

Hamilton's voice draws my attention back to our call. "Can you believe soon our friends may have a baby, a tiny human to be responsible for. I can't believe we are old enough to be parents, can you?"

Hamilton's words hurt. I am a parent and he is a parent—he just doesn't know it yet. I will turn his world upside down when I share Liberty. I mentally shake those thoughts away. Today is not the day for this.

"Yeah, just think in December we will have three married-couple friends, Adrian's pregnant, and by then Bethany might be, too. That will only leave Savannah, you, and me as the singles of the group."

"Speaking of being single," Hamilton's face grows serious. "Have you been on any dates?"

Seriously? I thought we were sort of a long-distance couple. I thought when he kissed me and told me he loved me that he wanted me as more than a friend. Is he asking as my friend, or as someone interested in me? I find his question as confusing as his actions at Adrian's reception. Our one night together confused me and even a year later, I grow more confused with each passing month. I have no idea where we stand. I don't know if I am in the friend-zone or not.

I school my features as best I can. "With everything I've shared about student-teaching, lesson planning, tutoring, walking at night with Alma's puppy, and Bible study when do you think I've had time to socialize or date?" I tilt my head to the side glaring his way. "How about you? Any new prospects in the arm-candy or trophy-wife area?" I throw his question right back secretly hoping he will confess his feelings for me and we might forget this game of cat and mouse he seems to be playing.

"Touché," he raises his palms out towards me on the monitor.

Of course, his answer doesn't tell me his plans or feelings. He doesn't reveal anything. I could just scream—I'm so frustrated by his actions. Soon he admits his exhaustion and we end our call. I remind him he's got this—he will do great on the mound tomorrow. I wish him good luck and say goodbye.

I hope he finds sleep faster than I do. I go over my lesson plans for the next day as my college-advisor will be observing me in the classroom. I ponder his reason for asking if I had been on a date. Is he contemplating a date with someone in Chicago? Is that his reason for asking? I feel more confused than ever. Will I ever know where we stand or what to do?

I'm excited to watch tomorrow night's game. I'm excited both teams have made it so far this season. I hope for Hamilton to have the game of his life. I imagine him pitching in The World Series in mere weeks. So many great things are occurring all around me, yet I focus on the darkness in my life. I don't like keeping a secret from Hamilton. It festers and grows inside me stealing the happiness I should be feeling on a daily basis. With my rambling thoughts, sleep evades me for several hours.

Later, I dream of a life Hamilton and I might have had if I told him I was pregnant from the start. Hamilton insists that Liberty and I attend the Wild Card Playoff Game. Ever superstitious he insists the two of us attend every important game during his career. In my dream, Hamilton reads a Cubs Baseball children's book while tucking in Liberty. As she sleeps he speaks to her of being his good luck charm.

Before the game, I see him at his locker. Family photos of the three of us, of Liberty playing with a rosin bag on the Wrigley pitcher's mound, and Liberty in his arms with Cubbie Bear at his side line his locker shelf. Hamilton kisses his index finger then presses it to the photo of Liberty before exiting the locker room.

I wake to pee at 4 a.m. interrupting my dream prior to the end of the game. I enjoy my dreams of our little family of three. They give me hope for our future life together if Hamilton doesn't hate me for my keeping the secret. I wish I had more of these dreams. I enjoy that I never want to wake up from.

64

MADISON

Unfortunately, it's raining outside, so we can't take Liberty and McGee for a walk. McGee doesn't like storms and stays close to Alma for protection from the thunder and lightning. At least, his fear means he isn't begging for a walk this evening.

Since tomorrow is Saturday and I am too nervous for tonight's ballgame, I opt not to give Liberty a bath—I will wait for tomorrow. This way she can bathe longer. She's grown to enjoy playing with her toys in the sink during bath time. Alma and I enjoy snapping photos of her as she smiles happily, and her face is framed by dark, tight ringlets.

I place Libby in her highchair and help Alma with our snacks. We chose several instead of a meal tonight. At the store last weekend, I admitted I would be nervous, and snacking might help me during the game. Alma then suggested nibbling instead of dinner. We take turns placing a few round cereal pieces on Libby's tray as we prepare popcorn, cereal snack mix, cheese and crackers, and chocolate chip cookies, along with our favorite fall snack of candy corn mixed with dry-roasted peanuts. We even make a small bowl of cereal rounds for Libby to enjoy during the game.

I carry several snack bowls to the coffee table while Alma places the cheese and crackers in the refrigerator next to a new bottle of wine for later. She offers to fix a cooler with drinks in it to take into the living room. I let her know I might need to walk between half-innings if I'm nervous, we opt to leave our cold snacks and beverages in the kitchen.

I scoop up my daughter, peppering kisses upon her chubby cheeks as we make our way into the living room. I set up her portable crib to keep her near for the entire game. Alma helps me record a video to put in my digital journal for Hamilton. I share our snack set-up, menu for tonight's game, and we record his littlest fan's game day attire. She wears a Cubs headband in her soft curls, a miniature Armstrong Cubs Jersey just like her daddy's, a diaper cover with Cubbie Bear on the seat, and little Cubs socks.

The pre-game show on the television discusses the Cubs and Hamilton's pitching. I point to him and prompt her to say daddy. Alma positions the camera just to the side of the TV pointed at me holding Liberty. Libby wears a huge smile wet with baby slobber. She extends her chubby little arms with wiggling fingers. "Da-da-da." One hand returns to her mouth. With two fingers inside she mumbles, "Da-da-da-da-da."

I look into the camera and inform Hamilton at seven months old, it is the only word she speaks so far. The three of us wish him luck and end this video journal entry. I place Libby on the floor seated with pillows surrounding her. I scoot her favorite toys within her reach, then place a kiss on the crown of her head. She smells of all things baby with oat cereal, and of course I love it.

I nervously munch on snack after snack as the game progresses. In the bottom of the fourth inning the score is still 0-0. Hamilton is on fire. His pitches baffle batters. He's given up only one hit. As he strikes out the next batter and we move to the top of the fifth inning, I hurry to the restroom—I don't want to miss anything.

Liberty finishes her bottle, I take her from Alma's arms and plan to rock her to sleep. Sitting in the rocker, I pull Liberty tight to my chest. "It's time for daddy's little girl to go to sleep." I kiss her temple then lay her in my arms. She extends an arm placing her hand on my chin. I love when she seeks comfort in touching me. With my free hand I lift and kiss her tiny hand. "Sweet dreams baby girl."

Libby's eyes grow heavy. Though my mind is on the game, I continue to rock her well into sleep. The Cardinals nearly score in the top of the fifth and again in the top of the sixth. Finally, the Cubs score as their clean-up hitter sends a homerun flying deep to centerfield. I know that one run is not going to win this game, but it's a start. I place my sleeping girl in her portable crib near the base of the steps. Walking to the kitchen I inform Alma, "It's wine time."

Frustration builds as the Cardinals begin to get one or two base runners each inning but fail to score. In the top of the eighth inning Hamilton's fastball fades a bit. The coach makes a pitching change after one out bringing in a right-handed closer. Although he should be proud of the job he did, Hamilton's body tells me he's upset. I smile knowing Hamilton will get credit for the win if the Cubs pull out a victory.

With our wine bottle empty next to our two glasses we nervously watch as the game moves into the top of the ninth inning Cubs 1-Cardinals 0. One run is not enough of a lead to believe the Cubs have won—they need three more outs. They can't let the Cardinals score. I'm too worked up to sit. I pace from Liberty's crib to the sofa and back while my eyes remain glued on the television.

After the right-hander strikes out the fourth batter this inning, Alma and I stand holding hands facing the TV. The score is still 1-0, there are now two outs, runners occupy first and third base with the number-four batter of the Cardinals line-up approaching the plate. I nearly scream when the Cubs choose to intentionally walk this renowned homerun-hitter. My free hand covers my mouth, so I don't wake my sleeping baby. The bases are now loaded—the Cubs need only one out. There is a force out at any base. They only need to cleanly field the ball and toss it to the nearest base.

In a risky play, a pinch-hitter is brought in for the Cardinals. The pitcher winds up and throws a fastball over the corner of the plate. I squat, and tears fill my eyes as the ball leaves the bat with a trajectory sure to send it far over the left-field fence. A walk-off grand slam, my St. Louis Cardinals advance to The World Series. Hamilton and the Chicago Cubs' season is officially over until next spring.

Once the shock of the final inning of the game ebbs, I contemplate shooting a text to Hamilton. What should one send her best friend after such a heart-breaking loss?

ME

Good Game

No. Delete. Delete. Delete.

> ME
>
> you threw a great game

No. Delete. Delete. Delete.

> ME
>
> I love you

Fuck a duck! I can't send that. No. Delete. Delete. Delete.

I stare blankly at my cell phone searching for words to comfort my friend. A tiny smile creeps on my face remembering it was a gift from Hamilton.

> ME
>
> You gave me this phone as a gift
>
> so we could be here for each other
>
> I miss you
>
> words can't express how much

Tonight, in my bedroom, I miss Hamilton more than usual. Our framed photo laughing on his tailgate rests in my hands. I recall sharing my clumsy hog lot story and his ensuing teasing. My finger traces his handsome face while I remember he gifted the framed photo to me during the scavenger hunt he created for me.

I miss this playful Hamilton. I miss the young man and the carefree times we spent together. Our former life in the small town of Athens quickly filled with work and grownup responsibilities.

I pray we will find our way back to each other. I hope fate will weave a road where we may find ourselves happy together with Liberty. While I hope we will be a couple, I pray he at least allows us to raise our daughter together.

65

MADISON

Hamilton's first full season in the MLB ended four days ago. Although I've texted him daily, I haven't heard from him. The students keep me on my toes while I am there, and I love every second of it, but I worry about him when I'm not at school. As I drive home today, I decide to call him tonight.

With no ballgames this week, Alma and I enjoy long walks each night after dinner with Liberty and McGee. On tonight's walk we enjoy our neighbors' fall and Halloween decorations. We wave as some work to rid their yards of the red, orange, and brown leaves. Luckily, we do not worry about leaves in Alma's yard as the lawncare company takes care of them once a week. McGee is content with his long walk and Libby yawns as we return home.

While I watch Libby enjoy her bath time in the kitchen sink. I shoot a quick text to Hamilton.

ME

can you talk?

While pregnant and the seven months since I've imagined ways to let Hamilton know about Liberty. I told myself I would tell him at the end of this season. Now that his season is over, I need to figure out when and how I plan to do it. I only have from now until February to carry this out. With Thanksgiving and Christmas in there the timeframe grows smaller still. Hamilton will spend time with his sister and mother in Athens for both holidays and he likes to report early to Mesa before spring training. I watch Libby in the sink still consumed by thoughts of Hamilton.

Noticing heavy eyes and pruned fingers, I lift my girl from the water and wrap her in a fluffy towel. While she sucks the water off her hand I dry her off before dressing her for bed. I carry her to Alma for goodnight kisses. Alma lays her book on a nearby table to hold Libby in her lap for a minute.

As I carry Liberty toward the nursery, I inform Alma I plan to write in my room and bid her good night. Once fast asleep in her crib, I head to my bedroom with monitor in hand. I place the monitor on the dresser by the door. It's close enough I can see the red lights if she wakes up and far enough away it won't be heard on my call. My little girl grows fast. I mean *our* little girl. Soon she will be crawling, pulling up, talking more, and walking. I've got to talk with Hamilton—he's missing more with each passing week.

I select Hamilton's name from my favorite contacts list and dial. It's 8:15 p.m. I am not sure if he will answer. I can't imagine why he hasn't responded to my texts for four days. I nervously wait as it rings three times and I hear Hamilton's deep voice on his voicemail message.

"Hi, just checking in. I figure you are busy with end of the season winding down. I hope you're alright. Please shoot me a text when you can. Bye." I try to sound light-hearted. I don't want him to know how worried I am about him. I haven't heard from him since the Cubs loss. I worry he's being hard on himself. Is he depressed his season is over? It's not like him to ignore my attempts to contact him. I don't want him to know how much I miss his texts and calls.

When not with my daughter or working on lesson plans, I've begun writing again. Journaling or creating stories consumes my free time. As sleep often eludes me, I find several hours each night to place my pen to paper. After many hours pass while writing, I fall asleep with no text or call from Hamilton.

66

MADISON

I'm on my knees wailing while tears drench my cheeks, chin, and neck. As his truck pulls from Alma's driveway, my life, my entire world leaves with him. Hamilton doesn't look my direction one final time. His mother keeps her eyes on the backseat avoiding me. I scream when I no longer see his red truck.

Alma and her daughter Taylor approach with words they hope will calm me. Through my sobs I see their mouths moving, but I do not hear their words. I don't want to hear them. Nothing matters—nothing will ever matter again. My world fades to black.

I feel cold metal upon my chest. I don't open my eyes—I can't. I hear Taylor instructing another to write a prescription. I hear a male voice but can't make out his words. A cold hand brushes my hair from my face and Alma whispers near my ear to come back to her. The dark emptiness engulfs me once more.

Warm light bathes my face, I internally debate covering my eyes with a pillow or opening them. My bladder urges me to wake if only for a moment. I open one eye. My room is empty. Opening my second eye I notice not only are my curtains open, but the wood-slat blinds no longer decorate the window with horizontal lines. I'm sure it's Alma's doing.

Sitting up every muscle in my body protests. I'm unsure how long I laid in my horizontal slumber. It doesn't matter. A quick trip to my restroom, then I will return to my protective blankets and forget about the world around me.

My eyes remain on the tile floor as I enter. Upon flushing my eyes remain down as I sip water from the faucet of the sink and pad back to the bed. I don't need to see my reflection I know how I look—I look and feel like walking death.

While my legs slide beneath the blankets, Alma darts into my room.

"I've brought water, diet cola, chocolate, crackers, and a ham sandwich." She gasps for breath. "My doctor visited yesterday morning. I've placed your pills on the tray. Taylor insists they will help."

I fluff my pillow, lay my head down, and close my eyes.

"Madison," Alma's stern tone is not one I've heard before. "You need to eat, you need to drink—it's been two days." She rips the blankets from my body. "I've allowed your hiding in bed long enough. It's time to take care of yourself. In order to fight, you need to be strong and healthy. Liberty needs you now more than ever."

67

MADISON

I bolt upright. I'm drenched head to toe. I brush my wet hair from my face as I frantically search my room. I dart from my bed to the nursery. I slap a hand over my mouth when a sob escapes at the sight of my sleeping daughter in her crib.

I pant as I attempt to take a full breath. She's here. Liberty is here with me. She's not with Hamilton. She's not in Chicago. I haven't lost custody of my daughter. It was a dream. It was a horrible dream. It was just a nightmare— my worst fears playing out in my head.

Unable to restrain myself, I lift my daughter clutching her to my chest. She remains asleep while I hold her close—we rock. The creaking of the wooden chair and her warmth at my chest calm my racing heart.

The next morning, I wake to texts.

HAMILTON

sorry I missed your call

I've been in meetings with coaches and my agent

Stan going through something.

I've been hanging with him at night, too.

promise to call soon.

(heart emoji)

These texts rest my concerns as he sounds okay just busy. I know Stan is another Chicago player. I am not surprised Hamilton is a leader on his team and helps other players out when needed. I'm happy to hear from Hamilton —my heart is marginally lighter as I start my day.

A week later, I cringe when my cell phone vibrates on my night stand while I change into my pajamas. The game ended ten minutes ago—he waited ten minutes later than I thought he would.

HAMILTON

are you up?

ME

you know I am!

HAMILTON

testy, aren't you?

I angrily stare at the cell phone in my hand. I know he is teasing, so I fight the urge to remind him his team didn't even make it to the World Series. I can't be that mean. The Cubs came so close this year, it was very exciting for him, the team, and for the fans. I know my disappointment at my Cardinals' loss is not the same as his loss with the Cubs. I jump as my phone vibrates indicating an incoming FaceTime call in my hand.

"Hey," I hesitantly greet awaiting more teasing.

"I'm sorry."

"Don't worry about it. I'm just tired and pissed that they couldn't step up on their homefield to win. It's not your fault." I slip under my quilt with my back leaning on pillows against the headboard.

"I'm sorry for teasing you. I know better than anyone how serious you take your Cardinals. They were one run away. Sometimes being so close makes the loss even more sour." I hear rustling on the other end of the line.

"What are you doing?" In the background I see pillows and his headboard.

"I just got done watching the game with Stan." The rustling is louder for a moment then he continues. "He messed up on our last road trip, his wife found out, and he's been crashing with me ever since. You won't tell the paparazzi, will you?" he teases.

"She's warming back up to him and has let him visit the kids a few times now." Hamilton sighs. I bite my lip as he wipes his hands down his tired face then runs his hands through his dark waves. "Some guys are so stupid. They forget about the great things they have at home and go hog-wild on the road. It makes me sick to be around it all and I'm not even married."

"If you don't approve of their actions, why are you helping Stan?"

"This was his first screw-up. He hangs with the guys and drinks before turning in each night. He had too much to drink following our victory before the Wild Card game. I guess when you hang around those type of guys, eventually you imitate their actions. Hold on a second." I hear a thump as he places the phone on something and I can only see a lampshade, then more rustling. I imagine him removing his shirt in that one-arm-above-the-head way guys do. When I begin daydreaming of his muscles and chest I reprimand myself for such thoughts.

"He came to my hotel room at 3:00 a.m. He was a mess—he immediately regretted his actions. We talked for hours not getting any sleep that night. He chose to come clean—he just waited until our season ended. Now he is paying the price." Hamilton makes a stretching sound. He's lying shirtless in bed now. I struggle to keep my thoughts on our conversation and not my desire to lie beside him. "I give it another week or two and she'll invite him to move back home. I don't mind having him here, but I'll be glad when I have the place to myself again."

I like the dark sexy scruff covering his jaws and chin. It's more than a five o'clock shadow but he's kept it groomed. I imagine it grazing my neck, my chest, and my thighs. When I slowly raise my free hand up to touch him, I snap my thoughts back to the present and our conversation. I scramble for something to say to keep my thoughts off the reactions my body has for my very sexy friend.

"Stan's got to be putting a damper on your entertaining the ladies." I tease hoping he does no such thing. But I know he is an athlete, he's famous, he's super sexy, he's single, and he's a man with needs. He's not a single-parent like me curbing my needs to earn my degree and care for our daughter.

"Right, I have no free time. Plus, I see the strain it puts on all relationships with all of our appearances and travel."

When he pauses, I jump in. "There are these things called no-strings-attached hook-ups." I slap my hand to my forehead. What am I doing? I want him. I want to be the one he wants. Why am I suggesting he hook-up with random women? I hate when my mouth moves before my brain filters the words.

His laughter tickles my ears. "Did you just slap yourself?"

Fuck a duck! He saw that? I am such an idiot. I'm still a novice when it comes to smartphones and relationships. He is so out of my league.

"Yeah, I thought a bug was about to bite me." Nice. Real nice. I'm in my bedroom and it's late October. Bugs have gone into hiding like I wish I could right now. Hamilton's laughter continues causing warmth to flood my body despite my embarrassment.

"I'm not like the others. I don't want paparazzi posting photos of me in print and on all of the gossip sites. Other players don't mind a different girl every week, but I like my privacy. I am not a playboy, and do not want to be portrayed that way. It's just easier to avoid it all." I watch as he changes positions. Is he trying to kill me with all of the noises he's making while seeing him chest bare in his bed?

"I guess I'm truly a small-town guy. I'm not interested in making myself available to a total stranger. Some of the women that flock around us are trying to hook themselves to a star. They stop at nothing. A few guys have kids in cities we travel to because they chose one night with a woman wanting an athlete to take care of them for the rest of their lives. It's so much worse than I imagined and heard about before being called up." Hamilton speaks through his yawn. "I find it hard to trust anyone. It's nothing like Athens, you know?"

"Yeah. Columbia is different, but nothing like the world you live in." His yawn causes me to yawn.

"How's your social life?"

"Right now, it consists of chatting online with fellow student-teachers about our placements and lesson planning. I'm finding a teacher can work from the moment they get home until the moment they give up to go to bed and still feel like they didn't get enough done."

"Let me rephrase my question," he chuckles. "Other than all things college and student-teaching how's the social life?"

"I still attend Bible study on Wednesday nights. We occasionally plan an outing like a movie or bowling for the weekend. Alma and I walk McGee each night and we talk with the neighbors. I've been invited to drinks on Friday's at four when we leave school by a few of the teachers at the middle school. I plan to go next week, although I am the only one not twenty-one yet." I shrug. I know they believe I am the usual college senior at age twenty-two or twenty-three. I don't like to flaunt my ability to move through my college classes faster than usual. "I'll be the only one ordering a tea with lemon."

"You should still go. It might lead into a good reference or them putting in a good word for you when you are applying for teaching positions." He's right—it's the reason I even considered going in the first place. Finding a job post-graduation is all about networking and putting myself out there. "Any dating?"

"Ham, I'm so hyper-focused on my student-teaching that I haven't given it a thought." It's a lie—I think about dating Hamilton every time I look at my daughter and while I lie in bed at night. "Besides, I am still young. There will be plenty of time to find Mr. Right after December." Speaking these words out loud puts a bad taste in my mouth.

Hamilton yawns again.

"You look like you need some sleep."

"I thought when the season ended, I'd be free to visit Athens and you down in Columbia. My agent has me booked for the next three weeks. We are meeting with companies for possible endorsement deals like Gatorade, Snickers Bars, Nike, a local car dealership, and a few more. The Cubs Organization has me making several appearances at area events and fundraisers. I even get to visit the children's ward at a local hospital and a few inner-city programs. I've been leaving the condo by nine and arriving back after six each day when I don't have a dinner meeting to attend. I'm not sure when it will slow down. My agent reminds me it's increasing my income and provides job security. I'm just ready for a vacation."

I mentally panic at his mention of coming down to Columbia. We need to arrange a time together as I plan to divulge my secret, but I can't have him just pop-in. I'm a bit relieved it seems he is too busy to plan a time for us to meet right now. I'll try to plan something when his world slows down in the months to come.

"Promise me you'll give me notice when you plan to visit Athens. I want to find time in my schedule to see you." I hope this will allow me to keep him away from Columbia until I have a chance to talk with him about our daughter.

"I promise," he speaks through a yawn. "I better let you go, you have school tomorrow and I have meeting after meeting."

"Try to get more rest, you look exhausted. I don't want you running yourself down and getting sick." I cringe at my nagging him.

"Okay, mom," he teases. "Sweet dreams."

I'm sure they will be sweet dreams of you, I think to myself as I place my phone back on the charger and switch off my lamp.

68

MADISON

Saturday is currently my favorite day. I don't even mind that I am awake by 7:00 a.m. It's my day to enjoy my daughter. I don't pick up my laptop or look at lesson plans the entire day—we fill our day with mommy-daughter activities. Currently we are in my bed chatting about our plans for today. I love her babbles. I ask a question and she answers me. It doesn't matter that I have no idea what she attempts to say.

"Should we go downstairs and make breakfast for Alma?"

"Da-ba-ba-ta-da," Liberty responds with arms and legs animatedly signaling her excitement.

When I rise from the bed, Libby lifts her arms to signal for me to pick her up. I scoop her into my arms and smoother her with kisses causing baby giggles to erupt. I have not a care in the world in these moments.

I secure Liberty in her highchair, place a few cereal rounds and two teethers on her tray, then speak to her often as I start the coffee and prepare the griddle for bacon. I look forward to a long walk to the park today, I will swing and slide with her as Alma takes photos and McGee enjoys the dog park. We are blessed with a sixty-five-degree day this first weekend in November—we must enjoy the weather while we can. Maybe we will eat a picnic lunch in the back yard, too. The fresh air will quickly wear out McGee and Liberty. I'll help Alma around the house while she naps. I live for these simple days.

"La-La," Liberty announces Alma's arrival in the kitchen loudly. McGee scurries to eat the cereal she knocked off her tray in her excitement.

"Good morning Miss Libby," Alma greets before pouring her cup of coffee. Libby jabbers right back to her with a piece of cereal visible on her tongue.

While my Saturday with Liberty allows me to genuinely smile and enjoy myself, as night falls my thoughts darken and all of the troubles in the world creep in. My thoughts move from troubled students, to miscarriages, to my mother, to my father's death, to the loss of my girlfriends and Hamilton, to my ever on my mind secret, to starving families, then to other atrocities from the nightly news.

As is my new habit, I bleed my feelings into my notebook each night. The lined white paper quickly fills with my treacherous thoughts. My remembering that today is my mother's birthday cut me open after Liberty's bath time. I've looked forward to tonight's writing for two hours now. I've needed to banish my thoughts onto the paper.

I spill every drop—I rid myself one by one. Tears stream as I confess my continued love for her after everything. I admit the guilt I carry for not trying harder to get her help. I should have enlisted the help of adults to force her into treatment at a rehab facility. I should have begged our family doctor to have her committed. As her daughter I should never have given up—I should have fought for her over and over to seek the help she needed.

Thoughts turn into words. Words form sentences and sentences form a story on paper. The younger version of me becomes my main character. Certain aspects of my life mirror the character while in many ways we are different. Page after page the story flows, grows, and with it my heart grows lighter. This is my therapy.

69

MADISON

Wednesday, Alma's three children with spouses and kids arrive to celebrate Thanksgiving. The full house is chaotic. As an only child it's a bit overwhelming. The siblings seem to have adopted me as a little sister. The children love Liberty and she enjoys little humans to entertain her, as well as, a second dog in the house.

I attempt to help Alma with the cooking but find her two daughters and daughter-in-law are much more proficient than me. I opt to help setting the table, corralling the kids, caring for the dogs, and taking care of the dishes. I take turns sitting at the kids' table with Liberty and the adult table at meal times. Taylor's two pre-teen daughters love caring for Libby. They claim they are practicing at babysitting.

While Alma, her oldest daughter Taylor, and youngest daughter Cameron begin work on the big meal Thursday morning after breakfast; her daughter-in-law Ava and I peel potatoes at the kitchen table.

Taylor informs our group, "My daughters are hinting they want a baby brother or sister now, thanks Madison." Sarcasm laces her voice.

"I think that is a lovely idea," Alma quickly responds.

"Seriously?" Taylor looks offended. "My daughters are almost grown, my career is on the rise, and soon we will have the house to ourselves. Why start all over with night feedings, diapers, and teething? I'd be fifty-eight when he or she would graduate high school. No thank you. They can just babysit and visit Libby to get their baby fix."

I chuckle. Both of Alma's daughters and her son are work-a-holics. Taylor meticulously planned the birth of her daughters barely twelve months apart after her two years of residency and prior to focusing on her cardio-thoracic specialty. Cameron is still single at thirty-years-old. She's an editor with a large publishing house in Dallas, Texas. She works long hours and frequently travels.

"It's Cameron's turn to give you grandbabies," Taylor informs Alma. "Trenton and I gave you two girls and two boys. It's time she marries and spits out some little ones." Taylor winks at me.

"First, I will not 'spit out' anything let alone a tiny human. You know for a physician you sure don't talk like one. Mom, I think you wasted money on her education." Taylor addresses Alma with the voice of a true youngest-child. "Second, I don't have to marry to have a baby. When I'm ready, I'll just have one."

Alma's sharp intake of breath and hand to her chest alarm me. I worry she doesn't feel well. Cameron on the other hand, knows exactly what her reaction means. "Mom, I want nothing more than to meet Mr. Right, marry, and start a family. I need to inform you, finding Mr. Right is more difficult than walking through land mines. I seem to find the creeps and phychos. So, if I feel the strong urge to start my family, I'll take care of it myself if a good male candidate isn't in the picture." Cameron smiles knowing this will not set well with her family.

"You must be looking in the wrong places. Have you tried online dating or Tinder?" Alma stands with hands on hips attempting to solve a problem for her youngest child.

"Mom!" Taylor shouts astonished.

Ava beside me spews her mouthful of iced tea all over the potatoes we've peeled on the table.

Cameron simply looks to heaven asking, "Why me?"

"How do you know what Tinder is?" All three women look my way instead of at Alma.

"Don't look at me, I didn't teach her about that app."

"Please," Alma addresses her children. "I watch television and movies, I read, I'm an educated woman, and I keep up on the latest trends. Besides two women in my Bible Study were chatting about their sons using Tinder to avoid long-term relationships and how they fear they will never have grand-children. I came home and Googled it." She points to Taylor and then to Cameron. "Your mother isn't ready to be put out to pasture yet."

Ava and I rinse the potatoes of her iced tea, then continue peeling. I love Alma's ability to still surprise her daughters. I've often thought of her as twenty-five-year-old brain in her sixty-five-year-old body.

"Just so you know Tinder is for one-night-stands, mom, not finding a long-term mate." Taylor states returning to her pie crust.

I excuse myself to check on Liberty while the women continue instructing Cameron on how to find a man. Libby sits on her blanket, she has a toy in her hand, I notice her head is bobbing slightly, when I am close I also note her heavy eyelids. My little girl needs a nap. The constant attention from the four other kids and two dogs is sensory overload for such a little girl. She lifts her little arms and hands toward me. I scoop her into my arms and we escape to the quiet of her nursery. Her head lays heavily on my shoulder up the stairs and into her room. While I change her diaper, she yawns and rubs her eyes with her chubby little fists.

Although she falls asleep quickly, I choose to rock her for several more minutes. I love Alma's family and am happy everyone came to visit. But I'm off from school and I have very little time with Liberty as they all take their turns. I plan to steal a few loves right now. In here, I don't have to make sure I smile at appropriate times—I don't have to fake happiness. I let my guard down and enjoy my daughter.

I play with a few of her stray ringlets—I'm happy she has Hamilton's dark curls. I gently run my fingertip over her eyebrows and little nose. She's growing too fast. I can't believe how big she is in my arms now. My baby is eight months old and crawling. This little one is very active as she explores and keeps Alma and me on our toes every day.

I place Liberty in her crib, turn on the monitor, and a sound machine, before I shut off the light and close her door.

70

MADISON

I find Cameron sitting on the top step, so I join her placing the baby monitor beside me. "Have enough advice from the married women?" I tease.

"They mean well," she states. "I wanted a few minutes to chat with you."

I'm caught off guard. I have no idea why she wants to chat with me.

"First, you must promise not to be mad." Cameron looks sternly my way. When I nod, she continues. "Mom shared two of your stories with me, you are a gifted writer."

"Wait, what?" Her mom? Alma? She did what with my stories? In late-September I began going through my old notebooks full of young-adult stories. The urge to write again was strong, so I purchased ten new notebooks, and shared a couple of my previously written stories with Alma.

"You promised not to be mad." Cameron sternly reminds me. "She told me you shared them with her. She loved them and shared them with me. You *are* a *gifted* writer. Mom says you haven't sent inquiries to agents or to publishing houses, is that true?"

"Umm," my mind still tries to process Alma's betrayal and Cameron's words. I shared four of the stories I've written over the past three years for fun. I mentioned it during one of the days we read while it rained outside. She insisted I let her read them. I never thought she would share them with someone. I sure didn't think she would share them with her daughter, an editor at a publishing house in Dallas.

"They are in my suitcase. I made a few, and I mean a very few edits and suggestions for you." When I don't react, she continues. "I think you should let me pitch them at next month's new authors' meeting. I'm confident one of our three publishing houses will pick them up." She turns my chin to face her. "You're mad. You can't be mad—you promised. You really have no idea how good they are, do you? Madison, readers *need* these books. The young-adult market needs more authors like you."

She places her hands on each of my shoulders, arms fully extended as she stares at my face. "I need you to hear me. I need your permission to pitch your books. I'd love to see your other stories, too. They are *much* too good to hide in a drawer or in a laptop file. Your students need these books. Let me help you, please."

"You really think kids would enjoy reading them?" I can't wrap my mind around her positive words on my writing. I transformed my thoughts and fears into stories as a form of therapy for me. I never intended to share them.

"Madison, yes your writing *is that* good."

"I write as a hobby at night when I can't sleep. I've always kept journals and even written some poems. I can't believe you are sitting here telling me you, an editor, want to pitch my stories. I mean, I've daydreamed about it a couple of times, but it was never something I planned to pursue."

"I'm not promising anything. I've worked with hundreds of writers, I've edited many manuscripts, and I believe your work is among the best I've seen. I am confident you'll find others interested in them. I work for the parent company—we have two smaller publishing houses that we also own. If you permit me to pitch these first two books, I feel one of the three houses will pick them up." Cameron's smile is infectious.

I am excited that she enjoyed them. I even feel hopeful that someone else might like them well enough to publish them. My stories contain characters based on little parts of me. In my seven stories I've written about the topics of an alcoholic parent, of losing a parent, of a smart girl attempting to not appear so smart around her peers, and of a nerd that wants to be in the popular crowd. All of my stories are based in one middle school with three different groups of friends. Writing about my life is therapeutic for me—maybe my books can help others in similar situations. Maybe Cameron really can help me. A hundred questions form in my mind.

"Let's take some time tonight after Libby goes to bed to go over the two I have. If you choose, you can rewrite and share an electronic file with me. I will print copies of the manuscript to share at the meeting. Then we will just wait and see if we hear anything the following week or two. When they pick up a new author it happens quickly. They call, set up meetings, explain the timeline, and the process. You will know before Christmas either way."

I agree to work with her later tonight. While Cameron returns down to the family, I remain on the step. I love Alma. I consider myself blessed to spend each day with her. However, at this moment, I'm still hurt. The fact that she didn't ask when she knew how private I kept them hurts. I know if she asked me, I most likely would have given my permission to share my stories with Cameron. I know it's the same outcome as if she did ask first. Cameron's reaction and confidence in my stories would still have surprised me. I know Alma only wants the best for me—I guess I can't fault her for that.

I allow myself a few moments to process the fear, the excitement, and to dream. I imagine two of my books get published. I envision local school and city libraries carrying my book. A bud of excitement blooms. I like the idea of being published. With Cameron's help it just might happen. My thoughts fade as my phone vibrates.

HAMILTON
how's the crowded house?

ME
busy

HAMILTON
wish you were here

ME
tell your mom and sis I say hi

HAMILTON
we consider you family, too

I should have insisted you join us

ME

I already made plans with Alma when you asked

your family likes you all to themselves

they don't see you enough

HAMILTON

I don't see you enough

ME

when do you head back to Chicago?

HAMILTON

Friday evening

two more weeks, then my calendar opens up

ME

maybe then we can get together. I'm done teaching

I just observe until Dec. 5th, then graduation

HAMILTON

I'll call Monday and we will get something on my calendar.

ME

I'll be very honored

Hamilton Armstrong's calendar

(Heart emoji)

HAMILTON

stop

you are more important than events on my calendar

I hope you know that

I have to do these appearances

I want to see you

big difference

ME

(heart emoji)

Alma needs my help. We will be eating soon

enjoy your family

HAMILTON

(hoart cmoji)

ME

(2 heart emojis)

With the busy house, the big meal, and Cameron's bomb about my books; I don't need to worry about an approaching get together with Hamilton to tell him he has a daughter. His proclamation of missing me and being more important than events on his calendar further confuses me. I have enough on my plate today and tomorrow. I decide to wait for the weekend to worry about Hamilton, his feelings, my feelings, and a December you're-a-daddy meeting.

71

HAMILTON

Sitting at the Thanksgiving table, I look from my mother, to my sister, to the empty chair. I should have contacted Madison in October. Then she would be sitting at our table, enjoying my mother's extravagant Thanksgiving meal.

We are her family. Since 8th grade Madison has been at our holiday table and a member of our family. I can't fault her for spending time with Alma's family. I abandoned her. We planned to attend college together and I bailed. In the hours after I was drafted I changed our plans and left her on her own for college. With no support from her mother and no other family she started a new chapter of her life without me.

My mother's voice draws my attention. "We miss her, too."

I realize I was staring at the empty chair Madison occupied every Thanksgiving, Christmas, and Easter for five years. I thought she would always be here, my friend, my adopted little sister. Although my feelings for Madison have changed, I still believe she belongs at our family table for the holidays. It's time for me to lay my heart out and share *all* of my feelings with Madison. If I want to share every part of my life with her, she needs to know before she applies for teaching positions after her quickly approaching college graduation.

My mother shares all she's learned about Madison's relationship with Alma and her children. Mom, through her many emails and phone conversations each week with Madison, knows more than I do. I'm glad Madison has found a safe family to live with while in Columbia but need her to know this family needs and misses her, too.

My mom clutches my left hand upon the table. "She knows we wish she was here."

Her words don't calm my thoughts. They only fortify me resolve to open up to Madison. I can't let another off-season pass without spending time ensuring Madison knows exactly how I feel, and I need her by my side.

72

MADISON

ME

R U awake?

HAMILTON

yeah, what's up?

ME

I have too much on my mind

HAMILTON

want me to call?

I hesitate in my response. I would love to talk to him about everything but hearing his voice over the phone before bed will just add more thoughts, although very pleasant thoughts, to my long list to worry about. Maybe he can distract me from everything else.

"Hey," I greet when he answers my call.

"Hi, why didn't you video call?"

"Are you crazy? It's after eleven on Thanksgiving night. We've been up and cooking since seven. I've chased dogs and kids most of the day. I'm exhausted, my hair is in a messy bun, and I'm in my pajamas."

"None of that matters to me and you know it. I've seen you…"

I want it to matter. I want him to desire me, to find me sexy, to think I am beautiful, and at this moment I am anything but beautiful.

"Spill it," his deep gravelly voice prompts. "What has your mind swimming instead of sleeping?"

I share how much Alma loves having her family here for the holiday weekend and how they've somewhat adopted me as a little sister. For an only child it is both comforting and overwhelming. I tell Hamilton about the four resumes and applications I've submitted for open teaching positions in the spring in the Columbia area. I convey my worry that I will have to wait until fall to find one. I share my conversation with Cameron about my books. Hamilton knows I write to relax and work through things in my life. He's very excited that I might be published. I speak of Bethany, Troy, her new pregnancy, and that she is keeping it from Troy. I'm both excited and scared for them. She so desperately wants to start a family. Then I talk about Adrian's pregnancy and the approaching wedding of Latham and Salem.

I leave out my confusion at his actions. Am I his friend? Or am I more? I also do not share that I have a life-altering secret I need to share with him and I'm worried how he will react. I don't reveal my insomnia is back and I fear the darkness of depression is creeping in again.

"So, you can see I have many reasons I can't fall asleep tonight." I roll onto my side with my cell phone between the pillow and my ear, then turn off the bedside lamp.

"You've always worried too much about those around you. You can't solve everything for everyone and I love your loyalty to family and friends. Let's focus on Madison's items in your list." He is both stern and caring.

"Have you applied to school districts outside of the Columbia Metro Area?" I wonder if his question includes areas very far from the Columbia area, like Athens. "I've only applied in the metro so far. As it is mid-year, most districts won't have openings until late-spring and summer when contract renewals occur." I don't share that I have free childcare and living accommodations here versus me moving to another town.

"Remind me again what endorsements you have."

Endorsements? Have I spoke of these enough that he remembers? It's not usually a term those outside of education use. "I can teach in Kindergarten through eighth grade. I have endorsements in Social Studies and Mathematics. I'd love to find a history or math job in a middle school." I roll to my back, once again holding my phone in my hand. Staring at my dark ceiling I wonder if he is doing the same in his room. Is he in pajamas or just boxers? Is his chest bare? Stop it! Focus Madison!

"I only have seven school days left in my student-teaching," I sigh before yawning. "I think I am too attached to my students. I will have spent fourteen weeks with these middle schoolers and I already dread never seeing them again."

"This is what will make you an excellent teacher. You care about their learning, their development, and them as people. The students lucky enough to get you as a teacher are blessed." His faith in my teaching abilities causes me to smile. He is my number one fan, just as I am his.

"I'm sure like anything else, it's a numbers game. The more resumes and applications you send, the calls for interviews will start rolling in." I hear his yawn through the phone prompting me to yawn. "Think back to middle and high school. Did we have a single teacher that graduated from the University of Missouri?" While I think he continues. "All of our teachers attended Missouri Western, Northwest Missouri, and Truman State—all excellent teaching programs but not the University of Missouri. I have to believe your degree will set you apart from other applicants when you apply outside of Columbia."

I had not thought of that. Why does he keep mentioning for me to apply outside of Columbia? He's not in Athens. We shared a desire to leave and never return. Does he want me closer to his family? If so, why?

"Now, about those books." Hamilton must stretch because I hear a satisfied groan escape him. It causes my belly to flutter as I imagine him without a shirt, his abs on display. "From what you've shared in the past, Cameron is accomplished—she's well known in the publishing community. If she feels your books are good, they must be. You need to believe her."

"Once the shock wore off, I did believe her. She both flattered and scared me. I had only thought of publishing once or twice and never looked into it. I had too many other things in my life that needed my attention. Now that she opened my mind to the possibility, I want it. I want it bad." I close my eyes for a moment. I Imagine my books on a library shelf, on a bookstore shelf, and in a school library.

"When is her pitch meeting?"

"The second week of December," I inform him.

"Wow, this could happen fast then."

We continue to talk about finding out by December 14th if they want to pick me up as a new author, about the meetings with me that might follow, and how this might all occur before Christmas.

Next our conversation moves to Latham and Salem's wedding. Hamilton will be in Athens visiting his mother and sister, so he will be at the wedding. At least I know ahead of time, so I can prepare for this encounter. I briefly flash back to my shock and reaction at seeing him at Adrian and Winston's wedding last spring.

We chat about how our group of nine have changed so much from high school graduation. Two couples are already married, and both are expecting a baby. Another couple will marry in December. Little does he know two members of our group already have a daughter.

Our yawns grow more frequent. We decide I am now ready to fall asleep and say good night. Our conversation did the trick—I immediately fall asleep to dreams of Hamilton and I together raising our daughter Liberty.

73

MADISON

My December calendar grows fuller each day. Yesterday was my last day in my student-teaching placement. With my mentor's approval, I planned fun educational games to play with cheap pencils, erasers, and candy for rewards —the students loved it. I left the building at the end of the day with an armload of gifts and cards. The math teacher, social studies teacher, and administrator I worked closely with surprised me by each handing me a reference letter to use as I apply for positions. It was both a sad and exciting end to my college studies. My graduation the fifteenth is quickly approaching.

This morning, I received a call for an interview on December 17th for a long-term substitute teacher position open in January. I'm glad my many resume and application submissions are starting to reap interviews just as Hamilton predicted. My goal is for a teaching position instead of that of a temporary substitute. Alma and I celebrated my first interview call by taking Liberty out to lunch with us.

Back home now, Liberty crawls across the living room, clutches tightly to the legs of my yoga pants, and pulls herself up to stand in front of me. "Ma-ma-ma-ma-ma," she greets.

"Hey, baby girl." I close then set my laptop aside before lifting her into my lap.

"Me-me-me," she babbles as slobber escapes both corners of her mouth.

She calls me ma-ma, Alma is la-la, and McGee is me-me. At nine months, she's really starting to express herself and navigate into all sorts of places she shouldn't. As Christmas draws near, I am anxious to see her imitate Alma's grandchildren in opening gifts and playing with new toys. It should be a fun Christmas followed by her approaching first birthday.

"McGee is outside going potty," I reply to her inquiry of where her friend me-me is. "Want to go let him in?" Liberty lifts her arms signaling she wants to go. When we enter the kitchen, she calls me-me as we approach the back-door. McGee raises his head from his large bone in the middle of the yard when we open the door. Libby again babbles me-me, and her friend runs toward us.

I kneel once we close the door to offer McGee some love. Still calling his name, Libby pats both hands upon me-me's back. I sit her on the tile floor while I grab a treat from the pantry. Aware of what I have, McGee sits a few feet from Liberty. I pry Libby's fingers open and lay the small treat in her palm. I help her extend her open hand. McGee ever patient remains seated.

"McGee come," I firmly state. He slowly approaches and careful not to hurt Liberty, takes the treat.

Libby squeals with glee and her legs flail on the tile floor. She loves licks from her puppy. We recently began assisting Liberty in sharing treats. Both Libby and McGee love this new trick. I decide to repeat it and set up my phone camera on a nearby chair to record it this time. McGee only gets one treat when he comes in. His ears perk up and he resumes a sitting position at the sound of me in his treat jar. Liberty opens her hand on her own this time. I still assist in extending the treat and I tell McGee to come. Liberty squeals before McGee even snags the treat this time.

I probably record too many common everyday items in my attempt to compile a video journal for Hamilton. In my keeping him from this part of Liberty's life, I attempt to record everything I can. Last week I purchased an external hard-drive and moved my video journal files onto it. I past the free space in the cloud I used in November. I don't want to risk my laptop as the only location of these important clips. Between the cloud and Dropbox, I have one copy saved online and now a hard-drive for another copy that I can pass along to Hamilton this off-season.

The only week Hamilton and I have free in December is the week before the wedding and now I have an interview that Monday in Columbia. I'm supposed to be in Athens that Friday for the bachelorette party. That gives me Tuesday-Thursday to tell him everything. Alma and I discussed it today. I now worry if his reaction is not as I hope, we might ruin the wedding weekend for our friends. I'm trying to decide if this is just another excuse I am creating to keep from having this difficult conversation with Hamilton or if I should wait until after the wedding.

I sit Liberty in her highchair, placing a small handful of her favorite cereal on her tray. Glancing at the wall clock, I note Alma should be home from her hair appointment soon. My cell phone rings in the living room. I ensure Libby is buckled safely in her seat before I quickly fetch the ringing phone and return to the kitchen. McGee lies protectively on the floor near the high chair.

I quickly listen to the voicemail message from an unknown number. It's Cameron calling from her work line, so I redial.

"Hi there," she greets. "Have a minute to chat?"

"Yep, sorry I didn't answer. I had to make sure Liberty was safe in the high chair, your mom is at the salon, and my cell phone was in the living room." I'm out of breath.

"I pitched your two books this morning," Cameron begins. Her pause worries me. "D.C. Bland Publishing will be contacting you in the next 24 hours to let you know they want you as their new author-of-the-year. This is our parent company—that's the big publishing house. They only take on one new author per year and they've chosen you."

My head spins. "Seriously?"

"I told you to be ready," she proudly reminds me of our Thanksgiving discussion. "When they call they will set up meetings and travel for you to Dallas so be ready for that."

"You just pitched, and they said yes?"

"No, they received a copy of the manuscripts two days ago. Several staff members read, take notes, and pass them to the next person. So, when I pitched at the meeting, they were already in love with your stories." Cameron speaks to someone on her end before returning to our phone conversation. "When I began my pitch, they interrupted asking for more information about you, the author, and not the stories they already loved. I told them you lived with my mother, were soon to graduate from the University of Missouri with a degree in education, were from the small town of Athens, MO, and were only twenty-years-old. I figure anything else is your story to tell."

"They asked to see your manuscript with my first edit notes. They were extremely impressed with the level of writing prior to the first edit. Honey, they are in love with your work. Prepare for much flattery when they contact and meet with you." I can hear Cameron sip from a beverage. "And best of all, they've appointed me as your editor. This means I will be at all meetings and we will get to work closely together. I can even have Bland Publishing pay for my trips to see you at mom's. How cool is that?"

I think Cameron is more excited than I am. In my wildest imagination I didn't see this coming, even with Cameron telling me it probably would. We chat for a bit and she makes me promise to call her once they officially call me.

I sit stunned at the kitchen table when Alma returns home. McGee barks and runs to the front door to greet her. I am just coming out of my trance when she enters the kitchen.

"La-la-la," Liberty greets Alma.

Alma looks at me concerned. I fill her in on the call I just received from Cameron. As her excitement builds, my shock wears off, and the reality of the information Cameron shared begins to set in.

74

MADISON

I lay my cell phone on the coffee table while Alma's bugged-out eyes stare at me for information. "I am flying to Dallas December 19-20th." I can't form any other words.

"Let me fetch my calendar. We have a busy week that week." I love the fact her cell phone and laptop have digital calendars, yet she still prefers a paper calendar posted on the kitchen wall to schedule all of her events. When she returns with a pencil in hand we discuss the rest of December. I graduate on the 15th, our all-church Bible study potluck is the 16th, I have an interview on the 17th, will be in Dallas the 19-20th, have a bachelorette party the 21st in Athens, and then Salem's wedding on the 22nd. She mentions her family will arrive the 23rd as I return from Athens.

"I think it is best if I stay here with Liberty while you head to Dallas. We can prepare for the holiday company and you can focus on your meetings."

I agree with her and thank her once again for all she does for Liberty and me. She suggests I call my friends and Hamilton to share my news. I don't have the energy to fill the girls in, so I text to see if Hamilton is free.

ME

text or call when you have a few minutes to chat

. . .

An hour later, Hamilton's video call rings my cell phone. I quickly signal from Alma to Liberty before heading for my bedroom.

"I assume you've heard something since you asked me to call." Hamilton's deep voice greets and every cell in my body stands at attention.

"Can't a fan just need to speak to her sports hero?" I tease.

"C'mon, I'm dying here. Share please." He sounds frustrated and desperate.

I share in great detail the call from D.C. Bland Publishing. I explain I am now flying to Dallas for two days and can't come to Athens early as we had discussed. He promises we will find time to visit after the holidays and before he heads to spring training in Mesa, AZ. Seems I've found yet another reason to avoid introducing Liberty to her father. I worry the longer I put it off, the worse it will be when I do.

Hamilton catches me off guard when he claims if he didn't have a meeting with PepsiCo, he'd fly to Dallas with me. Is that something he'd do as a friend? Maybe if we both lived in Athens he would accompany me as a friend, but he's in Chicago and I'm in Columbia. Maybe I am just wishful thinking that it means more than it does. I'm still hopeful. I'm not sure when I will get the opportunity to confess, but I am growing more and more hopeful that he is more understanding and happier than mad at me.

Holding my sleepy girl, I smile while wishing Alma a good night. She inquires the reason for my smile. I confess I've filled another spiral notebook. I'm such a nerd—I'm excited to write in a new notebook tonight. It's a blank slate and I'm giddy to create a new story on its pages. I take pride in the knowledge it's my tenth notebook—I'll need to buy several more soon.

75

MADISON

My college graduation is finally here. I can't describe the relief I feel that my hard work is over. I'm graduating two years earlier than my peers. Now, I need to find a district that will hire a twenty-year-old college graduate.

I gaze at the reflection in my full-length mirror. Alma took me shopping this week for a new dress. Of course, I protested claiming I wanted to just wear slacks and a blouse from my closet. Alma had none of that, insisting a big event requires a new dress. Ever the shopper, she dragged me to five stores before we found anything she loved. I'm not one to stand out, to wear daring or eye-catching attire that draws attention to myself. I didn't like the dress when she tossed it over the changing room door at me. I reluctantly slipped it on and immediately knew we had found my dress.

The red dress resembles the famous Marilyn Monroe white halter dress. It's snug to the waist and free-flowing from the hips to the knee. The crimson color is perfect for the holiday season and any special occasions the rest of the year. As graduation is inside and I'll wear a gold gown over it, Alma claims I will only need a cardigan to wear after the ceremony at the reception. We found sexy red heels and a matching cardigan at the same store.

Alma wraps on my open bedroom door. "There's mama," she attempts to calm Liberty.

Alma's daughters Taylor and Cameron along with Taylor's two daughters, flew in last night to surprise me for my graduation. They claimed it is a known fact that sisters must attend a baby sister's college graduation. I fear I might never get used to this large family atmosphere. Liberty has been going one-hundred miles an hour since she woke at seven this morning. She is in desperate need of a nap. I hope she falls asleep in the car and naps most of the ceremony. I'm hoping since the December graduation isn't as long as the spring ceremony, she won't need to leave the auditorium during the ceremony

"Why don't you pull a t-shirt on before you hold her. We don't want drool or spit-up to ruin such a beautiful dress." Alma never ceases to amaze me with her knowledge on all things.

With t-shirt on, I pull Liberty toward my chest and shoulder. She places an open-mouth drool-soaked kiss upon my chin before resting her head on my shoulder. I ask Alma to grab my heels and sweater from my bed as we head downstairs to join the others. Taylor offers to drive her rented mini-van and we all pile inside. Liberty is asleep before the end of the block—I breathe a sigh of relief. I want my daughter at my graduation. We've been through so much this year and I want to be able to tell her stories of attending my graduation as she grows up. I've worried since she missed her nap at eleven this morning, she might cry, causing someone to leave the auditorium and miss my ceremony with her. I can't seem to stop worrying.

Taylor looks to her daughters through the rearview mirror to the third-row seats. "Trenton, Cameron, and I all graduated from Mizzou."

"Do we have to go to Missouri?" They ask apparently thinking it is not something they want to do.

Taylor informs them they are free to choose the college best for them. She's just proud that I am following in my adopted-siblings' footsteps. It warms my heart that Liberty and I are welcome in this family.

One graduate stands between me and my diploma. I am nervous to walk up the steps and across the stage in my heels. I wish I hadn't let Alma insist I choose them over flats. At my turn I climb the four steps as my name is announced. I pose for my photo diploma in hand. I can hear raucous cheers

from my family and church friends. A deep male voice catches my attention. I quirk my head while exiting the stage to hear better.

Hamilton is here? Hamilton is here! He told me he had meetings this weekend and heads to Athens on Monday. He lied. Crap! If he is with Alma's family, he will see Liberty. My heartrate quickens. With her dark curls, brown eyes, and his smile there is no way he won't find Liberty's resemblance to him interesting. As I attempt not to fall down the steps to resume my seat, I chant 'please don't let him see Alma.' This week is too important and too busy to add the baby-daddy discussion with Hamilton to it. My ears ring and my head throbs as the ceremony drones on.

After the ceremony, I frantically scan the crowd as I wait for my row to be dismissed. My heart pounds against my chest wall. My ears still ring and I'm sweating. Finally, in the distant hallway, I see Alma in our pre-determined spot. I notice Cameron holding a still sleeping Liberty in her arms. I quickly scan the area unable to see Hamilton with Alma's family and my church friends. Perhaps I imagined his voice cheering for me earlier. A tap on my shoulder causes me to jump.

"Congratulations," Hamilton murmurs from behind me. I nervously turn to face him. He wraps me in a tight embrace whispering in my ear. "I knew you would do it. A college grad at age twenty." He slowly releases his hug, while keeping his hands on my forearms.

"Thank you," I whisper. My voice sounds weak. I fear he's seen Liberty with Alma. "I thought you had meetings this weekend." I worry what his next words might be.

"I couldn't ruin my surprise. You didn't think your number one fan would skip your graduation, did you?"

I smile up at him while inside I tremble like a Chihuahua.

"I can't stay long, I promised mom I'd be in Athens for dinner with pictures of you on your big day. She planned to attend with me, but she caught a terrible cold. She didn't want to be coughing loudly annoying the other proud parents at the ceremony." I can only nod at his words. Memphis planned to attend my graduation? My own mother didn't attend my high school or college graduation.

"Can we ask someone to snap a picture of us before I head out?" He looks in the nearby crowd.

Alma approaches and offers to take the picture after Hamilton hugs her and asks the favor. He pulls me tight to his side. His hot body and hands spark life to all parts of me. I hope I smiled in the photos Alma took. I'm not really in control at the moment. Alma points out her family to Hamilton and he waves at all the girls. I am thankful Taylor and Cameron keep Liberty at a distance and only wave back.

Alma gives us some space as Hamilton pulls me tight. He leans down to my temple placing a kiss then whispering, "I am so proud of you. I can't wait to see you at Latham's wedding this weekend. I love you." Another kiss is placed upon my temple before he pulls away waving before disappearing into the crowd.

I blink rapidly. Did that really happen, or did I just imagine Hamilton was here? My body is still hot where his hands and lips made contact. My blood hums through my veins. I'm grateful he attended but a few minutes are nowhere near long enough in his presence. I can't prevent the wave of feelings that flood my system. Excitement, happiness, lust, love, anxiety, fear, and dread hit all at once. It's more than I can take.

Alma slips a tissue into my hand before squeezing me tightly to her side. "You'll be okay." I nod. "Blot your eyes. The girls are anxiously waiting to see you."

I dab tears from the corner of each eye with shaking hands. Alma hugs me and whispers he didn't see Liberty, but it was a close call. She tells me this is not the time to dwell on it, we need to celebrate. Taylor and Cameron give me knowing smiles before joining Taylor's daughters. The noise wakes Liberty and she immediately stretches her arms to me.

Alma and Taylor snap several photos of us all before asking a gentleman nearby to take a few of our entire group. I'm on autopilot. My mind on Hamilton, I pose and attempt to smile when prompted. Taylor offers to take everyone to CC's City Broilers claiming she has a reservation. I am not in the mood to celebrate—Hamilton's attendance zapped everything from me, but I still find the energy to pretend for my family.

This is my first visit to CC's, I've heard Alma and many from church share about the divine meals they've enjoyed here. Cameron shares that their father insisted on dinner at CC's for birthdays and graduations. It humbles me that they include me in yet another tradition. My eyes are the size of saucers when I notice the prices on the menu. Taylor leans my way whispering her husband insisted they treat me to dinner here in exchange for my sharing an experience at Wrigley and meeting Hamilton with them while in Chicago a year ago. I'm cognizant of the fact that I paid nothing at Wrigley when I arranged to meet Hamilton. Taylor and her husband paid for the tickets and are now paying for this meal.

I order the lobster tail and petite filet with asparagus. On a trip to Kansas City once in high school, Adrian, Salem, Savannah, Bethany, and I splurged to eat at Red Lobster. We each ordered different items, so we could taste them all. Surprisingly I loved everything. This is definitely not a Red Lobster. I'm sure this meal will be among the best I've ever ordered. Taylor orders a bottle of wine for the table and sparkling water for her daughters. Before our meal arrives, they toast my graduation, upcoming job interview, and upcoming meetings in Dallas.

76

MADISON

As the approaching holidays and Salem's wedding draw near, I receive more texts from the girls in Athens. Alma's daughters and the girls left shortly after noon today. Alma is giving Libby a bath in the kitchen sink while I read the texts bombarding my phone this evening. The girls must have planned to all text me at seven.

ADRIAN

I'm officially 6 months pregnant!

I have trouble sleeping & I'm always horny

of course, Winston doesn't mind that part

ME

TMI

I quickly interrupt while trying to keep the images from forming in my mind. That's way too much information.

BETHANY

I'm 2 months pregnant!

I told Troy last night

he's freaked out & going to be over-the-top protective

I imagine Adrian and Bethany's kids growing up together. Bethany & I know my daughter is the oldest child in our little group. I find I long more and more each day to share my secret with the rest of these ladies.

BETHANY

Troy's 20th birthday weekend of wedding

accepted to the academy in St. Joe

starts cop school this summer

ME

(I text a pic of my college diploma)

It suddenly feels like bragging—I hadn't thought about that. Adrian chose to open her resale shop and not attend college. Bethany attended Athens Community College for a year before dropping out to provide childcare and become a mother. Salem attended a one-year LPN program at the community college and now works at the hospital. And Savannah works full-time as a bakery manager at the grocery store. I'm the only one to achieve my degree, but I'm glad they are all happy on their own paths.

ME

now for biggest news

ADRIAN

if you hooked up with Hamilton & didn't call

I'm gonna be pissed @ you

SAVANNAH

what's big news?

ME

publishing house in Dallas is flying me down

Dec. 19th & 20th to discuss publishing 2 of my

(book emoji)

BETHANY

what books?

SALEM

(book emoji) ?

Of my group of friends in Athens, Savannah and Adrian knew of my previous writings. While they never read any of them, I did share that I wrote stories in my spare time while hiding in my bedroom at home.

SALEM

what type of books are they?

ME

young adult

some middle school & others high school age

ADRIAN

did you write about any of us?

I regret mentioning anything during their texts. It would have been easier to chat at the upcoming wedding or not to tell them at all. I've opened this can of worms, so I have to continue.

ME

aren't based on any 1 real-life

characters have pieces of us

aren't entirely like any 1 of us

no need to worry

After congratulating me and wishing me luck on my trip to Dallas, Salem texts to remind us we have five days until her bachelorette party and six days until her wedding. The girls text excitedly for a few minutes about all of the details, when I will arrive, and the honeymoon.

Last but not least, Savannah texts that the bakery is incredibly busy for the holidays. She is taking Friday and Saturday off for Salem's wedding, so she won't fall asleep standing up at Salem's events. She hasn't had a day off since the second week of November and she can't wait for January when every-thing slows down again.

As we end our text session, my friends wish me good luck at my meetings in Dallas on Wednesday and Thursday.

Alma carries Libby bundled snuggly in her towel towards me. My tired girl smiles at me.

"Are you ready for bed?" I ask as I sweep her into my arms towel and all.

"She almost fell asleep in the sink," Alma claims.

As I secure a diaper on my wiggling daughter she giggles. I wonder if Alma imagined Liberty's sleepiness as she is very active now. In her sleeper, we begin to rock in the corner of her room. I tell her all about our busy week ahead.

"Da-da-da," my beautiful girl asks me. With baseball games almost daily for months, she's now gone quite a while without us pointing out or talking about Hamilton on TV.

I tell her daddy is in Athens. I realize she doesn't understand me, so I pull my cell phone from my back pocket and display the photo of Hamilton and I at my graduation. I point to Hamilton, "Daddy."

Liberty attempts to pull the phone from my hands. When that doesn't work, she points. As she points I say daddy or mommy depending on who she points to.

At this moment tears form in my eyes. I've let her down as a parent. I've kept her daddy away from her for much too long. Hamilton will be a perfect father and Liberty deserves to know him. I must find a time in January to talk to him about her. I can't let another off-season pass and keep my secret. I hand Libby her bottle and lay my phone on a nearby table.

As my daughter quickly slides to sleep, I imagine my conversation with Hamilton revealing Liberty as his daughter. As I have hundreds of times before, I attempt to think of all possible outcomes, the perfect location, and the perfect words to use.

77

MADISON

When I return home Monday, I check on Liberty napping in her crib before I change from my interview suit. I barely have my yoga pants on when Bethany pops on the screen of my ringing phone. I answer the video call.

"So, how did the interview go?" Bethany immediately asks making it clear her reason for calling me.

As I hang my suit in the closet and return my heels to the shelf I answer. "They hired me on the spot. I start on January Fourth. I'll be teaching social studies and current events at the middle school for at least five weeks."

Bethany smiles and claps the entire time I talk. She asks if she can tell the others in Athens and I give her permission. I am much too busy this week to worry about another long phone call to the girls.

"What does Libby think of her mommy's new job?" Bethany segues to her favorite part of our private video calls.

I walk into the nursery with the camera facing away from me. Although she was sound asleep only moments ago, she's standing at the railing of her crib smiling when I enter.

"There's my girl," Bethany announces through the phone. "Hi, Libby."

I lean my phone with camera pointed at Libby's face against the wall, while I change her diaper on the changing table. Bethany coos and babbles, but Libby looks at me. As soon as my hands are free, I position the phone, so Bethany can see my daughter again.

The two jibber and jabber for long minutes before Bethany claims she hears the garage door and needs to go before Troy walks in. I tell her I'll see her Friday and we end the call.

As I wrap Liberty's Christmas gifts 'from Hamilton', I fight tears while I imagine her big, strong father excitedly shopping then gift-wrapping them himself. Remembering the gifts, he gave me during my scavenger hunt the day he left Athens, I know what a great gift-giver as a dad he will be. I know my wrapping gifts from her dad will never make up for really having Hamilton in her life. This is another reason I must introduce the two before she gets any older.

I hurry to wrap the remaining gifts as I attempt not to think of Hamilton, his future relationship with Liberty, and my failures as her mother for keeping her a secret from her dad and his family. I climb into bed knowing I will struggle with sleep as the thoughts still swarm my head.

When sleep finally comes to me it's fitful with nightmares of losing Alma. Recently my fears of Alma's age and health infiltrate my dreams in horrible scenarios. Images from these nightmares haunt me when I should enjoy my time with her. I over analyze every ache she mentions, and her occasional memory lapses.

Friday arrives before I know it. I enjoy a slow easy breakfast with Liberty in her chair near me. When I arrived home last night she was already in bed for the night. I spent Wednesday and Thursday away from her and today I will leave for two days in Athens while she stays home again with Alma. Every day away from her seems like an eternity. I want to help my friends celebrate, but the thought of leaving my precious girl in an hour sickens me. I need to finally confess to Hamilton, so I'll no longer have to travel without her.

Alma allows me time alone with my daughter before offering to help me load my car for my next journey. I've only packed a small suitcase and a garment bag—Alma carries them to the car while I soak up another hug and smother Liberty with kisses. I've learned fast goodbyes are best and am soon on my way to Athens.

78

MADISON

Bluetooth interrupts my playlist over the speakers to announce I have a call just as I pull into the city limits of Athens.

"I just pulled into town," I inform Hamilton instead of saying hello.

"Good, I was worried."

"Why?"

He explains I mentioned the time I planned to leave Columbia and with that I should have arrived an hour ago. I can't admit that I needed one more hour with Liberty before I left on yet another trip. Instead I promise that my reason for running late is a great one that I will share over lunch with them in about twenty minutes as I am stopping for gas on my way through town. I've been busy this week—I still need to tell him all of my good news.

Before I park my car, Memphis and Hamilton walk my way. Hamilton opens my door for me. Memphis wraps me in a tight hug and Hamilton joins us.

"Guys, I can't breathe," I sputter.

They release me, help me with my bags, and lead me into the house. Just as I thought she would, Memphis has lunch ready for us. Hamilton whisks my items upstairs while Memphis orders me to take a seat. I don't dare disobey her. When Hamilton returns we eat.

"Spill it," Hamilton orders.

Memphis swats his right arm. "Hamilton Armstrong, where are your manners? I raised you better than that."

Smiling sugary sweet, Hamilton looks from his mother to me. "Madison, sweetheart, please share with the two of us about your interview on Monday and your trip to Dallas." Hamilton lays his politeness on very thick—I can only laugh. Memphis rolls her eyes at me. I've missed the two of them.

"The middle school hired me on the spot Monday. I start January 4th for at least five weeks teaching social studies." I smile at Memphis before taking a few more bites.

I didn't anticipate Hamilton's reaction. He runs over to my side of the table to hug me from behind while I remain seated. He claims we need to celebrate. I remind him we have bachelor and bachelorette parties tonight and a wedding tomorrow, we can celebrate there. Hamilton returns to his seat but doesn't resume eating. He awaits the rest of my good news. I take two more bites chewing slowly to make him wait a bit longer.

"D.C. Bland Publishing chose me as their new author of the year for the upcoming year. They plan to publish my first book by late-summer then slowly release my other books after that. Cameron will be my editor and contact person. She will get to travel to visit Alma and me on the company dime while we talk business. It all seems very surreal."

Both Memphis and Hamilton talk excitedly about this news. I try to answer questions when I can and promise to share more as I learn about it. Memphis requests to read my manuscripts prior to publication and I promise to send a digital copy to her soon.

After lunch we remain at the kitchen table to catch up on Hamilton's many endorsement deals and public appearances past and future. I feel at ease and comfortable at the Armstrong table. I wonder when I divulge my secret about Liberty if I will still be welcome and comfortable. If I am not, I pray Liberty will be.

Hamilton invites me to help him make a few repairs outside, but I opt to visit with Memphis this afternoon claiming I need to rest for tonight and tomorrow's activities after my travels to Dallas and drive to Athens this morning.

Memphis and I visit for a bit then quietly read while Hamilton busies himself outside. I'm half sitting half laying on the sofa while I read on my Kindle App. Memphis rocks as she reads her book.

"I hope the two of you will find some time this afternoon or tomorrow to talk." Memphis closes her book in her lap. I look up from my phone. "I'm a mom and a mom can sense when there is something up. The two of you..." She tucks hair behind her right ear. "I've tried not to interfere, but it's been a year."

She moves close beside me on the sofa. Holding my hand in hers she informs me she knows I'm hiding something. "It's more than just moving away to college. During your video calls and even now, your eyes give you away. I can tell you are happy to be here, but there is something you are holding back." She raises her palm out to me when I begin to speak. "Now, I won't push—it's your life. I just want you to know I am here for you. You can tell me anything—I'm here to help in any way I can. If you just need a shoulder to cry on or an ear to listen, I'm here for that, too. If you can't talk to me, I want to encourage you to talk to Hamilton. I realize he is very busy and usually so far away, but he's here today and tomorrow for you. He'll be here until after Christmas. I just hate seeing you hold back."

She takes a deep breath. "The same goes for him. Something is up. I don't know if it is stress, his team, his appearances, or what. I've tried a few times to get him to open up with no luck." She shakes her head then stands frustrated. "I feel helpless. I can see the two of you suffering a bit, but I can't fix it if I'm not let in."

Before she leaves the room, I call to her. "Memphis, you're right. I do have something I just can't share it yet. I'm still trying to work a few things out. I've almost called you a hundred times but am not ready quite yet." I take her hand in mine. "I know you are here for me. I need to share this with him first and it's never been the right time."

"It will never be the *perfect* time. Life is unpredictable. You need to get it off your chest before it festers too big to do anything about. I assume by him you mean my son." I nod. "Hamilton loves you—talk to him. It's the off-season. He has a while before he reports to spring training. Take a deep breath and then tell him whatever it is. You'll feel better just getting it off your chest."

I nod and return to the sofa. I don't open my phone. I can't read now. I should have known I couldn't hide from Memphis. I want to tell her. I could do it right now then ask her how to break the news to her son. In my heart I am ready for everyone to know, but I can't take the spotlight off Salem and

Latham's wedding. I can't do it with Liberty so far away—they will want to see her immediately.

Again, it's not the right time.

Memphis kindly gives me time to myself. She mentioned Hamilton is keeping something from her, too. I wonder if it might be about me. It could be work and his busy off-season schedule this year. I'm sure he knows he can talk to me if he needs to. I don't want to push it, though. As much as I want to know if his constantly touching and kissing me means something, I'm not ready for that discussion either. I close my eyes deciding to focus on Salem and her wedding activities. The rest will work itself out in time.

79

HAMILTON

As I walk back toward the barn, I remember anxiously awaiting Madison's arrival this morning. I wish I could turn back time. I'd sweep her into the barn immediately when she arrived. I'd kiss her breathless and while she caught her breath I'd spill my heart to her. I'd tell her I love her, I'd tell her I want her in my life every day, and I'd ask her to consider moving our relationship forward.

When she began to argue, I'd share I imagine us married, starting a family, and living in Chicago year-round. In my dreams, she teaches in Chicago, she's actively involved in the middle school, and often shares stories from school at our dinner table. I'd explain my strong desire to ask her to marry me, but realize we need to date, to solve our long-distance issues, and reconnect first.

I climb on the four-wheeler and peel out of the barn much to fast seeking the open pasture. As I drive my heart aches at her excitement of her new temporary teaching position. In my ear I hear mom saying, 'if you snooze you lose'. Because I hesitated in sharing my feelings, I can no longer share as it will make her choose career or me.

The excitement on her face and in her voice as she shared about her temporary job, I can't ask her to give that up to be with me. I want her near me and I want her happy. I know how hard she worked in high school, throughout the past year to earn her degree, and to secure this job. I can't cause her to lose that light in her eyes. I can't ask her to choose me over the temporary position.

I'm such an idiot. I'm out here zooming around on an ATV that my coach and agent would have a coronary if they knew about when I want to be with Madison. My goal is to spend as much time with her this weekend as I can. It's time to stop pouting, man up, and enjoy the weekend with Madison while I can be near her.

80

MADISON

The day passes quickly, before I know it, Hamilton drops me off at Adrian's house for Salem's bachelorette party. Tonight's festivities will be the exact opposite of the crazy event I planned for Adrian's bachelorette party.

"Uh-huh," Adrian shakes her head placing a hand on Hamilton's chest. "This is a bachelorette party; no guys allowed. You just hop back in your truck and drive your butt over to Troy's."

Hamilton grabs my elbow preventing me from entering the house. "Call me when you are ready for a ride home. I'll be here in five minutes," he whispers in my ear before he places a soft kiss at the corner of my lips then returns to his truck.

I stand on Adrian's porch waving as he backs from the driveway. His husky whisper ignited tiny fires throughout my body. My lips burn where his perfectly plump hot lips left his kiss. Adrian is mumbling something from the doorway behind me. I can't quite make out her words, but it sounds like such a cute couple. When I can no longer watch Hamilton, I'm ready to focus on the girls and start our party.

"You're the first to arrive," Adrian states with a giant smile on her face. As she hangs my coat in the entryway closet, she states drinks and snacks are in the kitchen. "So, Hamilton and you are staying with Memphis this weekend, how cozy." She waggles her eyebrows up and down.

"Stop it," I warn. "It's not like that and you know it. Nothing has changed. I'm just as confused now as I was months ago. I'm going along with the feelings he demonstrates. Seems we are very friendly friends."

Adrian cocks a brow. "How do you feel about that?"

"Confused," I answer honestly with a groan. "I'm confused. We've been close since eighth grade. He's still my best friend, and I am still his number one fan. I live each day anxiously awaiting a text or phone call from him. It feels good seeing him again today. Everything is smooth like it was in high school except for a kiss to my lips or cheeks from time to time. The kisses seem friendly, I assume that's what we are, just friends." I shrug and snag a diet cola from the fridge.

Bethany and Salem barge through the unlocked front door without knocking, announcing Savannah just pulled into the driveway. With the gang all here, it's time to start the party. Once we all gather around the kitchen island, Bethany shares the party plans.

"Ladies," Bethany raises her voice to get everyone's attention. "Tonight, we are keeping it simple. All drinks are non-alcoholic in honor of us two pregnant women. We will eat, visit, play games, watch movies, and snack. Nothing too wild as requested by our bride-to-be Salem." She motions toward our friend.

"Sounds great," Salem announces. "Bring on the food."

Adrian pulls deli trays from the refrigerator and I place the buns and condiments for sandwiches nearby. We open several bags of chips and two tubs of dip, then dig in. We choose to visit then watch the latest romantic comedy release. I enjoy every minute with my girls. I don't pretend here—they take me as I am. Although we talk almost weekly, I find there is still so much I miss out on.

"Things must be very different for you in Columbia."

I meet Salem's eyes before I answer. "Yeah, my life is very different. I haven't needed to use Tater Hill, Wilson Holler, or Coon Creek (*pronounced krik*) to give directions in over a year." I tease my friends.

"We know," Adrian chides. "you love it in the big city and don't miss Athens-life."

I don't correct my friend. I don't confide in my girls that I miss them and Athens. I can't tell them I long to raise Liberty in this small town. I don't share in my year away I've come to realize my distaste for Athens had much more to do with my mother and not small-town life as I believed.

An hour and a half later, Bethany starts our movie and we settle in with snacks on our laps. We chat and laugh the entire movie. I notice Salem keeps texting someone and looks concerned by the latest message.

"Everything okay," I whisper not wanting to draw everyone's attention to her.

"My mom says the boiler at the church isn't working. She's on her way to the church to meet a repairman. It's too cold to hold the wedding tomorrow without heat." Concern is written all over her face.

"Adrian is asleep, and Bethany looks ready to doze off at any time." I point in their direction. Savannah listens in on our conversation now. "We could call it a night to let the pregnant mommies rest and you can join them at the church."

Salem hesitates, but I decide to end the party for her. "Ladies, I think it's time to clean up the kitchen and let our future mommies get some sleep." Adrian's eyes snap open and we make quick work of the clean-up.

81

MADISON

I pull out my cell phone to call Hamilton for a ride as we planned.

"Mady!" Hamilton yells in greeting. Without pulling the receiver from his mouth he slurs to the men. "Guys, she's on the phone. Stop. Stop. Troy it's your turn." I can't make out Troy's words. "Bull shit!" Hamilton yells. "I call bull shit!"

Sensing something is up, I signal for the ladies to be quiet by putting my index finger over my lips and set my phone to speaker. The girls gather around to hear better.

"Hamilton, you suck!" Troy yells.

"Shut up and chug," Latham slurs loudly.

"Drink. Drink. Drink." The men chant for Troy.

Next, we hear Hamilton say, "Two fours."

Then Troy yells, "Bull shit."

Hamilton attempts to taunt while slurring, "Are you sure Troy, you'll have to drink if you're wrong."

"I call bull shit!" Troy reiterates.

Hamilton groans then seems to chug a drink while the other three chant. The ladies begin to giggle around me. We haven't heard Winston, but it sounds like the other guys are drunk.

"Hamilton," I call with a raised voice. We hear the game continue as if I am not on his phone. "Hamilton!" Still nothing from his end, so I hang up.

"Can someone give me a ride over to Troy and Bethany's house? I think I need to drive Hamilton home tonight."

Savannah offers to drive me, but Bethany chimes in. "Why don't the three of you ride with me? I bet Adrian will need to drive Winston and Salem you'll need to drive Latham. If I take you, then you'll only have your guy's car to drive." It makes perfect sense. We say our goodbyes to Savannah with promises to see her at the wedding before we pile into Bethany's minivan for the short drive to her house.

Although the phone call led us to believe all four guys were drunk, we were not prepared for the mess and how drunk they all are. Upon opening the door, the strong stench of beer greets us. Bethany's morning sickness hits— she darts to the bathroom with her hand over her mouth.

We watch from the doorway for a moment as they continue their game totally unaware we stand nearby. Winston sits with a stiff back as his head wobbles from side to side and he attempts to focus on his cards. I've never witnessed Winston and Hamilton in this state of inebriation. Troy and Latham often let go on the weekends, but the other two usually only enjoy a beer or two. Latham leans his head on his hand with elbow on the table. He struggles to keep his eyes open. While his cards lie on the table face-up in front of him for everyone to see.

We are standing behind Troy, but from his raised voice, animated actions, and mispronunciation of several words, it is clear he is drunk. Hamilton attempts to focus on the game and doesn't see us watching straight across from him.

"Hey guys," I greet.

"Hamilton look Madison is here!" Latham yells in his drunken state.

Hamilton looks at me, then picks up his cell phone. "Madison are you still there?"

I decide to play along by walking behind his chair. "Hi, Hamilton." I pretend to still be on his phone.

"Did you need something?"

I roll my eyes towards Adrian. "Hamilton can you come pick me up? Our party is over."

"Sure," he lays his phone on the corner of the table. "Guys I gotta go.

Madison needs a ride." Laughter erupts. Hamilton rises from his chair and trips over its leg. I grab his shoulders in an attempt to help him find his balance.

"Thanks Madison," he slurs.

I witness the moment he makes the connection. He looks at his phone then at me and back.

"You don't need a ride," he announces.

"No, but it seems you do," Adrian answers for me trying to stifle her laughter.

Winston realizes they are all busted. "It's Troy's twentieth birthday so we decided to play a drinking game." He speaks to Adrian as if she is his mother and just caught him drinking.

Latham extends his arms to Salem. "We ran out of beer, so we had to use Jack Daniels." He points to the open bottle on the table.

Ah-ha that explains how lit they are. Stupid boys, I've told them several times. 'Beer before liquor never sicker. Liquor before beer in the clear.' Seems they will be bent over the toilet tonight. It amazes me in just over three hours, Hamilton and Latham forgot they needed pick us up and drive home tonight. Winston drove himself over here, too. I'm even more glad we chose not to drink alcohol at our party tonight. Bethany and Adrian might have driven all of us home tonight if we had.

At this point we attempt to get three sets of keys from the guys. Bethany finds everyone's keys by the back door on a table and passes them to us.

I laugh so hard as I attempt to load Hamilton in his truck that I nearly pee my pants. It's like trying to help a sleepy four-year-old to bed, but he's over six-feet-tall and over two-hundred pounds. I roll his window down and encourage him to keep his nose near the fresh air as I drive. I don't want to clean up vomit from his truck tonight.

He's snoring when I park in Memphis' driveway. I shake him awake and remind him his mother is asleep, so we must be quiet on our way to his room. He tries his best to walk, but still leans heavily on my shoulders. His heavy boots bump the door frame on our way inside. I contemplate removing the boots in the mudroom or upstairs—I decide in his room will be easier. Much too loudly we make our way through the kitchen then up to his room.

He falls onto his bed placing his arm over his eyes. I shut off the overhead light and switch on the bedside lamp. Where to begin? I untie and slip off his heavy work boots. As I tuck them on the floor of his closet, he makes a groan before darting to the attached bathroom. I knew this would happen.

I place a wet washcloth on the back of his neck, then take a seat on the edge of the tub and rub his back while he heaves the contents of his stomach into the toilet. He's not quiet while puking. I cringe knowing Memphis surely hears him. I decide to peek into the hallway to let her know he is okay. I do not find her, and her door is still closed, so instead I fetch water and pain relievers from the kitchen.

When I return, Hamilton is sprawled out on the tile floor with the washcloth over his eyes. "Ham, I have some water if you want a sip." He groans rolls to his side and proceeds to vomit on himself and the bathroom floor. Great, now I will get the honor of cleaning his bathroom. I do my best to assist him toward the toilet just in time for the next round. After fifteen minutes his stomach seems to calm. With a fresh washcloth I wipe his mouth and chin.

"Ham, I need you to take a shower. You have puke all over and it might help you feel better." He doesn't respond.

I struggle to pull his t-shirt covered in puke over his head and in doing so I realize it's now in his hair. I try not to gag as I ask him to stand and remove his jeans while I turn the shower on. He struggles what seems like an eternity with his belt. It is clear I need to strip him the rest of the way. He's sick—I can do this. My fingers fumble nervously before successfully unhooking the belt then button on his jeans. I'm acutely aware of my knuckles brushing against his dark happy trail in the process.

My stomach somersaults as thoughts of slipping my hand further inside his jeans enter my mind. I imagine the thick, heavy weight of him in my palm, his reaction to my touch, to the movement of my hand…

"Mady, if you don't stop worrying your lip I'll have to rescue it myself," his husky whisper draws my eyes up his contoured abdominals then chest to his heavy-lidded brown eyes.

He's drunk. He's sick. Snap out of this Madison. You can't go there tonight.

Hamilton's fingers rest under my chin while his thumb pulls my lower lip away from my incisors. I wasn't aware of biting it.

"The shower is ready. Get undressed and hop in."

I sigh as he nearly falls over while attempting to remove his jeans. Placing my hands on the waistband of his pants I assist him in sliding them down his thighs. I urge him to put his hand on the wall before he steps out of each leg and his socks. I close my eyes tight as I stand back up.

"Okay, you in the shower," I order attempting to control my hormones. My body is alive. I fight the urge to press myself against him, to take him in my mouth, to seek a release for both of us. Though I try hard not to, my eyes glance down and my breath catches at the sight of his erect cock. Needing to remove myself from the room and my thoughts, I turn him toward the shower with my hands on his shoulders. I open the glass door and guide him through. When he places his two palms on the tiles under the nozzle allowing the spray to pummel his neck and back, I flee.

I squeal when Memphis scares me in the hallway on my way to my room. "Everything okay?"

I don't know if she means with me or Hamilton. "Hamilton drank too much, so I drove us home. He's been sick and now he's in the shower."

Memphis fails to hide her smile. It's clear she knows why I was darting from his bedroom. "You need anything?" When I can only shake my head, she bids me goodnight and returns to her room shutting the door behind her.

I hear the shower shut off. Crap! I didn't get the chance to regroup in my room. I debate turning in or checking on Hamilton one more time. I reluctantly return to assist him in finding his bed—I won't asleep until I know he is safe in his bed.

Peeking through the bathroom door. The dripping wet hunk of a man that is Hamilton Armstrong greets me. His hands are planted on the counter, a towel is secured low around his waist, and his eyes look to me in the large mirror.

"Feel better?"

He nods before squeezing toothpaste on his toothbrush then scrubbing his teeth and tongue. I lean in the door frame transfixed as his back, shoulders, and arms flex while he brushes. Hamilton clears his throat drawing my attention to his reflection. He smirks, yes, smirks at me. It seems he does feel better.

"Alright, I'm going to turn in. Please take the pain relievers and drink the entire water I put by the bed. Goodnight." I turn and head to his sister's room.

82

MADISON

I lean against the shut bedroom door allowing myself to slide to the floor. My mind still focuses on Hamilton's bare back and shoulders with water droplets glistening. His white towel secured low on his hips as it hints to what lies beneath. The eighteen months since I experienced what hid under his towel seems like only yesterday and at the same time an eternity ago.

I've replayed our time together over and over in my mind. His body, his words, and his touch are burned in my memory. Part of me desperately yearns for a repeat performance. It's been eighteen long months since I've been with him. My fantasies are no replacement for the real man only a room away.

I peel myself off the floor, slip on my pajamas, and crawl into bed. I unsuccessfully attempt to clear my mind of all things Hamilton. I flip from my back to my stomach and then from one side to the other unable to find comfort. After what seems like eons, I tiptoe to the bathroom in the hallway. I splash cool water on my face then pat it dry with the hand towel. As I return to my room, I sneak a peek into Hamilton's room to check on him.

"Hey," his sleepy voice calls as he lifts his head slightly.

"Just checking if you need anything." I twist the end of my tank-top around my finger.

"Having trouble sleeping?" When I nod, he slides over patting for me to join him. I stand frozen. "C'mon, I promise not to bite."

Hesitantly I move towards him. He lifts the covers and I slip under leaving plenty of room between our bodies. Having none of it, Hamilton wraps his arm around my waist and pulls my back snug to his front. I'm home. Wrapped in his warmth as his breathing evens out, I slide into slumber.

I fight the urge to wake as several slight tugs on my hair beckon me. Slowly I blink open my eyes adjusting to the morning light seeping in through the open blinds.

Hamilton's blinds.

Hamilton's bedroom.

The bottom falls out of my stomach at my realization I slept in his bed with his mother just down the hall.

"Good morning," Hamilton whispers from behind me. "How'd you sleep?"

His eager face shocks me. I fully expected a hungover, cranky Hamilton this morning. I planned to force a little hair of the dog down him in an attempt to help him bounce back for the wedding this afternoon.

Recalling his question, I answer. "I haven't slept this soundly in months." Guilt consumes me immediately. Being away from Liberty is equally responsible for the sound sleep as the proximity Hamilton is. I don't mind giving up sleep for her. I'd give up so much more if I needed to. She's my world and yet here I lie acting as if she doesn't exist.

"Hey," Hamilton whispers pulling my chin towards him. He searches my eyes. "What's wrong?"

I shake my head fighting the tears that threaten. He tucks my hair behind my ear. I'm sure my bed head is atrocious. I force a smile. "How's your head?"

Hamilton assures me my nursing skills last night scared off any hangover he might have deserved. I don't believe he feels no pain, but it's clear he feels much better than he should. I decide to remedy this.

"I washed your clothes and cleaned your bathroom last night, but I couldn't bare cleaning the cab of your truck in the cold and dark." I squeeze my tongue between my teeth on the verge of hurting to fend off a smile.

A long groan rises from Hamilton's chest.

"I'm sorry, I know I should have taken care of it immediately…"

"No, it's not your fault. You cleaned much more than you should have. I shouldn't have put you in such a position." He slides from his side of the bed.

He's fully dressed. Come to think of it I smelled toothpaste while he was next to me. "How long have you been awake?"

He sits on the bed beside me. He's been up for an hour or so, he even ate breakfast and got a tongue lashing from Memphis. She ran to town for a bit, so he came to wake me up. When he excuses himself to go clean his truck, I admit I was teasing. Before I can react, he tackles me on his bed, braces my hands above my head with one of his hands, and tickles my ribs. I squirm attempting to escape. I flail desperately in my attempts to evade him.

His dark brown eyes lock on mine and we freeze. I'm extremely aware of the alignment of our pelvic regions, the fact that he pinned my hands just like this the night we were together, and we are alone in the house. Every cell springs to life—my body hums. My nipples pebble in my thin tank, it suddenly feels one-hundred degrees in his room, and I can't peel my eyes from his.

"Breathe Madison," his husky voice growls just as he did our first time together.

Slowly he closes the distance between our lips. When I can take his slow descent no more, I fight against his restraint to meet him.

"Patience," he chuckles mere inches from my mouth. "We are in no rush."

Finally, he allows his plump, warm lips to meet mine. I moan and melt under him. I part my lips granting him access to more of me. His warm tongue strokes mine, stoking fires deep inside me. Always needing more, I lift my pelvis infinitesimally to grind against his. He tugs my lower lip between his teeth pulling back slightly and I grind again. He moves kissing behind my ear, licking, then blowing. His breath causes goosebumps on my damp skin. I tilt my head exposing more neck for his attention. My core is on fire.

"Ham," I beg.

"Yes?" He moves kissing my collarbone still pinning my hands above my head.

"Ham, I need…" He nips then kisses.

"Tell me what you *need*."

"Ham, please I need you, now, everywhere," my husky voice further demonstrates my arousal for only him.

He wastes no time. He releases my hands, pulls up my tank, and tugs off my boxer shorts. His eyes turn molten as he scans my body head to toe. I no longer have the tight body he's seen before. I have more curves at my breast and hips along with stretch marks. Suddenly I'm worried what he might find on his explorations. I throw my arms around his neck and pull his mouth to mine. My kiss is primal, needing him inside me now.

Hamilton pulls away, reaching for a condom. I tug him back.

"I'm protected and I'm clean." I stare into his eyes.

"Um," he hesitates. His eyes search mine. "I *always* wear a condom."

"I'm giving you permission to skip the condom. I get a shot every three months. I'm not going to get pregnant." *This time* I think to myself. "I've only been with you." I sound desperate as I try to talk him in to entering me.

"I'm clean." He clears his throat. "You really haven't been with anyone else?"

"Only you," I promise.

He throws my leg around his waist, gently places himself at my wet opening, then with eyes on mine slowly glides in to the root. I raise my other leg around him. As he finds a delectable rhythm, my eyes close unable to fight to keep them open any longer. My fingers dig into his shoulders and my head falls back into the mattress. Hamilton's mouth is everywhere. He kisses my lips, licks my neck, and sucks on my nipples. He slides one hand between us. At first contact I groan and grind into his fingertips. Quickly I wind tighter and tighter, growing closer to my release.

Hamilton trails kisses from my breast, to my collarbone while his stubble scrapes and ignites my sensitive skin. His hot breath fills my ear. "I'm not going to last, you feel so good around me, so hot, so…"

His words combined with his fingertips and to his thrusts are my undoing. I scream his name as my orgasm hits. I arch, I grind, I beg him not to stop. Every muscle tightens, my breath hitches and white flashes of light shoot in every direction behind my closed lids. "Y-e-s!" I growl.

Hamilton's hand on my hip bites into my flesh holding me as he pounds again and again. His other hand winds in my hair and pulls me toward his chest. With one, two, three more thrusts he shutters inside me. His veins pop out in his neck and his head looks to the ceiling. I feel his growl move from his abdomen, through his chest, and escape his open mouth.

"F-u-c-k," his breath comes in rapid pants as his every muscle relaxes over me. He falls beside me, breaking our connection.

I stare at the ceiling afraid to make eye contact with him. I really messed up. I need to tell him about his daughter before I allow myself to be confused by our relationship. As my breaths slow and my body relaxes, I worry how Hamilton will feel when he finds out I had sex with him while keeping his daughter a secret. Why am I making things worse instead of opening up to him?

"I haven't either," Hamilton states turning to face me.

I struggle to understand him. Did he speak while I was lost in my head? I turn toward him my brows raised.

"Since we were together, I haven't been with anyone else."

His words are a hundred-pound anvil to my chest. As if I needed anything else to complicate things, his confession is everything I want to hear. Tears pool and my throat closes tight.

"Mady, don't cry." Hamilton pulls me tight against his chest. His hands rub up and down my bare back. "Sweetheart, what's wrong?"

I shake my head. If it weren't for Salem's wedding, I could spill my guts right here, right now. I know lying naked in his arms is not how I want to share we have a daughter. I want to, I need to unburden myself of my secret. "I…" my voice quivers. I take in a deep breath then exhale. "I've got something major I'm working through. I need to plan some things out before I can share it with you." I glance into his eyes.

His brow is furrowed. "I can help you if you let me," he offers.

I have no doubt how he will help once he knows the truth. This is just not the right time. "Your mom asked me about it yesterday. I guess she can see I'm holding something back. I just can't tell the two of you, yet." His eyes beg me to open up. "I need some more time, I need to do something first, and then I promise I'll share it with you."

Internally I cringe at my words. I make my daughter sound like a burden, a complication that I am avoiding for the time being. I can't give any hints to my secret. I need to change the subject before I mess this up further.

"Your mom claims you are keeping something from us, too."

My words hang heavy in the air. He sighs heavily while scrubbing his hands over his dark stubbled face and into his hair. "I've just been so busy, it seems like I have no off-season that's all."

Although it's the truth, I know Memphis speaks of something bigger than this. I feel like a bad friend as I didn't notice until Memphis mentioned it. He does carry a burden. We used to tell each other everything. We helped each other come up with plans and ideas to solve our problems. Life was much simpler when we were in high school, visited our cemetery, and were available to each other 24/7.

Hamilton's long muscular arms wrap around me. "I hate being so far away from you most of the year. I want you with me—I need you in my life."

His confession fills me with hope and scares me to death at the same time. I can't contain the hiccupping sobs that overtake me. He kisses my forehead and nose before hugging me. One arm holds me tight against him at my shoulders, the other glides up and down my bare back.

"It's okay, we will find a way. I promise." I hear his words but continue to cry. "We will figure something out—we will find a way to make *us* work."

"You may not..." I wipe my running nose on the back of my hand and I gulp in air. "You may not want me when I..."

He interrupts me. "I will always want you. I've tried to think of every reason the past eighteen months not to be with you. I can't fight it anymore. You are all that I want, all that I need. There is nothing," He lifts my chin, so I must look directly at him. "and I mean *nothing* that you must work through and tell me about later that will change my wanting you." His eyes search for my understanding.

Through more sobs I attempt to speak. "You don't know that. It's big, it's huge. It's not something you will consider no big deal. You'll feel differently about me. I know you will. It's that bad."

He wipes my tears before engulfing my mouth with his. His kiss demonstrates his declaration to me. It proves his conviction as he attempts to swallow my fear, my guilt, and my doubt. He attempts to fill my heart and mind with his love for me and the knowledge that he will always want me. It's a passionate kiss, but not in a sexual way. His passion is for me and for us. My crying stops. I cling to the hope that there just might be a chance.

I squeal as Hamilton tugs the towel from my body. Our eyes lock in the vanity mirror. In his I find feral desire. He spins me, lifts me, and carries me back to his bed.

I giggle as he gently tosses me to the mattress then leans atop me.

"Hamilton, your mother will be back any minute." I attempt to be the voice of maturity in this moment.

He blatantly ignores my mention of his mother's return. Instead he removes his shirt and jeans while peppering kisses on my lips, my neck, my collarbone, and my ribcage.

At the sudden absence of his mouth, my eyes open. He's smiling while his eyes skim my face. His lips slightly part.

"You are so beautiful." His molten brown eyes sparkle. They match his dazzling smile. His dark wavy hair has grown too long—I can't keep my fingers from tangling in it. His dark stubble is more than evading the razor for a day or two. It's soft and prickly at the same time. His brown eyes, I could swim in their chocolate depths forever. And his body, oh his body, has only improved with time. Although always muscular and strong, it's now defined and powerful. He now sports dips and contours as his soft skin covers the rock-hard muscles. I rapidly blink to regain focus on Hamilton's words.

"Welcome back," he teases. "I've always known you are beautiful inside and out. They say absence makes the heart grow fonder—it's cheesy, but it's true." Hamilton places a gentle kiss upon the corner of my mouth. "It seems our distance apart caused my true feelings for you to surface."

"Or my sexual prowess on our one night together..." I attempt to tease, but he places his fingertips on my lips.

He replaces his fingers with his mouth. My brain grows quiet and I feel. I bask in every glorious sensation he awards me. I moan softly when his strong hands part my thighs and his hot tongue darts to tickle my clit. My back arches and my fingers clutch hold of his soft waves. His strong palm flattens to my abdomen in an attempt to halt my thrashing. His hot breath assails my sensitive nub when he blows for a moment before he lightly scrapes with his whiskered chin. I cry out at the overwhelming sensation. Sensing my approval, he repeats the warm wet lick, the hot breeze, then the tantalizing torture of his stubble—once, twice, and I cum.

Like a sniper's bullet I am not prepared. I scream as my every muscle tightens then spasms, my head burrows into the mattress, I grind my pelvis against him, and shatter into a sextillion pieces.

I'm lost in a sea of sensations while he nips, licks, and kisses his way over my stomach, my breasts, my neck, to my mouth. I lazily return his kiss.

I finally summon the strength to partially open my eyes. He's there, inches from me a proud smirk upon his face. I swat his shoulder begging him to stop. When he doesn't, I take our situation into my own hands, literally.

I firmly grasp him in my palm. My treacherous body outs me. I quiver. I'm trying to harness my inner-sex vixen and I quiver at the anticipation of his heavy cock about to enter me. I focus on my task. I watch his pupils dilate as I apply pressure with each stroke. I position my thumb upon the ridged nerve on the underside enjoying the groan I evoke while his eyes close. My fingertips slide the slick drop of pre-cum over his tip.

I gasp suddenly rolled over and impaled upon the cock I massaged in my hand the moment before. My fingertips bite into his pecs as I adapt to the full sensation. Hamilton's hands on my ass urge me to move.

While my hips grind, my eyes beg his to love me. I urge them to love me in spite of my secret, and to love me and our daughter. His eyes seem to be talking to mine at the same time.

Tears well in my eyes at the realization while our hearts and bodies communicate our eyes display the secrets we withhold. When wetness escapes to my cheeks, Hamilton's thumbs swipe them away as his fingers hold my jaws.

With an ab crunch his lips rise to mine. He presses his forehead to mine while whispering everything will be okay.

83

MADISON

Promptly at 3:00 p.m. the organ music announces it's time for us to walk down the aisle to witness Salem and Latham's vows. The church is toasty warm thanks to a service man agreeing to work off the clock on a Friday night to ensure the wedding would go on without a hitch.

As I walk down the aisle, my eyes find Hamilton looking sharper than James Bond in his black tux. He smiles warmly and winks before I turn to take my spot on the step leading to the alter.

The music changes, the crowd stands and Salem on her father's arm beams as she walks to Latham at the front of the church. I see a hint of tears in her eyes as Latham accepts her hand from her father. Latham looks scared to death, his face is pale, and he stands stiffly.

When I spoke to him earlier he seemed like the normal farm boy he is. He admitted to fighting his hangover all day but felt fine for the ceremony. I glance to Winston. He wins first-place for the worst hangover today. He still looks a bit green in his tux. Adrian complained about what a big baby he had been all night.

Hamilton and I walk out arm in arm. Once in the sanctuary Hamilton spins me towards him. He tells me how ravishing I look before kissing me passionately in front of all of our friends. This is not a peck on the forehead or the cheek. It's a panty melting-if I were wearing any, heartbeat skipping, melting into a puddle of wanton need, long smoldering kiss. I strain to reopen my eyes. Our group of friends stand statue still, mouths agape in shock by Hamilton's actions.

"Now, that's more like it," Adrian cheers while clapping. Walking closer to us she continues, "The two of you have skated around this for years. It was exhausting to witness. Now, sleep together and live happily ever after."

I bury my face in Hamilton's chest. My cheeks burn with embarrassment. We are in a church for goodness sake. The girl has no shame and most of the time no filter. When I finally pull away from Hamilton, I find our friends gathered tightly around us. It seems Hamilton's public profession of feelings for me is well received.

Adrian places us in a receiving line as guests begin to spill into the reception hall. Hamilton keeps his hand on the small of my back as we welcome Salem and Latham's family and friends. Salem kept her wedding small—the ceremony and reception are intimate for all in attendance.

As I enjoy dinner at the wedding party table, I realize for the first time that Salem and Latham are truly the epitome of high school sweethearts. It's the captain and quarterback of the football team falling in love with the head cheerleader. Many books and movies exist based on such a couple.

My mind then wanders to Hamilton and me. Not that we are officially a couple or anything. Yet. I hope we will be someday. We are the tumultuous storyline of the popular jock with the nerd. Hamilton as my high school friend thought his job was to pry me away from my books and laptop to attend events with him. I was his nerdy sidekick and he was my fun-loving, center-of-attention hero. Wow, our journey has yet to begin and I am already writing our story. I shake away my thoughts, drawing my attention back to the couple of the hour-Salem and Latham.

Music plays during the reception, however there is no dancefloor or first dance. Salem opted for the traditional meal, cake cutting, and at the end the tossing the garter and bouquet. With the holidays mere days away, she knew families were busy and wanted to keep the ceremony and reception short. I'm grateful as it allows me to return to Columbia at a descent hour. I long to hold Liberty in my arms.

Adrian loudly announces it's time for the single ladies and guys to gather. She escorts me to the front of the women beside Savannah. "You're next she whispers in my ear. You better catch the damn bouquet or feel my wrath."

"Pregnancy doesn't agree with you," I tease.

I have no intention of catching Salem's flowers. My life is complicated enough without everyone claiming I am the next to be married. It's time for me to focus on my new career and my daughter. And of course, Hamilton's public display of affection will haunt my thoughts for many months to come.

Latham lifts Salem's dress, removing her garter with only his teeth amidst cheers. He shoots it like a rubber band from his fingers. It lands on Hamilton's head. The white and red garter sits as a crown upon his dark locks. He quickly grabs it and hands it to a teenage boy standing beside him. Several adults inform him he can't pass it, he's the next to marry. Hamilton's eyes dart my direction. Giggling, I can only shrug.

Adrian makes a big production of adjusting the line of all the single ladies before she passes the bouquet to Salem. Of course, Savannah and I are front and center. Salem turns her back, as the crowd counts one, two, three she then tosses it over her head to the right of us ladies. It falls at the feet of a man before Salem's single cousin hurries to claim it. Yay, she's the next to marry.

Shortly after Salem and Latham make their escape, I say my goodbyes. Hamilton walks me to my car prolonging our goodbye. He promises to visit me before he heads to Mesa in January as he pulls me closer. He kisses the top of my head while holding me in the chilly air. He begs me to stay one more night and drive home tomorrow in the daylight, but I can't bear to spend another night away from Liberty. I claim I need to help Alma as her family begins arriving.

84

HAMILTON

I stand frozen in the church parking lot watching as my heart and world drive away. I mentally kick myself for only completing half of my goal this weekend. I'm not sure I successfully demonstrated how much Madison means to me. While I left no doubt my physical attractions to her, I didn't ask her to come to Chicago, to live with me, and start our lives together.

Instead, I let her excitement for her life and new job in Columbia keep me from telling her everything.

Now, I'll spend the rest of the off-season alone and pining for Madison from too many miles away.

85

MADISON

As I begin to drive through Athens, I head West instead of South. I drive unaware of my destination. Ten minutes later I pull into my mother's drive. It's 6:30 p.m. on a Saturday, I knew she wouldn't be home. I walk through the unlocked front door. Empty bottles no longer decorate only her bedroom. The living room and kitchen are cluttered with her remnants. My heart aches at the confirmation that nothing has changed in her life. My absence doesn't cause her to reach out or visit me. For my mother the entire universe revolves around her.

Briskly I flee from my former home to the safety of my car. I set my course for Columbia and my new family. A family that needs me, supports me, and misses me when I am away. A family I depend on as they depend on me. My new family and my new life far away from my mother.

Like my drive home from Adrian and Winston's wedding, my mind attempts to process my new reality, my lovely daughter, my new job, and Hamilton's actions. I count all of my blessings before I ponder all things to do with Hamilton. His kiss made it clear to everyone that he considers me more than a friend. I must wait for his next text or phone call to see where he plans our relationship to go. Long distance relationships suck. Will he really move us forward? Will he treat me like a girlfriend? How will our friendship change? I fear that he might follow through on his promise to surprise me with a visit before he heads to Arizona. I must arrange for us to meet in Athens if he mentions it again.

I know I should load Liberty in my car, drive to Athens, and immediately share my secret with Hamilton. I vowed to reveal our daughter to him prior to the start of next baseball season—I'm down to one month, now. I have two major focuses for January. I start my new job and I need to introduce Liberty to her father in the next thirty days.

Alma's home fills with family and excitement as Christmas morning arrives. Keeping her family tradition, we gather around the Christmas tree to open presents still in our pajamas. Alma dawns her Santa hat while passing out gifts. Her grandchildren make it their mission to teach Liberty to open gifts.

My daughter giggles and claps while watching others rip giftwrap to reveal the present beneath. The boys pull a corner open for Libby to grab. She simply looks to them to finish the task for her. Trenton and Taylor's children decide it's easier for them to open the gifts and allow Liberty to cheer them on. They assist in removing new toys from their boxes, so she may play with them.

I save her gifts from her daddy in my room to open later in front of the webcam.

Waking I groan. I lie completely still willing myself back to sleep, back to my dream. Of course, this never works. Now staring at the ceiling, I smile remembering the warmth of Hamilton's arms when he held me next to our Christmas tree. It's the kind of dream I never want to end.

Hamilton and I played Santa after our four-year-old daughter fell asleep. While he assembled her little bicycle with tassels, a bell, a basket, and training wheels; I filled her stocking and placed other gifts under the tree. We laughed and teased while reading and rereading the instructions to assemble the bike. He vowed to pay extra for assembly from now on.

With Santa gifts all ready, we each nibbled a cookie from Santa's plate and chased it down with milk. Hamilton pointed out we were positioned below the mistletoe. That's where I woke up. I was snuggled in his arms as we kissed under the mistletoe.

As upset as I am the dream ended, I'm grateful it wasn't a nightmare as many of my dreams seem to be lately.

86

MADISON

As I assist Alma dusting the house during Liberty's naptime, my cell phone rings with an unknown number.

"Hello, this is Madison," I answer. It's the principal from the middle school I'll be starting as a long-term substitute teacher in three days. I take a seat allowing myself to give him my full attention. As he explains they won't be needing me to cover this placement, a hot heavy weight lands in the pit of my stomach. I listen while he explains the male teacher I was to cover for will no longer need to take five weeks off for paternity leave. His wife gave birth three weeks early.

Tears sting my eyes as I assure him I understand that babies rarely arrive as scheduled and I hope he will keep me in mind for any upcoming subs he might need.

As I return my phone to my back pocket, I mourn the loss of the steady income I counted on for the next five weeks.

I return the duster to the pantry before filling Alma in on my disappointing phone conversation. I excuse myself to my bedroom as I need to register for as many substitute positions at the area school districts.

For the next three hours, I jump from website to website inputting my information and uploading my documentation. I download the two mobile apps most districts use so I am ready to receive alerts as openings occur.

Now I wait. Several schools restart classes from winter break tomorrow, so I need to be ready to quickly accept any openings that might alert me tonight or prior to seven in the morning.

I shoot a text to Hamilton as I head downstairs to join Alma and my girl.

ME

sub job cancelled

(sad emoji)

I say goodnight to Alma as I carry Liberty up to bed. Liberty and I rock for fifteen minutes before I lay my sleeping girl in her crib.

I slip into my pajamas before climbing into bed with a notebook and my laptop in hand. I start a random movie on Netflix, take my pen in hand, and start writing. Instead of continuing my story, I journal tonight. I fill pages with my disappointment. I complain now that instead of one school, one subject, and one group of students for five weeks, I will be at different schools, with different ages or subjects, and new students every day.

I'll no longer know if I work tomorrow or in three days—at times I'll get an alert or phone call then need to be at the classroom within an hour.

I looked forward to this long-term placement to make a great impression day after day. Now it might be harder to meet influential administrators at each building while I'm only there a day then not seen again for a while.

I really thought this was my lucky break. I wanted this chance to fit in as a part of a team, it's not easy to do that one day here and one day there.

I pout and wallow in my disappointment for several hours before finally falling asleep with Netflix still streaming on my laptop.

87

MADISON

Day after day and night after night, I attempt to accept sub positions when alerted to an opening. It seems many other subs are much faster than me at accepting a sub job. Over and over, I'm notified the position has already been filled when I reply to an alert.

After two weeks, I finally successfully accept a sub position. Tomorrow I am a kindergarten teacher in an elementary school on the far side of Columbia. Tonight, instead of fretting about my finances and ability to find a teaching position for fall, the worry of the unknown keeps me awake. The thought of successfully entertaining twenty-one five-year-olds for seven hours scares me. I should be excited to work and earn money, but I dread it.

Getting up early to drive thirty-five minutes across town exhausts me just thinking about it. I want easy. I want comfortable. I want to stay home with Liberty and not be seen in public, but I need to work.

88

MADISON

Try as I might, I cannot shake last night's nightmare. The images replay all day. It's one of my biggest fears. I often worry as I keep putting off telling Hamilton that I might pass the point of no return. In the dream, Liberty started kindergarten and I still hadn't introduced the two of them. I kept finding an excuse not to reveal his daughter to him. Today I've imagined my life as a single mother of a middle school and high school daughter. I draw on my own years without a father.

I don't want Liberty to watch her friends with their fathers and yearn for hers. I don't want her to go without. I don't want him to miss the little things in her life. As it is now, he'll miss the first two years. He's missed a lot already —I need to ensure he doesn't miss another year of firsts.

It's here. Today's the day all single, widowed, and divorced women dread most. We can't hide from our calendars—it's February 14th. Alma asked me not to accept a sub position for today. She has secret plans for the two of us while Liberty attends Mother's Day Out Preschool at our church.

As I walk down to breakfast, I silently hope our five hours aren't as painful as the commercials leading up to this holiday are to watch. As difficult as it is on us unattached females, it must be equally stressful for attached men. The ads guilt them into needing to buy their special someone jewelry, expensive perfume, extravagant floral arrangements, and luxury cars. While each ad reminds me like a slap in the face that I'm single, the ads must remind men they need to take out a loan to prove they love their women.

Alma playfully reminds Liberty our plans are a secret as I enter the kitchen. I approach the highchair and place good morning kisses on my daughter's cheek. I play along by asking Liberty what secret plans Alma confessed to her.

I realize Alma only wants me to enjoy the day, but we are different. She's known true love, she experienced decades of love with her husband. While I love, I have to experience a year with someone I love, let alone decades. While Alma reflects upon memories, I long to have a relationship I've read about or one the commercials portray.

I try multiple times to ask Alma about her plans. She's closed up tight like Fort Knox.

We walk Liberty into her classroom together. Alma says her goodbye in the hall before I walk Liberty in to her teacher. Once entering the classroom, it's as if I no longer exist. Liberty loves playtime with her friends. I worry she spends too much time in the company of adults. Seeing her interact with children her age does my heart good. She's outgoing, friendly, and kind to everyone.

As we return to the van, I ask Alma one more time about our plans. She zips her lips with pinched fingers and pretends to toss the key over her shoulder while wearing a sly grin.

With every turn through the streets of Columbia I quickly edit the list of possible activities she might be driving me towards. I breathe a sigh of relief when we park at a movie theater. If we spend two hours of our five free hours today at a movie, perhaps Alma's Valentine's Day plans won't be bad.

Alma purchases two tickets to a comedy containing one of her favorite hunky young male actors. She turns right instead of heading straight to our theater. I assume we need popcorn and colas, but instead of the counter she leans on the bar.

"Two long Island iced teas, please."

The bartender nods. He asks which movie we plan to see. He claims he's heard many great things about our comedy. As we prepare to leave, Alma shares our theater number and assigned seats, stating we'll need two refills each spread throughout our movie.

I can only shake my head when he agrees. Patrons usually exit a movie to procure a refill. This is so Alma—she's loved by everyone. It's hard not to entertain her. The bar staff will deliver our two sets of refills just as I will drink the three Long Island iced teas she ordered for me. It seems Alma plans to get me tipsy today.

We laugh so hard during our movie that I snort twice. I'm glad on a weekday the theater is nearly empty. Alma loudly cheers during her hunks nearly naked scenes further drawing attention to us. We spend most of the movie fanning our over-heated faces.

As we giggle and lean into each other in the lobby, a college-age male approaches. I recall seeing him at church functions. It seems Alma arranged him as our Uber driver until 3 p.m. today. It's now I realize neither of us should drive with the drinks we enjoyed. The alcohol didn't affect Alma enough to let me know where we head next.

Our driver easily escorts us to a strip-mall a couple of miles from the theater. Alma instructs him to pick us up at 2:45 p.m. I guess we will shop for the two and a half hours until we pick up Liberty at three.

As she planned our adventure today, I allow Alma to lead as we glance in each storefront. We pass two clothing boutiques and a hobby shop before Alma holds a door open for me to enter the Ink, Inc. Tattoo Shoppe.

I recall Alma confessing a few weeks ago that she's often thought of getting a tattoo. I thought about it several times since then, but never mentioned it to her. She must be ready to do it today.

When Alma state she's finally getting her tattoo and I can watch, I announce I want one, too. I love the large knowing smile that graces her face. "I'd hoped you would say that. Your first tattoo is on me."

"Hello, ladies," a thirty-something heavily tattooed blonde greets approaching the counter. "I'm Wyatt. Which one of you wants a tat today?"

I scan my eyes from his sandy blonde man-bun to just below his waist where the counter obstructs my view. He's muscular but not bulky—he reminds me of Latham in his build. I've always found tattoos sexy when they don't take up every inch of skin. It's clear Wyatt likes tattoos to express himself but hasn't gone overboard. Matching sleeves from mid-forearm decorate up to disappear under his short-sleeved black skin-tight t-shirt. They contain no color, just black and shades of gray creating the Filipino Tribal designs. His only other visible art catches my eye. Low on his neck a half-dollar size, black and red Star Wars design sparks my interest. I point toward his neck while asking if I might examine it closer.

Wyatt places his forearms on the glass countertop and leans toward me. Half the circle is part of the Rebels' Logo and half is the Empire's Logo. Three heavy-poured drinks disabled my filters. I trace my fingertips on the design while biting my lip.

"It's a Star Wars design," Wyatt states a sexy smirk on his lips.

It's clear he doesn't think I know. "Which way do you lean?" I whisper. Yes, I whisper. What's up with that?

Alma clears her throat attempting to pull me from my actions.

"Light Side vs Dark Side, Jedi vs. Sith, Rebels vs. Empire," I interpret out loud my voice stronger now. "I tend to lean to the Light Side while the Dark Side attempts to creep in at night." My hand covers my mouth as I realize how my words might be interpreted. Through my fingers I explain, "I struggle with depression. Its darkness threatens 24/7, but I'm weakest to its influence at night."

Wyatt's blue eyes darken with my words. It's easy to see he appreciates my extensive knowledge of Star Wars and its resemblance to my life. I believe he knows I compare my struggles with that of Anakin Skywalker's before becoming Darth Vader.

Alma interrupts. "Both of us want tattoos today."

Wyatt stands once again speaking to Alma. "Feel free to browse the walls and these portfolios for ideas. Either of you already have art?" His dark blue eyes scan my body for hints of previous work.

"I already know what I want for my first tattoo." Alma looks to me. "My friend might need help to decide on her first."

I shake my head. "I have an idea. Do you do original designs?"

"Noel, we've got virgin skin for you." Wyatt hollers toward the back.

A gorgeous young woman peeks over the cubicles smiling, then cheers before joining us in the front.

Wyatt and Alma chat for a bit, then he secures a page from a binder on the front counter to show her. She nods and the two disappear to his station while Noel pulls a sketchpad and pencils from under the counter. "What are you envisioning?" I watch her take notes at the bottom of the page as I explain.

"I'd like a left-handed pitcher gripping a baseball ready to throw a four-seam fastball." I admire her hazel eyes with artistically applied eye shadow to further make the green pop. Her left eyebrow contains to silver hoops with tiny blue and green striped beads. Looking down I marvel at the speed in which she sketches a baseball. I startle when she hollers for Wyatt's help.

"Show me how to hold a baseball for a..." Noel's eyes glance at the bottom of her page. "A four-seam fastball." Her voice rises with her last word. She's clearly not an avid baseball fan. It's not fair to judge her, as most women aren't as versed in pitches as I am.

"If you have a ball I can show you," I offer. "I'm not sure how to explain it without actually seeing it."

Wyatt produces a weathered baseball from a tub under the counter. I chuckle as it seems weird to find a baseball in a tattoo shop. Wyatt explains it was found in the parking lot and they decided to keep it for situations just like this. He expertly positions his hand to demonstrate, while looking to me for confirmation. When I nod, he admits he pitched a bit in high school. Knowing the difference between a two- and four-seam fastball leads me to believe he pitched more than a bit. His interest peaked, Wyatt stays to see the design I chose.

Noel returns to sketching, "Glad Wyatt's a lefty. It makes visualization easier."

"I'd like the fingers in black, red stitching on the baseball, and a royal blue #1 Fan on the face of the ball."

"Nice," Wyatt praises before returning to Alma.

Noel's dimples decorate her cheeks and her eyes twinkle before her hand returns to sketching. "I love creating permanent artwork that means something to my client. Can you tell me why you chose this design? The more I know the better I can help the image come to life."

I tell her about my best friend, our high school friendship, and his teams. I'm careful not to divulge his name or which MLB team he plays for. I only share enough to help her create my image. I'm aware assuming he's from Missouri, it wouldn't be hard to find a left-handed pitcher from Missouri currently in the Majors, but Noel doesn't seem the type to put that much work into finding out anything about a sport.

I marvel at the effortless ease in which she sketches my design. "Does he still know you're his number one fan?" I nod. "Cool." She turns her sketch to face me. "Maybe one day you'll share your tattoo with him and he'll fall in love with you as much as you are in love with him."

Noel is *very* intuitive. Or am I that easy to read?

As she ushers me to her cubicle she asks where I plan to place the design. I point to my left front jeans pocket. I explain I want to be the only one to see it. She shows me where to lay and instructs me to lower my jeans and underwear to reveal the entire area. I'm glad my body faces the wall, so I won't be on display to anyone walking by.

I listen as she tugs on her black gloves and explains the safety precautions while cleaning my skin. She asks me to place my fingertips where I want the top and bottom of the baseball. She places a tiny ink pen dot at these two locations.

With equipment in hand she asks me if I'm ready. When I nervously nod she mumbles 'virgin' while shaking her head and placing the needle to my skin. I grind my teeth while holding my breath as needles inflict sharp, scratching pain upon my skin. I let out my breath and relax my jaw as I now know what to expect in terms of pain level.

I can handle this intense scratchy feeling. I had imagined extreme pain like labor pains—this is much easier. I smile realizing Hamilton will be a permanent part of me. My tattoo will remind me of his high school, minor, and major league career while also reminding me the reason I chose to keep our daughter a secret for a few years.

To anyone lucky enough to catch a glimpse of my tattoo in the future, they will only believe I am a big baseball fan. Those who know me well will know that the left hand belongs to Hamilton and could be no one else.

Noel remains quiet as she works. I enjoy the rush of adrenaline the constant pain releases. I now understand how some claim tattoos may become addictive. I feel alive.

Hamilton's FaceTime call pulls my attention from my writing. My laptop clock tells me it's 9:30 p.m. I position my pillows against my headboard as I answer.

Hamilton shares about his first day of practice with the other pitchers and catchers as they reported today. He then wishes me a Happy Valentine's Day. We discuss as we had last year how much it sucks to be alone tonight. He asks how my day was.

"Alma planned a movie and surprise shopping trip for me today."

"What movie?" Hamilton repositions himself to lie on his side facing his tablet camera.

Instead of answering I blurt, "We got tattoos!"

I watch Hamilton thin his lips between his teeth and furrow his brow. I continue, "Instead of shopping, Alma wanted to finally get her tattoo, so I got one, too."

When he asks what I got and for me to show it to him, I explain it's in a private location and only meant for me to see. He begs a couple of more times before realizing I won't share details tonight.

I shouldn't have blurted it out. I knew I wouldn't want to share the details. I wanted him to know how daring I was today, but now I realize I will field questions about my tattoo until I cave and show him. I'm grateful Hamilton states he needs to turn in and ends our call.

89

HAMILTON

Madison got a tattoo.

Now said tattoo haunts me as I try to fall asleep. My sex-starved mind imagines its location. If it had been on her arm, neck, wrist, or legs she would have shown me, or I might have seen a bandage.

Maybe it's on her ribcage and curves under her breast. I groan remembering how fine her breasts are. I bet it's some saying or quote that means something to her. I imagine her lying in my bed. As I kiss her, I unfasten and remove her lacy black bra. I trail my lips down her collarbone and around her globes. A I plan to attend to her nipple, I freeze when I glimpse the script. I trace my fingertip over each letter. Madison wriggles as my featherlight touch tickles.

My mind leaps to another option. Perhaps her tattoo is instead a red heart with words upon a scroll woven through it. As I remove her red satin panties, I spy the tattoo low, and I mean low, on her abdomen near her right hip. Her tiny panties kept the treasure hidden. First, I trace the design with my fingers then my tongue while gazing up at her face through my lashes. Her head presses back into the mattress and her back arches in pleasure.

Why didn't I stay on the phone until she gave in and showed me her new tattoo? At least then I wouldn't imagine it on every part of her soft skin. The subject of the tattoo isn't as distracting as its location is for me. My mind constantly fantasizes about Madison before the mention of a tattoo. Now my previous knowledge of her body combined with a mysterious tattoo overload my senses.

I'm never going to fall asleep this way. I contemplate calling her back to find the answers to my tattoo questions. Even if we speak, I'd still be in my current state afterwards.

I decide I must take the matter into my own hands. Literally. I opt for a shower instead of my bed. When steam fills the room, I step inside my glass shower. The hot water immediately caresses every inch of my skin. I imagine the droplets are Madison's fingertips exploring every part of me.

I squirt a drop of body wash into my palm. Slowly I glide one hand over my erect cock and groan at the sensation. My eyelids close and my head tips back as my second hand joins my first. I tighten my fist working up and down as my right-hand swirls lightly over my crown.

After an hour and a half of fantasizing in my bed and a few pumps of my fist, I'm near the edge. I lower my gaze to my left hand pumping my cock and slam my right hand on the glass wall to balance myself. I lean into my palm, rising to my toes for my final thrust as I growl Madison's name. Cumming I shudder once, twice, then a final stream of semen spurts onto the glass in front of me.

With both hands pressed on the wall, I attempt to remain standing in the wake of my release. The shower stream pummels my back and water covers every part of me. I allow myself five minutes under the relaxing spray before lathering my entire body and rinsing off.

My mind remains on Madison when I crawl back into bed, but I'm at ease. Sleep sweeps me off to dreams of moving Madison to Chicago, getting engaged, and finally starting our lives together.

90

MADISON

I shoot up from my bed. Taking in my surroundings I find I'm in my room covered from head to toe in sweat. It felt real. It was my reoccurring dream of telling Hamilton about Liberty. In tonight's episode even after meeting her, he demands a paternity test. He accuses me of becoming pregnant on purpose to get his money.

My tight chest aches with the accusation and lack of trust. I'm hurt that my closest friend might ever believe I could do such things. I know keeping my secret will cause others not to trust me in the future, but I hope that everyone will believe me when I admit Liberty is Hamilton's daughter.

91

MADISON

It's now March and I cannot believe Liberty will be one this month. The first twelve months of her life flew by. As did the off-season in which I didn't keep my promise to introduce Hamilton to his daughter. His agent kept him busy claiming remaining in the public eye keeps him in demand. Hamilton complains his agent's favorite words are 'strike while the iron is hot.' Hamilton is now back in Arizona. I know. I know. I conveniently keep putting it off.

"Have a seat," Alma greets as I enter the kitchen to prepare dinner.

"Would you like me to start dinner first?" I try to interpret Alma's stern demeanor. Is she ill or in pain? I worry about her health more with each passing day. I fear what will come of Liberty and me should something happen to her.

"We'll order pizza after we talk."

Oh no. This sounds ominous. I take a seat across from her, place my arms on the table, and tip my head for her to begin.

"When do you plan to tell Hamilton?" Alma's eyes peer into mine. Alma knows Hamilton is already in Mesa, Arizona. He returned early just as he did last year.

"I guess I'll have to wait until next October to introduce Hamilton to her." I rest my chin in my hands with elbows on the table. "I'll tell him before

Liberty turns two. I can't let it go any farther than that." I inhale deeply. "Will you make sure I tell him before next Christmas?" Perhaps I can count on her to force me to keep my word. I know she will hold me accountable.

Alma rises from her chair. She remains silent until she returns with two water bottles. She slides one over to me. "That's a long time away, are you sure you don't want to travel to Mesa now?"

If I fly to Arizona this week or next, I'd interrupt Hamilton's pre-season routines. I'd need to take Liberty with me, so Alma would need to tag along. Regardless of Hamilton's reaction to my revealing he has a daughter, this close to his season would interfere with his performance for the months that follow.

"I can't upset his world right as his pre-season starts. This is life-altering news. He needs time to process it. I have to do it during next off-season." My eyes beg Alma to validate my reasoning.

"Then next October, November, or December it will be." I breathe easier knowing she agrees. "Let's formally invite Hamilton and his family here for Christmas. We have plenty of room for three more and once he meets his daughter he will want to be near her for the holiday."

I like the idea of my two families sharing the holiday.

"When I call Memphis," Alma continues. "I'll mention you feel torn between the two families at the holidays. Perhaps that will encourage them to accept the invitation."

We discuss reaching out to Memphis in July, securing a hotel nearby for Alma's children, and now that we have a firm date in mind we can plan in greater detail as fall approaches. Alma writes on her July calendar to call Memphis about Christmas. I create an event in my iCal. I also create the event in my countdown app for December Twenty-Fourth. This will keep a count of the total days I have until I need to meet with Hamilton. I hope I find an opportunity prior to Christmas to tell Hamilton, but if not at least with Alma's help Liberty will meet the rest of her family by Christmas.

I order pizza delivery while Alma runs Liberty's bath.

While enjoying our pizza, my phone vibrates alerting an incoming call from Adrian. It's after 7:00 p.m. I send it to voicemail hoping she'll text instead. With texting I'm able to reply when it's convenient for me and I have more time to think of my responses. Texting allows me to enjoy more time with Liberty.

At the next commercial break, I excuse myself as tears begin to sting the back of my eyes. I've cried too much lately. Liberty's new achievements cause me to cry. Missing Hamilton and my friends bring tears. Just now, a cell phone commercial brought the tears I struggle to control. I pour myself another glass of wine before blotting my eyes and wiping my cheeks. I take a couple deep, calming breaths before returning to the front room.

I'm greeted by Alma's concerned eyes. I blame these tears on hormones. She raises her brow not buying my excuse.

I sip my wine as Liberty enjoys her final minutes of playtime before bath and bed time.

Liberty's birthday is this weekend. Glancing at my cell phone I peruse my list. I've planned a simple First Birthday party for the three of us. I still need to wrap her gifts and pick up the cake otherwise, I am prepared.

Liberty's voice travels through the baby monitor alerting us she's awake from her afternoon nap. I tuck my cell phone in my pocket as I ascend the stairs. On the third step, my phone rings. I pause to answer.

"Adrian is in labor," Salem's excitement is clear. "Her water broke at ten this morning and labor is progressing quickly now. They cleared the room of everyone except Winston and Adrian's mother." We chat for a bit and Salem promises to call as soon as she has news.

I scoop Liberty from her crib into my arms. She places her hands on each side of my face and plants a wet baby kiss near my mouth.

"Adrian is having her baby today," I inform my daughter. "Her birthday will be two days before your birthday. Isn't that exciting?" Liberty claps her hands as if she knows what I say.

I opt to spend my entire evening with Alma, Libby, and McGee. I check my phone often throughout the evening. As more time passes I worry about complications and shoot a text to Salem.

ME

any news?

SALEM

they wheeled her in for a C-Section over 30 minutes ago

promise to text soon

I tuck Libby in bed by eight and immediately pour two glasses of wine. After two full glasses of wine, I decide to retire for the night at 9:30 p.m.

At ten, Salem texts that Adrian and baby girl are tucked safely in their room. Both mom and baby are happy and healthy. My friend doesn't know it yet, but her daughter's birthday is two days before my daughter's. My thoughts drift to the years ahead when my secret is revealed. I imagine joint birthday parties as our girls grow up one year apart. Bethany is now five months pregnant with a baby due in July. Her son or daughter will only be four months younger than Adrian's daughter. Recently Salem revealed they are trying to conceive. Last year's theme was weddings, this year's theme is babies. With all but Savannah and I married, the rest of our gang moved on to starting families.

92

MADISON

As I arrive home from my day as a middle school physical education teacher on Friday, a rental car is parked in front of Alma's house. We weren't expecting company, at least not that I knew of. As I walk up the porch steps, Cameron opens the front door and Liberty toddles out to greet me.

"Momma," Libby cheers as she wraps her arms around my leg.

I lift her in my arms while walking toward Cameron. "What are you doing here?" I suddenly worry we had an editor's meeting I might have forgotten.

Cameron steals Libby from me. "I couldn't miss my niece's first birthday."

I shake my head. When will I ever learn to expect these family surprises? After dinner a knock at the door has Alma hopping from her chair. Trenton, Taylor, and their families spill into the house. Alma's grandchildren scramble to Libby playing on the floor.

"Am I the only one surprised here?" I ask Alma.

She explains they planned during the Christmas visit to surprise Libby and me for her first birthday. Tears well in my eyes as I realize the only thing missing will be Hamilton.

Mid-morning Saturday, Bethany's video call rings my phone. She immediately asks to see the birthday girl. I attempt to chat with Bethany as I follow behind Liberty with camera in hand as she plays with the other kids.

Bethany shares that Troy's over-protectiveness has reached a new level. At five months pregnant he now worries about pre-term labor, Bethany falling due to the size of her belly, and hurting the baby while having sex. He doesn't want her driving and insists to drive her anywhere she needs to go. He's scheduled drop-in visits each afternoon by his and her parents, to make sure she's okay.

I try to help her understand he's an excited first-time dad. He's trying to protect his family and although it's a bit over the top, he does it because he loves her. I encourage her to express her frustration and for the two of them to plan ways to let him know all is okay throughout the day, while allowing her to continue her daily activities. I mention she could text him often sometimes even just an emoji to let him know all is well.

With pregnancy hormones always in control, Bethany mentions sending him an eggplant emoji and several others to suggest he hurry home and carry her off to bed. I reprimand her for talking about sex on Liberty's birthday phone call.

At the mention of my daughter, Bethany complains she had to share her attention today with Alma's family. I corral my daughter in her nursery allowing Bethany a few minutes of Libby's attention and to wish her a happy birthday before we end our call.

To ensure no other random phone calls interrupt Liberty's party, I text Hamilton setting up a call with him after nine tonight when I am alone in my bedroom. This allows me to enjoy Liberty's birthday without the worry he'll call and wonder what all the family is doing here this weekend.

Weeks later, the bathroom mirror cruelly reflects my image back at me. With little sleep last night, I opted to skip washing my hair to lie in bed fifteen extra minutes. Dark circles like bruises under my eyes broadcast my weeks of insomnia. I make it through each day with caffeine constantly in hand.

By 8:00 p.m. I'm ready for bed. Once there, sleep refuses to arrive. Some nights I lie eyes closed in the dark for hours in hopes of sleep. As that fails, most night I write. I figure I won't be able to sleep for hours, I might as well be productive.

My new curse is a mind constantly creating two or more stories at once.

The more I write the more story ideas spark to life. For every story I complete two more take its place. I have one notebook containing lists of future story ideas—it's growing fuller by the day.

I'm proud of my notebooks full of stories. I figure if I can't sleep, I should be productive. Writing unclogs my head, works through my issues, and helps lighten my dark moods.

A FaceTime call vibrates my phone. It's Hamilton. It's been almost a month since our last call. I prop my phone on the pillow beside mine as I answer.

His tired brown eyes and a lazy smile greet me. "Hey."

"You look sleepy," I force a smile hoping it hides my own exhaustion.

"I needed to see you before I fall asleep tonight," he confesses. "I didn't wake you, did I?"

"Nope. I haven't been sleeping much." I yawn, "How was today's practice?"

Our conversation flows from our plans for the week, to what little we've heard from Athens, to how much he misses me. Hamilton apologizes for how busy he's been and states. I'm always on his mind. We close each sharing an 'I love you'.

I'm not sure the true meaning of his three little words. Once I believed we were becoming more than friends, as time passes and the distance between us grows ominous although we continue to say, 'I love you', I worry the meaning has dissipated.

Opening my phone, I confirm I'm not imagining it. Hamilton's texts transition to fewer texts and are farther apart. Last week he texted two times and this week we've only chatted once.

I scroll farther back. As I read our past conversations, I witness our interactions from Adrian's wedding all sweet and lengthy morph to quick chats of work and school then only a couple of words. Our long texts chats and calls now more often than not read 'I love you' or 'I miss you'. As time passes, we withdraw but continue to let each other know we still think of each other.

It' easier this way. Although I miss him so much it hurts, of now it's easier to hid Liberty with fewer calls where he might hear my secret in my voice or written on my face. I don't like hiding her—I regret keeping my secret. I'm taking the chicken way out to make it easier on me.

93

MADISON

I pull my cell phone close as I attempt to open my eyes. The April sunshine is bright through the blinds I forgot to close last night. It's 9:15! I hop from my bed and hurry to Liberty's crib. It's empty—Alma must already have her downstairs allowing me to sleep late. A gift every mom loves.

I find Liberty in her high chair munching on her cereal and Alma reading the newspaper with coffee in hand nearby. I pour a mug of coffee while I wait for my toast to brown. Liberty cheers when the toaster pops up.

I secure my hair in my usual ponytail. It allows me to go an extra day or two between washing it. I spend my extra minutes each morning lying in bed or cuddling Liberty.

Today I wear a long-sleeved T-shirt under my blouse. Along with added warmth, it fit better over its thickness. I need to ask Alma to help me shop for more this weekend. Just the thought of shopping exhausts me. I sigh as it's a necessary evil.

Today I cover high school woods class. I'm nervous thinking of all the ways teenagers can injure themselves with tools and saws while under my care. If I were more secure financially I would only select positions I felt comfortable in. Subbing three or four times a week will not fill my checking account and let me be picky, so today I will be a high school woods teacher.

I check Hamilton's texts from this morning. As I know his baseball schedule, Hamilton now texts me only the reasons he's too busy to call. 'Photo shoot tomorrow', 'hospital visits today', 'dinner and contracts tomorrow with' this company or that one—his texts are meant to let me know how busy he is when he can't call. Instead they further prove me right in allowing him more time to acclimate before I reveal his daughter to him.

At dinner I relive our outdoor day. I wish I could plan more days like this with Liberty and Alma. I'm lost in memories and thoughts.

"Madison," Alma interrupts our silent dinner. "Are you feeling okay?" She tilts her head and furrows her brow.

I inform her I'm fine just tired. My appetite grows smaller when I'm tired, and I've been tired a lot lately.

"You rarely eat. Your clothes are starting to hang on you. And you weren't heavy to begin with."

I hear her real meaning. She's worried. My constant lack of energy and appetite worry her. She's reaching out in hopes of pulling me out of my ongoing funk. I don't mean to worry her. I need to make an effort to ease her worries.

I cringe when Hamilton's FaceTime call rings late Sunday evening. The Cubs were home this afternoon—I should have realized there was a small chance he'd call tonight. I glance around my bed covered with notebooks scattered around me before I accept the call on my Mac with a smile upon my face.

"Wow," his warm masculine voice hugs me from afar. "You're writing I see."

"Let's chat for a few minutes then I'll let you get back to work so you don't forget what you are writing." Hamilton licks his lips before beginning. "How are you?"

Wow. Please tell me he didn't call for idle chit-chat. I don't have the patience for this.

"I'm good, just busy."

"Madison," Hamilton's tone pierces my outer armor. "It's me. I may be busy and too many miles away, but I see you. I see more than you want me to." He clears his throat and runs his fingers through his hair. "I know *it's* back and it is time you start treatment again."

My eyes sting as tears threaten. I've tried to text more than call as my appearance hints I am struggling. Hamilton and Memphis have been down this road with me a few times in the six years they've shared their home with me.

"I know you don't need me to point out how I know. So, let's move on to discussing what's going on and how we plan to work through it."

My hackles rise, and I prepare to tell him it's none of his business. How dare he try to help me from his perfect life in the spotlight high in his condo overlooking Chicago. I want to fight, I want to hang up, I want to be alone with Alma and Liberty. But I'm too tired to fight against him. I'm tired of being tired.

I wipe my tears before I nod. It's all Hamilton needs to know I'm in need of his help yet again. He offers to make appointments with my physician and counselor for me. He knows Memphis helped with this in the past.

"I saw a counselor down here last winter. I'll go online and schedule an appointment." As much as I want to curl into a ball and hide in my bed 24/7, I know from past experiences talking helps, and I need to get better for Liberty. She deserves me at my best.

"Don't!" Hamilton's adamancy startles me. "Don't go there. It's not the same and you know it."

Of course, he knew I'd compare myself to my mother. Her depression and her alcoholism took her from me after dad's death.

"You are stronger than her," Hamilton promises. "you seek help when you need it. You do what it takes to get better." His eyes attempt to slip through my armor—they implore me to believe. "Do you want me to call Doc in Athens to get a referral? He attended Mizzou—I'm sure he knows someone close by you can see. I know you hat the side-effects, but the meds have worked in the past for you."

"I'll call doc in the morning." Hamilton tilts his head while squinting. "I promise I will call.' I put as much feeling into my words as I can. He contemplates my sincerity. I realize he is remembering me making promises in the past I didn't keep. "I'll send you a pic of my script."

Hamilton apologizes. He explains he trusts me but knows the illness might prevent me from following through. Someday I hope to be deserving of his trust. Until I share Liberty with him and begin to see my way out of the current darkness, I am not worthy of his trust.

Hamilton vows to check-in more often. He urges me to email or text anytime about anything. Although he may not be able to reply right away he promises he will read them. He asks my permission to talk to his mother about tonight's conversation. When I agree, we say goodbye and I return to writing my current story.

94

HAMILTON

Stan approaches my area in the locker room minutes before we take the field. "We still on for our post-game celebration?" he keeps his voice low not wanting teammates to invite themselves to join us.

I nod while my eyes scan our surroundings. No one seems to care about our conversation. "The Mrs. Okay with you not coming straight home from the game?" The last thing I want is for her to kick him out again. I rather like having my condo to myself.

"She knows *how* we are celebrating and agrees I shouldn't allow you to celebrate alone." Stan pats me twice on my shoulder. "Let's go start the season of in the win-column."

I follow Stan and our teammates from the locker room onto the field. Crowds at Wrigley Field are always loud, but this Opening Day crowd is electric. Their excitement carries over from our successful season last year. We were one win away from the World Series. It's contagious. My muscles spark to life as I am introduced. I wave to my fans before assuming my position for the National Anthem.

I sing every word as I remember myself on the ballfield in Athens as our announcer played a recording of the high school choir singing these same words. I love the game of baseball as much today as I did years ago.

"Here we are," Stan parks his Land Rover in front of Ink, Inc. "You know when you mentioned wanting to get a tattoo on opening day, I thought it was pretty lame." Stan pulls his eyes from the tattoo parlor and turns to face me in his driver's seat. "I mean the guys head to bars and nightclubs. But the more I thought about all the trouble they get into, I realized this is a much safer celebration."

"The less you hang with those guys the less trouble you get in at home," I tease remembering Stan's one-night stand last October and his wife's reaction that led to him inhabiting my sofa for several weeks.

"We gonna stay in the car like a chicken shit or are we gonna man up and ink your skin?"

I punch Stan's shoulder and exit his vehicle. I position myself with my back toward Ink, Inc. quickly take a picture, type 'celebrating our win', post it to Snap Chat as my story as well as, send the snap directly to Madison.

'Want me to play the role of your Instagram boyfriend to take several pictures throughout your celebration?" Stan teases. "First, we'll pose you with your hands in the shape of a heart. Then…"

"Finish that statement and I'll send a pic of you standing near a random woman to your wife."

"Not cool, man."

"Neither was your Instagram boyfriend comment." Stan pats me on the back and we enter the parlor.

95

MADISON

Alma and I share our plans for the day. It's supposed to be a warm late-April day, so I propose a long walk to the park. Alma likes my plan. When breakfast is over, I carry Libby up to change from her pajamas. We giggle and play as she attempts to run around in only her diaper. Eventually I win and wrestle her into her first outfit of the day.

Liberty and I are still laughing as we approach the top of the stairs at the same time Alma opens the front door. We made so much noise I didn't hear the doorbell. I stand frozen holding Liberty in my arms as Adrian stares at me while holding her baby carrier. My heart pounds loudly in my chest as my palms begin to sweat. Her eyes are locked on mine, there is no way she doesn't see us.

This is karma for not divulging my secret by now. I knew this day would come, I just wanted to control the narrative. I mentally berate myself for not telling Hamilton already. I gather myself as I descend the stairs. Liberty waves at our guests. Alma recognizes Adrian from our many video calls and stands frozen in the doorway. I'm sure she's as shocked as I am.

I hug Adrian awkwardly with Libby on my hip and over her baby carrier. "What are you doing all the way down here?" My voice squeaks showing my surprise. "Alma, please help Adrian come inside."

Alma snaps back to the present inviting Adrian to come in while assisting her with the diaper bag. I keep Libby on my lap to prevent her investigating the new baby.

"I missed my best friend. I spend too much time at home alone, so I decided to drive down and surprise you." She tilts her head while squinting at Libby. "But you win. Your surprise beats my surprise visit." Adrian pulls her daughter, Isabella, from her carrier.

Here we go—I can avoid this no longer. I allow my squirming daughter down and she toddles close to Adrian to get a better look. Liberty places her palms on Adrian's knees while she peeks at the sleeping infant. Alma excuses herself to the kitchen for drinks.

"She looks just like Hamilton," Adrian blurts before I may explain. "Funny though, my friend denied on more than one occasion having 'taken a nap' with him." I want to smile at her signaling air quotes with her free hand while talking in code.

"I didn't lie. I promise. If you look closely you will see there is no way that I 'took a nap' with anyone in the off season. It happened in early June before he went to Des Moines. I've wanted to tell all of you, but I have to wait until I tell him."

"Momma," Liberty's voice draws my attention. She points at the tiny baby in Adrian's arms. She looks back to me and nods her head. This is her way of asking permission.

Adrian sensing Libby's desire to see the baby suggests, "Let's give the baby to your mommy and I will help you get closer." Scooting next to me on the sofa Adrian extends her six-week-old daughter to me. "Bella, this is Madison," Adrian's voice morphs into the tone of a mother.

I cuddle her tiny, bald baby. "Hi, Bella." My free hand straightens her tiny pink headband. No doubt Adrian places it on her head so others know she is a girl. "She's so tiny."

"I'm sure this one was once that tiny," Adrian retorts while lifting Libby into her lap so my daughter can see.

"Actually, she was 9 lbs. 3 oz and 23" long at birth. I don't think Bella is quite there yet. I didn't get the opportunity to hold anyone this tiny." I smile at Adrian. "Liberty, this is mommy's friend Adrian." I point and Liberty smiles. "Adrian, this is my daughter Liberty. We call her Libby."

Adrian greets Libby, but my daughter is more interested in the tiny one in my arm. She points at Bella then looks up at Adrian. "Can you say baby? Baby?"

Libby shakes her head then extends her arms. I imagine she thinks Bella is a baby doll like the ones we play with most evenings.

"Libby go get your baby and show it to Adrian." She climbs down and toddles to her toy basket beside Alma's rocking chair. She doesn't show it to Adrian. Instead she plops down and proceeds to pull every toy out of the basket onto the carpet around her. Her short attention span allows me to talk to Adrian.

96

MADISON

"So, Hamilton doesn't know?" Adrian prompts raising her brow.

I explain to Adrian the events that occurred after the bonfire party his last night in town. Then I share my fear the day I took the pregnancy test. "After my initial freak out, I realized if I told Hamilton I was pregnant he would give up baseball and takeover the farm in Athens." I glance down at Bella before I continue. "You know I'm right. There is no way he would have chased his baseball dream and I couldn't be the reason he gave it up. I plan to tell him. I planned to tell him this past winter, but he was so busy that Salem's wedding is the only time we could get together. I didn't want to take away from Salem's special day and I can't tell him over the phone. I wanted to let him settle into Major League Baseball so when I introduced Liberty to him, he would consider continuing his baseball career."

"Adrian, I love him so much it is killing me to keep them apart." I don't fight my tears. "He wouldn't have given it a second thought. He would have taken over his family farm so that he could provide the security and financial support we would need. Then every time he drove by the ballpark or watched a game on TV he would have resented me for getting pregnant. I just couldn't steal his dream from him." I wipe my tears as I clear my throat.

"Liberty turned one on March 10th. I was so excited when you gave birth to Bella two days before Libby's birthday. During all of our video calls when Bethany and you discussed your children growing up together, I longed for you to know about my daughter and realize our children are just a year apart."

Adrian wipes tears from her eyes. I know it is the post-partum hormones as my friend Adrian is too strong to cry. I knew she hates feeling weak, so I ignore them.

"She's gorgeous. I love her curls and her dark eyes. And she has her daddy's height, too. There's no way anyone can deny she is Hamilton's little girl." Adrian pulls her eyes from Libby playing on the floor and returns them to me. "It's got to be hard looking at her every day and her reminding you of Hamilton while he is so far away."

I share with Adrian our love for watching Hamilton pitch during Cubs games. I tell her about the many video-journal clips I have created for him. I share how Alma assists me in caring for Libby while I am on the phone with Hamilton or the girls, how she cares for her when I must return to Athens, how her three children have adopted me as their little sister, and how I struggle every day to plan a time and way to talk to Hamilton.

"I've purchased a twelve-month calendar and keep it on my desk in my room. I asked Alma to ensure that I introduce Liberty to Hamilton before the end of the year. Each day I cross off knowing I am getting closer to the day I will tell him. He'll be done with his season in October. I will then have two months to make it happen." My tears return.

"Adrian, I've put it off for too long. I worry by delaying another year, I may hurt any chance I have of being with Hamilton after he meets Liberty. I've always intended tell him. I only postponed so that he could settle in the MLB. I love him, and I want him to play baseball. I just couldn't take that away from him." Tears trail down my cheeks—I wipe them before they can fall on a sleeping Bella. I lift her tiny head, so I can place a kiss upon her forehead.

"He loves you, too." I lift my eyes from Bella in my arms toward her mother. "His kiss at Salem's wedding proves his intentions. He wants you." Adrian pauses to wave at Libby when she turns her way. "Did Hamilton share anything while the two of you were at his mom's? Any clues to how he wants the relationship to work?"

Liberty stands and toddles to me. "Dada?" She points at Adrian. My adorable daughter heard Adrian refer to Hamilton by name. "Dada?"

I extend my arm around her waist and lift her into the open side of my lap. "Yes, Adrian said Hamilton."

Libby waves at Adrian. "Dada..." She continues jabbering words that I have no idea what she is saying.

Adrian smiles at me. I tell her about the photos of Hamilton we keep visible and how we watch him pitch and point to him on the TV. With her short attention span, Libby slides down and turns to me. She says Alma's name and I let her know she can go find Alma in the kitchen.

While I look at Bella I answer Adrian's questions. "We didn't discuss a relationship, per se. He was very drunk when I got him home on Saturday. He barely made it to his bedroom before he began vomiting. He laid on the bathroom floor and got sick all down the front of him. When he took off his t-shirt it got in his hair. I had to undress him and put him into the shower. He was better after that, so I went to my room. I couldn't sleep. Hours later, I went to the bathroom and popped my head in just to check on him. He was awake and spotted me. Knowing how I struggle to sleep, he invited me to lay beside him." I shrug and sigh before I share the rest of the events from the next morning. Of course, Adrian asks for every detail when I confess we had sex again. Unlike her, I don't share in great detail.

"So, he laid that kiss on you in front of all of us to let us know he loves you. But he didn't plan out times for the two of you to meet, date, and stuff?" Now knowing all the details, Adrian seems as confused as I am.

Liberty runs into the living room announcing Alma's name. Alma follows her, places drinks on the coffee table, announces I have hogged Bella long enough, and steals her from my arms.

Later, as we eat a light lunch Alma prepared Adrian fake pouts across from me. When I inquire what's wrong she asks if Bethany has already met Liberty. I remind her Bethany's trip to Columbia was a surprise and I didn't plan for her to learn my secret before anyone else. I ask if Bethany knew Adrian was driving down today and she states she only told Winston at breakfast this morning. Good. I hope Bethany would have called to warn me if she knew what Adrian had planned.

Our afternoon together flies by. Adrian plays with Libby while Alma and I take turns holding Bella. Mid-afternoon Adrian leaves in order for her to arrive home before dark. At the end of it all, I'm glad Adrian surprised me today—I'm glad she now knows. Bethany and Adrian's reactions give me hope that Hamilton, his family, and my other friends will understand my reasoning when I introduce Liberty.

97

MADISON

My attempt to remain far, far away from Athens on Mother's Day weekend fails this year. I plan a day trip on Saturday to attend Troy's graduation from Athens Community College and Bethany's baby shower. When I agreed to attend, I informed my friends that I would not be spending the night—I claimed I wanted to spend Mother's Day with Alma when really, I plan to spend the day with my daughter. Of course, Adrian and Bethany know my real Mother's Day plans.

I recently developed a new addiction—I enjoy listening to audiobooks of my favorite reads. After I read a book once and sometimes twice, I download it on Audible. I listen via my phone while I drive, clean, or lay in bed at night. On my drive to Athens today, I am enjoying Cambria Hebert's *Hashtag Series*. I've already read the series twice. My three-hour drive flies by as I enjoy the stories yet again.

I hit town twenty minutes before the graduation ceremony is slated to begin. I stop quickly to refill my gas tank for the drive home later today. At the college, I park along the street and slip into my saved seat with five minutes to spare.

Our gang does our best to embarrass Troy. Adrian blows her air-horn while the rest of us cheer loudly. Troy turns to the crowd points in our direction then raises both hands in rock-devil-horns while sticking out his tongue.

Many in the crowd laugh at his antics. We on the other hand know we didn't embarrass him in the least.

Following the graduation ceremony, Troy and Bethany's family join us at the Christian Church for lunch and Bethany's baby shower. Their parents decided to combine the two celebrations into one event. Bethany's mother arranged for it to be at their church as it was one of the only venues big enough for both families and our group of friends.

Bethany looks amazing at seven months pregnant. Today I've seen first-hand the extreme level of Troy's overprotectiveness. Bethany shares new stories every time we talk, but seeing it live in person makes it more ridiculous. Bethany's parents drove her to and from graduation. Troy immediately places her in a chair, then waits on her hand-and-foot. She's only allowed to stand for her frequent visits to the restroom—even then Troy hovers.

I realize Bethany and Troy love spending time with their families, but this baby shower is out of control. I attempt to do a headcount but fail twice as people move around visiting and paying no attention to Bethany opening her two eight-foot tables full of gifts. If I average the two headcounts, there are at least forty people here. Young children run between chairs and tables unsupervised by their parents. Older relatives stand on one side loudly carrying on their conversation about The Farmer's Almanac's predictions for this summer, fall, and what it means for the crops. I struggle to focus on my friend and the reason we are all here at this moment. When their nearby conversation moves to recent deaths amongst their friends, I can take it no more.

"Excuse me," I interrupt as I approach their group. "This is Bethany's baby shower. Her *first* baby shower. I drove over three hours to be here today. This is not the time to discuss death and funerals loud enough they can hear you in the sanctuary. Please move your conversation outside or sit down and quietly watch Bethany and Troy open the baby gifts." I stomp back to my chair, throwing a glare over my shoulder. I dare them to defy me, but I hope I didn't upset Bethany—she's the only one I care about. If anyone else didn't like my actions they can suck it. I want to celebrate with my friend.

When the elderly group grab their coats to leave, Bethany blows me a kiss before she returns to opening the baby stroller Alma and I purchased for her. It's the same model we use with Liberty as we walk McGee. I hope she enjoys it as much as I do.

Opening the baby gifts takes as long as Troy's graduation ceremony.

Bethany rolls her neck and Troy massages her shoulders. She rubs her lower back and removes her ballet flats to wiggle her toes. I hope both families witness her exhaustion and leave soon. I hug Bethany and apologize for my outburst. Troy assures me I wasn't the only one annoyed. I inform Troy he needs to get her home in the next thirty minutes. She needs to put her feet up and be waited on for the rest of the day. I mention a massage would be a nice touch, too. I hug Bethany one more time, she whispers in my ear to hug Libby for her, and I leave.

98

MADISON

I know I shouldn't drive by. I already know her car is there, yet I find myself driving by the corner bar. Just as I thought. It's not even 4:00 p.m. on a Saturday and she is drinking. I'm not surprised she's here—I am only surprised by what I do next.

I park my car in the tiny gravel lot and walk into the Black Jack bar. The smell of stale beer and smoke assault my senses. My eyes struggle to focus in the dark space. The walls and ceiling are all painted black. The tables, chairs and bar stools don't match—some are even held together with gray tape. I easily spot my mother. She's leaning on the bar with a man on either side of her. The bartender and two men look my way as I enter. My mother doesn't bother turning her head.

Henrietta, the bartender, claims she's happy to see me back in Athens. I don't want her to get her hopes up. I don't plan to stick around. I won't be available for her to call to pick up my mother. That hasn't changed.

Even with Henrietta greeting me by name, my mother doesn't acknowledge my presence. I figure it's because she has already had too much.

I call to my mother, when she doesn't turn, I tap her on the shoulder. The man on her left places his arm out to steady her as she jerkily turns to look over her shoulder my way. Her eyes barely open and she speaks not a word.

"Just stopped in to say hello. It's been almost two years and I haven't

367

heard from you. I'm glad to see you're not dead, nothing has changed, and you're still having fun. Guess I will stop by here to say hello in another two years." I hate my cold words.

I leave the bar and return to my car with my head held high and shoulders back. She doesn't define me. I am a good mother. I love my daughter. I'll never abandon Liberty the way my mother abandoned me years ago. I don't cry as I drive through Athens. I have no tears left for her just as she has none for me. I must be crazy to hope she will ever change. I was crazy to drive over here and go inside. It won't phase her, and she doesn't deserve my time.

I decide to treat myself hoping to change my mood before the long drive home. I purchase some cheese tots and a vanilla diet cola from the Sonic Drive-In. With a drink and a snack, I return to my audio book and head to the place I want to be most—Liberty is my everything.

99

MADISON

Our plan seems to be working. I limit my substitute-teaching to three days a week. Every day, I schedule me-time like showering or soaking in the bathtub, reading a book, giving myself a manicure or pedicure, doing things for me. Liberty greets me at the door each afternoon I teach. Her unconditional love and contagious smile bring light to my world.

On the days I don't teach, I attend counseling appointments then Liberty and I take a quick nap together enjoying our sleepy cuddles. With our naps I'm not tired all the time and still get a full night's sleep most nights. My depression meds are working. They make me feel like I'm living my life in a thick haze, but my new doctor likes the progress I've made. He claims we will adjust my dosage again soon.

Our evenings contain walks through the neighborhood, meals at the table, and a fifteen-minute break after every hour spent on work. With Alma's help, I better schedule my work and personal times. I will always need to work evenings and weekends to plan lessons or grade papers, but by balancing work and personal time, it seems easier.

It's a long uphill battle. I'm constantly struggling to swim against the current, but with the help of Alma and Hamilton I have the stamina I need. My days and nights contain more light than darkness now. With each passing week, the darkness continues to shrink. I can see a light at the end of the tunnel and I can fight this battle for me and for Liberty.

100

MADISON

I smile down at my sleeping daughter comfy in her crib. I tuck a wispy curl away from her closed eye. She plays at one-hundred miles per hour all day then crashes hard at nap and bed time.

My phone rings loudly from my bedroom. I turn off the lamp and pull the nursery door halfway as I return to my room.

"Hey, I thought you might be dodging my call tonight."

Hamilton's voice wraps me like a fleece blanket. I assure him I was just out of my room and not avoiding him. I sit yoga-style on my bed. I place my cell phone on two pillows in front of me, so I can relax my arms.

We chat about Hamilton's travel today and tomorrow's game in Arizona. I share about my week teaching summer school and the many teaching positions I continue to apply for in hopes of securing a job for fall.

"Don't get too hung up on the job search," concern laces his voice. "Remember it's a numbers game. You should reward yourself for each one you apply for."

"Ham, I'm good. Really." I know he worries I might slide backwards. "I met with my doctor today. We've lowered my dosage for the second time. I'm on the lowest dose now. I still see my counselor twice each month. I feel good —I really do. I'm not trying to fake that I'm good for your benefit."

With Alma's help, I've mastered scheduling time for myself every day. I balance work, motherhood, and personal time. I continue to marvel at Alma's wisdom. I've started to fill a notebook with all the things I've learned while living with her.

"I believe you. It's just I know how excited you are to teach, and I hate that you haven't been offered a contract yet."

"About that…"

I'm glad Hamilton brought the topic up. I share that recently my work with Cameron and D.C. Bland Publishing I've enjoyed focusing more on my writing. Part of me feels guilty for seeking a degree in education and not using it to help children.

Hamilton states my young-adult books might help students experiencing similar situations. I'm using my degree in a different way. He claims when I earn my spot on the NY Times Best Sellers List I will reach more people than I could in a brick and mortar classroom.

I love that Hamilton supports my writing and possible career change. Sometimes I forget he is my number one fan.

"Why are you smiling?"

At my words, his sexy smile morphs into his patented smirk. Like it always does his smile, dimples, and dark stubbled jaw spark a fire in my belly while dampening my panties. My heartbeat quickens. I fight the urge to fan my overheated face aware that Hamilton can see me.

"You come alive when you talk about your writing. It's sexy."

"Sexy?"

Hamilton smirks but doesn't explain. My mind reels as my body continues to react to the words and sight of the man I love upon my phone screen. Hamilton quickly ends our call arousing my suspicion I might affect him as he does me.

I'm aware I won't be able to focus on writing or sleep until I remedy my current situation. Instead of fantasizing Hamilton in bed with me as I pleasure myself, tonight I imagine he's masturbating to thoughts of me while I masturbate to thoughts of him.

101

MADISON

In late-June during the last week of summer school, my administrator interrupts my class stating I have an important call. My mind races to Liberty with Alma and hundreds of horrible things that might have happened.

"I'll cover your class. I was told you need to check your cell phone."

I grab my phone from the outside pocket of my laptop case and dart from the room. My fingers scroll through several missed calls and texts from Alma, Adrian, and Salem. Once outside, I stop to read the texts in the order they were received. Bile rises in my throat, my legs give out, and I sit on the sidewalk.

"Adrian..."

"Madison, oh thank God, it's Bethany. Someone side-swiped her mother's car, her water broke, and she started having contractions." Adrian struggles to catch her breath through her tears. "Troy called on his way from St. Joe to tell me they were transferring her to North Kansas City Hospital. I can't remember what he said the reason was. I'm terrible at this, I'm sorry. I should have written everything down, but I was in shock. Madison, it's too early." Sniffles fill my ear. She can't lose this baby, too."

"Adrian," I firmly interrupt her hysteria. "She'll be okay. She's made it thirty-six weeks. Yes, it's early, but in Kansas City they see this more often." Through the phone, I hear Adrian's breathing slow. "It's a good thing they didn't keep her in Athens. The sooner she gets to the city, the better it will be for the baby. Now, is Winston with you?" Adrian states he is on his way home and Salem is on her way over, too. I ask about Bella and Adrian tells me she is napping.

"Okay, I'm going to stay on the line until Winston or Salem arrive. Honey can you go get a drink of water? Bella's going to need you when she wakes up." I try to distract Adrian from her frantic thoughts. I listen as she makes her way into the kitchen, opens the refrigerator, and guzzles from a water bottle.

"What now?"

"I don't know. I don't think I can drive to KC today. Alma's been with Liberty all day and I have to teach summer school for two more days. I'm sure Winston will drive Salem and you down, so the two of you will have to give me updates."

"Madison…" Adrian's faint voice pauses for a hiccup.

"She'll be alright. She's taken good care of herself. Both Bethany and the baby will be fine."

"Promise?" Adrian whispers. I hear the sound of a door in the background. Adrian calls to Winston. There's a muffled sound against the phone over which I can hear Adrian's sobs again. The sound against the phone grows louder.

"Madison," Winston's deep voice greets. "What can you tell me?"

I share what I was able to get from Adrian, which isn't much. I mention Salem is on her way to meet them. He tells me he'll drive the girls down to the city and he'll send me updates. I thank him, ask him to take good care of my girls, and to drive safely.

I take a moment to gather myself in the restroom. I lift a little prayer up for Bethany, Troy, and the baby. As I exit planning to return to class the final bell rings—classes are over for the day. I slowly make my way back to the classroom as students scurry out the door. With each day this week their excitement grows to begin summer like their friends.

On my drive home, my thoughts are on Bethany and Troy. I don't allow myself to think of them losing their baby. I need to be at home, holding Liberty in my arms until I hear an update from KC. I desperately need the comfort Alma and my daughter will provide.

102

MADISON

Hours pass. I busy myself playing in the back yard with Libby and McGee until storms threaten. Inside we play with building blocks and read several books. At 7:00 p.m. Alma encourages me to shoot a text requesting an update. I decide to send a group text in hopes that one of my friends has a moment to let me know if there is any update.

ME

anxious to hear if you have an update

Moments pass. I force the fear that attempts to overtake me back to the pit of my stomach. I ask Alma to keep an eye on Libby while I take a minute. I slip out to the back porch. A summer storm brews around us. Angry, dark clouds approach from the west, the winds pick up speed, and the temperature drops ten degrees. It would be easy to let this tumultuous weather influence my mood, but storms don't bring me down—they rejuvenate me. As a child, I thought I would like to be a weather-chaser and study meteorology. I've always been drawn to changes in the weather.

My silent phone in hand, I say another prayer. The wind picks up again and rain begins to fall from the oppressive clouds above.

"Mama," Liberty's soft voice calls from the screen door.

I turn to find her palms flat on either side of her face pressed to the screen. She's not smiling—she senses my mood. I open the door, scooping her into my arms and place a kiss on both her cheeks. I point to the clouds and rain while talking to her about the weather. I extend her fist over the railing of the porch allowing several sprinkles to wet her palm. Liberty squeals pulling her hand back giggling. As her mother, I love experiencing the world for the first time through her eyes. Libby extends her palm wanting me to help her catch the raindrops again. Her innocence and eagerness to explore lightens my heart.

When I place Libby on the kitchen floor while I latch the back door, she runs to the front room yelling for Alma. I smile knowing she babbles to share about the raindrops with Alma. Of course, she doesn't have the vocabulary yet, but she will continue as if we understand her. I follow behind her and share the raindrop story for Alma.

We bathe Liberty, place her in pajamas and each read a book to her before she finally falls asleep. Alma meets me at the bottom step with a glass of red wine. We settle in our favorite reading spots for the rest of the night. I understand my friends are scared, but with each half hour I don't hear from them my fears begin to replace my positivity regarding Bethany's baby. It's another hour before I receive a reply to my text.

WINSTON

it's a girl!

Bethany is fine, baby in NICU

Adrian will text soon

At the sound of the text alerts, Alma moved beside me to read with me. We breathe a sigh of relief. Alma fetches the bottle of wine from the kitchen suggesting we have another glass to celebrate before we turn in.

Later in my room, Adrian and Salem text me. They report Bethany is exhausted but healthy and happy. Salem calls me claiming it is too much to text. As Winston drives back to Athens, Adrian and Salem fill me in on speaker phone. Bethany's daughter is tiny and the doctors state she might be in the Neonatal Intensive Care Unit for a couple of days while her tiny lungs struggle to provide oxygen and she fights jaundice. She weighs 4 lbs. 8 oz. and they haven't shared her name yet.

My girls report Troy is an even bigger mess now than he was during the pregnancy. He's torn between his daughter and wife's room. They have no idea how he was able to drive to the hospital when he left the police academy in St. Joe today. I explain he must have had his guardian angel on his shoulder the entire way and the girls agree.

Adrian shares Winston went to a nearby store for food and toiletries for Troy. He plans to decide in the morning if he can leave for the academy or not. He's much closer from the hospital than he is driving back and forth to Athens.

I claim I need to get to sleep so I can face my fifteen students in the morning. I thank Winston for driving my girls before we all say goodbye. I send a text about Bethany and the baby to Hamilton and inform Alma in her room before I turn off my light. With good news from KC and two glasses of wine in me, I quickly drift to sleep.

Over the next three days both Troy and Bethany text us photos and updates. Their daughter, Jameson or Jami as they will call her, improves every day. Troy continues to attend the police academy each day and spend his evenings with his girls. Bethany is discharged on the second day—her family secures a hotel room nearby for Troy and her to sleep in when they are forced to leave the hospital each day.

103

MADISON

As little Jameson begins day number seven in North Kansas City Hospital, an alert signals I have a text messages from Bethany.

BETHANY

going home today

Jami weighed 5 lbs this morning

my mom going to stay with me until the weekend

then Troy will be home

please give us a day or two to settle in

then we will text/call you

(heart emoji)

In the weeks that follow, Bethany continues her video calls to see Liberty. Now, I also get to see Jami during our calls. Bethany is the mother I always knew she would be. She's bubbly all the time. She makes her own wet wipes which probably means she will make her own baby food in the months to come. She even uses cloth diapers—I cringe at the thought. As a stay-at-home mom she is able to spend much more time on parenting than I was. I am happy for her.

She continues to care for two other children during week days. She shares Troy loves the police academy and shares stories of bruises from handcuff training, as well as, the pain of pepper spray training. His training runs from 8-5 every week day. The toughest part is the three hours he spends on the road each day. He's committed to making it work for the 23-week course. Then he will wait two months for his twenty-first birthday to be eligible to work as a police officer. The Athens police department plans to give him more hours as a dispatcher while he waits. His dream is becoming a reality.

I'm happy that busy with his long days of training, Troy now enjoys time with his wife and daughter instead of his former overprotective ways. The new parents enjoy every moment of parenthood. Troy jokes about the long nights, dirty diapers, and spit-up. With large families nearby and frequent visits from friends Bethany and Troy overcame the heartache of a miscarriage and now have found their happily ever after.

104

MADISON

With summer school now over, I plan to enjoy my free time with Liberty and Alma. I still have no teaching contract for fall. Instead of continuing to apply for positions, I am focusing on my writing.

My work continues with Cameron and Bland Publishing. My first book will release next month with another to follow in September. The next two books are tentatively scheduled for January and April of next year. My unplanned venture into the world of an author is amazing. I find myself writing a bit every day often at night after Liberty falls asleep. I created a "To Be Written" Note on my phone that I am constantly writing new story ideas when they pop into my head and later enter them into my ideas notebook. While I continue to morph my previously written young adult stories for publication, I have new ideas for new adult and romance titles in my future.

My friends in Athens are crushing this adult thing. Winston and Adrian continue to run successful businesses while raising their beautiful daughter Bella. Adrian sneaks in a private video call from time to time while Winston golfs to catch a glimpse of Liberty and ask for parenting advice.

Salem loves her job as an LPN and helping Latham on the farm every moment she isn't at the hospital. She shared they are expecting a baby in February in our last text session.

Savannah continues to work fifty hours a week in the bakery. She offers to babysit on date nights for the other couples, while she seems to enjoy her single life. She and I are the only single ladies remaining in our group.

The ladies and I continue our Sunday evening video calls, but instead of weekly we talk on the first Sunday of each month. It's still only for us girls, but now Bella and Jami join us from time to time. Adrian and Bethany remain the only two friends that know about my daughter. Our friendships have strengthened by sharing parenting stories while they keep my secret.

The Chicago Cubs continue to have a record season. They currently lead the division by ten games. The World Series Talk grows more with each passing week. I hope this is the season I get to witness Hamilton pitch in the World Series. Alma, Liberty, and I watch every game Hamilton is on the mound. On nights he doesn't pitch the games are still on, but we listen more than we watch. Go Cubs!

Alma enjoys her busy life. We walk in our neighborhood and to the park. She is healthy and active in the church. My work with Cameron allows her to visit Alma more than ever before. Frequent visits from her three children and four grandchildren are her favorite times. With my help she's started video calls with her family and still joins me on mine with the girls in Athens.

The idea my college advisor had for me to live with Alma while attending college continues to prove advantageous for both of us. I would be lost without her guidance and help with Liberty. As our bond strengthens, I grow closer to my new adopted family. I can't imagine what my life would be like had I not met Alma. With her support I've completed my degree and, in a few weeks, will be a published author. Her time spent with Liberty eases my stress and saves me tons of money. She's introduced me to a supportive church family along with my new adopted siblings. My life is full because she's in it.

McGee and Liberty are best friends and partners in crime. They keep Alma and me on our toes both inside and outside the house. We enjoy our walks, playtimes, and frequent cuddles with both of them.

Hamilton and I continue to chat or text several of times per week. We haven't been together since Salem's late-December wedding, yet I think we are a couple in our own way. Hamilton now tells me he loves me and misses me during every call. He shares much more about his relationships with coaches and teammates and asks more details about my writing and new adopted-family. Although we live far apart we are closer than we've ever been, except for the gigantic secret part of my life I still keep from him.

Over the past two years my life took a different path than planned. It's not how I imagined life away from Athens—it's better in so many ways. I'm not sure what my relationship with Hamilton will be when I share about our daughter this winter. For now, I enjoy his distant love and presence in my life via our phones. It's not a conventional relationship, but I'm happy, hopeful, and it's all I have time for in my life right now.

TAILGATES & FIRST DATES

The Locals #3

105

HAMILTON

I glance at my phone one more time—she texted again.

MADISON

I want to be a fly on the wall of bullpen 2nite

World Series (baseball emoji)

Have fun!

(heart emoji) you

I glance around the locker room to ensure no one's watching. I don't want the guys to have fodder for teasing.

ME

wish you were here

(heart emoji) you

I'm beginning to worry. if I'm this nervous for game one, how nervous will I be when I am the starter in games four and seven? I turn my cell phone off then tuck it into my suit jacket in my locker. I kiss my index finger and press it to my favorite picture of Madison. In profile, she's looking at me and laughing on the tailgate of my truck near the start of our senior year.

I miss her laughter, and I miss her attending all of my games. I miss her.

"Time to go," Stan yells through the locker room. "That means you, too." He swats my ass with his ball glove.

Side-by-side we walk, the last two to leave the locker room. "You ready for this?" I ask the centerfielder.

"Waited for this my whole life." Stan states the obvious.

I wish my dad were here. I scan the crowd, noticing many fathers with sons in the stands. There's an empty seat somewhere that my dad should be sitting in. I wish he were alive to see me pitch in the World Series. I like to think he's on my shoulder. I miss our long talks—I could use his advice. In my heart, I know what he'd tell me.

First the World Series, then focus on making Madison mine.

Madison

It's really happening–tonight the Chicago Cubs play the New York Yankees in the first game of the World Series. Alma and I plan to order pizza again—we must keep our post-season tradition alive. I take Liberty and McGee to the park for a couple hours in hopes of wearing them out.

Hamilton will pitch in the fourth and possibly seventh games in the series. My stomach flip-flops every time I remember that Memphis and I have tickets to game four in Chicago. Last night, Alma's daughter, Taylor, called to brag that they have tickets to games three and four. I wish we could find a ticket for Alma, but I'm glad she'll care for Liberty while I attend the game.

As if I'm not nervous enough, my phone buzzes non-stop for an hour. My high school friend in Athens is first.

ADRIAN

I'm so nervous

I can't sit still

I've cleaned entire house

Y isn't Ham pitching tonight?

ME

he's slated for game 4

ADRIAN

bummer (sad emoji)

I'll still watch

Next, I hear from Alma's oldest daughter, the heart surgeon in Chicago.

TAYLOR

hosting 6 couples

for tonight's game

can't wait for game 3&4

Wrigley will be rockin'

ME

6 couples?

You're crazy (tongue sticking out emoji)

TAYLOR

Potluck

Easy Peasy

ME

Are you off tomorrow?

TAYLOR

no, I can't be off the day after all 7 games

my elective surgeries rescheduled

Cubs fans, lol

ME

that's good

lighter week then?

TAYLOR

yes!

gtg

ME

Go Cubs!

(fingers crossed emoji)

(baseball emoji)

Two other friends in Athens, Bethany and Salem, text that they are watching tonight's game at Winston and Adrian's house. The last texts are from my only single friend in Athens.

SAVANNAH

watching game @ Adrian's

may not last long

can't be myself

with little ones nearby

will go home yell & cuss

hard to censor myself

ME

I understand

I yell @ the TV

Good Luck!

(4 leaf clover emoji)

With each new text conversation, my nerves grow exponentially. I turn the volume up on the TV as the pregame show begins. Alma bakes cookies in the kitchen, claiming it helps calm her nerves.

"Liberty," I call toward my daughter as she plays with blocks on the carpet. "Let's go help Alma in the kitchen."

She wastes no time standing to follow me into the kitchen. I scoop her up and buckle her safely in her highchair near the table. With one pan already in the oven, the kitchen smells divine. Nothing compares to the smell of fresh baked chocolate chip cookies.

"Wow!" I stare at the large mixing bowl of dough resting on the counter near Alma. "That's not one batch is it?"

"It's three batches," Alma admits. "I needed to fill two hours until game time." She shrugs as she places balls of dough on two more cookie sheets.

I chuckle. "That should keep you busy until game time." I open the refrigerator door, scanning for a snack. "When should I order dinner?"

When Alma shrugs again, I decide to go ahead and order the pizza on my phone, "All done. You keep on baking. The pizza will be here in an hour."

106

MADISON

"Want anything from the kitchen?" Alma asks with our empty paper plates in her hands.

"I could go for some of your cookies."

Liberty toddles behind Alma and McGee brings up the rear as the group enters the kitchen. During the commercial break, I quickly make a trip to the restroom. While I wash my hands, my cellphone vibrates.

SAVANNAH

I'm headed home

too much talking

distracting

ME

3 innings

shocked you lasted that long

SAVANNAH

need to yell

someone's gotta score soon

ME

cheer loud!

SAVANNAH

I will

I tuck my phone in my back pocket on my way to help in the kitchen.

"Let's go," Alma instructs her two little shadows.

"Need me to carry the cookies?" I offer.

"I've got it, if you help Liberty carry her treats."

I look at my daughter's hands. One clasps her cup, the other tightly grips a bone for McGee. He walks beside her with a careful eye on the treat she carries. I love his patience with her—they truly are best friends.

We settle back into our seats for the fourth inning. The Cubs score two and the Yankees score one. Liberty finally falls asleep during the fifth inning, so I carry her to bed during a commercial break. In the bottom of the sixth, the Yankees tie it up. By the top of the seventh, I'm pacing and turn the volume up as Alma heads to the kitchen to bake the final batch of cookies. *If I'm this nervous now, how bad will I be when Hamilton pitches?*

On my path back towards the TV from the front door, I glance towards the kitchen. My stomach plummets as I watch in slow motion as Alma's feet slip out from under her. I cringe when the hard bump sounds as her head makes contact with the table before she lands on the tile floor and a loud groan escapes her mouth.

I wake from my trance, darting to her side, silently praying she'll be okay. McGee licks her flushed cheeks; I shoo him away. My role model suddenly looks old and frail on the floor. "Don't move!" I order as I roll up a kitchen towel and place it under her head. She groans weakly again as her hand clutches her right hip.

"I...can't...move," she stutters between labored breaths.

"Then don't try to move." I assume my motherly tone. My insides quiver with fear for my friend; my future hangs in the balance. I muster all the strength I can to help her through this. "You hit your head, too." I gently walk my fingertips down the back of her head until she winces. I glance down at my fingers. They're wet with fresh blood, so I am quick to pull them out of

Alma's line of sight. Rising, I inform her, "I'm calling an ambulance. Don't move." I rinse my hands before returning to her side.

"9-1-1 what is your emergency?" the calm, male dispatcher greets.

"My friend fell...she bumped...bleeding." The words stream much too fast from my aching throat. "her head and is bleeding...I think she hurt her hip."

"What is your address?"

I rattle off our address and Alma's name and age and am informed an ambulance is en route. The calm, male voice instructs me to assist Alma in holding a cloth to her head wound. Moments pass as if they are hours. My heart races, and my hands tremble. He remains on the line with me even when I hear the sirens and get up to unlock the front door. When the ambulance pulls up, I greet the EMTs on the front lawn.

I lead the way back inside as the EMTs follow with duffels on their shoulders. Nervously, I watch as they assess her vitals, press on her hip, then peek at the head wound.

"We'll need to transport her to the hospital," the older EMT states while rising to stand beside me. "She needs stitches and an X-Ray of that hip."

I nod. It's all I can do. My sinuses burn as tears threaten. I can't let them fall—if they start, I'll never get them to stop.

"You're welcome to ride with us..."

"My daughter is upstairs." I frantically look from Alma to the front room and back. I pat Alma's forearm. "Liberty and I will follow the ambulance to the hospital."

Mid-groan, Alma nods.

"This should help with the pain." I watch as the EMT injects pain meds into her IV.

One first responder stays with Alma while the other fetches the gurney. I decide to quickly gather Liberty and our bag so I'm ready to leave when they do.

I throw a few items into the diaper bag from the nursery before I lift Liberty into my arms. Back downstairs, I drop the bag at the landing before grabbing both my purse Alma's on the way into the kitchen. Alma's eyes are heavy with sedation as the two guys, now joined by a female and another male, maneuver her onto the stretcher, strap her in, then raise it up with guard rails secured.

"I'm Hale," the female states. "Can I help you to your vehicle? You have your hands full." She gestures to Liberty and my bags, but her pleasant smile does little to calm my racing thoughts. "Let me carry…"

I decide to entrust our purses rather than Liberty to her care. The weight of my daughter keeps me from spiraling out of control. *I can do this. Alma needs me to keep it together.* In the living room, I ask her to grab the diaper bag before I lock and pull the door shut behind us. Outside, neighbors gather on the sidewalk in front of the house.

I use the key fob to unlock Alma's minivan. As Hale places our bags in the passenger seat, I approach our next-door neighbor, Mr. Edwards. "Alma fell. It might be her hip. Would you be able to let McGee out before bedtime if you don't hear back from me?"

Just as I knew he would, he tells me not to worry. He will dog-sit until he hears from me tonight or tomorrow. He's done this before, and Alma trusts to leave her spare key with him. I thank him and head for the minivan as the ambulance doors close on Alma.

The ride to the hospital seems to take forever. I whisper cuss words as the ambulance barrels through a red light, and I must stop. I sit idly as only one car moves through the cross street and the light remains red. *C'mon. C'mon.* My stomach somersaults as I accelerate at the green light. I attempt to wrangle my thoughts from Alma to the road and cars around me. At the next intersection, I zoom through on yellow, not wanting to wait for another red light.

I worry for my friend. *This is exactly why her children wanted someone to live with her. Her children! Crap!* I instruct hands free to dial Taylor, but Alma's daughter does not answer her cell phone.

"Taylor," I barely recognize my quivering voice. Clearing my throat, I try again. "Alma fell. I called an ambulance. We are on the way to the hospital. I'm going to call Trenton next. If you don't hear from him, call me when you get this message."

"Call Trenton." I order. I'm anything but patient as the car speakers echo the ringing of his phone.

"Hello," his deep voice answers.

"Trenton, Alma fell. I'm following the ambulance to the hospital. She needs stitches on the back of her head, and they need to x-ray her hip." I gulp in a breath as I turn into the hospital behind the ambulance. *Crap! I can't park in the ambulance bay.* I frantically search for a nearby parking lot.

"Madison, is she okay?" Anguish is heavy in his words.

What kind of question is that? I just told him I called an ambulance. No! She is not okay!

"I mean, do you need me to book a flight? I can be there in…three hours."

"She was in a lot of pain. They gave her meds and it seemed to help. She didn't talk much, but her eyes seem to understand." I try to calm his fears while mine run out of control. *Alma means everything to me. She has to be okay.*

"I'm at the hospital now." I slide the two purses into my backpack that doubles as a diaper bag. "I left a message for Taylor. Can you call your sisters and fill them in for me? I'll be in touch as soon as I know anything."

I sense Trenton's hesitation. Since his father's death two years ago, he's tried to step up for Alma. I'm sure he wants to be here. "Text or call with any details. No matter how small they might be. I'll call Taylor and Cameron, then I will pull up flight information in case I need to hop a plane tonight."

I open Liberty's door. Having already pulled the stroller from the back, I quickly pop it up and lock the wheels. Liberty barely stirs when I move her from the car seat to recline in the stroller. I drape a blanket from the sunshade to prevent the interior lights from disturbing her.

I almost forget to lock the van on my way to the Emergency Department entrance. The automatic doors of the hospital swoosh open, and I enter a bustling waiting area.

Careful not to roll over any toes, I slowly maneuver the stroller to the reception desk.

At my turn, I state I followed an ambulance in with Alma for stitches and possible hip injury. The staff member taps a few keys on her keyboard before excusing herself to the back hallway.

Do I stay here? Should I take a seat? I'm not sure if she's done with me. I look around the waiting area as if someone there knows what I should do. The sound of a door buzzing then unlocking startles me.

"Come on back," the staff member instructs. "She's in the second bay on the left." I follow the direction her arm points and thank her.

Alma lays in a hospital bed, her eyes closed when I peek through the drawn curtain. Her skin has a grey hue instead of the normal pinkness. Monitors beep as wires and tubes attached to her body to machines on both sides of her bed. She looks posed instead of comfortable. Her arms are too perfectly placed at her sides, on the blanket that covers her lower body.

"Alma, I'm right here." I pat her forearm to ensure she can feel me beside her, and her eyes open a sliver. "Hey. How you feelin'?"

Alma opens her mouth. Only a moan escapes as her eyes search the room, struggling to find me.

"It's okay," I sooth. "Don't talk. Just rest. Liberty and I will be right here if you need anything."

The sharp scrape of the metal curtain hooks on the rod slice the silence as a nurse quickly moves to Alma's bedside.

"I'm Madison," I greet anxiously. "How is she?"

"Are you her relative?" The nurse doesn't pause her deliberate actions to look my direction.

I open my mouth to explain my relationship and quickly realize if I'm not family, I might be asked to leave. "I'm her daughter."

"The doctor hasn't been in yet. I'm starting an IV with fluids and pain medications." She glances to me with a warm smile.

Good. She's not the Nurse Ratched type.

"Doc will be in here next. We'll know more then." As quickly as she came, she exits.

I slide my backpack into an empty chair just as my cell phone vibrates in my back pocket. It's an ESPN alert. The Cubs won four to three in nine innings. *Good thing Hamilton wasn't on the mound tonight.* I forgot all about the baseball game. Wanting something to do to fill the minutes while I wait, I shoot a text to him.

ME

Congrats on the win!

Alma fell, we're at hospital

stitches & hip x-ray, will keep you posted

I slide my phone back into my pocket as four people in scrubs step into Alma's area. The man in the white coat scrolls through screens on his tablet while barking directions to the others. One holds a stethoscope to Alma's chest while another prepares a blood pressure cuff at Alma's arm. The third person quickly jots down results on a paper chart.

My head spins with directions, numbers, and terms that I don't understand as they fly around me. I peek into the stroller; Liberty sleeps as if she's home in her own crib. I wish I were as oblivious to the situation as she is.

Two of the nurses assist in propping pillows behind Alma's shoulders. Her pain meds seem to have kicked in; she doesn't react to any movements. They tilt her head to expose her cut to the doctor. I watch as another nurse injects the numbing agent along the cut then as stitch after stitch closes her wound.

Pleased with his work, the doctor exits the room to assist the next patient. "The nurses will assist you from here," he throws over his shoulder as he walks away.

"We've stopped the bleeding," the male nurse addresses me. "We're taking her down to x-ray. She'll probably be gone an hour or more." He nods as the other nurses wheel Alma's bed from the area. "You're welcome to stay here or out in the waiting room. Get yourself something to eat, relax, and we will bring her back as soon as she's done. If you're not here, we will look for you in the waiting room."

I smile and nod. I have no intention of leaving Alma's area. Trenton, Taylor and Cameron are counting on me. I need to update her kids—I send a group text.

ME

Alma in x-ray

I'll text when hear anything

TAYLOR

Thank you

Thank God you were there

TRENTON

Thanks for update

I can catch a 10:30 or 11:45 flight

Just say the word

CAMERON

Trenton, mom's okay, chill

ME

I'll text soon

I note the time is just after nine before returning my phone to my pocket and scanning my surroundings. I pull my phone out again. I need to write; I need to record my feelings. In my Notes app, I attempt to record everything I feel in this moment. My fingers fly across the keyboard of their own accord.

Lost, alone, afraid, deserted, vacant, void, childlike, unworthy, left behind yet again, destined to be alone, in a cave, a hole, as deep dark chasm, deserted island, dark, scared, weak, at war, abandoned, failure, falling, in limbo, I want to hit something, I want to scream at the top of my lungs, I want to yell "Why me?", needy, sad, devoid, bankrupt, helpless...

Unaware an hour passes, I'm still lost in my thoughts and app when Alma is returned.

"How'd she do?" My voice is weak, foreign to me.

As the two nurses scurry to return Alma's bed and IV, one shares. "She's sedated. Results should be available soon." And with that, they are gone.

The curtains form a modicum of privacy as I approach her bedside. "Alma?" I try to wake her, but she doesn't stir. I worry. *Should she be so out of it? Is she really in so much pain that they must knock her out?* "Liberty and I are still here. I've texted your kids. They're worried." I sigh deeply. *Is she hearing any of this?*

Dr. Anderson enters, startling me.

"How's she doing?" His voice cuts through the tension.

Confused, I look his way. *Why is my Ob/Gyn here?*

"How are you holding up?" He looks around the room, assessing Alma's status. "I overheard at the nurses' station that one of our own is here. There are still several of us teaching that worked with her husband for years."

"She hasn't really said much since the fall," I state, hoping he will ease my worries. "Should she be able to carry on a conversation while on the pain meds?"

Dr. Anderson looks from me to Alma. He rubs her forearm then pats it a few times. Seeing no reaction from her, he moves closer to her head. "Alma?" He pauses. "Alma, can you hear me?"

"I know she's in pain, but why did they knock her all the way out?" I ask, voicing my concern to him.

"Everyone reacts to medications differently," he explains. "I'll check on the dosage."

I realize he hopes to make me feel better, but it does little to rest my concerns—I fear something is not right.

"How about you," he glances to the stroller. "or Liberty? Do you need something to drink or a snack from the cafeteria, a vending machine?"

I simply shake my head. My stomach roils at the thought of food.

"I'll be back in a bit." Dr. Anderson smiles, pats my shoulder, then disappears beyond the curtain.

I look to my phone again, hoping to pass the time faster. Unfortunately, 45 minutes pass, seeming like hours. The sound of the curtain opening rescues me. Two nurses move around Alma, taking vitals and making notations.

"She'll need surgery," a nurse states without looking my way. "We'll be admitting Alma, and surgery is scheduled for 11 tomorrow." Now they both sympathetically look my way. "You're welcome to stay until we settle her into her room."

I nod. I'll definitely stay.

"Visiting hours are over, but we will sneak you up with us for a few minutes." The male nurse raises his chin towards the stroller. "Your little one must be able to sleep through anything."

"Alma and I wore her out at the park today, so she'd sleep through most of the ballgame tonight." I shrug as sadness rushes over me. *Our plans for a World Series game one party completely failed tonight. Looks like I'll be watching the game alone tomorrow night.*

"Who do you root for?"

"I have a friend that plays for the Cubs." *A friend. Friend? Hamilton is still my friend. He can be more and still be my friend, right?*

"Armstrong," he states. Surprised, I nod, and he continues. "I played against him for two summers."

"What team?" I ask, repositioning myself in the uncomfortable chair. "I attended all of his games."

He played for the Moberly American Legion team. We discuss two memorable games between Athens and Moberly at Districts before he excuses himself.

Helplessly, I follow behind as they transport her upstairs. Thirty minutes later, Alma is situated in her private hospital room for the night. I say goodnight and push Liberty back towards the elevator. My feet feel heavy as I approach the van. I move Liberty carefully and fasten her safely into her car seat. Once buckled in my own seat, I connect my phone to Bluetooth and call Alma's kids.

Trenton answers first. We wait a moment for the girls to join the call.

"Alma's tucked into room 408 for the night. Hip surgery is scheduled for 11 tomorrow."

Trenton interrupts me. "Did Mom ever gain consciousness?"

"No. Dr. Anderson checked her dosages, but he didn't seem worried. He claims they are ensuring she is comfortable." I try to sound like I believe this explanation.

"I'm booking my flight now," Trenton states. "I'll arrive about 10."

Taylor rattles off flight times. She talks out loud as she works through the timelines. "I'm flying into St. Louis. I land at 7:15."

Trenton jumps in. "I land about the same time. We can meet at baggage claim and share a rental."

I focus on the drive home through the dark, desolate Columbia streets.

"Cameron," Taylor calls to her baby sister over the phone lines. "What do your flight options look like?"

"I've got something I need to work out before I can book a flight."

Trenton and Taylor urge Cameron to book a flight and just call in to work tomorrow. Clearly, they don't understand her hesitation.

"I'm home," I butt in, ready to end this call. "I've got to get Liberty inside and let McGee out." I don't hide my exasperated sigh. "I'll talk to you in the morning."

107

HAMILTON

> MADISON
>
> Alma has hip surgery
>
> tomorrow at 11

ME

how are you holding up?

I dial her phone before she can respond.

"Hello." Her voice sounds so small.

"Are you home?" I ask in almost a whisper. I know she'll hear me as I speak into the mic and wear my earphones.

"Yes," she yawns. "I've been home about 30 minutes. How about you?"

"I'm on the bus back to the hotel," I explain in a hushed voice. I try not to draw the attention of the entire team.

"I'm good," Madison lies.

"Um, Madison, it's me. You don't have to appear to have it all together. Tell me the truth." I already know the truth.

"I'm scared. What if something happens during the surgery? She's acting weird on the pain meds. Things go wrong in surgery all the time, and with her age, there's more of a risk." She sucks in a shuddering breath. "What if she's not strong enough to walk after the surgery? What if she can't come back home? She looks so frail lying in the hospital bed."

"How is she acting weird?" I ask concerned.

"Since the fall, she hasn't spoken a single word," Madison releases a frustrated sigh. "She groans in pain, but she hasn't spoken. They keep her so high on pain meds, she's out of it. Her eyes search the room and never focus on any one thing." Madison pulls in a deep breath. "I worry it's her head injury. I mean, she should say something or mumble. She doesn't even try to speak."

"You want them to give her enough meds to keep her out of pain, right? Ask her kids. Maybe she reacts this way to strong pain meds. It's natural to worry. She's important to you. I know you can't just turn it off. Remember, the doctors and staff see this all the time. They know what to look for, and they are taking good care of Alma. You need to make sure you are strong for her. You need to be sure to eat, stay hydrated, and get enough sleep so you can help her on the other side of her surgery. She'll lean on you more for a while. You know?" I try to be the voice of reason when Madison's anxiety and fears threaten to engulf her.

"Yeah," she agrees.

"Yeah?" I chuckle. "Is that a 'Yes, I understand and will take care of myself'. Or is that a 'Yeah, I'm done talking on this subject'?"

"You're right. I'll focus on what needs to be done and have faith it will all be okay," she murmurs.

"We're at the hotel. I should let you go." I rise from my seat, grabbing my bag.

I want to talk to her for hours, but I have big things going on this week.

"Okay. Good luck tomorrow night. I assume I will watch the game with Alma in her hospital room," Madison sighs.

"I love you, Madison," I state.

Loud hoots and cat calls surround me. The teammates standing near me holler, "We love you, Madison!"

"So much for a private conversation." I laugh.

She giggles. "I love you, too," she states before we disconnect.

108

MADISON

I drop Liberty off at the Mom's Day Out program at the church at 8:30 on my way to the hospital. Oblivious to Alma's issues, Liberty quickly joins her little friends playing on the carpet of her classroom. I'm glad she hasn't picked up on my stress. She deserves to play without a care in the world.

When I walk into Alma's private room later, Dr. Anderson sits at her bedside. For a moment, I wonder how he knew to be here. My brain quickly assumes since he's on staff and formerly worked here with Alma's husband, he has many ways to know when a friend is admitted for surgery.

"Good morning," he greets, rising to offer me the chair.

"Hi. Has she spoken to you this morning?" I cringe at the sound of fear in my voice.

"No. They're keeping her sedated to avoid pain. Did you contact the kids?" Again, he gestures for me to take the seat he vacated.

"Yeah. I called them last night." I sit, pulling my knees toward my chest and wrapping my arms around them. "They should all arrive before her surgery." I squeeze Alma's hand in mine. *Is it my imagination? Did she just squeeze my hand back?* I repeat the gesture. This time I feel nothing.

"I've got rounds, but I will back before her surgery. Do you need anything?" Dr. Anderson places his large hand on my shoulder, drawing my attention from Alma toward him.

"No. I'm good. Thanks."

Alone with Alma, I rub her forearm while I speak to her. "I'm here. Liberty is at church, but she'll be here when you get back from surgery. I hope you can hear me. I want you to be strong. I need you to fight. Hip surgery can't keep the Alma I know down," I bite my lower lip, hoping she can hear me. "Liberty and I need you. Remember that and don't doubt how much we love you."

I wipe the tears from my cheeks before grasping her hand again. The rhythmic sound of the beeping heart monitor lulls me into a trance.

"Knock. Knock."

I squeal. Trenton, Taylor, and Cameron stand at the open hospital room door. I clutch my chest in an attempt to keep my racing heart from exploding.

"Sorry. We didn't mean to scare you," Taylor states, walking to her mother's bedside.

Trenton joins her while Cameron comes to my side. Wrapping her arm around my shoulders, she whispers, "How are you holding up?"

I nod as I reply, "I'm fine." I look toward Alma. Her children are calling to her, attempting to stir her consciousness. "She still hasn't been alert enough to speak."

Taylor assumes the chair I previously occupied while crooning to her mother. Trenton gently rubs Alma's cheek from the other side.

I need to give them time alone, so I make my way to the door.

"Where do you think you are going?" Cameron calls to me as she jogs to my side in the hallway.

"I need a break," I fib because I feel out of place. With Alma unwell, I fear my spot in my adopted family will fade. "I'm going to the bathroom and getting a drink."

She tucks her hand in mine. "I'll join you."

"Don't you want to visit with your mom before her surgery?" *They just got here. Shouldn't she want to spend time with Alma?*

"Like you said, she hasn't been lucid enough to talk. I'm sure my siblings will let her know I am here." She tilts her head at me while we wait for the elevator. "I'm not good in these situations. My siblings take over, and I get in trouble for everything I say or do. Besides, you've been by yourself—I'll keep you company."

We step into the elevator, and the doors slide shut.

"Where to?" Cameron asks with her finger poised to press a number for a floor.

"I'm not sure."

"I thought you needed a bathroom break and a drink," Cameron reminds me.

I shake my head. "I just needed to give them privacy."

"Uh-uh," she scolds. "They don't need privacy. You're part of this family now, and you deserve to be in the room as much as I do."

Her words do make me feel a bit better.

"Let's find the cafeteria," she suggests. "I could use a snack and a decent cup of coffee. I'm sure you could use a pop. The caffeine will do both of us good."

When the nurses enter to whisk Alma off to surgery, her room is crowded. Dr. Anderson stopped by to visit as he promised while Trenton, Taylor, Cameron, and I all stand nervously watching the clock in anticipation of the surgery. We take turns kissing Alma's cheek or patting her arm as they push her out the door.

Dr. Anderson assures us she is in excellent hands before exiting. Unsure what to do, the four of us stand lost in the now nearly empty room.

"I need to go pick Liberty up from church," I explain, gathering up my purse. "I'm going to run by the house to let McGee out. Can I bring you anything?"

Trenton and Taylor plan to eat in the cafeteria and sit in the surgery waiting room. Cameron asks to join me on my drive.

Exhausted from her playtime at church, Liberty still sleeps in her stroller when the nurses wheel Alma back into the hospital room. The medical team scurries to situate her and record vitals. Taylor and Cameron squeeze into the room and stand by my side.

"She's getting so big," Taylor whispers, peeking into the stroller.

"I still can't believe she's one-and-a-half," Cameron states. "She's so tall and smart."

"Too smart for her own good sometimes," I agree. "She and McGee can be quite the handful when they play." I turn from Alma to face the women. "This week, we lost track of them for a split second. We followed Liberty's chatter to find them in Alma's bathroom. Liberty stood in the bathtub with both hands on the knobs to the faucet with McGee sitting nearby."

"Were they going to take a bath?" Cameron giggles.

"Well, Liberty wore only her diaper. Her clothes were strewn in the hall and on the bathroom floor. Whether it was just one or both of them, someone planned to get wet." I shake my head and turn to face Alma's direction again. "Thankfully, she can't turn the knobs yet."

"Oh, just wait." Taylor places her palm on her cheek. "The twins used an entire bottle of bubble bath in the tub once. We had bubbles everywhere. Liberty will keep you on your toes, but you won't want it any other way."

The three of us chuckle as the staff finish with Alma and Trenton enters. "The surgery went as planned. She should be waking in the next half-hour or so," The female nurse states as she adjusts the call button on top of Alma's blankets. "Press the nurse call button when she wakes or if you need anything." With that, we are once again alone with an unconscious Alma.

109

MADISON

Liberty and I keep Alma company in the third inning of the second World Series game. Taylor and Cameron left to get dinner for our group and let McGee out. Trenton is taking a walk to call his wife and kids with an update. The afternoon was smooth; Alma woke, said a couple of words to us, then nodded off and on. The staff claims she's progressing nicely, and they plan to assist her with walking a bit in an hour or so.

The score is one to one; the Cubs are tied with the Yankees. Liberty sits in my lap, pretending to read one of her books. Alma, alert at the moment, watches the game with me.

"Coming to the plate is the designated hitter for the Cubs, Hamilton Armstrong," the announcer states. "A bold move on the part of the coach." A second announcer explains Hamilton is a pitcher and usually a pitcher doesn't hit in either league for another pitcher.

I stand, placing Liberty in the chair. I glance at Alma; she wears a smile. "He's hit well all season." I state the obvious and Alma agrees.

My nerves are through the roof. Hamilton isn't supposed to pitch for two more games. Now that he's active in this game, though, I have even more butterflies in my stomach than I did before.

The first pitch is a ball brushing Hamilton back from the plate. That's a dirty move. The opponent is sending a message. I wonder if they studied

Hamilton's hitting from the regular season. He likes outside pitches and crowds the plate to get a better swing at them. The second pitch is a slider across the outside corner of the plate for a strike.

"C'mon, Hamilton!" Alma croaks.

I wonder if her pain meds are wearing off. I'll need to call the nurse after Hamilton hits.

Hamilton crushes the third pitch that looks like a fastball. As he sprints to first, the ball flies deep into left field. It bounces off the wall with an advantageous hop away from the leftfielder. Hamilton continues to second and the runner on third charges towards home. As Hamilton slides safely into second for a double, the ball soars toward the catcher at the same time as the runner slides across home plate. It's close.

I hold my breath as I await the call from the official. The Cubs runner returns to step on the plate as the catcher scrambles to find the baseball. He returns the ball to his glove and attempts to tag the runner. The head umpire signals safe. The Cubs now lead two to one and Hamilton gains an RBI. He beams on second base when the camera zooms in on him.

I hop up and down, trying to refrain from cheering at the top of my lungs. "Yes!"

"Da-Da!" Liberty cheers from the chair behind me.

"Yes, Daddy got a double!" I inform her as I scoop her in my arms to celebrate. We high five Alma and dance at her bedside.

Alma cringes as she coughs. I return Liberty to the chair. "Are you okay? Do you need more meds?" I've tried not to hover all day as her children are overly protective.

Alma doesn't answer. I decide to press the nurse's call button just in case. Alma coughs again. Her eyes search the room as her mouth opens.

"Alma," I call to her. "What's wrong?"

Her mouth moves as if she's trying to speak, but no sounds escape. She's in distress. I press the call button again. Something is wrong; I know it. I dart toward the hallway, not leaving the door frame.

"Help!" I scream. "We need help in here! Hurry!"

A nurse exits another patient's room, running my way. I scoop up Liberty and stand at Alma's bedside. Three nurses gather around her as I move against the wall so they can work. The head of her bed is lowered while one nurse calls to Alma, attempting to get her to answer; the others record vitals.

In the blink of an eye, a nurse pages for assistance. I'm unable to make out the announcement as tears cloud my vision. *This can't be good.*

"Miss," a voice calls. "Miss, I need you to step into the hallway." A nurse places a firm hand on my shoulder to guide me out of the room.

"What's happening?" I wail, unable to restrain my emotions.

The nurse returns to the room without a reply. I lean against the wall, my eyes raised to heaven. "Please. Please help her," I beg God.

"Ma-Ma?" Liberty's tiny hand pats my cheek.

I attempt to pull myself together—I don't need to scare her. I kiss her cheek then pull my phone from my pocket. I open the group text from yesterday.

ME

Get back here!

NOW!

I don't look for a reply; I tuck it back in my pocket. "It's okay," I sooth Liberty, rubbing her back. "The doctor and nurses are helping Alma right now. We're okay." I hope my words console her more than they do me.

A raucous at the end of the hall draws my attention. "Sir!" a female voice yells. It's Trenton. He doesn't acknowledge her. Instead, he runs towards us.

"What happened?" He gasps for breath.

"I don't know. One minute we were high-fiving Hamilton's double, the next she couldn't utter a sound and looked confused." I shake my head. "I paged the nurse but had to run in the hall to yell for help."

Trenton extends his arms for Liberty. I don't want to give her up; she anchors me in this chaos. She leans toward him, so I relinquish her. Trenton pats her back while murmuring that everything will be alright. I'm not sure if he's directing it towards Liberty, me, or himself.

"Taylor and Cameron were already on their way back when you texted," he explains still breathless. "They'll be here any minute."

Several long moments pass. I retell my account to the girls, and we all stand scared, hoping for an explanation soon. Liberty wiggles down to sit on the floor near my feet, playing with my cell phone. When it vibrates, she extends it to me. It's an ESPN alert. The score remains two to one in the top of the seventh inning. The World Series game is no longer in the forefront of my mind. I return the phone to my daughter.

After what seems like an eternity, Trenton peeks his head into Alma's room for answers. The rest of us remain frozen in the hallway, staring into space. Trenton emerges as Alma is wheeled from the room with several staff members flanking both sides of her. I refrain from reaching to her as it's clear they are in a hurry to their destination.

"They're taking her for an MRI," Trenton states.

"A stroke?" Taylor asks, and Trenton nods.

In my shock, I didn't think to ask her what might have happened, even though she is a cardiologist. She probably had a pretty good idea all this time. Sobs escape Cameron as her legs go weak, and she slides down the wall to the floor.

Liberty immediately approaches. She places her hands on Cameron's cheeks. As is her way, her dark brown eyes search Cameron's. I wish I could shield Liberty from all of this. It has to be confusing. I'm selfish; I want her with me when I should have secured a babysitter.

"O-Tay?" Liberty asks.

In her own little way, she is trying to make Cameron feel better. I gnaw on my lip. *How do I explain this to someone so young?*

Taylor states she'll fetch the food from the car and be right back. I don't offer to help her carry. I can't move. If I move, I might react. If I react, I might lose what little control I'm hanging on to.

Trenton brings two more chairs into the hospital room then urges Cameron, Liberty, and I to take a seat. *I didn't even notice him leave. I wonder where he stole the chairs from.*

As she promised, Taylor returns with food, and we eat in silence for a bit. Trenton turns on the game to find it's still two to one in the top of the ninth.

"I'd like the Cubs to score a couple here." Taylor snaps our silence.

"They can win by a run," Trenton teases, trying to ease the tension.

"I'd feel better with more of a cushion for the end of the game." I agree with Taylor. It would make the win seem safe.

I busy myself with pinching off pieces for Liberty, eating my slice, and watching the end of a game that I can't get excited about. We watch the postgame celebrations as the Cubs secure their second win in the series. In our room, there is no cheering, only fake smiles when we make eye contact. It's clear our thoughts are with Alma.

I opt to keep Liberty in my bed tonight. I know it's selfish; I can't be alone. She sleeps peacefully next to me as I prepare to send an email update to Hamilton.

From: alwayswrite@gmail.com
To: armnhammer@gmail.com
Subject: Fly the W

Congrats on the single, double, and two RBIs. I watched the game tonight in Alma's hospital room. It was hard not to cheer at the top of my lungs when you hit the double to steal the lead. You brought a large smile to Alma's face as we high-fived.

Just think, the next 2 games are in Chicago. I bet Wrigley will be lit. Alma's surgery went off without a hitch we were told. She was alert off and on all afternoon. But, halfway through tonight's game, she had a stroke.

Trenton was calling his family somewhere for privacy, and the girls went to get us dinner. One minute, Alma was cheering, and the next thing I know, it happened. I was so afraid, and I'm still scared to death. The doctor confirmed it was a stroke after the MRI but stated it would take some time to know how much damage it caused. As visiting hours were over, he urged us to go home and promised us more answers in the morning.

Like an idiot, I looked up strokes on the internet—now I will never sleep. It's hard enough for someone her age to recover from total hip replacement. Add a stroke to it, and it might be impossible. I know her kids are all worried about it, too.

I'm sorry to deliver such upsetting news on the eve of an awesome win for you. I feel I need to keep you posted.

I'll email you tomorrow when we hear from Alma's doctor.
Love,
Madison

110

HAMILTON

I close Madison's email, placing my phone back in my coat pocket. I guess I won't text to ensure she is up then call her like last night. My excitement to share tonight's game with her evaporates.

My head in my hands, I hunch forward, elbows on my knees. An acrid taste fills my mouth, and my stomach feels heavy. The overwhelming need to comfort Madison feuds with my need to celebrate with my team.

My mind races with possibilities. The team flies home tomorrow; our next game is in two days. I could hop a flight tonight and be in Columbia when she wakes up. Since I start game four, I could spend the entire day with her and fly home in time for game three.

Coach will understand when I explain what's going on, that my head isn't here with the team, as it is. I'll promise him a clearer head in time for my start in the fourth game.

Coach's voice floods my brain. "I'm counting on you to hit in any given game. Your bat is hot, and we'll use it. We may use you as the DH or a pinch hitter, so be ready."

As much as I love Madison and want to help her through this tough time, I cannot abandon my teammates. I hope she understands.

"Yo," Stan nudges my shoulder, standing in the aisle beside me.

"Sorry." I shake my head and rise from the bus seat.

"Where's your head at?" he inquires.

"Madison wrote me. The woman she lives with suffered a stroke during our game tonight."

"Dude, I'm sorry." He lowers his voice as we exit the charger bus at our hotel. "How bad is it? Did the hip surgery cause it?"

Unable to keep emotion from my voice, I open her email, passing my phone for him to read.

"You need to be there, but you have to be here," Stan states, understanding my dilemma.

At the lobby, most of the team heads to the bar to continue the celebration. Stan suggests we head up to my room.

"She's your number one fan," he reminds me. "From all you've shared, it feels like I know her. Madison wants this for you. She'd pitch a fit if you missed any part of the World Series with your team."

He's right. She'd kick my ass if I didn't enjoy every minute of this week.

"Take some time," he orders. "Text her, call her, whatever, just make sure she knows you're with her in thoughts and prayers. Then, join the team for drinks. I'll meet you down there."

Then, he's gone. I'm alone in the empty, much-too-quiet hotel room. I place my suit jacket in the closet, remove my tie, and unbutton my top button before rolling up my sleeves.

With cell phone in hand, I stare out the window. The lights sprawl out as far as the eye can see.

I choose to return her email, hoping she's already asleep. She'll need all her strength to help Alma and her family get through this.

111

MADISON

In the two days since Alma's surgery and subsequent stroke, Taylor and Cameron hurry home for work and to rearrange their schedules for another trip to Columbia. Trenton works via the internet and reschedules many of his appointments from Alma's hospital room. Alma's physicians informed the group that due to the severity of her stroke; she will be transferred to a long-term care nursing facility. While they expect her to make improvements, they are confident that she will not be able to return home. Once the shock wore off, Trenton and Taylor discussed some major decisions they need to consider as soon as possible. Not wanting to face the truth, I excused myself from such a discussion. Cameron wasn't far behind me. Although she claims her older siblings rarely listen to her opinions, I believe she tries to avoid these situations.

Tonight, is game three of the World Series. Taylor and her spouse have tickets. I'm supposed to attend tomorrow night's game with Memphis, and she promised to call today for an update on Alma. I'm writing on the deck, watching Liberty and McGee play in the backyard when my phone rings.

"Hello," I greet, placing my laptop to the side. Quickly, I click the save button before shutting the lid.

"How are things?" Memphis wastes no time.

"They're transferring Alma to a nursing home this afternoon." My voice conveys my anguish in this development. "Trenton is with her. I opted to stay home."

"I'm sure her kids found her the best facility, and she will have the best care available." Her words do little to ease my worries. "How are you?"

"Scared." It's true. I'm scared of everything.

"Trenton plans to fix a few things then put Alma's house on the market," I sigh dejectedly. "I need to start searching for a new place to live."

"Will you stay in the Columbia area?" I detect a hint of wistfulness in her voice. "You're done with college, and your writing career allows you to live anywhere. Have you considered leaving Columbia?"

I close my eyes for a moment. I hadn't thought of this. I've only made a list of things I need to do to move out—it didn't occur to me that I can move anywhere. This revelation makes my decision even more daunting. I need to choose a state and town before I can start apartment hunting.

"I'm sorry," Memphis interrupts my thoughts. "It's a big decision, and I just made it bigger."

"No, you're right." I sigh again. My eyes follow McGee as he chases Liberty with the ball in her hand. "It should make it easier to move, but deciding on a location is more than I can handle right now."

"You are more than welcome to stay with me in Athens while you consider where to move. I mean, I'd love for you to move back to Athens, closer to all of your friends, but I understand if you still want distance from your mother."

The thought of being close to Memphis in the absence of Alma is comforting, but I'm not sure I am ready to move back near my mother. I've liked not worrying every day about her drinking, her arriving home safely, and what she is up to. Distance did wonders to ease that anxiety that haunted my life. *Does living near Memphis and my friends outweigh living near my mother?*

"I'll have to think about it. Thanks for the offer." A real smile slides onto my face for the first time in days. "I might plan a trip up to visit when things calm a little here." I clear my throat, preparing to deliver my next news. "Memphis, I think I'm going to have to give up my ticket to tomorrow night's game. It just doesn't feel right to go with all that Alma is going through down here."

"I was actually going to ask you if you still wanted to go," she confesses.

"Of course, I want to go. I mean, it's the World Series, and Hamilton will be pitching. I don't want to miss it, but I need to be here to help Alma settle in at her new place." I roll my head and neck, seeking to release some tension. "I don't know yet when her daughters will be back, and Trenton plans to head back to Tennessee for the weekend to visit his family. I don't want Alma to be all alone in a nursing home without someone to visit her. I know I can't do much, but I can keep her company."

"I knew you'd want to be there for her."

"Do you think you can find someone to go with Amy and you on a day's notice? I'd hate for the ticket to go to waste." I hope Hamilton's sister will take someone in my place.

"I'm sure Amy's 'friend' will gladly go," she chuckles.

"She claims they are still just friends?" I try to remember if it has been a year now that Amy and her guy friend have been glued at the hip. Memphis' words not mine.

"Oh, one minute in the room with the two of them and it's clear to see he is not her friend." Humor laces her voice. "My daughter is just in denial. She won't even admit they are friends with benefits. I've made it very clear I wouldn't have a problem with it—she just prefers to be in denial."

"Well, whatever he is, I'm glad he can use my ticket."

"He played American Legion ball with Hamilton for two summers. Amy hinted last week that she wished she asked Hamilton to send him a ticket, too." Memphis clears her throat. "I'm sure he will be thrilled to attend."

"And since it's an overnight trip, maybe Amy will finally confess they are a couple," I tease.

"I didn't think about that. I wonder if she will share a room with me or him." Memphis giggles. "Oh, this could be so much fun. I'll get to watch her squirm."

"Be nice," I scold. Liberty is laying in the grass with her head on her arm. I fear my girl is in need of a nap. "Well, I need to let you go. I've got stuff to do and more to consider now."

We say our goodbyes before I whisk McGee and Liberty inside for an afternoon nap.

The Cubs won last night, so tonight's game could end the series if they win again. I'm sure this adds more pressure to Hamilton's appearance on the mound. I tried to talk to him last night after the win and again this morning, but the team is keeping him very busy. I did get to hear from Taylor about how exciting it was in Wrigley last night. I'm glad Memphis and Amy will be there tonight for Hamilton. I'm very jealous. Adulting sucks sometimes.

Liberty and I drive home for a few hours to relax before we return to watch tonight's game with Alma. She's in a private room, but it is very tiny. It's hard to keep Liberty entertained inside the four walls for an entire day.

I open my phone to see if I've missed anything while I move around the house, picking up and packing toys for tonight. Looking at my last text to Hamilton, I realize he hasn't texted me since yesterday morning. I purse my lips, contemplating sending him another text, when my phone vibrates.

SAVANAH

got time to chat?

ME

yes, call me

I promptly answer my ringing cell phone. "Hey, girlie. It's been too long. What's up?" I fake excitement.

Savanah and I were close in high school; we bonded over our difficult situations at home. While I struggled with the loss of my father and my mother's drinking, Savannah's mother struggled to support the family. Savannah babysat as much as possible until she turned sixteen, then she started working at the grocery store for money. From that point on, she purchased her own gas, insurance, and clothes. She works hard for her money and strives to provide a better life for herself.

"Oh, you know." Savannah mutters something about an idiot driver before returning to our call. "Work, eat, sleep, work, eat, sleep. It's the story of my life." She lets out a long sigh.

"So, plan another vacation," I suggest. "I heard you snagged a nice rack a few weeks ago during bow season. When are you taking off again for gun season?"

"I have a vacation planned the second week of November. Then, the bakery gears up for the Thanksgiving and Christmas busy season. Don't worry, I still get as many vacation days in during deer season as I can."

I struggle to think of what to say next. I know Savannah has a reason for calling. While she participates in our group calls, she never calls me herself. We text occasionally, but for her to call me, something must be up. I need to wait until she's ready to share.

"I could use some of your iced cookies right now. Just talking to you gives me a sugar craving." We laugh together.

"I need to vent," Savannah blurts.

"Have at it." I anxiously wait to hear the issue.

"People in Athens suck." She pauses.

I hear her car beep as she opens her door, then turns off the ignition. Her breathing increases as she walks.

"Sorry, I just got home. Where was I? Oh yeah, I hate how people are rude to anyone not from around here. You know?"

"Tell me about it. You know it's one of my pet peeves."

"Today, I was helping a customer with his donut order. Ol' Lady Humphreys walked right up to him. She introduced herself to the guy. I'm sure my chin hit the floor when she told him that she'd overheard he was looking to buy a house and that it was a bad idea. She actually informed him it would be smarter to rent as he would only be here a year or two. 'People like you don't last long in Athens,' she told him." Savannah imitates the old woman then groans. "It's like she rules the town, and she came in to inform him he'd need to leave soon."

"I'm not all that surprised."

"I hear all of the gossip at the store. People come in to visit all the time. I waste over an hour a day visiting with shoppers. My boss reminds me it is PR, and I need to stop what I am doing and visit with them. I listen to everyone complain that we don't attract new businesses. Well, duh. New businesses and people will not stay if we don't welcome them." In her voice, I sense her frustration growing with her volume.

"So, who was the guy?" My curious mind needs to know. *Is he an upstanding citizen? Is he a criminal? Why was Ol' Lady Humphreys keen on speeding his exit from Athens?*

"He's a new history teacher at the high school. He comes in a couple of times a week for a donut before school. There's absolutely nothing wrong with him."

"Except he wasn't born in Athens or the surrounding area," I quip.

"Right!"

"So, he's a donut addict?" I clutch on to the nugget of information my friend didn't mean to share.

"Oh, you know, he's always in a hurry, so he grabs breakfast on the way to school several times a week," she quickly back pedals.

Wouldn't it be quicker at the convenience store or McDonald's drive thru? He's not coming in for the donuts. He's interested. This is so awesome! I cheer internally for my friend. I do not let her know my real thoughts—I don't need to scare her.

112

MADISON

We arrive at Alma's room an hour before tonight's game. I unpack a wide variety of activities for Liberty throughout the room. As Alma is already in bed for the night, I don't have to worry about her falling over any of them.

The head of her bed is raised to allow her to easily chat with us and view the TV. With arms up, Liberty signals she wants me to lift her onto the bed.

"Be careful," I prompt.

Liberty sits facing Alma and blabbers. Alma smiles and listens as Liberty shares a story of some sort. After a minute, she wiggles her way off the bed, back to her toys.

"She...happy..." Alma's slurred speech is difficult to understand. The stroke has caused her to lose mobility in the left side of her face. She struggles with word choices and is easily frustrated when she can't communicate.

"She played in the yard again today." This makes Alma smile. "We've been very lucky this October. She didn't need a jacket again today." I pat her arm as I move the chair closer to her bedside. "She was probably telling you I gave her a bath before we came tonight." I swirl my finger in circles near the left side of my head. "This mom went crazy and changed our nightly routine."

A sound resembling a laugh comes from Alma. "Ham...Ham...he...pitch."

"Yes, and I'm too nervous. Memphis sent this picture." I show her my cell phone and the photo of Memphis and Amy with Wrigley in the background. I reach into my backpack. "I smuggled you in some chocolate chip cookies Liberty helped me bake today. You know we have to keep making your lucky cookies so the Cubs will win." I cringe remembering Alma fell while making her last batch of lucky cookies.

Liberty approaches. "Wib-Be."

She's letting us know she needs a cookie. I break one in half, knowing she will want another one later during the game. She smiles toward Alma then returns to her baby doll on the blanket covering the tile floor.

I find the announcers annoy me before the first pitch is thrown. I turn the volume down a bit more. I want to listen occasionally but seeing the game is more important to me. The game begins as all the others have this week with the National Anthem. Tonight Maroon 5 performs.

Next, two little boys throw the ceremonial first pitches from the mound. The balls barely make it halfway to the catcher. Tears well in my eyes when Adam Levine encourages the two to pick the balls up and throw them the rest of the way home. I absolutely love that he didn't do it for them, rather assisted them in making accommodations to be successful. On the second throw, each ball hit the catcher's mitt. This is why I love this singer.

This week, I've watched as Taylor and Trenton did things for Alma instead of helping her do them. It's important that she learn a new way to do things for herself. I'm going to make it my mission to talk to her kids and assist her in finding success on her own. I'm sure she still wants to be independent as much as she can, and we can help her.

"That's...guy...girls like you..." Alma slurs, frustrated with her impaired speech.

"Yes." I lock eyes with Alma. It's important that she know, despite her frustration, she can communicate effectively. "'Girls Like You'." It's the song and the video we both love by Maroon 5.

I smile, remembering Alma dancing around the house with me one day when we were cleaning to my Maroon 5 playlist. We took a break, and I showed her the video that the band made to go with the song. We discussed the message of empowerment it shares and attempted to name all the famous women in each video. Our short break turned into over an hour of enjoying music and videos together. I hope we continue to make more memories like that.

"When the Cubs win tonight," I only half tease. "We will crank up our song and dance."

Although she shakes her head, believing she can't dance, I know the feisty, fun-loving, try-anything Alma is still inside her.

"What? Are you afraid I will dance better than you now?"

Alma's garbled laughter is music to my ears.

Hamilton pitches a near perfect game, though you wouldn't know it by my nerves. The closer we come to the end of the game, the more anxious I grow. He racks up 12 strikeouts and gives up no walks or runs as we start the eighth inning.

Alma is napping at the moment, and Liberty sleeps on the blanket in the corner of the room with Cubbie Bear tucked under her arm. Alma drifted off a few times, and I attempted to cheer quietly during her naps. I probably should have packed up and left at eight when visiting hours ended. I know Alma needs her rest, but I wanted to watch the entire game with her as if she hadn't had a stroke.

The vibration of my cell phone on the bedside table wakes Alma. I pretend I didn't notice she fell asleep as I pick it up.

TRENTON

I'm back in town

ME

I'm with Alma

watching game

TRENTON

I'll go to the house

past visiting hours

ME

permission to stay late

> say you're here to pick us up

> watch end of game with me

TRENTON

> okay

> I'm 5 min away

The game remains scoreless in the bottom of the eighth. I desperately need the Cubs to score. My nerves will not survive extra innings. Alma's face lights up with Trenton's arrival.

"Bottom of the lineup, not a promising place to score a run," Trenton shares.

"Ham...Hamilton," Alma mumbles to refute his statement.

"She's right," I chime in. "Hamilton is not your average pitcher batting ninth in the lineup." I give Alma a thumbs up.

Trenton smirks. He knew what he was saying. He wanted to get a rise out of us women. We played right into his plan. He winks at me.

Hamilton stands in the batter's box with a full count. I hold my breath as the pitcher winds up, then delivers. His upper body twists, his thighs bulge, his bat cracks, and the ball flies. It soars over the infield and continues over the outfielders.

I rise from my chair. I throw my arms straight up in the air. Internally, I am screaming, "Go! Go! Go!"

The ball's trajectory arcs down past the outfield wall. Stunned, I look to Alma then Trenton. I feel my eyes bulging as my chest tightens and burns. Breath, I need air. I suck in an audible breath. As life returns to my lungs, I begin to react.

"He hit it out of the park!" I hop in place. "Hamilton hit a homerun out of the park in the World Series!"

Trenton hugs me then his mom. I raise my hand toward Alma. Shakily, she lifts her arm to give me a high five. The right side of her face smiles while the left droops. Our celebration continues until Hamilton resumes the mound at the top of the ninth. Trenton adjusts the TV volume.

"Armstrong returns to start the ninth," the announcer's baritone voice states. "It's rare for a starting pitcher to throw an entire game in the Majors."

The second commentator adds, "Armstrong has only thrown 76 pitches. He hasn't shown any signs of arm fatigue. I'm impressed the coaching staff allows Armstrong to go the distance."

Worried about his arm, my mind calculates pitch counts. With three strikes per out and three outs per inning, a pitcher theoretically could throw nine strikes per inning for nine innings. If my mental math is correct three times three times nine is eighty-one. I remind myself Hamilton has thrown seventy pitches in a couple of games this season when he was pulled by the sixth inning. I tamp down my over-protectiveness by telling myself his coaches would not keep him in the game if it might hurt his arm.

The first Yankees batter hits a fly to right-center field where Stan easily catches it. The fans at Wrigley go wild. Goosebumps prickle my skin with the realization that with two more outs, the game and the World Series will be over.

Hamilton walks the second batter. The commentators rationalize that his arm is showing signs of fatigue, and the weight of this game is taking its toll on his concentration. I attempt to block out their words.

Hamilton bounces the rosin bag in his hand while looking toward the runner on first. He positions himself on the rubber and looks to his catcher for the sign. He shakes his head once, twice, then a third time. Catcher's don't like to be shook off like that. *C'mon Hamilton, listen to him, and work together.* Finally, he likes the sign he's given and nods. He glances towards first as he comes set on the rubber.

Hamilton's fastball targets the outside corner of the plate. The batter swings, making contact, and the ball bounces towards the shortstop. The shortstop fields the ball, throwing to second as he falls backward. Hamilton darts to back up the first baseman while the second baseman places his right foot on the bag then throws to first.

The ball arrives at first, simultaneously with the runner who is stretching his stride to cross the bag. Hamilton throws his arm and closed fist over his shoulder, signaling the runner is out at the same time as the official signals.

All air evaporates from the room as Alma, Trenton, and I are frozen. We don't make a peep or look to each other. Our eyes are glued to the screen. A double play means the game is over, and the Cubs win.

The network replays the play at first from three different angles. It's close, however from the outfield camera angle, we see the ball in glove with the infielder's foot clearly touching the bag a moment before the runner's right footsteps onto the bag.

I don't allow my body to celebrate—I don't allow my mind to go there. I wait with bated breath for the official to make his ruling. The head umpire behind Homeplate clenches his fist in the air. Out. Out? Out!

I don't hear the announcers or the crowd at Wrigley. I only hear Alma and Trenton cheering. *They did it! The Cubs did it! They won the World Series in a four-game sweep. Hamilton pitched an entire game. The Cubs are World Series Champs!*

Two members of the nursing staff remind us to keep it down as most residents are asleep. They congratulate Alma on her team and her friend winning while reminding us to go soon before their shift ends.

I pull out my phone, needing to text Hamilton.

ME

You did it!

World Series Champions!

Fly the W, Cubs Win!

Great game!

I (heart emoji) you

I know he won't see my texts for hours, maybe not until tomorrow. I'm sure Chicago will party all night, as will his team. I hope he joins them—he deserves to celebrate. His homerun and pitching led to the final score of one to nothing.

113

HAMILTON

"He's out!" I signal while jumping up and down and shouting.

The official closes his fist and raises it above his shoulder. "Out!"

Out! That's three! Game over! We win!

We win. We won the World Series. Every muscle in my body flexes as the infielders swarm me. It takes all my strength to remain upright. I can't risk injury on the bottom of a dogpile. Adrenaline courses through my veins as warmth engulfs me.

I struggle to pull in a breath and tears stream down my face. I'm crying. I'm freakin' crying. On one of my upward jumps, I notice our large group gathered in the infield. The bench clears and coaches join in our celebration on the field.

Television cameras and the media begin to infiltrate our mob, seeking photos and interviews. Staff from the head office begin corralling us this way and that for the networks. T-shirts and hats declaring the Cubs World Series Champs fly through the air with orders to put them on.

Two sports announcers with camera in tow approach; I close my eyes and attempt to catch my breath. Madison comes to mind. She stands in front of me, excitement oozing from her every pore. Her dazzling smile reaches her bright eyes and beyond. She bounces on her toes, too excited to stand still. It's easy to see her arms twitch, needing to hug me. She's the only person I want to celebrate with in this moment and the one too far away to do so. She had a ticket to tonight's game. She was supposed to be here. I'm glad she's with Alma in her time of need, but it doesn't stop me aching for her to be with me.

"Hamilton," frantic sports personalities greet while their camera persons scramble to find the perfect angle. "Great outing tonight. How does it feel to be World Series Champions?"

What a dumb question. I'll have to answer it just like every other ball player has over the years.

"It's been an amazing season. This is a great group of guys. We worked hard all season long and never lost sight of our goal. I'm proud to be a Cub." I hope that doesn't sound too cheesy.

"With a World Series win, how will this affect next season?"

"We'll prepare for next season as we do every year." I attempt to keep sarcasm from my voice. They really do ask dumb questions in these post-game interviews. "Perhaps we'll earn another ring to join this season's." I wave five fingers at them.

"I understand that your mother and sister were in attendance tonight. What does it mean to you that they witnessed you pitch in the final game of the World Series?"

"I'm always happy when my family can attend. I wouldn't have made it this far without their support over the years." My thoughts dart again to Madison. "A special person couldn't make it tonight. Although I wish she were here, I know she's celebrating with us in her thoughts."

"Hamilton is this a new romantic interest?" the over-eager announcer asks.

I smirk, raise my palm up, and walk away from the interview. I've said too much. I only wanted Madison to know I am thinking of her in this monumental moment. I don't want the press to hunt her down or follow her around.

With each of my next three interviews, I struggle to keep thoughts of Madison from becoming my answers.

"You have that faraway look in your eye," Stan claims as he and Delta approach through the raucous crowd.

I hug an excited Delta.

"You were on fire tonight," she states, patting my back. "Why isn't your family down here with you?"

"I invited them, but Mom prefers to celebrate privately at the condo later," I explain.

"That's not who you were longing for," Stan prods. "Did you get another update?"

I shake my head–it's much too loud to continue this conversation. When the next media crew approaches, I wink at my friend before composing myself yet again. I don't attempt to move Madison from my mind this time. There's no need to fight it–I can't deny I need her here. She's a big part of my life, she means everything to me, and it's time I told her so.

114

MADISON

Trenton offers to drive Liberty and I home, claiming he will return for his car tomorrow. He even helps me pack the abundance of toys I drug to Alma's room. He carries Liberty to the van and deftly buckles her in the car seat. Once home, he carries her to her crib, tucking her in for the night. He's a great adopted uncle. Liberty needs more male role models in her life like him.

I attempt to wipe the smile from my face as I lie in bed later. My thoughts return to Hamilton's performance in tonight's game. I imagine him celebrating in the locker room with his teammates. *I wonder where they went when they left Wrigley tonight. Did the owner plan an after party at some expensive venue?* Wherever he is, I want Hamilton to enjoy the moment. This is a once-in-a-lifetime moment; well for most it's once in a lifetime. Maybe the Cubs will repeat next year or the year after that. Perhaps Hamilton will collect another World Series ring or two during his career. There's no way I'll miss his next World Series. I won't be in another state–I'll celebrate with him every step of the way.

Baseball season is over, and in two days, it will be November. I only have two months. This time I will do it. Although, the joint Christmas with Alma and Memphis' families is no longer happening, I promised Alma, we set a deadline, and I will keep my vow. Liberty will meet Hamilton by Christmas. I will come clean and deal with the repercussions.

I'm sure Hamilton will be busy for several weeks until the World Series hype dies down. That gives me a couple weeks to plan a time to meet and the perfect words to explain we have a daughter. You'd think I would have figured it all out in the two years following my positive pregnancy test, but I've found it difficult. It seems finding the right words to say I'm sorry, share the reasons for my actions, and not lose the love of my life vexes me.

Add to that the fact that I need to find a new place for Liberty and I to live, and my life is very complicated right now. Memphis mentioned staying with her while I figure out my next move. In order to do that, I need to speak to Hamilton about Liberty first. I know I don't want to be here when the realtor starts showing the house to potential buyers, so I need to figure something out fast.

Last week, I felt safe as Alma and I shared this happy home. With one fall, one accident, my entire world shifted. I can't stay in this house. Liberty and I need to come up with a new plan and life that no longer depends upon Alma.

Alma is my pillar, my foundation, my friend. Now everything seems to crumble around me. I feel her loss more with each day she's away from home. Once again, I'm alone trying to find my place in the world. The 18-year-old me thought my college degree would secure my place and path. I even thought leaving Athens for college would ensure I left loneliness behind. How silly of me to think that something like that could change.

Fate is cruel. Our loving family ended with my dad's death. My once loving mother transformed into a tortured soul. It brought Hamilton into my life in middle school then tore him away with the draft. It brought Alma into my life, and now she falls away. *Where will it lead me now? Who will be the next to make me love them only to be ripped from my life? Will the cycle ever end?*

Realizing it will be hours before my mind allows me to sleep, I turn on my lamp to write. Without Alma's help, when will I find the time to write? While Liberty plays by herself, she still does require my attention–when I write, my mind is on one track. I can't watch her and write at the same time.

Try as I might, I can't think of anything but Hamilton. Instead of my story, I decide to send Hamilton an email.

From: alwayswrite@gmail.com

To: armnhammer@gmail.com
Subject: Freakin' World Series Champs

The word congratulations isn't big enough. You and the Cubs are World Series Champions!
You dominated the mound with every pitch. I'm so proud of you. (That sounds stupid & maternal.) You've worked hard for many years, and tonight, it showed.
I'm so sorry I wasn't there. I hope you know that. I wanted to be there so bad. It's not the same watching it on TV.
Alma stayed awake for most of it. Trenton came back for the last inning. The three of us struggled to celebrate quietly for your home run and again at the end of the game.
I'm home now and can't quiet my mind. I'm lying in bed, celebrating. I'm imagining you celebrating in the locker room and at the after party. I hope Stan kept you from leaving early. You've earned the right to party with your team all night (scratch that), all week long.
I must admit, I laughed at your post-game interviews and the silly questions they always asked. You smiled like a kid on Christmas morning.
You're a celebrity, and I often forget that. I'm not sure how you handle it. It's gonna change now. You'll have trouble walking down the street or going to your favorite restaurants from now on. Your hand is gonna get tired from all the autographs you'll be signing.
Don't let it go to your head, or I'll drive to Chicago and knock you down a notch or two. Remember what you were like in Athens and how much your favorite players influenced you. Oh, and I need an autograph, too.
Alma still stutters and slurs her words. She becomes frustrated when she can't get the words out. The staff mentioned she'll be transferred to a rehab facility or nursing home soon. While they state she'll improve, she'll never be able to return home. Trenton is meeting with a realtor about the house. Taylor and Cameron are letting him handle everything.
I'm so glad Memphis and Amy were at Wrigley for the game. I wish they could have stayed more than one night. I'm sure they wanted to celebrate with you. Amy's "friend" saw a great game with my ticket. Does she admit he's her boyfriend yet? Memphis and I laugh about her denial.

I really should do some writing and let you sleep or celebrate. I'm sure from this email you can see my thoughts are all over the place.

Love Ya,
Madison
P.S. I'm still your #1 fan.

115

MADISON

Liberty calls to me through the monitor. "Ma-Ma."

I want nothing more than to sleep late today. The adrenaline high of the World Series game took hours to fade. I wrote until two a.m. knowing Liberty rarely sleeps past seven.

I'm surprised to find Trenton already up and working in the kitchen as Liberty and I enter.

"Good morning," he greets without looking up from the laptop and legal pad in front of him on the table.

"It won't be good until after 10 or several cups of coffee," I mumble. Although I'm up with Liberty daily at 7, I am definitely not the morning person she is.

"There's a huge article about your man on the cover of today's paper." He motions toward the paper opposite him on the table.

I secure Liberty in her chair and hand her a bowl of luke-warm oatmeal and a spoon, knowing full well she will opt to use her fingers instead. With coffee in hand, I focus on Hamilton's cover story.

As the journalist describes the plays in last night's game, I relive them in my mind. I'm lost in the excitement and staring at the photo of Hamilton's teammates surrounding him on the mound at the end of the game.

In a perfect world, I would've been at his game. I'm bummed I gave my ticket away, but I know my place was with Alma yesterday.

"Madison," Trenton calls to me, breaking my trance. I look to him, confused. "Your daughter's done eating."

I look up from the paper and can't help but giggle at the sight of my daughter covered in oats.

"On a positive note," I tell Trenton while moving to the sink, "her bowl is empty." I wet two paper towels. They won't be enough, but it's a start.

Liberty sucks on her fingers while I begin at the top and work my way down. I free her springy curls then wipe down her face. The doorbell rings as I start at her elbow and wash to her fingertips.

"Can you get that, please?" I ask Trenton as my hands are now covered in oatmeal paste. I continue removing cereal from my daughter until a throat clears behind me.

"Madison, it's for you." Trenton steps by me to take Liberty from her chair.

A gruff male voice greets me as I turn. "Madison Crocker?"

All air flees my lungs and my hands fly to my mouth. Bile rises in my throat and I fear my worst fear has come to fruition.

"Yes," I assure both officers now standing in Alma's kitchen.

One shifts nervously. "Ms. Crocker, I'm Officer Blackburn. We're here in regard to your mother…"

"What's she done now?" I blurt. "And how much is the bail?" Heat floods my veins. I fume, and I don't even know what I'm fuming about.

"Ms. Crocker, there was an accident."

I knew this day would come. Her repeated attempts at drunk driving after late nights at the bar could only lead to this. *Please let there be no one injured. Please let there be no one else involved.*

"Ms. Crocker, a neighbor drove by her house twice this morning. He called the Sheriff's office in Athens because the front door stood open both times." He adjusts his hat before returning his hand to his belt loop.

I hear the officer's words but cannot process their meaning.

"Ms. Crocker, your mother passed away last night." He clears his throat with a horrifying half growl, half croak. "Now, they aren't sure of the specifics and are currently investigating."

I hear my heartbeat in my ears. Suddenly, I'm sweating.

Dead. My mother is dead. I can't believe it. She's dead. I never get to say goodbye.

What happened? How did she die? Was she in pain? Did she think about me? She was alone. I never wanted that. I never expected this.

"Madison." Trenton grips my shoulders, bending down to look directly into my eyes.

I shake myself out of my thoughts. "I'm sorry," I look toward the entry to the kitchen. The officers are no longer there. "Where'd they go?"

"Sit." Trenton pushes me down into his chair. "Drink." A bottle of water is forced into my hand. "You need Taylor or Mom right now. Anyone is better than me." He laces his fingers together, hands resting on top of his head.

"I'm fine," I inform him. "It just caught me off guard for a minute."

"Try five minutes," he states. "They didn't have any other details but wanted you to know that the house is roped off as a crime scene. The sheriff's department is retracing her steps of the previous 24 hours and anxiously waiting on the toxicology screen results."

I thank him for stepping up for me and brush my fingers lightly over Liberty's cheek before she darts from the room.

"Can you keep an eye on Liberty while I pack?"

"Madison, you don't need to pack right now. Take a minute. Take an hour. Hell, take all day. There's no rush. You can drive to Athens tomorrow." Trenton's frustration over not knowing exactly how to assist in this situation exudes from him.

"I need to keep busy," I explain. "I think better while I work. It will only take 30 minutes."

When he agrees, I excuse myself to pack upstairs. Unsure if I will be away a couple of days or a week, I pack several outfits for both Liberty and me. I fight the tears that threaten as I grab my writing materials for the sleepless nights that lie ahead and pack a separate suitcase of toys for Liberty.

It doesn't escape me that as I pack now for a trip to Athens, soon I will be packing for a permanent move from this house. I've become very comfortable in Alma's home for the past two years–it will not be an easy move.

Looking to heaven, I ask for mercy. "Please. I've had enough," I whisper. Alma's fall, her stroke, my need to move, and now my mother's death press down on me. I feel so helpless...It's too much. I want to roll up into a little ball and hide for a day or two. That's an option I don't have. I must be strong for Liberty, I need to help Taylor, Trenton, and Cameron, and as her only relative, I need to make funeral arrangements for my mother.

I pat my cheeks and mentally tell myself, "Suck it up, Buttercup."

I make two trips, carrying our bags down the long staircase. I find Trenton entertaining McGee and Liberty in the sunroom. I take advantage of their distraction to load the mini-van with four suitcases, a portable crib, a cooler for drinks and snacks, and my purse; it takes several trips.

The two-hour drive to Athens gives me much too long to think. With Alma in the hospital, I have Liberty with me. The big secret can no longer hide. All of Athens will soon meet my daughter.

Looking back, I wouldn't change a thing. I requested a favor—Hamilton granted my favor, and we followed through on our plans. If I changed anything, I wouldn't know Alma and her family, I wouldn't have my degree, I wouldn't be a published author, I wouldn't have watched Hamilton pitch in the World Series on TV, and I wouldn't have Liberty. I leave pieces of me everywhere. Some break off–some I willingly give. Part of my heart remains in Athens and part now resides in Columbia. A large chunk of my heart lives in Chicago.

I allow tears to fall as I drive.

For two years now, Hamilton and I chased our dreams, were apart, but kept in touch. Hamilton is my oldest friend, my best friend, my go-to-person, my emergency contact, my voice of reason—I cannot lose him.

My thoughts swirl to my mother. I assumed I'd have another 20-plus years to work things out with her. Of course, I imagined she'd eventually seek help for her addiction. She'll never meet her granddaughter. She'll never give me advice on being a mother.

I swipe away the river of tears, covering my cheeks. I need to mentally prepare myself to bury my mother while introducing Liberty to her dad and grandma. I shake my head; this will be a week from hell.

As my used Honda Accord carries me through the main streets of Athens, I feel the eyes of the locals assessing me. A car with an unrecognizable driver will cause the rumor mill to kick into overdrive. Several residents glue themselves to their police scanners. They will have shared that the sheriff was at Mother's farm and that the coroner was summoned. Law enforcement agents on the scene often share a few details with their families, neighbors, or friends. Privacy is not practiced in this town. The town of Athens, Missouri runs on the spreading of gossip.

Placing the car in park at the small grocery store, I cringe knowing inside I will be recognized. Within an hour, more than half of Athens will know I have returned for the funeral with a little girl in tow. It will spread like wildfire, everyone in this little burg knows the reason I am here most know of my strained relationship with my mother and assumed I would not show.

I assist Liberty from her car seat, and we walk hand-in-hand into the small market. I lift her into the child seat of the shopping cart while reminding her we only need a few items today and plan to return again tomorrow. The sweet smile on her cherub face warms my heart.

As we make our way up and down all eight aisles of the store, I place the items we might need this afternoon or tonight in the metal cart. Liberty requests macaroni and cheese for supper, so I purchase a box along with margarine and two-percent milk. I buy a case of diet cola—caffeine is a necessity for me. I procure cereal for breakfast and tissues, just in case there is none when we arrive. At the pharmacy section, I place a bottle of Benadryl in the cart to assist my sleeping before making my way to the check out.

Liberty enjoys looking at the varieties of candy placed conveniently as we wait our turn. She understands these are not items we consume except on special occasions. One might claim this is indeed a special occasion–I see it as much needed closure to a traumatic portion of my past. It's come much too soon. Every time I try to process her death, I long to run to Alma, but I can't.

"Madison Crocker," a much-too-high voice greets. "How long has it been?"

I close my eyes, bite my lips, and attempt to gather myself to politely greet her. I slowly turn around with a fake smile upon my lips find, a former classmate, Waverly Fleming behind me. Her grocery cart overflows with processed foods. Two toddlers sit in the child seat of the full cart, their fingers gripping the push handle. A boy about seven stands behind the cart next to his mother. In his hands, he holds four chocolate candy bars.

"Waverly, how have you been? Are these your children?" I attempt to be polite and interested in her life.

"The twins are my oldest; Mom is in the car with my youngest," she answers then points to the boy, "This is my husband's son. I'm so sorry to hear about your momma, my Aunt is the night dispatcher at the sheriff's office. She shared the tragic news with us at breakfast at Mom's. I am glad you came back to town. Will you be here long?"

"I'm here to make her arrangements; that's all," I claim not wanting to share too much for the gossip mill.

"Is this your daughter?" Waverly points as she asks the question I've been dreading.

"Yes, this is Liberty," I twirl her dark curl around my finger.

"She's adorable," Wendy draws out, her voice rising an octave.

Fortunately, it's now my turn at the register. As I place our few items on the black conveyor belt, Liberty waves at the little ones behind her, and Waverly continues talking. She fills me in on all the latest gossip on my former classmates. I pretend to listen as I block her out.

Waverly and I graduated together from Athens High School. It seems she married right after high school, choosing to remain local. In the two years I've been away, she has given birth to three children. In this small rural town, it's common for women to choose to forego college to start families immediately.

Once I pay, I wave goodbye to Waverly, quickly escaping with Liberty to my car. I'm sure she is not the only one that recognized me. Others will also be spreading the news of my arrival. I will be a hot topic as I have Liberty with me for the first time.

Liberty runs playfully through the grass ahead of me. Out of the city, on this seldom traveled gravel road, my constant, watchful eye is unwarranted. I know this, but I can't turn off my mother-hover gene. I attempt to corral her closer to the front door.

I freeze fifteen feet away, taking in the scene in front of me. As promised by the officers this morning, bright yellow tape hangs as a makeshift fence to keep non-law enforcement out. The front door is closed. I imagine it open, picturing the scene as it looked when they found her... Somewhere inside, my mother lay for hours, alone. *Was she in pain? Was it quick? Did she long for me?*

While Liberty sits nearby playing with sticks, I peek in a window. It's dark inside, and I can't make out anything. I should have known stopping here was a bad idea. I want answers to so many questions I fear I will never find answers to.

I long to visit my favorite spots, the cemetery across the road and the tree-house Dad built for me. I need time to think. I fight the urge to help Liberty climb up into the treehouse in the backyard with me; instead we climb back into the van. I pull from the gravel driveway with a pit in my stomach. I don't want to spend tonight in the motel room with Liberty. Athens only has one motel and to say it is lacking is an understatement. It seemed like a good idea when I made the reservation this morning, but now, I don't believe it is.

Instead of turning towards Athens, I head in the opposite direction. I've taken this road a million times. The farther I drive from my mother's home toward my new destination, the lighter I feel. I can do this–we can do this. It's time. I can take this sad situation and make it somewhat better.

When I place the van in park, my stomach drops, and my heartbeat quick-ens. *I'm really doing this. Take a breath. Just like pulling off a bandage, quick is best.* As I ease my driver's door open, Memphis steps out her back door.

"I'm so glad you're here," Memphis greets, opening her arms for me.

When I pull from her embrace, I ask, "Can I stay with you?"

"Psst," Memphis swats at me. "You know you are always welcome here."

"Well, I need to tell you something first." I signal for her to stay put as I back toward the vehicle. I open the back, driver's-side door, unbuckle then lift Liberty from the van. "Liberty, this is…"

"Grandma!" Memphis stands beside us; tears fill her wide eyes as her left hand presses against her chest and her right fans her face. "Oh, my!"

I'm not surprised; it's easy to see the resemblance between Liberty and Hamilton. She looks like his sister, Amy, as a little girl.

"Libby, this is Na-Na." I point as I speak. "And this is Liberty."

"Wib-Be," Liberty tells Memphis while pointing to herself.

"Yes, Libby," I point to my daughter. I love that she's attempting to intro-duce herself.

"Hi, Libby."

I absolutely love the smile on Memphis' face. It gives me hope.

"Mommy," Liberty places her hand on my cheek to get my attention. She then extends an arm towards Memphis.

"Um, this might be a little weird," I nervously tell Memphis. "Can you let Libby touch your face for a minute? She does this thing where she likes to look in your eyes." I love when Liberty does this to Alma and me. I hope Memphis will allow her to do her thing.

I step closer to Memphis. Liberty raises her two hands, placing them on each of Memphis' cheeks. Although I can't see it, I know her eyes are peering straight into her grandmother's. I witness tears form in Memphis' eyes while she smiles at Liberty. I'm not exactly sure what Liberty looks for when she does this, but happy with what she sees, she lets go of Memphis and looks around the farm.

"Mow-Mow!" Liberty claps. "Mommy, Mow-Mow!" She points at two kittens near the house. She wiggles trying to climb down.

"She's saying meow." I ask Memphis, "Are they somewhat tame?"

Memphis nods. "Let me get one for you."

I lower my daughter to the ground, and I hold her near me. Liberty claps as Memphis approaches the kittens. She wiggles harder to escape my hold. I release her as Memphis walks back with a kitten in her hands. She sits in a nearby chair, and Liberty quickly approaches.

"Mow-Mow," Liberty calls then giggles, placing her hands over her mouth.

"You want to touch it?" Memphis gently asks.

I slowly ease Liberty's hand out to touch the fluffy kitten. She tugs her hand back immediately after contact. With her hands over her mouth, she giggles.

"Our neighbor has an older, male house cat," I explain to Memphis. "He hides from her. This is the first cat she's ever seen up close and touched." I shrug. Growing up on the farm, touching animals was the norm. I suddenly feel embarrassed that my daughter has never touched a cat and need to explain it to Memphis.

"Libby," Memphis calls to her. "Want to touch it again?" When Liberty nods, she slowly extends the kitten toward her.

Liberty slowly holds out her hand. She hesitates within an inch of it. Memphis gently pets the kitten with her free hand and encourages Liberty to pet it just like she does. Liberty places her hand near the kitten's ears and rubs down its back. She imitates Memphis' petting over and over.

I love watching the world through my daughter's eyes. Her sense of wonder and desire to try new things amaze me. I hope to foster this in her and encourage her to be a life-long learner.

"Mind if I unload while the two of you..." I motion from Memphis to the kitten.

She nods, and I carry in the portable crib, our luggage, the cooler, the groceries, and the backpack. After my last trip, Liberty now sits in the chair with a proud smile upon her face while Memphis helps her hold the kitten in her little lap.

"Look at you!" I praise.

On Liberty's next pet down the kitten's back, a little meow emits. Liberty's eyes bug out as her mouth forms an "O". She quickly looks from Memphis to me.

"Mow-Mow!" Liberty announces.

"Yes, I heard the meow," Memphis states. "The kitty likes you. Cats meow when they are happy."

Liberty proudly nods at her grandmother's words.

"Libby," I bend in front of my daughter. "It's time to let the kitty go back to its mommy. We need to eat dinner. Aren't you hungry?" I nod trying to encourage her agreement.

Memphis rises, takes the kitten from Liberty's lap, and lets it down near the house. We watch as the kitten jogs towards the other cats near a tree in the backyard.

"Let's go see what Grandma has for dinner." She extends her free hand to Liberty.

"I bought some food on my way through town," I say as I follow the pair into the house.

Memphis shakes her head. "Nonsense. I'm sure I have something. We can save your food for tomorrow." She lifts Liberty to stand on the counter in front of her as she opens a cabinet door. "Hmm..."

Liberty points, and Memphis pulls a box of macaroni and cheese from the shelf. I nod, telling Memphis it works for dinner.

"Before we cook, let's go wash our hands." I say and Liberty hurries to follow me.

"Pod-de! Pod-de, Mommy!"

"Okay," I acknowledge. "Potty first."

I assist with removing her leggings then her Pull-up. It's still dry. She's really taken to this potty training. I lift her up to sit on the toilet seat then step back to wait and listen.

"Big girl potty already?" Memphis asks, approaching the restroom door.

"I tried it once a week ago, and she enjoys it. Sometimes she's wet overnight or after a nap; otherwise she potties in the big girl potty. I know at one-and-a-half, it's early. I anticipated her fighting me. I thought we'd attempt it once or twice a week for several months before I focused intently on it," I chuckle. "I should have realized she'd be tenacious in potty training, just like she is in everything she does. When she attempted to feed herself and walk, she demanded to do it on her own and didn't give up."

"Shh!" Liberty places her finger over her mouth. Her eyes grow wide as the sound of urine hitting the water fills the quiet room. When finished, she claps and cheers, nearly plunging into the toilet.

"Wow!" Memphis looks to Liberty. "You are a big girl."

Liberty nods. I help her finish the task and redress before we wash our hands. I squirt a small dab of hand soap on Liberty's hand then mine.

"Ready?" Liberty nods and I begin. "A-B-C-D..."

Memphis joins in, singing the alphabet song with me as Liberty and I rub soap over our hands. When we finish the song, I turn on the warm water, and we begin removing the bubbles from our hands. I dry Liberty's hands, and she helps dry mine. I scoop her up, and we return to the kitchen.

Liberty sniffs her hands then gestures for me to smell them. At Alma's, we use unscented soap. Memphis has a sweet pea hand soap, and Liberty won't stop sniffing the sweet scent. In the kitchen, she urges Memphis to smell her hands.

"Smells good," she tells Liberty, much to the joy of my little one. "I have a bottle under the sink. Would you like your own bottle of the soap?"

Liberty nods excitedly and claps.

Memphis pulls an old highchair from the utility closet. "I pulled it down from the attic to use when Amy brings the twins over."

"How often do they visit?"

"A couple of times a month, she brings the boys over for a change of scenery." Memphis places two plates and a bowl on the table. "They are a handful now that they can walk. Sometimes, they are too much for even the two of us to keep an eye on."

While I prep a salad, Memphis keeps an eye on the macaroni on the stove top, and Liberty entertains herself, eating dry cereal in the highchair.

"I'm sorry," I blurt. I can't wait, and Memphis hasn't asked. She hasn't pried for details. I need to know how she really feels about my actions.

"Uh-huh. You don't owe me an apology." Memphis leans back against the counter beside the stove with a wooden spoon in her hand and arms crossed. "You've given me a happy, healthy grandbaby. You made decisions you thought you had to. You sacrificed, and I'm sure you struggled. I now understand why you separated yourself from everyone you knew; it was to give my son his dream." She stirs the pasta, lays the spoon on the counter, and approaches me at the table. She places her hands on each of my shoulders. "Thank you for giving me a granddaughter. I might be biased, but I believe she is absolutely perfect."

I love her words but find it hard to believe she isn't mad at me for keeping my secret for so long.

"I kept a video journal during my pregnancy and after." I hope my videos prove I always planned to reveal Liberty to Hamilton and his family. "I'll give you the login information after dinner so you can view them. I know it can never make up for the time I robbed from Hamilton."

The timer interrupts my explanation. Memphis preps the macaroni, I fix each of us a drink, and Liberty talks to herself. We fix our plates and eat in silence for a bit.

116

HAMILTON

I pour myself into bed at 10:30. The past few days begin to wear on me. The appearances and the interviews take their toll. Tomorrow, my day begins promptly at 5:00 a.m. at the local network via satellite with ESPN on the East Coast.

My cell phone vibrates on the nightstand.

MOM

Madison is staying with me

her mother died

& she needs you

ME

I'm slammed with interviews

MOM

I know

ME

services scheduled?

> **MOM**
> sheriff still investigating
> rumors of foul play

> **ME**
> let me see what I can arrange

> **MOM**
> it's a family emergency
> Cubs will understand

> **ME**
> I'll let you know

My heart aches, and my chest feels heavy. It's not like my upcoming interviews will ask any questions I haven't already answered five times in the past twenty-four hours. I want to be with Madison. I decide to shoot a text; if I don't hear back, then I'll email my publicist, Berkeley, to see if I can get out of the appearances.

> **ME**
> are you up?

> **BERKELEY**
> yes, want me to call?

I dial her number instead of replying.

"Hello," Berkeley answers, always perky. "What's up?"

I'm sure the late hour leads her to believe I have a problem. "There's been a death in the family, and I need to get to Athens." It's not a total lie. Madison has been a part of my family since eighth grade.

"I'm sorry, Hamilton. Who passed away?" Berkeley quickly inquires. "How's Memphis?"

"Madison's mother passed away yesterday." I prepare for her stating the obvious--that she's not family.

"Just a second," Berkeley pauses, and I hear her murmuring to herself as she opens the calendar on her iPad. "Okay. Hmm. Okay. Maybe. No, that can't work. Okay…"

Realizing I could be on the phone for hours trying to help her rearrange each appearance, find a replacement for me, or cancel a function, I decide I'm going, no matter what. I've been the perfect client, public figure, and player. I've done everything asked of me and never been a no-show. I need to do this for Madison–I need to do this for me. I'm going to do this.

"Berkeley." I interrupt her thought process. "I'm packing as we speak. I'll be in Athens by morning. I need you to take care of everything for me."

"Sure." I hear the frustration in her voice. "How long do you need?"

I'm relieved she didn't fight me on this. "A week?" I run my hand over my face. "I'm not sure. Mom says she's not handling it well. Law enforcement suspect foul play. She can't schedule a funeral until the investigation is complete and they release the body. Let's say a week. I'll keep you updated."

"Um," Berkeley hedges. "Okay. You've got to be tired, and it's over a six-hour drive. Can I talk you into waiting until morning to drive?"

I groan. She's right. The smart thing to do is wait until morning.

"Can I ask a favor?" Berkeley clears her throat and quickly continues. "Can you do the ESPN gig at the station in the morning? I won't be able to get anyone to replace you in the next six hours. You could leave Chicago by nine and be in Athens around dinner time."

I release a deep, audible breath. "Yeah, if you can get me out of everything else, I can be there in the morning."

"Good. Pack quick and get to sleep. We don't want dark circles under your eyes on ESPN."

I agree with Berkeley and say goodbye. I pack a bag and hang my suit over it in the closet before climbing back into bed.

ME

I'll head out in the morning

text when I'm on my way

MOM

Thank you

ME

be there by dinner time

MOM

she'll be glad to have you here

ME

gotta be up @4 am

need sleep

talk to you tomorrow

MOM

I love you

ME

(heart emoji)

117

MADISON

I barely keep my eyes open as Memphis clicks another video entry in the journal I created for Hamilton.

"I'm gonna go lay Liberty down for the night," I state after my next yawn.

"Why don't you turn in for the night, too?" Memphis' words catch me off guard. I thought I was hiding my exhaustion. "I'll just be here, watching Liberty grow before my eyes. You've created a terrific chronicle of her life. Get some sleep. I'll see you in the morning."

I nod and carry Liberty upstairs. I hesitate at the door to Amy's room. I set up the portable crib in the corner earlier. I look to my pajamas on Amy's twin bed. This is not where I need to be. I turn, walking back down the hallway.

I step into Hamilton's room. "This is Daddy's room," I inform Liberty.

"Daddy," my sleepy toddler murmurs around the two fingers in her mouth.

I sit her on the bed Hamilton used for 18 years of his life. "I'll go get a book; you stay right here." When Liberty nods, I grab the bag I packed for her from Amy's room and return with it in hand.

I choose one book then slide onto the bed, urging Liberty to lay beside me. I open the book, and she begins playing with one of the curls that frame her face. As I read, her eyes grow heavy and eventually close. I shut the book midway, rolling to face my baby girl.

My head lays on Hamilton's pillow just as his has so many times before. The heady scent of him surrounds me. It wraps me like a warm blanket, letting me know everything is going to be okay. In my heart, I know Hamilton will love and accept Liberty on sight. It's his feelings towards me that I fear. I know he loves me, but I'm unsure if he will continue to love me when I share Liberty with him. Now that Memphis has met her, Hamilton will learn about our child very soon. I can no longer hide her. As more people in Athens meet Liberty, I risk Hamilton finding out from someone other than me, and I can't let that happen. I need a plan, and I need it now. I grab my phone.

ME

I'm @ your mom's

I know you're busy

will you be @ funeral?

I plug the phone into the charger and quickly fall asleep.

The first day of November arrives with heavy dread as I slip from Hamilton's bed. I quietly take care of my morning business in the attached bathroom then sit on the floor, leaning on the bed, and open my cell phone.

I don't see a text from Hamilton. The timestamp shows I texted him at 11:15 last night. It's now 7:00 a.m. I guess he could have been asleep and not have seen my text yet. I turn as Liberty stirs on her side of the bed.

"Good morning," I call to her, a smile upon my face.

"Na-Na?" She sleepily rubs her eyes and stretches.

"Let's go potty, then we can go down to see Grandma."

I follow along as Memphis tours the farm with Liberty in her arms. We pet the horses and prepare to bottle-feed a calf. Liberty enjoys making each animal sound with Memphis. I marvel at the ease at which the two have bonded.

I know it will be the same with Hamilton. I dread his reaction to my betrayal. I fear he won't forgive as easily as his mother.

I force my mind to focus on my daughter feeding the calf in front of me. I snap a couple photos with my phone. Lifted by her grandmother, Liberty tips a large bottle into the mouth of the week-old calf. As the calf nurses and nudges, it reminds me of helping my dad with chores on the farm. I shadowed him as often as I could. My favorite memories are riding the tractor with him. Maybe tomorrow I'll take my daughter on her first tractor ride.

"We should clean up," Memphis suggests. "We'll need to leave soon for the funeral home."

I'd forgotten all about the appointment Memphis made for us to discuss arrangements for a funeral. She's promised to help me every step of the way, and I'll surely need her help.

118

HAMILTON

My mother's house comes into view. I find it odd that no vehicles are in the driveway. Mom knew I'd be here for dinner, and it's 5:30 p.m. That's weird. I shoot Mom a text before I exit my parked truck.

ME

I'm here

where are you?

I decide to carry my bags inside while waiting for Mom's reply. The house is dark. I turn on a light as I walk through the kitchen and upstairs to my room. I hang my suit in the closet and place my duffle on the bed. A stuffed toy lays on a pillow. Amy must have left it last time she had the twins over to visit Mom. I check my phone as I descend the stairs. Still nothing.

ME

hello?

MOM

sorry, I'm at store

be home soon

I peek out the kitchen window at the sound of a vehicle coming up the lane. I don't recognize the light blue minivan. I walk outside to greet the stranger. Perhaps they're lost and need directions.

As the van parks, I recognize Madison in the driver's seat. I approach, a smile on my face.

"Hey," she greets, exiting from the driver's seat. "This is...a surprise." She doesn't sound like herself. Her hands shake as she plays with the zipper on her jacket.

Why isn't she coming to me? A surprise? Why didn't my mom tell her my plans? Mom said she wasn't handling her mom's death very well, maybe Madison forgot I was on my way. She stands frozen in place, pale as a ghost.

"I told Mom I would be here for dinner." Unable to resist any longer, I wrap her in a tight hug. In her ear, I whisper, "How are you doing?"

She shakes her head, unable to answer me. She pulls away as tears stream down her cheeks. "Let's go inside." Her voice is shaky and barely above a whisper.

As we enter Mom's kitchen, I turn her to face me.

"Madison, you're scaring me," I confess. "Please talk to me."

Her cell phone beeps from her pocket at the same time mine vibrates in mine.

MOM

I'm leaving store now

please talk to Madison

tell her how you feel

give her some good news

I quirk my head to the side, trying to interpret Mom's texts. *Does she mean our conversation last Christmas? Does she want me to share everything we talked about then and in the year since?*

"That's weird."

I lift my head at Madison's statement. "What's weird?"

"Your mom just texted me, and I quote, 'Make Hamilton tell you the secret.' What does she mean?"

Damn it, Mom. She leaves me no choice. My pulse speeds up and my palms sweat.

Dark shadows lie beneath Madison's sad eyes. Exhaustion and stress darken her beautiful face. "Um..." I rise, walking to the refrigerator. "I'm going to have a beer. You want one?"

"No, thank you."

"So..." I pause, trying to decide how to start. "Last year, last winter, I had a long talk with Mom about my life in Chicago." I sit and take a long pull from my beer. "Okay. I'm going to share some things with you, but you have to promise you won't be mad at me."

"Mad at you? Why would I be mad at you?" She tilts her head, her eyes imploring me for answers.

"I didn't share some things with you. I didn't share them with anyone until I told Mom last Christmas." I shrug apologetically. "I live in a town with millions of people, and I am alone. When I leave the ballpark, I'm alone. I eat alone, I watch TV alone, and I live in a large condo all by myself." I groan on my exhale. *Thanks Mom. Is this really why she texted me to come here?* I attempt to take in a calming breath.

"It's hard to trust anyone I meet. I learned in my first short season in the Majors that people want to use me. Other players, women I meet, and even businesses want to exploit my celebrity for their gain." I run my fingers through my hair. Madison nervously picks at her cuticles while her eyes are on me. She doesn't look away. I continue before I chicken out.

"I quickly learned it's just easier to avoid these situations. It's so different from life here in Missouri. So, if I'm not working, I'm home alone. Mom, Amy and you are the only people I trust aside from my agent and publicist. It's the way it has to be."

Madison places her palms on the table in front of her, leaning in my direction. "What about Stan? You talk about him and his family sometimes." The corners of her mouth curve slightly. She perks up a bit at the chance to help me through this.

"Yeah, I hang with him and the family from time to time. But as you can imagine, they are busy, and I don't want to be a nuisance." *Wow! I sound pathetic.* "I spend most of my free time imagining you with me."

Her cheeks pink infinitesimally as her eyes grow wide. I smirk, knowing what she thinks I meant.

"When I walk down the street, I imagine you walking beside me. I daydream about you being at the condo when I return from a road trip." I draw in a deep breath, preparing for the big reveal. "So, last winter I asked for Mom's help."

I shift in my seat to pull the tiny black velvet box from my front pocket. "I've carried this with me since January." I fall to one knee in front of her.

Madison's hands fly to her mouth. Her eyes grow wide, and her breath hitches.

Smiling, I continue. "My life changed on my last night in Athens. I've missed you more every day since. I can't tolerate my life, any life, without you by my side. Madison Crocker, will you save my lonely existence and marry me?" I extend the open ring box toward her.

I attempt to regulate my racing heart. *I did it. I finally admitted everything. I've placed my heart in her hands.*

"Ham," she whispers as large tears flow down her face. "I have to tell you something first."

"No, you need to answer me. Then you can tell me anything you like."

"Hamilton, I'm afraid you may not want to marry me after I tell you..."

I realize the exhaustion I recognized earlier on her face was also fear.

"There's nothing you can tell me that will make me change my mind." I need her to trust my love.

She shakes her head vigorously. "You say that now, but I need you to know..."

The door swings open; I witness true fear in Madison's eyes before she turns. A tiny girl toddles into my mom's kitchen like she owns the place. I'm still kneeling as she rounds the table on her way to Madison, her chocolate curls bouncing with each step.

"Mommy, ice-me. Ice-me." She extends her tiny jacket covered arm, allowing Madison to remove the plastic grocery bag.

Madison's attention is glued to the child. Warmth speeds throughout my body and my heart drums in my chest. My brain rapidly processes the fact Madison is a mother. Instantly, I know the child; I've seen her before. She's a mirror image of my sister, Amy. I peel my eyes from the darling girl to my mother, standing behind Madison. Mom beams and nods. I open my mouth in an attempt to draw more air into my burning lungs.

"Grandma bought you ice cream?" Madison asks the child.

The girl nods once before clapping.

"Ice cream after dinner," Mom reminds the toddler and places several small tubs of ice cream into the freezer.

The little girl proudly carries her own tub to Mom, and she tucks it away with the others. I glance back to Madison. She stares anxiously at me.

This is it. This is the secret she mentioned so many months ago. She wasn't raped as I worried when she fell deep in her depression. This is the secret she worries will cause me not to love her. This is the reason she didn't reply to my proposal moments ago.

I move the ring box from the table into my open palm and extend it in her direction. She shakes her head, tears falling faster now. "I love you more now than I did minutes ago. I love everything about you. Please?" I choke on the words I need to say. I attempt to clear my throat. I hate the hoarse sound of my voice when I continue. "Marry me. Let me love you. Let me love both of you. I'm lost without you."

I pull my grandmother's ring from the box. Slowly, I slide it upon her left ring finger and lock my eyes with hers. She doesn't refuse my action. She doesn't argue.

My mother claps excitedly as I rise. I pull Madison from her chair into my arms. "I'm sorry I hurt you," I whisper. "I can't imagine how scared you were. I didn't know..."

She pulls from my embrace. "I didn't want you to know." She shakes her head. "I mean I didn't want to tell you right away. I wanted you to chase your dream, and you did. It was even better than my wildest dreams. I needed you to settle in before I told you."

Wait. What? She's protecting me. I failed to protect her on our first night together. And she thought she needed to protect me?

453

"I…" I begin, but Mom interrupts me.

"Let's wait 'til later tonight to share all the details," she points to the little one she's holding. "I've got a hungry granddaughter to feed."

Granddaughter. She has a granddaughter. I have a daughter.

As a tsunami of emotion floods over me, the little girl squirms free and walks toward me. I squat in front of her, never taking my eyes off of her. She extends her tiny hands to my face. Her dark eyes scan mine. I marvel at her actions. She's never met me, yet she peers into my soul like she knows me. This precious miniature version of my older sister standing before me, eyes scanning mine. But what is she waiting for? What should I do? What would a dad do at this exact moment, meeting his daughter for the very first time? How old is she? I scan this confident little person still clutching my face from head to toe. She could be one or maybe… My thoughts stop in their tracks when her perfect lips grace my cheek with a kiss.

She steps back, pointing to her chest. "Wib-Be," she says.

Wib-Be? Fear engulfs me. She's trying to tell me something, and I don't understand. I look to Madison for a lifeline.

"This is Liberty, or Libby." Madison smiles for the first time tonight.

Liberty points to me. "Daddy."

It's not a question. Her voice doesn't rise at the end of the name. *She knows I'm Daddy. How can that be?*

She turns to her mom when I don't respond. Madison picks her up, quickly placing a kiss on her chubby cheek. I remain frozen in my squat, and my hands tremble.

"I think Daddy needs another drink." Madison looks from me to Liberty. "Should we get him a drink?"

My daughter smiles my way, nodding. Her smile melts me to a puddle. I've never seen anything so beautiful, so perfect. Instantly, she's my whole world, the center of my universe. I try to remain calm and look casual as my world has just doubled in size. Instead of one woman, I now have two.

"She's a miniature Amy," I blurt.

They turn back from the fridge with a beer for me while my mom pulls me into a hug.

"Isn't she perfect?" Mom whispers into my ear before pulling away.

"Daddy," Libby calls to me as Madison extends the cold beer bottle. "Pod-de!" her little voice yells without warning.

I marvel at the speed in which Madison sweeps her into the bathroom and closes the door. I look to Mom, my brow furrowed.

"Potty training," Mom beams proudly. "She's smart."

"She got that from her mom," I state.

Mom waves a paper plate at me. "She gets her looks from you."

"Um," Madison calls from a slightly open bathroom door. "Libby wants Daddy to watch her."

Watch her potty? Is that allowed? I'm a guy. Stone-still, my wide eyes beg Mom for guidance.

My mother turns me in the direction of the bathroom and gives me a shove.

"Should I...?"

"You're her Daddy. It's okay if you're her dad." Mom states, understanding my hesitation. "You'll be by yourself with her, so you better get used to it."

"Daddy!" My daughter waves at me.

I stand frozen awkwardly in the door frame. It feels pervy to watch a child sit on the toilet.

Liberty's movements cease as the sound of pee fills the tiny room. The widest smile I've ever seen glows as bright as the twinkles in her dark eyes. She claps at her success. When her tiny bottom sinks, Madison quickly saves her from falling into the water. That was close.

I'm lost in the routine as they redress, squirt soap on hands, sniff the soap, and sing the alphabet song. *How will I ever learn all of this? There's got to be a book. I'll ask Mom about it later.*

Libby raises her freshly washed hands in the air, signaling for me to lift her up. When I do, she places her tiny hand near my nose. I inhale the scent as she giggles.

"She's enamored with your mother's sweet pea hand soap," Madison explains. "We don't have it at Alma's."

Libby again places her hands on my cheeks. This time her eyes don't examine me. She places a kiss on my lips.

Again, this tiny girl knocks me to my knees. Her kiss, her acceptance of me, her calling me Daddy within minutes of meeting me is humbling. Suddenly, everything I've accomplished pales in comparison to creating this perfect, tiny person.

Madison and Mom fly around the kitchen, distributing paper plates, napkins, pizza and drinks for everyone while I hold my daughter in my arms, never wanting to let her go.

119

MADISON

I snap Liberty into her highchair, placing a paper plate in front of her. From mine, I cut tiny pieces of cheese pizza then slide them onto hers. I tear a piece of thinly sliced ham for her and move her toddler cup of milk within her reach.

As I turn toward our table and my plate, I find Hamilton staring at me. "What?"

He shakes his head. "I've got a lot to learn," he murmurs, brow furrowed.

"You'll be fine," Memphis assures him. "Most is common sense, so you will be fine."

I guess I didn't think that Hamilton might feel overwhelmed by all of the day-to-day parenting activities. I worried about all the important moments he missed and created videos to help with that.

"Believe it or not," Memphis continues, "you've watched parents your entire life. All that info is stored deep in your brain and will slide to the front as you need it."

I know it may not help with his current fears of knowing what to do and when, but I feel I need to share now. "Ham, I've created a video journal for you. It has videos from my growing belly, the birth, first words, first steps, and attending Cubs games."

His eyes sparkle.

"I know it can never make up for the moments you missed, but I wanted you to be able to see her life up 'til now." I shrug apologetically, knowing my videos will never be enough.

He reaches across the table to hold my hand, tilting his head. He opens his mouth to speak but is interrupted.

"Daddy!" Liberty raises her little voice and extends her hand to him.

Hamilton takes her hand just like he holds mine. She smiles at him and continues to eat with her free hand. I chuckle. Seems Liberty will be jealous of the attention her daddy gives me. His hands will be full, and I love it.

"I watched four hours of videos last night," Memphis brags. "I couldn't take my eyes off the laptop screen. I even had to rewind and watch several of them a second time."

Hamilton looks from his mom to me, a crooked smile upon his face. His brown eyes dance with excitement.

"I'll give you the site and log in tonight." I smile, knowing he's excited to view them. "You can watch on your phone or computer anytime."

"Don't start if you don't have an hour to two," Memphis warns. "It was hard for me to shut them off to sleep last night."

I love that she enjoyed them so much. I hope Hamilton will, too.

"Cubbie," Liberty wines while Memphis and I clear the table.

I place the leftover pizza in the refrigerator then turn to face Hamilton, who's holding Liberty. One of her hands twirls a curl while Hamilton spoon feeds her the ice cream, her head on his shoulder.

"Liberty," I attempt to draw her attention from her father's large bowl of ice cream to me. "First bath time, then Cubbie bear."

Memphis announces, "It's bath time! I love bath time."

Liberty lifts her head from Daddy's shoulder, and she slides from his lap, abandoning the shared ice cream. She looks over the edge of the bathtub as I run warm water and place a few of her favorite bath toys inside. Happy with what she finds, she hurries back to Hamilton. "Daddy," she clutches his right hand in both of hers. "Baff!"

Hamilton promises, "You go. I'll eat my ice cream quick then come watch you in the bathtub."

My daughter, happy with his promise, runs toward the bathroom yelling at Na-Na the entire way. It may be very crowded for three adults to watch her in the tiny bathroom tonight.

I shut off the water, strip Liberty, and prompt her to potty before I place her into the tub. As she always does, she begins swimming, splashing, and blowing bubbles immediately. I step back to allow Daddy and Grandma to witness the bath time fun.

As they enjoy Libby and her bath time play, the pit in my stomach grows. Soon, Liberty will be asleep, and Hamilton and I will be alone. It'll be our time to talk.

I want him to tell me honestly how he really feels. He needs to yell at me or throw something. He should say he'll never forgive me. I deserve his ire. I deserve it all–I cheated him out of a year and a half of Liberty's life. I stole moments; although I tried to record many, it's not the same. I didn't give him a choice–I chose for him to go after his dream rather than be with his daughter. I'm selfish. How can I hope for him to keep loving me?

120

HAMILTON

Wrapped in a towel, Liberty stands on a matt outside the tub while Madison attempts to dry her springy ringlets. I shake my head. It's like I'm looking at Amy in our childhood. It's uncanny.

My cheeks ache from smiling so much. My heart swells tight in my chest. I never dreamt I'd know such love. The shear amount of love I hold for the two girls in front of me overwhelms me.

"Daddy," a sweet little voice calls as her arms reach upwards. Now in a Cubs nightgown, I lift her into my arms. "Cubs," she points to the front of her chest.

"I love your pajamas," I respond.

"Daddy gave you those for Valentine's Day, didn't he?" Madison prompts, and Liberty nods in agreement.

I go along with it and add the gift to all the questions building in my head.

At Madison's prompting, we say good night to Grandma before I carry my daughter up to bed. Liberty's head rests upon my shoulder as we climb the stairs, Madison following behind.

"I set her crib up in Amy's room," Madison states, placing a hand at my side.

"Daddy's," Liberty demands.

For the life of me, I don't understand.

"Her books are in your room," Madison explains.

I hold Liberty in the center of my chest, unsure what to do next.

"Cubbie!" Liberty points to the stuffed toy on my bed.

Unsteady in my actions, I lower her onto my bed where she hugs the bear tight to her chest and rests her curls on my pillow. I sit carefully on the edge.

Madison approaches, a couple of books in hand. Without a word, she slides between Liberty and the wall.

"Pick a book," she prompts, holding three books above them.

Liberty points to the weirdest book I've ever seen. Madison lays the other books down and settles into the mattress, opening the cover.

"Daddy sweep," my daughter demands, patting a pillow.

Madison turns her head and smiles encouragingly. It's clear they have a routine. I feel like I am interfering.

"Wib-be wead,"

Will I ever learn this new language? I feel lost with no translation manual.

"Okay, Libby can read to Daddy." Madison throws me a life raft by interpreting.

"Wib-be wead" equals Libby read. That makes sense. Maybe I'll get the hang of it after all.

Liberty begins to point at each photograph in this four-by-six book and declares who is in each photo. The first photo is Madison then Alma. I look at the picture of Alma holding Liberty. It's the same woman I've seen a few times while Face-Timing Madison. Next is McGee then my mom and me. So, this is how she recognized me tonight. Madison shared photos of me to help my daughter connect. It's all coming together now.

A giant yawn engulfs Liberty's entire face.

"Can I read?" I offer to allow her to fall asleep.

Her approving nod clutches my heart. Surely not all kids are this agreeable.

I steal peeks frequently at Liberty's tired eyes as I read the label secured at the bottom of each picture. The book contains photos of my family, Alma's family, and all of our mutual friends from Athens. I continue to read a few more once she loses the battle to keep her eyes open.

I move my glance to Madison to find her eyes glistening with tears. I lay the book down, my hand moving to her face on its own. Gently, I caress her cheek.

"She's perfect," I whisper in an attempt to keep from waking Liberty.

"Far from perfect, but I know what you mean," Madison corrects.

"I'm sorry I didn't protect you." A lump forms in my throat.

Madison's hand covers mine on her cheek. "You never hurt me."

"You were alone, pregnant, in a new city, a new school, with no money, I..."

She places a finger on my lips to silence me. Slowly, gently, I kiss her fingertip before pulling her finger away.

"I should have been there. If I had visited during my off-season as I promised, I would have known you were pregnant," I clear my throat. "I would have helped Mom with the farm and cared for the two of you. You didn't have to do it all alone." Tears wet my cheeks as I spill my heart to the woman I've loved for so long. "Please forgive me," I beg. "I've known for a long time that I should have taken over the farm after Dad's death. A good son would have."

"Ham," her voice cracks. "I'm the one that needs your forgiveness. I didn't tell you. I wanted you to have a career in the Majors and didn't want to be the reason you gave that up."

I long to pull her into my arms as her sobs strengthen. "Shh," I urge. "I know why you kept the secret. I'm just sorry I didn't protect you better on our night together. I never meant for this." I swipe tears from her cheeks. "You allowed me to earn a World Series ring." I smile at her. "Tonight, we admitted we'd rather be together than apart. We've both apologized. We're good, right?"

Madison nods, a slight smile upon her lips.

"Now, what's the update on your mother's investigation?" I ask.

"I can't," she whimpers. "Distract me. Tell me all about the World Series."

Her tears dry and eyes grow heavy as I play with her hair and share everything I remember about our celebrations. I stare at my fingers in her hair as I talk. When she no longer asks questions, I find her eyes closed.

She snores softly. I study her relaxed face. I don't like the dark shadows under her eyes. She hasn't been sleeping. Taking care of Liberty and Alma while watching ball games each night has taken their toll.

She needs sleep. I tug my phone from my pocket and snap a picture of my sleeping girls. I stare at them for several long moments. My world will never be the same.

Realizing I neglected to get the login information from her before she fell asleep, I tiptoe downstairs to see if Mom's up. I can't wait to see the videos she rants about.

121

MADISON

My head swims with all I learned at my family's lawyer's office today. Hurt slices through me with the secrets my mother kept. Why wouldn't she tell me? With my dad's death, the farm was paid in full. I never knew this. My mother had a thousand more dollars per month that she apparently squandered on her drinking. A tiny part of me hopes she didn't spend it on alcohol but on something responsible. Maybe I will uncover it in the days to come, but I'm not holding my breath.

Also, with my dad's passing, a trust fund was created for my secondary education expenses. Why did she not tell me this? I get why she didn't tell me at age 13 it existed. Perhaps she wanted me to strive for good grades and thought if I knew my education was paid for, I wouldn't care about the grades. But she didn't tell me my senior year, at graduation, or when I moved in with Alma in Columbia. I worked my butt off to get straight A's. I took all of the dual credit classes I could while they were free in high school to save me money. I saved my money from babysitting and my part-time job. All the while, she knew more than 50,000 dollars gathered interest in the Athens Bank while I scraped for every penny I could save. I nursed my twenty-year-old, beat up car along for years to save money. I didn't have an air conditioner in the ninety and one-hundred-degree July and August days. Why? Why would a mother do that to her child?

Top that off with the fact that I didn't know my dad's parents' farm remained in our family. As of now, it's in my name. I'm 20 years old, and I own two farms, free and clear. Fortunately, when my dad passed, their farm waited in a trust until I turned 18 instead of transferring to my mother's name. This farm is valued at over 1.5 million dollars and constantly growing. I became a millionaire at age 18 and didn't even know it. The land and the old farmhouse are rented on a year-to-year basis. All of the income from the property rolls back into Crocker Farms, so it's constantly growing for me.

Their lawyer, now my lawyer, states I need to decide what to do with my parents' farm as soon as possible. He offered to help me rent the land and the house or sell it. My grandparents' farm has already signed contracts for the next 12 months, so I have a year to decide whether to continue with it kept in the trust or to sell. Hours later, my head still swims with all I inherited years ago and this week along with all of the responsibility and decisions that lie ahead.

I sat quietly during the meeting, taking it all in, while Hamilton asked several questions. He shared the contact information for his financial guy with the lawyer and seemed to understand the ins and outs of the financial mumbo-jumbo.

I'm grateful he's with me. When the funeral is over, I plan for him to walk me through it all and give me some lessons. It's important that I understand it all to ensure a better future for our daughter.

"Mady," Hamilton's voice calls to me. He stands outside my open passenger door. We've arrived at the sheriff's office.

"Sorry." I shake my thoughts from my head, preparing to face news of my mother's death inside these walls. "I'm not sure I can handle much more."

He pulls me into a tight hug. "I'm here." He places a long kiss to my temple. "After this, I'll take you to Liberty." He tucks my hair behind my ear. "We can hold 'Mow-Mows' and eat ice cream."

I love the speed with which he's learning everything about Liberty. Looking into his eyes, I see he believes once we're at Memphis' farm in the presence of our daughter that all will seem better. He's right—when Liberty is in my arms, the present and future seem less daunting.

I take his hand, shut my door, and allow him to lead me into the county sheriff's office. We don't need to introduce ourselves. Several office staff members, Athens Police Officers, Highway Patrol Officers, and deputies swarm Hamilton. Rumors of his return to Athens tipped them off that he might arrive with me today. They congratulate him on the Cubs winning the World Series, ask for autographs, and pose for photos with him.

It's easy for me to forget he's a famous athlete. When I'm with him, he's still just Hamilton. It isn't until we go out in public and he's surrounded by adoring fans that I remember he's more than just my hometown boy now. He glances my direction with an apologetic look. I smile, letting him know it's okay. Watching him with his hometown fans eases my mood.

"Ms. Crocker," the sheriff greets, extending his hand. "I'm sorry about all of that." He nods towards Hamilton.

"It's fine; he needs to come home more often. Most of them were his fans before he left for the Major Leagues."

"Guys!" He yells through the office. "Mr. Armstrong, please join us as we head to my office." He shoots a stern look to the crowd.

Hamilton assumes the seat beside me while the sheriff closes his door and seats himself on the other side of his desk. Moving a file folder from a tray to the empty area in front of him, he begins.

"In our investigation, we have interviewed several people that saw your mother on October 30th." He's careful to keep the crime scene photos covered. "The coroner suspects she was poisoned, and we are still waiting on the tox reports. They should be in later today or tomorrow." He sighs, clearly not wanting to share the next part. "Arnold Ballwin confessed to having a sexual relationship with your mother for the two months prior to her death."

Well, I wasn't expecting that bit of information. I thought he'd share a suspect list, the events of her last day, time of death, but not that my mother was having sex with the married owner of the bar she practically lived at.

"He confessed to entertaining your mother around four p.m. on the 30th. Then, she went to the Black Jack, and he waited an hour before he arrived at the bar. Apparently, this was common on the days his wife would open and close the bar." He closes the folder. "Several people verified your mother arrived at the bar around 4:30 and remained until closing. Arnold was said to leave the bar at 10:30 p.m. We confirmed with neighbors that when he arrived home, he stayed until his wife arrived home after the bar there all night."

"We have two more interviews this afternoon. Arnold's wife, Henrietta, was the last to see your mom when she closed the bar at midnight. She is one we will be talking to this afternoon." The sheriff takes turns looking at

Hamilton and me as he talks. "Your mother's car wasn't found at her home. We found it still parked around the corner from Black Jack Bar on the thirty-first. We are trying to piece together the events that occurred when she left the bar, how she got home, and what happened when she arrived home."

Hamilton squeezes my hand in support.

"I hope to have more information to share after today's interviews and the tox results. I'll call you around dinner tonight to give you an update." With that, the sheriff escorts us back to our car and sends us on our way.

"Thoughts?" Hamilton prompts as we drive home from Athens.

What a loaded question. My thoughts. Well, right now, they are all over the place. "Part of me doesn't believe she was poisoned. Or at least not by anyone but herself. I mean, why would anyone do it? They didn't steal anything; her purse and phone were found still in her possession." Hamilton nods in agreement as I continue. "I could do without knowing she was sleeping with Arnold."

"I know," Hamilton cringes while keeping his attention on the road.

"Honestly, I'm more upset with all she kept from me." I lean my head against the window, not seeing the farmland passing by. "I struggled through high school then even more the past two years, and I didn't need to. It blows my mind that she never told me. Why do you think she did that?"

"Honey, you will never know why. Just like so many other things she's done. All you can do is focus on what you plan to do now that you know about the two farms and the trust fund." He quickly smiles at me before facing the road again. "It's important that you take care of yourself and then do a little good with it. You know?"

I love that he gets me. Several people in Columbia took care of me when I thought had nothing. I need to find a way to pay it forward while thanking them for all they did for me.

"It's overwhelming," I confess. Lifting my head, I take his free hand. "Will you please help me with the farms and financial stuff?"

"If you want. I meant it when I said we'd discuss it with my financial guy. He really helped me organize and plan; I'm sure he will have lots of options for you." He squeezes my hand reassuringly. "First thing is you need to decide if you want to keep each farm and if you plan to live at either one."

I pull my hand from his and turn in the seat, pulling my knees up, facing him. "I plan to live with my husband."

Hamilton squeezes my knee. He tears his eyes briefly from the highway. His face says all I need to know. He likes my statement a lot.

"I don't know if I will ever live on either farm, but I think I'd like to keep them, at least for a while." I shrug and purse my lips. "I thought I would have to sell the farm since I couldn't keep up with the payments. Now that I know it's paid off; I want to keep it. I have many great memories of my dad on the farm. Even the last seven years didn't erase the fun I had with Mom and Dad before that."

"So," Hamilton summarizes, "I'll contact Foster; he can get in touch with your lawyer and share some options with you."

"Um, with us," I correct. "As a couple, what's mine is yours."

"I get that, but…"

"No buts!" My voice raises sternly.

Hamilton's sigh lets me know he doesn't plan to argue me on this topic right now.

"I'd like to plan a get together with the entire gang," I state, staring out the window once again.

"To tell them we're getting married?" he assumes.

"Well, yes," I agree. "I need to tell them about Liberty."

He swiftly pulls to the side of the gravel road and puts the truck into park. He turns to face me. "I assumed they already knew."

I shake my head, internally cussing my burning sinuses.

"Adrian and Bethany only know because they surprised me in Columbia," I confess. "I swore them to secrecy until I could tell you."

He pulls me onto his lap and holds me tight. As I cry into his shoulder, I feel him pull his cellphone from his back pocket. I'm still trying to stop my tears when my own phone vibrates.

He chuckles. "Group text. It's from me."

I wipe my eyes, struggling to read my cell phone through them.

HAMILTON

bonfire tomorrow

7 @ farm

ME

hope to see you

SALEM

we're in

ADRIAN

count us in

BETHANY

what can I bring

ME

nothing

SAVANNAH

(thumbs up emoji)

When we pull up to the house, Memphis and Liberty hold two kittens in their laps on the porch swing. Liberty's big wave greets us as we exit Hamilton's truck.

"Daddy, wook!" She hollers. "Mow-mow. One. Two." She points from her lap to Memphis'.

As we near, she lifts her kitten, presenting it to him. "Daddy do."

Without missing a beat, he cuddles the kitten in one arm and lifts Liberty into his lap on the swing with the other. I take some pictures of the three of them and a few more including Memphis and her kitten.

"Hop over here and let me get a family picture," Memphis orders, passing the kitten to me.

I want to argue. I'm sure I look horrible. I haven't worried much about my hair or makeup since Alma's fall days ago. I'd imagined our first photo of the three of us to be during happier times.

"Someone hasn't napped yet," Memphis pretends to whisper.

Liberty's eyes dart to mine. She knows she must nap every day. "Mow-mow, nap," she nods as she speaks.

Memphis explains, "We decided to pet the kittens then take a nap." Liberty still nods. "We just played with the cats too long."

Liberty's face awaits my verdict, eyes locked on mine.

"Daddy." I lean forward, looking toward Hamilton, hoping he'll play along. "Does your kitty look sleepy?"

He lifts the kitten to eye level. "What do you think, Libby? Is this kitten sleepy?"

Liberty nods.

"Here Grandma," I suggest. "You help the kitties go take a nap, and I'll help Libby."

"Bye, Mow-mow," she waves over my shoulder as we enter the house.

After she potties, we sing the ABC song and rinse our hands.

"I'm going to make a few calls while you lay her down if that's okay?" Hamilton asks, peeking into the bathroom.

I nod and carry my sleepy girl upstairs.

"Hey, sleepy head," Hamilton greets as I slink into the kitchen.

"I can't believe I fell asleep," I croak.

"Apparently, you needed it," he teases.

"What's all that?" I point to a legal pad and papers strewn in front of him on the table.

Hamilton explains he called his money guy and the firm jumped into action. He points to an email. "Seems your grandparents' farm has been in the family over 100 years." His eyes continue to read the email. "He has forwarded the information necessary to have it listed as a Century Farm. Once confirmed, you may display a Century Farm sign on the property."

Pride grows within me. For so long, I believed my family history and my connection to them passed with my father. I'm finding my connection to my family through the land quite appealing.

"Foster will be at the lawyer's office at 10 tomorrow morning. He'd like to meet with you after lunch, if that's okay."

I nod. He's been a busy man during my nap. The sooner I begin understanding my new financial situation, the better. For now, my head continues to swim with too much information and too many possibilities. I crave for the order and normalcy I knew as my life a week ago.

Hamilton moves toward me; I sense he's something else to share with me.

"I asked him to do something else," Hamilton hedges, takes a deep breath, then continues. "I want my name on Liberty's birth certificate. Foster says it's easy, as long as you're okay with it."

In his eyes, I see worry. Does he seriously think I would fight him on this? Why wouldn't I want it? I tried to put it on the certificate when she was born, but I couldn't.

"I tried to do it when she was born," I explain. It's important he knows this. "Since we weren't married and you weren't with me, the law wouldn't allow me to list you as her father. I was able to give her your last name, but it was all I could do at that time."

He chews on his thumb nail while I explain. "So, I can?"

"I'd always planned for you to be on her birth certificate," I murmur, my throat tightening. "You've always been her father. I made sure she knew that. I'm glad you're wasting no time. I'm just sorry I took so long…"

He silences my apology, his lips smashing to mine. He wastes no time pressing his tongue between my lips, seeking entrance. He consumes my mouth, just as he consumes all of me.

122

HAMILTON

Looking at my watch, I sigh. She's just awakened, and I need to leave. With all that she's got going on in her life, I should really stay here with her.

"What's wrong?" Madison's brow furrows.

"I need to run to town for a bit," I admit reluctantly. "I bought something a month ago with the promise to pick it up my next time in town." I run my hands down my face. "It should only take an hour."

A small smile slides upon her face. "You should go. We'll be okay." She tightens the messy bun on top of her head.

"You can come with me." The words fly out of my mouth. I should have considered it earlier. "Liberty should come, too. I can't wait to see her reaction."

Although I purchased the puppy to keep me company in Chicago, I love that all three of us can share it now. What little girl wouldn't love a puppy?

Madison mulls over my offer for a few moments. I watch as she processes the rest of the day and an impromptu trip to town with Liberty.

"Okay," she sing-songs. A flicker of excitement appears on her worn out face. She grabs a backpack then informs our daughter we're going for a car ride.

I park beside the two trucks in the gravel lot. I spot Marshall and his mother across the park. It seems like yesterday we were playing ball and she attended every game.

"Pway!" Liberty squeals when the playground comes into view. "Mommy, pway!"

Madison widens her eyes in my direction. I promised a surprise and gave no details.

"I'm going to talk to Marshall for a minute." I point in his direction as I talk. "You can play for a bit." I jerk my chin towards the playground equipment.

Madison squints, trying to read me. I love her reaction to my mention of a surprise. It places a smile upon her face and a pep in her step, if only for a little while.

Approaching Marshall and his mother, I can't pull my eyes from the fluffy ball of black and white fur at the end of the leash. I kneel, and the Siberian Husky puppy pads my way. While I pet my new friend, Mrs. Harris informs me of the shot records and paperwork in the envelope she holds. I'm picking the dog up two weeks earlier than planned, but she assures me I won't have any issues.

Marshall and I chat a bit about the final World Series game he attended with my sister and Mom. It's clear he would have liked attending the after parties with me instead of heading back to the condo with them.

"I promised my girls a surprise, so I better head over there." I motion toward the playground. We say our goodbyes, and I walk toward the playground with my puppy in one arm and an envelope in the other.

Madison notices the puppy immediately and shakes her head at me, a huge smile on her face. I bend down, placing the puppy in the grass as I walk the final yards toward them.

"Daddy!" Liberty waves from the bottom of the small slide. "Puppy!"

Cute little girl squeals emit as she toddles toward me, her little hands waving at the puppy.

"Who's this?" Madison inquires as she squats and extends an open hand for the puppy to sniff.

Liberty stands just out of reach of the fluffy creature. Clearly, she longs to play, but waits for confirmation it's okay to do so.

"This is our new puppy," I explain. "She's gonna need a name."

As if sensing Liberty's apprehension, the puppy sits between us, its little tail wagging with anticipation.

"Libby, come pet our puppy," I urge calmly.

She looks to her mom. With Madison's nod, she slowly walks over and plops down near the eager puppy. She's immediately awarded kisses on her cheeks. Giggles fill the air–they're music to my ears.

"So, we have a husky puppy," Madison murmurs, nudging my shoulder.

"I reached out to Marshall a month ago to see when his mother would have her next litter. I made arrangements to pick her up when I came to Mom's for Thanksgiving." I pull my eyes from our happy daughter and her new friend. "I figured if I picked her up a little early, it might help entertain Liberty for you this week."

The light in her eyes and her megawatt smile assure me; Madison is glad I did.

"Liberty," I call to the little girl on the ground with a puppy on her chest. "Let's go show Grandma our new puppy."

"What should we name her?" Madison asks as she buckles Liberty into her car seat and I secure the leash to the seat belt beside her.

"I have one name I like," I admit, opening the driver's door. "But we can..."

"What is it?" she interrupts.

"Indie," I respond. "Indiana from the Indiana Jones movies." I smile sheepishly.

"We named the dog Indiana." Madison recites the line from the movie. "Indie it is," she states.

I love that we share similar tastes in movies.

Amy's truck is at the farm when we arrive. When Mom mentioned she'd be over today, I immediately started dreading her arrival. I love my sister, but when she's upset, she doesn't handle it well. I realize Madison is not new to our family. I worry that Amy will let her have it for keeping my daughter, her niece, a secret for nearly two years.

I notice Madison's spine straighten and shoulders move backward before she exits the truck to pull Liberty from the car seat. She's preparing for battle– I ready myself to allow her to fight her own battles while I also protect her.

I lead Indie to the nearby patch of grass. "Go potty," I prompt and wonder how much harder it will be to potty-train at four weeks instead of the normal six weeks.

My eyes track Madison as she carries Liberty into the house. Distracted, I'm unsure if the puppy went potty or not. I decide to risk an accident rather than let Madison face Amy alone.

Liberty anxiously waits at the door. "Puppy!" she squeals and points. "Na-na, puppy!"

I hand her the red leash, and she proudly parades her puppy to Mom. I hear Amy's raised voice in the front room. My mom gives me a knowing look as I pass her in the kitchen.

Madison stands, arms folded across her chest. Amy's a couple of feet in front of her, hands on her hips, in a wide stance.

"You'll get no money," Amy spits. "If that's what you're after, you're barking up the wrong tree. You'll have to share custody."

"Amy, I didn't plan to get pregnant, nor do I want any money." Madison's voice is low. "I love…"

Amy throws her palm out towards Madison's face, halting her words. "Don't play dumb. You hitched yourself to my brother years ago. You wanted him to be your way out of your miserable life in Athens. I've been on to you for years." She waves her finger in Madison's face. "I won't allow you to hurt him, and we'll be demanding a paternity test."

I can't allow her tirade to continue. "Enough!" I step beside Madison, tugging her tight to my side. "A paternity test? Really?" I swing my arm wide toward the kitchen. "Why don't you take a quick peek at your niece before you spew more crap."

As Amy stomps over to the doorway, I whisper in Madison's ear, "I'm sorry. Are we okay?"

She only nods. She's trying to keep a tight hold on her emotions. She doesn't want Amy to see she's rattling her.

"She's trying to protect you," Madison murmurs. "I've hurt her with my secret, and she needs to let me know it. I'm ready for it." She fakes a smile up at me.

Realizing several minutes have passed, I look to the doorway but don't find Amy. I guide Madison with me into the kitchen.

"Mommy," Liberty greets and points. "May-me!"

My sister sits crossed-legged on the linoleum floor, building blocks in her hand and a big, dopey grin on her face. It's clear she loves that Liberty knows her name.

When Amy's eyes meet mine, I inform her, "Madison created a book with all of our photos. They read it before naps and at bedtime." With my stare, I hope she understands Madison never tried to keep us from knowing Liberty.

Amy's slight nod acknowledges my statement. I won't delude myself by thinking she'll apologize and move on. She'll be rude a couple more times before she moves on, but the worst is over now.

123

MADISON

My phone rings after dinner. Seeing the sheriff's number on the caller ID, I choose to answer on speaker phone. "This is Madison," I greet. "Hamilton is with me, and I've put you on the speaker."

"I have an update," the sheriff informs. "Although the toxicology report hasn't arrived, we have a suspect in custody and a signed full confession."

I feel as though I've been punched. I attempt to pull in a breath without success. I pull my knees to my chest and wrap my arms around them. This allows me to gulp shallow breaths.

Standing behind my chair, Hamilton rubs my shoulders and asks, "Who confessed?"

Memphis enters the room, fetches me water, and encourages me to sip. When Indie and Liberty run into the room, she herds them back into the front room. Amy assists her in blocking the doorway.

"Henrietta confessed she knew of her husband's affair. She admitted to driving your mother home from the bar that night." He clears his throat. "She also admitted to slowly poisoning your mother's drinks each night at the bar with a variety of toxic houseplants. Seems the Athens Garden Club recently had a presentation on dangerous houseplants for pets and humans. She listed five plants in her home she added over and over to your mother's drinks at the bar. She even confessed to ordering two Oleander plants on Amazon that will arrive later this week. She planned to use them to finish the job if the other houseplants didn't work."

"Does this mean you will release the body to the funeral home?" Memphis asks for me from the doorway.

Hamilton moves to squat in front of me, holding my hands.

"Yes, I've already contacted them to officially release the body. With her confession, we do not need to wait on the tox report as it may not screen for the poisons she confessed to using. The house has also been cleared for you to enter."

"Thank you." My timid voice breaks. I take another sip of water before speaking again. "I appreciate all your department has done to quickly solve this."

My mind boggles with the words "poisonous houseplants." I didn't even know houseplants could harm a human. Seems weird to have such items out in a living space. He said Athens Garden Club. My mom was a member of the garden club. I wonder if she and Henrietta attended the same meetings. Repeated poisoning. I guess my mother's copious amounts of alcohol made it easier to poison her repeatedly night after night.

"Hey," Hamilton's soft voice calls to me. "Let's take a minute and go upstairs. Amy and Mom will play with Liberty."

I don't resist as I allow him to lead me up the stairs. He pulls me through his room into his bathroom. He places a stopper in the drain and proceeds to fill the tub with hot water. Walking to his shower, he removes his shower gel, and squirts it into the stream of water. White bubbles quickly multiply beneath the spout while he adjusts the water to a tolerable temperature then turns back to me.

"A nice, long soak in a warm bath is just what the doctor orders for you after the day you've had." He flashes his boyish smile at me. "You climb in. I'm going to fetch you a large glass of wine." He places a warm, heavy kiss to the corner of my lips before exiting his bathroom.

Turning toward the vanity, I cringe at my reflection. The weight of the day shows on me. My eyes are tired, and dark circles shadow below them. I place my hair in a messy bun on top of my head, strip, and slide beneath the blanket of bubbles into the decadently warm water. I rest my head on the back of the tub and place my toes against the opposite end. I submerge myself from the neck down, relaxing in the warmth.

As promised, Hamilton returns with a large glass of rosé. Without a word, he places it on the edge of the tub, lights two candles, turns on a playlist, and turns off the bathroom light before he leaves.

"Ham," I whisper while he spoons me in his bed.

"Yes," he murmurs back.

"I'm sorry." Even at a whisper, my voice quakes. "I'm sorry I kept Liberty from you and your family. I can never make it up to you."

He spins me in his arms and silences my apology with his lips upon mine. While I want to fight him to finish my apology, my traitorous body succumbs to my desire for him. He kisses me senseless, only pulling away when I gasp for breath.

"Now that you can't speak," he begins, "listen to me. I love you. I've always loved you, and I will always love you. You don't need to apologize to me. I know why you chose to move away from Athens and care for Liberty on your own. I believe it when you say you always planned to tell me; your videos are proof of that. It hurts me when you think you need to apologize, because if I had protected you that night, you wouldn't have had to make such a big decision on your own."

I begin to protest, but he places his fingers upon my lips, silencing me. "If I had protected us better, we wouldn't have that precious little girl in our lives." He points his thumb over his shoulder at Liberty, sleeping in the portable crib on the other side of his room. "If we changed one thing, it would change all of them. I've only known her a day, yet I know I don't want to live in a world without her in it." He lifts my hand to kiss my fingers. "You've apologized too many times. I accept your apology, just as you've accepted mine."

He rolls me to my stomach, placing his hand under my shirt upon my back. As he rubs his fingertips up and down, he whispers, "I love you, can't wait to marry you, and to live as a family."

He rubs my back until my mind drifts off into dreams of the three of us happily living in Chicago.

My worry grows the closer we get to seven. Of course, Hamilton doesn't stress at all. I remind him that I'm the one that kept the secret and told lies to cover it. He was innocent in it all.

As the caravan of four trucks stir up dust on the gravel lane, I nearly experience a panic attack. Memphis distracts Liberty in the house until we are ready for her to make her big appearance outside. On the porch, watching them park, Hamilton kisses me. It starts sweetly and quickly heats. His lips surround mine, his hot tongue tangles with mine, so deep and so long I forget where we are.

As my thoughts come back into focus, our friends stand in front of us, clapping.

"We're engaged," Hamilton declares, squeezing me tight to his side.

Adrian lifts my left hand, and they admire his grandmother's ring.

"It's about damn time." Troy pats Hamilton on the back with a loud thump.

Hamilton turns to me. His furrowed brow and tight mouth signal his confusion by Troy's statement.

"They've been looking for this since Salem's wedding," I whisper, raising an eyebrow.

His face lights up, recalling our interactions and dancing that night.

"When's the big day?" Bethany inquires, beaming.

"It's new, and we have other stuff to focus on this week." Hamilton answers to fend off further questions.

We usher our friends to the chairs circling the fire pit in the backyard. Excited conversation flows from our engagement to jobs to Bethany and Adrian's little ones.

"We have another surprise," Hamilton announces, rising to his feet.

Bile rises in my throat; I actually feel my airway tighten. Not now. I need to visit with our friends for a while and then ease into it. But with his declaration, it has to be now.

He prompts me to stand from my chair, looks into my eyes, then whispers, "You can do this."

I watch as he leaves our circle and enters the house. I turn back to the group, finding all eyes anxiously waiting on me.

"I've needed to tell you something…" I pause as their attention shifts from me. Turning, I see our daughter waving to the group from her daddy's shoulder. When I spin back around, seven pairs of eyes await my explanation. "This is Liberty. Libby, these are Mommy and Daddy's friends."

"Befan-ney," she squeals before wiggling down from Hamilton. "Baby?"

I grab her around the waist and lift her away from the fire. As we walk to Bethany and Adrian, I explain the babies stayed home. Liberty's lower lip protrudes in disappointment.

"Maybe you can come play at our house later this week," Adrian offers.

Of course, this raises red flags amongst our other friends. "I didn't share this with Hamilton or with any of you. I wanted Hamilton to be settled with baseball before I introduced him to our daughter." I take a few calming breaths. "Bethany and Adrian made surprise trips to see me last year, so they were sworn to secrecy until I could tell Hamilton." I look at Winston and Troy. "Please don't be mad that they kept my secret."

The guys nod at me.

"So, an engagement and telling your secret to him, when did this all happen?" Savannah asks, standing with hands on her hips.

"Memphis arranged alone time for us last night," I begin. Savannah's hurt, I can sense it.

"She tricked the two of us into being the only ones here at the farm for an hour last night. Madison didn't know I was coming. Mom urged me to talk to her, knowing I've been trying to find the time to ask her to marry me since last Christmas," he shrugs with a crooked smile. "Once I proposed, Madison told me everything." He wraps his arm around my shoulders and tugs on Liberty's curls.

"Just last night?" Savannah seeks affirmation. "So, Hamilton you've only known…"

Nodding, he confirms, "24 hours."

This appeases some of Savannah's anger at being left out of the loop. We're close and keeping this from her causes some damage. I'll need to find time for just the two of us after Mother's funeral.

"Well look-y here," Memphis greets the group in her backyard. "Libby, your bath is ready."

Excited, Liberty wiggles this way and that until I pass her to Grandma. I instantly miss her calming effect on my emotions. Hamilton's arm squeezes me tight, as if he senses my hesitation in letting her go. Memphis and Liberty say good night to our guests on their way back inside.

We truly have the best friends. The rest of the night flows easily. They have a million questions about my life in Columbia and Hamilton's World Series week. Slowly, as time passes, my nerves calm, and my heartbeat regulates. When I can't stop yawning at about ten, I'm disappointed that our guests begin to leave. I've missed every one of them. I've missed our group and just hanging out. I'd like to do it more often, but if I move to Chicago with Hamilton, I'm not sure that will be possible.

Two days later, while Hamilton makes some calls, I shower, put on the appropriate black attire, fix my hair and apply my makeup. I'm nibbling on a granola bar and fresh fruit for a mid-morning breakfast, knowing I won't feel like eating at the meal provided by the church later. I even played blocks with Liberty until Amy arrived. Although she's still giving me the cold shoulder, she's nothing but kind to Liberty. I'm thankful she's able to stay here with her while we attend the funeral this afternoon.

I'm avoiding Amy's scowl and stares by hiding in the kitchen until Hamilton comes back inside or Memphis is done getting dressed. I've enough to cope with today; I don't need to verbally spar with her again. I know with time she'll work through her anger, and we will be friends again.

Unable to be alone any longer, I walk out to Hamilton in the driveway. He's explaining he needs one more day, then he will spend a few days in Chicago before heading back to Athens. It's clear they want him available for much more than he wants to commit to.

"I need to go; I have a funeral in an hour. I'll look at my calendar tonight and let you know which events I'll attend." Hamilton's tone further expresses his firm stand on this matter.

"Sorry." He pulls me into him, wrapping his long, strong arms around me tightly. "I'll be in Chicago two, maybe three, days next week. I need to make one more call. It should be quick; stay right here." He keeps one arm snug around my waist as he connects his next call.

"Sheridan," Hamilton greets. "Just got off the phone with Berkeley." He listens to the voice on the other end of the line.

"Yes, the funeral is today. I informed her I will be in Chicago for two, maybe three, days next week. Then, I will need to come back to Athens." During the pause, he places a peck on my forehead.

"Of course, she did. Anyway, I'm filling you in so that you can ensure the other members of the team cover for me as I have family matters to tend to. It's not like I'm at Disney World…" His agent must have interrupted him.

"I'm just wanting to make sure the club knows there was a death in the family, and that I am not on vacation. It's not too much to ask as I've jumped through every hoop up until this week." Again, he pauses to listen.

"Okay. Thanks." With that, he places his cell phone in his pants pocket.

Without a word, he guides us back into the house.

"There they are!" Memphis calls, and Liberty runs toward us.

"She thought you left already," Amy explains with a smile for me.

124

MADISON

We're at the church for lunch. Somehow, I made it through all of the hugs and kind words shared by most of the town of Athens at the funeral. I left the ceremony just as my mother had planned it. I would much rather have had a private burial and been done with it, but if this was her last wish, I granted it.

My mother hadn't been active in the church or community for many years. Visitors attended her funeral for the woman she used to be and to give me their support. Fortunately, there were only the minister, Hamilton, Memphis, and I at the graveside. A fitting goodbye to the mother that only yelled at me when she wasn't ignoring me these past years.

Memphis insisted I allow the ladies of the Lutheran Church to serve a lunch for us. She reminded me that, once, my entire family was active in their church. I invited my girlfriends and Hamilton's family to join me here, since I have no other family to accompany me.

Hamilton and I are first in line to fix our plate. He scoops food onto mine for me. I'm not hungry, but I know he and Memphis will make me eat. The brisket and homemade mac and cheese look good; the rest of it I will pass on.

Memphis sits by Hamilton. Adrian, Salem, Savannah, and Bethany sit across the table from us. They do their best to distract me with their conversations while the quiet church ladies frequently refill our water and tea glasses.

I lay my fork down after a few bites. Hamilton squeezes my shoulders and whispers, "You should eat a bit more."

Reluctantly, I nibble some more. I don't taste the food; I only eat it so I'll have energy to play with Liberty tonight.

"Pardon me," a lady approaches. "Madison, your phone has been ringing nonstop in the kitchen."

I rise to take my phone from her. I must have left it in my purse—I hadn't even missed it. Odd. I've three missed calls from Trenton and one voicemail. I click on the voicemail then lift the phone to my ear.

"Madison, I know your mother's funeral is today. Crap! I thought it was over by now." The voice barely sounds like Trenton. "This can't wait any longer. Mom suffered another stroke this morning and passed away about nine. Call me when you get this so I can share the plans with you."

My legs buckle and the tile floor reaches up to slap me.

"Madison!"

It's all I hear as darkness engulfs me.

"Madison," Memphis firmly calls to me.

I struggle to open my eyes. They're too heavy as I try again. They open but a fraction. The bright lights burn; I close them quickly.

"Madison," Adrian calls this time. "Honey, we need you to sit up and open your eyes."

I use all my strength to raise my hand to shield my eyes before I slowly open them. I blink several times before they focus on everyone hovering above me.

"There you are," Memphis greets. "You gave us a scare. Here, sip some water."

No sooner do I swallow the water than I feel my stomach lurch. I crawl from the group, rise, and sprint to the restroom. At the toilet, I lose everything I just forced down. My stomach empty, I continue to dry heave for several more minutes. The pain in my abdomen does not compare to the pain in my heart.

I thought my world was falling apart before; now it has truly crumbled. Alma passed away, and I wasn't there. I didn't get to say goodbye.

A cold, wet cloth is placed on the back of my neck as I still bend over the stool. Hamilton's large hand warms my back. He doesn't say a word, just allows his nearness to comfort me.

In the hall, I hear Memphis direct Adrian to thank the church ladies, explain what has happened, and say goodbye for us.

When I attempt to rise, Hamilton scrambles to assist me. I splash water on my face and pat it dry with the paper towel he hands me.

Memphis returns, pressing an ice pack to my scalp near my forehead. "Doc says to bring you right over. I think you need stitches."

I want to argue, but I don't have the strength. They help me to the car, buckle me in, and I watch as the town of Athens passes by the window. While Memphis drives, I hear Hamilton making calls in the back seat. I recognize the words "death", "Columbia", "not next week", and "make it happen". I don't even attempt to make out his meaning.

Memphis removes the ice pack from my forehead, claiming we'll ice again in an hour. Liberty stands from her cars on the floor to take a closer look. She didn't like that I was hurt. It took both Hamilton and Amy to distract her so I could rest nearby on the sofa.

"Mommy," she soothes, patting my shoulder. "Ow-wy." She points to my head. "Tiss?"

"Um, Hamilton." I call across the room to him for assistance.

He approaches, brows raised, unsure what she's said.

"Tiss, Daddy?" She asks him the same question.

"Honey, it hurts too much to kiss it," I explain.

"Libby, you can kiss Mommy somewhere else to make her feel better."

I smile. He's getting it. He's thinking like a Daddy now.

"Kiss me here." I point to my cheek.

My strong-willed daughter does me one better. She kisses both my cheeks and then my mouth before she blows a kiss at the five stitches along my scalp. I feel the tickle of her breath across the exposed stitches as Memphis returns to tape a fresh gauze over the wound.

I wince as I rise to a sitting position. Hamilton and Memphis hover closely, frowning at my movements. "I'm fine. I need to call Trenton then pack."

Hamilton shakes his head. I'm ready to fight when he speaks. "I've already talked to Trenton and Taylor." He sits beside me, and Liberty promptly climbs on his lap, wanting to care for me. "I told them we would text when we leave here at about 6."

Liberty reaches up to touch my cheek. I smile at her sweetness. "I'm okay."

"Taylor and Mom talked. We think it's best if Libby stays here with Grandma. There have been many changes for her this week, and Taylor worries returning to Columbia might confuse her even more."

I want to argue; I need her with me. I need her to help me. But I know they are right. I need to protect her more than I need to use her to calm me. I nod.

"If Mommy and Daddy go to a meeting, can you stay here with Grandma?" I search my daughter's face for any sign of fear. This will be her first time spending the night alone with Memphis.

"Na-Na!" She beckons toward the kitchen as she climbs off Hamilton's lap.

Memphis enters the room to face her.

"Ice-me?"

That little devil. She's not worried about spending the night without me. She's already plotting an ice cream celebration with Grandma. If Memphis isn't careful, Liberty will walk all over her kindness.

I laugh at her antics. It makes my head hurt, so I immediately stop. I look away from Hamilton's gaze as I don't want to be babied. I rise to pack and get on our way. I need to be with Alma's family.

125

HAMILTON

I feel as if my heart rips in half as I kiss my baby girl goodbye. In 48 hours, she's become everything to me. As one half of my heart remains at the farm with Liberty, the other half of it aches for Madison.

She slumps in the passenger seat beside me. The light that Liberty and Indie brought back to her face a day ago is nowhere to be found. The woman I love lethargically sits an arm's length away. I feel as though I'm losing her with each mile we drive.

I fiddle with the radio. "What would you like to listen to?"

She slowly turns toward me; her beautiful blue eyes are now empty pools. I caress her cheek with my free hand, but she doesn't lean into my touch. Glancing in her direction for a brief moment, I cringe at her haunting eyes and distant stare. I choose an oldies rock station, turning the volume down to be barely audible.

The entire family greets us on the porch as we pull into Alma's driveway. A wide, genuine smile hops upon her face. Gone is the haunted look. As I exit the driver's seat, Taylor's girls and Trenton's boys surround Madison in a group hug. Waves are exchanged, and Trenton assists me in carrying in our bags.

When the front door closes, McGee trots excitedly to Madison. I bend down to give him loves. In his excitement, on his hind legs, he knocks her onto her butt and slathers her with wet kisses. I wonder what will happen to him now that Alma is gone.

I bend to pet McGee, rescuing her from his love. She clutches her aching sides from her laughter.

"Everyone, this is Hamilton Armstrong." She swings her arm wide towards me.

McGee's magical kisses sparked more life into her.

"Duh!" one of the boys shouts.

"We all know who he is," another boy states.

Two girls whisper and blush near Taylor, who I met at my debut at Wrigley.

"Okay, well then," Madison acts offended. "Hamilton pay attention. We will test you later." She prepares to introduce me to each family member.

"Let me," I interrupt, pointing. "Trenton, his sons Grant and Hale. Let's see, I think I remember hearing Grant is the oldest. So, you must be Hale, right?"

The boys nod in silent awe that I know who they are.

"And you must be Trenton's better half, Ava." She melts under my smile. Madison is shocked I've guessed correctly so far. She's talked of each of them often in our calls over the years I bet she didn't realize I paid attention.

"Taylor and her husband I met at Wrigley." I wave in their direction. "I assume those were your two giggling girls that ran from the room before I could get to them. And last but not least, you must be Madison's editor, Cameron."

Madison beams proudly at me. I've made a great impression with my knowledge of a family I've never met.

"Let's head to the kitchen," Taylor invites. "I'm sure you could use a drink and perhaps something to eat."

I place my hand in Madison's as we follow Alma's children to the kitchen. Madison's breath catches at the sheer volume of food on the counters and table.

"Mom's church family and neighbors have delivered food off and on all day," Cameron shares. "I hope you are hungry, because I can't eat another bite." She chuckles, rubbing her belly.

"We ate a sandwich before we left," Madison states. "I would like a snack, though." She skims her eyes from container to container, peeking under some lids, and groaning at the desserts.

"Check the fridge, too." Taylor orders.

The overwhelming amount of food is a true testament to Alma's love. Her activity in the community easily placed her dear to the hearts of many.

I slide a paper plate into Madison's hand. As I place odds and ends on my plate, I make suggestions for her to fill hers. We sit at two small spots cleared at the table while Trenton sits nearby, and his sisters lean on the counter.

"The funeral service begins at 10 at the church," Trenton shares while we nibble. "Burial will be in the church cemetery. Then, we will be served a meal inside the church."

In Trenton's eyes, I see the pain he attempts to hide.

"We've asked the praise band to play during lunch." Taylor smiles proudly. "Mom always liked the services they performed during." She shrugs.

Madison can't help the welling tears. She tries to bite them back, but they flow down her cheeks. I wrap my arm around her shoulders and squeeze. She lays her head on my shoulder as she wipes them away with her left hand.

"Oh! My! Gosh! Oh my gosh!" Cameron squeals, jumping up and down.

Everyone's eyes fly to her to see what is wrong. The thunder of the children running down the stairs fills the air with her continued squeals as she fans her face. The four kids freeze by their parents, afraid of what is affecting Aunt Cameron.

"I can't believe you!" She stares at Madison. "You little…"

I witness her search for an appropriate word in the mixed company. For the life of me, I don't know why she's squealing at her.

"I can't believe you didn't tell us," she brushes one index finger over the other in my direction. "Shame on you for holding out."

"What?" Taylor asks.

At the same time, Madison asks, "Cameron, what do you think I did?"

"Um…" She holds out her left hand, pretending to display a ring.

Crap! With her mother's death, my meeting Liberty, and the murder investigation, she forgot to tell them we got engaged.

"Oh!" She stands, walking toward Taylor and Cameron. "I'm sorry. Things were crazy the past couple of days."

"Oh." Cameron acts like her apology solved everything.

"So, how did it happen? When?" Taylor asks.

"What happened?" Grant asks still confused as to why his aunt screamed.

"Aunt Madison and Hamilton are engaged!" Cameron tells the kids.

The kitchen fills with cheers, high fives, and congratulations. Taylor awards the four kids a dessert to help us celebrate then sends them up to finish their movie before time for bed. It's easy to see she wants them out of the room to get all the details of my proposal.

Madison moves to the refrigerator for another water, bringing me one back with her. "I have to say, Memphis was the instigator."

I nod in agreement then kiss her temple. "You'll need to start from the day before, so they understand Mom's meddling."

"Okay." She sips her water to ease her dry throat. "I planned to drive to the motel in Athens. Suddenly, the thought of Liberty and I spending hours in a tiny, outdated motel room didn't appeal to me. When I pulled out of the driveway, I headed towards Memphis' farm. It only took a few minutes. She opened the door as I stepped from the van."

"I introduced her to Liberty and asked if I could stay with her. Of course, she was glad I was there." She looks to me for the next part.

Taking her cue, I continue. "Mom texted me after Madison and Liberty turned in for the night. She only typed that Madison was struggling with her mother's death, and I really needed to try to come to Athens." I smirk. "I wanted to be there; it's just the Cubs had me booked solid with World Series appearances day and night." I shrug.

"The next day, Memphis arranged for us to meet with the funeral home. The weird part was that she wanted to drive two separate vehicles." Madison shakes her head. "I figured she needed to run an errand, and she didn't want Liberty and I to be with her for it."

I jump in. "I had texted Mom when I left Chicago, stating I would be at the farm by dinner. I arrived, and no one was home. So, I texted her again. She claimed to be on her way home."

Patting my forearm, Madison shares, "Memphis sent me on home, stating she and Liberty needed to stop by the store. When I pulled in the driveway, I was shocked to see Hamilton there. Memphis had not told me he would be coming. We went inside and both our phones vibrated with texts."

I look to Madison before continuing. "Mom told me via text she would be home soon, and I needed to share the thing with Madison that Mom and I had talked about several times since last Christmas. I confessed to being lonely and to wanting her with me in Chicago. I shared that I spoke to Mom about it last winter and had been trying to find the perfect time."

"He fell to his knee and pulled out this ring." She wiggles her fingers, allowing the diamond to catch the light. "It was his grandmother's ring."

"But wait," I order over the oohs and ahs. "She didn't say yes."

"I wanted to say yes." Madison turns to face me. "You know I wanted to say yes."

I nod.

"I told him I needed to tell him something, and he might not want to marry me when I did," Madison explains.

"I promised her nothing she would share might change my wanting to marry her." I defend.

"That's when Memphis and Liberty walked in the kitchen," she announces.

"Uh-huh," I agree. "This little girl bounds into the kitchen hollering, "Ma-Ma" and climbs right into Madison's lap."

"He's still kneeling in front of me, staring at a younger version of his big sister," Madison adds.

"Long story short, when Mom calls Liberty over to put the ice cream in the freezer, I slide the ring on Madison's finger while asking her to marry me again." I look into her eyes and silently whisper, "I love you."

"I gave in," Madison finishes.

"No, you didn't!" Cameron argues. "You've wanted to be with him since the day we met you. You said yes because you're head over heels in love with him."

"And you're going to live happily ever after," Ava swoons.

"And raise a gaggle of future Cubs players," Taylor adds.

"Wrong." Trenton chimes in. "Cardinals players." He smiles, proud of himself.

"I forgive you for forgetting to share with us." Cameron is serious now.

"You did have situations pulling you in several different directions, and I'm sorry I overreacted when I spotted the ring." She smiles shyly. "You've shared so much, and I was overwhelmed that something so big and so right finally happened for you."

126

MADISON

"I have a bit of business I'd like to go over with you before tomorrow." Trenton gestures for me to sit on the nearby sofa. "We want tomorrow to be a day of celebration and remembrance. Thus, I've already sat with my sisters regarding the will."

I look to Taylor and Cameron. Both smile and join us in the living room. Hamilton takes my hand in his as he sits beside me on the sofa.

"Mother, as you know, was very fond of Liberty and you." He clears his throat before continuing. "She amended her will with a clause that her house can't be sold until you and Liberty find a place to live. She wants you to have a place to stay while you make other arrangements. And the three of us agree. We all love you like a little sister; we want to make sure you are taken care of, and we hope you will allow us to continue to be in your life."

Tears fill my eyes. I want to speak, but words are caught in my throat. Hamilton's arm moves around my back and pulls me closer. I take a few moments to gather my thoughts and a couple of deep breaths.

"Liberty and I will be staying with Memphis while I take care of a few things in Athens. Then, we'll be moving to Chicago to live with Hamilton," I assure my adopted siblings and pause to fight the tears threatening to spill from my eyes.

"With all Madison has do deal with due to her mother's passing, we haven't had time to iron out all of the details," Hamilton jumps in for me. "She decided she'd move to Chicago; beyond that, we have much to discuss and plan."

"When I met with my parents' attorney," I explain, "I learned that I have a trust fund that I should have been given access to to pay for college, my parents' farm is paid off, and I also inherited my grandparents' farm that is doing quite well." I take in a deep breath while scanning the room. "Not knowing any of this before, I have several pressing financial decisions to make. The reason I'm sharing now is that I want you to know I don't need you to wait on me to make a decision about the house." I pin my gaze on Cameron. "Liberty and I will be taken care of and have a new home just waiting for us to move into."

"We will be neighbors!" Taylor claps and cheers. "You'll love Chicago. I'll show you all my favorite stores. And I'm sure the girls will want to babysit anytime you two want a day or night out."

"If we can return to business..." Trenton looks sternly at Taylor. "Mom made arrangements to leave her van for Liberty and you," he states, smiling.

"She detested your car," Taylor adds. "I can't tell you how many times she worried it would strand you on your way to or from campus. She even mentioned wanting to buy you a vehicle."

"I told her you were independent and would never allow her to purchase a vehicle for you," Trenton continues. "So, this is her way of making sure you have a safe vehicle to drive and leaving you no room to argue."

Alma's children chuckle.

A tiny smile graces my face. "It's rare that your mother doesn't get her way."

"I have all the documents you will need to transfer the title into your name." He motions to a file folder in his lap.

I didn't expect to be in Alma's will. We've only known each other for two years. Although I loved her like a mother, I had no intentions of being enveloped so deeply into her family.

"She also awards you her entire library."

"What?" I blurt. "No, I couldn't. Cameron, you work in the book industry; they should be yours."

Cameron shakes her head. "You've never seen it, but my library puts Mom's to shame."

"You should look through it; there may be something each of you would want. You get first choice." My voice cracks the longer I speak.

"We can look through them when we are finished here," Taylor promises. "But Mom has given us books over the years."

"As I was saying," Trenton takes control of the conversation once again, "we can make arrangements with a moving company to box them up and ship them to you when we sell the house."

My eyes dart to Cameron. Previously, she shared her growing desire to move back to the area with me. She hates the thought of selling her parents house to strangers. She hasn't told her siblings she wants to buy the house. She shakes her head so only I notice. I need to help her open a dialogue soon.

Trenton passes a small, sealed envelope to me. I recognize the stationary as Alma's. "Mom left this for you, and she has one more item in her will for you." Trenton's eyes scan the room. "McGee!"

Thump-thump. Thump-thump. McGee trots down the staircase, sliding to a halt in the center of the hardwood floor.

"Mom wants Liberty to keep McGee," Trenton beams proudly.

With his statement, my shaky hold on my emotions crumbles. Tears swim steadily down my cheeks and a whimper escapes. Alma's really gone–we're parceling out her belongings and taking little pieces of her. Her thoughtfulness knows no bounds.

"Um," I look from Trenton to Hamilton. "I don't know if I can…"

Hamilton squeezes me as his lips graze my ear. "We can handle two dogs. I can't imagine keeping Liberty from her Me-Me."

He's so awesome. I don't know how I would have made it through meeting with my parents' lawyer or listening to Alma's will without him. I'm overwhelmed by the adult decisions thrown at me. In less than two weeks, I've lost my home, lost my mother, introduced Liberty to Hamilton, got engaged, learned I'm a millionaire, decided to move to Chicago, gained a puppy, lost my surrogate mother, and learned I get to keep McGee.

In Hamilton's gaze, my fears subside. "We can handle two dogs." His words play on repeat in my head. McGee is trained, and, thanks to Alma, I'll be able to train Indie. As the smile sweeps upon my face, I nod at Hamilton.

"I guess we will be a two-dog family!" I cheer. "McGee, come." Rubbing my hands under his chin, I murmur, "Liberty will be so glad to see you. Yes, she will."

McGee leans into my scratches. I've missed him the past few days.

"And with that, our business is done." Trenton passes me the folder, containing my copy of the will, before rising to put away his copy of the will. "Who needs a refill?"

While Taylor and Trenton fix drinks in the kitchen, I sidle up beside Cameron. "I think now is a good time to discuss you buying the house."

Her eyes grow wide, and she shakes her head.

"Trust me. They'll be okay with it."

Trenton hands a water to Hamilton before resuming his seat, interrupting my pep talk. Taylor hands a drink to Cameron, and I pounce.

"I have a potential buyer for the house," I announce.

All eyes pivot to me, and Cameron looks ready to flee.

"Are you open to all offers on the house?" I look from Taylor to Trenton. Both nod. I look to Cameron; she doesn't speak.

"Cameron has an interest in moving to Columbia." Bomb dropped, I move to Hamilton's side, smiling proudly.

Taylor cranes her neck around the men, looking at Cameron. "I didn't know that." She looks at me then back to Cameron. "Why didn't you mention it to me?"

I know why, but I'm not telling her–I hope Cameron doesn't tell her either. She needs to focus on buying the house, not start an argument with her older siblings.

"It's a recent idea. I just bounced it off Madison first." Cameron lies. "I spoke to my boss about transferring the to KC office and working from home as often as possible."

"Do they allow others to work from home?" Trenton inquires.

"It's becoming the norm to work from home and come to the office only for meetings." Cameron straightens her shoulders.

I see her preparing to stand up to her two older siblings. She's used to defending her decisions from their overprotective, been-there-done-that ways. "At first, I couldn't see anyone else living here. But then, I remembered last year looking at houses in Denver and New York City for a change of scenery.

I'm tired of Dallas. It's just not my kind of place." She smiles at me before looking to Taylor. "And our talk last Thanksgiving with Mom telling me it's my turn to give her grandchildren got me thinking. I can't see myself raising a family in Dallas."

"Can you see yourself raising a family in Columbia?" Trenton teases.

"A family is a few years off, but I could see myself with a family here." She swings her arms wide. "I mean, it was good enough for us. It should be good for..."

Taylor interrupts, "You to find a man and have a brood of your own."

"Let's not get hung up on my future family." Cameron shakes her head. "I'm not sure what you plan to list it at, but I have a large chunk saved for a down payment. I figure my house payment should be less than the 2000 a month I pay in rent now." She shrugs. "So, let me have it. What do you think?"

Taylor wastes no time. "I love the thought of the house remaining in the family. You'll be closer to me, and, if you get to work from home, I think you should go for it." She winks at her little sister.

Cameron raises her eyebrows when she looks my way before facing Trenton.

"I have concerns," Trenton states. "I'd hate for you to suffer a setback at work by moving here. You've created a name for yourself in Dallas; you might have to start over in the Kansas City office, and, if you work from home, that might be difficult."

He pauses, allowing his worries to sink in. "This is a large, old house for one person. It will need maintenance and repairs. You won't have a super to call and fix everything like you do in the apartment."

Cameron nods with each point he makes.

"If this is something you've thought about and want, I will support your decision. Just be sure it's not just a decision you are making in grief. None of us want to sell this house; we want to hold on to the memories as long as we can." He clears his throat, taking a moment to collect himself. "I like the thought of you relocating to the Midwest, and I'm glad to hear you are thinking of a family." He chuckles. "I was beginning to worry that you would be the crazy, single, old lady with litters of cats and hordes of books."

Everyone laughs at the image he creates. I love that they supported Cameron and didn't just brush off her idea as an immature notion. They tend to struggle to see her as an adult instead of their baby sister. Cameron beams—any fear she had that they wouldn't support her has evaporated.

"The realtor is coming tomorrow night," Trenton states. "I'll call and cancel that appointment. We can take care of this transaction ourselves." The proud smile he wears is priceless—he likes the idea of Cameron living here.

127

HAMILTON

"Ham," Madison turns to face me as soon as I close the bedroom door, "we've got a lot to talk about."

"I know. It's been a busy week." I pull her towards the bed. "In a perfect world, my proposal would have led to us making decisions about our future immediately." I pull a knee between us on the bed. "Or at least discussions over the next couple of days. I felt like you needed to focus on other things, and we would get our time to chat later," I explain.

She nods. "It's been one thing after another, hasn't it?" She curls both legs between us and grasps my hand. "I'm exhausted, but we need to talk about some stuff."

"I've described the condo to you and the pet services we have available. We can handle two dogs." I intertwine my fingers with hers in her lap. "I need to be in Chicago in three days. I'd like to take the two of you with me when I go back. I know you have stuff to arrange in Athens, but most of it can be taken care of over the internet and phone."

"Okay," She agrees, much to my surprise. "I'm ready. I'm ready to see where we will live. I'm ready to make us a home. From your description, I have an image in my mind. I'm sure it pales in comparison to reality."

I pull her tight against my chest, her head tucked under my chin. I kiss the top of her head. "I've waited so long to take you to Chicago with me. You have no idea how much I need you there." I lower my chin, so my lips graze her ear. "I love you." My husky voice breaks.

My heart jackhammers against the wall of my chest. With each passing day, our new life becomes more real to me. For so long, I wanted us to be a couple, and now we officially are. We are engaged! She's going to marry me!

Never taking my hands off her, I reposition her to an arm's length away. She looks up into my eyes, and I melt even more. This sexy-as-hell woman is mine.

"You've dealt with a lot this week. I've made some calls trying to prepare for your arrival in Chicago." I hesitate. I'm unsure how she will handle this news. "Berkeley, my publicist, found a four-bedroom condo upstairs from my current one. It's similar to mine only with two more bedrooms for us."

My eyes search her face. "I've asked her to get a bedroom set similar to mine and a sectional for the living room. She rented them for us. We can return them and pick out our own or purchase them. I thought it might be an easier transition for Libby if we didn't live in my condo for a week then move to another one. This way, we can settle her in one time. We'll still need to buy furniture and decorate, but it will be ready for us to sleep in on our first night in Chicago."

Heat floods her cheeks. She pulls away from my touch to stand across the bedroom. Heavy stones sink to the pit of my stomach.

"Mady," I plead. "What did I say to upset you?" I make to stand.

She raises her palm, directing me to stay away. My breathing stops. Talk. Talk to her. We need to talk this out.

"Berkeley picked out our home?" she spits. "Berkeley bought our bedroom set?" "I'm not sure I like the idea of a strange woman making such intimate decisions for us. I want us to make these decisions together," she growls.

"I'm sorry. Maybe I'm being irrational. My life is out of control. I need to reign it back in. I want to be in control and planning our life together can do that for me. I mean," she pauses to draw in a shaky breath, "I don't even know this Berkeley." She rolls her wrist, waving her hand in the air.

I stride toward her, not allowing any space between us. "I chose the condo, not her. I looked at the floor plans online. She only called the leasing agent to secure it. I love everything about my condo: the location, the layout, the design, the amenities, and the security." I run my thumb over her lower lip, eyes boring into hers. "You've seen the interior during our FaceTime calls. You seemed to like it, if I recall. I'm just trying to make it easier on the three of us."

She nods. It seems the red-hot rage cools slowly within her.

"We don't have to keep the bedroom set." I let out a frustrated sigh. "I'm so used to Berkeley arranging things for me, I didn't even think what it might be like for you. She's my publicist, my assistant. Nothing more. There has never been anything between us, not even a spark. We can sleep on the floor by the portable crib or on the sofa. We'll return the furniture and, together, select our own."

I don't want to say she blew this out of proportion. I'm not sure if she's jealous or what. I bet the fact that Berkeley was a part of my Chicago life when she wasn't hurts. I need to be more sensitive. I can't jump in, make a call, and decide everything.

"It's okay," she whispers. "One less move will be easier on Liberty. I want the three of us to be comfortable on our first night in our new place. I'm glad you arranged all of this. I am." She places her hand over my heart. "It's going to take some time for me to get used to you having money and people that work to make your life easier. I'm used to doing everything myself and making my own decisions."

"You have money, too," I smirk.

"It's surreal to me. I may never get used to it." She shakes her head.

"As my wife, my money is our money. You're the reason I entered the draft in the first place. Liberty and you mean everything to me. I've already made arrangements. Soon, you'll have paperwork to sign that adds you to all my accounts. During the season, life is hectic. Much of what Berkeley did for me, you will be able to do for us. I leaned on her a lot while I was on the road. I'll lean on you from now on," I promise.

I press a kiss to the corner of her mouth. "I love you. We both need to get used to the changes. We're no longer single; we're a couple, a family. Forgive me?" I'm lost in her eyes.

"There's nothing to forgive," she whispers, fiddling with the envelope Trenton handed her earlier.

"Want me to read it to you?" I offer, feeling helpless.

She nods, extending it to me.

I carefully open the sealed envelope; I'm sure Madison will want to keep this forever. I pull the handwritten note from inside and unfold it.

"Madison, I need you to help keep my secret," I read, eyes peaking up to hers.

She shrugs, not knowing what secret Alma speaks of.

"In the garage, behind the red toolbox, are two boxes labeled 'cleaning supplies.' I need you to sneak them into your car without my children finding them. What you choose to do with them is up to you. I can't bear the thought of my three children finding them. They will not understand my addiction to steamy and erotic romance novels as you do. I feel it's best if we protect them from years of therapy if they were to envision me reading such books."

Through her tears, Madison laughs a real laugh. It seems her heavy heart grows light. My eyes sparkle through my tears. I fold the note back into the envelope and tucks it in her bag.

"If you can stop laughing," I tease, "you can distract the family, while I go get the two boxes. If they ask, just tell them I forgot to bring in something."

She wipes her wet cheeks and squeezes the remaining tears from her eyes as she quells her laughter. Leave it to Alma to lighten her mood. She wouldn't want Madison to cry so much over her. She'd tell her to focus on her daughter and her recent reconnecting with me. She'd urge her to open one of those sultry romance stories and lose herself in it. She's going to miss her so much.

I can't fall asleep. I hold Madison snug against my body, her back against my front. I can't hold her close enough. She's mine.

I struggle to hide my body's reaction to her. With all she's dealing with, I can't act on my desires. She needs time to cope with the death of her mother and Alma and time to accept moving to Chicago. She needs time to help Libby adjust to our new life. There will be plenty of time for the two of us. We'll have a new home to christen. I adjust myself while trying not to wake her.

We haven't even been on a first date. I need to plan one. I can't expect her to marry me if we haven't even dated. One might argue that all the time we spent alone in high school were dates. I must plan a first date and a second; I owe her that much. I'll ask Berkeley to make us reservations. No! I can't! I need to do this myself. This is not a task to involve Berkeley in. It's important that Madison knows I planned our date, every part of it.

128

MADISON

On our drive back to Athens, I replay parts of Alma's service in my mind.

I smile as I remember Hamilton slipping his hand into mine as a silent symbol of support. It gave me strength and hope. As warmth encompassed me, I felt as though Alma was happy to see us together.

"I had a thought last night." Hamilton breaks into our quiet ride. "We need to find a farmer to rent your parents' land, someone we trust to make the improvements needed."

His eyes leave the road for only a moment, and I nod.

"We also need to find a reliable renter for the farmhouse. We don't want to constantly vet new renters." His words echo my recent thoughts on the matter. "I know one couple unhappy in their current situation. They would make great renters for both the house and the land."

Who could he mean? He's rarely in Athens. How does he know a reliable renter? A wide smile forms as I realize he's speaking of Latham and Salem. I've shared during our phone calls how Latham and Salem moved into the farmhouse when his parents retired to move into Athens. His brothers were not happy about it. Living on the family farm, they saw Latham as boss in their father's absence. They started arriving late and leaving early. They fight Latham at every turn if their father isn't around. Latham and Salem spend nights and weekends working their butts off while his brothers are in Athens with their wives.

I smile. Hamilton's idea sparks hope within me. "Do you think Latham would consider it?"

"I'm not sure how fed up he really is with his brothers. It's worth mentioning."

"I know Salem is unhappy," I state.

"I thought we might invite them to join us for dinner while we're in Athens. We could tell them we have an offer for them to consider. We still need to work out the logistics. Perhaps we don't charge them rent for the house–it could be part of Latham's salary. We could offer him a salary to fix the fences and outbuildings along with working the land. It's not a large acreage, but it needs a lot of work. I thought he might also be able to help at Mom's since the farms border each other. She works too hard, and I'd like her to be able to come to Chicago to visit anytime she wants to."

"I think it's worth discussing with them before we advertise for renters," I agree.

"In time, Latham could even oversee your grandparents' farm, too." Once again, he meets my eyes briefly. "I mean, if you choose to keep all that land, too. You should text Salem and see if they are free tonight or tomorrow night. We could discuss this before heading to Chicago."

"I'll text her now."

ME

what are you doing tonight?

Hamilton & I want to go out to eat

SALEM

I'm off today

ME

we could meet at Pizza Hut

SALEM

I'll pull Latham in

to shower at 5

ME

meet at 6?

SALEM

yes

"It's done," I inform him proudly. "We're meeting them at Pizza Hut at six."

I step from Memphis' truck; my feet feel like anvils as I approach the front door.

"One hour," Memphis' words soothe. "We just need you to give us a few instructions. Then, once you give Salem a tour, you are free to take my truck and go." She squeezes my shoulders while she looks into my eyes. She attempts to share some of her strength with me.

I nod. Why is it all of the happy memories hide deep behind the horrors of the past six years? Why can't I focus on the three of us happy here on the farm?

Four of her church friends greet us on the small front doorstep. Memphis mentioned this ministry to me, and I clung to it like a lifeline—there's no way I could ever clean out my mother's house. I'm barely able to step inside without losing it. So, when Memphis described a group of ladies at her church that volunteer to box up, throw away, and donate households for families that lost a loved one, I gladly accepted the offer. I scan the empty boxes, crates, and trash bins littering the large, front yard.

"Madison, we understand this is difficult for you," a silver-haired woman much older than Memphis begins. "We only need a few directions from you, then we will begin."

"As you can see," a blue-haired, short, pleasantly plump woman explains, "we've labeled boxes for important papers and photos." She points to the two large stacks of labeled boxes. "We will remove all photos from their frames before boxing them up. We will place the frames in these tubs for donating."

My head swims as they continue to explain the process, just as Memphis had a few days earlier. Soon, we are walking through the entire house as I point to items I wish to keep. I'm not surprised there isn't much I want. I don't think any furniture was kept in our family for generations. My mother decorated with a modern theme in my early childhood, and nothing ever changed. I ask to keep my books, my favorite cereal bowl from my youth, and two wedding dresses hidden in a closet. I don't even know who they belonged to.

The women promise to keep anything of importance for me to look through at my convenience. They hope to finish by dinner tonight but state they might need a few hours tomorrow afternoon to clean after removing everything. I'm just grateful I don't have to stay here to see any of it.

Memphis guides me back to the front yard at the same time Salem and Latham pull into the driveway. I do my best to fake a smile for my excited friends.

129

HAMILTON

I excuse myself, claiming I need to work on the tractor in the barn. While the girls play in the front room with Mom, I sneak some supplies out the kitchen door with me. I load all the items I need on the four-wheeler, making two trips to the cemetery to deliver everything. I toss some of the items over the fence and carry the small grill over with me. Once set up, I step back to take in the scene. I try to see it from Madison's point of view for the first time.

It's our favorite spot. I figure it's the perfect location for our first date.

"Daddy!" Liberty squeals, running to my open arms. She jabbers on with all the stories of her day.

My smile grows as her animated chatter continues. I react to her words as if I understand. When her tales dwindle, she lays her head on my shoulder.

My heart bursts wide open with her love. I've waited so long for the day Madison and I could be together. Finally, our life together begins, and my daughter makes it even more special.

"Mommy and Daddy are going out." I tug on one of her springy curls. "Can you be a big girl for Grandma?"

Liberty lifts her head, frowning at me.

She wiggles her way down from my arms and runs over to Madison.

"Mommy, no," she whines with her arms in the air.

When Madison picks her up, Liberty clings tight to her mommy. Madison softly attempts to soothe our now crying girl.

Madison's eyes plead with me. I feel her pain. So much has changed for our little girl in the past week, it was only a matter of time before she began to show the effects. Suddenly, I have no desire to take Madison on a date. I want only to assure my girl that everything is alright.

Sitting on the sofa, Madison rubs her free hand up and down Liberty's back. She attempts to pull the tiny, clinging arms from around her neck.

"Libby, honey," she soothes. "Mommy and Daddy will only be gone for a little while." She kisses Liberty's hands. "We need you to be…"

Liberty squirms down from her mommy's lap and runs to me. "Daddy, no!"

The trails of tears on her chubby cheeks combined with her pouty lower lip are my undoing.

"It's okay, Mommy and Daddy won't…"

My words cease at Madison's glare and shaking head as she approaches.

Pulling Liberty's hands into her own, Madison whispers, "Grandma needs help with McGee and Indie. She knows how to take care of the kitties but doesn't know how to take care of the dogs." She purses her lips, pretending to contemplate the dilemma. "Can you be a big girl and help Grandma? You'll have to teach her how McGee does his tricks. Indie needs to go outside to potty and will need a treat before bed. Grandma doesn't know which treats to give him."

Liberty's sobs subside. Madison wipes her runny nose with a tissue. Sensing her persuasion working, she continues, "Grandma will need you to help her run your bath and put toys in the water."

I feel Liberty's nod against my shoulder. My heart still burns at the thought that my plans caused this.

"Maybe Grandma will read you three books tonight at bedtime," I suggest.

Liberty lifts her head. Her puffy, red eyes look into mine. Tears coat her dark lashes. Instead of a pout, a slight smile decorates her lips.

"How about it? Can you be a big girl and help Grandma for a little bit?" Madison asks.

Without a word, Liberty escapes my hold. She toddles toward her grandma, extends her hand, then tugs her to the kitchen.

"I'm sorry." I meet Madison's gaze. "I didn't think she'd... I mean, she's seemed happy with Mom."

"She's tired, that's all." Madison wraps her arms around my waist. "She chased after two dogs and the kitties all day. This happens when she's too tired. She'll be fine with your mom tonight."

Her words should make me feel better. She has more parenting experience than I do. I'm reminded, again, that I'm playing catch up.

In the kitchen, Liberty stands on the counter, pulling mac and cheese from the cabinet for Mom. She smiles as she hops back into Grandma's arms. Mom whispers something before Liberty waves goodbye with a smile on her face.

"Get out of here," Mom orders. "We'll be fine."

It seems she's ready to start dinner now.

Madison smiles in my direction. "You take free time whenever and wherever you get it." She shrugs. "I don't remember making plans for tonight."

I move closer, taking her hand in mine. "We're going on our first date."

Madison freezes in shock. I drop the bomb, not giving any details. I'm sure she hadn't even thought about us dating. She's excited to marry me–I don't think she planned on the usual traditions that come before a wedding. I don't plan on waiting long, but I can allow us a few dates before we tie the knot.

"I should go change then," she offers, unable to keep the smile off her face.

"No," I say quickly, not letting go of her hand. "The only thing you need is a sweatshirt."

It's the first week of November in Missouri–the weather is mild.

I pull her towards the door, tossing a sweatshirt at her as we pass through the kitchen. We say goodbye to our daughter, and excitement builds at the knowledge of the evening I've planned for us.

I motion for Madison to climb on the four-wheeler. She hesitates for a moment before sliding on the back.

130

MADISON

"You drive," he urges. "We're going to the spot where we began."

The weight of his words warms me. We began the night I asked him for a favor; we met in the cemetery, and it changed my life forever.

Approaching the chain link fence surrounding the site, I notice twinkle lights hanging from the oak tree in the center. Beneath them, blankets and pillows cover the dead grass. A small grill holds flaming logs, a cooler and crockpot sit nearby. It seems Hamilton has been very sneaky this afternoon.

"Ham..." I choke on my words.

He pulls my back tight to his chest while wrapping his arms snuggly around me as I take in the scene. "I've thought about a first date for a couple of days now. Movies, going out to eat, dancing, driving to Kansas City…none of those seemed perfect."

I spin in his arms, placing my hands on his cheeks. "This is perfect."

He chuckles. "You don't even know what I have planned."

"It doesn't matter. It's you. It's me. It's our special spot. That's all it needs to be perfect."

"Should we climb this fence so we can start our date?" Hamilton suggests.

We lay stretched out on the blankets and pillows, our bellies full of loaded grilled cheese sandwiches and tater tot nachos Hamilton prepared ahead of time for us. I could only groan when he offered to make s'mores for dessert. We decided to save those for later.

"Savannah called me today," I state as we stare up at the clear night sky. Of all our friends in Athens, she's the only one I haven't found the time to share a meal within the days I've been back.

"What's she up to, besides deer hunting?" He plays with my hair.

"Remember the donut guy I told you she's mentioned a couple of times?"

"The history teacher, right?"

"Yes, well," I cuddle a bit closer to his side, "he asked her out. She claims it's not a date, but it's a date. He asked her to be his plus-one to the faculty Christmas party the first weekend in December."

Hamilton smirks in my direction.

"She said he made it sound like she'd be doing him a huge favor by not making the new guy attend all by himself."

"So, she's going?" he asks, surprise in his tone.

"She told him she'd think about it," I smirk. "But she's going. I told her to call him tomorrow, claiming she shouldn't leave him hanging in the wind too long. It'll be a weird first date. She'll be attending with all of her teachers from school, every one she ever had. The principals, the coaches, and even the secretaries will be there. I mean, she's an adult now, but they all knew her as a kid in school. It will be weird, but he promised they would make an appearance and slip out early."

A silly smile covers my face as I stare at the sky. She wouldn't mention it to me or consider the date if she didn't like this guy. I like the idea of Savannah having the hots for someone. She's been on her own for so long, it's time she lets down her guard to let someone in. Several moments pass as I imagine her happy.

"So..." Hamilton rolls to face me, breaking the silence of a chilly evening.

"Okay." I roll to face him; my hand rests on his chest. "I want to elope. I don't see any reason to plan anything big. We don't have a lot of family, so we should keep it simple; we should plan it before you head to spring training in February."

"Uh, duh!" He laughs.

"Okay, Mr. Obvious. When?" I retort.

"The weekend after Thanksgiving," he deadpans without missing a beat.

Wow! He's thought about this more than I have. That's a couple of weeks away.

"I see the wheels turning in your mind." Hamilton taps my creased forehead. "What are you thinking?"

I only stare at him.

"Eloping means we have no planning to complete," he explains. "We just need to pick a date, arrange for a license, and bam!"

"Bam? Seriously? Like it's that easy." I release a breath I didn't know I was holding in. "We have to decide where. Like, in Missouri or Chicago? What are we going to wear? Who will be our two witnesses?"

"Easy," he chides. "I only meant you aren't a bridezilla. But I'm beginning to rethink that."

Lucky for him, he doesn't laugh at his own joke.

"If we pick a date, then we can pick where. The rest will fall into place. So, what do you think about after Thanksgiving? Mom and Amy will be in Chicago to help with Liberty."

I shrug noncommittally.

"C'mon," he urges. "Give me something to work with here."

I sigh deeply before engaging in the conversation. "In the next week, I'll be moving Liberty and me to Chicago with you." He smiles proudly at my words. "We'll be moving into a bigger condo, buying furniture, decorating, and stocking the cupboards. We're hosting 11 people for Thanksgiving, which is only two weeks away. That's a lot to do, and there's not much time to do it in. We have to make sure that with all the changes, we help Liberty adapt to her new world." I can't hold back the shrug that escapes.

"I see." Hamilton's thumb caresses my cheek, distracting me. "I think the keyword to remember there is 'we'. You're not alone anymore. I will be helping you. I only have a couple of appearances on the calendar. Taylor offered to help you shop, too. I know I've explained how the condo has delivery services. We'll pick out the furniture, and they will place it in the spot we tell them to. We'll also have Miss Alba, our housekeeper, to help with grocery shopping and keeping the place organized. I think you will find it much easier than it would be to start a new house in Athens. Trust me, we can do this.

"Besides, if you get stressed, I will run you a hot bubble bath and deliver glass after glass of wine for you to enjoy by candlelight."

I snort unladylike. "You've forgotten our daughter. There's no way she will leave me alone for a long, relaxing bath."

"Ah, but you forget, although I am new to the role of Daddy, I am quite adept at playing with Liberty. I will situate you in the bath then read her two stories, and she will fall asleep. You'll have plenty of peace and quiet while you soak." His sexy smirk makes an appearance. "Then, I'll lift you from your bubbly retreat, slowly dry every inch of you, and deliver a sensual massage in our bed. I'll have you relaxed in no time." He smiles proudly as his hands slip under the back of my sweatshirt.

"Perhaps you can rid me of stress," I admit. "We still have much to discuss, so don't try to distract me right now with your sexy smile and tantalizing touch."

Hamilton removes his fingers from my skin, returning one to the safety of my cheek. "When you envision eloping, what do you see?"

I quirk my mouth to the side while I think. "I see you in jeans and a nice shirt. I'm in a simple dress. And no flowers."

"Do you care where we do it?"

I shake my head.

"I'd like to fly to Vegas on the Friday after Thanksgiving. We could elope Friday night and stay until Sunday for a short honeymoon. Mom and Amy can stay at our place with Liberty."

"Ham, flying to Las Vegas over the holiday weekend is too expensive."

He doesn't respond with words. He simply smiles as his gaze wills me to get his message. I stare back until I remember I have money now.

"It's new to me," I defend. "You can't just expect me to stop worrying about money–I've counted every penny for so many years. I can't just shut that off and start spending your money."

"Our money," he corrects. "And you recall our meeting with your family's lawyer; you have plenty of money of your own now, too."

I hedge. He's right. It's still hard for me to process that I'm a 20-year-old millionaire. It should comfort me that Liberty and I have plenty to live on, but I have no idea how to use it, save it, or get used to it.

"You deserve a mini-vacation." Hamilton interrupts my thoughts. "You've focused on your degree, raising Liberty, and caring for Alma...it's time you take a little 'me' time. No one will fault you for that. You've had a rough go of it these past few weeks. Two nights in Vegas, just the two of us, might be just what the doctor ordered."

I slowly nod as I imagine it.

Hamilton beams. "It's settled then, we'll elope in Vegas. I'll arrange everything."

"I'm going to need your help," I state. "I get so hyper-focused on tasks that I often forget to have fun."

"Evidently, you've forgotten my job has always been to drag you away and force you to have fun." He bops me on the nose playfully. "I realize we have a lot to do in the next couple of weeks. There are others willing to help, and I will make it my personal mission to make sure you have fun at least once a day."

My attempt to hide my yawn fails as it lasts several seconds.

"Okay, it's time I take you home and tuck you into bed. We have a long drive home tomorrow. I imagine we will need a ton of patience to drive six hours with a toddler."

"One: you have no idea." I raise a finger as I count off. "We will need to make frequent stops." I hold up another finger. "Two: It's awfully presumptuous of you to think I will sleep with you on our first date." I smile innocently.

"Ah, ah, ah." He wags his finger in front of my face. "I said tuck you into bed not have my wicked way with you by ravishing your body until the wee hours of the morning."

Another big yawn overpowers me.

"Let's go." He pulls me up and passes blankets for me to carry. "I've kept you out past your bedtime."

"It's barely 10 o'clock," I protest. "I don't know why I'm so tired all of the time."

Hamilton simply nods, causing me to wonder what he thinks. *Am I tired due to stress? Am I exhausted from the emotional upheaval in my life?* No matter the cause, Hamilton's support and understanding means a lot to me.

131

MADISON

"We're here!" Hamilton announces. "Our new home awaits."

When he exits the truck, fear floods my every cell. I sit frozen in the passenger seat; a sudden queasy feeling fills my belly.

Hamilton's voice talking to someone draws my attention. Turning my head, I find him speaking to a tall, gorgeous blonde in a see-through silk blouse and a tight, navy pencil skirt. He waves for me to join him. Reluctantly, I slide from my seat, leaning against the truck door.

"Hand me the dogs. The three of you head on up, and I'll have everything brought up for you," the blonde orders, pointing.

I stand slack-jawed as Hamilton obeys. He passes the two dogs on leashes to her before returning to carry Liberty over to me.

"Let's go see the new place," he murmurs. "Berkeley will take care of our stuff."

She has a name. This is the infamous publicist, Berkeley. This is the person he allows to handle his personal affairs and make decisions about our new home, even about the bed we will sleep in tonight.

I want to release my inner rage. I want to scream and stomp my foot. I want to yell, but I don't want to embarrass Hamilton. I don't want him to feel he needs to hide his interactions with her from me. I don't want to teach Liberty that type of behavior is okay. So, instead, I wave to Berkeley as I allow

Hamilton to lead me by the hand, across the parking garage to the waiting elevator.

My mind buzzes with the sheer size of this complex. It's not a city block; it's bigger. Hamilton had mentioned the center courtyard containing two dog parks as well as a playground for children. I imagined small spaces. Given the immense facade I witnessed upon pulling into the garage, the courtyard must be large.

I'm going to be living in these buildings of splendor with doormen. I'll have dog sitters, maid service, and nannies available at my beck and call. There's a pool, fitness center, gymnasium, and running track on site. This is now my home–this is now my life.

In a trance, I enter our condo while Hamilton holds the door for me. I scan the enormous space, void of decoration, void of all furniture but a sectional sofa and enormous television. I note a few toys strewn on the sofa; that's a nice touch. The kitchen counters are bare. There are no rugs on the dark, wood floors.

Hamilton owns no furniture–Berkeley rented a bed and sofa for us until we purchase our own. He has no dishes, no pans, no utensils, and I'm not even sure he owns any towels. Our shopping list looms large in my mind. Thanksgiving is only 10 days away. We'll need so much before our company arrives–my head swims.

I startle when warm, firm lips surround mine. Hamilton's strong hands secure me in place. I'm vaguely aware of Liberty trotting around the large open floor plan, cheering at the top of her little lungs. Hamilton's hot tongue slides across my lower lip, seeking entrance. I part my lips but a sliver. It's all the permission he needs–quickly our kiss heats. My mind plants itself firmly in the present.

Too soon, Liberty tugs on Hamilton's jeans, interrupting our kiss.

"Hey." Hamilton quickly lifts her between us. "What do you think of our new home?"

Liberty pats Daddy's cheek as if she understands.

I take a moment, spinning to take in my surroundings. It's a large, open floor plan. The kitchen area, with a large island, sits opposite the floor-to-ceiling windows. Outside, Chicago twinkles in the night, stretching out as far as the eye can see. A sunken living room area faces the windows. Opposite the kitchen, a dark wooden door promises a room behind it. Maybe it's a bedroom or an office.

Hamilton leans over my shoulder, whispering, "Welcome home."

Goosebumps cover my neck where his warm breath caressed. My belly flutters. "We're home." A large smile adorns my face. It's all I hoped for. It's better than I imagined. I am giddy with the possibilities this space provides for us, for our family.

The sound of a toilet flushing travels down the hallway. Hamilton's brows dart up, telling me he didn't expect a guest. I quickly take Liberty from him and stand behind his large body. The sounds of a giggling girl cause me to peek around his shoulder.

"Surprise," a female voice greets with little conviction.

"Hamilton!" a younger voice screams, and her little feet run to his outstretched arms.

"Aurora!" Hamilton spins her in a circle before placing her back on the floor.

"You're early," the female states, standing behind Aurora. "The guys just went down to get the food delivery. We planned to surprise you with a meal when you arrived. Sorry, our timing sucks."

Hamilton blows it off as no big deal.

Liberty squirms to escape my hold. Without a care, she approaches Aurora, and the two play with the toys on the sectional.

"Um, Hamilton..." the gorgeous female waves her index finger between herself and me. As he doesn't understand her, she prompts, "Why don't you introduce us?"

Before he can start introductions, the front door beeps as the entry code is entered and swings open. I recognize Stan; he plays baseball with Hamilton. I assume the young man with Stan is his son, so the woman and girl must be Stan's wife and daughter.

"The gang is all here," Stan states, placing several plastic bags of takeout cartons on the kitchen island. The boy places two bags of beverages on the island, too.

"You must be Madison." Stan extends his right hand to shake mine.

"And you, Stan, are the reason my Cardinals didn't have any baserunners in the playoffs," I tease.

"My glove was on fire. What can I say?" Stan's chest puffs out, and he beams.

"This is his wife, Delta, his son, Webb, and daughter, Aurora." Hamilton motions to each of them as he speaks. He pulls me tight to his side. "This is Madison, and over there is Liberty."

"Your fiancé, Madison," Delta corrects. "Girl, let me see that ring." Her flawless, mocha hand, with an immaculate manicure, beckons mine.

"You've already seen the ring," Stan reminds his wife.

"Not on her finger," Delta informs, her tone clearly letting them know there is a difference. She oohs and ahs for a bit, remarking that it's a gorgeous heirloom.

"Let's eat," Stan demands, already filling a paper plate. "Hope you like Italian," he calls in my direction.

"What will Liberty eat?" Delta asks at my side.

"We stopped at five to stretch our legs and keep to her schedule. She's already eaten." I smile. "Thanks for asking, though."

"Ours have already eaten, too," Delta confesses. "Aurora wanted to drop off a few toys for Liberty to play with until hers are unpacked, and we knew you'd be too tired from the drive to worry about dinner."

"This is so kind. Thank you." My words don't seem to be enough for their gestures. "I was so focused on getting here then settling Liberty in before bedtime that I didn't even think of our dinner."

"Thank you," Hamilton directs towards them both.

"How old are your kids?" I ask Delta while she follows me through the line of boxes. When my plate is full, I move to the other side of the island to eat.

"Webb just turned 13, and Aurora is 4," she beams as she occupies the empty countertop beside me. "Liberty is two, right?"

"Libby will be two in March," Hamilton corrects.

"She's got your height." Delta peeks over her shoulder at the two girls playing on the sofa.

"Along with his hair, his eyes, his dimples…" I add.

"She has her mother's smarts and stubbornness," Hamilton interrupts.

I want to argue, but he's right. When I look at our daughter, I only see the ways she looks like Amy and him—I don't see myself in her. So, I only smile at his words.

Stan's eyes dart between the two of us, looking for any sign I'll argue.

Aurora and Liberty play together as if they've done it a million times before. I love my daughter's ability to instantly accept others into her world without any hesitation. I dread the day she learns from anyone to prejudge others.

After dinner and the quick cleanup, the adults move to the sectional and the toddlers to the living room floor. Webb occupies the corner cushions between his mother and father; he's enthralled in his e-Reader. Although I participate in the adult conversation, I long to know the book he's reading. I catch a break when Stan and Hamilton begin to discuss tomorrow's public appearance.

"Webb," I call across the room, "what are you reading?"

He sits still, not acknowledging my question. If it weren't for his eyes looking from his mom's lap to his dad's and back, I might think he didn't hear me.

"Webb," Delta prompts, "Miss Madison asked you a question." She places her hand in the space between his face and the e-Reader.

Webb looks at his mom, sees her touch her finger to her nose, then looks in my general direction. The simple signal reminds him to make eye contact.

"It's a book by John Green," he states. His eyes quickly return to his mom's hand atop his e-Reader.

"I love his books," I reply. "Which is your favorite?"

As Delta hasn't withdrawn her hand, he looks to her before glancing back to me. "I'm reading *Paper Towns*," he states.

"I like *Looking for Alaska*, but *Will Grayson, Will Grayson* is my favorite book of his." I wait several moments for his response.

"This is the first John Green book for me." His eyes connect with mine for the first time.

Hamilton mentioned Stan's son was on the Autism spectrum during our phone calls last year. I know Webb's eye contact is a challenge and smile at his small connection with me, a total stranger, during our conversation.

"What other books do you enjoy reading?" I ask, wanting to continue our interaction.

His eyes return to the e-Reader. "I want to buy two books by a new author, but my parents are making me learn patience." He looks in Stan's direction. "I put my name on the waiting list in the school library. I'm never going to get to read it or the one that follows it. Two times they checked it back out before looking at the waiting list."

It's easy to see that he is frustrated with the long wait for his book and breaking the rules by not following the waiting list order probably caused an issue for him.

"What book is it?" Hamilton inquires, returning to the conversation as I head to the kitchen for another bottle of water.

I notice Webb looks to him without hesitation, making it clear the two have a connection. "She's a new author and has two books so far." His eyes never stray from Hamilton's. "It's M. Crocker."

Hamilton chokes on his laugh. Stan and Delta stare wide-eyed at him, eyebrows raised.

I quickly turn, staring into the fridge with my back to the group. I want to confess; I'm the author, and I want to hand him a book. I pretend to search the fridge for an item. His parents want to teach him patience.

"Webb," Hamilton's voice cuts into the room, "what do you know about that author?"

I pull a water bottle out, shutting the refrigerator door. Leaning against the island, I take a sip, facing the living room.

Webb rises from his seat, moving closer to Hamilton. He swipes a few times on the e-Reader then moves the device toward Hamilton. "She's a new author this year. So far, she's published two books. The publisher claims two more will release next year." Webb swipes one more time. "Here she is..." His voice trails off.

I watch as Webb's posture grows stiff. He grabs his e-Reader from Hamilton and returns to his corner of the sectional, safely between his parents. He doesn't look to Hamilton or me; he averts his eyes from everyone in the room.

Delta leans over, glancing at the author photo on the screen. "No way!" Her eyes are alight with excitement as she smiles in my direction. "Hamilton told me you were an author. I assumed it was Chicklit or romance." I stand frozen as she approaches me.

"What am I missing?" Stan looks around the room, lost in the conversation.

Hamilton clues his friend in. "Madison is M. Crocker. She's the author Webb is waiting *patiently* to read."

Stan looks my way, slack-jawed.

Delta nudges my arm with her elbow, joining me at the breakfast bar. "So, not just an author. You're the hot, new, young adult author causing a buzz in middle schools everywhere."

I met her only an hour ago, and I already see the twinkle in her eye and pride on her face for my work. I'm going to like this woman.

"You should give Webb a book," Hamilton suggests. "I know you have a few copies in a box over there."

My wide eyes attempt to signal Hamilton that he is crossing a line. I chance a glance at Delta.

"You don't have to," Delta states, still smiling with excitement. "I mean…"

"I don't want to step on your toes," I explain. "I know it's important to follow through on the patience lesson."

"Oh, forget that." She lowers her voice for only the two of us to hear. "Webb has waited three weeks, and they keep checking out the book without following the waiting list. I think we've drawn enough patience from him. I mean, if you have a copy you can find easily, I'm sure he'd love it." She shrugs, attempting to make light of the situation.

"Ham," I call toward the guys, "would you mind finding the box labeled 'office' for us?"

He doesn't hesitate, heading straight for the boxes. Stan rises to assist him; a hesitant Webb joins them. Although no emotion graces his face, by approaching the boxes with the men, Webb shows he is interested in their task and my book.

"Ta Da!" Hamilton cheers. "Webb, come help me open the box."

I marvel as Webb hands his e-Reader to Stan and joins Hamilton at the box with "office" in large, black print on the sides. Hamilton lifts two flaps, and Webb immediately lifts a book from inside as if it's the Shroud of Turin or the Holy Grail. He shows no emotion, but his actions convey his excitement.

"Bring it over here, Webb," Delta motions towards him.

He slides beside his mother, my book cradled to his chest. She pulls it from his grasp, looking at the cover and then the back. Webb glances my way but averts his eyes quickly.

Delta taps his nose before prompting, "What do you say to Miss Madison?"

Webb directs his eyes to mine. "Thank you." His eyes return to the book.

"You need to wait until tomorrow to read it."

At his mother's words, Webb taps his wrist as if touching a watch. Stan immediately directs Webb to accompany him down the hall.

"Is that his tell?" I look to Delta. Hamilton smiles at me from her side.

"Yes. Tapping his wrist signals his teacher, his aide, and us that he needs a minute." She sighs. "I'm sure he's angry he can't open it now and hide in its pages until he finishes it in one sitting." She attempts a smile for me. "He's excited to read it but has school tomorrow. It's another lesson in patience."

I place my hand on her forearm. "I understand. He's awesome. It's clear he is close to Hamilton, and he engaged with me, a total stranger in his first time seeing me." I smile at my new friend. "I know it's challenging."

She pats my arm and a genuine smile graces her face. "We have our moments. He's working so hard every day. It's all him."

Taking the book in hand, I find a pen in the kitchen. I sign my name on the title page. When Webb begins to read, I hope he'll find my signature.

I know Webb must work every day to fit into *normal* society. I also know his parents struggle with every decision, every event, every interaction he has outside his family. Webb's acceptance of Hamilton and even me tonight is a testament to the safety he feels with his parents, the skills they assist him with daily, and using his timeouts any time he requests one. I've learned a lot about Hamilton's friends, my new friends, tonight.

132

MADISON

With Liberty tucked safely in her portable crib in the room next to ours, I fall on our king-sized bed. Hamilton emerges, fresh from a shower, in his shorts as he snags a t-shirt from his bag. I admire the sculpted contours of his muscular abs and chest. My eyes delight in the sight of a new tattoo near his heart. I place my hand over my mouth to hide my shock when I realize he's going to flip when he finds my tattoo.

"I hope you aren't too upset they were here tonight," Hamilton states, sliding his shirt over his head.

"At first, I was," I confess honestly. "I wanted our first night to be the three of us. Delta was right though; we didn't plan for food or drinks. Besides, I had fun. They're easy to talk to." I yawn before continuing. "I'm nervous to meet your teammates and even more nervous about meeting their wives and girl-friends." I quirk my mouth to one side. "Stan and Delta seem normal, and I absolutely love their kids."

Hamilton nods in agreement, a large, lopsided smile on his face.

"You failed to mention Webb really likes you."

"I told you I hung out at their place quite a bit. I never know how he feels about me, but I keep treating him as I would any other kid. It seems to work." He shrugs.

He makes light of his connection to Webb. I know he understands the struggles that child and his parents face, and I decide to drop it.

"We have a big day tomorrow," he murmurs.

"Yeah, I'm exhausted just thinking about it."

"To sleep you go!" He swats me on my butt.

I giggle as he slides into bed and pulls me against his hot, solid body. I turn to face him and wrap my arms around his middle. I rest my head on his left shoulder.

"I love you," I whisper then yawn.

"Get some sleep," he whispers into my hair. "We have a big day of shopping tomorrow."

I nod.

He spins me in his arms before pulling my back snug to his front. "I love you, too. I can't tell you how good it feels to finally have you here with me." His hot breath tickles my ear.

In mere moments, I drift asleep.

Liberty leaps from my arms with the opening of our door. She jibber-jabbers as she walks into the space.

"Is that so?" Miss Alba responds as if understanding Liberty's every word, even though they only met this morning. "Would you like a snack?" She stands with hands on her hips a wide smile upon her face. Her brightly colored dress is protected by her apron. Hamilton assures me, I'll love her. So far it seems I will.

Liberty promptly nods and raises her arms towards Miss Alba. She lifts Liberty, and together, they browse, first in the pantry then in the refrigerator.

"Fresh fruit. That's the perfect snack after a busy day of shopping." Liberty nods to Miss Alba's statement and patiently waits as she's secured in her highchair. Once the bowl of diced fruit lies in front of my hungry daughter, Miss Alba addresses me. "What can I get for Momma?"

I shake my head. "I can get my own." I'm relieved to find a bottle of water in the door to the fridge as we don't have glasses yet. "Looks like you've had a busy day shopping today, too." The pantry is full, and the refrigerator contains many options as well. "I'm sure that took over an hour at the grocery store."

Miss Alba nods. "I love my job!" She smiles.

It's weird, allowing someone to shop for us.

"Let's set up your cell phone calendar to sync with the home calendar," Miss Alba suggests, pressing a few buttons on the refrigerator door.

A large screen within the stainless steel door reveals a list of tabs across the top.

"I press the calendar tab like this," she instructs. "This calendar will show Hamilton's travel schedule, the dogs' schedule, Liberty's activities, my schedule, and your work schedule. With the individual tabs, we can view each separate calendar and make additions to them" She smiles while awaiting my show of understanding. When I nod, she continues, "Let's look at Liberty's calendar. In red are possible activities. Let's pretend she will be going to this tumbling activity tomorrow at three. When I press and hold it, the color changes to black. Black calendar events indicate her planned activities, and they show up over on the combined calendar, too."

I press a few tabs, viewing various calendars as Hamilton walks up behind me.

"Let's ask the dog walkers to take the dogs down at six tonight," he suggests over my shoulder. "Wanna put it on their schedule?"

I open this calendar, press today's date, and six o'clock, holding it until it turns black.

"Perfect," he praises.

"So, now what happens?" I ask, looking from him to Miss Alba.

"At six, one of the guys will ride the service elevator up and take both dogs down to run for a while at the dog park," Hamilton explains.

Miss Alba adds, "When the service elevator pings over here," she points to the elevator doors in the utility room off the kitchen, "they'll announce themselves before walking in. If no one is here, they'll still enter and get the dogs."

"Too easy," I reply.

"They make it all that easy for us," Hamilton states.

"The combined calendars will help me plan meals and clean areas of the condo," Miss Alba informs. "The list tab is where you place any special requests from the store. You can also leave me notes of meals you prefer or guests you'll be entertaining."

"Got it," I assure.

She presses a few buttons. "There. I've sent you a link to your phone, so you can schedule from it. If you enter a phone number for the iPad or email address right here," she points to a button for me, "you can send a link to connect it to all your devices to schedule from them."

"Very high tech," Hamilton assures me. "When we hire a nanny, her calendar will join the others."

I give Hamilton the look, to which he just glares back at me.

"We'll talk about it later," he smirks.

"Follow me," I demand, striding to my empty office.

"I guess we are talking about it now." Hamilton attempts to make light of this. "Open your calendar to the children's activities."

I do as he instructs. I'll humor him for a bit.

He leans in over my shoulder. "She'd love swimming lessons, tumbling, story time–she'd like all of these activities."

I nod in agreement.

"Even if we signed her up for only two of these, they meet three days a week." He moves to face me. "That would cut into your work time. If you were still teaching, Liberty would be in daycare or preschool from seven-thirty to four, five days a week. Writing is your job now; a nanny will give you more free time to write and allow Liberty to make new friends in the building."

"I guess we could look into it, but I'm not making any promises," I grumble. I've survived almost two years without a nanny. I leaned on Alma to care for Liberty while I attended classes. My mind tries to calculate the hours Alma cared for Liberty each week.

"I love you, stubborn woman," he states prior to kissing my forehead.

After dinner, the long day begins to take its toll on me. I long to prop myself up on a few pillows in the corner of the sectional.

"This way," Hamilton urges as we walk down the hallway.

I hear the sound of running water in the master bathroom. "What's up?" I pause, looking up at Hamilton.

"Liberty and I have a surprise for you." He continues to maneuver me towards our bedroom with his hand firmly at the small of my back.

"Sup-pize!" Liberty jumps up and down on our bed as I enter my room. "Sup-pize, Mommy!"

I climb onto the bed and begin jumping with her. Liberty wraps her little arms around my legs, and together, we fall to the mattress, giggling. She wiggles her way up my body.

She points to the master bath. "Sup-pize, Mommy!"

I crane my neck. Hamilton bends over the sunken tub, turning off the faucet. He dips his hand in, testing the temperature.

"Perfect," he declares, looking my way. "Your bath awaits." His long arm gestures above the tub.

"What's all this?" I lift Liberty, walking towards him.

"Libby and I want some Daddy-Daughter time, so we thought you could relax in here for a bit." He extends his arms, and Liberty quickly climbs into them. "Let's light the candles for Mommy."

I stand in the doorway as the two position six candles around the tub, counting out loud as they light each one. The faint scent of vanilla wafts in my direction. My eyes shift from my daughter; Hamilton's sexy smirk says it all. He loves when I use vanilla body wash and body spray. His eyes stare hungrily at my lips. It's clear he has plans for after my bath.

"Bye-bye," Liberty announces as they vacate the room, turning off the light as they pass.

I dip my fingers through the bubbles, testing the water. I'm pleased to find it hot and deep. I remove my clothes, placing them in the hamper. I lift one foot over the edge into the tub then the other. I slowly lower my body below the bubbles into the blissful heat. I don't move while it acclimates. Goosebumps prick upon my shoulders despite the heated air. The hot bath causes the warm air to seem chilly.

I extend my legs, placing my toes near the waterline. With arms braced on the edge where cream bathtub meets oatmeal and chocolate tiles, I gradually lean back, my eyes closing, submerging myself to my chin in the divine warmth. Tiny bubbles pop near my ears as I swirl my arms beneath the water.

Opening my eyes, I notice a hand towel, cradling earbuds, next to a glass of white wine. Condensation on the glass signals me that the wine is cold. Raising the glass to my lips, the chilled liquid starkly contrasts the heated water. The refreshing, fruity wine is another point scored by Hamilton. I realize Miss Alba must have helped purchase the wine. But Hamilton thought ahead to place it in the refrigerator for tonight. He remembers I like wine in the evening from time to time.

Curious, I lift one ear bud gently, placing it in my right ear. A 1980's power ballad plays as I scan the bathroom for a device it's connected to. I find nothing. While Warrant sings "Heaven", a deep calm slides over me. The wine, the bubbles, the warmth, the candlelight, and the melody coaxes the last month's stress from every bone in my body.

Madison

I rest my head against the tub and close my eyes. I lift one foot, letting my toes peek out from the water. I lift it higher and higher to rest it on the spout. Slowly, the foam glides down my shin and over my exposed calf. As the bubbles pop, the sensation prickles my heated skin. I immerse the foot beneath the tranquil water.

Opening my eyes, I reach for my wine again, taking a deep sip. I savor the blend of apples, citrus, and peaches as it refreshes my mouth and throat. I return the glass to the tile tub edge and raise my other foot to enjoy the tiny bubbles popping, releasing even more tension.

My muscles loosen and my thoughts evaporate as the alcohol affects my head. I stir the remaining bubbles by gliding my hands just below the surface. I further unwind by removing one earbud to enjoy the sloshing my waves create.

I notice my empty glass is full again. My sneaky man must have tiptoed in. As I consume more wine, I sit up, allowing the bubbles to explode on my back and shoulders. Goosebumps form, chilling my skin. In three long gulps, I down the wine before exiting the warm, soapy haven to rinse in the shower.

I choose a warm temperature from the dials before I step under the spray. I allow the stream to pelt my scalp, spinning for the water to fall on my face, my back, and my chest.

I wipe the water from my eyes before I open them to find the vanity lights on and Hamilton leaning against the counter. I wipe a large circle of water drops from the shower door. Hamilton smirks, arms crossed over his chest. My nipples come to full attention as warmth sinks past my belly.

He strides towards the shower door, snagging a heavy, terrycloth robe from a nearby hook. I turn the water off, anxious for what he plans next. He opens the glass door, robe opened for me to easily slip my arms into it. The soft, fluffy material engulfs me.

"I told myself to give you a few nights to settle in, but I can't resist you any longer," he growls into my neck. His humid breath taunts my sensitive skin.

I tilt my head, exposing my neck. He nips and sucks playfully. He palms my chin, turning me into his kiss. His mouth devours mine. I pivot, positioning myself tight to his chest. My hands tug at his belt, exposing my urgent need.

He carries me to our bed, laying me out before him. His jaw ticks as his hands deftly open the robe. I watch through hooded eyes as he scans down my body.

When his brows raise and lips part, I know he's spotted my tattoo. I expect his eyes to find mine or for him to speak–he does neither.

"Do you like it?" I whisper. It's almost identical to the one he has over his heart. Although we never planned it, we chose similar tattoos.

He crawls onto the bed, his fingers tracing the lines. I watch his eyes fill with lust, rubbing my upper thighs together slowly to ease my growing need. After several moments, I attempt to sit up, needing to touch him.

With one forceful hand, he prevents my movement. He climbs up my body, a feral look in his dark eyes.

"Do you like it?" I whisper again before wetting my suddenly dry lips.

His eyes track the motion of my tongue. "It's the sexiest tat I've ever seen," he growls before attacking my lips and tongue with his.

He pulls his mouth from mine. "I imagined a design placed here." He licks the area behind my ear.

Lowering himself, he nips my collarbone on his descent. "I fanaticized of script along here." His thumbs graze under the curve of my breasts before he nips and sucks each nipple.

He tugs my arms from the robe I forgot I was wearing and flips me over as if I weigh nothing at all.

I flinch as his warm mouth licks down my spine. "I imagined a delicate, vining floral design here."

He palms one ass cheek and bites the other. After my squeal, he informs, "The thought of one here haunted me for hours at night."

He plants kisses on the back of each knee before lifting one foot into the air. "I imagined an animal or four-leaf clover here." He lightly runs a calloused fingertip over my ankle.

With both ankles in hand, he twists my legs, prompting me to roll over. Like a large cat, he prowls up my legs to my waist.

"I spent countless hours and too many sleepless nights fantasizing about your secret tattoo and its location." He licks the perimeter of the baseball then kisses its center. "This is the sexiest gift you could ever give me."

I pull his mouth to mine. As our mouths collide and tongues dance, I feel him squirm as he removes his pants. I fist the hem of his shirt and tug it up and over his head, breaking our kiss only when necessary.

"We match," I state.

That's where our tattoo exploration and conversation end. Hamilton carries out his plan for our bodies to reconnect.

133

MADISON

When my alarm sounds, my body aches in protest as I stretch. It's the delicious reminder of a long rendezvous with Hamilton last night. My muscles crave a long, hot soak in the tub, but I'll have to settle for a long, hot shower.

I groan, remembering the hours of shopping planned for me today.

"It won't be that bad," Hamilton calls from our bathroom.

I crawl down the bed, excited at the prospect of ogling my naked man. I groan again when I find him already dressed with Liberty sitting next to him on the vanity.

I want nothing more than to crawl under the covers for a few more hours of sleep. But my day awaits.

Only 40 minutes after I kiss Hamilton goodbye, our doorbell rings. Since the doorman didn't call ahead, it must be a resident or someone on Hamilton's pre-approved list. *I need to see who he has on that list.*

With Liberty behind my legs, I hesitantly open the door.

"Oh, hello." I greet the last person in the world I want to see at our door.

"Hello," the super-peppy Berkeley greets and enters without my invitation.

"Um..." I'm not shocked she's here but shocked by her boldness. "Hamilton's already left."

"Oh, I know," she states, squatting carefully in her heels and pencil skirt. "Hi, Liberty. How are you today?"

My daughter looks to me for direction. I smile and nod, anxious to see her reaction.

Not one to disappoint, she barely lifts her hand in a half-wave then darts back to her toys without a word.

Gracefully rising to stand, Berkeley seats herself on the sectional she secured for us. I follow her lead and take a seat.

"What brings you by today?" I ask, wanting to hurry this awkward visit along.

"I didn't want to intrude on your first night in Chicago," she begins. "So, I thought I'd drop by today and introduce myself."

I'm at a loss for words. What do I say to that? She's Hamilton's employee, not mine. I have no reason to talk to her.

The service elevator beeps, signaling Miss Alba's arrival. Liberty takes off running to greet her.

"Good morning," I call from the sofa.

Miss Alba returns my greeting, Liberty in her arms. "Oh, hello, Berkeley," she adds.

I can't read the tone with which Miss Alba greets Berkeley. It seems flat; maybe she's not a Berkeley fan.

"What brings you by?" Miss Alba inquires.

"I needed to officially introduce myself, and I hope I have a solution for Hamilton's family," Berkeley proudly replies.

Miss Alba raises her brows at me before releasing Liberty to the floor.

"What problem do you have a solution for?" I ask, dying to know the real reason for Berkeley dropping by when her boss is not present.

"First, let me share my card with you," she offers, flustered by my forwardness. "I work for the Cubs and Hamilton, but if you ever need anything, feel free to reach out. I was new to Chicago four years ago. I know what it's like to be all alone in a new city." She quickly corrects herself, "I mean, you're not alone, but I'll help if I can."

Whoa. So, she's really here to be nice and help me? I won't let my guard down that easily, but, given that Hamilton trusts her, I'll keep an open mind. I thank her for the card.

"I wanted to talk to you in person about a nanny for Liberty," Berkeley states, looking toward my daughter playing with blocks near my feet.

"I'm not convinced we need a nanny." I tell her the same thing I've told Hamilton several times in the past week.

She moves beside me and pats my knee like we've known each other for more than 48 hours. "Nonsense. You'll need time to write and a sitter to watch her while you attend the Cubs functions. Anyway, I have the perfect nanny for you."

My eyes widen as she ignores my protest and continues.

"Slater is a trainer for the Cubs and lives here in your building. His fiancé, Fallon, just graduated with a degree in Psychology and moved in with him. She's filled out the paperwork and plans to nanny as she slowly works on a master's degree. She knows the ins and outs of the Cubs life, and who's better than a psych major to care for a child?"

I nod. She sounds too good to be true.

"I've met Fallon a couple of times over the past two years. I've been talking to Slater the past two weeks, and this just seems like a perfect fit."

My head swims. I recall the information Hamilton shared about the services the condos offer. They keep a large staff of screened nannies and back-ups available for tenants.

"I thought we could invite Fallon over this morning, just to see if she might be a good fit for your family." Berkeley's timid smile lets me know she's really not trying to force me to make a choice. "Can I text her? The two of you could chat, and she could play with Liberty a bit."

"Would you like a drink?" I need a moment to mull this over.

"No, thank you," Berkeley responds.

As I approach the refrigerator, Miss Alba moves to my side.

"Nannies don't usually live in the building," she whispers so only I can hear. "It might be worth meeting her before another family grabs her up."

Every part of me trusts Miss Alba's advice. Maybe Berkeley isn't as bad as I imagined.

I sip from my water as I return to the sofa. "Text her. I'd love to meet her."

I smile genuinely at Berkeley. "I'm still not convinced we need one, but it can't hurt to meet her. If she's free before one, she can come on over."

I move to the floor with Liberty and her block towers.

Berkeley welcomes our guest, motioning to the sectional.

"Madison," she introduces, "this is Fallon."

I wave at our new guest.

"And this little princess is Liberty." Berkeley squats, accidentally knocking over two of her block towers.

"No!" Liberty points at Berkeley and stands, hands on hips. "No, pin-thess. Me Batman." Finished with the conversation, she marches to her room.

"Umm, excuse us." I follow my headstrong daughter down the hall. I'm sure she's looking for her costumes, and we haven't unpacked them yet.

"Follow me," I instruct her, continuing to my room.

From my large suitcase, I pull out her Batman costume. I hold it up, and Liberty grasps my arms as she steps into the pant legs before sliding her arms into each sleeve. I tie it behind her neck.

"I'm gonna go back out to talk to Fallon," I inform her. "I hope you'll come out and play with us."

As I walk down the hallway, I hear her tiny feet following behind me. I seat myself on the sofa, smiling proudly as Liberty stands in the center of the sectional, her hands on her hips, shoulders thrown back, and chin up.

"Batman," she states.

"I love your costume," Fallon says, moving to sit on the floor. "What does Batman do?"

Liberty wastes no time demonstrating as she speaks. "Wun, jump, fwy…"

"Careful," I remind her as she climbs upon the sectional and hops to the floor.

Liberty takes Fallon on a tour of the house, points out her toys and books, and even demonstrates McGee's tricks for her. The two are fast friends. When they return from Liberty's room, Fallon prompts her to tell me what she's learned.

"Hola, Mommy!" My pretty girl waves proudly.

"Hola!" I wave back.

"She's bright," Fallon informs. "I'm fluent in Spanish and thought I'd teach her a word." She waits for my reaction.

"I love it. She's a sponge; she'll soak it up quickly." I smile.

Fallon stays for an hour, during which Liberty and I fall in love with her. We're still visiting when Taylor arrives to escort us shopping. We plan for her to nanny four days each week with other hours as needed.

Shopping with Taylor is as bad as I expected. We have much to buy, and shopping is my least favorite thing. I'm thankful Liberty sleeps through most of it, and, in the end, I'm glad Taylor is along. She proves to be a great help. However, once we climb off the elevator back at the condo, I can feel the exhaustion already setting in. "I'm hungry," Taylor tells me as we open the door. "Lucky for you, I've already prepped lunch!" Miss Alba chuckles from the kitchen. "Go get washed up while I set it out."

As we fill our plates with sandwiches, chips, and items from a relish tray, we share our shopping adventures with Miss Alba.

"Just before you returned, maintenance phoned to state your furniture arrived. They'll be bringing it up the service elevators soon." She looks to me for approval.

"Libby, did you hear that?" I lean towards her highchair. "Your new bed is here!" I clap my hands excitedly, and Liberty joins me.

"Wow, you've got a busy day," Taylor states.

"I'm sure I'll be exhausted tonight," I reply.

"Nonsense," Miss Alba tisks. "The guys will place it all where you want it and even assemble the beds for you. You only need to instruct them where to put it all."

"Hamilton will be home soon," Taylor reminds me, patting my forearm on the marble island. "He can help direct them for you."

As if summoned by her, Hamilton emerges through the front door at that moment.

"Daddy!" Liberty cheers with a cheese cube in her hand.

"What have we here?" He smiles at the four of us around the kitchen island.

"Take a stool," Miss Alba offers Hamilton. "Furniture is on the way up. You need to eat quickly."

Without argument, Hamilton tosses his coat on the sectional and strides to the empty barstool near Taylor. Our conversation returns to the morning's shopping and plans for the furniture while we enjoy our meal.

"Thank you." Hamilton shakes the three maintenance men's hands as they board the service elevator off the back of the kitchen.

When the doors close, he maneuvers himself through the waist-high stacks of boxes bordering the walls of the kitchen and dining room. All of our purchases from this afternoon have been delivered, too.

"Why don't the two of you take a break?" Miss Alba offers. "I've got dinner ready. The furniture is all in place. You can relax a bit before you begin opening all the boxes."

Hamilton hedges, but I am ready to eat and sit for a spell. "The new sheets will be done soon in the dryer, and most of the new dishes are now clean and dry." I wrap my arms around his waist. "I need to sit and eat."

He looks down into my eyes, assessing me. "Then we will eat. You know, the rest of this can all wait until tomorrow."

I shake my head–the thought of waking to so many full boxes tomorrow doesn't sound enticing. "Eat, rest for a minute, and then we will open the rest of the boxes."

He holds out a barstool for me, and I slide upon it. Miss Alba places Liberty into her chair while I begin cutting up a tender chicken breast for her plate.

"I can stay if you'd like." Miss Alba looks to me.

Hamilton shakes his head as I quickly respond. "Thank you for offering, but there's no need. We will work a little more before we call it a night." I smile. "There will be plenty left for you to help with tomorrow morning."

We work for just over an hour. Hamilton opens each box, and I wipe a cloth over each item before finding a location for it to grace in our new home.

I admire our work. Furniture now fills each room while the walls and ledges hold decorative frames, vases, and artwork. This recently vast, empty space now looks like a home.

Hamilton wraps his arms around my waist from behind. As I melt in his warm embrace, he whispers in my ear, "Once the trash and recycling are removed, our home will be ready for company."

I turn my lips to his cheek, placing a warm peck upon them. "They arrive tomorrow."

"You're exhausted," he murmurs softly into my messy hair. "Let's tuck Libby into bed before we wash off all of this day and rest for our company."

Hamilton

I turn on the shower, allowing the spray to warm up before we enter. Madison attempts to run her brush through her tangled hair. I stand, frozen in awe of this gorgeous woman of mine. Her life has been uprooted and her world completely changed. She's taken every blow with her chin high, always looking for a solution.

In the past two days, she and Liberty have moved with me to Chicago and helped me create a new home. She shows no fear, although I know she feels it just as I do. She's determined to start her new life here with me, and I love her even more for agreeing to do so.

Her eyes lock onto mine in the large mirror. She tilts her head to the side and quirks a smile at me. Unable to abstain any longer, I close the short distance between us. I place my hands upon her jaws and press my lips to hers. Our kiss begins slow but quickly becomes feverish. When she gasps, I slip my tongue into her mouth. My left hand entwines in her long locks, insisting she remain tight against me. My other fingers trace along her jaw, down her delicate neck and collarbone. I need her, but not here.

"Let's shower," I whisper as I begin to tug her t-shirt off of her.

We make quick work of our clothes, and I guide her ahead of me into the steam-filled stall. My hands remain on her hips while she leans her head back into the spray, wetting her hair. I fight the urge to run my hands up her abdomen to her breasts that lunge towards me while her back arches.

She pulls her head from under the spray, opening her eyes. In them, I see her desire, and my control crumbles. My lips seek hers in a punishing kiss while my hands knead her breasts and pluck her nipples into tight buds. She moans into my mouth, causing me to press myself against her soft flesh from thigh to chest. The water slickens our skin, and my erection continues to grow for her.

Behind her back, I pour shower gel into my hand. Starting at her shoulders, I slowly slide my hands up and down her arms then glide them over her chest. Again, her head falls back as her lips part. I allow one hand to trail down her breastbone, over her navel, to the soft mound above her entrance. I love that she waxes but leaves the landing strip. I gently tug on the short hair.

Madison

I jump back to life, turning in his arms, quickly lathering my hands with soap, while he massages my back. I spin, my hands flying to his cock between us. Gently at first, I glide my slick hands over him then slowly increase my grip with each stroke.

His hands press against the glass wall behind me to steady himself while he pumps into my fists. I've never showered with anyone. I've seen my share of sexy shower scenes in movies and read them in erotic romance books, but this is more than I ever imagined.

A low growl climbs from Hamilton's chest moments before he grasps my wrists, removing my touch from his erection. He holds my wrists above my head with one hand as we allow the spray to wipe all soap from our bodies.

His eyes are liquid pools, staring into mine, reaching to my soul. My lips part, and my tongue darts out to moisten them.

He pounces–his lips on mine inform me playtime is over. I'm spun around, and he places my hands on the glass. He lifts one of my knees, allowing my foot to rest on the shower seat, opening me up to him.

My back arches when he glides his bulging cock between my cheeks, down toward my entrance. He growls in my ear to keep my hands on the wall just before he slides into me in one swift motion. He's still, allowing me to stretch over him after his intrusion. I lean myself back into him, craving the contact of his chest against me, needing more of him, all of him.

He begins pounding in and out of me in a hard, steady rhythm. The sounds of our wet bodies slapping together fill the shower enclosure. I grind myself by swiveling my hips while he remains deep within me.

I feel the pelting water move from my backside. I'm so in the moment, into the sensations and momentum, that I didn't notice his hand leave my hip and move the shower head, adjusting the stream of water. I squeal when the spray connects with my sex while he's deep within me. Thank goodness for hand-held shower heads.

Hamilton slows his pistoning as he begins swirling the shower jets over my sensitive lips and swollen clit.

"Oh, oh… Ham," I groan as my body speeds from 60 miles per hour to over 100. "Hamilton…" I gasp for small breaths as the sensations overwhelm me. "So close."

Hamilton leans his torso onto my back, his mouth suckling at the nape of my neck. He stills the circular motions of the spray, now targeting it directly on the center of all my nerve endings.

"Yes!" I scream, feeling my release near. My core clenches, my muscles strain, and the tight coil prepares to release.

Hamilton nips my neck, and I fall apart. Wave upon wave racks through me. He doesn't still; instead, he continues to drive into me, the showerhead tormenting me.

My orgasm doesn't wane; my forehead hits the wall as tremors overtake me. Feeling me quake, Hamilton drops the showerhead to the tile below. His hands plant on my hips as he drives into me hard once, twice, and I feel him shutter as he grinds his release deep in me. While he trembles and sputters within my channel, my body turns to gelatin. My knees bend; my hands and head slide down the wet glass as I start to fall.

Hamilton withdraws, increases his grip on my hips, and steadies me. His arm around my waist tugs me to him, and he wraps another around my chest, gripping his hand over my bicep. My head falls back upon him.

Our rapid breaths begin to sync with each other as we fall deeper into each other.

134

MADISON

DELTA

what are you up to today?

Me

prepping for company

some writing

DELTA

I'm on my way to pick you up

we're taking Liberty shopping

ME

okay?

I'll have doorman send you up

I only met her a week ago; I'm not sure what to make of this spur of the moment shopping trip. I let Fallon know she may have the rest of the day off.

543

Liberty exudes more enthusiasm than I for our impromptu outing. She greets Delta at the door with cheers.

"What is all of this about?" I ask while we stand in the kitchen.

"Hamilton didn't tell you about today, did he?"

I recall our conversation last evening. He mentioned two events today: a public appearance and a meeting with his team. I shake my head.

"I figured as much." she smiles. "They had to R.S.V.P. a month ago. I knew he wouldn't remember this is a family event."

My eyes bulge. *Family event with the team? I'm not ready for this.*

"We've got this," she states. "It's a pre-holiday party for the Cubs organization and their families. We shake a few hands, gossip, eat a meal, take a few photos, and slip away at the first moment we can."

She must sense my fear. "I promise that I will not leave your side, unless Hamilton is with you."

"I..." My hand covers my lips. "I have nothing to wear."

"Duh," she laughs. "I knew you needed something new to wear. Thus, our shopping trip, silly." She wraps her arm around my shoulders. "Don't be upset with Hamilton. I'm sure if the R.S.V.P. came through now, he'd include you in all of it."

I shrug. I don't blame him, but I don't really know how I feel about it. Perhaps scared is the best way of explaining it.

Upon entering the department store of Delta's choosing, we are whisked to a large, private dressing room area. Beverages and snacks appear along with three saleswomen.

"Did you see what Hamilton took to wear?" she asks.

"A blue dress shirt with a Cubs-colored tie," I inform.

"We're looking for royal blue party dresses for Madison and Liberty," Delta points as she instructs. "Not cocktail, though."

Liberty toddles from mirror to mirror, enjoying the view as she giggles and waves.

The saleswomen nod before setting out on their task. I marvel at the large area–I've never seen a dressing room quite like this. I've never shopped in a store like this.

Delta places her hands upon my shoulders as she bends to make eye contact. "It's my treat today. Let's have fun." She mistakes my shock for worry.

"Delta," I murmur, "it's not that. I mean, it is, but it isn't." I look toward the ceiling as I struggle to compile my words. "Money isn't an issue. I'm just new to it. That's all." I smile, not wanting to ruin her gesture. I lower my voice near a whisper. "Since my father's death, I've struggled for every penny. My mother fell into depression and sought to ease her pain in bottle after bottle. She didn't reveal that I had a college fund, didn't share that the farm was paid off or that I had inherited my grandparents' farm. Weeks ago, I learned I should never have worried about money. I spent years scraping every penny I could from part-time jobs. When not at school or work, I studied. I took several college classes while in high school and took the CLEP test to earn others. My grades earned me a full ride. I lived with a charitable woman who provided free room and board for Liberty and me." I lift my eyes toward Delta's. "I have money. Hamilton has money. I'm just not accustomed to it. I shop at Target." I laugh.

"We are not that different, you and me." Delta places her hand upon mine. "I didn't inherit money, but marrying Stan rescued me from a shanty in Louisiana." A small smile climbs upon her face. "I understand it's hard to spend more money on things, but you deserve nice things and to attend these events."

I nod as racks of dresses roll into the room.

"Now for the fun part!" Delta stands, extending an arm to me. "You try on yours, and I'll help Liberty into hers. We'll meet out here by the mirrors with each outfit."

I enter the changing room as several dresses are placed over the door for me. I revel in the bright blue fabrics, some solid, some floral. I slowly inspect each as I place the hanger on a hook. I draw in a deep breath, vowing not to glance at the price tags. I need a dress worthy of being at Hamilton's side.

I wait at the three-way mirror. I turn this way and that, admiring the solid wrap dress, its length falling just above my knees.

"Mommy!" Liberty calls as she runs excitedly toward me. She sways side to side, enjoying the full skirt with layer upon layer of wavy tulle. The bodice is a simple tank ornamented with large, threaded flowers with rhinestones in the center. A large bow decorates her waist, a large rhinestone adorning it as well. "Wook, Mommy!"

The royal blue suits her dark curls and twinkling, brown eyes. The matching lace-top anklets and patent leather Mary Janes perfectly finish the look. I love it; it's fancy, yet appropriate for a little girl. Her excitement is contagious. While she admires herself in the mirrors, I look to Delta.

"I think I found my dress." I shrug, embarrassed. I feel I am trying on clothes, waiting for my mother's approval.

"Uh-huh," she shakes her head. "You must try them all on."

I cross my arms across, tapping my toe. "This is the perfect dress. There's no need to try on the others."

I slowly spin with outstretched arms for her inspection. I love the simple structure, the flow of the fabric, and the fit at the waist. It's blue screams Chicago Cubs. It's a dress I will happily wear again.

"Why don't you go look at the rack of dresses and tell me if you see one you like more than this one," I suggest to my friend. "I'll assist Liberty in trying on her next dress."

We return a few minutes later with Liberty proudly swirling in a long, blue satin dress with lace tulle and an ostrich feather adorning the flower broach at her right hip. Although she looks lovely, I dislike this choice. My daughter looks five instead of nearly two. I humor her as she parades into the common room, posing for Delta and the sales staff.

Delta agrees with my initial dress selection. After modeling two more dresses, we decide on Liberty's first dress. She squeals with glee when I inform her that she gets to wear it out of the store. I've remained in my new dress and adorned it with the matching heels and jewelry they offer.

I shakily hand over Hamilton's Amex to cover our bill. I remind myself we now have money to afford such things. I attempt to focus on how the two of us look and Hamilton's surprise when we arrive rather than the large amount we spend.

After picking up the kids from school and quickly changing at home, Delta delivers us to the event. I try to hide my nerves as we ascend in the elevator. I should have texted Hamilton to let him know we'd meet him. I fear what it might look like when we arrive separately.

With a ping, the elevator doors announce our arrival. I prompt Delta and her family to lead the way. Liberty proudly walks at my side as the hem of her dress sways down the long hallway toward the party.

"Delta," Stan's deep voice calls as he exits the elevator.

Turning, I find Hamilton standing bewildered beside him.

The two girls run towards their fathers; Webb remains at our sides. With daughters dancing at their feet, the men quickly join us. Hamilton opens his mouth, but Delta stops him with an extended palm.

"I thought you might forget this is a family event, so I delivered your family for you." She smiles proudly.

His eyes dart to mine, apology clear on his face. "I didn't know. I promise," he pleads.

I nod. "Delta said you had to RSVP last month; it's no big deal."

Hamilton's gaze sweeps over my entire body. My skin prickles at his attention and the lust I see in his gaze.

"It's new." My nerves are evident in my voice.

"I like it."

"Daddy!" Liberty interrupts, drawing Hamilton's attention from me. "Daddy, wook!" She spins in a circle, causing her dress to billow out further.

"You look very pretty." Hamilton smiles proudly at her. "Both you and Mommy are very pretty."

Liberty lifts her arms; Hamilton scoops her up. She places a kiss upon his cheek while wrapping her arms tightly around his neck.

"Shall we?" Stan gestures toward the nearby entrance.

I observe Delta closely and follow her lead. Hamilton removes his hand from the small of my back, securing the backpack on his free shoulder.

"I'd like to introduce Madison and our daughter, Liberty," he proudly announces before returning his hand to my back.

I smile and shake hands with the team's owners and management each time Hamilton introduces the two of us. Liberty even extends her little hand to shake.

"Mommy," her little voice calls to me as she points to the small backpack Hamilton holds. "Cubbie Bear?"

I assume she's feeling overwhelmed in this crowd of strangers and wants her bear to hold. I easily pull it from the backpack still on Hamilton's shoulder. When I extend it, she quickly cuddles it to her chest.

"I recognize this pretty face," a gruff voice announces from our right. "This is Hamilton's number one fan. I told you about her; she's from his Des Moines debut."

Hamilton allows the three men to enjoy a chuckle prior to continuing his introductions to the coaches.

"I hope this means you've joined him in Chicago," the pitching coach states. "We could use an extra set of eyes to keep Hamilton in tip-top shape."

Over the loud chuckles, Hamilton informs, "Madison has finished college, and we've just moved into our new place." His hand on my hip pulls me snug to his side.

It doesn't escape me that the way Hamilton has introduced us tonight implies we've been a couple. It's no one's business; I'm glad he isn't drawing attention to the fact we aren't wed, and he didn't know he had a daughter a week ago.

"Daddy, wook!" Liberty squeals, pointing across the large room. "Cubbie Bear!" She animatedly points with one extended finger before using her hand pressed to his jaw to turn his head.

"Excuse us," Hamilton begs of the coaches. "She's a huge fan."

His hand slips from my hip before he lowers Liberty to the floor. Quickly, his hand grasps mine as we hurry to follow our daughter who is running towards the Cubs Mascot, calling loudly to Cubbie Bear.

I now regret not teaching her that the Chicago Cubs mascot is Clark. The plush toy she clutches in her tiny hand now is the Iowa Cubs Mascot, Cubbie Bear. Although it's their minor league team, the two mascots are different.

She freezes five feet from the oversized bear. Her little head cranes upward to marvel at the life-size version of her plush friend. She extends her tiny free hand and waves.

Clark quickly returns her greeting before kneeling to her level. Liberty extends her Cubbie Bear, proudly showing it. The mascot places his large, furry hand over his mouth and bounces to mimic laughter.

Liberty grabs Hamilton's hand and pulls him closer with her. Many one-

and-a-half-year-olds enjoy mascots from safe distances but fear them up close. Not our daughter–I marvel at her inquisitive nature and fearlessness. Clark stands as she draws near, so Hamilton lifts her into his arms. The mascot pats her on the head. Liberty leans forward to kiss his cheek.

A female photographer wearing three large cameras, urges us to pose as a family with the mascot. While I stand on the right of Clark, Hamilton holds Liberty on the left side. With one camera and then a second, she rapidly snaps several photos then excuses herself.

"Libby is kissing him in half of the photos," Hamilton whispers when I return to his side. I shake my head as we approach Stan's family.

"That was adorable," Delta states. "Libby, who was that?" She points at the mascot.

"Cubbie Bear," Liberty replies, extending her stuffed toy.

"His name is Clark," Webb states matter-of-factly, staring at his hands. Beneath them is the copy of my book.

"Cubbie Bear!" Liberty argues, wiggling her stuffed bear towards him.

"In Des Moines, the I-Cubs mascot is named Cubbie Bear," I tell Webb, hoping he'll drop the argument without drawing more attention to us.

"Hamilton pitched for the Cubs minor league team there for a month before he moved to Chicago," Stan informs Webb.

"Can I see your Cubbie Bear?" Webb inquires, looking toward Liberty.

Leaning forward from Hamilton's grasp, she places her beloved bear in Webb's hand for inspection. He turns it over then looks to Clark and back.

"They aren't the same." He passes the toy back to Liberty. "I like your Cubbie Bear better."

Happy with his approval, Liberty nods firmly.

Hamilton leaves me with Delta to speak with teammates, and Stan follows. Aurora invites Liberty to join her and a few other girls near the windows. They have dolls spread out everywhere as the sun sets in the background. "You may read for 30 minutes," Delta tells Webb.

He quickly rises, book in hand, and escapes to read by himself on the floor.

"I feel like a million eyes are burning my back," I confess.

"Oh, everyone is looking and speculating why you are here with Hamilton." She leans closer and lowers her voice. "Can you blame them? Hamilton keeps to himself. The team and fans know very little about him. Now, suddenly, he arrives with a hot woman and little girl in tow." She purses her lips. "It will wear off. Hamilton and Stan are probably setting the guys straight as we speak."

I sneak a peek. Hamilton stands, facing a group of guys with his back towards me. The men are hanging on his every word. I turn around, searching for Liberty. She's not with Aurora or Hamilton. I scan the room. She's seated near Webb while he reads. She doesn't seem to be bothering him, so I leave her be.

"Would you mind keeping an eye on Libby while I join Hamilton for a bit?"

Delta nods as I rise. When I approach, undetected by him, I slip my arm under his and lean in close.

"Hello," I greet the group of wide-eyed men as Stan simply chuckles. "I'm Madison."

"Oh, we know who you are," a tall, muscular, blonde states.

He is promptly slapped on the back of the head by the pitcher next to him.

"What he should have said is, 'we're the idiots you've heard cat-calling in the background as Hamilton attempted to speak to you on the phone.'" I quickly recognize him as a closing pitcher.

"Hamilton's not a chatty soul, but he has spoken of you." This comes from the third baseman.

"I haven't witnessed Hamilton smiling so much; it's clear you're good for our ace," the tall, muscular blonde states. I finally realize he is the backup catcher.

Glancing to my left, I find the gaggle of women staring daggers in my direction. Not wanting to insight a riot, I excuse myself, claiming I need to check on our daughter. I don't need anyone to think I'm flirting with their man.

Liberty still sits beside Webb as I return to Delta at the nearby table.

"If your goal was fewer eyes upon you, you failed." Delta stares back at the group of ladies across the room.

"I only wanted to meet the team. They can inform their women."

I refuse to peek at the women. Instead, I look toward Hamilton. A wide smile graces my face as he approaches. At the last moment, he swerves toward Liberty and Webb.

"I miss that," Delta states longingly.

"Miss what?" I ask, still watching as Hamilton kneels by the children.

"The whole can't-stand-to-spend-a-minute-away-from-each-other, beginning-of-a-relationship feeling."

I peel my eyes from Hamilton. "If you ever want Hamilton and me to watch the kids so the two of you can go out for adult time, you only need to ask." I love the smile I bring to her face.

"That's very generous of you." Her smile morphs into a smirk with wiggling eyebrows. "Maybe in a few weeks, after you learn to hold the honeymoon hormones in check between the two of you, at least while others are around."

I shake my head as Delta giggles and my cheeks pink. I do attempt to keep my hands and lips to myself while in the company of others. Apparently, I have not succeeded while in her presence.

"Here comes Hamilton," she announces. "I'm sure all of five minutes have passed since you last made contact with one another."

"What are the two of you smiling about?" Hamilton teases. "Wait. I don't want to know."

Liberty climbs upon my lap, Cubbie Bear in one arm and her other hand twirling a curl. It's a clear sign she is tired.

"We should go soon," I inform Hamilton. Turning to Delta, I continue. "She gets whiney as she gets tired. It's not the type of thing I want anyone here to see."

"Mommy, poddy," Liberty whines.

"We'll be right back," I inform the group before quickly escorting my daughter to the hallway.

"I'll go, too." Delta rises and joins us, keeping her promise not to leave me alone this evening. She takes a seat in the hall near the restroom door while Liberty and I enter.

135

HAMILTON

Incessant vibrations from Liberty's backpack interrupt my conversation with Stan. I pull Madison's cell phone from the outside pocket. Cameron's name lights the screen.

"Hello," I answer.

"Hamilton?" Cameron's voice greets. "Is Madison there?"

I excuse myself from Stan and head toward the hall. "She's with Libby in the restroom. We're at a function. Can I have her call you back on our way home?"

As I emerge from the room, Cameron replies. "It's pretty important. Can I speak to her for just a minute?"

"Hold on," I instruct. "Delta, please tell Madison she has an important call."

Delta rises without delay, entering the restroom. She holds the door wide; I see Madison and Liberty at the sinks. Delta helps wash Liberty's hands as Madison returns to me.

"Who is it?" She pulls the phone from my hand as I mouth, "Cameron."

"Hello?" Madison can't hide the apprehension in her voice.

I watch as concern fades from her face, replaced by excitement.

"Daddy!" Liberty screams, running in my direction.

I catch her as she hops into my arms, quickly pulling her to my chest. My eyes remain on Madison as I hug my daughter.

"Daddy." Liberty's hands clasp the sides of my face, directing my eyes to hers–she assesses me for a moment. A wide smile graces her face just before she places a kiss on my lips.

I smile down at her as she scans my face once again. This perfect little angel holds my heart in the palm of her hands. I never knew such a love could exist. I thought nothing would ever compare to the love Madison blind-sided me with, but. when Liberty bolted into my mother's house mere weeks ago, my heart swelled. Instantly, I knew an even greater love.

I toss my daughter skyward–she squeals with glee. I spin us in circles, enjoying the carefree happiness it brings. When we stop, I direct her attention to Madison.

"Mommy's talking to Aunt Cameron." From the corner of my eye, I notice Liberty's nod. "Mommy's pretty when she smiles. Isn't she?"

Liberty pulls her eyes from her mom to mine, nodding in agreement. She begins to wiggle, so I allow her down to the floor. She scurries over near the floor to ceiling windows. Her hands and nose press upon the glass; she marvels at the spectacle that is Chicago at night.

Delta passes by, placing a hand to my forearm. "I'll watch her."

I nod then return my attention to Madison as she ends her phone call. Her free hand fans her face. Her eyes are wide and sparkling, her smile, broad and radiant. Moments pass before her eyes focus on me mere feet in front of her.

"Cameron…" she attempts to speak through excited breaths.

"What did Cameron have to say?" For the life of me, I can't imagine what could be so important to interrupt our evening and draw such an excited reaction from my fiancé.

"I…" Madison fans her face again as she swallows hard between her shallow breaths.

"Through your nose," I urge. "In and out, in and out."

A moment passes.

"I'm a USA Today Bestselling Author!" Her voice cracks as she smiles, tears welling in her eyes.

I whisk her up, placing kisses upon her lips while we spin in circle after circle. She pulls her mouth from mine to squeal. I hear Liberty's laughter and clapping nearby. I slow our spin and place one long, soulful kiss upon her lips. The kiss grows deeper, and soon, we're lost in one another. I feel her warm tears as her cheeks press to mine. Liberty interrupts our inappropriate celebration.

"Daddy, me turn! Me turn!" She demands.

Madison's palms push away from my chest, so I gradually release my hold upon her hips. She remains close while I scoop up our daughter.

"Mommy's famous!" I share.

The three of us cheer as we share a group hug.

Several long moments pass with our family in own little world. Faint murmurs draw my attention to the nearby seating area. Delta and the photographer croon over the display screen on her bulky camera.

Madison is the first to investigate; Liberty urges me to follow. As the camera turns for our inspection, I catch a glance of our family celebration captured for eternity.

Madison

"You took these?" My voice fills with concern. "For what purpose?"

"These will be only for you," the female photographer quickly explains. As she rambles, it is easy to sense her need to defend her actions. "I didn't mean to intrude. I just happened upon a sweet moment between father and daughter." She deftly scrolls to the photos of Liberty and I while Madison took her call. "I'm hired to take promotional photos for the organization, but these won't be included. The scene called to me—I couldn't resist. The excitement continued to grow, and I had to record it for you."

She gulps in a breath before continuing. "I wasn't close enough to hear anything; my zoom allowed me to capture the image without intruding. Please scroll through all of them." She passes the camera to me, while Hamilton peers over my shoulder.

"I ask her to get a pic of the four of us each year at this event, so I can use it in our Christmas cards," Delta adds. "Give Madison your card," she urges the photographer.

"Here. If you contact me, I'll send you all of the files." She pauses, drawing in a nervous breath while Hamilton takes the extended card. "I've started my own business. If you'd like, I could play with some of the images. You know, so you could blow them up or stretch them on a canvas."

I can't tear my eyes from the images. Shakily, I nod. "Yes, please."

"Madison received very exciting news during her phone call. I'm grateful you caught the moment for us." Hamilton's smile eases her mind.

"You have quite an eye," I compliment. "We'd love to have these images. Thank you." I pass the camera back. "Don't lose that business card."

Hamilton bites his lip as he makes exaggerated motions tucking it into the outside pocket of our backpack.

"I'm dying to know," Delta blurts. "What are you celebrating?" Her eyes ping pong from mine to Hamilton's and back.

The photographer attempts to excuse herself, giving us privacy. Hamilton holds his arm blocking her escape. "M. Crocker," he gestures toward me, "is officially a USA Today Bestselling Author." His chest swells with pride. "She's worked hard for this honor; she should be proud and shouting it from the rooftops."

"Oh. My. God." Delta rises, wrapping herself around me tightly, rocking back and forth.

"Congratulations!" The photographer shakes my hand when Delta finally releases me.

"My editor called to let me know it will be announced this week. We can't publicize it until the paper officially prints the updated list. So, no social media posts." I point my finger sternly at Delta.

With hands defensively between us, Delta promises her lips are sealed.

"We should say our goodbyes. Libby needs her bed," I tell Hamilton.

At my words, he notices the weight of our daughter's head upon his shoulder. Her eyes are half-mast, Cubbie Bear is tight to her chest, and her fingers spin in her curls. She's sweet in her relaxed state.

"Would you mind snapping a picture of her?" he whispers over Liberty's head to our photographer friend.

While photos are captured, Delta gathers her family.

Hamilton presses the elevator call button as Stan, Delta, and kids approach.

"Congratulations," Stan whispers.

I assume Delta spilled the beans and instructed him to keep it a secret. I smile back. The elevator pings, and we all climb aboard. I notice Webb standing beside me, holding my book. A bookmark marks his place midway through the story.

"What's your favorite part of the story so far?" I ask him.

Webb's eyes remain downward, and he holds the book tighter.

"The main character," he answers without explanation.

My eyes widen, my breath catches, and I will my body not to react further when he slides his hand in mine between us.

"She's like you, but you aren't alone. I am your friend, Madison." He entwines his fingers with mine.

I lick my lips, eyes darting toward Delta's. I witness the same revelations there. I was a stranger to Webb a week ago. Social interactions with others, especially new acquaintances, are difficult for him. Personal space and contact with others are learned, not a natural reaction. His understanding of the similarities between the character in my book and me along with his empathy and proclamation of friendship are a huge achievement for him. I do my best not to make a scene.

"Thank you, Webb," I whisper as my voice feels trapped in my throat. "I can't wait to discuss it with you when you finish the book."

He pulls his hand back to his side, inches from mine. "I'd be done if Mom didn't only let me read it for an hour a day."

Again, I bite my lip. This time, it prevents my smile. I keep my eyes from the other adults. I'm sure they are fighting the same battle as me.

While exiting the elevator, we say our goodbyes, promising to talk tomorrow. Hamilton escorts me to his vehicle within the parking garage. While he secures Liberty in her car seat, I slip into the front passenger seat, tears rolling down my cheeks. Strong in the elevator, I no longer win my battle holding the emotions back, and I don't try to hide them.

Hamilton pulls onto the street before he notices. "Honey, what's wrong?"

Guys can be so oblivious sometimes.

"Webb," I sob. "That was huge, you know?"

Hamilton nods.

I wipe my tears, realizing he doesn't understand it all. I raise my cell phone and FaceTime Cameron.

"Hello," she greets as her face lights my screen. "How was your first Cubs Event?"

I do my best to keep my tears from sounding in my voice. "We had fun. The photographer took amazing photos of the three of us. I can't wait to show them to everyone."

"Are you in a car?" Her face scrunches as she moves closer to her screen to see clearly.

"We are on our way home," I respond. "I had an interaction with a young fan tonight that I couldn't wait to share with you."

Cameron's face lights up. In the small inset, I see the streetlights flash light upon my face occasionally.

"One of Hamilton's teammates has a son that I gave a book to last week," I begin.

"Stan's boy. I remember you telling me about the night you met him and found he longed to read your books," Cameron shares. "He's on the spectrum, right?"

"Yes," I reply. "This evening, our two families shared an elevator as we were leaving the event. The elevator car was full, but not so crowded we were touching." I smile and goosebumps prickle my skin at the memory. "I noticed Webb held my book, so I asked him what his favorite part of the book was so far."

"He kept his eyes turned down and simply stated that he liked the main character. I loved his answer. It was his true thoughts, and I imagined the confused feelings someone with autism might feel as they read of such a lonely girl, struggling through high school." I raise my hand as I recall his next actions. "I felt his palm slide next to mine. He touched me, and that's huge for him. Still not looking at me, he stated 'She's like you, but you aren't alone. I'm your friend.' Then, he clutched my hand in his for a moment before pulling away again."

"Wow!" In the well-lit kitchen that I once lived in with Alma, I see the tears forming in Cameron's eyes. "He understood it all. That's so cool."

"Right?" This is why I needed to call her. I needed someone else to understand what Webb's words meant for him, as well as for my writing. "Even with his social challenges, he understood the pain I wrote about. Having met me, he assumed I wrote about a real part of my life, and he demonstrated empathy in a manner he's been working on with his parents and his teacher."

"It's your validation as an author," Cameron states.

"Exactly! It means more than the online reviews. They mean the world to me, but they are anonymous. I know this boy; I know the constant struggles he faces in his daily interactions." My tears have dried; I'm overcome with happiness. "If I've reached Webb, then I'm reaching other readers as well. They understand my story."

"I'm glad you now believe what I and many others have stated about your work for months now. You may be the only author that being named to the *USA Today Bestselling Authors' List* wasn't validation enough. You had to hear directly from a young reader." She chuckles. "I'm glad that you finally see. I'm happy you called to share with me, because I need to ask a favor of you."

"You know I'd do anything for you," I remind my adopted sister.

"Um..." Cameron fidgets. "What time does your flight leave for Las Vegas?" Wide-eyed, she clenches her teeth.

I glance at Hamilton. We fly to Las Vegas on Black Friday to elope. Surely, she won't mess with my wedding for a favor.

"We fly out at 11," Hamilton answers for me. "What do you need?"

"Our world-renowned author backed out of his book signing today," she groans, fisting her fingers in her hair. "He was to be at a Chicago bookstore all day Friday." She bites her lip, hesitant to continue. "I know it's a busy and exciting day for you, but I thought maybe we could squeeze in an hour or two with you signing books to appease the store owner." With hands on either side of her head and palms toward the camera, Cameron proceeds, "I realize you're not a morning person, so I'll majorly owe you for this. Maybe we could schedule the book signing from seven to nine that morning. This could start the buzz for your new book, releasing in January. What do you think?"

I look to Hamilton for guidance. It's a busy day, a busy weekend.

Removing his eyes from the road for only a moment, Hamilton smiles and nods.

"I think we can make it work," I tell Cameron. "Will you make all the arrangements?"

"Of course," she quickly replies. "I'll email you all of the details, and I'll owe you big. So big."

"I'll make sure you make good on it, too. Cameron, who's there?" For only a moment, I spot a man without a shirt walk behind her.

She quickly turns the phone and herself so my view will be obstructed from any further visions.

"Oh." Her eyes seem to search for an explanation. "I have a dripping pipe in the basement. I asked the neighbor to check it out for me."

"That didn't look like Mr. Edwards," I inform her.

She rises. In the background, I see she moves through the kitchen then down the steps into the basement. Her finger covers her face in my view before the camera angle switches to show the basement.

"Dalton, is that you?" I recognize him immediately; it's Mr. Edwards' son. He works with his father in the family construction business. Alma told me he left college many years ago to help his dad through a cancer battle and to take over the family business.

"Hey, Madison. How's Chicago?" Dalton waves, a smile on his face, dimples and all.

"What happened to your shirt?" I tease.

Dalton points to the pipes overhead. "Fixing pipes is wet work."

I nearly choke at his words.

Cameron returns the camera to her face view. "Behave," she scolds. "I'm lucky he lives next door. I planned to duct tape the area until I returned from Thanksgiving with you."

Dalton's voice interrupts from across the room. "I'm glad she mentioned the drips to my father. If I hadn't checked on it, she would have returned to a flooded basement."

Cameron rolls her eyes. "I think he exaggerates, but I am glad he had time to fix it tonight for me."

Hamilton

"I'll tuck her in," I offer.

Madison nods, fixing a water in the kitchen while chatting with Indie and McGee at her feet.

"The guys let the dogs out an hour ago, so they are ready for bed," I inform as I carry my sleeping daughter to her room.

I turn on the small bedside lamp then pull back the blankets. Liberty barely stirs as I lay her on the bed. I contemplate waking her for the bathroom or covering her up as is. I decide her dress wouldn't be comfortable sleepwear, so I gently lower the zipper and remove it. I unbuckle her black shoes and tug off her frilly socks. Pulling up the sheet and comforter, I tuck her in. My little girl looked like a princess tonight.

I was proud to introduce Madison and Liberty to my teammates and coaches tonight. While Madison encourages Liberty to ignore gender norms, it pleases me she chose such a pretty dress for this evening. I place a kiss on her chubby cheek as McGee assumes his position at the end of her bed. I pat his head before heading out; I pull her door closed until only inches remain open then go in search of my fiancé.

"I love this dress," I state, my eyes locking on her reflection in our bath-room mirror.

Madison stands at the vanity, removing first her earrings and then her necklace. She turns towards me, smiling.

"Why this dress?" she asks coyly.

I spin her around to face the mirror as I stand behind her. My hands at her hips, I press into her back. The softness of her bottom surrounds the hardness of my erection. I stifle the groan rising in my throat. I slide my hands to her shoulders, keeping my eyes on hers in the mirror.

"Blue is definitely your color," I whisper, my lips near her ear. My fingers trace the edge of the fabric as I continue. "The neckline taunted me all evening. This hint of cleavage continually called to me, wanting me to uncover the body hidden beneath."

Madison's lips part, and a tiny gasp escapes. I tease the skin exposed at the top of her breasts. My hands slide over her shoulders and then just under her arms. As I trail them slowly down her ribs, Madison's head falls back on my shoulder while her heavy-lidded eyes remain on my reflection.

"It falls just above your knees, revealing only a hint of thigh," I confess. "When you sit," I sigh deeply and return my fingers to grip her hips, "it slides up to expose more, and my mind wants your thighs wrapped around my waist while I bury myself deep inside your warmth."

"This tie at your hip..." I allow my groan to escape as my fingers play with the thin fabric. "My mind wondered if I tugged on it, would the dress allow me access to all that lies beneath?" I pinch the free end of the tie, preparing to tug and find out.

She places her hand on my wrist, applying pressure, causing me to pull the strings apart. Her free hand quickly unties a smaller tie on the opposite hip when the front of the dress falls open.

My lips play at her ear and exposed neck as my hands slide the dress from her shoulders. While nibbling at her collarbone, my eyes take in the silky blue dress circling her feet in the bright blue heels. My gaze trails up her long legs, past her red lacy panties, over her bare stomach. It lingers on her tattoo before continuing to her heaving breasts peeking out of her red lace bra.

She pulls away, spins in my arms, and our mouths collide feverishly. Tongues tangle as her hands make quick work of my tie and front shirt buttons. Her soft fingers slide up my chest, over my shoulders, and down my arms until they are stalled in the attempt to remove my dress shirt.

I chuckle before pulling away. As I unbutton my cuffs, she deftly removes my belt and unfastens my pants. My head falls back, and I bite my lip when her long fingers snake below my boxers and clutch my cock. Already, I am close. This woman affects me in every way.

Madison

"I need you now," I beg through a whisper. My nipples threaten to slice through my bra, and my panties are soaked. "I can't wait. Here," I demand.

Hamilton slides my panties quickly down my thighs. My hands steady on his shoulders while I step out of one side then the other. Suddenly, he lifts me to sit on the vanity; I squeal as the cold tile connects with my heated backside. He steps back, slipping off his shoes and making quick work of removing his boxer briefs and dress pants in one swift motion. I giggle as he places his hand on the counter after nearly losing his balance attempting to remove his socks.

"Find that funny?" he growls, pulling me to the edge and spreading my thighs.

I shake my head, no longer in the mood to play. *I want release, and I need it now.*

His large hand cups the nape of my neck, pulling my mouth to his. His free hand unlatches my bra; I moan into him at its release. My pert nipples pebble further in the chilled air. My teeth lock on his plump lower lip while the pads of his thumbs graze each nipple. The sensitive buds become rock hard–his contact now on the precipice of pleasure and pain.

"Ham, please," I whimper, digging my nails into his back.

Wearing his trademark crooked smile, he continues teasing me. I need him; I need our connection, now. I quickly slide my hands down the taut planes of his chest and abdomen. His smattering of dark hair guides my fingertips further south toward the treasure I seek.

I wrap one hand around the velvety skin covering his steely girth. When my other hand joins the first, I begin stroking him from base to tip. I see his smirk has disappeared. His eyes are half-mast, his lips parted, and his head falls back. Now, he will give me what I need. While I pump, I pull him toward my eager center.

When his sensitive, mushroom-shaped tip meets my wet entrance, Hamilton takes control. One of his hands replace mine on his shaft while the other secures my hip. Looking at him, I witness the carnal desire grow on his face as he watches his cock slowly impale me. Seated entirely within me, both hands on my hips, his forehead now pressed to mine, he whispers, "I love you."

My hands fly from his shoulders to his jaws. "I love you, too." My voice is a needy plea as I rotate my hips.

Taking my cue, he finds a slow, constant rhythm, gradually raising each of us toward climax. He lowers his mouth to my shoulder, gently biting down on my muscle. It's primal–it only hurts a minute before it turns to pleasure. As he gradually increases his bite, I not only reach my peak, but I tumble from its cliff.

"Yes!" I cheer in a drawn-out growl as my thighs grip his waist like a vise. My core spasms, my internal muscles gripping his cock.

He curses, pumping into me three more times before he shudders, his forehead on my shoulder. We hold each other tightly while we regain our breath and float back down to earth.

"That was…" I'm the first to speak.

Hamilton interrupts, "I'm not done with you yet." His smirk is back.

I moan as he disengages our joined bodies and giggle when he scoops me up, carrying me to our bed.

136

MADISON

I groan when my alarm summons me from slumber before eight. I stretch and remind myself family begins to arrive for the holiday today. The flashing lights on the monitor signal Liberty is awake in her room, too. I slide one foot towards the floor then another. I shiver as the warm comforter no longer protects me from the chilly air.

As I approach the door to our master suite, I call down the hall, "Libby, Mommy's up."

She squeals, and I hear her speak to the dogs as I await her arrival.

"Hola, Mommy," she greets. I groan internally that she's a morning person.

"Come shower with me," I invite, and she runs past me towards my bathroom. She enjoys standing on the shower seat while I use the hand-held nozzle to clean her. I'm nervous to leave her unsupervised and usually speed through my showers. Today, I need to enjoy the warm shower spray before my busy day begins. I turn on the water to heat while I place my robe and towels just outside the shower for us.

"We get to go to the airport to see Nana and Amy today," I inform Liberty.

Her face lights up. "Nana!"

"And Aunt Amy," I remind her.

"Nana and Amy, my house," she cheers, and I join her.

"You can show them your big-girl bed and your books," I explain. "We will take our shower, eat breakfast with Miss Alba, then drive to the airport to pick them up and bring them to your house."

Liberty nods as I speak.

I'm verifying everything I might need is in Liberty's backpack when my cell rings on the kitchen island, and Delta's name appears on the screen.

"Good morning," I answer.

"I'm downstairs. Can you tell them to let me come up?" Her voice sounds both desperate and excited.

"Yes. See ya soon."

"Delta's coming up," I inform Miss Alba before calling down to the lobby.

"Deltha!" Liberty yells from her highchair.

"You need to hurry. Finish your breakfast so we can go get Nana and Aunt Amy," I remind her.

I barely have time to contemplate why my friend showed up unplanned before she raps on the door. Miss Alba answers while I tuck a fresh bottle of water into the side pocket of the bag then secure it over my shoulders.

"Hi," I greet as I clean Liberty's face and let her down from the chair.

"I realize you are busy today," Delta begins. "I stayed up half the night and finished your book."

I slip Liberty's coat on while glancing up at Delta.

"I have questions, so we need to talk," she states. "I'll drive you to the airport so we can chat."

I smile, shaking my head at my new friend. "You're welcome to ride to O'Hare with us, but I need to practice driving in Chicago."

We say goodbye to Miss Alba, and Delta helps me load Liberty into Hamilton's SUV. *Well, I guess it's my SUV now, too.*

I type our destination into the navigation before we pull from our spot and exit the parking garage.

"Are you sure you can talk while you drive?" Delta teases. "Relax. I'm sure you've driven on interstates before."

"Yes, but interstates weren't six lanes or bumper to bumper," I defend my nervousness.

"So, the prank on the middle school principal in your book," Delta begins her interrogation. "Did that really happen and were you involved?"

"Yes and no," I answer.

"Okay, so was Webb correct to assume you and the main character are one in the same?"

"No character is solely based on someone in real life," I state as I merge lanes, preparing for the upcoming turn on the navigation screen.

"Uh-uh," Delta shakes her head in my periphery. "You're not getting away with any official statements given to you by the publisher. I'm your friend, and I deserve answers."

I glance in my rearview mirror, glance at Delta, then return my eyes to the traffic in front of me. I clear my throat before I answer. "There are many similarities between the character and me," I confirm.

"Okay. Thanks for not spilling your guts," she deadpans.

Silence falls upon the vehicle as I ponder an honest answer to share.

"Let's not compare me to the character." I turn my blinker on as prompted by the voice in navigation. "I'd much rather spill my guts on a sofa with drinks in hand," I confess.

"Okay, so let's just focus on the Madison now living in Chicago." Delta glances over her right shoulder. "You can merge if you hurry."

I do so, anticipating the next turn on the screen.

Delta sits quietly for a bit.

"I realize Stan and I threw ourselves in your face on your first night in town. I hope you know that we think the world of Hamilton and want you to know we are here for anything, so don't hesitate to call, text, or drop by."

Several quiet moments pass.

"Delta," I begin, but the navigation interrupts, stating we have reached our destination. After driving around a bit, I find a parking spot and quickly claim it before someone steals it.

I place my hand on Delta's forearm before she can exit the vehicle. "I promise we will find a time, just the two of us, to share our pasts. And you didn't throw yourselves at me. I've enjoyed the time we've spent together. Things are moving fast, what with prepping the house and Thanksgiving this week, so we haven't had a lot of laid-back, get-to-know-you time."

She nods, smiling at me.

"We don't have time right now, so here is the *Cliff Notes* version. My characters are a mosaic of the students I went to school with. My father died before my eighth-grade year; my mother, in her depression, became an alcoholic. The only family I had was my mother, and she was rarely sober. I often felt alone in the world. I had a few friends, but as I couldn't drive anywhere and they all lived 15 minutes away in town, I spent much of my time alone in my room or on the farm. I bumped into Hamilton, literally, and he lived on the farm beside ours. We began hanging out, and, with his help, I had friends around me and felt less alone." I sigh deeply in preparation for her reaction and extricate myself from the driver's seat.

Delta walks over to my side. "I just need to know," Delta fidgets, "do you feel isolated or alone now?"

I shake my head as I zip the front of Liberty's coat and place her in the stroller. "I haven't felt that type of loneliness in years. I'm actually excited about the new life we're building in Chicago. And I'm glad to have you as my friend."

"Sounds like a Hallmark movie. Enter the cheesy, up-beat instrumental music," Delta razzes and pulls me in for a quick, tight hug. "Okay, so we got that cleared up. Let's go get the family."

I scan the crowd of holiday travelers scrambling around the airport–meeting Memphis and Amy may be harder than I anticipated. Delta and I maneuver the stroller as best we can towards the baggage claim where we planned to meet and anchor ourselves by a large pole to wait.

After a few moments, Liberty begins waving animatedly. My eyes follow hers. Leave it to my baby girl to spot Memphis before the two adults.

"Na-na!" She yells, wiggling against the seatbelt restraint of her stroller.

Memphis strides toward us, still waving at her granddaughter. I unbuckle and lift Liberty. "Just a minute, Grandma will be here in just a minute." My words do little to soothe her.

"There's my girl," Memphis croons with outstretched arms.

Liberty leans towards her with arms extended. I release my hold, allowing the two to celebrate their reunion. Memphis peppers kisses over her cheeks, nose, forehead, and chin, causing her to giggle.

When the two settle down, I scan the nearby crowd and ask, "Where is Amy?"

"Hamilton asked her to pick up something from an airport shop," Memphis informs, shrugging. "She'll be here in a minute. We're supposed to grab our bags."

I guide our group toward the moving conveyor belt. Memphis describes the bags, and we anxiously wait for them to appear.

"Excuse me," a loud, female voice rudely calls from behind. "What's an aunt have to do to get a hug from her favorite niece?"

Amy stands behind our group with hands on hips in faux annoyance, three large, brown, paper bags on her arms. Beside her, we find the two large suitcases we were waiting for.

"Amy!" Liberty squeals, stretching out her arms.

Amy places her bags on the nearby luggage handles before hugging her mini-me.

"Let's move toward the car," Memphis encourages our group. "I'm ready to escape this crowd."

Madison

"Liberty..." I free her from her car seat in the parking garage. "Take Grandma's hand and show her how to use the elevator." I wink at Memphis.

I assist Delta and Amy with the luggage, and we follow Liberty's lead. She pushes the elevator call button then smiles proudly at our guests. Inside the elevator, I lift my daughter to press number 14. Liberty cheers when the elevator stops on our floor. This time, she takes Memphis and Amy by the hand as we walk into the hallway. At our door, Liberty releases her holds and knocks on the door.

Miss Alba opens, anticipating our arrival. "Hola," she greets. "Miss

Liberty, who are your guests?" I love that she supports us in encouraging Liberty's independence.

"Na-na," Liberty points. "Amy."

Miss Alba holds the door as our guests and their luggage enter the condo. I bend down next to my little girl, removing her coat.

"Why don't you show Grandma and Amy your room?" I suggest, knowing they want a tour of the entire place.

Liberty takes their hands once again and guides them down the hallway.

"I should get out of your way," Delta offers.

"You're welcome to stay as long as you want," I invite. "If the kids are at school and Stan is out, stay and visit with us."

She looks from me to Alba and back. "You sure you aren't too busy preparing for the meal and company tomorrow?"

"I think Miss Alba has already bought everything we need. We're gonna sit around and visit." I make pouty lips. "Please?"

"For goodness sakes!" Delta swats at me playfully. "Stop acting like a 2-year-old."

"Then it's settled," I state. "Can you find us something fun to drink while I go check on them?" I motion down the hallway.

As conversation begins between Miss Alba and Delta, I follow the sound of Liberty's squeals to the master bedroom. Memphis and Amy laugh as Liberty jumps up and down on my bed, her arms swinging as she points to my attached bathroom.

"What is going on in here?" I pretend that I don't like what I am seeing.

Memphis rescues her granddaughter from the mattress. "Libby was just telling us about your shower. She says she likes taking a shower."

"Would you like to see the rest of the condo?" I ask, motioning towards the hallway. "Liberty, show Grandma and Aunt Amy where they will sleep and then to Mommy's office."

Liberty nods, smiling and clapping her hands. She wiggles down and trots to the hall. "Nana here. Amy here." Liberty points to the spare rooms as she continues on to the front room.

"Maybe she'll let you actually look in the rooms before bedtime," I tease as they follow my daughter.

"Toys," Liberty points. "Food. Office." Done with her tour, she enters the kitchen and asks Miss Alba for water.

"We're making margaritas," Delta announces, throwing her hands into the air. "Well, actually Miss Alba is making her famous margaritas." She claps her hands.

"Keep an eye on Libby. I'm going to give a much slower tour to my guests." Delta nods.

I usher Memphis and Amy into my office. "It's still a work in progress." I explain the unorganized shelves and boxes still in the corner. "I've actually found a few hours to write."

"When?" Memphis asks as she takes in the view from the windows behind my desk.

"Are you taking some poor neighbor kid's Adderall?" Amy asks, straight-faced. "There is no way a normal human can furnish a place this size, buy all the little things to make it livable, attend functions, care for a toddler, and find time to write in a week."

Memphis admonishes her daughter.

"Hamilton insisted on keeping Miss Alba fulltime as well as a nanny," I admit, embarrassed. I chance a glance at Memphis, worried how she will react. It's Amy that surprises me.

"I'm glad he did," Amy states. "He leads a busy life. You deserve time to work as much as he does. There's nothing wrong with hiring help."

Now, I feel bad that I forgot that Amy's a nanny. She works for a young woman that now has guardianship of her twin nephews who are a little older than Liberty.

"I didn't mean..."

Memphis interrupts, placing her hand on my shoulder. "It's important to ask for help when you need it. You're an amazing author, and Hamilton knows it's important that you continue to write." She hugs me tight to her side. "It took me a while to understand the crazy life and schedule Hamilton keeps. It may seem unnecessary now, but come baseball season, you'll be glad you have 2 extra pairs of hands."

Uncomfortable with the serious tone our conversation has taken, I finish showing them the rest of the condo, and we end the tour by dropping off luggage in each of their bedrooms.

"I'm ready for one of your famous margaritas," I call to Miss Alba as we return to the kitchen island.

"Be warned: she has a heavy pour," Delta states before taking a tiny sip from her margarita glass. "I'm glad I talked you into adding these to your shopping list." She clinks her manicured nail, complete with rhinestones, against the glass.

Miss Alba doesn't apologize for her recipe. Instead, she fills a salt-rimmed glass for Memphis, Amy, and me.

"Is there anything else you would like me to help with before I leave?" Miss Alba murmurs, leaning closer.

"No. You've helped so much already," I look at my Fitbit, noting the time is now one p.m. "What are your plans for this afternoon? Do you have a lot of baking to start on?"

She hedges for a moment before speaking. "I'll wait on my husband in his office. He plans to leave early today. I'll begin my baking in the morning. We eat late tomorrow afternoon and evening."

"You should stay and visit with us until he's done," I invite, taking her by the hand and squeezing. "You'll be more comfortable here than in his tiny office for hours."

"I'll just watch my telenovelas..."

"Stay with us," Memphis pleads. "You've made margaritas; stay and enjoy them with us."

With Memphis' words, I believe Miss Alba begins to consider the invitation.

"Peaz," Liberty begs from the hem of Miss Alba's dress.

She scoops her up in her arms, spinning her once. "Of course, I will stay with you, Miss Libby."

Yes! Thank you, Liberty. My heart warms; I enjoy spending time with my new family and friends. We move our festivities from the kitchen island into the living room.

"We seem to have lost Memphis," I inform the crowd.

"It was all of 10 steps," Delta muses.

"Libby, I have a present for you," Memphis calls as she emerges from the hallway. She chooses the empty cushion next to me, places her glass on the nearby sofa table, and waves a book at her granddaughter.

Liberty loves books. She springs from her blocks on the floor to climb on her grandma's lap. Her little hands caress the hard cover as her eyes take in the boy, girl, and dog on the weathered exterior.

"This was my favorite book when I was a little girl," Memphis informs her. "Can I read it to you?"

"Me read," Liberty states with attitude.

She's everything I'm not. She's confident and goes for what she wants with reckless abandon. I love her independence and attitude. That is, when she's not throwing it back at me.

Her little fingers gently open the cover, turning to the first page. She glances up at Memphis, points her index finger, then begins. "This is..." She pauses for Memphis' help.

Memphis looks to me, surprised. When Liberty repeats herself, she supplies in a shaky voice, "Jack."

Liberty nods and continues, "This is..."

"Kim," Memphis says, short of breath. She can't take her eyes off of Liberty, but she can't help looking at me. I'm no help, however. I'm just as shocked as she is.

"See Jack. See Kim," Liberty's little voice continues.

While Liberty turns the page, my mind explodes. She's never seen this book before—no one has read it to her before. She points to each word as she reads each sentence. They are choppy, but she reads them. She won't be two for four more months, and she's reading. I didn't just imagine it, right? When I return my focus to the guests in the room, I find every pair of eyes on me—they seem as shocked as me.

"Did that just happen?" I ask the room.

Everyone nods, wide-eyed.

"Miss Libby," Miss Alba calls. "Come help me take the towels to your bathroom, please."

Liberty gently passes the book back to Memphis before climbing down to shadow Miss Alba. I'm grateful for the distraction she offers so we may discuss the situation.

"That's not normal." Amy simply states what we all struggle to comprehend.

"Have you read that story to her before?" Delta asks Memphis.

When Memphis shakes her head, she looks to me. I also shake mine.

"Reading starts at about age five. For some, as early as four," I recall from my education classes.

"Webb told me Libby read to him last night. I assumed she pointed to an 'a' or 'I', so I didn't ask him for the details," Delta shares.

"Read what?" My mind reels.

Delta only shrugs; she's no help. *Why does my chest feel so heavy? She read a couple sentences. It's not like she's sick or hurt. Why does this feel like a bad thing, and why am I fighting tears?* Memphis pats my thigh as Liberty storms back into the room.

"Libby," my voice cracks nervously, "what book did you read to Webb last night?" I hold my breath, waiting for her answer, for any answer, for any idea how to handle this.

"Mommy's book," she proudly answers. Her little hands are now poised on her hips.

"Mommy's book?" I parrot. "You read from my book?" I rise from the sofa, approaching her in the center of the floor.

Liberty nods once, still smiling. In a trance, I walk into my office, snag a book from the shelf, and hold it near her.

"This book?"

Liberty points at the cover as I hold it out. "Mommy's book."

"What did you read?" I can't believe I am asking my baby girl this. Of all the things I worried about as a mother, this was not even on my radar.

"Ten." Liberty pulls the book from my hands, slowly turning page after page.

I help her turn to page ten. Liberty shakes her head at me. I quickly flip to chapter ten.

Liberty points to the large, bold numbers at the top of the page. "Ten."

"Can you read this to me?" I'm not sure what I want to witness. *Do I want her to read it word for word? Or do I want her to point to one word and be done?*

Liberty sits on the wood floor, the book in her lap. She points to the first word of chapter 10 and begins. "The sun..."

She's reading. Again. She is actually reading. Really reading. *Now what? Do I encourage this new skill? Do I start teaching her?* I'm lost. I wish Hamilton were here. I know he wouldn't know any better than I do, but at least he could hold me.

Liberty has closed my book and moved back to her building blocks. I remain sitting on the floor but spin to face the women. My face must say it all.

"Ladies," Miss Alba stands, "bring your glasses to the kitchen. It's time for more margaritas."

We follow her directions. In the kitchen, we may discuss without tiny ears listening.

"It's important not to panic," Memphis states.

At least I knew that much. I've kept my panic hidden on the inside. So far, that is. *More. I need more. What's next?*

"We shouldn't make it seem unusual. We don't want her to be ashamed. She should be proud."

I stare at Amy–her words shock me. She's right. I just thought it would come from Memphis or Delta. They are mothers; Amy isn't.

"Taylor will be here later this afternoon. She might have contacts to talk to about it," Memphis mentions.

She's right. Of course, she is right.

I nod, words eluding me at the moment. Inside, I have hope. We're making a plan. I need to find a specialist to discuss this with. Hamilton and I will find one.

I slap my palm to my forehead.

"What was that for?" Amy chuckles while Delta pulls my forearm back to the table.

I am such an idiot. *Why didn't I think of it before? She should have been the first person I reached for.* I raise my cell to my ear.

"Hello," Fallon greets.

"Fallon, I'm sorry to bother you on your day off," I begin while still trying to find what I want to say. "Would you have a few minutes to stop by? Something important just happened with Liberty, and I'd like your input."

Fallon promises to arrive in a few minutes. This is good. Fallon studies these types of things–she'll have resources for us.

"Who's Fallon?" Amy blurts the minute my phone disconnects from the call.

"Fallon is our nanny. She lives in the building." I turn to Delta. "You've met her; she's the trainer's fiancé." Turning back, I explain, "Slater is a trainer for the Cubs, and Hamilton's publicist introduced us."

"She's a sweetheart," Miss Alba informs the group. "On her first visit with Libby, she taught her to say hello in Spanish."

My cell phone vibrates loudly on the counter in the silence of the kitchen.

HAMILTON

call me when you get a chance

(heart emoji)

ME

(thumbs up emoji)

I sip the last of my drink, wiping away the salt from the corner of my lip. Liberty still plays with her blocks. I ask the group to keep an eye on her while I make a quick call.

"Hello." Hamilton's deep, cheerful voice causes me to smile.

"What's up?"

"Hold on," he instructs as I hear rustling on his end of the line. "I didn't know what you girls were up to, so I thought it might be best to have you call me when it was convenient for you," he explains, his heavy footsteps echoing in the background.

I can't tell him about today's events over the phone–I need to do that in person.

"Liberty's playing blocks while we are visiting, so it was a good time." I sink into my leather office chair and swivel to look out the floor to ceiling windows at the lively city of Chicago. "Taylor and the girls should be here in an hour. Your mom and Amy are relaxing after their early flights this morning. Where are you? It sounds like you are in a cave."

"I'm in the stairwell," he chuckles. "We are in between events here, and I wanted some privacy. This was the nearest door I found."

Privacy? Is this bad?

"The P.R. lady stopped me in the hall this morning. She met with the photographer from the function last night and loved the photos of the three of us with the mascot and the one we posed for. They are working on a holiday promo and asked our permission to use the images for the Thanksgiving and holiday season message."" He pauses to catch his breath.

My mind races. *Publicity for the Cubs. Photos of our family. Do I want Liberty in the public eye?*

"I've emailed you the three images they would like to use. I also attached the release we must sign if we agree to give permission."

I sense the hesitation in his voice.

"You've mentioned keeping Liberty off social media posts and stuff to protect her; I'm okay with it either way."

"I'm opening the email right now," I state as my fingers maneuver the mouse over the attachments. "Ahh, I love the mascot shot."

"Which one?"

"Both, but where she's kissing the mascot is my favorite." I continue on to the image of the three of us in front of the Cubs logo. "These are good. I can't wait to see the others she took for us."

"P.R. stated the commercial would just say, 'Happy Thanksgiving' or 'Happy Holidays to your family from our Cubs family.' They have photos of a couple more families. I think Stan and Delta are in one," Hamilton concludes.

"I guess they can," I begin. "I don't see anything wrong with the photos. Has Delta allowed them to use pictures in the past?"

"Yes," Hamilton quickly replies. "I remember Stan complaining about Delta forcing him to pose for photos of the four of them so she could use them in holiday cards and the Cubs using the same photo, causing her to take a different picture. He hates posing for pictures. Action shots don't bother him; it's the standing still and posing that he detests."

"Do we both have to sign this release?" I ask as my finger hovers over the print icon.

"Yes, but we can sign it digitally," he explains. "If you place your mouse over the signature line, she says it's easy."

"I see. Okay. I've signed it," I announce. "Can you sign it while you are there today?"

"Yes." His voice echoes in the stairwell. "I'll swing by the P.R. office and do it before my next meet and greet. I should be done about two today."

The echo disappears, and I can tell by his breathing that he is walking again.

"Text me if you need me to pick up anything on my way home," he offers.

"Okay. I love you." It still makes me smile, knowing I get to profess my love for him publicly now. It's taken us so long to get to this place–I'll never take it for granted.

"I love you, too, babe," Hamilton whispers before disconnecting our call.

I jump when Memphis' voice calls to me from my office door.

"Here you are! I asked Libby where you were, and she just shrugged. She loves playing with those blocks, doesn't she?" Memphis hovers near the corner of my desk. "What are you working on?"

I pivot my laptop screen toward her, displaying the mascot photo first. "Hamilton called. The P.R. Department needs our permission to use three shots of our family in upcoming ads." I scroll through the three photos.

Memphis' face lights up at the images.

"That is so sweet!" She points to Liberty kissing Clark, the mascot. "I love how her hands hold his face so he can't pull away from her." She turns her face from the screen to me. "Are these by the same photographer that you were telling me about?"

"Yes. I can't wait to see the other photos," I state.

When the doorbell rings, Liberty sprints from her toys, excited to see her cousins.

"It's probably Fallon," I inform my daughter, raising her into my arms. "Let's see."

Fallon smiles as we open the door.

"Hola!" Liberty immediately reaches for her. She plants a noisy kiss on Fallon's cheek. "Pway?"

Fallon lowers Liberty to the floor. "I need to talk to your mommy for a bit, then I will come play with you."

Happy with the promise, Liberty scurries back to her blocks on the wooden floor across the room.

"What's up?" Fallon asks, voice lowered.

"Let's move over here." I return to the barstools and my friends. "This is Hamilton's mother, Memphis, and his sister, Amy." I motion in their direction. "And you've met Delta, right?"

"Yes. We've met a few times," Delta answers.

Fallon says hello to my guests, nervously climbing onto an empty barstool. "I've called you here to help with something new we've noticed with

Libby. I want you to have some time to help us research strategies moving forward to assist her the best we can." I'm rambling.

I sip from my glass. Before I can offer one to Fallon, Miss Alba slides a freshly made margarita in her direction.

"Okay," Fallon begins after her first drink. "You've gotten ahead of yourself. I'm happy to help, but I need to know what we are talking about. What have you witnessed?" Fallon pivots on her seat to gaze at Liberty across the room.

"She can read," Delta stage whispers, not wanting the little one to hear.

Fallon looks from Delta to me, brows raised.

"Let's start with the details," I direct the group. "Memphis brought her favorite book to share with Liberty. Liberty has never seen the book before today. She demanded to read instead of Memphis. We thought she would tell a story from looking at the pictures only."

A tear forms in my eye. *This is not something to cry about. Why am I getting so upset over it?*

"Liberty used her index finger to point to each word as she read it."

"Here," Memphis interrupts, sliding the book to Fallon. "She read the first two pages."

Fallon opens the book, flipping through the first several pages. She closes the book, sliding it back to Memphis.

"Delta's son, Webb, told Delta last night that Libby read to him. Of course, we didn't think anything of it. But, after reading for us, we asked questions." I pause as Amy opens my book to chapter 10. "She told us this is the part of the book she read to Webb last night." I give Fallon time to read the passage. A few silent moments pass.

"What do you think?" Delta asks, breaking the silence.

"First, understand that although I majored in psychology, I am still working on my graduate degree." Fallon scans the group for understanding. "I do have many resources I can look to for assistance, but we may need help from more than one source.

"As you are close family and friends, I'm sure you already know that Libby demonstrates advanced linguistic levels for a 2-year-old. This might be because she spends much of her time in the company of adults, but when I asked for background information from Madison, I found Liberty, like her peers, has spent three days per week with children her own age."

Fallon pauses for another drink. My mind is dying to hear what she thinks, and mentally, I will her to hurry up.

"Two days a week at Mom's Day Out and time in the church nursery on Sundays is comparable to other children's interactions outside the home for her age. As Libby and I began attending playgroups and tumbling this week, I've noticed she interacts appropriately with children near her age. The ways she interacts with adults varies greatly from the way she interacts with young children. She's learned to speak at the level of the company she keeps."

Fallon smiles sheepishly. "I've already spoken to a professor about this, and I've started seeking other studies on children with her linguistic abilities. I'm not going to focus on this topic now as it's not what has you concerned today. It is, however, important that you understand most children that are advanced linguistically do not interact well with peers and often prefer to stay with the adults at playtime."

A wide smile forms upon Fallon's face, and she lays her hand on mine. "She's a bright child. I'm sure we've all witnessed this. We need to understand her talents and encourage her in the areas she prefers." Looking straight at me, she continues. "You've mentioned noticing Libby quietly observing certain situations. You stated it was as if she was taking in all that was going on around her. Perhaps she was learning. Children are little sponges, soaking up everything they see and hear."

"I need to interrupt." I lift my hands in the air in front of me. "I'm sorry." I stand; I can no longer sit still. "My mind has been racing since I heard her read. I've been playing over events from the past year. I may be overanalyzing everything, but prior to the end of October, Libby spoke a few words and sounded more baby-like. She did often sit quietly, taking in all going on around her." I chuckle. It sounds fake. "I don't know why it didn't faze me at the moment, but she started talking more, said more words correctly starting right around Halloween. 'Ma-ma' became 'Mommy,' 'Da-da' became 'Daddy,' and so on."

Memphis rises, pulling me into a hug. "You have had so much on your mind with the passing of your mother and Alma–It's been a stressful time."

She's trying to make me feel better, but I don't want excuses. Liberty is my daughter. I should have celebrated a new milestone in my daughter's life. I should have documented it in her baby book. Regardless of the events in my life, she is my daughter, and I am her mother; I should have recognized each change.

Fallon encourages me to resume my seat beside her. "Children can sense moods around them. Libby knew her mommy was upset. She knew changes were occurring around her. Her home changed, she met new people, she visited new places, and she was around adults during this time."

She pauses, letting us process her words. "Perhaps, during the changes around her, Libby began her transition. She began communicating at a higher level to cope with her new surroundings."

Fallon turns, facing me. She places her hands on my shoulders and stares into my eyes. I fear what she plans to say next.

"I hope I don't overstep my boundaries or upset you, but I need to state the obvious."

I nod for her to continue.

"In the past 30 days, Alma moved from the only home Liberty knew. You drove to Athens, to a different home for a few weeks. Although she had seen photos, she met Memphis and Hamilton for the first time. She watched her mom cope with the death of two women and then moved into a new home in Chicago, meeting new people at every turn." Fallon lifts my chin, directing my eyes back to hers. "Children are resilient. Libby seems to be adapting well to all of the changes. We need to adapt to changes in her, too." She places her arm across my shoulder as we turn back to the group. "Libby can read three years before her peers. She speaks better than other 2-year-olds. She's also much taller than kids her age. As her family, we need to be aware of all of these things and any others that appear. She doesn't now, but she may struggle to fit in with other children if they notice her abilities. We shouldn't shelter her–we need to nurture her talents and foster relationships with other children. I'm going to speak with all of my professors and conduct research on my end. You should continue to read to her and allow her to read when she volunteers."

We all agree with Fallon's assessments. I feel a bit better knowing we have a plan and someone training to be a professional guiding us. I struggle to rejoin the group conversation as my mind swirls.

Fallon leans into me, adding as an afterthought, "The next time you see Taylor, you should talk to her. She can guide you to professionals in the medical field with much more training and experience than me."

"She'll be here." I look to my wrist. It's four. She should already be here. I glance at my cell phone screen to see if I missed anything from Taylor. Nothing. That's odd. "She should be here any minute." I raise my voice for the entire group to hear. "It's about to get much louder and more crowded. Taylor and the gang are due anytime."

Proving that children are sponges, taking in their entire surroundings, Liberty rises from across the room. She hops up and down while clapping and cheering. Taylor's twins dote on her; she's excited to see her cousins.

"I should get out of your way," Fallon states.

"No, stay. I mean, if you're not busy, we'd love for you to stay and chat." I smile at my new friend and nanny. "What are you and Slater doing today?"

"He's working until dinner," Fallon admits. "I've just been reading."

"What book are your reading?" Memphis asks, always looking for her next great book.

Fallon blushes. "I'm reading a published paper on 'Social Media Behavior, Toxic Masculinity, and Depression'."

Memphis laughs. "I won't be adding that to my 'To Be Read Shelf.'"

We join in her laughter.

"Well, I believe you need rescued from so much excitement," I state. "Stay with us for a bit. Drink margaritas, gossip, cook, or sit with me and watch these fabulous women cook." I motion to the group.

"Maybe we should give Madison lessons while we cook this afternoon," Amy suggests, teasing.

"Amy, behave," Memphis scolds.

"No way am I cooking today or tomorrow," I state emphatically. "Thanksgiving is a major meal, and I don't want to go down in history for ruining any part of it." I wave my hands back and forth in front of me. "When I set off the fire alarms..." I look up. *Do we have fire alarms? I'm sure we do.* I search for the nearest one while I keep talking. "The dogs would go nuts, the kids would scream, the guys would never let me live it down...it's just not going to happen."

Miss Alba looks directly at me. "I will give you cooking lessons once a week, starting next week. No pressure, just easy dishes."

Her tone leads me to understand there is no room for debate on this topic. I half-smile and nod.

Turning back to Fallon, I insist she stay. "Surely this group is more interesting than your fun reading at home."

Fallon agrees to stay. We celebrate by filling everyone's margarita glasses.

"Delta, what are your plans for tomorrow?" Memphis asks.

She sips from her margarita. "We don't have traditional Thanksgiving dinner."

"Wow," Miss Alba jumps in. "So, what do you serve instead?"

Delta looks down at her hands, fiddling with her glass. It's clear she does not want to answer.

My eyes dart from Miss Alba to Memphis to Fallon.

"Last year, we fixed Mexican," Delta murmurs. "Tomorrow, we're fixing pizza."

"Why do you do that?" Amy pries.

Delta chuckles, "It's just the four of us, so it's silly to fix a huge dinner."

"So, it's not because you can't cook or avoid the holiday?" Amy pries further.

Delta simply shakes her head.

"So, join us," Memphis offers. "We have too much food and plenty of room. The kids can play together, too."

"I don't know," Delta hedges.

"You're eating with us," I state. "If I have to, I'll call Hamilton to get Stan to agree."

Delta smiles.

"Good. That's settled." I squeeze her hand before turning my attention to Fallon. "Would Slater and you like to join us?"

Fallon chews on her lower lip for a moment. "I don't think your table will hold us."

Miss Alba answers for me, "They're bringing up tables and chairs from the meeting rooms."

"Please. Say you'll join us," I beg with a smile.

"Unless the paper you're reading is more exciting," Amy adds sarcastically.

Fallon's eyes float around our group. When she looks back to me, she nods.

"Yay!" I clap. "My new Chicago family will all be here!"

The doorbell echoes through the space. It's about to get louder. Let the holiday begin.

Taylor, her twin daughters, Trenton, his wife, Ava, and their sons, Hale and Grant, spill into the front room. Their arms are full of groceries, pots and pans, board games, and electronics. One of the delivery staff wheels a metal cart full of more goodies. Silly me. I thought we had most of the stuff we needed for tomorrow.

"Everything to the dining room table, please," Taylor instructs her minions.

I approach my new guests as Liberty leads McGee and Indie from her bedroom. I begin passing out hugs, and they take turns petting the dogs and kissing Liberty.

Trenton murmurs before releasing our hug, "I'm ready for adult time. Can you help your big brother out?"

"Okay." I raise my voice above the crowd. "Kids grab your electronics and follow me. Trenton, I'll need your help for just a sec, please." I draw out the word while making a praying gesture.

The troops follow me down the hallway. "This is Libby's room. You are welcome to play in here." I point as I walk, "This is now the game room. Trenton, will you make sure the game system is hooked up right for me? I moved it this morning after Hamilton left; I thought it would be simple, but the two TVs are different. There are so many cables."

"I've got it," Trenton states.

I elbow him before I exit the room. "I'll have a special drink waiting for you in the adult room when you're done."

He returns to the kitchen moments after me. I slide him the beer Ava stated he would enjoy.

"Make yourself at home." I motion to the front room. "You can have the entire living room to yourself. We will try not to be too loud over here baking and stuff."

"And stuff?" Trenton teases.

"I have no idea what all of this needs." I swirl my hands at the dining table, the island, and the counters. "I'm just here to…"

"Look pretty," Trenton teases, messing up my hair.

"You," Taylor uses her mother tone, "to the living room. Find some boring guy show to watch. Summon one of us when you need a beer; otherwise, don't bug us."

Trenton does his best to pretend he's being punished as he settles himself on the sectional in front of the large flat screen.

I assume a bar stool at the island and enjoy chatting with the ladies while they scurry around, prepping relish trays, bread, noodles and desserts for tomorrow's meal. I do my best to keep beverages full for everyone and monitor the kids in the playrooms.

"What do we have here?" Hamilton shouts when he returns home.

Memphis and Amy swarm him with hugs.

"Hello, beautiful." Hamilton snatches me from the group, placing a long, somewhat inappropriate kiss upon me.

"Hamilton," Taylor chides. "There are children in the house."

His thumb wipes the corner of my mouth as he displays his crooked smile. He looks around. "No kids in the area." He pulls me back into his chest.

I place my palms flat against him. "Why don't you go say hi to the kiddos then entertain Trenton? He's been the only dude in the chick zone for over an hour now."

"Hey," Hamilton greets Trenton. "Can I get you another beer?" When he nods, Hamilton pulls two beers from the fridge. "Hey Amy, where are you hiding the popcorn?"

"What popcorn?" I ask him.

"I asked Amy to buy some Garrett's popcorn for us to munch on. You haven't tried it yet; you're going to love the Chicago Mix."

Amy pulls the three large, brown bags from her guestroom. Miss Alba makes quick work of producing three large bowls and filling them with cheese, caramel, and a mixture. I watch as she quickly scoops smaller bowls and delivers them to the children's rooms with waters for everyone.

"You're off the clock," I remind her. "Sit down and have another drink."

She attempts to argue, but Hamilton speaks up. "You're a guest; enjoy yourself."

With a wide grin, she sips from her glass.

Taylor plops in the seat next to me with a big sigh. I wrap my arm around her shoulders, laying my head on her.

"I can't believe Cameron changed her flight. Did she give you a reason?" Taylor shakes her head. "I bet it was work."

I shake my head, fighting the urge to smile.

"I see that." She points at the twitching corner of my mouth. "You know something. Spill it," Taylor demands.

"She's dealing with the plumber," Hamilton answers, unaware of his slip up.

"What plumber?" Trenton asks, joining us in the kitchen, a fresh beer in hand.

"Is something wrong with the house?" Taylor prods, rising to stand by Trenton.

I bet they don't realize they gravitated to each other to become a united front to interrogate. I suddenly realize how Cameron must have felt every time they badgered their baby sister. "First of all, I called her about my book last night–that's how I know. She didn't call me," I explain. "I saw someone walk by while we were Face Timing. She carried the phone down into the basement to let me see the neighbor, Dalton, fixing the pipe. I guess it was only a drip, but he said it might have flooded if she hadn't called him," I shrug. It doesn't seem like the big deal they make it out to be.

"Dalton Edwards?" Taylor smirks. "So, is she staying while he makes repairs or…" She wiggles her eyebrows suggestively.

"I mean, he was shirtless, but that's because it was wet from the drip," I continue sharing what I was told. "Just because he's cute and she's single doesn't mean they hooked up."

"Yes, it does," Trenton states, and Taylor laughs.

"What am I missing?" I stand with hands on my hips.

"They were high school sweethearts," Taylor smiles slyly. "They dated from ninth grade until college."

"I never should have let her move back to Columbia," Trenton spits, shaking his head. "I forgot he lives with his dad next door."

"Just because they have history…" I start being the voice of reason.

"Oh, trust me. They'll hook-up," Taylor sighs.

"Please," Trenton pleads. "Can we not discuss my little sister's sex life?"

We all laugh at his discomfort, and I scramble to change the subject.

"All done?" I ask, a bit ashamed that I'm not more involved in the baking process.

"All set until we start the turkey in the morning," Memphis states from across the island. She takes the margarita Amy hands her.

"That's the last of the margaritas," Amy announces to the room before sticking her head into the fridge.

She emerges with a bottle of water. She looks from the glass water bottle to me with raised eyebrows before she takes a sip.

Sitting back down, Taylor confides, "Fallon spoke to me about Liberty reading. I texted a friend from work; she's a child psychologist. She'd like to meet with you. She'll look at her calendar on Monday and set something up for the two of you."

I lift my head. "Thank you."

"It's a good 'problem' to have." She makes air quotes. "I dealt with a biter and a five-year-old that wet the bed every night."

I raise an eyebrow in her direction.

"The joys of parenting," Taylor shrugs. "We work with whatever pops up."

"I'm exhausted," I confess, falling onto our bed after 10 o'clock.

"I'm glad Mom suggested turning in early," Hamilton smirks, leaning his body over mine.

"We do need to be up for Taylor by seven in the morning," I remind him.

"Some of us are always up by seven," Hamilton teases as his nose gently guides along my neck.

"Ham," I half moan, half protest.

He presses himself up on his straightened arms as if doing a push up.

"Let's place a bookmark in my intentions. What's had you distracted all day?"

I bite my lip. I should have known I couldn't hide this from him. I roll my eyes before I begin.

"It's that bad?" he asks.

"No. I rolled my eyes because I hoped to keep it from you until we were alone. I thought I did a better job hiding it," I admit. "It's nothing bad, just a parenting challenge for us."

His eyes morph from full of desire to concern for our daughter. He sits up on the bed, pulling a folded leg between us. I prop myself up, crossing my legs in front of me.

"Webb told you that Libby read to him last night, remember?" When he nods, brows furrowed, I continue, not wanting to worry him any longer. "Well, it turns out that Liberty really did read to him. Libby can read."

He tilts his head to the side. "Read?"

"Let me back up. Your mom brought a book she liked as a child to read to Libby. She brought it into the living room, and Libby hopped onto her lap. When your mom offered to read it to her, Libby demanded to read it. We all watched, expecting her to pretend to read." I shake my head at the memory.

"Ham, she pointed her little finger and read every single word as if she were in kindergarten or first grade." I rub my tired eyes while I wait for him to respond.

His lips pull to one corner of his mouth while his eyes roam around the room, unfocused. He's thinking.

"Delta mentioned Libby reading to Webb last night. So, we asked Liberty what book it was. It was my book." I smile proudly. "She stated she read number 10. When we turned to page 10, she said that wasn't it. I turned to chapter 10, and she again pointed her index finger and began reading from *my young adult book*."

"So, it's not…" he pauses. "She really can read?"

"It seems so," I reply. "I called Fallon to come over. I figured she could provide some help and research for us. And Taylor is arranging a meeting with a friend of hers that's a child psychologist."

"Can I go with you?" Hamilton asks.

"Of course," I quickly answer. "We need to work together, learn together, and help her."

Tears well in my eyes and proceed to flow down my cheeks.

"Honey, what's wrong?" Hamilton brushes his thumbs to wipe my tears away. "Did something else happen?"

I shake my head adamantly, but inside, I know there is.

"Madison, something has you upset, and I have a feeling it's not that our little girl can read." Concern engulfs his features. His eyes dart over my face, reading my emotions.

"I'm her mom," I cry. "I'm her mom, and I missed signs. I was too caught up in my own drama and didn't even notice..."

Hamilton squeezes me to his chest and lets me sob. He doesn't pry; he doesn't interrupt. He lets me work through my overwhelming emotions in my own time. After several long moments, my bawling subsides.

"She changed," I share. "While I was dealing with Alma's fall then stroke, my mother's death, and then Alma's death, our little girl reached milestones, and I didn't even notice. She started using more words. She changed from baby talk to that of a big girl, and I didn't notice until today. It took me a month, and if she hadn't read to us today, I still wouldn't notice."

Hamilton doesn't speak. He offers no words to contradict mine. He places one warm peck to the corner of my lips. Then, another on the other corner. His next kiss is followed by a sweep of his tongue along my lower lip. Without conscious thought, my body opens for him. He doesn't rush, and he doesn't dominate. He slowly caresses my tongue with his.

As my tongue begins to dance with his, his hands move from my back to my hips. My chest, no longer squeezed to his, begins to heave. The repetition of my nipples grazing his firm muscles triggers another response from me—one deeper and lower on my body. My blood hums, pulsing heavily through my veins.

Hamilton pulls away from my mouth, resting his forehead against mine, our heavy breaths between us. Slowly, we calm. He opens his eyes. We stare deep into each other.

"You are an awesome mom," Hamilton states and squints as his eyes drill his statement home.

I pinch my lips between my teeth. "Fallon and the girls reminded me of everything I had on my plate in the last month. Fallon thinks with all of the changes in her surroundings and in reaction to my emotions at the time,

Liberty began using her advanced language skills to better communicate with all of us. She doesn't do it at playgroup."

"So, what kind of changes are you talking about?" Hamilton inquires.

"Before Alma's fall, she used words like Ma-ma and Da-da; they changed to Mommy and Daddy. A pretty big difference," I admit.

"I never got to hear her say Da-da."

"Ham, I'm sorry. I should never…"

He places two fingers over my open lips to silence me. "I'm just realizing out loud that what I hear now, what I think is baby talk, isn't." He hugs me tight. "Promise you won't laugh?" When I nod, he continues. "I freaked out," Hamilton confesses. "The night I met Liberty, I freaked out. I couldn't fall asleep, even with the two of you lying in bed next to me. I got up, woke my mom up, and we talked for a few hours."

His eyes search my face for my reaction. I give him my warmest smile. *I'm not sure what this has to do with our current situation.*

"She told me that all parents make mistakes." He taps the end of my nose with his index finger. "She admitted Dad and she made many mistakes. She stated that the two of us would make them, too. We just have to do our best as parents and learn from our mistakes."

It hurts a little that he didn't talk to me. I'm glad he talked to Memphis and that she helped him, but I long to be the one he leans on. *Did he go to her because I kept my secret from him?*

"What's going on in that pretty little head of yours?"

I paste a smile that I don't mean upon my face.

"Promise me you won't dwell on this," Hamilton pleads.

I fight it internally. I know I need to let this go so I can focus on Liberty moving forward.

"I'll promise if you'll do something for me," I counter.

Hamilton

. . .

Is she giving me an ultimatum? This woman. She's everything to me. They are everything to me. There is nothing I wouldn't do to be near her. I'd even give up baseball if it meant I could live the rest of my life holding her, loving her, being near her.

I nod, anxious to hear what she wants.

"Can you ask your mom if she would consider traveling to Vegas with Liberty?" She smiles sweetly, a glint in her eyes. "I want Liberty there when we elope."

How did she find out? Did I leave anything out for her to see? Maybe she overheard a phone call with Berkeley. But I was careful, very careful. I didn't text or talk on the phone in the condo for fear she might hear. One of her friends must have spilled the beans.

"I wanted to elope so my side of the church wouldn't be empty at the wedding," she explains. "I've thought about it, and I need Liberty with us; she's my family."

Madison seems nervous. *Or is she afraid of my reaction?*

"And I'm feeling guilty for not allowing your family to attend the wedding. I want Memphis and Amy with us." She shrugs sheepishly.

My smile widens–my surprise is safe. I'm not the only one hesitant to leave our little one this weekend. I've wanted to ask her a million times.

"Why are you smiling?" she inquires.

"I want them there, too. I'll speak with them first thing in the morning," I promise.

"Now, let's get you showered." I smirk as my eyes scan her head to toe. There's no way I'm letting her shower alone.

137

MADISON

What is that incessant noise? I roll over, covering my ears with my pillow. As I still hear the noise, I groan out loud. Suddenly, it stops. Hamilton pulls my pillow off my ear. I open one eye in his direction with another groan.

Hamilton chuckles. "Taylor will be here in 15 minutes."

When I groan and cover my head with his pillow, he full on laughs at me.

"Maybe a shower will help wake you up," he suggests. "I know you took one last night, but it might make this morning easier for you. I'll go get you coffee. You get up."

I peek from under his pillow as he leaves our bedroom. Part of me wants to grab him by his belt loop and tug his jean covered ass back into bed and have my way with him–morning sex would help me wake up. Maybe I should mention that to him for future reference.

As I approach the kitchen, Hamilton extends a large travel mug of coffee to me. I accept it, not convinced it will perk me up the way he intends it to. I hold the cup at my side, cozy up nice and close to him, and whisper, "thank you," while batting my eyes up at him.

I find solace in the warm, sensual kiss he gifts to me. I wrap my arms snuggly around his waist, even with my coffee in hand. His warm heat and his hard, muscular body soothe my soul. I melt in his touch, enjoying the hot friction our tongues produce, longing for that friction to continue between my thighs.

A throat clearing behind my back pulls our mouths from one another. I don't need to turn. Hamilton pulls his smile from me towards his sister.

"Good morning, Amy." He laces his words with sarcasm.

"You two need to learn some self-control," Amy spits, passing on her way to the coffee pot. "Some things should not be seen first thing in the morning."

"Bacon will be ready in five minutes," Memphis interrupts, changing the subject.

Hamilton ushers me to a kitchen stool with his hand on my lower back. Memphis pulls yogurt and fresh fruit from the refrigerator, placing them on the island.

"I brought donuts!" Delta motions to the large box of pastries before sliding a stack of paper plates our way.

Hamilton fixes a plate of yogurt with fruit and another with a glazed donut, yogurt, and fruit. It's easy to know which plate mine will be; Hamilton rarely indulges—he strives to keep his body a lean, powerful machine.

While I chew my first, sweet bite of the donut, I watch Liberty eat her banana slices with her fingers. I pinch a bite of my donut and place it on her tray; her little eyes light up.

"Your cell is vibrating." Hamilton slides it towards me.

TAYLOR

we're here, be up in a minute

ME

I'll open the front door

"Taylor and Cameron are on their way up," I notify everyone.

With guests beginning to arrive to help with the cooking, our Thanksgiving Day officially begins. Excitement builds in my belly despite the early hour. I open the front door, anxiously watching the elevator. When it opens, Cameron exits, followed by Taylor.

"Good morning," Cameron sings, briskly approaching me. She wraps me in a tight hug, rocking me back and forth. "I'm so ready for a weekend off. Let's start this party!" She proudly pulls orange juice and vodka from her large purse.

"She's got a four-day weekend. You'd think she won a Powerball jackpot," Taylor teases as I guide them into the condo.

"I hate to be Debbie-Downer," I tell Cameron, "but you are working tomorrow morning. Remember? You asked me to do a book signing on Black Friday."

"Of course! I didn't forget." She rubs my upper arms. While keeping her arms upon my shoulders, she locks eyes with me. "I owe you big for saving my behind tomorrow. I realize it complicates your day of travel, and I can't thank you enough for squeezing it in for a couple of hours."

"You promised it would be fun," I remind her. "I don't get up before six a.m. for just anyone."

"I realize that. That's why I owe you *big*." Cameron turns to the small crowd in the kitchen. "Let it be known that I, Cameron, will owe Madison Crocker big for an entire year."

The group brushes off Cameron's words. Memphis and Delta fill Taylor in on what's presently cooking and what's next and show her the list for the day. Hamilton helps Liberty sort her blocks by colors in the living room while the two dogs look on from nearby.

Cameron finds champagne flutes in the kitchen to create her screwdrivers. She passes them out then joins me on the stools at the island.

"I should pour your screwdriver over your head," Cameron murmurs from my side. "Trenton and Taylor spent an hour last night discussing Dalton. Seems someone mentioned he was helping me in the basement." She pretends to be angry.

"Sorry," I whisper. "I swear I didn't know that the two of you had a history. I'm sorry they grilled you about it. How bad was it?"

Taylor interrupts, "We didn't grill her. Trenton expressed some concerns about repairs on the house. And the two of us simply cautioned her to take things slow this time with Dalton."

Cameron rolls her eyes at me, expressing her frustration with her older siblings' interference. In our past conversations, she's shared their constant attempts to over-analyze her decisions, guide her career, and mention that she needs to start a family. It has to be hard being the baby of the family.

My cell phone vibrates on the kitchen island. I rise from the hallway floor where I've been playing with race cars with Liberty.

WEBB

I'm ready to come work with your books?

ME

you may come anytime

tell your dad

On his last visit to the condo, Webb was mesmerized by my empty office shelves and box after box of books to populate them. Delta mentioned he loves to sort and organize items and offered to let him help me. Now he's probably pestering Stan to bring him over to get started.

Two hours later, I peek into my office and watch Webb put two more books on the shelf. He'd noticed all my empty shelves the last time he was over and begged me to let him organize my books. I'm happy to see him loving the work. "Webb, do you need anything?" I ask.

"No," he answers without interrupting his task. He pulls out another book and slides it onto the shelf. "No, thank you," he corrects himself.

I slip from the room, leaving him to his preferred task.

"I wish I could do that," his mother states from beside me. "Imagine what I could accomplish in a day with his laser focus," she teases on her way to resume helping the cooks in the kitchen.

Was she checking on Webb, or was she checking on me? Oh well. No big deal.

I'm just glad her family is joining us today and that she is helping cook in my place.

I'm so happy that I can't stop smiling. The gang is all here. Hamilton and Stan return from working out and finish their showers prior to Fallon and Slater arriving. A few minutes later, Taylor's husband and girls arrive with Trenton's brood.

The kids play in Liberty's room or with electronics in our room, occasionally popping out for a nibble or a drink. The men flip back and forth between college and NFL football games in the living room. They even agree to lower the volume when Delta hollers in from the kitchen area.

When the service elevator pings open and the dog walkers peek in, I'm surprised it is already 11. I round up the dogs and make the guys promise to fix a plate and stay a bit when they return at one with McGee and Indie.

Delta, Taylor, Memphis, and Amy buzz around the kitchen. Their intensity increases as we are nearing our one o'clock meal time. I rise from my stool, sliding the eight-foot folding table and small card table into place. Ava and Fallon join me in placing the autumn orange table cloths on each. The three of us make quick work of setting the table, taking care to put out the center-pieces that Taylor's daughters made. Once we finish, I stand back and admire our work. The fall colors work well together.

I know better than to offer to help with the final cooking preparations. Tensions in the kitchen rise–the last thing they need is for me to burn something.

"Can we place anything on the tables yet?" I ask the three cooks. "We could put condiments on the tables and set the rest up in a buffet line," I suggest.

A look of horror from Taylor leads me to believe it's a stupid idea.

"With eight at the long folding table and four at the card table, things are tight," I explain.

Memphis crooks her head to the side, considering my idea. Delta stays out of it.

"I guess it would work," Taylor admits.

"The whole point of today is to enjoy our company," Memphis reminds us. "It'll be nice to have some space at the tables."

"Then it's settled." Taylor claps her hands together. "We can place the butter, jelly, salt, and pepper on the tables. The rest we'll spread out on the island."

Ava, Fallon, and I begin following Taylor's directions. We leave space for the large turkey platter and ham plate then place the green bean casserole, mashed potatoes, and other sides on the island. Ava moves the bar stools against the wall while I organize the desserts at the other end of the island. Pecan pie, cherry pie, pumpkin pie...

"Time to eat," Memphis announces from the kitchen.

Delta fetches Webb from the office while Amy collects the children from the playrooms. Memphis and I help direct the younger kids to the smaller tables. Amy, Cameron, and Delta offer to sit with the children while the rest of the adults take seats around our dining table. All conversation ends when we are seated.

I look around at my guests and squeeze Hamilton's hand which rests on my thigh under the table. When I stand, all eyes focus on me.

"We don't want our meal to get cold, so I'll keep this short." My guests chuckle at my words. "Thank you for coming and sharing Thanksgiving with us. I've felt alone for so long. You'll never know..." I struggle to clear my throat before continuing. "You mean more to me than you will ever know. In the past month, my family and friends have grown exponentially. My life is full and so is my heart. Thank you for accepting Liberty and me in your lives. We may not be blood relatives, but I consider each of you my family."

My throat closes tight as tears threaten. I return to my seat, ready for all attention to be off of me. I didn't expect to spill my heart today. I'm not prepared for the overwhelming feelings of acceptance and belonging that blindside me.

Hamilton's hand rubs up and down my thigh. He knows it's not easy for me, and I love that he's trying to soothe me secretly under the table.

"Let's say grace; please bow your heads," Memphis suggests.

After her lovely blessing, we assist the children in filling plates then take turns as couples filling ours. Light conversations circle each table. I love my family. I hope it is always this easy.

We excuse the children as soon as they finish eating. Amy, Fallon, and Delta pull their chairs to the large table, and we enjoy staying, nibbling on dessert, and chatting for another hour.

Eventually, the guys begin to hint that there are football games to watch. Memphis, as the matriarch in attendance, releases the men as the elevator pings, and the dogs sprint inside.

I usher the guys in to fill a plate and allow them to eat in the living room with the men and the football games. Luckily, they don't argue and fit right in. I thought we'd have to deliver a plate to them; I'm glad they felt welcome enough to come up as we suggested.

We round up the dishes. Delta places silverware, glasses, and as many serving bowls as she can into the dishwasher. I realize now how smart it was of Ava to load the dishwasher twice during the day. We only have a few large bowls and platters to hand wash. I scrub, Fallon dries, and Memphis puts them away. It takes little time to finish the task.

"I'm having a second piece of pie," I announce, snagging a paper plate and plastic fork.

Delta, Memphis, and Fallon join me in a second serving of dessert. While we snack around the island, I lean towards Taylor. "What's going on in there?" I ask, tilting my head toward my office.

Taylor's daughters' giggles can be heard clearly in the kitchen. I believe the only other person in the office is Webb, and I'm worried we might need to rescue him.

"They've entered the 'into boys stage,'" Taylor states, smiling. "They flirt every chance they get. I think my husband is going to go insane before they even reach 16."

"You can't blame him." I bump my shoulder against hers and admit, "It can't get any easier as they get older. I'm already dreading how fast Liberty is growing."

We both turn as the girls wave bye to Webb from the office door then walk to the fridge for a water. They attempt to tell secrets, but we can hear them.

"Who are the guys sitting with Dad?"

"What guys?"

"Look!" She turns her twin's head to the sectional in the living room.

Then, their eyes meet ours and they race down the hall, giggling the entire way.

Taylor rolls her eyes, sighing dramatically. "I see nothing but drama in my future."

"I hear ya," I agree; she has her hands full. The twins are only 13 years old. I can only imagine what they'll be like at age 16 or 18. My mind imagines Liberty at age 16, driving and dating boys. I bite my lip while imaging Hamilton's stress as boys show interest in his little girl. He seems easy-going, but I imagine he won't be when our daughter's dating phase comes into our lives.

"I'd like to bite that lip," Hamilton whispers hot against my ear.

Surprised, I jump. I was so lost in my daydreaming that I didn't hear him come up behind me. He looks quizzically at me.

"I was daydreaming about Liberty," I murmur.

He rubs his hand up and down my back. "She's not dating until she's 30."

Apparently, Hamilton paid attention to Taylor's daughters, too.

When our last Thanksgiving Day guest leaves, Memphis directs Hamilton and me to go pack while she and Amy pick up. We only agree because there isn't much left to clean.

"Can you believe we fly to Vegas tomorrow, and in two days, we'll be married?" I ask Hamilton as we lay our toiletries out to pack in the morning.

"I'm ready," he quickly replies. "We're still getting married in t-shirts, right?"

I nod–I love the idea of us wearing our favorite baseball shirts. I'm not a traditional girl. I want to elope. It'll be quick and we'll be comfortable.

138

HAMILTON

I wiggle the tinkle bell on the end of the elf cap then allow it to touch Madison's cheek. Her eyes squeeze tight, her nose wrinkles, and her lips purse.

"Stop," she gripes. "Make it stop!"

"I would, but Cameron is counting on you. You promised her, so you need to get up," I remind her, safely out of arms' reach.

"Fine," she spits, sitting up with the. "What the..."

Her eyes look to me. They struggle to focus then process the sight of her husband. I'm prepared for this reaction. I give it five minutes, then she'll spring up and join in the fun.

"Oh my gosh!" She covers her open mouth with her hand. "What are you doing?" She laughs.

"It's Black Friday," I begin to explain. "You usually decorate your bedroom and car today."

Her eyes grow wide with the realization of holiday fun to come.

"You start playing Christmas music on Black Friday," I add. "I thought since you had a book event and couldn't decorate at home, I'd find a way to let you celebrate your favorite holiday."

"You're wearing that to my book signing?"

"Umm, no. *We* are wearing this to your book event." I wave her costume. "I ran the idea by Cameron, so we are all set."

She looks from the costume to me.

"Seriously?" she asks again. "You are really going to wear that in public with me?"

She said 'with me;' I knew she'd like this idea. She's even perking up–I might just make a morning person out of her after all.

I wiggle the costume in hopes she hops up soon, and she does. She takes the hanger from me then leans in close.

"I'm kinda diggin' the tights," she murmurs. "Can I lift the hem of your jacket and check out your package?" She flutters her eyes at me while making duck lips.

"If you get any closer to my package, we will be late, and Cameron will kill you," I say through gritted teeth. This woman tests my restraint constantly.

"Okay. I'll leave your package alone for now." She turns, shaking her beautiful behind into our bathroom.

Think about Grandma, puppies, and ice cream. I attempt to prevent the tenting of my tights. These tights show everything. I didn't think this through when I picked out these costumes.

I sit on the bed and open my social media to distract me from the fact that Madison is naked mere feet away from me right now. I scroll through all of the Thanksgiving posts I ignored for the last 24 hours. I haven't posted for over a week; I should post something today.

I walk over to our full-length mirror, hold my phone in front of me, and snap a photo of everything from my elf hat to booties. I open Instagram and post the picture. I type, "Elfin' around Chicago today. Stop by Lake Street Books 7-10am. #LakeStBooks #BlackFriday #ArmAndHammer" Next, I tweet the same post on my Twitter account.

"We need to leave in the next 10 minutes," I call towards the bathroom as I wheel the two suitcases to the hall, and I park them at the front door.

Madison

He bought us elf costumes to wear on Black Friday. He must really love me. I absolutely love the costume. The dopey grin I'm wearing in the mirror matches it perfectly. *I better not grin like this all day, or my fans will think I'm a weirdo.*

I look one more time front and back in the mirror. Liking what I see, I enter the bedroom. *Where'd he go?* I peek in on Liberty before I head to the kitchen for coffee and a protein bar.

"I've got your breakfast." Hamilton waves a bar and travel mug my way. "You can eat in the car."

I nod and follow—we have a tight schedule today. I can't fault him for hustling me along. In fact, I'm grateful he's helping me this morning.

"Our car is waiting downstairs," he mentions as the elevator plummets to the ground floor.

We pause for a photo with the doorman prior to joining Cameron in the back of the car. She's laughing and explaining how the crowd will love our holiday themed attire. Seems we will enter through an employee entrance, meet the owner, arrange the signing table, then open the door to shoppers and fans.

"I'll have to go around a few blocks to get access to the back of the store," Our driver informs us. "Looks like you have a lot of fans."

His words puzzle me. I peek out the window of the car to see a line from the front doors of the bookstore, down the block, around the corner, and blocking the alley entrance.

"Is there another author appearing today?" I ask Cameron.

"No." She pats my thigh. "These are your fans, silly."

"There's no way they're all here to see me," I state.

I did notice the crowd seemed to be a mix of teens and adults. They are the right demographic for my genre, but at a book signing this early on Black Friday, they can't all be for me.

I look at Hamilton. "What's up with your phone?" It won't stop buzzing. His phone never buzzes this much prior to seven.

He tugs his phone out of his elf jacket pocket. "I posted a pic on social media this morning," he confesses. "I guess I make a great elf. Everyone's sharing and commenting."

"Oh my gosh," I laugh. "Your teammates are going to save the picture and use it against you. You know that, right?"

He nods. "It's worth it. I wanted to promote your book signing."

"Wait. What?" Cameron leans forward to see Hamilton. "What exactly did you post?"

Hamilton opens Instagram before passing his phone over for us to read.

"I knew the fans weren't all here for me." I breathe a sigh of relief.

"Trust me, they're here for you." Hamilton squeezes my shoulders. "I promoted your book signing."

"I love you," I whisper.

He believes they are here to see me, but many are coming under the guise of my signing to see him in the elf costume. If it helps me sell a few books, I'm glad he posted it. I'm actually a bit relieved that I don't draw this big of a crowd. I want readers, but I'm not looking for mobs to stalk me everywhere I go.

When the driver parks the car, we quickly hop out and slip in through the back door.

"Hello! I'm Cameron with D.C. Bland Publishing." Cameron extends her hand to shake.

"I'm Mr. Richmond." He shakes Cameron's hand.

"I thought I'd be meeting with…"

He interrupts Cameron, "I'm the assistant manager; the owner had a family emergency yesterday, so I'm filling in." He motions for us to follow him through the backroom and out onto the sales floor. "We've placed a table for you here to the side. I noticed a line formed outside, so I arranged these felt ropes to guide those interested in your book signing to line up over here. This way, they won't interfere with our Black Friday shoppers."

It might just be my nerves, but I feel like Mr. Richmond doesn't want me here today. Cameron made it sound like the owner was elated that I was filling in for the true crime author that baled. Mr. Richmond acts like my signing event will be small and in the way of the regular business.

I will not let him ruin my signing. I will not let him ruin my signing. I chant inside my brain. My nerves ratchet up another notch. This is my first, big city signing. I've been to a few small, independent bookstores. I've never signed at a store of this size, and this is Chicago for goodness sake.

With Hamilton's help, Cameron and I cover the table, stack books, set up the backdrop and my banner, and place a sign at the end of the velvet ropes so guests know what the line is for and where to line up.

"The books you pre-signed are in these two boxes." Cameron motions to the opened boxes at my feet. "If the line is long and a fan doesn't fill out a card for a personalized autograph, you can hand them one of these as you speak to them for a minute."

I nod my understanding.

"Hamilton, will you help me offer these to guests in the line," Cameron points to a stack of cards and ink pens. "If they would like a personal message with the autograph, they should fill one of these out to hand to Madison when it's their turn. Encourage them to print legibly."

"Yep! Let me know if there's anything else I can do to help," Hamilton answers. He tucks a handful of pens and a stack of cards into the pocket of his elf jacket. He leans across the table to me. "Can I get a kiss before the public enters, and there can be no elf PDA?"

Cameron excuses herself. It's a good thing there was a table between us. Our kiss, while hot, remains PG-13.

"The doors will be opening in five minutes," Mr. Richmond announces without looking in our direction. He peeks out the giant windows, trying to gauge the length of the line formed outside.

I open and close my right hand a few times in an attempt to stretch out my fingers for the three hours of autographs that lay before me.

"Stop worrying," Hamilton murmurs. "They already love your book. They're going to love its author, too. And with that cute little elf costume, they'll love you even more."

I love his words, his enthusiasm, and his support for me. It's weird having him as my number one fan. I've always been his fan; now the tables have turned. I guess I'm not surprised he supports me. It's just new. For that matter, being a published author and holding my own book signings is also new to me.

Hamilton

. . .

It's been a busy first hour–time truly does fly when you're having fun. And I am having fun. I wish I could spend more time with Madison, but I'm enjoying my interactions up and down the line of anxious fans waiting for her autograph.

I had no idea my two social media posts would spark so much interest. Lucky for me, the Cubs fans that arrive today also seem to truly be interested in Madison's books, too. The only people here to see me and not the books are my teammates. I didn't expect any of the guys to be up this early, let alone dress and come find me.

I'm sure one of them saw the post and called the others to wake them up. I can handle it. Let them save the picture and try to embarrass me with it in the future. I'm doing this for my girl. A successful signing and a happy Madison will make it worth their teasing in the future. I would not have posted the pic of me in the costume if I didn't expect it to be seen.

The guys have even started posing for pictures for people still in line outside. The fans chat about the Cubs, and my teammates find a way to bring up Madison's books with each of them. I'm going to owe them big for this. They've helped me hand out free copies of Madison's two books to lucky fans. We've signed Cubs gear, posed for individual and group pics with fans, and even posted a few on our social media platforms.

"Excuse me." A deep, male voice demands my attention. "Who's in charge here?"

I turn around to find a group of eight police officers scowling. I don't think we are breaking any laws here, but it's not my place to decide.

"The bookstore assistant manager, Mr. Richmond, and an agent from the publishing company are inside," I promptly inform them. "If you'd like, I can take you to them." I motion toward the bookstore doors.

"Hamilton Armstrong?" one officer asks, squinting at me.

I extend my hand to shake his.

"Are the Cubs to blame for this crowd?" another officer asks.

I notice their scowls have morphed into smiles.

"Maybe," I reply. "My girl is signing copies of her book until 10 today. I decided to dress up and join her. Some of my teammates had come down to razz me, and they stayed to entertain the crowd while the fans wait. We didn't mean to cause any traffic issues," I apologize.

"We'll spread out along the blocks to ensure traffic continues to flow and no one stands in the crosswalks," an officer offers. "Beats working the strip malls with crowd control today."

All the officers chuckle and agree.

"Thank you." I shake his hand. "Let me know if you'd like to meet the author or snap a photo with some of the team."

Madison

As I speak to a teenage girl and her mother, I sneak a glance at the long line that seems to have no end.

"Look who I found!" Cameron's cheery voice draws my attention behind me.

"Hola, Mommy!" Liberty calls from her stroller.

"Hi, guys" I greet Memphis and Liberty. "Can you believe the turnout? Isn't this crazy?"

"One hour left," Cameron murmurs near my ear. "I'm showing these two around before our driver takes them to the airport."

"Wish I could visit," I apologize to Memphis.

"No, you don't. Don't apologize for working. Being busy means talking to fans and selling books." Memphis hugs me before returning to Liberty's stroller. "We just wanted a peek."

I wave to them then quickly return to the next female in line.

"I apologize. My family dropped in for a second," I tell the 20-something woman as I shake her hand.

"Your daughter is adorable," she states. "My students are raving about your books. I planned to snag a copy for my classroom. When I saw on social media that you would be signing today, I couldn't miss it."

"What grade do you teach?"

"I'm an eighth-grade literacy teacher," she informs me.

I raise my arm, signaling for Cameron to return to me. I ask her to get two unsigned books to donate to the middle school. She quickly pulls them from behind a partition.

"Here are two copies for your classroom or the school library," I explain, handing them to the teacher. "This way the autographed copy can remain in your personal library."

"You are so kind." She blushes.

"I love to encourage young readers whenever I can. I'm also a former teacher, so I know about funding shortages and the price you pay to create your classroom."

"Thanks again. My students will be thrilled."

Hamilton and his teammates gather around my signing table. Cameron lets me know we are in the final 10 minutes of the signing.

The line still expands out the door and down the block. I feel bad for those that waited in line so long and won't get to meet me. Part of me wishes I could stay.

As if she's reading my mind, Cameron murmurs, "The owner called me, excited about the turn out. He's offering coupons for 10 percent off a purchase to everyone still in line as we leave. Hamilton and the guys are going to go pass those out right now." She quickly hands little cards to the men who quickly start passing them out to everyone.

"Can I walk down the line and thank them all for coming?" I ask her. "I feel like they should at least see me after waiting so long."

I sign the next book then rise. I utilize my teacher voice to thank everyone for coming and apologize that I can't stay. I encourage them to make sure they get a coupon then move farther down the line to repeat the process.

Several fans snap photos of me with their phones as I wave and talk. When Hamilton approaches, more cameras pop out. Everyone cheers for us to pose together as the two elves. We continue to work our way down the line and even pose with the men in blue. Hamilton posts that photo on his social media and tags the Chicago PD.

Before I know it, Cameron approaches to whisk us inside, through the back room, and to our waiting car. The assistant bookstore manager thanks us and informs Hamilton that if the Cubs or his charity ever need donations or books to be sure to contact the store. It seems the large crowd softened his heart towards having me there today.

Cameron shares some sales numbers and stories with us as we travel to the airport. Then, she passes us our duffle bag. While she and the driver focus on the road ahead, Hamilton raises the partition, and we change into our travel attire for the flight. I would have loved flying in the costumes, but Hamilton doesn't want to draw attention to himself. I hadn't thought about it, but he wants to disguise himself so we can enjoy our weekend without cameras or fans.

"It's clear you don't change on the go very often," I chuckle as I am finished, and Hamilton still struggles.

"I'm a bit bigger than you," he states. His long legs stretch to the floor board in front of me while he remains in his seat, attempting to pull up his jeans and fasten them.

"Excuses. Excuses."

When he finishes, he lowers the divider. Cameron informs us we are pulling into the airport. My nerves ratchet up a notch. I'm not afraid to fly. It's just that this is the first time I'll be flying with Liberty. Hamilton purchased stand-by tickets for Memphis and Liberty on our flight. He claims someone won't show up, and they'll fly with us. Although I've researched flying with toddlers online, I'm still very nervous about it. *What if they don't get on our flight?* Memphis will be stuck in a busy airport with her for who knows how long.

Taking in the multiple lanes of bumper to bumper traffic and airplanes taking off, I worry we may never find Memphis and Liberty in this post-Thanksgiving crowd.

When Hamilton slips something black from the duffle bag, my jaw drops. He slips on a pair of small, black, rectangular framed glasses and a Cardinals ball cap. *He doesn't need glasses. And couldn't he get in trouble if he's spotted in a Cardinals hat?*

"What?" He smiles at me.

"Since when do you need glasses?" I sputter in shock.

"I don't," he replies. "This is my travel disguise. No one would ever expect me to wear a Cardinals hat. I thought I'd use the glasses like Clark Kent does."

"Clark Kent didn't improve his looks by wearing the glasses. They made him look nerdy," I pant. "You look hot in glasses. I hope I don't get into a fight when women can't keep their eyes off of you."

His smile widens. "So, the glasses don't help my disguise?"

Oh, they help. They help make it harder for me to keep my hands out of his hair and off his face. My panties grow wetter the longer I gaze at him.

He chuckles. "I figured you'd like the hat." He places his thumb upon my lower lip. "Please, stop biting this. We need to meet Mom and catch a flight. If you keep biting your lip, I'll instruct the driver to drive a bit further and raise the divider. We'll miss our flight and worry my mom."

"We can't have that," I whisper.

"Here we are," the driver announces.

Hamilton opens the door and guides me out. Before he lets go of my hand, he asks, "Is it the hat or the glasses that have you so hot and bothered?"

I only shrug.

Hamilton accepts the two carry-on bags before tipping the driver. We hug Cameron goodbye and enter the airport.

"Mom plans to meet us at our terminal," Hamilton reminds me, understanding that I might be worried about finding Liberty in the mayhem.

Hamilton and I opted for carry-on bags to avoid the crowds and waits at the baggage terminals. He promised I'd have everything I need when we arrive in Las Vegas–I'm trusting him to know what he's talking about. He guides me through the masses, through the TSA Pre-Check, and to our terminal like a pro. I guess it helps to be over six feet tall and muscular to fight the crowds. He acts like a blocker on the football field, and I simply follow close behind.

"I see a stroller," Hamilton calls over his shoulder.

I follow his index finger. There they are. What a relief.

"You made it," Memphis greets. "I promised Libby she could get out of the stroller when you arrived."

"Hey, sugar." Hamilton immediately unbuckles Liberty and lifts her up.

"Need go potty," Liberty attempts to whisper, but we all hear her.

"Hamilton, do you mind watching all the stuff if I go with them?" Memphis asks, motioning to her carry-on and our backpack near the stroller. "I'll put my bag in this seat to save it for me."

"Have you checked in at the counter yet?" he asks before we leave.

"Yes. They will call me up before boarding," Memphis shares.

"I hope you get to take our flight." I verbalize my big fear. "I don't know what you'll do if it's full."

"It will all work out," Hamilton promises. The corner of his mouth twitches.

Hamilton

My girls return at the same time the flight staff announces we will begin boarding soon. I know Madison has worried about the four of us getting on the same flight. It's time I set her mind at ease.

"Mom, they called your name," I lie.

She smiles before taking her tickets up to the counter. I keep an eye on Madison as she watches my mom's interactions at the counter. I hate that I've caused her stress in trying to perpetuate my surprise.

My mom turns towards us, giving a thumbs up. I hear Madison release the breath she's been holding. Mom and I had this all planned out. We only pretended she had stand-by tickets.

"We're all set," Mom announces when she returns.

I pull the tickets from her hand then pull out our tickets to compare. "We're just across the aisle from you," I announce, adding excitement to my voice.

"Really?" Madison perks up.

She allows Liberty to stand on her own. "Stay with us, or we'll need to buckle you back in the stroller."

Liberty walks in the small area in front of our three seats, pointing to random items and chattering. The travelers around us seem to enjoy her banter, so I allow her to continue. The more energy she burns now, the better she will sleep during the flight.

"Those glasses…" Madison whispers huskily in my ear.

"You really like them that much?" I chuckle at her silliness.

"Plan on wearing them to bed tonight," she whispers. "And tomorrow night."

I shake my head.

"What was that Kenny Chesney song I used to tease you about?"

"She Thinks My Tractor's Sexy," I remind her.

"Now, she thinks your glasses are sexy," she twangs, still in a whisper.

I roll my eyes.

Madison

Memphis insists she will be fine helping Liberty settle in during the pre-boarding.

"They'll be fine." Hamilton pats my arm reassuringly.

"I just worry about the booster seat in the small seats. It won't be as roomy as the SUV to install," I explain.

"Honey," Hamilton leans forward to better face me. "we're in first class. There will be plenty of room for the booster, and Libby won't be able to kick or bump the seat in front of her. She'll nap. You'll see."

First class? Is he kidding? I love that he wants to treat us to a nice trip, but we don't *need* first class. I don't even want to know how much these tickets cost.

139

MADISON

I roll over and flop my arm out to find I'm alone. I crack one eye, searching the room for Hamilton; he's nowhere to be found. I raise myself on two elbows, quirking my ear to listen for sounds in the bathroom. Nothing. I grab my phone from the charger. It's 9:30 a.m. *Where could he be?* Maybe Liberty is awake.

I tie my hair in a messy ponytail, pull on a t-shirt and sleep shorts, and make me way out into the common area. I find Memphis and Liberty; still no Hamilton.

"Mornin'. Have you seen Hamilton?" I ask, wiping at the corner of my eyes after a big yawn.

"Good morning!" Memphis wears a huge smile. "He went down to work out. Said he'd be a couple of hours, and I should let you sleep."

My nose leads me to the dining table. I spot the remnants of Liberty and Memphis' breakfast. *Bacon.*

"I'll order you some," Memphis offers. "Bacon, fruit, muffin. Anything else?"

"That sounds perfect." I place my hand on my belly as it growls in answer. "Make it a double order of bacon," I add.

Memphis nods before picking up the hotel phone to order room service. I plop on the sofa, tucking a throw pillow to my chest. Liberty plays with a toy car that flies across the ceramic tile floor with ease, causing her to giggle.

Two hours. Who works out for two hours while in Vegas? He's crazy, but I love him. If it's nine now, he should be back about eleven. By the time he cleans up, we will need to fetch some lunch for all of us.

I'm lazy for the rest of the morning. My breakfast of double bacon is divine, the sofa is comfy, and I have no desire to shower or even move for that matter.

At 10:45, Memphis suggests I shower and get dressed before Hamilton returns. It takes all of my strength, but I peel myself from the sofa cushions and slide my stocking feet across the tile toward our room.

The shower feels sublime. The water pelting my back and neck works out all of my kinks. I opted for a cooler temperature in the hopes that it would wake me up, and it does. I feel revived when I emerge, dressed and ready for the day. When I open my bedroom door, I freeze on the spot, raising my hands to the wood frame for support.

The room is full. Full of my friends and new family. *How can this be?*

"Surprise!" the group shouts, clapping and jumping up and down.

Still in the doorway, I scan the room, looking for Hamilton. I only find Memphis walking towards me.

"Hamilton planned everything," she explains. "He made arrangements to fly all of us out here weeks ago." She searches my face.

Tears well, and I'm finally able to leave the door frame. As I walk through the group, each woman greets me with a hug and excited words about my wedding tonight. *Wedding? I thought we were eloping.*

"You look like you need a stiff drink," Adrian states, thrusting a flute of orange liquid my way. "Mimosas. So, you're still eloping. Hamilton wanted your family and friends to celebrate with you."

I'm still confused. "Who's all here?" My voice croaks.

"The guys are spending the day in a suite with Hamilton. They're keeping him from seeing the bride on his wedding day. Memphis insisted on that tradition."

I look at Memphis then back to Adrian. I chug my drink then place the glass on a nearby end table.

"So, all of the guys came, too?"

"Yep," Adrian answers while refilling the glass I just abandoned.

Taylor walks up to me. "Are you nervous?"

"I wasn't until now," I confess.

"Oh please." Cameron approaches swatting at me. "It will still be the two of you with Elvis up front."

She acts like it's no big deal. Now, we will have an audience. That changes things a bit.

"Aunt Madison, can we see your wedding dress?" Taylor's daughter asks from across the room.

"Um..." I begin to walk in her direction. "We opted to not dress up. I'm not wearing a dress." At least I hope I'm not. *Surely Hamilton didn't change that without my input.*

"We brought our Cubs shirts," Taylor reminds her daughters. "That's what everyone is wearing to the wedding.

"I'm going to have a gown like Belle's in *Beauty and the Beast* when I get married," the other twin states.

"You better start a wedding fund in addition to a college fund," Cameron teases her older sister. "Sounds like the girls will want all the bells and whistles at their weddings."

"Tell me about it; their father is already dreading the day," Taylor teases.

"So, how long is everyone staying in Vegas?" My head is full of so many questions.

While waiting on our toenails to dry, Salem mentions she has a hilarious ER story to share.

"Now, I'm not sharing any names, so we aren't breaking any HIPPA laws," Salem starts.

"Athens is a small town. I'll figure it out," Adrian brags.

"Shut up, or she won't share!" Bethany draws closer, excited for gossip.

"Anyway..." Salem points her finger at Adrian to shut her up. "A guy came in with hives over his entire body. He even had hives you-know-where." She wiggles her eyebrows while avoiding words that might draw youngster's attention.

Our group shares wide-eyed shock and giggles.

"While I asked questions, trying to understand the reason for his extreme allergy attack," Salem shares, "the guy tells me that they were trying to get pregnant, and his wife wanted to try to spice things up a bit. She slathered him in honey, massaged him a bit, then hoped to take her time licking it all from him, finishing in a very special spot." Salem blushes.

"So, he didn't know?" I ask. "I mean, honey is a common food."

"He claims he's never consumed honey," she states. "We gave him a shot of Benadryl and urged them to abstain until *all* redness and hives disappeared from his privates."

"No baby-making this month for them," Savannah blurts, causing wide-eyes from Taylor's twins across the room.

We burst into raucous laughter.

140

HAMILTON

My hands are shaking–I'm nervous. At any minute, the woman I love will walk through those doors. Today, I'll lock her into my life forever as my best friend, my wife, and the mother of my children.

I'm way too hot in this jacket, but I can't take it off and reveal the surprise beneath until Madison stands beside me. It's my final statement of love and support for her. She's my everything, and I plan to show her in every way possible.

My breath catches in my throat as the double doors open. I crane my neck in search of Madison in her gaggle of girls. The doors close quickly behind them, leaving me without a glimpse of her or Liberty. In scanning the room, my eyes lock with my mother's–she smiles and winks to let me know all is well. It does little to calm my nerves. I need to see Madison; I need to hold her hand.

Madison

Liberty and I stand alone in the large foyer. I nervously fluff her tutu that Aunt Amy purchased for her. She looks sweet in her little black and white striped umpire shirt, black tutu, and zebra-striped tights with black Mary Janes. Amy spared no expense in securing the perfect outfit for our wedding. We planned for Hamilton to wear a Cubs t-shirt and for me, a Cardinals t-shirt. Liberty, as our referee, is a perfect addition. I'm glad Amy took it upon herself to dress our daughter appropriately.

Well, it would have been a perfect picture for the three of us had I not decided to change things up at the last minute. Don't get me wrong; I'm still a humongous Cardinals fan, but I love Hamilton. At the altar, I plan to surprise him by unveiling my Cubs jersey.

When the ladies surprised me today, I learned they all brought Cubs attire. It would not bother me to be the only one sporting a Cardinals shirt, but I thought it might be nice to surprise Hamilton by showing my support of him and his team on our special day. I'm not even wearing my usual Cardinals tank underneath it to protect my skin.

The door opens a crack, and Trenton squeezes through.

"Did our nieces talk to you today?" he asks as he approaches.

I smile as I nod, remembering Taylor's daughters informing me they asked their uncle to walk me down the aisle.

"Well then," he extends his elbow, "shall we go get you married?"

I slip my arm under his elbow before prompting Liberty to walk in front of us to her daddy. Trenton opens the door, and I catch my first glance of Hamilton. As we step into the chapel filled with our closest family and friends, I only have eyes for my man. Subconsciously, I bite my lower lip as we slowly close the distance between us. I feel my temperature rise with his deep brown eyes upon me. My skin prickles as thoughts of what tonight will bring flood my thoughts. My cheeks flame, and my breath catches when Hamilton's tongue darts out to dampen his lips before his signature smirk shines. He's thinking about tonight, too.

Liberty hugs her father's leg as Trenton releases my arm, placing a kiss on my hot cheek.

"Let us begin," the Elvis impersonator states.

Hamilton raises his index finger, halting the magistrate. His fingers grasp the zipper of his jacket then slowly lower it down. I quickly follow suit with my own sweater, curious what he has under his. In unison, we remove them, letting them fall to the floor at our feet.

Laughter engulfs me as tears fill my eyes. We couldn't have planned this any better. Hamilton stands before me in a Cardinals t-shirt. He's shaking his head at me.

"I wanted to surprise you," I murmur.

Adrian, in the front row, heard my admission. "You mean the two of you didn't plan this?" A full belly laugh sounds as she slaps her thigh.

"We didn't plan this," Hamilton announces to the crowd.

"Great minds think alike," Memphis calls from her seat in the front amidst the laughter of our friends.

Taking Liberty's hands, Hamilton and I face Elvis to exchange our vows.

Before I know it, we are back at our suite, celebrating with our family and friends. Caterers bring us appetizers and beverages. With plates in hand, we mingle with our brood. I grab Hamilton's bicep to steady myself. Hamilton places his large hand over mine, looking down to access my reaction.

"What's wrong?" His eyes search mine for clues.

Unable to talk at the moment, I point toward his sister, Amy, across the room. She holds Liberty in her arms while chatting with the guy beside her. The guy. The we're-just-friends guy that she denies is her boyfriend.

Hamilton chuckles. "Yeah He's been with the guys all day. Mom texted me that no one is allowed to chat with Amy about it. I think Mom worries Amy will get mad and dump him if we do."

"Can you dump someone you're not dating? I mean she's adamant he's not her boyfriend," I tease.

"Be nice," he prompts. "They attended the World Series together and now our wedding; I think it's safe to say they are a couple." He shrugs, quirking the corner of his mouth.

"I won't say a thing, but I think we should start a pool. The person that picks the month she officially admits that she has a boyfriend is the winner," I suggest.

"We are so totally doing that!" Hamilton leaves my side and approaches the guys from Athens who are standing near the alcohol in the corner.

141

MADISON

Upon returning to Chicago, our life does not slow down as I'd hoped. Fallon and Liberty submerge themselves in activities. They attend playgroup, tumbling, and swim lessons held in our building. I've observed a few times; Liberty seems to love playing with her peers. I'm settling into a new writing routine four days a week. Delta insists I leave one day a week open to run errands, go shopping, or just hang out with her. She ensures that I enjoy my new city and make new friends, and I love her for that.

I squeeze in a couple of hours to write this morning before my girls arrive. Our home will be crowded for the next 48 hours. My four friends, along with their two daughters, are driving up for a Christmas shopping trip. I don't look forward to shopping, but I do look forward to the time we will spend together.

"Lunch time," Miss Alba states, peeking her head through my closed door.

I save my document before shutting my laptop for the rest of the week.

Entering the kitchen, I find Fallon at the island and Liberty already in her highchair. Miss Alba sets out a bowl of fresh salad, sandwiches, and berries. We eat quietly in anticipation of guests arriving in the next hour.

Although I gave them the rest of the week off, Fallon insisted on playing with the three girls both days, allowing the grown-ups alone time to gossip, shop, or relax; Miss Alba insisted on cooking and keeping up with the dishes for us. I realize they will be paid for their time but am glad they want to ensure it's a great visit.

Liberty and I stand in our open door, anxiously watching the elevator. When it pings, Liberty hops up and down, clapping. I can't resist recording her; she's too darn adorable. With the swooshing sound of the doors opening, Liberty darts in its direction.

"Here, Mommy!" she squeals, still clapping.

"Well, hello Liberty," Adrian greets as she carries Bella into the hallway.

I'm not surprised to see a staff member wheeling a cart loaded with luggage, diaper bags, strollers, and portable cribs. It's not easy traveling with little ones.

"I need alcohol," Savannah states near my ear before vanishing inside the condo.

I bet the six-hour ride with two little ones and a pregnant Salem taxed her patience. I'm a bit surprised she took the time off and agreed to make the trip.

"Got to pee." Salem waddles past me.

I instruct the man where to place the luggage in one guest room and thank him for his assistance. And just like that, the house is noisy, busy, crowded, and I wouldn't have it any other way.

Miss Alba hooks Savannah up with a delicious margarita. Once Adrian and Bethany get their girls settled in with Fallon and Liberty in her room, they seek Miss Alba's famous margaritas, too. Salem opts for water while rubbing her baby bump.

"So, how was the date?" I nudge Savannah as I plop down on the sectional next to her.

"Yes, finally," Adrian whines. "We've been asking for almost a week, and she has divulged nothing."

"I promised to share with all of you," Savannah defends. She makes an exaggerated effort to settle into a comfy position as we all wait. A wide smile slides upon her face before she begins.

"Start at the beginning, and don't leave anything out," Bethany demands, always one for gossip.

"It was an ugly sweater holiday party held at the principal's house. Lincoln found matching his-and-hers sweater vests for us to wear. They were hideous." She pauses to pull up the photos on her phone for us to see. As we pass the phone around, she continues.

"We stayed at the faculty party an hour. That was 45 minutes too long for me. Of course, every teacher shared stories with him about me. It was all good until the high school teachers started talking of my ditching, pranks, and poor attitude.

"The P.E. teacher spilled some rum punch on her chest, so I reached into my purse to hand her a moist towelette that I stuck in there the last time I had barbecue. I was in the middle of a conversation, so I didn't pay much attention when I handed it to her." Savannah shakes her head. "When the guests around us broke into whispers and laughter, I looked at my hand to see what was so funny. I grabbed a condom instead of a towelette."

"Oh my gosh! That is hilarious!" I snort.

"I bet half the teachers nearly fainted," Adrian adds. "Crusty old hags."

"My face flamed; I'm sure I was bright red," Savannah admits. "When we were at his place, we had a good laugh about it, but in the moment, it was horrifying."

"Um, can we get back to the sex?" Salem urges.

"Fine, we had sex," Savannah huffs.

"Well, it couldn't have been good if that's all you can say about it," Adrian states.

"What if I told you I stayed both Saturday and Sunday night at his place?" Savannah counters.

"Details. Now," Bethany demands.

"I'm not going to give you any specifics other than it was so good, I spent 24 hours at his place," Savannah shares.

She just told me all I need to know. My girl has found herself a guy. *Yay!*

While she continues, I notice the goofy grins on Savannah and Lincoln's face as they stand with an arm around each other's back for the photo. The sweater vests are hideous. Paired with red bell bottoms and a polyester shirt, the vests are too colorful, the design is too busy. She went all out for him–she likes him more than she's let on.

"We went back to his place where he made lasagna with garlic bread for us. We watched Netflix…"

"You watched Netflix and chilled?" Adrian blurts. "OMG!"

"No, we didn't," Savannah defends while blushing.

"Yes, you did," Bethany states. "I know for a fact you spent the night at his house."

Several of us gasp at this news.

"How the hell would you know that?" Savannah rises, hands on her hips.

"I stopped by at eight on my way to the grocery store," Bethany states, like she does this all the time.

"You nosey little…"

I cut Savannah off before this becomes a fight. "Enough!" I wave my hands in front of Savannah's face to get her attention. "Ignore her, and continue with your story," I urge. "I've been waiting to hear all about it. Please?"

Savannah throws herself back into the sofa cushions with a huff. "Anyway…" She throws a glare at Bethany. "We watched old sitcoms, making fun to the hairdos and clothes. He bought wine, but we ended up drinking beer all night." She chuckles. "We drank too much beer."

"Anyone need a refill?" I offer on my way to the kitchen.

Miss Alba assists me with filling the three margarita glasses.

"Yes, Bethany, I did end up staying all night," Savannah sighs. "I didn't plan it; in fact, I made myself promise before he picked me up that I wouldn't sleep with him."

"So, what if you slept with him?" Bethany chimes in again. "Was he good?"

When we return from our afternoon of shopping, the girls can't thank Fallon enough for keeping their daughters. While I struggled to find the perfect gift at the perfect price, they arrive back at my place with bundles of bags. I don't enjoy shopping, but I enjoyed their excitement in securing gifts for their families.

"I'm home," Hamilton calls as he enters.

"Daddy!" Liberty squeals, running to greet him.

He sweeps her up, kissing her until she can't stop giggling.

"Stop," she wails, squirming in his arms.

When she wiggles free of his grasp, she pulls him to the toys on the floor and points out Jami and Bella to him.

"Hamilton, are you ready for the estrogen invasion?" Adrian teases.

He greets the women one by one and assures us he can handle all of us.

During dinner, Salem shares photos of the work she's completed on the inside of my parents' farmhouse while sharing stories of Latham's work on the outside. I'm amazed how a coat of paint can change the appearance of the inside of my childhood home. She's lightened it up with her choice of colors and blinds instead of drapes. I like that it looks like a happy home once again. I'm glad their family will fill it with happy memories once again.

The rest of our visit passes much too fast. Before I know it, Liberty and I are waving goodbye to the Athens gang as they drive away. We promise to visit as we drive to Columbia for Christmas.

Madison

Hamilton clocks my mood the moment he arrives home. "It's not easy to say goodbye, is it?" He brushes my hair over my shoulders, placing his palms on the back of my neck. He pulls me into his chest, holding my tight.

I don't need to admit I've laid on the sofa for the past hour, wallowing in my sadness. He knows me all too well.

"Let's put Liberty to bed early tonight," he suggests, steering me towards her bedroom.

She's tired from playing with her two guests; it should be easy for her to fall asleep. I'm exhausted, but suddenly, my blood hums in anticipation of Hamilton's real intention for tucking Liberty into bed early.

An hour later, I melt into Hamilton's arms, my head upon his chest, and our warm comforter over us. Sated from our shower, my eyes are heavy and my muscles loose. The culmination of the busy day shopping coupled with the vigorous shower sex threatens to carry me off to sleep. Hamilton's fingertips lightly caress my arm, further encouraging the sandman carrying me away.

"When is your next shot?" he murmurs lazily near my ear.

I bolt upright, turning to face him where he still lays on his pillow. Sleep is no longer knocking on my eyelids as my mind flies. I visualize my calendar while staring at our headboard. I visited Dr. Anderson prior to Alma's fall. October...November...December...I snag my phone from the nightstand on my side of the bed. My thumbs fly over the screen through my iCal.

"Crap!"

Hamilton chuckles from his pillow. "I didn't mean to cause the cyclone that just occurred inside your head," he states.

"I messed up," I explain. "I need to request Liberty's and my medical records. I can't believe I didn't think of that while planning our move. We need to find a pediatrician we like before she needs her next immunizations, or, heaven forbid, she gets sick."

I widen my stare at the still very relaxed Hamilton in bed beside me. "I have to schedule a new patient appointment and probably get a physical with my shot within the next two weeks."

"Okay," he smiles.

"Okay? Seriously? You don't understand," I inform the smirking man beneath me. "It takes a month or two to get a new patient appointment with good gynecologists."

Hamilton stretches his long arm; placing his hand on the back of my neck, he pulls me down beside him. "What if you don't get another shot?"

My eyes search for his meaning. My trembling hand covers my mouth. *He couldn't mean that, could he?* My eyes close as I take a deep, steadying breath.

"Ham..." My voice quakes with the revelation of his question.

"I know it seems too fast," he begins to explain. "I'm ready. We're ready. Liberty is nearly two; she'd be close to three by the time a baby would arrive."

He places one finger firmly against my lips when I begin to speak. "Amy and I are closer to four years apart. Don't get me wrong; I love my sister, but we were never into the same things. The age gap meant I was always the pesky little brother. I want our children to be close. Maybe they could even play on the same sports teams one day."

All of my arguments dissolve at his words. He's given this lots of thought.

He's imagined himself with our children and, I'm sure, even envisioned coaching them.

"How…" I swallow, trying to calm my shaky voice. "How many…?" I find it hard to voice my question.

I witness Hamilton attempt not to laugh at me. His lips move from a smile to turn under his teeth and bite down.

"I know you wouldn't want Liberty to be an only child like you are," he correctly assumes. "There were two of us, and I always wanted a brother. I think three or four would be a good number."

Three or four? Could I endure four pregnancies? Envisioning it in my mind, I realize future pregnancies would be different than Liberty's with Hamilton by my side. *In a perfect world, it could be two of each, but what if it were four girls? Or one girl and three boys?* My eyes widen as wild, younger versions of Hamilton tear through my future house while Hamilton works.

"What's going on up here?" Hamilton taps one finger to my scrunched forehead.

"You see us with four kids?" I squeak.

"I can see it, yes. You're the one that does all the work for nine months, so I understand if you only want two." Hamilton's finger moves from my forehead to lightly brush my cheek.

"And you're ready now?" Before he can answer, I continue. "February means January, December, November." I tick them off on my fingers. "January means December, November, October."

Hamilton raises an eyebrow. "What are you doing?"

"I'm taking the month we might become pregnant and counting backwards three months."

"Why?" Now his brow is creased.

"If we get pregnant in January, I would deliver in October. If it happens in February, it would be November," I explain. "If we're really going to try to get pregnant, I want to deliver in the off-season, so you will be with me."

His face lights up. "So, we're doing this?"

"I'm just thinking out loud for now," I state. "If I don't get my shot in December, I'd have to see a doctor, but I assume we could try in January. Of course, trying doesn't mean we'll be successful. If we actively attempt to get pregnant in January through April, I could deliver before you had to report for spring training the next season."

Hamilton flips me onto the mattress, propping himself on his forearms above me. His eyes assess me, then his mouth smothers mine in a deep, all-consuming kiss that makes my toes curl and my body spring to life.

"It only took one night for Liberty." He dawns his sexy, crooked smile.

I swat his chest, but his proximity prevents the desired effect.

"We won't be that lucky next time," I muse. "But trying is also fun."

"Should we practice right now?" he whispers, his lips grazing mine.

I slide my hand between us in answer to his question.

142

MADISON

I place my left hand on Hamilton's bouncing knee.

He immediately stills, eyes finding mine, and whispers, "Sorry."

I knew he would be on edge when he struggled to fall asleep last night. I tried to assure him that she's happy, healthy, and we'll learn how to help her at this appointment—it's all positive and nothing to worry about.

"How long has she been back there?" Hamilton murmurs, squirming in his waiting room chair.

I look at my cell phone screen before answering. "Almost 45 minutes." I rub my hand up and down his back. "Taylor said they'd play, talk, and read. It takes time."

My words clearly don't soothe my anxious husband. He rises from his chair, pacing along the back wall of the waiting room. A couple of the others in the room give me knowing smiles.

"Liberty's parents," a male nurse calls from the now open door.

Hamilton takes my hand in his as we follow the nurse down a short hallway. He squeezes my hand too tight. I squeeze his twice. He loosens his hold before moving his hand to the small of my back.

The nurse knocks three times on a closed door before he opens it and motions for us to enter. I quickly take a seat; Hamilton follows my lead.

"You have a dynamic young lady," Dr. Conway smiles and greets from across her large wooden desk. Her blonde hair is sleek in an intricate knot at the back of her head. A white doctor's coat covers her navy, silk blouse and matching pencil skirt. "I apologize for the wait. Liberty entertained us, and we lost track of time."

A proud smile slips upon my face. I made it my goal as a parent to raise a confident girl. I don't want her to sit timidly in class, downplaying her academic abilities. Liberty won't be a demure princess, waiting for her prince to rescue her, protect her, and make her happy.

"During our time in the toy area, she answered my questions easily and demonstrated her moxie," Dr. Conway smiles.

"I'm sorry to interrupt," Hamilton butts in.

I cringe. Why can't he wait for the doctor? I'm sure she'll answer all of his questions if he just has patience.

"Where is Liberty right now?" he demands.

The smile widens on the doctor's face. "She's in the playroom with two other children and a couple of my medical students."

Hamilton nods his acceptance.

"I'm going to share technical terminology as I explain my findings. You will hear words that might scare you, but please listen to my entire explanation before you jump to conclusions or ask questions." She looks towards Hamilton, hoping her last words sink in.

"Liberty has hyperlexia." Dr. Conway looks to both of us before continuing. "It's a fancy word for children that read much earlier than their peers. There are conflicting studies on children with hyperlexia. Some doctors believe all hyperlexic children fall on the autism spectrum. I'm among those that believe not all hyperlexia cases are autistic. Although some display 'autistic-like' traits and behaviors, they sometimes gradually fade as a child gets older," Dr. Conway pauses, allowing her diagnosis to settle in. "Are you familiar with the autism spectrum?"

Hamilton nods, and I answer, "I've read a lot about it in my teacher education courses, and we have a close friend with a son on the spectrum."

"Have you witnessed any 'autism-like' behaviors in her?" The doctor leans back in her large, burgundy, leather chair, steepling her hands in front of her.

Hamilton's worried eyes dart to mine. While staring at him, I search my memories. I shake my head when I look back to Dr. Conway.

"I want to be clear; I do not believe Liberty is on the spectrum," Dr. Conway smiles. "We may find some behaviors as we observe her more closely, but I feel these are not permanent behaviors. I'd like for both of you to keep a journal or notes on your cell phones. Note anything you feel is odd or not her normal behaviors. Also note if she is tired, hungry, scared, over-stimulated...any shifts in her environment. This will allow us to uncover trends, triggers, and situations that bring certain behaviors."

Placing her forearms on the desk between us, she continues, "Liberty is a delightful young lady. She didn't shy away from strangers or our strange office situation. While her ability to choose and speak words is advanced for her young age, they are normal for conversation. What I mean is, I don't find that she misuses words or struggles to express herself. She seems to understand the meaning of words and uses them correctly." The doctor smiles while shaking her head. "During our play time, she began asking my staff questions. She wanted to know why doctors wanted to play with her and if they liked Spiderman."

I pinch my lips between my teeth. That's our girl, always wanting to learn.

"We allowed her to choose the first book to read. Then, to ensure she hadn't memorized it as it had been read to her in the past, we chose two other books. She *can* read, and when asked questions about her reading, she seems to comprehend as she reads. This is important, because many children with hyperlexia can read most books placed in front of them, but they do not understand what they read."

"Checking for understanding," I whisper.

Hamilton leans forward, turning his head to mine in question.

"Yes," Dr. Conway confirms. "It's important that we check for understanding while Liberty reads. As she selects chapter books, we need to pause and check for understanding often."

"So..." I need to verify my understanding. "We should work with vocabulary words, context clues, and check for understanding, just like a teacher does for the appropriate level she is reading?"

"Yes," Dr. Conway affirms. "With your education and that of your nanny that Taylor mentioned, I feel confident. Liberty is lucky the adults in her life are equipped to nurture and challenge her. Hamilton, I'm sure this seems confusing, but it's easy."

"I…" He runs both hands through his long, dark waves. "I just need to know Liberty is okay."

I place my hand on his bouncing knee.

"Hamilton," Dr. Conway's soft voice soothes, "Liberty is a healthy girl on target in every area we observed today. Often hyperlexic children shy away from peers. They prefer interacting with adults over playing with children. Liberty quickly introduced herself to the two children in the playroom. She picked up toys and joined right in, even with adults still in the room. We also assessed her motor skills. Many times gifted or advanced children exhibit slower physical abilities than peers. Liberty did not display this. Physically, she is on track if not a bit more coordinated than her peers. Perhaps this is hereditary as her father is a talented athlete."

I find myself biting my lips again as the doctor's cheeks pink when Hamilton's crooked smile dazzles her. *My man is quite the charmer.*

"It's clear the two of you challenge her both physically and intellectually." Dr. Conway glances at the notes in front of her before continuing. "I don't like to label children, especially those under the age of seven. When you go home and look up hyperlexia on the internet, you will see the terms advanced, gifted, talented, savant, Mensa, and many others. You will read about IQ levels and their meanings. Labels tend to place children on one targeted path rather than allow them to just be kids. It's important to expose children to normal childhood activities, even if they show a propensity to excel in an area. In the past, some of my patient's families opted to begin testing the child immediately. Often, these children are then guided down one narrow path based on one facet of their abilities instead of allowing others to further develop. As Liberty enters kindergarten, it will be important to discuss her abilities with educators, but until then, I believe it is important that, while nurturing her talents, we continue to challenge her in a variety of subjects and activities. Well-rounded children become well-rounded adults that thrive in our society."

"So, we should continue to take her to playgroup, tumbling, and swimming lessons while we encourage her to read and ask her questions while doing so?" Hamilton inquires.

"Exactly," Dr. Conway states. "Remember to take notes should any difficulties arise so we might evaluate these situations, but otherwise, raise her like a normal little girl. Her diagnosis of Hyperlexia Type 3 doesn't need to disrupt her normal childhood."

"Would it be possible to get a copy of your notes and diagnosis to share with our nanny?" I ask, wanting Fallon to have everything. With her training, she will understand all of this even more than I do.

"If you'd like, you can sign a form allowing us to share all our records with her now and in the future," Dr. Conway offers. "It's my understanding she's working on her graduate degree in psychology."

I nod.

"I'll have my receptionist get the appropriate signatures." She jots a few notes on the pad in front of her.

"Fallon, our nanny, seemed very excited when I told her we had an appointment with you. Seems you come highly recommended," I share. You never know if Fallon might need Dr. Conway's help furthering her career, so I want to place a seed for future use.

"Taylor speaks highly of Fallon," she informs us. "You hit the nanny jackpot with that one. I would like for Fallon to join you on future office visits. She is an important part of Liberty's daily life and including her will also help Liberty."

As our appointment wraps up, a million thoughts fly through my mind. I want to rush home to scour the internet but know that will only further overwhelm me. I'm sure Hamilton has a million questions, too.

"Let's go find Liberty," the doctor suggests, rising from her office chair and motioning us towards the door.

She points out the observation window through which we see our daughter building a block tower with another girl. A boy sits nearby with a toy truck in his hands.

When we enter the playroom, Liberty immediately glances in our direction. "Mommy, Daddy watch!" She points to the tower of blocks. "Go!"

At her signal, she and the other girl scoot back from the tower as the boy rams his metal truck into its base. Blocks tumble to the carpet below as all three kids cheer. Hamilton and I join the other adults in the room in clapping.

"Libby, it's time to go," Hamilton calls to her.

"Bye," she waves to the children then to the adults. "This was fun."

Hamilton looks to me wide-eyed and surprised by her comment. While we stressed as parents over the doctor's analysis, our little girl had fun. She didn't find the doctor's questions or tasks stressful.

"Let's go home and have more fun with Daddy," I encourage as we each take her little hands in the hallway.

143

HAMILTON

"We're all loaded," I announce from the kitchen island when Liberty and Madison emerge from the restroom. "Are we ready?"

"I'm ready," Liberty states while Madison slips her winter coat over her arms.

"Are you sure you have the dogs' schedule straightened out?" Madison asks, pulling out her Notes app on her cell phone. She scrolls through her massive list for this trip to ensure we aren't forgetting anything.

"Yep. The guys know we are gone and plan to check in on them extra times to keep them from getting bored," I restate for the third time today. "Would you like a water for the road?" I ask as I pull one for me from the refrigerator door. When she nods, I grab her one.

"Okay, let's hit the road," I cheer, motioning for Liberty to lead the way to the elevator.

Now five hours into our nearly seven-hour drive, I long to stop and stretch my legs, but I don't want to wake a napping Liberty. We've stopped once to eat and use the restroom; it's my hope that we can make it the next hour and a half before we must stop again.

"Do you mind if I change the station?" I ask Madison.

She's typing away on her laptop, so I assume she won't mind if I turn it to country music. Singing along with my favorite songs will help to take my mind off of my squirming legs and tight back. I don't mind her pop music and rock stations, but for this last leg of the trip, I need to hear Luke Bryan, Blake Shelton, Luke Combs, Jason Aldean, and maybe a little Carrie Underwood. The first station I scan to is just what I'm looking for.

While Madison dives deeper into her writing, my mind sings along as we head down the interstate. They're expecting snow later tonight, but so far, Mother Nature gifts us with clear roads.

The music worked. I gently nudge Madison in the passenger seat, alerting her we have arrived. She places her closed laptop on the floorboard before stretching her arms above her head and her legs out in front of her. I force myself to keep my eyes on the city streets when all I want is to knead my hands into her muscles and help her relieve the tension.

"Sorry, I fell asleep," her raspy voice croaks before she takes a sip of her water. Looking out the front window, it dawns on her where we are. "We're here!"

She bounces in her seat like a red, rubber ball. Christmas is her favorite holiday and spending it with family is her new favorite tradition. I love that after so many years, she's surrounded by friends and family at all times.

"Liberty," she calls into the back seat while tugging on her little arm. "Liberty, we're here."

I see a bit of movement from her car seat in the rear-view mirror and the sound of clapping fills the air.

As soon as the SUV parks, Liberty announces she needs to potty at the top of her lungs. Maybe I should have stopped an hour ago. I hope she can make it past everyone inside before she has an accident.

"I'll carry her in real quick while you say hello to everyone," I offer. "Then, she can come back out and say her hellos."

Madison nods as we step from the vehicle. Cameron, Taylor, and Trenton swarm us to assist with unloading.

"Cameron, potty!" Liberty demands.

"I've got her," Cameron states, briskly crossing the porch with Liberty in hand.

I rub my hand down my face as I slowly shut the bedroom door behind me. Madison's sleepy eyes greet me from her former bed. I tug my t-shirt off over my head. When my eyes reconnect with hers, I find the laziness replaced with desire. I can't help myself. My shoulders straighten and my abdominals tighten. Subconsciously, my body reacts to her need, her want, and her invitation.

As I approach the bed, she extends her right hand. Fingers entwined with mine, she pulls me next to her as she slides to the other side of the bed.

"What a mess," she murmurs. "I've never seen so many presents in all my life."

"We went a little overboard," I confess.

"I think they all did," she laughs. "We'll need to set limits for next year."

It was worth it to see the excitement on Liberty's little face. Her eyes danced while inspecting each new gift-wrapped box in front of her. She delighted in the possibilities hidden in each. At first, she tried to neatly pull the paper from the gifts, then Trenton's sons demonstrated the fastest way to rip the paper from the boxes. She giggled and cheered as the scraps of paper piled up and new toys, books, and clothes stacked around her.

"She was fun to watch," Madison states, reading my mind.

"That she was. Mom and Amy seemed to have a good time, too," I add.

Madison nods, a wide smile slipping upon her lips. She's up to something–I squint my eyes at her.

"I have one more gift for you," Madison whispers.

"Oh, you do, do you?" I growl, positioning myself in a plank position over her.

She bobs her head up and down while biting her lower lip, eyes looking up at me through her lashes. My hands slip under the hem of her t-shirt, tickling the skin near her navel.

"As of tonight," she pauses her whisper, hoping for a dramatic effect, "we are officially baby-making."

Giggles escape from her as I swiftly free her from her sleep shorts and t-shirt. I'm a man on a mission.

TAILGATES & TWISTS OF FATE

The Locals #4

144

MADISON

I slowly close my laptop after saving my newest writing. Five more chapters. I've been a busy girl this morning—I smile to myself. As I open my office door, I find Miss Alba buzzing around the kitchen, the scent of fresh baked cookies in the air.

"You're alive," she greets as I snag water from the refrigerator. "Fallon and Liberty should be back from playtime soon. Are you ready for lunch?" She places the hot pan of chocolate chip cookies on a cooling rack before looking to me.

"I'll wait for them. Have you seen my cell phone?" I scan the counters and tabletops.

Miss Alba smiles, pointing toward my bedroom.

I find I left my phone on my nightstand when I climbed out of bed this morning. I am so involved in the new book world I've created that I can't wait to start writing each morning. I swipe my thumb across the screen, bringing it to life as I walk into my bathroom. I freeze at the vanity. I have five missed calls and two texts from Savannah with no voice messages and a text from Hamilton wishing me good luck with my writing.

SAVANNAH

where are u

I press the buttons to connect with Savannah. "Hi. Sorry," I greet when she answers. "What's up?"

Silence. I glance at my phone screen to ensure the call is connected.

"Savannah, you're scaring me," I admit.

"I'm freaked out myself," she murmurs so low I can barely hear her.

"Talk to me. How can I help?" I cringe at the fear in my own voice.

"I screwed up," she sobs. "I'm such a freaking idiot. I did the one thing I swore I would never do."

"Sav, I'm sure it's not as bad as it seems," I soothe. "But, I need all the details if I'm going to help."

"I'm pregnant." Her voice is flat. She's been sobbing. She sounds defeated.

I freeze. "How sure are you?"

Her voice raises an octave. "What do you mean, 'How sure are you?' Pregnant. It doesn't get more real than that."

I shake my head. "Have you taken a pregnancy test, or are you just a few days late?"

"I've got four positive pregnancy tests on the counter in front of me," she yells.

Well, that's pregnant. My mind quickly jumps to the first weekend in December, her first date with Lincoln, five weeks ago. Although I no longer live in Athens, I'm pretty sure I'd know if she had been with anyone else.

"Madison," she whispers, "what do I do?"

"Oh, honey, it's going to be alright," I promise.

"I need you here." Her words slice through me.

In my mind, my calendar for the rest of the week and the weekend flashes. I could drive to Athens; there's nothing pressing keeping me in Chicago.

"Let me check in with Hamilton, then I'll call you back," I promise.

"I love you," Hamilton whispers into my hair as my head presses tight to his chest. "Call or text when you're ready for me to pick you up. And don't worry about us. Liberty will be spoiled by Mom from the moment we arrive at the farm."

His chest vibrates as he chuckles. Part of me doesn't want to let go of him, but I know Savannah needs me. So, I must. Liberty naps in her car seat as I reluctantly pull away from my husband and wave as he pulls from the driveway. When I turn, Savannah opens her front door; she was watching through the window.

"Hey," I call as I approach the house. Immediately, I wrap her in a tight hug. I rub her back as she sobs into my shoulder. I don't interrupt her; I allow Savannah to cry herself out as we stand just inside the closed door.

"So, this is what you experienced the summer before college?" Savannah begins as she plays with the saltines on her paper plate. "I don't know how you kept it to yourself. You did it all with fortitude. I can't imagine doing this with the strength and grace you did, all by myself.

"First of all," I explain, "I was scared to death. I was staying with Memphis at the time, because my mom was entertaining strange men at the house; Hamilton was in Des Moines. I felt like everyone could read the fear on my face. I told myself I had two options: one, go to college and not come back. Or, two, move away and not come back. I knew I would eventually tell Hamilton, and I couldn't return to Athens until he knew about our baby."

Savannah nods. "How did you know you made the right decision? That you could do it on your own?"

I chuckle. "I didn't—I was winging it every step of the way." I take down my hair and run my fingers through it before I secure it in another pony tail. "I was scared to death."

Tears fill her eyes again. "I've become the one person I vowed I'd never emulate." She wipes away the tears on her cheeks. "I can't be like Mom."

"Stop! I won't have that," I order. "First, you didn't hunt Lincoln—he courted you. Second, you didn't deceive him and manipulate him by purposefully getting pregnant to tie him to you. It was an accident, and you aren't going to use your pregnancy to hurt him."

At the sound of a car door shutting, Savannah's hand flies to her chest, her eyes widen, and she peeks out the front window. "It's Lincoln! I can't... I haven't answered his texts or calls." She shakes her head. "There's no way I can speak to him in person."

I rise from my chair. "I'll go talk to him."

Savannah freaks even more.

"I'll keep your secret," I promise as I walk through the front door.

After exchanging greetings, I motion towards his vehicle. "Can we sit in your car?"

Lincoln nods, returning to the driver's door.

"It's just too cold outside," I say as we climb into our seats.

With his hands resting at the top of the steering wheel, Lincoln stares ahead at Savannah's house. "Is she in there?" He sounds depressed.

I nod. "She's going through something major, and it's stirring up ghosts from her past." I attempt to explain Savannah's recent behavior. "When she called, I dropped everything and drove down here to help her for a few days."

Lincoln swivels to face me, his knee in the seat between us. "She could have called me; I would have helped her." Frustrated, he runs both hands through his short hair, locking them together behind his head. "She won't answer my texts or calls. I just don't know what I've done wrong." Lincoln shakes his head, returning his hands to his lap. "I've been spending every weekend with Mom; her chemotherapy makes her very sick and weak. But, I've been texting Savannah often and calling her, too."

"You did nothing wrong." I urge him to hear and believe me. "Savannah needs time to work through this. She's processing it, trying to get her head on straight, and then she'll reach out to you—I promise." I pat his knee. "Please be patient."

Lincoln's concern shows on his face. He really cares for her, and he doesn't understand why she isn't leaning on him in this time of need. It's taking everything for him to refrain from barging into her house. I need to throw him a bone here.

"Let's plan on the four of us eating dinner here tomorrow night. I can't promise she'll be ready to open up by then, but she'll be ready for a distraction and your company."

"Promise me you'll let me know if I can help in any way," Lincoln implores. "And text me what to bring for dinner. I can buy all the groceries—anything she needs."

"Let's exchange phone numbers," I offer, opening my contacts. Once I have his number, I shoot him a text, so he has mine.

On my way back inside the house, I shoot a text to Hamilton.

. . .

ME

I'm gonna stay here tonight

HAMILTON

I'll drop off bag as take Mom to store

ME

(heart emoji)

Savannah and I enjoy an evening like we often shared in high school. We sleep on the living room floor, having enjoyed pizza, breadsticks, and copious amounts of chocolate chip cookie dough before baking cookies and watching several movies.

Sounds of Savannah moving around the house wake me the next morning. "What should we have for breakfast?" she asks from the kitchen, her elbows leaning on the countertop.

I bite my lower lip, my eyes looking to the ceiling as I attempt to diagnose what my stomach's in the mood for.

"I started a pot of coffee," Savannah says.

"Um…" I walk towards her, trying to choose my words wisely. "Pregnant women are encouraged to avoid caffeine." I purse my lips to the side, waiting for her arguments.

"Duh," she says like a petulant teen. "Since I can't drink it, I make it for the smell."

"Hopefully you won't have morning sickness where the smell of coffee roils your stomach," I state. "I'm going to fix toast. Do you want some?"

While I lower two slices into the toaster, I realize I need to talk to her about dinner plans for tonight. We have tons to cover today. "Okay. You've freaked out, you've sobbed for hours, and you've spent a lazy evening avoiding the topic." I glance at my friend, judging how she reacts to my words before continuing. "Now you need to start making decisions. First, an important one: do you plan to carry the baby to term or not?"

My insides tighten as I worry about her answer. I love Savannah and will stand beside her whatever she decides. It's her right to choose, but I hope she wants to have the baby.

A small smile appears on Savannah's lips before she answers, "I'm having the baby. There's no other decision I can live with."

Internally, I cheer. "Next important decision: will you keep the baby or give it up?"

Savannah's lips part, displaying a wide, open-mouth smile. "I love you," she laughs, shaking her head. "You think of everything. When I close my eyes, I see me raising the child." She bumps my hip with hers. "What's next?"

I return her hip bump. "Next decision: are you doing it solo or with Lincoln?" I lock my eyes on hers, hoping to see any hints she may display that her words won't reveal.

"Do you have a list?" Savannah asks through laughter.

As I butter the bread, she sits at the table with a glass of orange juice for each of us. I slide the plate of toast in front of her after I lower my own to brown. I'm famous for my lists; it's no surprise she thinks I prepared for this talk. I tap my temple with my finger as I speak. "The list is up here. Now, stop stalling and answer. We have lots to cover today."

"I can't keep Lincoln from his baby," Savannah confesses. "If he wants to be involved, he will be."

"Wow! Look at you!" I golf-clap in front of me. "You've made so many tough decisions already." I slide into the chair across from her, toast in hand. "And you were worried you couldn't do this on your own."

Shaking her head, her mood drops. "How hard will it be to tell Lincoln?" She squirms a bit in her chair. "Our situation is different from yours with Hamilton, but how hard was it?"

I can tell by her demeanor that she's really worried about this. I can't make light of this topic; she needs honesty and help. "Well, Memphis intervened for me, and I'm glad she did. I went over a million scenarios in my head and still didn't know how to do it."

We sit silently for a few minutes as we eat our toast and wash it down with juice.

"Why don't we cook dinner here tonight? Hamilton and I will join the two of you as a buffer, and you can ease into telling Lincoln," I suggest, feeling a little guilty for planning the dinner yesterday before I talked to her about it.

She doesn't immediately answer. We consume the rest of our breakfast, placing our plates and glasses into the sink. As I rinse the dishes, Savannah leans against the counter nearby.

"Okay, but…" she holds her index finger between us. "We need to practice what I'll say over and over between now and then."

I promise to help her, and she texts to invite Lincoln to dinner as I look over her shoulder.

SAVANNAH

wanna join me for dinner tonight

@ my place with Hamilton and Madison

LINCOLN

yes, what can I bring

SAVANNAH

beer for you guys

LINCOLN

can't wait to see you. I miss you

(heart emoji)

SAVANNAH

5pm

(heart emoji)

145

HAMILTON

I'm haven't been at Savannah's 10 minutes when she claims she needs a guy's perspective. That must be the real reason Madison asked me to arrive an hour before Lincoln. I want to ignore Savannah and bury my nose in ESPN in her living room. She wants me to share how I would have preferred for Madison to tell me about her pregnancy.

This is a heavy topic for pre-dinner conversation. Honestly, I've never contemplated other ways Madison might have told me about the pregnancy. My mind reels with possible scenarios. I come to the conclusion that there was no perfect way in the situation we were in.

Savannah needs input, though, so I answer honestly. "Like a bandage—quick and rip it off. Don't draw it out; just blurt it, so he can react, cope, and then make plans."

Savannah seems to like my answer. Madison mouths "thank you" from beside her. It's clear to see both women are stressed about Lincoln's arrival for dinner. Savannah's situation has to have brought up memories from Madison's pregnancy and our situation. I'm here as a buffer. Lincoln isn't even here, and the atmosphere is too heavy. I need to lighten the mood.

"Did Madison tell you we're trying to conceive?" I ask as I side-hug Savannah.

"What?" Savannah squeals. She jumps up and down when I release her.

"No way!" She turns to face my wife. "We're going to be pregnant at the same time! This is so cool."

There. My job is done. The girls chatter excitedly as they move about the kitchen, setting everything out for dinner while I return to the sofa and ESPN.

Thirty minutes later, I offer to answer the door when Lincoln arrives since the girls are busy in the kitchen. "Come on in." I exaggerate the motion with my arm as I open the door.

"I have gifts." Lincoln raises the two six-packs of beer in his hands.

I resist the urge to encourage him to shotgun two of them in preparation for the dinner conversation. We're not close, however, and I'm unsure how he will react to Savannah's announcement. I pull out two of the cold bottles, placing them on the coffee table before I encourage him to place the rest in the refrigerator; I'm sure he's more comfortable here than I am.

"Can we help with dinner?" I ask after I take a long pull from my beer. "Savannah, I'm sure you're a great cook, but we need to keep an eye on everything Madison touches," I only half tease.

"Be nice!" Savannah swats me with a tea towel. "Madison's making the salad." She raises her eyebrows and bugs her eyes at me. "Everything else goes in one dish in the oven, so there's really nothing else to do."

"Sounds like we're being exiled to the living room," Lincoln states before he kisses Savannah's cheek and walks away with me.

My mind can't focus on the television. Now that Lincoln's here, I'm nervous for them both. Seeing Savannah's life play out in front of me, I can't imagine the turmoil Madison must have faced on her own. She was pregnant and alone, far from her mom, my mom, and all of her friends. I say a prayer of thanks that Alma and her children were placed in Madison's life in her time of need. I should have been there for her. She needed me, and, although I understand the choices she made to allow me to follow my dream and settle into my career, I wish things could have been different.

Lincoln fetches a second beer for the two of us. I watch out of the corner of my eye as he whispers something in Savannah's ear, causing her to blush. It's clear he can't keep his hands off of her, and judging by her reaction, she's just as in to him.

"Can I get you ladies a beer or a glass of wine?" Lincoln inquires.

The three of us glance nervously at each other, worried declining alcohol might tip him off about the pregnancy. I can't think of anything to say to move the conversation away from alcohol.

"Dinner's almost ready, and I think I'd rather have water with it," Madison says without missing a beat.

"That sounds good," Savannah agrees, clearly glad her friend sent her a life line.

"I'll set the table," Lincoln offers without batting an eye at the reason the women are avoiding alcohol.

"I'll help," I state, placing my half-empty beer on the counter. I can't let him outdo me in front of the women.

The two of us joke as we place the plates, silverware, and water glasses on the table. I make a big production of exclaiming over the salad Madison created as I set the large bowl in the center of the round table. Lincoln joins me in examining it, ensuring she didn't ruin it. Madison takes it like a champ; I love that she can take a joke and dish it back, too.

"Take a seat," Savannah directs as she removes the glass dish from the oven.

Madison places a trivet on the table, and Savannah places the hot dish atop it.

"Dinner is served," Savannah announces and plops in a chair beside Madison.

I take the seat across from my wife, and Lincoln sits in the remaining chair across from Savannah. Lincoln offers to say grace, then Madison passes her salad masterpiece to the right. With greens on all four plates, we dig in, and Savannah decides to go for it.

"I'm pregnant," she blurts, fear in her eyes.

Lincoln's lettuce-covered fork freezes mid-air, and a deer-in-the-head-lights-look adorns his face.

"I'm sorry," Savannah murmurs, tears spilling onto her cheeks. Gravity tugs them toward her chin as she bites her lower lip.

Several quiet moments pass before Lincoln wakes from his stupor. "We're pregnant?" He wipes his hands down his face. "Give me a minute," he begs. He looks from me to Madison before locking eyes with Savannah.

She nods, wiping tears away.

"I can see how this could freak you out," he says finally. "I wish you'd have been able to tell me first," he confesses, "but I'm glad you reached out to

Madison for help to process it." He looks to Madison apologetically and shrugs. Looking back to Savannah, he continues, "Please tell me... we're keeping it." His eyes search her face nervously.

Unable to speak, she simply nods.

Lincoln releases the breath he held as he rises from the chair. When he walks past Madison, he pats her shoulder, before squatting beside Savannah. At first, his voice is a whisper, but his volume increases the longer he speaks. "I want to be involved in the pregnancy and after. I'll be as involved as you'll let me. I'd like to marry you, but I understand it's no longer the norm to get married in our situation." He shrugs, purses his lips, then continues. "I'm a little old-fashioned on this one. I'd like to marry you," he raises his hands to halt Savannah's reply, "not because you're a woman or weak, but because I love everything about you. I forced myself to only come into the store for doughnuts three days a week, so I wouldn't seem to be stalking you. I've enjoyed every minute we've spent together, all our texts, and our long evening phone conversations. It's killed me not to spend every waking hour away from work with you. You're a strong woman, and I understand your need for space and to make your own decisions. I respect and love that about you." He pulls out his cell phone, swipes through a few pics until he finds the one he's looking for, then shows it to Savannah. She gasps, her hand flying to her lips. "I planned to give this to you on Valentine's Day; it's in my sock drawer right now." He draws in a long breath before asking, "Will you marry me?"

I stare wide-eyed and open-mouthed across the table at Madison.

"Wait!" Savannah freaks out. "What?" Her eyes ping pong from the cell phone screen to Lincoln and back. "You bought me an engagement ring already?"

Lincoln timidly answers, "Yes."

Looking to Madison, Savannah asks, "Did you..."

Madison interrupts, "I swear I didn't tell him yesterday." She crosses her heart.

"I bought it two weeks ago with Mom in Kansas City," Lincoln informs. "Her cancer diagnosis proves life is unpredictably short. I figured we'd be engaged for a year or so, but yes, I planned to propose to you on Valentine's Day." He bites his lower lip in anticipation.

"Yes!" Savannah jumps from her seat. "Yes, I will marry you!" She wraps her arms around Lincoln's neck, peppering kisses on both cheeks.

I've never witnessed this behavior from her. Savannah's our withdrawn friend. She rarely shows emotion and never acts like the girly-girl that stands before me.

"This isn't the pregnancy hormones talking?" Lincoln teases.

Savannah swats the back of his head.

"Too soon?" Lincoln laughs.

The three of us nod, grinning.

I enjoy dinner with our friends after that. Once we help rid up the dishes and load the dishwasher, Madison and I escape, leaving the couple to talk, plan, and celebrate.

Our task complete in Athens, we plan to head home tomorrow.

146

MADISON

Boy, when they called it the Windy City, they were not exaggerating. I make sure my coat is zipped, my hat is on securely, my gloves are in place, and my scarf covers any exposed neck while I mentally prepare myself for the walk from my vehicle into the store. On the count of three. One. Two. Three.

It takes all my strength to push the car door open against the wintery gale. I glance at the pavement; there's no ice, so I set one foot then the other down. I toss my purse strap over my shoulder, lower my head, and push toward the doors.

I could have stayed home—I should have stayed home. No one in their right mind runs to the grocery store for chocolate in weather like this. I tried to tell myself that Miss Alba could get it tomorrow during her bi-weekly grocery run, but my cravings grew greater as yesterday passed—I woke this morning jonesing so bad that I had to venture out.

I don't remove my layers inside the store. I quickly grab two bags of fun-size candy bars from the candy aisle and a large sea salt and milk chocolate bar near the register. Pleased with my pillaging, I extend my debit card in my glove-covered hand then scurry back out into the cold.

The light-weight plastic bag billows loudly in the wind. Just over halfway toward my parking spot, the gale picks up. My hat flies from my head. I try to snag it with my free hand as it begins to fly away. Not paying attention to the ground, I slip on a patch of ice and fall to the pavement with my feet in the air; my right shoulder takes the brunt of the impact.

"Fuck!" I shout at the pain radiating from my shoulder up my spine to my head and neck.

I lay motionless on the cold concrete, assessing the extent of my injuries. I turn my head side to side, and, although it hurts, I'm able to move it. The same goes for my arms, so I slowly sit up, look around to see that no one witnessed my fall, then stand. I curse at the minuscule patch of ice then trudge on to my nearby car.

When I attempt to pull the driver's door open, my right arm and shoulder protest. I messed them up good. Once I'm safe inside with the heater blasting, I remind myself I have lots of chocolate in my possession. Chocolate will make it all better.

On the short, four block drive, I find my neck tight and it difficult to turn my head. I do my best, utilizing the driver-assist mirrors and blind spot detectors to maneuver my way safely back home. I find it hard to extricate myself from the SUV in our parking garage. Every movement seems to jar my spine, shoulder, and neck. The pain is now a constant that worsens with any movement. The final steps from the elevator to my front door seem to take light years, but I make it safely inside with my chocolate treasures in hand.

"Oh, dear!" Miss Alba waddles over at the mere sight of me. "What happened?"

I blow the hair from my cheek, trying not to move my arm to do so. "The wind... ice patch..." Every breath in and out causes pain.

She snags my chocolate, placing it on the nearby counter. I attempt to protest but she shushes me. She tugs off my gloves, letting them fall to the hardwood floor and unzips my coat.

"Easy," she warns as she tries to slide the sleeves down my arms without me moving. "Where does it hurt?"

"Everywhere," I whine.

Coat in her hand, she stares expectantly.

"My shoulder, back, neck, head, and arm," I inform while inwardly berating myself for braving the weather for a stupid bar of chocolate.

"I'll run you a bath," she states. "Should I call Hamilton? Do you think you need a doctor?"

The look in her eye dares me to lie to her; it feels like she's scanning my tissues and bones, like she's able to know the extent of my injuries. I want to lay down. I need some pain relievers. The thought of bundling up to go see a physician brings tears to my eyes—tears that Miss Alba immediately spots.

"Let's soak you in a warm tub, take some acetaminophen, then see how you're doing," she says, guiding me down the long hallway toward my bathroom.

"Mommy!" Liberty yells as I pass by her open bedroom door.

"Libby, Mommy needs to lie down." Miss Alba's firm voice stops Liberty in her tracks. "Fallon, can you help us for a moment?"

I'm leaned against the vanity while Miss Alba fixes my bath water, and Fallon helps me slip out of my clothes. Two pills and a glass of water are handed to me. In my pain, I don't even think to protest and try to undress myself. They guide me into the warm water, easing me down until my head rests on a towel upon the edge.

"Thank you," I murmur.

Liberty's voice grows louder as she walks into my bedroom. "Miss Alba put her in bath. She's crying."

"Liberty!" Fallon scolds. "Give me the iPad."

I hear rustling before opening my eyes to find Hamilton on the screen Fallon holds in front of me.

"I'm on my way," he states frantically. "What happened?"

"I fell, but I'm okay…" I want to protest his coming home, but the Face-Time call disconnects as he enters his truck. "Guess Hamilton will be here soon," I say dryly.

I want to be upset that Liberty called Hamilton after we've repeatedly discussed she's not to make calls without an adult's help, but I desperately want him home with me.

"Hamilton just sent me a text," Fallon informs me. "He's asked Slater to drop by on his way home in an hour to look you over." She chuckles. "I should have thought of that."

I don't fault her. The thought of contacting her fiancé to come assess my injuries didn't cross my mind either.

I melt in the warmth of the tub, not moving, willing my pain to evaporate before my husband arrives home.

Hamilton

I can't get to Madison fast enough. I will the elevator to climb faster. I sprint through the house toward the bathtub. Indie and McGee bark loudly at my chaotic actions. Miss Alba shushes them away with her apron, leaving me alone standing over my wife.

Slowly, Madison opens her eyes. "Hey," she whispers.

I crouch at the edge of the tub. "Hey," I whisper as I softly brush hair from her forehead. "What can I do?"

She shakes her head, freezing with a groan when it causes pain. "I fell. That's all. I'll have a bruise, but I will be fine."

"I feel so helpless," I murmur.

"It's a silly accident; these things happen. Liberty's gonna get hurt, I'm gonna get hurt, and…" her eyes dart around the bathroom. "There's no wood, so I can't continue my statement."

I love the smile that slides on her face. It gives me hope that her injuries aren't too bad if she can still smile. My girls are my world; today, I realized that I can't protect them from everything. I try to be all they need, give them everything, and prevent anything that might hurt them. Today, I'm reminded I'm mortal and unable to protect them 100 percent.

"Want some wine?" I ask, my hand playing with a tendril of her hair. "It might relax your muscles."

"I guess," she whispers, closing her eyes.

Slater digs his thumbs into the area directly below Madison's shoulder blade. A garbled groan escapes her, further solidifying the pit in my stomach. He's adjusted her neck, shoulder, back, and hips, claiming the fall messed with all of her alignment.

"I'm done torturing you." He pats the bed beside her. "I don't think anything is broken; you'll be bruised, though. The adjustment will help, but it will make you sore, too." He looks from Madison to me. "Alternate hot and cold packs to the shoulder area, take pain relievers, and give it four or five days. If the pain isn't easing by then, I'd see a doctor for x-rays. I think you will see improvement in a couple of days."

"Thank you," Madison mumbles into the mattress.

She hasn't moved since he stopped working on her muscles. Her eyes are hooded; maybe she needs a nap.

"I'll walk you out." I motion for Slater to head to the hall. "She insists she doesn't need a doctor. I'm glad you came by."

"Calmed your nerves, didn't I?" He smiles, patting my back.

147

MADISON

Days later, walking to our bathroom, I glance at our calendar for the day. Fallon and Liberty are out most of the day, and Miss Alba will be shopping this morning.

ME

it's go time

(baby emoji)

(heart emoji)

There. That should do it. I better hop in the shower in case Hamilton decides to come home early. With steam enveloping me and hot water pelting my skin, I remind myself not to stress over conceiving. Hamilton says it has to happen this month since he flies to Arizona during my next month's ovulation window. He takes his baby making very seriously. I prefer to adopt the motto that it will happen when it's supposed to and not before. Besides, stress impedes the conception process.

I'm not a morning person, but it's easier to get up and around on days my temperature spikes. While sex with Hamilton always rocks, during the ovulation window, we mate like bunnies, and I can't help but be perky.

I'll miss this come next month. Too soon, Hamilton will be in Mesa, Arizona, for spring training while Liberty and I remain in Chicago. I'm getting the hang of this big city life but have no desire to be a single mom in this city. I mean, I'm not alone; I'll have Fallon and Miss Alba to help me through the week. Delta promises that she'll help me cope with this part of Hamilton's career. After six years, she claims to be a baseball-widow pro.

It's just that Hamilton was a staple in my life for five years, and I've become accustomed to him in my everyday life again since October. I like the person I am with him nearby. I love the family life we've created here in our new home. I worry more for Liberty than I do myself.

Hamilton

I end my work out the moment Madison's text arrives. With three days of constant sex when she ovulates, I'm the luckiest man alive. Our regular sex life is out of this world; baby-making time elevates it to out of this universe. My wife is hot, and her libido matches mine perfectly.

As I ride the elevator from the gym back to our place, I send a couple of texts.

ME

please take the day off we want the place to ourselves today

MISS ALBA

I'll shop tomorrow then

ME

thanks

MISS ALBA

I'll say a prayer for the 2 of you

I love that Madison feels close enough to Miss Alba to talk to her about us trying to conceive. Next, I need to alert Fallon and Liberty.

ME

please text before returning from class

If no reply–give us more time before coming home

FALLON

we'll hang at my place today

ME

that's great

thanks

FALLON

I'll text you before dinner

ME

thanks for understanding

Madison, standing near the kitchen island in one of my t-shirts, nibbles on fresh fruit as I close the front door. The animal side of me surfaces at the sight. I don't hesitate to approach her, and, thrusting my pelvis against her backside, I growl and nip the exposed area between her neck and shoulder.

She doesn't squeal or pull away; instead, her butt grinds against my rock-hard cock as her head falls back against my chest.

While my mouth nips and sucks on her neck, my hands deftly slide the hem of my shirt over her hips, finding her bare beneath. I growl in approval. With one hand, I lower my workout shorts while my other teases her entrance. Her hot, wet folds further flame my desire. With my palm between her shoulders, I press her towards the counter before my hands grab her hips, pulling her butt to me. Sliding my cock through her folds, my need to be inside her cannot be delayed. I bury myself, balls deep, in one powerful thrust. I growl as her inner muscles grasp my shaft in damp heat. I don't move for fear the sensation might catapult me over the edge.

My jaw tightens when Madison's hips grind in a circle, seeking friction from my movements. My fingertips bite into her hips as I try to summon the strength not to blow my load.

"Ham, please," she pleads, continuing her grinding.

Sweat beads upon my brow as I slowly withdraw before plunging deep inside her. Knowing I won't last long, I seek to speed Madison's climax. Using the pad of my thumb, I assault her swollen bud.

With her palms flat on the granite island, her head flies back, her face toward the heavens. "Y-e-s," she moans as I continue my devilish massage on her clit while unable to control my animalistic need to thrust toward my climax.

"Yes, yes…" Madison screams. "Hamilton!" She falls into bliss, and I allow myself to follow.

The contractions of her orgasm milk every last drop from me. I shudder, and my knees wobble as her body massages mine.

She slowly slides herself off my cock. With hooded eyes, she grins slyly up at me. "Welcome home, honey," she teases.

I playfully swat her bare behind, evoking a squeal from her.

"Finish your breakfast. I'll go run us a bath," I say, pulling up my shorts.

"Um, what about Liberty, Fallon, and Miss Alba?" she asks, wide-eyed.

"I've texted everyone," I smirk. "We have the place to ourselves until dinner." I brag, proud of my planning.

Madison's wide smile warms my soul. She clearly approves of my foresight.

A little groan escapes as I stretch my arms over my head. I find Madison remains asleep beside me. Glancing at the clock, I realize we've slept an hour and a half. Our kitchen sex, followed by a long, erotic soak in the bubbles, clearly wore the two of us out.

My stomach tightens as the weight of our situation sets in again. It has to happen now. The next time she ovulates, I'll be at spring training. I'm sure we can slip away a time or two, but we won't have non-stop access to each other. While I tease that it only takes once to knock her up, I realize it's a numbers game. The more times we have sex during her ovulation window the better our chances.

Should she get pregnant in February, I won't be around when she finds out. In a perfect world, we'd conceive during this three-day period and learn we are pregnant before I leave on February 15th. We'd have a week to celebrate together and plan.

I'll need to speak to Fallon, Miss Alba, and Delta before I leave for Mesa. Pregnant or not, both she and Liberty will need their support.

I make a mental note to plan a dinner with a couple of my married teammates for ideas for the upcoming spring training and season. I'll need to learn the ins and outs of wives and kids visiting and me sneaking home for a day or two. They'll be able to tell me what works and what doesn't. The more prepared we are the better it will be.

My cock twitches at the gorgeous sight of my wife sprawled out beside me. As all blood leaves my brain flowing southward, I decide I should wake her up, carry her to the shower, and take my time washing every inch of her. If she sleeps much more, she'll struggle at bedtime. Besides, Liberty will come home in an hour.

148

MADISON

"While you're up," I call to Hamilton in the kitchen, "can you bring me a water?"

Returning from the bathroom, he diverts to the kitchen. When I hear the refrigerator door, I rise from the sofa, seeking a better vantage point for his reaction. Turning from the fridge, he smiles at me from the island.

"If I was getting your water, why did you get up?" He tilts his head to the side.

I furrow my brow and point. "What did you put in the oven?"

"Nothing," Hamilton states without looking in that direction.

"But the oven light is on," I point, insisting he look.

With one hand planted on the island, he leans towards the oven. When he notices the light is indeed on, he moves to open the door. "It's a bag of buns..." He keeps his back to me as he pulls them out. "The light is on, but the oven isn't on." He turns to face me, confusion upon his face.

"Why did you put the buns in the oven?" I play with him.

"I didn't," he states adamantly. "Do you think Miss Alba did it by accident?"

I can't have him placing the blame on her. "No, I've been in the kitchen several times this afternoon, and it wasn't on." I fake anger toward him. "You did it."

"I didn't!" He waves his hands in front of his chest while imploring me to believe him. "Who would put buns in the oven?"

"A bun in the oven..." I allow my voice to trail off.

"More than one bun in the oven," Hamilton corrects, his voice rising. "I didn't put the buns in the oven."

"Yes, you did," I state, placing my hands on either side of my navel, trying to get the message across.

Hamilton starts to argue. But, when he sees my hands, he freezes. Behind his wide eyes, I sense his mind reeling.

"We have a bun in the oven," I giggle nervously, patting my flat belly.

Hamilton stumbles back against the counter next to the stove. His face pales and his eyes are still wide as saucers. He grips the counter on either side of him, his knuckles turning white.

"We..." he scrubs his brow. "You're..." his voice trails off as he stares at my abdomen.

"We," I state, running into the kitchen to pull his right hand toward my belly, "are pregnant!"

His left hand quickly joins his right, splayed wide on my stomach. "Pregnant?" He whispers, not meeting my eyes. He's enamored with our tiny peanut deep inside of me.

Several moments pass while I wait for him to process our new condition. Eventually, his head turns up. Slowly, he cups my cheeks, eyes locked on mine.

"We're pregnant," he murmurs huskily. "You're carrying my baby. That's so..." He grabs my hand, tugging me to follow him toward our bedroom. "Sexy."

With his hand at each hip, he gently lifts me to sit at the end of our bed. Briskly, he locks our door, turns the baby monitor on and volume down, flips the lights off, and returns to stand in front of me. I scoot backwards into the middle of the bed as his heavy-lidded eyes devour me in the muted light from the nightlight in our bathroom.

My insides heat under his gaze. Unable to endure the anticipation, I seek to speed his seduction by removing my shirt and then my sleep shorts. When I tuck my thumbs in the band of my panties, Hamilton orders me to stop.

Goosebumps prickle my skin at his stern voice. He's never been an alpha in the bedroom, and I'm surprised I like it. I feel my breasts grow heavy in their red lace cages. Between my thighs, I feel my wetness as my body seeks his touch.

Through my parted lips, I beg in a whisper, "Please." I need him; I long for his body pressed against mine. I seek the friction only he can provide. I raise one hand, my fingers curling in a come-here motion.

His lips in a sexy smirk, he makes a production of slowly grasping the hem of his t-shirt and easing it up inch by inch. My eyes follow the trail of hair below his navel until it disappears under the low waistband of his sweats. I wet my lips as my thoughts imagine tugging off his pants to find his swollen cock. I would wrap my fingers around the base and as I squeeze, I'd stroke his length, gently swiping my thumb across his soft head then stroke back to the base. My tongue darts out again as I imagine a glistening drop of pre-cum and long to lap it up.

"Madison," Hamilton's voice is a low, guttural growl in warning.

I scold myself to remain in the present. His thumbs slip under the elastic waist of the sweats and slowly slide them down his hips. His rigid cock pops out, pointing in my direction. I slide myself toward him, but he orders me to stop. A squeak escapes my throat. I want to defy him. I need to touch him now.

With a mind of its own, my right hand leaves the comforter and slips over my navel, then under my red, lace panties. I whimper at the sensation of my fingers grazing my sensitive bundle of nerves, and Hamilton's darkening eyes as they witness my actions.

In record time, his sweats are sailing through the air towards the closet, and my husband crouches, his hands on either side of my calves. It's clear he's about to pounce, and my body sparks in anticipation.

I slide one finger inside, causing my head to fall back. Slowly, I glide it in and out, my palm causing a slight friction over my clit with the movement.

With eyes closed and head thrown back, the warm wetness of his tongue upon my inner thigh draws a groan from my chest. His nose and warm breath followed by soft kisses ignite a fire in my core as they approach my center. While I continue fingering myself, I feel his heated breath against my damp panties. Yes! Yes! Yes! Please, I want your mouth, your tongue, your lips down there. I need your mouth, now.

I freeze my ministrations when his long fingers slide my panties down my thighs. His breath caresses my hot flesh and wet lips. I lift my head, opening my eyes to take in the majestic view of my husband's head between my thighs. Grinning at me, he moves his gaze to my center and places his fingers around my slick index finger. He urges me to withdraw and slide back in. Over and over he assists me in my masturbation.

I groan in protest when he pulls my finger free, raising it to his mouth. His lips clench tightly as he sucks my wetness from the length of my finger. He nibbles the tip of my finger, his eyes locked on mine. Frozen in his trance, I don't react as he slips one finger through my wetness then inside me. My eyes close as a second finger joins the first, my muscles stretching around him.

"Y-E-S," I moan when his tongue presses firmly upon my clit as his two fingers curl to stroke me. "I'm… Ham… I…"

I can't speak; I can barely breathe. I'm a tightly wound coil about to release. My pelvis lifts, pressing into his hand and mouth. I grind myself against him. He suckles my clit, and I explode. My back arches, my breasts swell, and my orgasm splinters me into a million pieces.

Hamilton

Madison's inner walls greedily constrict in spasms around my fingers. I gently stroke her again which causes her body to twitch. All her muscles flex as wave after wave of her orgasm flows through her. She sinks into the mattress as her body turns to mush. Her eyes are closed, her lips parted, and her hand slowly caresses her shoulder, between her breasts, then back.

I slowly withdraw my fingers and crawl up her languid torso, placing kisses upon her skin. She arches into me as my lips close around her hardened nipple. As she moans in pleasure, I release it, blowing my hot breath over the wet peak. I repeat my actions on the other breast, coaxing more moans from her.

Internally, I fight my need to bury myself deep inside her. I want to make slow, sweet love to her. I rationalize that we've got all night as I rub my rock-hard cock through her wet, heated folds. Her gentle pelvic push toward me informs me she seeks me like I need her right now. Leaning on one forearm, I look deep in her eyes as I position my head at her entrance.

A wicked gleam in her eyes, she digs her nails into my ass cheeks, urging me to enter. Not one to deny her anything, I slam deep in one thrust, eliciting a throaty groan from Madison.

149

MADISON

I'm in ecstasy. Hamilton's buried deep within me as my muscles stretch to accommodate his length and girth. I love the fullness. I feel complete. I relax my grip on his butt, ready for him to move. When he remains motionless, I lift my head, searching his face.

Hamilton's eyes are closed tight, his brow beads with sweat while his jaw clenches tight as his shoulders and arms strain.

"Ham, what's wrong?" Fear floods my brain, worried he's hurt himself.

He merely shakes his head, not opening his eyes.

"Hamilton," I plead. "Look at me."

Slowly, his lids raise, revealing fear. I lift my hands to his jaws, rubbing my thumbs back and forth.

"What's wrong?"

Again, he shakes his head, rolling off of me. I dig my heels into his glutes, hugging him tight as he rolls to his back. I smile proudly at my success in the maneuver. Hamilton caresses my cheek with his left hand while his right plants on my hip.

"I..." his voice cracks. "I don't want to hurt you."

"You aren't hurting me," I reply, pressing my palms against his pecs, preparing to grind my pelvis into him.

His free hand flies to my other hip, preventing my movement. "I don't want to hurt the baby," he whispers, his eyes pleading with me.

I move my hands to his face; my eyes implore him to hear me. "You won't hurt the baby. Honey, sex is safe for the entire pregnancy." I lower my mouth to his. "I promise."

I pepper his lips with kisses, hoping he will engage with me. I slide my tongue along his lower lip and breathe a sigh of relief when he allows me entrance. I coax his tongue to mingle with mine as I try to assure him it's safe. I lay my forehead on his as I gasp for breath. My eyes search his for under-standing. I push my luck, grinding slowly against him. Pain and fear return to his eyes, so I stop.

"To hurt the baby, you have to hurt me," I explain gently. "When you make love to me, you don't hurt me. So, you won't hurt the baby." I try not to sound condescending. I remember how nervous I was during my entire preg-nancy with Liberty. Our eyes lock, I wait for his understanding.

I lift a bit then slide back down his still rock-hard cock. His eyelids droop, and his lips part. I repeat my movement, raising another inch then impale myself once again. When he doesn't beg me to stop, I grind into his pelvis. I allow my head to fall back as the friction stimulates my swollen clit.

I lift, fall, and grind myself over and over as my fingertips dig into his chest to anchor me. Emboldened by Hamilton allowing me to take charge, I lift my left leg over his torso to join my right. He lifts his head, interested in my intentions. I wave playfully over my shoulder as I slowly continue to spin. Once my legs position on either side of his hips, I raise and lower myself, allowing our connection to adapt to the new angles of our bodies. I place my palms above his knees as I rock forward then back. I gradually pick up speed as I repeat the motion. In my new position, tilted forward at this angle, my clit rubs against his balls on my downward thrusts. With each tantalizing graze, I move closer to my quickly approaching orgasm.

Not wanting to leave him hanging, I decide to speed up his release, too. I scrape my nails lightly up the inside of his thighs, eliciting a low growl. Still riding his cock, I grasp his thigh with one hand, lightly tickling his balls with my other. At his intake of breath, I have him right where I hoped. I grind myself repeatedly into his pelvis, rubbing my bud against him. I lightly tug on the hair on his sack.

In the blink of an eye, he ab curls to a sitting position. One hand cups my breast while the other strokes then flicks my over-sensitized clit. "Cum," he growls, pressing the pad of his thumb in a tight circle.

My body obeys, every muscle in my body heats, my core clenches, and I fall over the edge. White light flickers behind my eyelids. Tremors shake my thighs and abdomen, prolonging my orgasm as Hamilton, hands on my hips, glides me slowly up and down his shaft.

Hamilton

Madison's gentle tugs and caresses of my balls spark a fire at the base of my spine. I feel my impending release, and I need her to cum before I do. My cock, like Vesuvius about to erupt, I bolt upright. With one hand, I pinch and pull at her nipple. With the other, I carry out a full-on assault of her clit. At my command, she cums.

As her orgasm begins, I rock her up then down. Her inner walls spasm, taking every drop I have to give. I feel her body turn limp and lift her from me, laying her at my side. I curl into her, placing kisses upon her exposed neck. She mews at my touch, melting into me with a contented sigh.

"I love you," I whisper.

"We're having a baby," she giggles, clutching my forearm on her stomach.

Releasing her, I guide her onto her back. Slowly, I slide down her torso and place my hand upon her stomach.

"Right now, there's a tiny human growing in here!" My voice drips with excitement.

Madison tucks a second pillow under her head, allowing her eyes to meet mine. She smiles wildly at my statement.

I move my mouth near her navel. "Hello in there. I'm your daddy."

Madison attempts to cover her giggles at my conversation with our new little one. It may look stupid, but I don't care. We're having a baby, and I'm going to be an involved daddy every step of the way this time.

"What?" I place my ear against her. "Yes, she is the best mommy. She'll take very good care of you." I kiss her belly before continuing. "And I'll be doing everything I can to take care of her while she takes care of you. If you have any special requests, let us know."

Her giggles morph into a full body laugh, jiggling her stomach.

"Hold on in there," I call through my hands which form a circle at my mouth. "Madison, you're creating an earthquake. Contain yourself."

I place my ear against her tummy again, pretending to listen to our newest family member.

"Get up here," Madison demands as she tries to catch her breath from laughing.

150

MADISON

"Did you learn about that position in one of those romance books you like to read?" Hamilton murmurs with a boyish grin.

"Maybe," I tease. "It's called reverse cowgirl."

"You should give that author a good review," he chuckles into my neck.

"I already wrote an awesome review," I inform him. "I don't think other readers want to read about my sexual experimentation."

"I don't know...it might sell a lot more books." Hamilton slips out of bed and pulls on running pants.

"Where are you going?" I pout with my lower lip protruding.

"I'm going to check on Libby and get you something to drink," he states, tossing my t-shirt into my face.

When he opens the bedroom door, Indie and McGee are lying on the floor just outside. They run to Liberty's room. Hamilton continues to the kitchen as I slip on my night clothes. I turn the volume up on the baby monitor at my bedside table.

"I go potty," Liberty's voice states over the monitor.

I make my way into her room. She's in the bathroom, talking to the two dogs. It's so cute how she talks to them all the time. I lean on the door frame. "Hey," I greet.

She smiles sleepily back at me. Finished with her business, she washes her hands without singing a song and slides back into bed. I slip under the covers next to her, running my fingers through the curls framing her face.

"I love you," I whisper.

Hamilton

With water in hand, I peek into Liberty's room to ensure she climbed back into bed. I beam at the sight of my two girls sleeping. I can't believe Madison fell asleep that quickly.

I snap a photo, unable to let this moment pass. Madison's head is on Libby's pillow and the comforter over her, Liberty's hand resting in hers between them on the mattress.

Walking back into our room, I decide that I can't sleep by myself tonight. Far too soon, I'll be on the road, sleeping alone in hotel beds. I snag my pillow and wrangle our comforter from our bed. On Liberty's floor, I create a makeshift sleeping bag with the comforter. I toss and turn for far too long before I head to Madison's office for a book she had mentioned when we first spoke about trying to have another baby.

I scan five shelves before I spot it. According to Madison, it's the holy grail of information on pregnancy. Wrapped in the blanket, head on the pillow, I fidget a bit to find comfort on the floor. I open to the first chapter and read.

Madison

My eyes flutter open to the sounds of Liberty's muffled giggles. "Shh," she orders behind her index finger. I follow as she rolls over and points to the floor next to her bed.

I don't believe my eyes. Hamilton is sleeping on his back with a pregnancy book resting open on his chest.

Liberty rolls back to me, hand on mouth, to hide her giggles.

"Mommy fell asleep with you," I whisper. "I bed Daddy was lonely."

My daughter nods, her springy, dark curls bounce in every direction.

"Who's making so much noise?" Hamilton growls before chomping at Liberty's neck like a monster.

Her melodic giggles fill the air as Hamilton tickles her ribs, stomach, and feet.

"D-a-d-d-y!" She struggles to speak through her laughter.

"Daddy what?" Hamilton asks, grinning.

"D-a-d-d-y, s-t-o-p!" she spits out.

"Stop what?" He teases, resting his hands on the mattress beside her.

"Stop tickling me," she orders, as her hands rest on his cheeks. Serious for the moment, she peers into his eyes, while holding him still. "Why you read baby book?" One little hand moves from his cheek to point at his book on the floor.

Hamilton's worried eyes dart to mine for clues on how to answer her. Not wanting to see him struggle, I jump in to assist.

"Daddy, bring your book up here," I say as I position Liberty closer to me.

Hamilton lies beside her, a tight fit for the three of us in her twin bed. I hold the closed book up for all to see.

"What... to..." she starts reading. "Mommy help."

That's her way of asking for help with tough words. I point to each word as I say it in the rest of the title.

She points to the picture. "Baby." Her lips purse as her little brain processes.

I have no idea what she'll come up with.

When I nod, she squeals as she hops up and down on the bed. "Baby brover! Baby brover!" she sings.

I guess we'll discuss this now instead of in the second trimester like I had planned.

"Libby, sit." I pat the bed. "Let's talk."

She takes a seat between us, eager to listen.

"Do you know what a secret is?" I begin, and she nods. "Well, Mommy, Daddy, and Libby need to keep the baby a secret. Can we do that?"

Again, she nods, hanging on my every word.

"Do you enjoy opening presents?"

She nods to answer me again.

"Presents are secrets. We don't want to tell anyone, so it will be a surprise, right?"

"The baby is a present," Liberty confirms, pressing her index finger to her lips. "Shh."

"Yes." Hamilton finally joins the conversation.

Unable to pay us any more attention, Liberty climbs from her bed to enter the bathroom.

"How many chapters did you read?" I inquire, passing the book back to my husband.

"I made it to the end of the 3rd month," he admits, looking embarrassed. "The more I read, the more confused I became."

"I read it 2 or 3 times before I could wrap my head around it all," I confess. "I can't believe you slept on the floor."

"I can't believe how fast you fell asleep last night," he counters.

151

MADISON

Walking to the kitchen after my shower, I find Hamilton has Liberty in her chair while he fixes breakfast.

"We will need to help Mommy," he says to our daughter as he shuts the fridge door. "She must take naps with you--"

"Um..." I interrupt. "I think you're getting ahead of yourself. Naps are when I'm as big as a whale."

Liberty looks to me, confused.

"As the baby gets bigger in Mommy's tummy, my belly will get big," I explain.

With no reaction, she turns her focus to the oatmeal Hamilton places in front of her.

"Since the baby is a secret," I glare at him, "we probably shouldn't talk about it all the time." I tilt my head towards Liberty, and Hamilton takes the hint, winking at me.

We place our finger to our mouths in unison. "Shh."

Liberty mimics our gesture and joins us. "Shh."

I know this will not last. There's no way Liberty will keep the fact that we're having a baby a secret.

Hamilton places my favorite mug in front of me on the island. I wrap my hands around it and inhale the earthy aroma. There's nothing like the smell of coffee in the morning. My mind runs through the list of foods and beverages I must avoid while pregnant. Coffee and Diet Pepsi will be the most difficult for me. But, just like with Liberty, it will be worth it to deliver the healthiest baby possible.

I lift Liberty from the highchair; she runs to her toys the second her feet touch the hardwood. As I dump my coffee down the drain, I pull out my cell; I need to make an obstetrics appointment.

When the receptionist answers, I state my name and date of birth then ask to make an appointment. While I wait for her to open the schedule, my eyes meet Hamilton's; in his, I see both excitement and fear. I can't wait to experience the next nine months with him.

The receptionist comes back on, telling me they had a cancellation this morning at 11, so I quickly accept it. I look to Hamilton as I disconnect the call.

"Can you go with me at 11 this morning?" My smile grows with his.

"I'll call Stan and let him know I can't workout." He already has his cell phone in hand to do so. "I'm gonna skip our workout, today," Hamilton tells Stan when the other man answers. "Madison's pregnant, and we have a doctor's appointment."

Seriously? It's barely been twelve hours, and he's already blabbed. So much for keeping it a secret for a couple of months.

"Hamilton!" I scold, hands on my hips.

At my words, he realizes what he's done.

"Crap. Stan, it's supposed to be a secret." He scrambles to cover his mistake. "Can you keep it a secret for now, please?" Hamilton places his phone on speaker. "Madison's here. You're on speaker, now."

"You two get your stuff together. I won't tell a soul," Stan promises. "I'm in no hurry to start the baby-fever that will sweep through the team. Been there. Done that."

"Really?" I ask. "Baby-fever?"

"Yes, even Delta catches it," Stan states, exasperated. "The wives and girl-friends all hound partners, trying to conceive, and sometimes, trying to get pregnant without consent. So, yes, I'll keep your secret. Just give me a heads up before you tell Delta. I need to be prepared," Stan promises and Hamilton ends the call.

"I'm sorry, babe." Hamilton wraps his arms around me.

"I understand your excitement, but it's common to wait two or three months before telling friends and family in case something happens," I remind him. "We haven't even seen the doctor to confirm the pregnancy."

"I know," Hamilton says, kissing my temple. "It just came out. I'll try to control it. I promise."

I nod, hoping now that he told Stan, he'll be able to keep the secret, at least for a couple of weeks.

"Madison Crocker," a nurse calls from the open door.

I take Hamilton by the hand, pulling him behind me as we follow the nurse, who takes my weight, and enter the exam room. He stands nervously beside me as I sit on the end of the exam table, and the nurse records my vitals. She urges him to take a seat in the nearby chair while I give a urine sample in the attached restroom. I must bite my lips, hiding my amusement at his nervous discomfort.

After a routine exam, Dr. Humphreys asks the two of us, "Any questions?"

I shake my head, looking to Hamilton for him to ask away. He hesitates for a moment before he speaks up.

"I'm worried about..." Hamilton begins, pausing to find the right words.

Dr. Humphreys chimes before he can finish. She's experienced in the worries of new fathers. "Madison's first pregnancy was an easy one. Nothing has changed since then, so there's no need for any restrictions."

Hamilton nods once. "She attends yoga twice a week. We've started weightlifting to tone areas she thinks need work." He shakes his head, not finding any fault with my body. "She carries our daughter, and Liberty weighs 30 pounds. I worry it's all too much."

"I see." Dr. Humphreys smiles at us both. "The most important rule is to rest. Madison is young and healthy; as long as it causes her no discomfort, then I see no reason for her to stop her normal activities."

She looks to me on the exam table. "No hot yoga or any poses that cause you strain. I'm sure the instructor can give you modifications to any poses you might need. Light weights with several reps are better than heavy weights. As you will remember, you will tire easily and need to rest more than normal. Often with a child at home, expecting mothers find they are much more tired than in the previous pregnancy."

Dr. Humphreys looks to Hamilton. "You should encourage her to rest often each day. If you notice she seems worn down, it's important that you allow her to rest, and intervene if she refuses."

Looking back to me, she continues, "Madison, it's my hope that you'll listen to your body when it tells you to rest. I'll give Hamilton my cell number. If he feels you aren't resting enough, I'll expect him to call me. I'll ask him to clear your schedule, and I'll visit you at the house, placing restrictions if I need to."

"I won't overdo it," I promise the two of them. "With our nanny and housekeeper taking care of everything, I'll take it easy."

Pleased with my promise, Dr. Humphreys asks Hamilton if he has any more questions. She sees the reluctance on his face and answers his next question before he asks it.

"Intercourse is safe during pregnancy." She only looks at him. "As you will find in many pregnancy books, it's important for couples to support each other through these nine months. It's safe as long as it doesn't involve risky behaviors."

She rises, walking toward Hamilton. "You will worry; all the knowledge in the world will not cure that. You know your wife. You'll be able to see when she's tired. You'll sense when she needs to eat or should drink more water." She pats his arm. "I'm sure you can handle this. You'll be a great expecting father."

As we schedule our next appointment in four weeks, Dr. Humphreys informs the staff to try to schedule our appointments when convenient with Hamilton's ball schedule. I take this moment to hand them a list of dates when Hamilton is available.

"I know we're asking a lot," I state. "I've taken the liberty to offer dates for the monthly appointment and then the weekly appointments near the end."

"I'll work on this today and tomorrow," the receptionist states. "We should be able to schedule on all of these dates. If we need to adjust them, we can, but if all goes as planned, you'll already have appointments that work for the two of you."

"Fabulous!" I smile widely.

Hamilton hugs me tight to his side. He won't admit it, but ensuring our appointments fit his schedule means the world to him.

152

MADISON

I slam my cell phone down on my desktop with more force than I intended. Why isn't Cameron returning my calls and texts? I flip through three pages of notes. How will I ever get all of this done in the next two weeks? I imagined by the third book I wouldn't find the weeks leading up to a release as stressful as before. With all the changes since September, my life seems to be busier with each passing week. I open my digital calendar, scanning today and tomorrow. Fallon and Liberty plan to attend several classes and play groups. That will allow me to focus in my office. I need selfies to post; I detest posting videos and photos of myself, but I've got to promote myself to ensure sales.

The doorbell interrupts my pity-party. Glancing at the clock in the corner of my laptop, I see it's 1:15. Who could be here?

"I'm here to save the day!" Cameron's voice sings as she approaches my office door. "Who's the best editor in the whole world?"

I shake my head as she prances into the room, her hands in the air.

"You're interrupting my mini-freak out session," I state. "Guess I know why you haven't returned my calls and texts today."

"Well, from our conversation yesterday, I felt you needed my help in Chicago, not via the phone and internet in Columbia." She shrugs as if it's no big deal. "Stand," she orders.

I hesitantly rise from my desk chair. "Why am I standing?"

"Because we need to decompress a bit before we buckle back down," she states as if I should have already known this fact.

Cameron strides into the kitchen like it's her house, passing right by Miss Alba. She opens the pantry then the refrigerator. She lays crackers, two types of cheese, and a bottle of wine on the island. She opens her mouth to speak, but her buzzing phone interrupts her.

I wait while she taps out a text reply.

After a large drink from her wine glass, Cameron turns on her barstool to face me. "What has you the most stressed?"

I stare as she swallows two big gulps of wine. "How was your flight?" I ask, wondering why she's chugging her drink.

"Are you trying to change the subject?" She chuckles, holding a slice of cheese and cracker halfway to her mouth.

I tilt my head and point to her nearly empty wine glass. "It's like you're trying to break the record to down it."

"I'm just glad to be here with you," Cameron shrugs, picking at her cracker. "Now, answer my question." She looks sternly in my direction.

"Um..." I release a loud huff. "I want to write. That's it. Everything else pulls me away from my writing. I have so many ideas I want to put out there, and I can't when I'm forced to post to social media."

Mouth full of crackers, Cameron nods.

"I continue, my fingers fiddling with the stem of my glass. "This week, I'm supposed to post selfies teasing for release day and the cover reveal of the next book. I need to build the hype with hints or sneak peeks of the new release, but I'm not creative enough to take good photos. And, filters baffle me."

Miss Alba refills Cameron's glass and sneaks a nibble of cheese from the tray.

"I've tried to assist with the posts, and my assistant uploads some, too." She thanks Miss Alba for the refill. "But, your fans want photos of you. They crave personal posts to learn more about you. That's hard for us to do from Missouri."

I sigh heavily. Guess I'm stuck taking selfies this week and next. "Can you at least help me? I don't know what to wear or how to pose."

"Maybe it's time we look into adding a personal assistant and publicist to your team," Cameron suggests and pops a slice of cheese in her mouth.

"Like what Berkeley does for Ham?" I ask, unsure I need all of that.

She washes down her last bite before speaking. "Perhaps only part-time for now. I don't believe we need anyone full-time, yet. Let's invite Berkeley over to get her input and see if she knows anyone to hire."

Pursing my lips, I digest her words. Berkeley is an expert in this area. I slide my phone open to send a text.

ME

when you have time we need to discuss my need for a publicist

BERKELEY

I'm free now

ME

now's good

BERKELEY

(thumbs up emoji)

"She's on her way over," I inform Cameron.

Two hours later, a huge weight has lifted from my shoulders. Berkeley plans to work with me as my part-time publicist. When my needs grow to be more than she has time for, she'll help me hire a full-time assistant.

Cameron explained the calendar and necessary posts leading up to the book's release. Berkeley promptly arranged a photo shoot with several clothing changes here in my home and office for use in future posts. We ordered a small desk for the corner of my office. Berkeley will use it half the day Tuesday and Friday when she's here. Cameron will sit at it when she's in town. It warms my heart that Liberty can use it to read and color as I write in the office. While I often need silence as I work from time to time, I'd love to share the space with Liberty. I can't stop smiling. With Berkeley's help, I can focus on writing, and that makes me happy.

"Why am I so nervous to ask him?" I say, fiddling with the fringe of the throw pillow in my lap. I mean he's my husband, I'm not asking for his permission. I just want his input before I commit to it.

"Should we ask Berkeley to be here?" Cameron asks.

"No, we've got this," I state, trying to believe my own words.

At the sound of the keypad on the front door, goosebumps develop from head to toe. I take in a steadying breath then turn in my seat to face the door. I rest my arm upon the back of the sofa, leaning towards him.

"Hey," I greet when he enters.

"Hello, ladies," Hamilton smiles with a small wave before Liberty runs into his arms.

While Hamilton talks with his daughter about her day, Cameron and I pull out table service and the meal Miss Alba prepared. My nerves skyrocket while I busy myself.

"Dinner's ready," Cameron announces.

Hamilton places Liberty in her highchair then takes a stool at the island beside her. Cameron smirks at my nervousness to discuss my job with him. I know he's a nervous, expecting father—I'm not sure how he'll react to our plan.

I sit by my husband while Cameron opts to stand across from us. We eat as easy conversation flows.

"Let's talk book tour," Cameron announces. "We've tentatively planned appearances for May and June."

Hamilton gives her his attention as he continues to consume his grilled chicken stir fry.

"We've planned morning show and book store appearances to coincide with the Cubs schedule during both months," Cameron informs us, glancing from Hamilton to me.

"She'll be five months pregnant," Hamilton reminds us. "She'll get tired easily and will need to rest."

Cameron nods. "We propose that Fallon travel with us. She'll have nights with Slater, so I'm sure she'll be interested."

She slides an itinerary toward Hamilton. "Items in bold are Madison's book tour. The rest is optional."

"I wouldn't have to attend the Cubs games that you aren't pitching," I jump in. "When I'm tired, I'd stay at the hotel."

"I appreciate that the tour was planned to coincide with my schedule." Hamilton points as he counts silently. "Correct me if I'm wrong, but in May and June months, you'll travel to seven cities plus Chicago for seventeen appearances."

Cameron nods.

He turns on his stool to face me. "Your number one priority is taking care of yourself for the baby. I know press for the new release is important. I'm worried that the schedule is too aggressive, though. You'll spend a lot of time in the air, and I worry how that will affect you and the baby."

Cameron's eyes lock on mine. I interpret that to mean it's my turn to convince him.

"Would you feel better if I discussed it with Dr. Humphreys?" I offer. "If she had no reservations for the travel and the schedule, would you be okay with this plan?"

My husband plays with my hands between us. Cameron talks with Liberty in between bites, giving us some time.

"I know I tend to overreact," he explains. "This pregnancy is overwhelming, and I feel like I can't control so much. I worry about everything. Things that used to be common, everyday activities are now dangers in my mind. Slipping in the shower, wrecking your vehicle on your way to Delta's, and even carrying Liberty worries me. It's all out of my hands and scares the crap out of me." He laces his fingers with mine and his eyes bore into me. "I'd feel better if Dr. Humphreys was aware of the plan and weighs in."

I love that he opened up about his fears. I am aware he feels out of control and hates it. I do my best to ease his worries but refuse to remain at home on bed rest. Things can happen anywhere, at any time, to anyone.

"I'll call the doctor tomorrow," I promise.

"We'll table it until I hear back from the two of you," Cameron states, placing her empty plate in the dishwasher.

Hamilton kisses my hand, before returning to his meal.

153

HAMILTON

My excitement grows as I get closer to home. I can't wait to surprise the girls with the rest of the day off. Traffic cooperates, and I make it home in record time. I drum my fingers against my slacks as I wait for the elevator to climb the last five floors. I have no idea what we will do this afternoon—spending quality time with my two girls grows more important as spring training draws near.

Upon entering, I find the front room and kitchen vacant. The door to Madison's office is closed, and Miss Alba is absent. I stride down the hallway, following the sound of Fallon and Liberty's voices to her bedroom. I peek my head in the doorway, finding them dancing and singing along to a children's song in Spanish.

"Daddy!" Liberty launches herself into my arms.

"Hola," I laugh.

"Hola, Daddy," she returns.

I look to Fallon. "My schedule opened up, so I thought I would spend the afternoon with my family."

She smiles as she turns off the music on Liberty's iPad. "Liberty and I plan to head to Toddler Time in 15 minutes." She wrinkles her nose. "I heard loud metal music, and Madison singing at the top of her lungs about an hour ago. Not sure writing went well this morning. Now that it's quieter, and the door is shut, I wouldn't interrupt her if I were you. She has that deadline for her first six chapters approaching."

I've sensed Madison's tension rising the past three days; add that to Fallon's assessment of this morning, and I don't think it would be wise to interrupt.

"I guess the two of you get to entertain me at Toddler Time," I tease.

"Libby, your daddy is going to the playgroup with us," Fallon states.

"Yay!" Liberty cheers, clapping in my arms.

"I need to change. I'll meet you in the kitchen in two minutes," I inform Liberty as I place her back on her bedroom floor.

I've run in this gym several times since I moved to Chicago. Somehow, it never seemed this large until I saw 10 two-year-olds darting here and there. I kiss Liberty on her cheek, then she runs over to a little boy and girl in the middle of the gym. I immediately notice my daughter is a full head taller than both of them. Scanning the entire room, I notice she towers over all the kids.

A whistle sounds, and every child attempts to freeze in place—several require a couple more steps to slow their momentum in order to stop. The female instructor in black yoga pants and a Chicago White Sox t-shirt calls them all to the center circle. I won't hold her shirt against her. I follow Fallon's lead as we take a seat behind Liberty. Other moms or nannies do the same. Of course, I am the only adult male in attendance—I don't mind; I'm glad my career allows me to hang with my little girl from time to time.

While the teacher talks to the circle of children, one little boy toddles over, pointing at me.

"Hi," I smile, unsure what I should do. When the child merely stands a foot in front of me, I try another tactic. "What's your name?" He shakes his head at me before returning to his circle of friends. I look to Fallon, confused by the interaction.

"He doesn't talk much. Liberty's verbal skills are higher than the normal two-year-old," she reminds me.

Prompted by the instructor, we stand to sing "If You're Happy and You Know It". I look around the circle of kids as they attempt to clap and stomp at the appropriate times. I am hyper focused on any talking I hear for the rest of the class and during the free play time. Liberty pulls two friends by their hands in my direction.

"My daddy," Liberty tells the two girls.

"Hi," I greet with the softest voice I can muster.

The blonde girl waves with a shy smile; the other sucks on her thumb.

"Ma-ma." The blonde points to two women standing near the wall.

"Is that your mommy?" I ask.

She nods her head before darting away, the other girl walking behind her. I realize in that moment the only words I've heard spoken by children other than Liberty were "ma-ma". I observe Liberty talking to the children and them shaking their heads or following her instructions.

"Are you having fun?" I ask my daughter.

"Yes. Come pway wiff me," she directs, extending her little hand toward me.

I look to Fallon to see if I can. With her nod, I rise and follow behind Liberty. She picks up a red, rubber ball and bounces it toward me.

"Were those your friends?" I ask between bounces.

She points to each girl and says their names. She continues around the room, naming each playmate as they scurry about.

As we make our way back to our floor, I realize that after this class, I better understand our visit last December with Dr. Conway and the gap in abilities between Liberty and her peers. My lack of time spent with little ones led me to believe all children were speaking like our daughter. Now, I see how unique she is. I'm glad her playgroup friends don't treat her differently, because she talks; they accept her as she is.

154

MADISON

The weeks fly by. I can't believe Valentine's Day is only four days away.

"Delta's on her way up," I inform Fallon and Miss Alba at the kitchen island. My nerves ratchet up a notch as the important conversation rapidly approaches.

At the sound of the doorbell, Liberty hops up and down, cheering. When I told her I invited Delta to join us for lunch, she declared we are having a girl party.

"Liberty," I attempt to gain her attention, "you can open the door, now."

My daughter loves "big girl" tasks; opening the front door is one of her favorites. I'd never allow it if we didn't have the doormen and other security features in our building.

"Hola," she shouts, opening the door for our guest.

"Hola, Libby," Delta greets. "What are you wearing?"

I close the door behind our guest as she kneels in front of Liberty. My strong-willed child demanded to wear her Spider-Man costume with a black Batman cape. She shed the hooded mask only moments ago, and her hair is a wild mess.

"I'm 'pider-Man," she informs Delta, spinning to enjoy the fluttering of her cape.

"I see!" Delta attempts to stifle her laughter.

"We've been reading about superheroes," Fallon explains. "Libby and I made a list of the new costumes she'd like to have." She spreads her arms apart, demonstrating it's a long list.

"Webb loves to read comics," Delta states. "Libby, maybe he would let you read a few."

Liberty claps her hands excitedly. Her love of reading continues to blossom. On our frequent trips to the bookstore, we've begun sampling new genres.

Miss Alba pushes a tray of sandwiches and wraps onto the counter, announcing it's time to eat. Fallon helps Liberty into her chair, pushing up her red and blue sleeves and arranging her cape over the back. My three friends join me on bar stools as we fill our plates with salad, fruit, and light sandwiches. While we dine, our conversation smoothly flies from one topic to another. It only pauses when Hamilton walks through the front door.

"Daddy!" Liberty yells with a mouthful.

Fallon quietly reminds her it's not polite to talk with her mouth full of food. Hamilton bends to place a kiss on my cheek. I rise to fetch him a plate so he can join us. Before I can turn or take a step, his hands splay upon my belly.

"What do you ladies think of our news?" he asks the group.

All eyes stare at his hands on my stomach. Fallon's jaw falls open. Miss Alba smiles as if she already suspected, and Delta jumps from her stool to embrace me in celebration. I bug my eyes out at Hamilton. For once, he understands my nonverbal gesture.

"Oops!" He raises his palms to the group. "I've ruined Madison's announcement."

"Ladies, please excuse my husband," I tease. "This isn't the first time he's blurted it out. It seems Libby keeps a secret better than her daddy."

"Libby," Hamilton calls across the island, "do you have a secret?"

Liberty smiles before placing her index finger over her lips. "Shhh," she stage whispers.

"Can you tell Fallon, Delta, and Miss Alba our secret surprise?" Hamilton encourages.

Her little brown eyes dart to me, seeking my approval. I nod, and she claps. "Mommy has my brover in her tummy," she proudly shares.

"We're pregnant!" Hamilton gleams proudly. "And, Libby wants it to be a baby brother."

I love the joy that lights his face as he talks about the pregnancy. He's like a little boy at Christmastime. He can't help but smile and talk about the pregnancy while he anxiously awaits the moment the baby arrives.

"So, that's the reason for our luncheon," I explain. "We're still in the first trimester. It's early, but we wanted to share our news with each of you."

"I'll leave for spring training next weekend," Hamilton continues. "I want Madison to have a support system in my absence. I'd like you to be my eyes and ears; you'll be around her often, and I'll be limited to video calls in the evening." He places his hands upon my shoulders, squeezing them. "Can you help me make sure she rests when she needs to and takes care of herself?"

Nodding, my friends gladly accept Hamilton's task. As if I'm not standing mere feet away, they begin to talk strategy without me.

"I'll be here every weekday morning and several afternoons to play with Libby," Fallon states. "I'll also be available any other time to help with Libby or run errands with her."

"Of course," Miss Alba chimes in, "I'll keep up the house, stock the cabinets, and make sure she eats as she should."

Delta pats my hand on the counter. "I'll ensure she doesn't stay locked up in her office twenty-four seven. I'll plan stuff for us to do." She quickly looks to calm any of Hamilton's concerns, adding, "They'll be short outings that won't be too strenuous. We'll lie around binge-watching mindless shows and movies, we'll brave the cold for a dessert, we'll find a movie to go to, and stuff like that." She looks to the other women in the room. "If you ever need, I can cover for you any day or night."

"It seems you've all got this planned out." I try to hide my anger that I'm being treated like a child and not the adult I am. "Can we finish lunch?"

Delta pulls her bottom lip into her mouth.

"This isn't my first pregnancy," I remind the group as I slide back into my chair. "I'm capable of knowing when I need to relax and eat; all I want is some company while Hamilton is away."

"This isn't the first time I've upset Madison by trying to protect her," Hamilton admits coyly. "I don't want to tie her to the bed for the entire nine months, but it would definitely take care of most of my fears."

Raucous laughter erupts—even little Liberty joins in. Hamilton furrows his brow, unsure of the reason. I laugh so hard tears form in my eyes, and I must excuse myself before I wet my pants.

As I step down the hallway, Delta can't help herself. "Surely, she wouldn't mind if you tied her to the bed for an hour or two."

I hurry the final few steps to the bathroom as I giggle. Now, Hamilton understands his slip up. I'm sure his cheeks are red with embarrassment. Knowing Delta, she will mention this many times in the upcoming months.

155

MADISON

"I expect you to take it easy today," Hamilton reminds me.

I know he only wants to look out for me, but I find his constant reminders to take naps tiresome. As the Women of the Cubs Valentine's Gala draws near, he's become more vigilant.

"The committee meets for an hour this afternoon," I remind him. "The others will do all the set up and decorating tomorrow. My only job is to dawn my gown and read the script at the event."

I've informed him of this several times this week, but he needs my assurance that I won't overdo it. We have a busy nine days ahead of us. Tomorrow night is the Valentine's Gala, then we'll enjoy the final days together before spring training. On Thursday, we drive to Missouri where Liberty will stay with Memphis while Hamilton and I head to Kansas City for Savannah's wedding weekend. Finally, on Sunday, I must drop Hamilton off at the airport headed for Arizona before Liberty and I drive back to Chicago on Monday.

"I love you," he reminds me, explaining his constant worry.

"I know," I whisper into his chest; my hands clutch as his unzipped coat. "Delta is picking me up, and I should be home in time to nap with Liberty."

I've come to enjoy our quiet cuddling in Liberty's bed at nap time. It's easy to drift off with her in my arms.

Hamilton

Stepping from the shower, I catch a glimpse of Madison in her red gown in our bedroom. I wrap a towel around my waist before peaking my head out for a better look. She stands in front of our full-length mirror, turning this way and that. She tilts her head and scrunches her mouth, taking in her reflection. She's a vision in this form-fitting gown. She slips her feet into the red stilettos I begged her not to wear. I argued her feet will ache from standing on stage for hours. She informed me she could endure a little pain to look worthy of my arm for the evening. She spins, looking over her shoulder into the mirror. I'm sure she sees faults where I know none exist. Madison catches me in her periphery.

"Hey." She shyly smooths out the dress, walking toward me.

I feel my eyes bug out, and my mouth goes dry. I've no idea how I will keep my hands off her for the next five hours, let alone tolerate every man in the place ogling her on stage all evening.

"Is that what you plan to wear?" She points to the towel around my hips. I love that her pupils dilate, and her pink tongue peeks out to lick her lips. She keeps me in a constant state of arousal; it's only fair that I occasionally have the same effect on her.

"I had to get a closer look at you," I confess, planting my hands on her hips, pulling her closer.

"Uh uh," she protests. "You're wet. You'll ruin the gown." She pushes away with her palms against my chest, but I notice her fingertips betray her by digging in.

"I need to start on my hair and makeup if we have any chance of leaving on time," she complains, disappearing into the bathroom.

I remain in the bedroom for a moment. I need to gather myself. I need to dawn my tux, but all I want is to lift the red dress to her waist and lose myself inside her warm heat. This will be the longest night of my life.

"Ladies and gentlemen," Madison greets, elegantly gracing the stage with the microphone in hand, "welcome to the fifth annual Women of the Cubs Valentine's Gala." She pauses for the crowd's applause.

I peek from stage left as the spotlight highlights my dazzling wife. It amazes me she's able to take the stage with all the attention centered on her. She's fearless.

"You're asking yourselves, who is this lady in red, and why is she keeping us from our dinner, right?" Laughter erupts. "My name is Madison Armstrong," she states. "I bet you all know my husband, Hamilton Armstrong."

She turns in my direction; that's my cue. I force my feet to walk towards her at center stage, but they feel like lead weights. I'll take a pitching mound over this any day.

"Hello," I say into the mic. "I'm not the only talented pretty face in the family, am I?" I strive for humor in my attempt to get the focus off me and back on Madison.

I wait for the applause to die before continuing with our planned script. It's on the tip of my tongue. I've practiced it a hundred times with her this week. However, at this very important moment, I can't remember what comes next. Madison slips her free hand in mine as a show of support, but I still have nothing. "Speaking of family, we're expecting our second child in October."

Instantly, I know I should have stayed silent instead of scrambling for something to say to fill the silence.

"Sorry," I whisper into Madison's ear before placing a peck on her cheek. I've definitely messed up again.

Madison places a palm on my chest, urging me to exit the stage as she points.

"Well, that definitely wasn't in tonight's script." She makes light of my announcement. "I guess the cat's out of the bag. He's talented with the strike zone, but secrets are his kryptonite."

The crowd loves her impromptu joke. Who knew she had the gift of improv?

"The rumors are true. Hamilton Armstrong will appear in the live auction following dinner. He's been elusive in the past, but try as he might, he couldn't say no to me."

More laughter and applause fills the ballroom. I feel silly for worrying all week about how hard it would be for her as the master of ceremonies tonight. I make my way back into the ballroom, assuming my position for the upcoming portion of the evening.

Madison informs the guest the bars are open as is the silent auction bidding. She encourages the crowd to mingle with the players and coaches as they view the wonderful items up for auction for the next hour.

I watch as she's swarmed when she exits the stage. I love that the crowd is drawn to her just as I am. I catch her quick glance in my direction before she engages with them. Delta comes to her side. She's proving a great friend, and I'm glad she will have Madison's back while I'm away. Eventually, I excuse myself to join my wife, still corralled near the stage. She takes my hand, and I follow her on stage to make the dinner announcement.

"We're back," she draws out in a sing-song voice. When the guests quiet, she continues. "I made Hamilton promise not to speak before I allowed him back on stage." Laughter fills the large room. I didn't expect to be the butt of her jokes this evening.

"If you'll find your way back to your assigned seats, the wait staff is ready to serve us dinner. You'll continue to get text alerts on any items you are watching or placed a bid on. If you find the alerts annoying, bid high. Then, you won't have to compete with so many others." Cheers and laughter prevail. "Remember, our goal this evening is fundraising, so dust off your purses and wallets. Don't be shy; we want your money. I'll be back after dinner, and who knows, maybe I'll let this big guy talk by then."

While the crowd enjoys her teasing, we exit the stage to join our table and special guests.

"The silent auction will close in one minute. If you're quick, you have one more opportunity to bid on any items you like," Madison announces after dinner. "Do we have any ladies in the house?"

A few boisterous women yell out or cheer.

Madison places a hand on her hip as if upset. The pose pushes her bare shoulders back and the exposed portion of her breasts out. I quickly avert my eyes back to the crowd for fear I might tent my pants for all to see if I continue to enjoy my view from above her.

"That was lame," she reprimands the women. "I need all the females to stand up. C'mon. Stand up." She lifts her hands up, encouraging them to rise. "Okay, shake out your arms like this." She demonstrates, and the women in the crowd mimic her motions. "Okay. Now that we are up and our blood is pumping again, I think you're ready for what comes next." She pauses to take a quick breath. "Who's excited to bid on the Cubs players in the live auction?"

This time, the women scream, jump in their heels, and clap excitedly.

"Now, that's what I'm talking about!" Madison exclaims, grinning.

Placing her hand on my right pectoral, she slowly slinks around my side, behind me, and appears on my other side. Her hand caresses my body as she circles. "One lucky bidder will win four hours with this fine specimen of male athletic talent." Her voice takes on a sexy purr.

This is exactly why I never agreed to participate in the auction before. Well, this and the fact I liked to arrive in Mesa early. Madison promised it wasn't a meat market. So, why do I feel every female eye undressing me under the extreme heat of the spotlights?

"We have 10 volunteers in this year's live auction. And you didn't hear me wrong; we've negotiated four hours for use. The details for the auction and rules are located in the program at your seat. Ladies, I'm sorry. You can look, but you can't touch."

Many groan audibly.

That's my cue to exit the stage.

"I know; I know. It sucks, but the gentleman sitting beside you wouldn't like it," Madison reminds them.

"Please take a look at the details before bidding. The back of your program is your bidding number. Remember to raise it high until the auctioneer staff records your bid."

156

MADISON

I introduce the catcher as the first player up for auction then relinquish the microphone to the auctioneer. Backstage, I join Delta who is sipping from a water bottle as the bids climb higher and higher. When the amount surpasses the winning bid for him last year, I return to stand beside the auctioneer on stage. Eventually, the bids cease, and I'm handed the microphone once again.

"$75,000! Your stock rose a bit from last year," I state as the catcher exits the stage.

"Up next, from the Cubs center field, is Stan the Man," I announce before allowing the auction to begin.

Delta hops up and down nervously backstage. She told me the players are very competitive on the amounts bid in the auction. Last year, Stan was the third highest; this year, he hopes to be number one. The guys have been talking trash to each other, and he wants to shut some of the younger players up.

I choke on a gulp of water when his bids instantly climb past last year's amount. Delta celebrates nearby, not worried at all as I sputter and cough. Moments pass before I catch my breath.

"Can you believe it?" Delta whisper shouts. "I wish I could see Stan's face."

"I better get back out there." I excuse myself. I need to be on stage when this bidding stops.

"Going once. Going twice. Sold for $150,000," the auctioneer announces before passing me the mic.

I grab Stan's arm as he tries to leave the stage. He reluctantly stands beside me. "Wow! $150,000! That's going to go straight to his head," I tease.

Stan shifts his weight from one foot to the other nervously.

"Let me look at you," I say as I walk in a circle around him as if I'm inspecting him. "You do clean up nicely. Delta's a lucky lady."

I dismiss Stan and assume my place center stage. "I have a surprise I was saving for after the live auction, but I feel after a bid of $150,000, I should tell you now. An anonymous donor will match each winning bid tonight to each player's charity!"

I smile proudly as the large crowd reacts. "As you bid tonight, you will be raising funds for our charity and the individual player's charity, so keep up the bidding."

The auction continues for the next seven players. Although the bids are high, Stan is still leading with the highest bid with only one player left to auction.

"Alright, I need everyone to stand up. C'mon, stand up." I point from table to table, urging compliance. "This is our version of the seventh inning stretch."

"Now, put your right foot in. Now, put your right foot out. Now, put your right foot in and shake it all about..." I sing into the handheld mic.

The crowd joins in. "You do the hokey pokey, and you turn yourself around. That's what it's all about," we sing together.

I applaud, and they join me. "That was awesome. I didn't think you'd really do it. This. Crowd. Rocks."

"Take your seats; we're not done yet," I announce. "If you've been counting, we've auctioned off nine players. For those keeping track in your program, you know who's up next."

A couple of the guests shout, "Armstrong!"

"You've been very generous in your bidding this evening. Let's keep it going for one more player. I know you've got money left. I bet some of you have been saving all your bids for this last player."

I turn to signal for Hamilton to join me on stage. "Honey, I have something I need to tell you before the bidding begins."

Hamilton looks a bit worried. We practiced at home; he knows the script for his introduction, and I am not following it.

"I can't bid on you," I state, pouting. "I would if I could, but wives aren't allowed to."

Hamilton smiles, relief apparent on his face. I'll have to ask him what he thought I might say when we get home.

"I understand." He leans in to speak into the mic in my hand.

"This is his first year entered in the live auction. Our daughter, Liberty, and I think he's pretty special, and we've quickly learned in the months we've been in Chicago that you like him, too." I squeeze and release his hand. "Remember, your bids raise money for our charity as well as his charity. So, bid up and bid often."

I kiss him on the cheek, wave to the crowd, and pass the mic to the auctioneer as I seek the water my dry throat craves backstage. Delta quickly stands at my side.

"Do you think Hamilton will raise more than Stan? I mean, let's be honest, Hamilton is more popular."

"Don't worry. Stan has reason to brag amongst the guys. He was second and had the high bid all night. If Hamilton goes higher, it's only because he's last and the crowd's more generous at the end of the night. I only hope they bid high enough that Hamilton doesn't regret me convincing him in to be in the auction," I confess.

The anticipation is building backstage. The planning committee, their men, and other players are gathering for the approaching big reveal of the total raised tonight. Not only is it crowded, but it's loud.

"Let's listen," Delta pulls me closer to the side of the stage so we can hear.

We are only able to see one-third of the crowd from stage left. The auctioneer is chanting quickly as I try to make out a number. I think he just passed one-hundred thousand. I relax a little. It's a figure Hamilton can be proud of. My hand flies to my mouth as the number continues to rise rapidly.

"We've raised so much money!" Delta leans into my ear to speak. "Way more than last year."

We share huge smiles. Since Delta chairs the committee this year, this is her victory.

"Going once. Going twice. Sold for $200,000!" The auctioneer's words interrupt my mini celebration with Delta.

I clip-clop my way back to center stage in my heels just in time to snag the mic. "Holy Moly!" I draw out. "Someone has a big fan."

Blushing, Hamilton tucks his hand in mine.

"Who's ready to hear the total raised this evening?" I taunt the crowd. "Wow! Listen to you party animals." I glance to the side of the stage. "I'd like to invite the members of the planning committee and their men to the stage."

Just as excited as the crowd out front, they scurry onto the stage, forming two lines, women in front and players behind them.

"While the accounting team checks and double checks calculations, I'd like to thank each one of you for attending tonight, for bidding during the silent auction, and for your generous bids during the live auction." I take a quick breath, peeking stage left for a sign we are ready.

"Okay, here we go," I announce, turning sideways to glance at the large screen behind us. "This year's total is…" I pause for dramatic effect while waiting for the figure to appear. "$2,575,979!"

Confetti falls from the ceiling while the guests stand to clap and cheer our success. Hugs and high fives are exchanged by all.

157

MADISON

I glance at my phone. 8:00 a.m. Faint sounds of Hamilton and Liberty sail through the air from the kitchen. Groaning, I force myself to roll from my bed and pad down the hall.

"Good morning," Hamilton smiles, teasing me about my hate for mornings without using any words.

I merely grunt as I fill my mug at the coffee pot and plop onto a stool near Liberty. She's eating her Cheerios and fruit with her fingers. With each bite, her chin and fingertips stain red with strawberry juice. She's so cute. I pull out my phone and send a few pics to Memphis and Amy. Even though it's Sunday, I decide that if I'm up, my friends should be, too. I send a group text to my girls before placing my cell phone on the counter.

"Want some breakfast?" Hamilton asks, fighting another smile.

He knows peppy, morning people annoy the heck out of me. In the presence of two of them at the moment, he tries to refrain from being too irritating. It's a simple gesture, and I love him for it. Love him so much that I reciprocate after 10 p.m. each night when he's tired, and I will still be up for hours.

I close my eyes and bask in the aroma of coffee, knowing that Hamilton carefully watches that I don't consume the caffeine. I should probably confess that I did allow myself a sip earlier this week. While I still love the smell, my taste buds have changed already in my pregnancy; I actually gagged from the small sip. It's probably a blessing. As busy as this week has been, I might have consumed more than a cup a day if I still enjoyed the beverage.

Rising from my perch, I open the pantry. "I'll nibble on a few saltines for now. I'll have cereal after a while."

Concern covers his face.

"I'm not sick," I quickly promise. "When I'm tired, I get a little queasy. It will pass." I pat his arm as I bite the corner of the cracker. Sitting on my stool once again, I groan, placing my head in my hands.

"What?" Hamilton hovers, always worried about me and the baby.

"I forgot to grab a water," I whine.

He holds his palm out to me before turning toward the fridge. "Would a ginger ale sit better on your empty stomach?" he calls, head buried inside.

"Maybe," I answer. Sometimes, the sugar content does more harm than good. Since I'm more uneasy than usual, I decide ginger ale is needed this morning.

His worry still written on his face, Hamilton slides the small can my way.

Trying to squelch his trepidation, I nibble on a cracker and wash it down with small sips. Slowly, my heat flash fades, and my stomach accepts my offering.

When my cell vibrates, Hamilton looks at the screen. "Savannah," he states, handing the phone across the island.

"I sent her a photo of our messy daughter," I explain before reading her message.

SAVANNAH

got a sec?

can I call?

ME

yes

"Hello," I greet when Savannah's call connects.

"I'm at my wits end," she begins. "My morning sickness now lasts all day, every day. I know you said you didn't really suffer from it with Liberty, but..."

"Honey," I interrupt. "I only felt it once in a while. What's going on?"

"Every smell, every taste sets me off." Savannah breathes a deep, audible sigh. "Valentine's week is one of my busiest in the bakery. How am I ever going to make it through?"

I hear tears in her voice. She sounds defeated—not like my strong, independent friend.

"Is Lincoln with you?"

"Yes."

"Put me on speaker phone," I order. "From all that I've read, there's nothing to cure your morning sickness, but there are things you can do to minimize it."

"We're ready to do anything," Lincoln states.

I love that he's invested in the pregnancy.

"I'm a bit queasy this morning myself," I admit. "I only feel this way when I've overdone it. I'm tired and a bit stressed with all we have scheduled this week. I'm nibbling on saltines and sipping ginger ale as we speak. Are you getting enough sleep?" I ask, already certain of her answer.

"She's staying up later and waking up earlier." Lincoln rats her out.

"We need more sleep when we're pregnant, Savannah," I admit. "If you aren't sleeping as much at night, you need to take a nap or two during the day. I'm guilty of it, too. Lincoln, this is where you can lend a hand. Remind her to take breaks. Offer to cuddle on the couch, rub her back while watching a show so she can fall asleep, and go to bed earlier with her. You can always get back up or watch TV after she nods off."

In the background, I can hear Lincoln stating he can help her with that.

"When you're busy, it's important to nibble throughout the day." I continue to offer advice to my friend. "Small meals or snacks more often keep the blood sugar levels even. I almost ended up in the emergency department on IV fluids in my third trimester," I share. I've not told Hamilton or Savannah this. "I was scrambling to finish as much in my classes as I could before I gave birth, and I spread myself too thin. My doctor lectured me while he hooked me up to fluids in his office. I imagine you're doing the same this week. You're scrambling to get ready for the holiday at work and your wedding this weekend. You need to take care of yourself before you take care of everything else."

"We've read about all of this, and I remind her of it every day," Lincoln states. "She refuses to listen to me."

Savannah doesn't argue with his words.

"Savannah, you need to take breaks, naps, and snack. You have employees that can cover for you at work. Let them take on more tasks to lighten your load. You stated you wanted a simple ceremony, so let Lincoln take over any last-minute details."

Hamilton approaches and puts in his two cents worth. "I hope my wife will listen to her own advice." He smiles my way before continuing. "Both of you are creating a tiny human. You don't need to do everything else on top of that. Lincoln and I want to help; we just need you to allow us to."

I want to swipe Hamilton's sheepish smile from his face. He's proud of himself. He's made his point, and he knows it. He warned me all last week to take it easy and delegate while prepping for the gala. I didn't listen, and today I'm paying for it.

"Yeah, I get it," Savannah's voice breaks. "I'm just not used to having physical limitations. You know?"

"Pregnancy reminds us we are mere mortals," I tease, knowing exactly what she means. "We can still do it all and have it all. We just need to pace ourselves."

Lincoln jumps in, "So, we need to rest more, eat more, and delegate. Funny... seems that's exactly what we read in the pregnancy handbook."

I cover my mouth. I can only imagine the death stare Savannah is shooting his way after that comment.

"Lincoln, you might want to reread the section on pregnancy hormones," Hamilton laughs.

"Okay," Savannah chimes in. "I think we've covered everything. Thanks for talking me off the ledge."

"Anytime. Even if I don't know the answers, I'm here for you," I remind my friend.

We say our goodbyes, promising to call mid-week for final details on the upcoming weekend.

Hamilton wastes no time. "How's the stomach now?"

When I give him a thumbs up, he positions a bowl, spoon, and cereal box in front of me before he grabs the milk from the refrigerator. It's clear that today I will be waited on hand-and-foot. I'm sure I will be resting, too.

158

MADISON

"We should plan something fun tonight," Hamilton states as he finishes running pomade-covered fingers through his long, curly hair. His eyes meet mine in the bathroom mirror.

"I'll plan something," I promise as I lay my head against his shoulder.

"I want to keep Liberty with me every moment I can," he confesses. "I really don't want to leave the two of you." He places a kiss atop my head.

I turn to face him. "I know. But, time will fly." I place my hands on his chest when he turns to face me. "You'll FaceTime us each night if you don't get in too late. Before you know it, 10 days will have passed, and we will be in Mesa to visit you." I rise to my tiptoes and place a kiss on his lips. "Baseball is your job, and you love it. We'll make it work; you'll see," I reassure him.

Hamilton brushes hair from my eyes. He leans his forehead to mine. "I love you. I wanted you in Chicago for so long, and now that you are here, I don't want to leave you."

"You're not leaving me." I stare into his chocolate eyes. "You're traveling on business; that's not leaving us. I promise we'll get through it. I'll make it as easy on you as I can."

I search his eyes for his understanding. Baseball is everything to him. I don't want him to give it up to be home with us each night. He'd hate a nine-to-five job behind a desk. I want him to play the game he loves for as long as he can. Liberty and I will support him every step of the way.

Madison

When Fallon pops her head into my office to notify me that Liberty is down for her afternoon nap, I save my document before following her to the kitchen island.

"Can the two of you help me move something?" I look from Fallon beside me to Miss Alba across the island.

Of course, they agree.

"I'd like to slide the mattress from my bed to the floor in front of the sectional." As we walk down the hallway, I explain how the three of us can slide the mattress on its side on the hardwood floor. With no lifting, we should be able to maneuver the king-sized, pillow-top mattress.

"Now what?" Fallon asks after we position the mattress perfectly on the floor in the u-shaped opening of the living room sectional.

"I can do the rest," I state.

"What are you planning?"

"Tonight, is Liberty's last night with Hamilton at home," I explain, plopping down on the sofa cushion nearest me. "I'm surprising them with a family sleepover. I don't want Liberty in our bed. I'm afraid it might become a habit, so we are having a pajama party out here tonight." I swing my arm wide in the space.

"I'm going to prop tons of pillows against the side of the sectional. We'll watch movies, read books, have a tea party, and all three of us will sleep out here tonight."

The large, genuine smiles on their faces demonstrate their approval.

"I'm going to do a few things," I continue. "I plan to tell Liberty all about it when she wakes up. We'll put on our pj's, then I'll have her help me choose movies. We'll pick out some books. She'll help me set up her little table for the tea party and carry some of her favorite toys."

I rise from my seat. "The three of us will make our own dinner and snacks tonight. Hamilton and Liberty will have non-stop daddy-daughter time."

"The two of you," I look in their direction, "can head out for the day. Take the rest of the afternoon off, and don't forget to clock out at your normal time. Liberty and I can handle the rest."

I wave goodbye to my friends and begin the process of collecting every pillow I can find for tonight. I search the pantry and fridge as I decide on our snack and dinner menu for the evening. I check the list on my phone before ducking back into my office to write until Liberty wakes.

Liberty's cherub voice sounds across the monitor on the corner of my desk. My baby girl is up from her nap. I quickly save my work then head to surprise her.

"Did you have a good nap?"

Liberty looks up from rubbing Indie's belly. She nods sleepily. She's a morning person just like her daddy, but she wakes from naps like her mommy. In these minutes following her nap, she looks more innocent than usual. Her little mocha eyes droop sleepily. Her dark curls dart this way and that, unruly. This is our cuddle time. I enjoy the moments she's slow to move, knowing that too soon she will be a spitfire of energy, playing.

I join her on the floor, stretching out beside her. "Wanna help me with a surprise party for Daddy tonight?"

Instantly, her brown eyes glimmer. She claps her tiny hands, nodding as she smiles. All traces of sleepiness evaporate. She kisses Indie on her snout before placing her hands on the floor to raise her little body to stand.

"We're going to have a pajama party tonight with Daddy," I announce, enjoying her delighted reaction. "Let's put on our pajamas, then you can help me get it all ready for Daddy."

She extends her hand. I take it, allowing her to believe she helps me to stand.

"Which pj's do you want to wear?" I hold up her pretty pink gown and her pale blue giraffe set.

Always knowing what she wants, Liberty shakes her head at me, her unruly curls swinging in the wake. She pushes past me, climbs her step stool, and hunts through her drawer.

"Dis one," she announces proudly, holding up the soft, two-piece set Amy gave her for Christmas.

I should have known she would want to wear her Cubs pajamas to a surprise party for her daddy. I think if she had her way, every item she owned would have the Cubs on it.

"Okay. You put them on while I go put on my pajamas," I prompt.

"Cubs, Mommy," she calls to me as I walk out of her bedroom.

I peek my head back in, smiling and giving her a thumbs up. She wants me to wear the pajama set she found for me on one of our many shopping trips with Delta. I've worn them around the house but always remove them prior to climbing into bed. I'm much too hot at night to wear those long pants during sleep, but I will sacrifice tonight.

Liberty bounds into my room as I slip the top into place. She climbs onto our bed, planning to jump. She notices the mattress is missing and tilts her head at me in question.

I scoop her into my arms. "Come to the living room, and I will show you where my mattress is." As I walk, I share my plans. "Tonight, you will sleep with Daddy and me in the living room." I point to our makeshift bed on the floor before letting her down to investigate. "We'll have our party here tonight," I state.

Liberty walks from one side of the mattress to the other before climbing up on the sectional. She looks to me, smiling. When I don't reprimand her for standing on the sofa, she hops to the pile of pillows on the mattress below. I love the squeal she emits.

I lay down on one side of the mattress. "Mommy will sleep right here tonight."

Liberty squats nearby. She points to the pillow beside me. "Wibby?" When I nod, she continues. "Daddy." She points to the pillow on her other side, and I nod in agreement.

"What movies should we watch tonight?" Crawling to the television cabinet, I open the doors for her to choose.

She doesn't point or flip through the DVD cases. She efficiently plucks out five of her favorite movies and hands each to me. I love that *Mulan, Cars,* and *The Sandlot* join the two movies featuring a princess. I've made it my mission to instill in my daughter that life is not a fairytale, and women don't need strong men to rescue them in order to be happy. Besides, Hamilton will tolerate these three films.

"Let's pick out some books to read with Daddy tonight." I extend my hand and guide her to the bookshelf in her bedroom.

The first book she pulls from her shelf is a children's book with a Cubs theme. It's a favorite that she allows Daddy to read to her. She chooses a few more picture books and two of her new first grade readers.

As I carry the books, she pushes a tub with some of her favorite toys behind me. In the living room, she places one of her baby dolls on a pillow and her Cubbie Bear on another. With hands on her hips, she looks to me for further direction.

"Libby," I call toward my little one playing on the mattress with her dolls. "Daddy's home. Are you ready to surprise him?"

I close my writer's notebook, placing it on the counter, and position myself near the front door. Liberty trots over and takes my hand; she's unable to stand still. She bounces from her tiptoes to her heels over and over. She listens intently for sounds outside our door.

"Here he comes," I whisper when I hear Hamilton tapping in the code on our keypad. "Ready?"

Liberty's wide, brown eyes glimmer up at me as she nods, a huge smile upon her face. A giggle escapes as the door opens in front of us.

"Daddy!" Liberty squeals, extending her arms toward her father. "Sup-pize, Daddy! Sup-pize!"

Hamilton hugs Libby to his chest, kissing her cheek, then he looks to me for a clue. I motion for him to follow me into the living room. Liberty points excitedly at all that we've prepared for our family fun night.

"What's all this?" Hamilton asks, looking from Liberty to me to the bed on the floor.

Liberty wiggles in his arms until he puts her down. She runs onto the mattress then hops up and down. She spins in a circle with arms straight out at her sides. When she stops spinning, she points to her pajamas and mine.

"Jama party," she informs her daddy. She points to a pillow on the far left. "Daddy." She points to the middle pillow. "Wibby." She points to the pillow on the far right. "Mommy and baby brover." She turns to face Hamilton, a proud smile upon her face.

Hamilton's brow furrows in my direction.

"We are having a pajama party tonight and sleeping in the living room. We've chosen movies, books, and toys for the evening so we can enjoy the hours we have left."

He smiles approvingly, "A pajama party? That sounds like fun."

"Libby, shouldn't Daddy go put on his jammies?" I prompt, hoping to get some alone time with him. "Let's get some treats. You work on tricks with McGee and Indie while I help Daddy find his pajamas."

Safely out of Liberty's earshot, I explain my plans to Hamilton. "I wanted Liberty to sleep with us tonight but feared she might start a bad habit if she slept in our bedroom. So, I created a way for the three of us to sleep outside of our bedroom. We'll let her stay up late—she can sleep on the long drive to Athens tomorrow." I know I'm rambling.

As Hamilton removes his shirt, my breath catches. I only see his back—his strong, sexy-as-hell back. I marvel as his muscles flex with his movements. As if he senses my ogling eyes and thoughts, he turns to face me, t-shirt in hand and smirk upon his lips. I use all my strength to remain seated on the bed while my body yearns to rub against him like a cat.

This is Liberty's night, not mine. Tonight, she gets all of Hamilton's attention. I have to press down my needs until we are alone in the hotel tomorrow night. I can do this for my daughter. I can do this for him.

I dart into our attached bath, busying myself by running a brush through my hair before securing it into a high ponytail. "I thought we would fix dinner together, watch a movie, play with her toys, read a book, and cuddle as we watch another movie," I explain.

I watch in the reflection of the mirror as he approaches. He's in his blue, plaid, flannel pajama pants, slung low on his hips and a snug light blue t-shirt. I wet my lips as I take in the faint outline of the ripples of his abdominals. I long to remove his shirt, run my fingertips along his defined muscles, and fantasize about following his happy trail below the band of his bottoms.

"Stop that," he growls at my ear, his warm breath tickling my exposed neck.

In the mirror, I find my hand raised as if reaching out to touch him, my lips parted, and my chest heaving as I breathe. Stop that! Tonight, is Liberty's last night with her daddy. I need to be strong.

I glance at the time on my wrist. 10:05 p.m. Our little girl fought sleep for over two hours past her usual bedtime. I smile at the sight of her cuddling Cubbie Bear between her and Hamilton's chest. His strong arms hold her to him, her head upon his chest as the end of The Sandlot plays before us. I smooth a few curls behind her tiny ear.

"I'm going to miss this," Hamilton murmurs.

I find his eyes on mine. They do not hide his sadness, his hesitation, and his tiredness. It's been a busy week, and a much busier weekend awaits us.

"You'll FaceTime us in the evening," I remind him, knowing our plan does little to soothe his sadness. "She loves video calls. We can read books, talk about our day, and count down the sleeps until we can visit."

He nods.

"We'll make it work." I hate my words as I attempt to make it better. "Spring training will fly by. You'll see."

Again, he nods. On his face, I see the battle he fights within; I see his fight to control his emotions. He's trying to be strong for us just as we are for him.

159

HAMILTON

Liberty and Madison sleep the first several hours of our six-hour drive to Athens. I worry in my absence that Madison will not rest as she should; even though I've asked several people to keep an eye on her, it's my job as her husband to care for her during our pregnancy.

I've listened to my teammates talk about juggling baseball and family; it just never hit home until now. I'll be the one they tease for ducking out early to call home. I'll be the one not hanging out after practice in order to speak to my daughter before she falls asleep. They'll say I'm "whipped," and I will love it. I'm proud to be married. I'm proud to be a father. I hope I can juggle my traveling for work and being an involved parent.

Liberty coughs for the second time since she's been asleep. I hope she's not coming down with a cold. I hate the thought of Madison adding illness to her plate in my first week away. Madison stirs. Her groggy eyes greet mine before I turn my attention back to the interstate stretching out before us.

"I hope she's not coming down with something." She parrots my thoughts.

I'm truly amazed at the mother she's become; while I struggle to learn all that a parent needs to know each day, she seems to come by it naturally. Even asleep, she hears her child's cough, and her maternal instincts kick in.

"She's coughed twice," I report.

"Could just be a new tooth, but I'll keep an eye on it," Madison states, adjusting her seat to a more upright position. "When it's convenient, I need to pee."

Of course, she does. I've been fortunate she slept so long. The rest of our journey will require hourly bathroom breaks. I don't complain. This will be one of the things I will miss in the weeks to come.

My girls squeezed another 45-minute nap in during the final leg of our trip. It's amazing that they don't wake up immediately when we pull onto the gravel road. "Sleepy heads," I call into the quiet cab of the SUV. "We're pulling into the farm."

In the rearview mirror, I witness Liberty stretch and groan in her car seat in the back. I smile at her lack of energy; she wakes from naps like her mother, slow and grouchy.

Madison looks in the mirror on the visor, wipes drool from the corner of her mouth, and groans. "That's definitely not sexy."

"I love you just the way you are," I state.

"You just wait until I've gained 40 pounds, have constant gas, and can't find a comfortable position for more than 15 minutes. Then, you'll see just how lovable I am," she offers.

I look forward to it. The videos of her pregnant belly with Liberty safe inside were the most beautiful I'd ever seen of her. I can't wait to splay my hand on her swollen abdomen, feel our child move within her, and treat her like the queen she is. I missed all of it with Liberty. I'm anxious to experience it all this time around.

Mom greets us in the driveway; it seems she just can't get enough of her granddaughter. I love that I've given her this gift—that we've given her Liberty. We worried that after the Valentine's Gala, she'd hear from someone else, but she didn't. I can't wait to share our news with her today or for October to get here to introduce her to another grandchild.

She opens the back door and releases Liberty from her seat before Madison and I exit the front. I signal for Madison to follow them inside, but she still follows me to the back for the luggage.

"What do you think you are doing? Because, I know you're not attempting to carry one of Liberty's two bags into the house," I only half tease.

When she huffs her sexy little huff, I prompt her to carry the backpack we use as a diaper bag. It's my attempt to let her help without over-exerting herself. I swat her playfully on the behind as we join Mom near the house.

"I have a surprise in the barn," Mom states. "We'll be back in a bit."

I move to follow; Mom stops me in my tracks.

"Stay. We'll be right back," she smiles.

In her smile, I read that she knows I'm reluctant to let Liberty out of my sight during our last moments together. I hate that I am that easy to read.

Madison excuses herself to use the restroom yet again as a cell phone rings on the kitchen table. Amy's face graces the screen.

"Hi," I answer.

"Well, that answers my question," Amy chuckles. "We're 10 minutes out." She disconnects without a goodbye.

I guess I need to come to grips with the fact that my final minutes with my daughter will not be as I'd hoped. Once Aunt Amy arrives, Liberty will have little time for me nor care that I'm leaving her tomorrow.

Madison

"Everything okay?" Hamilton asks, knocking lightly on the bathroom door.

"Yes, I'm just freshening up after the long car ride," I lie, frantically wiping tears from my face. I splash cold water on my eyes and cheeks, hoping to erase the redness. In the mirror, I find my eyes are still puffy. I can only hope Hamilton doesn't notice. He doesn't understand how pregnancy hormones affect me.

Slowly, I open the door, walking into the kitchen.

"There she is," Amy greets, swiftly wrapping me in a hug.

I notice the twins she cares for, running around the kitchen table when Memphis returns with an excited Liberty.

"Mommy, baby kitties!" Liberty announces upon joining us.

Amy's boyfriend chases the twins into the front room with the promise of toys. Liberty follows behind, not about to let two boys have all the fun. My head spins with all that surrounds me.

"Well, I'm waiting," Memphis prompts, arms across her chest and toe tapping on the linoleum.

My eyes dart to Hamilton in hopes he knows what his mother means. He shrugs back at me.

Memphis laughs, her eyes holding in tears. "When I told Libby about the baby kitties in the barn, she told me she had a surprise, too."

I smile. "Honestly, I figured Hamilton told you over the phone," I inform my mother-in-law. "He's had a difficult time trying to keep the secret. Liberty has known for three weeks, and you're the first person she's told."

"I wanted to tell you in person," Hamilton apologizes, embracing his mom. "We're having a baby in October."

"That's fast," Amy deadpans from across the room.

Hamilton turns away from his mother, a smile glued upon his face.

"Amy, be nice," Memphis admonishes.

Emotional, I take the nearest kitchen chair and fan my overheated face. Without missing a beat, Hamilton slips me a bottle of water, and his mom holds an ice pack to the back of my neck.

"Would you happen to have any saltines?" I ask a concerned Memphis.

"Of course," she replies.

Amy fetches a sleeve of crackers faster than her mother can. "Morning sickness?"

"Now, didn't you say that you didn't have that with Liberty?" Memphis moves the ice pack to my forehead and allows me to hold it myself.

"Just a couple of times, like, only when I'm tired. I think I'm a little car sick," I confess. "I tried to sleep most of the ride."

"Your driving that bad, bro?" Amy punches Hamilton playfully in his right arm.

"There's nothing wrong with his driving," I defend.

Hamilton smiles my way. "Anything I can do?"

I wish there was a way he could solve this for me. He wants so much to help. I worry he feels helpless. At this early stage of pregnancy, there isn't much for him to do. That will change by the third trimester.

As the hot flash fades, I place the ice pack upon the table. I nibble on another cracker and sip water. The increasing noise level from the front room draws our attention. The twins burst into the kitchen at full speed like a herd of cattle.

"Freeze!" Amy demands in a loud, authoritative mom-voice, causing me to flinch.

Amazingly, the wild boys freeze in their tracks. They stand wide-eyed, waiting for Amy to continue.

"We don't run in Memphis' house," Amy reminds them, bending to their eye-level. "Now, go play with toys in the living room, and use your inside voices."

The twins return to the front room. I decide Liberty might be out of her comfort zone with these two, so I excuse myself to join them, and the other adults soon follow.

Liberty hands a vehicle to both boys. The three roll their toys over the carpet, chatting and making car sounds. I keep my attention on the children while Memphis talks with Hamilton excitedly, timing the baby's birth for the end of the season, and wanting to know about his travel plans on Sunday. I hear the conversation but focus more on the interaction between the children. Liberty holds her own. I'm ever mindful of her interactions with peers, as Dr. Conway discussed. The boys are one year older than her and seem to accept her.

"Feeling better?" Hamilton murmurs, leaning towards me.

I nod.

The rowdy boys begin arguing over a toy tractor. They scuffle and yell.

"Fweeze!" Liberty yells with hands on her hips.

Surprisingly, the twins freeze, looking up to where she stands. Memphis and Hamilton burst out laughing. I cover my mouth with my hand in an attempt to prevent my giggles.

"That's my niece," Amy boasts.

"Whoa," Amy's male friend, Marshall, smiles. "She truly is a mini-Amy." He turns to face Amy. "I just had a flash of you as a child."

No one contains their laughter now. Although Amy tries to act offended, she doesn't succeed in hiding her amusement. Liberty simply takes the tractor from both boys, keeping it for herself, and hands them other vehicles. They return to their play, the boys a bit calmer now.

"As much as I hate it, we need to get back on the road," Hamilton states, standing.

"I'm going to make another trip to the bathroom," I announce, exiting the living room.

"Maybe we'll make it all the way to the hotel without having to stop," Hamilton teases.

I call from the bathroom doorway, "I heard that!"

I take my time in the bathroom, washing my face and patting it dry. I'm tired and my hormones are getting the best of me. I hope Hamilton takes care of his goodbyes with Liberty and Memphis before I emerge. I'm sure I'll be a blubbering mess if I witness his final goodbye with our daughter.

160

MADISON

We pull into the hotel shortly before six. I'm slow to step from the vehicle, and I take a moment to stretch my aching muscles. It feels more like I ran a half-marathon than rode in an SUV all day. Hamilton keenly watches my every movement and subsequent expressions.

"I'm okay," I promise. "Just spent too many hours in the car today."

"Let's get checked in so you can relax a bit before the rehearsal dinner." Hamilton guides me with a firm hand on the small of my back. With his other hand, he rolls our luggage behind us.

I stand in line at the reception desk while another family checks in. A ping signals the opening of the elevator doors; with loud conversation, Savannah and Lincoln's families spill out.

Savannah quickly spots me. I wave, and she scurries in my direction, wrapping me in a tight embrace.

"Savannah, you're squeezing my bladder." I beg for her to let up.

"Let's pee." Savannah tugs me by the hand. She turns to Lincoln and his family. "Pregnancy pee; we'll be a few minutes."

Inside the small bathroom made for one, she locks the door then leans her back against it with a sigh. Unable to hold myself any longer, I assume a seated position on the toilet.

"That bad?" I ask my stressed-out friend.

"You have no idea," Savannah answers.

"So, fill me in. What happened since we talked yesterday morning?" After I flush, I wash my hands, looking to Savannah in the mirror.

She rolls her eyes in my direction before taking her turn on the toilet. "My wedding dress arrived." Her tone tells me that this has been one of the worst things so far.

"Oh no," I face her while drying my hands. "Does it not fit?"

Flushing, Savannah washes her hands near me at the sink as our eyes lock in the mirror.

"It's hideous," she informs. "It's a white muumuu like my grandmother used to wear. Sure, it has some lace and a flower or two, but that doesn't help."

My friend looks as defeated as she sounds.

"I wanted to elope, but Lincoln agreed to a tiny ceremony to appease his mother. She offered to make all the arrangements while I dealt with Valentine's Day in the bakery. Now, I'm paying for it," she sighs, rubbing a hand down her face. "The guest list tops out over 150. She's planned a ceremony, a dinner, and even hired a DJ for dancing."

My mind reels with this new information. Unsure how to help, I rub my hand up and down her arm.

"The wedding dress resembles a tent." Her voice cracks as her emotions take over. "It's a giant, white, circus tent. It's so big that it will still fit when I'm nine months pregnant!"

She tugs her cell phone out of her pocket, scrolling through photos. She passes the phone to me. She's not exaggerating—it's a muumuu. Certainly not a dress any women would choose for her wedding dress. What mother would pick this for her son's fiancé?

"Sav," I murmur and clear my throat. "We'll fix this. First thing tomorrow, we'll visit a dress shop. We won't stop until we find the perfect dress for the wedding she planned." I wipe tears from her cheeks. "I will not let you wear a muumuu to your wedding. Understand?"

Moments pass before Savannah nods.

"I can't uninvite her guests or cancel the catering, but I can promise you that our Athens crew will help you enjoy the DJ."

Savannah laughs through her remaining tears. "So, if I can make it through the ceremony and dinner, I'll have fun?"

"Knowing Adrian," I whisper in her ear, "she'll find a way to help you enjoy the wedding and dinner, too. C'mon," I urge. "Lincoln and Hamilton will worry if we don't leave the bathroom soon."

After one more swipe away of the tears, Savannah takes a deep, calming breath, fanning her face, and we open the heavy bathroom door.

"I was about to send a search party," Hamilton's deep, concerned voice greets us mere steps from the bathroom. "Everything okay?"

"When a girl's gotta go, a girl's gotta go," Savannah spouts sarcastically.

Hamilton's eyes dart to mine, silently seeking a sign. I give a tiny smile and nod to inform him all is okay.

Lincoln approaches, followed by his family,

Before he speaks, his mother bites out, "Finally. Come on now; it's time to start the rehearsal."

I thought we had an hour. I hoped to freshen up in our hotel room and change out of my travel clothes. Hamilton senses my dilemma.

"I'm sure they'd understand if you need to go to the room for a few minutes," he whispers.

"It's okay," I lie. "Would you mind taking up our bags?"

"Do you need me to bring you anything?" he murmurs, not drawing attention to our conversation.

"I'd like my water bottle," I confess. Keeping it nearby will ensure I stay hydrated. We can't have the matron of honor suffering from fatigue and morning sickness. Savannah will be counting on me to be her buffer.

The sound of Lincoln's mother rudely clearing her throat alerts us she's displeased with my delay. Hamilton softly kisses my forehead before turning me towards her. With a gentle shove, he sends me on my way.

"What's wrong with Savannah?" Hamilton whispers in my ear as we sit at a large table with Lincoln's sister and parents in the nearby barbecue restaurant.

"For starters, the smell of spices and smoked meat is turning my stomach." I admit. "I'm sure it's upsetting her stomach, too, as she suffers from morning sickness constantly now." I sip from my water glass before leaning closer to his ear. "They didn't listen to her and Lincoln's plans for the wedding, and, to top it all off, they chose a hideous gown for her to wear."

"Seriously?" he whispers back.

I nod. "We're taking her emergency dress shopping in the morning. I'll be damned if I let them treat her this way."

The next morning, we sneak out on our mission to find a wedding dress. "I'll text you updates," I inform Lincoln and Hamilton.

Savannah and I watch for a moment as they start toward the restaurant around the corner to wait for us.

Inside a bridal shop, I immediately explain the situation to the saleswoman. She's appalled and enlists two other women to help us search their inventory. Savannah admits she's not a fan of dresses and wants nothing flashy. They escort Savannah into a dressing room. I almost laugh as they scurry this way and that, placing options over the door for Savannah to try on. Wanting to help, I begin browsing a nearby rack.

I've found it! In my hands, I hold two white pantsuits. These will be perfect for Savannah. I quickly return to the dressing room door and knock three times.

"Savannah," I call. "I think I found the perfect one. Well, I found two."

Savannah cracks the door a couple of inches; on her face, I see her desperation. I pass the two hangers to her.

"I want to see them both," I state, letting her know she will no longer try on items without modeling for us.

The moments that pass seem to take forever. I'm anxious to solve this issue for my friend.

"I'm coming out," Savannah announces, opening the door.

"Oh Savannah," I gasp. "Does the smile on your face mean you've found your wedding dress? I mean, suit."

Savannah turns one way then another in front of the three-way mirror. Her smile reaches her eyes and color has returned to her cheeks. The clerks return sharing their approval, and Savannah's glow grows brighter.

"It's not very traditional," Savannah states, worried what others might think.

"Anything goes in weddings nowadays," the saleswoman declares. "A bride last week chose a green dress."

Savannah and I smile wide-eyed at one another.

"You look perfect," I state. "This is your wedding—your special day. You should wear what you're comfortable with. Something that makes you feel like a princess on your special day."

The women agree.

"I'll take it," Savannah proudly states.

As she slips into the changing room, I call after her, "I dare Lincoln's mom to comment on your choice. I've got your back on this one."

"I don't want to cause a scene," Savannah calls back through the door.

"Oh, there won't be a scene," I assure her. "I'll get my point across discreetly I promise."

I text the men to share our good news.

ME

we found one!

HAMILTON

already

ME

it's perfect

stay put we'll come to you

we're hungry

HAMILTON

CU soon

Hamilton and Lincoln tease us about our eclectic food choices while Savannah and I nibble. Between the two of us, we ordered two appetizers and two meals to share. Of course, we will not eat half of it. It seems we craved a variety. They should just be glad we were hungry and not sick in the restroom.

"I'm wondering if I might ask another favor of the two of you," Lincoln asks as the waiter clears our table.

"Of course," Hamilton promptly replies.

"Savannah and I would like to elope and hope you'll be our witnesses." Lincoln leans in, placing a kiss at Savannah's temple. "We searched the internet last night."

"We found a site called *KC Weddings 2 Go,*" Savannah raises two fingers as she speaks. "They have a chapel in Independence, it's a 15-minute drive, and we booked for one o'clock."

Hamilton looks at his phone. "We better get on the road then," he states, rising from the booth and extending a hand to assist me.

"And you were worried about what they'd think of your choice of attire for the wedding?" I tease a now blushing Savannah.

"We still plan to go through with my mother's ruse of a wedding this evening," Lincoln informs. "We just wanted to do it our way."

"I love it," I announce.

Hamilton leans in close; his whisper tickles my ear. "We'll hurry back and squeeze in some alone time before the guests arrive tonight."

Warmth settles in my belly with his words. I want nothing more than to dart back to our room right now. My pregnancy hormones kick in—the slightest touch revs my engine quickly.

I look from one side of the room to the other, needing to relieve myself before our next adventure. "We should…"

Hamilton speaks at the same time, "You should use the bathroom."

Savannah and I head to the restroom amidst all of our laughter.

161

MADISON

Hamilton passes our keys to the valet and quickly ushers me into the hotel. I do my best to keep up with his quick steps. He presses the button, summoning the elevator. Once. Twice. Then, even, a third time.

"What time does the Athens gang plan to arrive?" Hamilton asks impatiently while we wait.

It's clear that I am not the only one anxious to spend as much time as we can together.

"Four o'clock," I answer as a ping alerts us to the arrival of the elevator.

We've got under two hours before we must be dressed and back downstairs. With the shutting of the doors, Hamilton pounces; my breath catches as I'm pressed to the wall. Hamilton's body pins mine, his hot breath caressing my cheek as his lips approach. He holds nothing back. I struggle to breathe while his lips and powerful tongue pummel mine.

"Ham," I moan, trying to get his attention. I press my hands firmly against his chest.

Only inches apart, we stand, gasping. I slide along the wall, placing space between us. He turns, a worried look upon his face. I hate that his mind instantly fears the worst in every situation. He's constantly worried about the baby.

"We should wait until we are safe in our room," I explain.

Unable to control all of his urges, Hamilton pulls me tight against him, kissing me once more. At our floor, I quickly start for our room. I hear Hamilton's heavy steps quickly approaching, so I squeal and run for our door.

I fumble with the key card which allows Hamilton to catch me. His large hands grip my hips tightly. He spins me to face him, my back plastered to the hotel room door. My heartbeat and breath quicken. I press my palms into his muscular chest, playfully attempting to push him away.

Hamilton refuses to move. He presses closer still, devouring my mouth in his. My head swims as the majority of my blood flows toward my center. My body heats, my chest heaves, the hairs on the back of my neck prickle, and a throbbing ache emanates between my thighs. I want him to take me here in the hallway, against this door. His molten eyes lock on mine; he deftly slides the key card through the lock. A beep sounds. Giggling like a teenager, I flee into the room with him on my heels.

Hamilton stalks towards me near the foot of the bed. I feel like a gazelle as a lion approaches on the Serengeti. His brown eyes smolder, fixed on mine. My lips part, and my blood feels electric, pulsing through my veins. In a trance, I sit on the edge of the bed. My hands grasp the bedspread; anticipation electrifies my every cell.

He pulls me by the upper arms to stand in front of him. His mouth covers mine, probes it, while his hands frantically seek to rid me of all my clothing. Mine follow suit, bumbling with his belt and waistband. It feels like years rather than days since I last felt him within me.

Hamilton

Madison lies pressed to my chest; my arms wrapped around her body. Her shallow, even breaths are the only sounds within the dark room. I only meant to hold her for a moment; I know we must prepare for tonight's event. As quickly as she fell asleep, I know she needs to rest. So, I push down the urge to ravage her one more time before our friends arrive.

Eyeing the time on my phone, I see that I've let her sleep as long as possible. I comb my fingers gently through her light brown hair, causing her to stir. Madison's eyes flutter while her face registers confusion.

"You dozed off," I inform her. "I was going to wake you up in a few minutes."

She sits herself up against the headboard and attempts to curtail her sexed hair.

"I should get ready," Madison states sleepily.

Still naked, I slip from beneath the sheet and head towards the bathroom. "I'll turn on the shower for you."

The warm spray started, I shut the shower door to allow the stall to fill with steam, but Madison's hand stops me. She slips past me, naked, pulling her disheveled hair into a bun atop her head. Joining her, I stand just outside the spray. Beads of water glisten upon her shoulders and back. My hands rise to secure her hips; they pause in mid-air. We need to be downstairs soon; I shouldn't let my selfish needs interfere with her supporting Savannah this evening.

I squeeze a dollop of body wash into my palms then proceed to slather her shoulders. My hands cover her back, trailing further and further down. I debate internally whether to continue soaping her bottom. I hesitate but only a moment before my body acts. I stare as my large hands slather her soft skin. They splay, and my fingertips press into her cheeks.

Madison's head falls back against my shoulder. Wasting no time, my hands seek her hips, pulling her tight to me. I watch the spray sprinkle upon her chest, her nipples puckering at the sensation. My cock swells, tucked pleasantly in the crevice of her ass. She grinds her bottom against my pelvis, the slickness of the soap easing the movement. My hands climb up her sides. My fingertips glide over the wet skin covering her ribs. In the pitter-patter of the water, I hear her mew. It's my undoing. A primal need consumes me, and I lose all control.

First, I spin then plant her against the glass shower wall. My palms flat on either side of her, I stand, arms fully extended, admiring the gorgeous woman before me. My erection mimics my arms, reaching towards its target. As my eyes sweep over her thighs and swollen mound, my cock twitches. It strains to reach her. It seeks her warm heat surrounding it.

Lost in my desire, I flinch when first one, then a second hand grasp my shaft. My lips part and eyelids grow heavy as I watch her eyes focused on her task. Her tongue darts out, swiping her lower lip. I'm the luckiest man alive to be loved by this magnificent creature.

Madison

I can't be late; Savannah needs me to act as a buffer between her and Lincoln's mother and sister. I need to protect her from their reaction to our secret, morning shopping. I quickly slip on my dress and heels. In a hurry, I apply minimal makeup.

"Should I go down and greet our friends?" Hamilton asks, leaning against the door frame between the bed and bathroom. "I can let them know you'll join us soon."

"I didn't want to get my hair wet," I spit in his direction before returning to my task. "That's why I pulled it up before I got into the shower." My eyes glare at him in the mirror.

The jerk has the nerve to smirk.

"Smirking sexy will not get you out of this one," I admonish. "There's no way to dry and style it in the next 10 minutes. I'll have to pull it into a pony-tail." I scowl.

I hear the sound of the hotel room door closing behind him. What. The. Hell? I'm the one upset, and he storms out without a word? My ire increases and bile rises in my throat. I pull my brush through my tangles much harder than necessary. Tears form in the corners of my eyes. I will not cry. I will not cry. I have no time to touch up my makeup if I do.

A faint beep alerts me to Hamilton's return. I quickly blot a tissue to each tear then return to brushing.

"We've got our work cut out for us," Adrian professes.

My breath catches. "What…"

"Hamilton claims he let you nap longer than he should, and you need help fixing your hair." She smirks at my reflection. "Judging by your severe bed head, the clothes strewn haphazardly, the twisted sheets, and the bomb that exploded in here," her arms sweep toward the water and towels on the tile floor, "I assume sleep is not the culprit."

Wide-eyed, I gape at her as heat floods my face.

"Blushing. It must have been really good," Adrian teases, taking my brush. "Let's create maiden braids."

She doesn't wait for my approval. She begins braiding and twisting. I relax on the bench as my friend whips my hair into shape.

"Thank you." I place my hand on top of hers.

"You can pay me back by giving me every steamy detail later tonight," Adrian states.

She's not kidding. My friend will badger me all evening for every sexy morsel.

Hamilton

Madison's not mad at me. She's worried she might be late, letting Savannah down. I'm sure by now Adrian has helped her with her hair, and they'll be joining us soon.

My phone vibrates in my slacks pocket. The screen announces Berkeley's call.

"Hello," I murmur, turning away from my friends and taking a few steps away for privacy.

While my friends from Athens converse loudly, I attempt to listen to Berkeley's words. Latham approaches, concern on his face. I hold my hand out, halting him.

"Berkeley, I need to go now. Handle this and inform me of every step. If I don't answer, text me the details. The ceremony starts in 20 minutes." With my hand on my forehead, I draw in a long, calming breath. "I want to press charges." I disconnect the call.

"Everything okay?" Latham asks.

I nod. "It will be."

It better be. I'm not sure how Madison will react to this. She already struggles to adapt to our new life. I can't let my public persona disrupt her life or that of our daughter.

Following Latham back to the group, I glance to my right. The female front desk clerk from check in is staring at me. It has to be her. She's the only staff member that's recognized me. Her name tag stated she was the assistant manager. I'm sure that allowed her access to the security tapes. Just how much money did the gossip show offer her for the footage?

I turn my attention to the elevator when it pings, anxious to see Madison. I need her near to calm my anger. Adrian emerges, immediately gathering the group to join the other wedding guests in the ballroom.

My brow furrows. Where's my wife?

"Madison will be down with Savannah shortly," Adrian mentions in passing.

I glance at my phone screen before tucking it into my front pants pocket. Berkeley's good at her job. She'll handle this. I only hope she's able to stop it before the show airs tonight.

162

MADISON

"Here we go," Lincoln grasps Savannah's hand. Signaling to Hamilton and me, he urges, "You two go on in. We'll join you at the front in a moment."

I squeeze Savannah's hand. We share a smile, and I wink. We're about to reveal a betrayal, and I know Lincoln's mother will not appreciate it. I remind myself to not make a scene as I protect Savannah from the fall out. My friend is happy, and that is all that matters.

Hamilton opens the door, the crowd quiets, and all eyes fall on us as we make our way down the makeshift aisle. At the front, Hamilton places a chaste kiss upon my lips before we part, awaiting the arrival of the bride and groom.

The guests stand when Lincoln and Savannah appear. Audible gasps are heard at their beauty. My eyes are locked on Lincoln's mother and sister. Seated in the front row, they have yet to notice Savannah's attire.

Lincoln escorts his lovely wife slowly up the aisle. Lincoln's mother's hand flies to her mouth, and his sister leans close to speak in her ear. They've noticed Savannah is sans muumuu. My friend beams. No doubt she's more comfortable and confident in her pantsuit.

At the front, they turn to face the crowd. Lincoln leans in to whisper in Savannah's ear. She pats his arm, and they turn to face the minister. Lincoln releases her arm and steps towards him. They speak quietly for a moment which ends with a nod from the preacher.

With a microphone in hand, Lincoln faces the crowd, smiles at Savannah, then announces, "There will not be a wedding."

Murmurs sweep through the crowd as heads turn from one to another. He waits for the reaction to wane before continuing, "Savannah and I are already married."

With this news, the crowd sighs with relief. His mother and sister look offended while his father simply smiles with hands folded in his lap.

"We took a trip this morning and eloped," Lincoln states before kissing Savannah's cheek and holding her hand. "We hope you will now join us for our reception. My mother and sister planned a delicious dinner and secured a DJ for dancing. Thanks again for coming. Let the fun begin!"

The crowd cheers while Lincoln's family approaches the newlyweds. Hamilton joins me, standing behind Savannah and Lincoln in solidarity.

"Congratulations." Lincoln's father hugs his son, patting him hard on the back. Next, he hugs Savannah. "Welcome to the family."

"Where's the dress I spent hours hunting?" His sister's snotty tone causes my hackles to rise.

"Stop!" Lincoln demands.

"I can't believe you disrespected the hours we spent putting this together for you," his mother whines. "I need to sit down; I'm not feeling well."

The strong woman I observed yesterday suddenly disappears as she attempts to seem frail. She portrayed a healthy woman until Lincoln's announcement. I imagine she's faking it as she didn't get her way. Father and daughter fuss over Lincoln's mother; we wait and watch.

Lincoln's sister walks towards Savannah. "This is all your fault," she points towards Savannah and me. "We scrambled to plan this wedding for you. We shopped online for hours and in several bridal shops to find the perfect dress for you. And what do you do? You're ungrateful. You ruin everything."

I step in front of Savannah, but before I can speak, Lincoln jumps in.

"You love the dress," he pokes his sister's shoulder. "Your fiancé is here. Go put on the 'perfect dress,' and let's have your perfect wedding right now."

Her lips, covered in bright red lipstick, open and close like a fish out of water. "Well... uh..." she sputters.

Lincoln tugs her arm towards the door, "C'mon. I'll escort you to the dress."

"It's not perfect for me," her shrill voice shouts. "It's perfect for her." She points at Savannah. "We did all of this for her."

"No, you didn't," I spit. "Savannah and Lincoln asked for a small wedding. Savannah stated she didn't want her mother to attend. They asked you to keep it simple." I stand nose to nose with her. "You didn't listen, or you didn't care."

I point to Lincoln's mother. "You planned a big wedding that you wanted. You invited her mother. You planned a large dinner and chose a hideous dress."

I take a quick breath. "The 'perfect dress' is a muumuu that old women wear. It resembles a white tent big enough to fit three women inside. You tried to humiliate her and don't even try to deny it." My index finger moves between mother and daughter.

Lincoln jumps in. "I gave in when you begged to plan a simple wedding for us," Looking to his mother, he shakes his head. "I decided last night that I wouldn't allow you ruin our special day and took matters into my own hands." He pulls Savannah snug to his side. "If you disrespect Savannah, you disrespect me. And I will not stand for it. I love Savannah, we're happy, and the two of you better get on board or get used to me not being in your life. Now, if you'll excuse us, my wife and I would like to go greet over 100 guests we didn't want at our wedding."

With that closing remark, Lincoln escorts Savannah towards the tables and their guests. Hamilton and I remain with the family. I want to make sure they don't plan to cause a scene.

Lincoln's father tells his wife to come enjoy their son's special day before he follows the newlyweds as they mingle through the guests at their tables.

"Let's eat," Hamilton suggests, guiding me toward empty seats near our friends.

I lower myself into the seat beside Adrian that Hamilton pulls out for me.

"I'll be right back," Hamilton states, walking to the doors.

I don't have time to ask any questions. I watch as he looks to his phone. I quickly look at my phone, worried I missed a call from Memphis regarding Liberty. I breathe a sigh of relief when the screen shows no missed calls or messages.

Hamilton returns a few minutes later with a large gift bag in hand. Now I know what he was up to. The photos we purchased of this morning's wedding ceremony have arrived. I wave for Savannah to join us at the table as Hamilton returns to my side. He hands the bag to the newlyweds.

Savannah pulls out the framed eight-by-ten print while Lincoln flips through the scrapbook of many more shots.

"How did you do this?" Lincoln asks, not tearing his eyes from the photos.

"Hamilton placed a rush order while I distracted you," I explain.

Our friends join in, congratulating the couple and enjoying the photos.

Again, Hamilton's distracted by his cell phone. I place my hand on his holding the phone. "Something wrong?"

He swiftly tucks his cell into his front pocket. Leaning in, he whispers near my ear, "I need to return a call. It should only take a moment."

Try as I might, I can't decipher the emotions on his face. Is it worry? Is it anger? Or is it something else? He slips out the door, leaving me worried about what might be more important than our friend's wedding. Slowly, conversation pulls my attention back to the room.

Hamilton

In my peripheral, as I hold my phone to my ear, I notice a gentleman striding my way in the lobby.

"It will not air," Berkeley promises. "Seems once I provided proof that it was your wife in the video and not some groupie, they no longer cared to distort the video for the purposes of the show."

"Good," I bite, frustrated. "And what of the copies of the video?"

"They assure me they have deleted them, and they apologize," Berkeley states. "They only ran with the story based on the false information the hotel staff member gave them. Hamilton, don't you have a wedding you should be at?"

"Yes, thank you." With her assurance that the matter is over, I need to return to the reception. I'm sure Madison is upset with me. We end our call, and I head to the ballroom.

"Excuse me, sir," an older gentleman standing behind me calls. "Mr. Armstrong?"

"Yes," I turn to face the stranger, the man that had approached while I was on the phone.

He informs me he is the manager of the hotel before apologizing profusely for the behavior of his assistant manager. I'm only half listening as Madison approaches the two of us. Without saying a word, she stands beside me.

"I'll comp your stay," the manager states.

"That won't be necessary," I respond. "We were able to squash it before any damage occurred. It is not the hotel's fault; the employee acted alone."

I feel Madison's arm slide along mine; then, her fingers curl into mine.

"We are responsible for the security and privacy of all our guests," the manager states. "I feel we need to..."

"It's not necessary," I interrupt. "I'm pleased with the prompt manner in which you remedied the situation. Let's just leave it at that."

"I'll let you return to your engagement," the manager offers before excusing himself.

Madison squeezes my hand. I release her to pull her to my chest, wrapping my arms around her body. I need to put her mind at rest. I'm sure she has a thousand questions, but I need to hold her. I've attempted to hold my emotions inside while I waited to hear the fate of the leaked video, and now it's all crashing down at once.

"So, is everything okay, now?" Madison murmurs into my chest.

"Yes." My voice cracks. I clear my throat. "The call I had to make was to Berkeley. She assured me that all is taken care of."

"Well then," Madison pulls back to look up at me. "Shall we go celebrate?"

I search her cerulean eyes. Does she really not need to know everything right now? Doesn't she want to know what happened?

Pulling my hand toward the doors of the ballroom, Madison informs me, "You can tell me what you've dealt with for the past two hours when we're alone in our room tonight."

"I love you," I profess loudly. In return, I'm awarded with a beautiful smile.

"Son," Lincoln's father greets me as we reenter the ballroom, "I'll make my announcement in a moment. I'd like you to stand near me when I do."

Madison's inquisitive eyes dart to mine. I didn't tell her about my previous conversation with him—I didn't see the need to. I offered my opinion. I didn't think he would include me any more than that.

"So many secrets," Madison smiles.

I shrug. "You'll love this surprise," I inform her as we follow him to the front of the venue.

With a microphone in hand, he asks for the guests' attention. Unfortunately, he holds the microphone too far from his mouth and the crowd's too loud in their conversations to hear him. The music is still playing in the background.

Madison pulls a chair from a nearby table and hops to stand on it. At the top of her lungs she announces, "Quiet!"

Instantly, the room is silent—my girl has a gift. She motions for Lincoln's father to continue.

"My wife and I would like to present our wedding gift to Savannah and Lincoln," he begins.

Madison pushes the mic closer to his mouth as he speaks.

His wife approaches with an open laptop. She passes it to Lincoln. I watch as tears flood Madison's eyes while she looks at the screen. Savannah and Lincoln stare in awe for a few moments before spinning the screen for the guests to view.

"We've purchased a home in Athens for the newlyweds," Lincoln's father announces. "We'd researched for a week. Then, with Hamilton's knowledge of Athens, we chose this lovely home. You can pick up the keys on Monday," he informs the couple.

The guests celebrate as Lincoln and Savannah share hugs with his family. Madison places herself directly in front of me, looking up with a wide smile.

"You've been a very busy man, Mr. Armstrong." She places hands on my jaw, pulling me in for a kiss.

Her warm lips on mine stoke a fire deep inside me. I return the kiss, running my tongue along her lower lip, begging entrance. She opens to me. Her body presses tight to mine as our tongues mingle. Her hands perch at my waist. The overwhelming sensation of them so near my cock coaxes a growl from deep in my throat. Summoning strength I didn't know I had, I pull my mouth from hers, resting my forehead to hers. My eyes remain closed as our breaths even out.

"When can we slip away?" I huskily whisper. I pray she feels as I do; I'm not sure how much longer I can refrain from ravaging her.

To my complete surprise, she whispers, "Let's say our goodbyes."

163

MADISON

The speed at which Hamilton shares our goodbyes thrills me. The anticipation of returning to our hotel room has built in me all evening. While I look forward to our alone time tonight, I know it means our goodbye tomorrow morning draws closer.

The girls giggle at Hamilton's urgency to leave the reception. I wish them all a happy Valentine's Day in hopes they'll remember it's our first as a couple.

As we wait for the elevator, Salem, Latham, Bethany, and Troy join us. I'm happy that, like us, they plan to enjoy tonight with no children. We make polite conversation with the other couples as we attempt to keep our hands and mouths off one another. The sexual tension is heavy inside the tiny compartment as it climbs.

When the ping signals our floor, we say our goodbyes to our friends before race-walking to our room. Hamilton doesn't chase me as he did earlier today; I'm disappointed when his hands remain in his trouser pockets while I unlock our door.

At the closing of the hotel door and the click of the lock, however, the air turns electric. I stand, frozen in his gaze. While riotous hormones hum through my veins, the weight of tonight enters my thoughts. It's our first Valentine's Day together. It's my first Valentine's Day with Hamilton or any guy for that matter. Tomorrow, I will drop my husband off at the airport for spring training. Forty-five days of Hamilton in Mesa, Arizona while Liberty and I are in Chicago. We plan to visit him in 10 days, but it's only for two nights. Tonight, is my last night with him, I plan to make it memorable.

I lower the zipper to my dress to my shoulder blades. Hamilton's molten, brown eyes devour my exposed collar bones. My skin heats, and my pulse quickens. I lower the zipper a few more inches down my back; then, I slip it from my shoulders. It quickly pools at my feet.

My skin prickles as the cool air bathes me. My right hand reaches to unfasten my bra, but he halts me; in two long strides, he's inches from me. Every part of me seeks contact with every part of him. His eyes scorch mine. When my tongue darts out to wet my lips, he pounces.

Immediately, his lips mash to mine, his hands are everywhere, and I'm totally naked.

"On the bed," he commands while removing his clothes.

I pull the comforter from the bed before laying on my back. My eyes take in the fine specimen of the man that I call my husband.

On all fours, Hamilton creeps up my body. Hovering above me, his eyes latch on mine.

"I love you," he huskily whispers.

I open my mouth to reply, but his mouth distracts me.

We're guttural moans, flailing limbs, groping hands, and shallow breaths as our bodies join, pushing us toward climax.

Struggling to catch my breath, I lie in post-orgasmic bliss as Hamilton enters the bathroom. I barely make out the sound of the shower over my breathing before he returns.

Taking my hand in his, he pulls me from bed and into the shower. I mew while his strong fingers massage my scalp, while he washes my hair under the warm spray.

Lost in my relaxation, I fail to notice Hamilton soap his hands and trail over my shoulders. As he caresses my breasts, I spark to life. The man pushes all of my buttons in the very best ways. Our shower turns hot, steamy, and sensual.

When we pour ourselves into bed, I fall asleep as soon as my head finds the pillow.

When the Sunday morning sunlight slips between the drapes, I fight the tears stinging my eyes. I mentally remind myself not to cry until I've dropped Hamilton off. I need to be strong for him.

"Good morning," he murmurs, pulling me tight to his chest.

"Mmm…" I moan, soaking in his warmth. "I love you."

He places a kiss upon the skin behind my ear. We hold each other without a word, dreading the next hour. I groan when Hamilton reaches to check the time on his phone.

"I need to shower, babe," he says.

I nod. Exhausted from our Valentine's celebrations last night, I decide to skip the shower. I drag my feet as I dress then pack my suitcase.

Emerging from the bathroom freshly showered and looking fine, Hamilton wraps his arms around my waist as he places closed-mouth kisses upon my nose and lips.

Without words, we communicate our reluctance to say goodbye.

I turn on the hazard lights when I park at the curb of the airport terminal. I hop from the driver's seat, meeting Hamilton on the sidewalk. I'm not supposed to leave the vehicle when dropping him off, but I don't care.

Hamilton's tired, chocolate eyes look down at me. I lick my lower lip before pulling it between my teeth.

"Ten days…" His voice cracks.

"Ten sleeps," I confirm, pasting a fake smile upon my face. "I love you. Text me when you land."

His warm, firm lips smother mine. Although we don't use tongues, it's one of the hottest kisses I've ever experienced. Too soon, he pulls away.

"I love you. Drive careful," he says, tapping his index finger to the tip of my nose.

With a baggage handler walking towards us, I wave before hustling back inside the vehicle. My heart is a heavy, burning weight in my chest. My sinuses sting as tears fill my eyes. I pull away from the curb, starting the long drive back to the farm.

An hour into the drive, I exit the interstate, preparing to drive on the slower, two-lane road the remainder of the trip. Checking it's clear, I pull from the stop sign onto the highway. As I barely accelerate, the SUV tires slip in the slick snow that's accumulated. I swiftly try to gain control as I fishtail a bit, breathing a sigh of relief when the car is moving safely again.

I note the dash shows it's 33 degrees outside as the precipitation continues to fall. The drizzle I'd driven through on the interstate turns more dangerous.

"Call Memphis," I command the car.

"Calling Memphis," the female voice confirms.

"Hello," her sweet voice greets on the second ring.

"Hi," I return, keeping most of my attention on driving. "I'm calling to let you know that I just turned onto Highway 6, and it's going to take me longer than normal."

"Slick?" Memphis asks I can hear concern in her voice.

"Yes, so I'm taking it slow." I confirm.

"Should you pull over and wait until the highway department treats the road?" she asks in her mom tone.

"I don't think it's that bad. I'll just slow down," I promise.

"Okay," Memphis says. "I'll let you go so you can focus."

The call disconnects, and I return all my focus to the driving conditions as my stress level rises.

Memphis and Liberty greet me at the door upon my safe arrival at the farm.

"You made it," Memphis cheers as my daughter claps.

"I could use a stiff drink," I inform her as I enter the kitchen. "I barely drove 40 miles-per-hour."

"Well, you can't relax with wine; how about a warm bath?" she suggests.

I shake my head; I only want to spend time with Liberty to distract my thoughts from already missing Hamilton.

"They've changed the forecast again," Memphis informs me later that afternoon.

I look at her phone as she scrolls through the next 24hours. Heavy snow-fall with blowing snow is now in the forecast.

"Mind if we stay a couple more days?" I ask.

"Of course not."

Twenty-four hours and six inches of snow later, the road-grader plows the gravel road leading to town. Latham cleared the lane earlier this morning, so we'd be ready to head to town when the main road was cleared.

Memphis plans to remain with Liberty while I drive to town to see my girls and pick up groceries. After assuring her the SUV has four-wheel drive, I promise I'll return prior to dark before she's okay with my expedition.

164

MADISON

I make it to Bethany's without any issues. I see my four girls in the open doorway as I exit the vehicle.

"I'm so glad you're here," Bethany greets, ushering me into her warm house.

"Yes, it sucks that it snowed, but I'm glad you get to stay a few more days," Savannah adds as we walk towards the kitchen.

"Hang on Bethany," I call from the back-entry way. "Do you have a side hustle I don't know about?"

"No, why?" she answers.

"What's this?" I ask.

Adrian jumps in saucily, "That's her new kink."

"It's not kink," Bethany bristles. "Troy saw that when he was doing construction on a local salon. They didn't want a third washing station anymore, and he remembered me going on and on every time I get my hair done about how good it feels when they massage my scalp." She smiles at his kindness. "So, he brought it home and installed it for me. And now, he offers to wash my hair." She shrugs like it's nothing special, although she knows it is.

"Kink. I told you," Adrian repeats.

"It has nothing to do with sex, so it's not kink." Bethany raises her voice, hands on her hips.

Adrian licks her lips, eyes dancing. "So, when he washes your hair, you guys don't end up in the bedroom, a closet, or in the bathroom right after?"

Bethany blushes with embarrassment.

"See? Kink!" Adrian winks, proud of herself.

At the first lull in the conversation, I announce that I'm pregnant. Although Savannah already knew, she joins my other friends in congratulating me. Our visit flies by, filled with catching up and teasing. Savannah plans to head home to nap when I say my goodbyes before heading to the grocery store.

As night falls, my sadness grows. I'll be spending Hamilton's first night of spring training in his bed at Memphis' house. I'll be surrounded by all his things, and it'll be that much harder. I frequently check the time and calculate the two-hour time difference while waiting for him to call.

I've successfully bathed Liberty and helped her pick up her toys by eight, when he FaceTimes.

"Hi, Daddy," Liberty yells into the camera.

I remind her she doesn't need to yell before we continue the call.

"I read all your texts," Hamilton informs me. "I'm glad you're stay with Mom instead of risking it."

"Daddy, wook!" Liberty points to the drawings she created with Memphis today while I was in town.

"Wow! Hey, did you put a surprise in my suitcase?" he asks our daughter.

Liberty giggles, nodding her head.

"Liberty and I sent a copy with you and brought a copy with us. We'd like to read with you each night when you call," I explain.

Our daughter's been infatuated with Alma's copy of Harry Potter and the Sorcerer's Stone for months now. I figured the thick book would be great to read as a family each night.

"Daddy," Liberty calls, entering the room with her copy of the book in hand.

"Are you ready to read?" Hamilton asks her.

"Let's go up to bed and read there," I tell Liberty. I carry her, the book, and the phone upstairs.

"Go," she demands as soon as her head hits the pillow.

I take a minute to lay the book on the bed above our pillows and turn her onto her belly so we're in the camera view, and I don't have to hold the heavy book, too.

"Haw-wy Podder and the...help Mommy," Liberty reads, pointing to each word in the title.

"Sorcerer's," I help.

"so-so-wes stone," she finishes.

I flip to chapter one as I hear Hamilton do on his end of the call.

"Can I read chapter one?" he asks, and Liberty nods.

I can't help my giant smile, watching Liberty point to words as Hamilton reads to us. Liberty lays her head on the pillow, no longer pointing to words after five pages. I position the camera, so Hamilton can see her on his next glance up from the book into the phone.

Noting her heavy eyes, his voice softens as he continues to read another page.

"She's asleep," I quietly inform him.

"Kiss her cheek for me," he instructs.

I keep us in the camera lens as I place a gentle kiss on her plump little cheek.

"I was shocked when I found the book," he confesses. "I'm glad you're awesome and planned a way for me to read to her all the way from Arizona."

"I miss you," I state as my voice quivers.

"I miss you, too. What did you do today besides draw with Liberty?"

I fill him in on the snow, my time with the girls, and building a snowman. He asks me to send him a picture of it tomorrow. After he shares his day, we talk about our plans for tomorrow. After my third yawn, he tells me to get some sleep. Of course, he reminds me that I'm pregnant and need my sleep before we end the call.

I turn off the light and cuddle close to Liberty. With happy thoughts of our family FaceTime, I fall into a peaceful sleep.

165

HAMILTON

Luckily, the weeks of spring training fly by. Madison and Liberty visit me on day number 11 of training. During their three-day visit, I spend every free moment exploring Mesa and holding them in my arms. Our little girl enjoys the swimming pool and warm weather. When we say our goodbyes, Madison promises she'll try to visit again during my final 30 days of training.

I miss our March obstetrics appointment. Madison records the visit, and I find it attached to an email when I'm done with practice. She was right; I didn't miss anything major.

A couple of days later, I struggle to focus on my pitching. It's Liberty's second birthday, and I want to be home with her. Talking to her on FaceTime tonight won't be enough.

"Armstrong," Stan calls to me from the practice field.

From the mound in the bullpen, I glance at my friend. He's pointing. I follow his hand to a section of the stands. I squint, my ball glove shading the sun at my forehead. It can't be. I blink as I attempt to process the vision before me.

In Madison's arms, Liberty waves. I glance over my shoulder to my pitching coach, wondering what I should do.

"Ten minutes then back here focused," he utters sternly.

I jog toward my family. My heart swells, and my arms crave to hold them. Liberty practically leaps from Madison's arms to mine on the field below.

"Sup-pize, Daddy," she squeals, wiggling fiercely.

My words stick in my throat. I squeeze Liberty, kissing her cheek to convey my excitement to see her.

"I hope we didn't interrupt your workout," Madison says, concerned. "I planned to observe from these seats until practice was over today."

I shake my head. "I wasn't focusing. I definitely needed a break to get my mind on throwing. Coach gave me 10 minutes."

Searching for field access, I motion for Madison to walk with me. I open a small door, and Madison steps down to the field beside me.

"Come to the bullpen with me," I instruct, placing a quick kiss to her temple.

I don't have to ask why they're here. I'm ecstatic they surprised me for Liberty's birthday. I don't have a gift for my girl, but we can take a shopping trip tonight. My thoughts settle, and Coach is pleased with my work out as the girls observe, mere feet away.

Madison

With writing my next story and two trips to Arizona to visit Hamilton, spring training passes quickly. Each evening, we video call. We share events from our days and plans for the next. We read pages from our book, and occasionally, Hamilton asks me to place the phone on my belly. He read about the baby's ability to hear sounds from outside the womb, and now he talks to our little one.

With spring training over, I'm excited for the new season. I prop myself up on three pillows at the headboard of my double bed. Watching Delta unpack, placing her items all over the hotel room, is both entertaining and exhausting. I decide to take this moment to check in at home.

ME

we're in St. Louis

what's up

FALLON

at tumbling

she says it's a PJ party tonight

sad my PJ's are sweatpants

ME

you should borrow mine

drawer 3 in tall dresser

FALLON

might take you up on that

ME

have fun

we're sightseeing

I love that Liberty feels comfortable enough for Fallon to stay with her while I travel. I wonder if she'll even miss me. I already miss my little girl. As much as I needed some girls' time, she would love traveling to an away game.

"Let's go," Delta orders. "We're burning daylight. If we plan to come rest before tonight's game, we need to get sightseeing now." She stands near the door, oversized purse on her shoulder and hands on her hips. I slide from the bed, slip my shoes on, and follow her out the door.

In the next four hours, we visit the Anheuser Busch St. Louis Brewery, the Gateway Arch, and Grant's Farm. While I've been here before, I've never been to the top of the arch or visited the Clydesdales. We enjoy observing the five-month-old colts interact with their enormous mothers. With our early flight this morning and sightseeing, I'm beat when we return to the hotel room.

After an hour nap, Delta and I dress in our Cubs gear then call an Uber to deliver us to Busch Stadium. She loves teasing me about cheering for the Cubs now instead of the Cardinals. An usher delivers us to our seats in the section with other player's wives, girlfriends, and family members that traveled for opening day.

Immediately, murmurs begin amongst the women.

Turning to Delta, I don't lower my voice. "Told you my t-shirt was too snug."

"Let them gossip." Delta flicks her hand at the wrist while she speaks. "A couple of them won't even be around by this year's All-Star Break."

"You are so bad," I scoff. "Can you make out what they are saying?" Curiosity gets the best of me.

"Something about how quick you got pregnant to tie yourself to Hamilton," Delta states. She doesn't hide our conversation. In fact, I believe she wants them to listen to us. "How dumb can they be? The two of you are married, unlike them. You already have a daughter together, so you don't need another baby if you want to tie yourself to him," Delta rants. "They just don't know what true love is. Not everyone is out to snag a man for his money. Some of us loved the man way before money entered the picture. That's why we'll be here for years, and they are temporary."

This is why I love her so much. No one gets anything over on her or her friends. Delta's lady balls are bigger than mine, and, at times like this, I'm grateful they are. The murmurs hush around us, and we focus on the field.

We watch a local 12-year-old sing the national anthem then locals throw out the first pitch. I'm glad we planned to arrive only a few minutes before game time. I'm nervous; I'm always excitedly nervous before the first pitch. My nerves continue to rise as the Cubs bat in the top of the first. In the bottom of the inning, I watch Hamilton warm up on the mound. I break down his every movement, during the wind up and as the ball crosses the plate. He looks ready.

As the first batter enters the batters' box, I grip the thin arms of my seat while I hold my breath. Delta pats my forearm in support when Hamilton comes on the mound. He nods at the catcher's sign, winds up, and sends the ball toward home. It wizzes by the batter and pops loudly in the catcher's mitt. The umpire signals while yelling strike. I note on the video board that Hamilton's fastball clocked at 100 miles per hour. That's a great way for him to start his fourth season in the Majors.

"You can breathe now," Delta reminds me.

My shoulders relax and my arms fall into my lap as I breathe in the excitement of the ballpark. I settle back into my seat and cheer for the Cubs. Between innings, Delta snaps a selfie of the two of us in our Cubs shirts. As I look at her photo, I note our hair blows wildly in the spring breeze. She shares the photo with me, and I text it to Fallon for Liberty.

When we make it back to the room following the game and a late dinner, I crawl into my bed before removing my shoes. I'm glad we planned our girls' trip for the first game of the season. While I enjoyed our trip, I wouldn't want to travel to every away game. I'm not sure how Hamilton does it.

166

MADISON

It's been five years since I last witnessed Hamilton's pre-game routine in person, and I'm giddy. Miss Alba is a veteran at preparing everything for him. I did ask her yesterday to help me fix his dinner for tonight. She patiently walks me through each step in baking his chicken breasts with his favorite seasonings and steaming the vegetables. Liberty helps us for a few minutes here and there until she becomes bored and returns to her toys.

At four o'clock, Miss Alba helps me write down instructions for the remainder of the meal prep before she leaves for the day. With a few minutes to spare before we expect Hamilton home, I help Liberty with her bath. She's excited to attend the home opener tomorrow, and we choose her outfit from head to toe, placing it near her dresser.

"Daddy!" she squeals, sprinting to the front door and into Hamilton's arms. "Come see my outfit for da game." She points him toward her bedroom.

"Why's your hair wet?" he questions as he carries her by me, placing a kiss on my forehead, before setting her down.

"My baff," she states like he should have known that answer.

"Oh... So you're all ready to come watch Daddy at work." Hamilton smiles, proud of her excitement.

"I made food," she informs him as they walk my way.

"Mommy made the food, Liberty helped, and Miss Alba ensured we didn't screw it up," I correct. "I'm glad you're home," I confess as he leans in for a closed-mouth kiss. I want to plaster myself to him while grinding a bit to hint I'm ready for some attention. But, it's the night before his first home game—I don't want to mess with his routine.

He deepens the kiss as his hands at my hips pull me closer to him. I don't protest; I melt into him, allowing him to take from me what he desires.

"Mommy," Liberty shouts near her highchair, "help!"

We break our kiss, and Hamilton assists her into the chair while I pull our food from the warmer.

Hours later, Liberty finally runs out of questions about tomorrow's game at Wrigley and drifts off to sleep. Hamilton and I took turns trying to put her down. Now, he stands, arms on either side of the bathroom door frame, as I finish my nightly routine.

"You're beautiful," his husky voice states before he wraps me up from behind.

We stare at each other in the large mirror. He keeps his eyes locked on mine as he lowers his mouth to nip below my ear. I tilt my head, enjoying his attention. Too soon, he releases me and pats me on my butt.

"We've got a big day tomorrow," he grins. "Better turn in."

As I follow him into our bedroom, I'm confused. Are we falling asleep, or does he plan to continue exploring my body with his mouth? My question is answered as he pulls his ball glove off the dresser, carrying it to his side of the bed. I bite my lip, trying to hide my grin as I watch him tuck it under his pillow. This is a tradition he started in middle school and still continues as an adult. There's still a little boy in his adult body, and I love him for it.

"What?" he asks when he notices I'm still staring.

"Should I give the two of you a minute? Want me to leave the room?" I tease, tucking myself under the blanket.

He tickles my ribs, causing me to squirm. Between my laughter and struggling for breath, I beg him to stop before he wakes Liberty, in hopes he'll quit his torture. Planking above me, he awards me his boyish grin, complete with dimples.

"I love you so much," he murmurs. "This finally feels right. The two of you here with me the night before a home game. I've imagined sharing it with you a million times."

He brushes hair from my face and caresses my cheek. Tears sting my sinuses while I look to him. He's my everything, my best friend for many years turned man of my dreams. He plants a sweet, hot, long kiss upon my lips before returning to his side of the bed. He wastes no time, tucking my back into his front after her turns off the lamp. I melt into him in the darkness. Safe, warm, and loved, I slip into slumber.

"I don't know why Hamilton protested so much," Amy says as we exit the "L" at Addison. "We made it here without any trouble."

When I heard that Memphis and Amy had never ridden the "L" on their previous trips to Chicago, I suggested we take the elevated train to the ballpark today. I don't need to tell Amy why Hamilton all but forbid us from riding the Redline to the game. He's protective of all of his family. He worries the Cubs fans might be wild on the train. The home opener is a holiday for many, and they party all day. Although our trip is problem free, I will not use this mode of transportation when it's only Liberty and me heading to the games.

Liberty talks a mile a minute as we walk the block to Wrigley Field. It's her first Cubs home game, and she's excited to cheer for Daddy. This morning, she fussed over her outfit and her hair; she wanted it to be perfect.

Hamilton snagged us passes to allow us on the field during team warmups. Memphis suggests that Amy carry Liberty while we descend the steps toward the field. In line near the batting cage, Hamilton spots us immediately. He greets us at the gate, pulling Liberty into his arms.

"I need my good luck kiss," he tells her.

Liberty promptly places kisses to his cheek then wraps her arms tightly around his neck. Pulling back, she places her palms on her chest. "See my Cubs?" she asks her daddy.

"You look pretty," he informs her. "I like your headband."

She smiles proudly then wiggles down. Amy moves to her side and takes her hand.

Hamilton bends down to Liberty's eye level. "You need to stay with Mommy and Grandma on this blue matt," he instructs her. "You can watch Daddy from right here like a big girl." She nods, and he returns to be next in the batting cage.

We watch as the coach throws pitches from behind a screen to Hamilton inside the dome of the batting cage. At first, he fouls a couple off. Then, he starts directing the ball to the outfield hit after hit. I'm transfixed by his power. Standing this close, I see his massive thighs flex and pivot to drive each hit deep. I watch his arms as they swing the bat with precision—I'm a sucker for his sexy forearms.

Luckily, Memphis snaps photos of Hamilton hitting and posing with our group while I can't take my eyes off my man. Amy skillfully entertains Liberty and prevents her from darting onto the infield. My little girl acts like she does this every day. I'm so proud of her. Several players walk over to speak with her. Stan greets her with high-fives and plays a little catch with her near the home team dugout.

Half the team gathers around her as she demonstrates how Hamilton pitches. She refuses to pitch until Stan squats like a catcher. The men love her bossy instructions to their centerfielder. They laugh and point as she mimics her daddy, stomping the mound at the white rubber before she winds up and throws left-handed to Stan. She laps up their cheers.

The first baseman asks if she's left-handed like her father. I shake my head before prompting Liberty to show Stan how Mommy pitches. Liberty moves the baseball to her right hand and stands facing Stan. As she's watched in my old softball videos, she mimics my fast pitch style, sending a pitch more like a pop fly to Stan. Again, her crowd cheers.

"Miss Liberty," Stan hands the baseball back to her, placing a kiss on her cheek, "we need to go to work now. Thank you for playing catch to warm me up for the game."

My daughter beams. Her dark brown eyes dance, and her smile lights up her entire face, framed by her dark-brown ringlets. She waves goodbye to her daddy, and we make our way back up into the stands.

For the next hour, we take turns walking with Liberty through the concourse all around the stadium. In order to be on the field with Hamilton, we knew we would need to entertain her for quite a while as we wait on the game. In between our walks, we enjoy the refreshments and snacks Hamilton arranged for us in the suite. As game time nears, my other guests begin to arrive.

Delta pulled Webster and Aurora out of school for the afternoon to attend their dad's game. We gave Fallon and Miss Alba the afternoon off. Fallon arrives minutes before Jasper escorts his nervous wife into the suite. It's Miss Alba's first ball game, and she mentioned that the large crowd of just under 42,000 fans scares her. I'm glad Hamilton surprised me with the suite; I enjoy sharing it with our close friends and family.

Our loud conversations grow silent for the National Anthem and ceremonial first pitch. I take a moment to absorb the Wrigley environment. On the outfield brick, the infamous green ivy begins to grow with the warmth of spring in the Windy City. In centerfield, the old-school, hand-turned scoreboard updates with scores throughout the league. Soon, the game will begin and traditional organ music will entertain and fire-up the crowd.

Hamilton pitches five innings, giving up only one hit and two walks. When Daddy isn't on the mound, Liberty and Aurora play in the back of the suite. She misses her nap time which concerns me for our trip back home. At the end of the game, we witness the raising of the W-flag before we find our Uber and make our way home.

167

MADISON

I lay my head on a towel at the back of the tub, letting the warm water and bubbles penetrate my tired muscles. I let the heat soak into my soul. I need it to wash away the last month of travel with my book tour and the Cubs. Although I put on a brave face for others, I'm exhausted and every muscle aches.

Memphis and Fallon care for Liberty, so I clear my mind, putting in my ear buds, letting the music carry me away. My eyes close, and I allow my arms to float languidly atop the water. I stretch my legs by pointing then relaxing my feet, one after the other. I press my shoulders back then forward a few times, relaxing the kinks. Moments pass too fast; soon, the water chills, and I must extricate myself from the once warm haven.

Standing, I wrap myself in my robe and carefully step from the tub to the soft bath matt. My reflection in the mirror shows dark circles beneath my eyes. Sleep. I need sleep, not just a night or two in my own bed. I need lazy, I need to lay on the sofa while binging TV, and I need cozy nights under the covers with Hamilton in our own home. It's time to recharge.

I climb onto my bed, sliding my legs under the comforter and propping my head up on two pillows. I snag my cell phone from its charger, opening my calendar app. I scroll through this week. Tomorrow, Hamilton has no game, and I have the day off from the book tour. The next day, there's no game; maybe, we can spend most of it at home, just the three of us. Then, the Cubs host the Brewers for three days before they hit the road again for a week. Looks like Liberty and I will have five days at home before our next seven days on the book tour.

I place my phone back on the charger before wrapping myself in the comforter and sinking into the pillows. I close my eyes for only a moment and fall asleep.

"Mommy, wake up," Liberty's melodic voice sings to me.

Opening my eyes, I find my daughter staring at me over the edge of my bed. I extend my hand to twist a dark, springy curl before sitting up. I pat the bed beside me, and her little fists grab the comforter, and she pulls herself up.

"Hi," I murmur, smiling at her large, brown eyes looking up to me.

She leans in, wrapping her arms around my waist. I revel in our hug.

"There you are," Hamilton calls from the bedroom doorway. "Did you wake up Mommy?" He tilts his head to the side with his question.

Liberty's hand covers her smile, her eyes still on mine through her dark lashes. She turns toward her father. "Saw-wy."

"What time is it?" I ask, craning my neck over her to check my phone on the nightstand.

"It's seven-thirty," he answers, closing the distance between us.

Seven-thirty? No way. I fixed my bath at two this afternoon. I closed my eyes for just a minute. Somehow, I slept for over four hours. I knew I was tired but had no idea I was that tired.

"Miss Alba and Mom urged me to let you sleep as long as possible," he states with a crooked smile. "How do you feel?" Concern covers his brow, eyes, and mouth.

"I was tired," I chuckle. "Guess I needed a long nap." I fidget with the terry-cloth robe, tightening it securely at my waist. "Did you eat?" I look from Hamilton sitting at the foot of the bed to Liberty.

"Daddy got pizza," she brags, eyes dancing.

"He did?" I draw out. "Did you save any for Mommy?"

Liberty's head nods proudly. She slides from the bed, extending her tiny hand for me to take and follow. As I climb from the bed and allow her to lead me to the kitchen, I worry about what my sleeping in my bathrobe might mean to Hamilton. I don't want him to worry about me. I want us to enjoy the time we have at home together. I glance over my shoulder to find him following close behind us.

I plop on a stool at the island, Liberty climbs on the one to my left, and Hamilton pulls the pizza box from the warmer. He slides a bottle of water, a plate, and a napkin in front of me. I lift the lid to the box, finding three pieces of pizza. One is cheese and two are barbecue chicken pizza, my favorite. Liberty claps when I smile at her.

"Do you want one?" I ask.

She simply shakes her head, brown curls bouncing, and slides down to the floor. She scurries over to the two dogs on the sofa to play.

I place a slice of chicken pizza on my plate before turning my attention toward my husband. He leans his bottom against the cabinet, his arms cross over his chest, and his eyes squint at me.

I attempt a smile for him which causes him to shake his head. I tilt my head to the side, urging him to talk. Perhaps he's worried that I missed dinner. I lift the slice to my mouth for a huge bite. The tangy, sweet sauce tantalizes my taste buds. As I chew, I motion for him to come closer. He leans on the island across from me, his arms extended towards mine. I take another bite then slip my hands into his.

"I love you," I say through my mouthful.

He shakes his head at me, a crooked smile upon his face. It's genuine. "I'm worried about you," he states, his thumbs caressing the back of my hands.

I swallow my pizza and sip from my water bottle to wash it down. "I'm tired and very, very happy to be home," I explain.

"And the baby?" he murmurs, concern lacing his words.

"She," I tease, hoping to ease a bit of the tension, "is safe and happy." I lean back in my chair, placing both my hands upon my baby bump under the robe.

Hamilton moves to my side, splaying his large hands over my entire belly. It's too early, but I'd love for our little one to kick right now. Feeling its movement would help Hamilton. It has to be hard to know there is a baby inside and be so helpless. I place my hands over his.

"In a month or two, you'll be able to feel her kick," I whisper, emotion clogging my throat.

His eyes move from my stomach to my eyes. They ping pong back and forth, searching mine. "I can't wait." His voice is quiet, somber, and full of emotion.

"I know." I lean over, placing a kiss upon the corner of his lips. "We are fine. I promise," I murmur before placing my mouth fully upon his.

His lips tenderly tangle with mine. The kiss is slow, gentle, and sweet. I long for more. I need more. I dart my tongue out, swiping his lower lip. Taking my cue, his tongue slides into my mouth. Quickly, the kiss becomes feverish, fast, and hard. When he pulls away, we struggle to catch our breath.

"Liberty," he pants.

One word. One name that says it all. He wants to continue. He needs to continue as much as I do, but Liberty plays nearby. My fingertips press upon my swollen lips, the memory of the kiss playing on a loop in my mind. I blame it on the pregnancy hormones, but we've been busy, we've been traveling, and we've missed each other.

Needing a barrier between us, Hamilton moves to the other side of the island as I finish two pieces of pizza. My eating seems to calm my over-concerned spouse's nerves.

"Go slip into your pajamas so we can tuck Libby in bed," he orders. "The sooner she falls asleep, the sooner we can turn in for the night." He wiggles his eyebrows at me, a sly grin upon his face.

I fall from my perch upon Hamilton's now sated cock to the bed beside him. I fight for the small breaths I pull in and out. My heart flutters frantically, and my body continues to pulse with aftershocks of my climax. Hamilton turns on his side, facing me. His hand tucks my wayward hair behind my ear before tapping me twice on the tip of my nose. I pry my sleepy eyelids open, looking up at him.

"I'm worried," he confesses.

"I know," I retort.

"I understand that pregnancy makes you tired, but I feel like the book tour is too much." He places his palm on my cheek, and his fingertips curl slightly at my ear. "It's important to you and the success of the book, so I wouldn't bring this up if I didn't have proof that you are overdoing it."

I nod once. My heart isn't breaking. I'm not upset at the thought of cancelling the rest of my appearances. What does that say about me?

"Madison..." Hamilton murmurs, snapping his fingers in front of my face.

My eyes focus on his face in front of me. "I'll call Cameron tomorrow," I promise.

He furrows his brow as his eyes search mine. "I anticipated a fight, an argument, or at least a discussion before you came to a decision," he admits.

"I'd be lying if I denied feeling exhausted today. I didn't mean to sleep for four hours. I mean, I didn't even have the strength to get dressed after my bath," I explain.

"I'm sure Cameron will understand," Hamilton states. "She's been with you daily. She's seen the same signs as Mom, Fallon, and I have."

I nod as tears form in my eyes, and my nose burns. I don't want to cry—I hate crying. It makes me feel weak, and I detest weakness. I close my eyes, drawing in a long, slow breath, hoping to calm myself. Hamilton knows this and refrains from soothing me. I lay in his arms, fighting to control my emotions. His large hands gently glide up and down my bare back, slowly lulling me to sleep.

"Ham," I murmur into his chest.

"Hmm," his hands still. I feel his voice vibrate as his throat presses against my head.

168

MADISON

It's official. I have a five-month-old demon soccer player growing in my uterus. Evidently, it enjoys night games. As I toss and turn, adjusting pillows between my legs and under my back, I realize this is the second week in a row that I am struggling with sleep. I decide I should be productive and head to my office. I'll work tonight and rest in the recliner tomorrow when the baby quits moving.

I stare at my current work in progress for several minutes. My writing mojo must be on vacation. I'm just not feeling this current story. I swirl my chair, looking out over the lights and sleeping city. As I clear my mind, a new story idea appears. Back at my laptop, I open a new document and let my fingers fly.

I loosely base the characters on Hamilton and myself. The male character is a ball player, and the couple are high school sweethearts. My storyline follows them from high school to college to the MLB. The words quickly pour from my fingertips.

"Hey." Hamilton's deep voice slices through the silence.

I squeal, jumping in my seat, and my hand flies to my chest. My heart pounds heavy against my hand.

"Sorry." He moves to my side of the desk. He arches an eyebrow. "What are you doing?"

"I figure since the baby won't stop moving and I can't get comfortable, I should write while I'm awake, so I won't fall behind," I explain.

"Looks like you've made progress," he states over my shoulder, pointing to my open laptop.

I save the document and shut the laptop. "It's a new story. The idea came to me tonight." I rise from my office chair, rolling my neck and stretching my back.

Hamilton splays his palms over my ever-growing belly. "Is he still kicking?" he asks, excitement upon his face.

He loves feeling our little one's movements. I'm glad we are finally to the part of pregnancy that he can experience.

"I think he or she has finally settled for the night," I reply, emphasizing the she. "Take me to bed."

"Okay," he responds with too much enthusiasm. "I love when you demand sex."

I close my eyes. Of course he'd go there. I should choose my words better. Internally, I debate stating I'm exhausted versus a quickie to relax me from head to toe. Sometimes, my hormones and endorphins activate my little kicker. Hamilton flies out for a four-game road trip tomorrow, so it's now or wait.

Hamilton taps my wrinkled brow. "What's going on in there?"

"I'm weighing my needs and the possibility that the baby will start kicking when I'm ready to sleep again," I share.

"I can go slow and easy," Hamilton offers with a crooked grin.

"I'd prefer a quickie and some sleep before Liberty gets up," I counter.

"So, it's not that you don't want me?"

"Oh, I want you." I emphatically state.

"Then, let's go; we are wasting time," he smirks. Hamilton tows me by my wrist through the house. I giggle the entire way.

169

MADISON

On the long drive to Athens, Liberty entertains herself by reading and watching movies on her iPad. As I shift positions often, my mind wanders. I can't believe the All-Star Break is here. This season and summer flew by.

Perhaps it's our crazy routines and the city life that causes time to fly. I wonder if adult life in Athens would be as simple as I remember it... I daydream about Hamilton and me living with Memphis, him helping with the farm and me writing on the porch swing while Liberty plays in the yard with our dogs and Memphis' cats. It's chummy in the old farmhouse, but we're family; I love it.

I shift, leaning against the pillows I brought propped on the passenger door. I imagine our friends hanging out on the farm and us at their homes in town. Hamilton helps with the American Legion baseball team during the summer while Latham covers for him on the farm.

Farms. Three farms. We have three farms. There's no way Hamilton, even with Latham's help, could handle all three farms. My daydream falls apart. Life wouldn't be simpler in Athens. I sigh deeply as I rub my lower back.

"Need me to stop?" Hamilton offers, observing my discomfort.

I shake my head. The more we stop, the longer the ride. The longer the ride, the more uncomfortable I become. I'm excited for our mini, four-day vacation; I just want to get the car ride over with.

Hamilton

It's our first full day in Athens; Liberty, Mom and I are up with the sun. We do our best to let my now six-months pregnant wife sleep as late as possible. We have a lazy morning before I must hit the road by noon. Liberty helps Mom load the dishwasher with our breakfast dishes, then I shuffle her into the bathroom to change into the outfit I brought down for her.

"Mommy is sweepy," Liberty states as we exit the bathroom.

"The baby makes Mommy very tired," I inform her.

"My brover makes her sweepy," she smiles.

Liberty and I refer to the baby as a boy which frustrates Madison. She reminds me often that it's important that Liberty knows it could be a girl or a boy and prepares for both outcomes.

As the clock nears nine, I enter my old bedroom. I brush hair from Madison's face and run my fingertips along her jaw. She stirs, stretches, and groans before opening her eyes.

"Mornin'," her gruff, morning voice greets.

"It's nine," I inform her. "I let you sleep in, but Liberty is getting restless. I thought after your breakfast, the three of us could take a walk."

Her smile ensures she likes my idea. Madison throws back the cover, her tiny baby belly peeking from under her t-shirt as it rides up. Who knew a baby bump could be so sexy? I adjust myself before offering her my hand.

"Easy, big guy," she taunts through her sly grin as she tugs the hem of her shirt down.

Her attempt to hide is in vain. Her abdomen tightly stretches her t-shirt, still allowing me to admire her body. I lick my lower lip as I tug her to her feet. When she turns toward the attached bath, I swat her ass, provoking a playful squeal.

"Want me to help you shower?" I offer, following behind her into the bathroom. "I could help you reach around your baby bump."

"Nice try." She pushes me away. "Go entertain Liberty; I'll be quick."

Five minutes later, Madison joins us in the kitchen, fresh faced and well rested. On its own, my body rises from the chair to greet her. I place a soft kiss to the corner of her mouth. My body pressed to hers. I move my lips to her ear and whisper, "Feel what you do to me?"

She swats my chest playfully. "Behave! Your mom and our daughter are right there."

I place my palm on her round abdomen. "Tonight, I will have you," I growl in her ear.

Her ravenous, blue eyes look up at me through her long lashes. Clearly, she has no objection with that statement.

An hour later, we swing Liberty by her arms as we walk through the tall grass in the pasture. Liberty's giggles are a beautiful melody on a partly sunny July morning. On the next swing forward, I scoop Liberty into my arms and secure her on my hip.

"Mommy and Daddy used to come here all the time," I inform her. "Mommy lived over there in that house." I point across the remainder of the pasture where Madison's old farmhouse is visible across the road.

"I liked to come over here to lay under that tree." I point to the large oak tree in the center of the cemetery. "I'd listen to the birds and watch the leaves. Sometimes, your daddy would find Mommy here, and we would talk for hours," I share, smiling at Liberty then at Madison. "Now, when we cross the fence, we need to be respectful…"

"This is a cemetery." Madison takes over my explanation. "The stones tell us about the people that went to meet Jesus."

Liberty nods, her face serious.

"We don't want to step on the grass in front of the stones," Madison continues. "Mommy and Daddy will show you where to walk, okay?"

Liberty looks from her mom to me before nodding. I fiddle with the chains that keep the gate closed. At six months pregnant, I can't allow Madison to climb the chain-link fence as we did in the past. When I get the gate open, Liberty squirms down from my arms, takes her mom's hand, and points to the stones as they walk the fence line.

I step between the headstones, squat, and invite Liberty to join me. "Libby, walk over here," I instruct, pointing.

I place my hand on the weathered stone, and she mimics my motion. Her little fingers explore the bumpy surface. "Want Mommy to read it to us?" I suggest.

When she nods, wide-eyed, Madison reads, "His name started with a W and his last name was Taul. These big numbers tell us he lived around here over 100 years ago." She indicates each line of text to our daughter as she reads. Madison's voice raises, helping Liberty understand 100 years was a long time ago. She's in teacher-mode, and I love it.

"This is my favorite headstone," Madison shares, placing her hand atop it with ours. "I did some research and learned that he fought for the North during the Civil War. His family owned a tobacco farm in Missouri and owned slaves. His two brothers fought for the South."

I stare, dumbfounded, at my wife. I knew this was her favorite headstone, but she never shared that she did research. Though, I'm not surprised. She's not the type to read something and move on; she likes to look up more information on things she knows little to nothing about. Liberty seems to have her inquisitiveness.

"What?" she demands at my staring. "So, I did a little research."

I nod. "You never told me."

"I just couldn't bear that all 45 of these people had no one visiting them," she says, shrugging. "I spent a lot of time here; I had to know who I was hanging out with. Didn't you ever wonder about their lives?"

"Maybe," I lie. To me, the cemetery was a place of peace and solitude, and I felt closer to God.

She bites her lip then continues, "I photographed the stones and did some research on an ancestry site. I found some living relatives that were eager for the photos and location of the cemetery."

I scoop Liberty into my arms, closing the distance between us, and I place a kiss upon Madison's cheek. "That's why I love you."

She shrugs it off as nothing when we both know she dedicated many hours to the project. Hours to help total strangers find a little connection to their past.

We guide Liberty to join us in laying on the ground under the large tree.

We point out a bird's nest above us and talk about the green leaves. Liberty points out a butterfly fluttering in the overgrown grass nearby.

"I miss this," Madison whispers.

I'm not sure that she meant to say it out loud, so I don't acknowledge her words. I know exactly what she means, though. Growing up, I never thought of the farm as quiet, but, comparing it to Chicago, it's peaceful here. Although there are many things to do on the farm, the urgency of the big city life doesn't reside here. I could be content living here; the question is, could Madison?

Too soon, it's time for our walk back to the house, so I can make my appointments in Kansas City this afternoon.

170

MADISON

While Hamilton attends two baseball clinics in the Kansas City area, I decide to take Liberty to some of our favorite spots on a treasure hunt. She enjoyed our trek to the cemetery with Hamilton this morning, so I've grabbed a backpack to hold all the treasures we find, an old county map from Memphis' junk drawer, and a cooler with bottles of water for our adventure.

"Libby," I call into the front room where she finished reading a book with Memphis a moment ago, "come here, please."

"Yes, Mommy?" She cranes her head to the side, wrinkles her nose and scrunches her little forehead, her hands on her hips.

I attempt not to laugh at the sassy way she stands, waiting to hear the reason I've summoned her. "We're going on an adventure," I state. "Here's our map and our backpack."

A smile lights up her face as she claps excitedly. "Na-na, too?"

"You can ask her to come along," I prompt, motioning to the front room. Having already discussed it, I know Memphis plans to come. I'm sure she worries that at six months pregnant, the July heat in Missouri may be too much for me. I really don't care about her true reason; I'm glad she'll join us.

Pulling Memphis by the hand, Liberty returns to the kitchen, marching past me to the door. I guess she's ready to head out. I pass the cooler to Memphis and wear the nearly empty backpack as we exit the house.

"Before we load up in the truck, let's look at the map." I encourage Liberty to hold it, loving the twinkle in her eyes at the thought of an adventure.

"We are here." Memphis places an "X" on the farm's location with the red Sharpie I pass her. "Can you find the red star?"

Liberty spins the paper map in her hands. Only a few seconds pass before she cheers, "I found it!"

Memphis nods and claps. "That's where we'll go first."

We climb into Memphis' truck and head down the gravel road. The rearview mirror fills with dusty clouds from the overly dry road. Although, I'm not driving very fast, visibility behind us is slim. I've forgotten about this. I might even say I've missed living on rural, gravel roads.

Ten minutes pass before I park along the blacktop road near the bridge. I smile, realizing this is a far cry from trying to find a parking spot in Chicago. There's no need to parallel park here. Memphis assists Liberty from her car seat, map still in one hand.

I point to the red star on the map. "This is the river. Let's put the map in our backpack, so you can use both hands to find treasures."

We stand in a small opening that borders the river. I pull the sunscreen from our backpack, and we slather each other up.

"Ready?" Memphis asks, and Liberty cheers.

"Daddy and I used to come down here to the sandbar when we were in school," I tell Liberty. "We liked to toss rocks into the water, go fishing, or light a fire and camp." I love how Liberty hangs on my every word.

I place my palm flat on the sand and decide it's too hot to slip off our shoes. I pick up a funny shaped river rock, extending it to Liberty.

"Look," I share. "See how this rock is speckled pink and white?"

Liberty nods her head as her tiny fingertips glide along the surface of the golf ball size stone.

"Pwet-ty," she states.

"Should we place it in our treasure backpack?" I ask, already unzipping the outer pocket.

"Yes!" She hops up and down, rock in hand, waiting for me to unzip.

"Libby, come quick," Memphis calls from the edge of the water, ten feet away.

Liberty jogs over to see what Na-na has to show her. I pull out my phone, snapping a quick picture of the two treasure hunters. Then, I open my texts and send the photo to Hamilton.

ME

know where we are?

we're treasure hunting

taking her to our favorite spots

"I sent this picture to Daddy." I extend my phone, displaying the photo of the two of them. "I thought he'd like to see you enjoying his favorite places around Athens."

"Look here," Memphis calls, and Liberty scurries to her side again.

I open my camera again, snapping photos of the two as they explore the sandbar.

"Look, Mommy!" Liberty's excitement is contagious.

In her palm, she holds a snail shell. I snap a closeup photo before we wrap it in a paper towel and tuck it in the backpack. We spread out on the large sandbar in search of our next treasure. I remain near the water line to ensure Liberty doesn't venture too close.

"Over here," Memphis calls to us.

She's sitting on a large log, firmly planted in the sand. It reminds me of the log Hamilton and I sat on at the bonfire his final night in town. It's where I asked him to do me a favor. I asked him to take my virginity before we headed our separate ways. I still can't believe I found the nerve to ask him or that he complied. It was the first domino in a long chain reaction that brought us to today.

Memphis assists Liberty in sitting atop the log with legs on either side. I take a picture of just Liberty then suggest Memphis scoot in behind her. After a few more photos, we head back to the truck, pull out the map, and head to the lake.

Our adventure continues with Memphis and me showing her the swimming area. We wade in the warm water at the edge of the lake. We visit Winston at the theater, and, as he gives Liberty a tour, we talk about the movies we watched as kids. At Sonic Drive-In, we order ice cream cones to enjoy as we head back to the farm. I pull over as we hit the end of the lane. For our last adventure, Memphis drives while Liberty and I ride the last quarter mile in the bed of the truck. I film her as the wind whips through her hair. She laughs and squeals as we hit a few bumps, and our bottoms hop from the wheel-hub.

I've given our daughter a peek into the life that Hamilton and I shared. I only wish Hamilton could have witnessed it. It's a life I took for granted and even resented until recently. Now, it's the life I long to give to our children. I love our life in Chicago and the opportunities it gives our daughter, but I think that life on the farm could make us happy, too.

171

HAMILTON

On our second day in Athens, I drop my girls off at Adrian's for a playdate while I visit Winston at his theater. He meets me at the door, locks it behind us, and guides me to his office. As I sit, I remind him that after spending most of yesterday in Kansas City, I want to hurry back to Madison and Liberty.

"I'll get right to it then," Winston agrees. "I've found another opportunity I thought you might be interested in. Your investment in the theaters proved profitable for us both, and I think this will be the same."

Since I've invested in his theaters, the improvements Winston has carried out have led to a rise in ticket and concession sales. I invested to help my friend; I wasn't sure I'd see any profits. It was a nice surprise when the theaters began showing me returns on my investment. I wonder if Winston plans to add on more theaters, build a restaurant, or upgrade to online ticketing.

He slides a real estate listing across the desktop to me. "The public golf course is for sale," he announces, excitement lighting his entire face. "Memberships are down, and it needs upgrades to the clubhouse and outbuildings. The course itself is in great shape; they have a fantastic groundskeeper who knows his stuff."

I'm shocked by the price—it's much lower than I anticipated. "This price includes everything?" I ask, pointing at the figure.

Winston nods excitedly. "I was thinking we could split it. It's a bargain. We could make some improvements, increase the number of memberships, and turn a profit in a couple of years."

"We should investigate the membership numbers over the past 10 years. I get that the numbers are down, but I would like to see how far they've fallen," I suggest, liking the idea more by the minute. "Perhaps we could do a membership survey as new owners to prioritize the improvements based on our customer's thoughts."

"So, you're in?" Winston asks.

"I'm interested," I inform him.

Winston tilts his head.

"Very interested," I explain. "Can you reach out to the realtor to request the financials and membership information? Hopefully it's digital, and we can review it this week while I'm in town. I'll get my guy working on it from his end... he may be able to get more information than they will share with the two of us."

Winston stands, extending his hand across the desk to me. Driving back to Adrian's, I'm excited to have another income opportunity in Athens.

On day three in Athens, we make the short trip to visit Salem and Latham. Liberty pouts the entire way as we wouldn't let her ride in the back of the truck. Madison started something there.

While Salem offers to give Madison a tour of the house, I motion to Latham, and we head outside to tour the farm. They've made many improvements since we asked them to move to Madison's parents' farm and take care of it for us. I knew it was a great idea, but I never imagined just how much they would accomplish in eight months. It's especially surprising since they welcomed their first child, Quincy, in May of this year.

"I believe we are ready to purchase cattle and a couple of hogs to get us started," Latham shares.

"Have you run out of things to do?" I tease.

"Actually, yes," he states, serious. "There are still a few little things here and there, but I don't have enough to fill my days."

"Mom says you've spent a couple of days each week helping her. Do you think you can continue that if we buy livestock?" I lean my forearms on the metal gate while I place one boot on the bottom rung.

"I see no reason why not." Latham joins me at the gate.

"Okay. Start attending livestock auctions." I pat him on the back. "I love everything you've done so far, so there's no reason to stop now."

My eyes drift across the road to the open pasture on my mom's land. "Could you see a house right there?" I ask, pointing.

"It's a great spot," Latham agrees. "Wait. Are you saying what I think you are saying?"

I keep my eyes on the area I've dreamed of building on since my teens. Many times, while sitting at the cemetery, I'd stare at Madison's farm and the flat pasture area between the two. On the backside, the pasture slopes toward creek bordered by trees. It's a great setting for a house.

Answering Latham's question, I admit, "It's just a dream. I haven't even shared it with Madison." I smile at him. "Just thinking of the future. I wouldn't even know where to find a construction company capable of building an entire home."

Always helpful, Latham informs me, "Troy moonlights with a couple construction companies in Athens. You should ask him."

I make a mental note to chat with Troy. Standing here, daydreaming, does me no good. I turn from the gate to face the house. "I think I've let Madison hold Quincy long enough. Let's go inside so I can take my turn."

On our last morning in Athens, Liberty and I descend the stairs to find Mom fixing a large breakfast. The scent of bacon hangs heavily in the air as Mom pours batter onto the griddle.

"I'm making pancakes," Mom sings as we move beside her.

"Why are there five places at the table?" I ask, sharing a piece of bacon with Liberty.

"Amy should be here any minute," Mom states matter-of-factly.

I know there's no way Mom called Amy this morning to set this up. Amy wouldn't have answered her phone. That means they planned this yesterday and didn't tell us. I hoped Madison could sleep late since we have a long trip back to Chicago this afternoon.

"I better go wake Madison," I complain.

"Let her sleep," Mom urges.

"She won't be happy if she comes down in an hour or two and we've spent the morning visiting without her," I argue before I climb the stairs two at a time.

An hour later, the five of us still sit around the table, our empty plates in front of us. Madison cleared Liberty's tray and placed a few toys on it to entertain her. I wonder if other two-year-olds would entertain themselves for this long in a highchair. The guilt of cooping her up in a car for six hours later today eats at me. She needs to run around while she can.

I extricate her from the tray and buckled belt, lowering her to the floor, allowing her escape. Immediately, she heads to the front room and all of her toys. Unfortunately, my mom decides to rid up the table once I get up. That was not my intention; I enjoy visiting at the table. It's rare that I get to slow down and relax like this.

I lean next to Mom at the sink while she rinses syrup off a couple plates. I pause. Her eyes are closed, and she's attempting to pull in long, calming breaths. I place my hand on her back, and her eyes fly open.

"What's wrong?" I ask, fear rising in my throat.

"I just stood too fast," she states.

It's possible, but I still worry. It doesn't escape me that she's getting older and health concerns will begin to pop up. It kills me that she lives here, so far from town, all on her own. Amy keeps busy five days a week with her job, and she's on the other side of the county. If anything happens, it's too far away. Mom doesn't always take her cell phone with her when she works outside. If something happened out in the pasture, it could be hours if not a day before someone found her.

With that thought, a heavy weight settles in my stomach. Chicago is far away, and I'm too busy during baseball season to keep an eye on her. Even if I tried to FaceTime her every day, I wouldn't know if something was wrong, and I wouldn't be able to get her help.

"Amy," I call across the kitchen, "let's take a walk."

All eyes look to me, concerned about my abrupt request. I plaster on a smile as I walk towards the door. It's all I can muster as my emotions continue to skyrocket. As soon as the door closes, I motion for Amy to sit on the porch swing.

"Have you noticed any changes in Mom's health?" I blurt, unable to keep it in any longer.

Amy simply shakes her head. That's not going to do it. I need her to talk honestly with me.

"Just now, she stood at the kitchen sink with her eyes closed, breathing funny," I inform Amy. I can't sit here; I feel like I'm about to lose it. I need to pace. "She claims she just stood up too fast, but all the color left her face."

Amy swings back and forth, taking in my words. "I haven't noticed anything. Maybe she's tired from your visit. It's all she spoke about for weeks."

I nod, but I still think something is going on. "I'm too far away and too busy to know what's going on. She's getting older, and she'll need our help more. I feel like my hands are tied for eight months of the year." I'm rambling, yet I feel like I can't express what I really want to say.

"We're together at least once a week, and we talk on the phone all the time," Amy reminds me.

"Do you think she'd tell you if she didn't feel good or was having strange symptoms?" I need to know we have a failsafe plan in place.

"She's a grown woman; she's capable of caring for herself," Amy states, unaffected.

"So, if she always felt tired, had trouble catching her breath at times, and takes a nap every day, do you think she'd mention it to you?" I counter. I'm growing frustrated by my sister's apparent lack of concern.

"Of course," Amy exclaims, offended.

"Well, for the last four days, that's the way it's been," I inform her, my hands at my hips. "She napped when Liberty and Madison laid down. In fact, she slept longer than they did each afternoon."

Amy furrows her brow, leaning forward with her elbows on her knees, no longer swinging.

"Madison told me that on their treasure hunt, Mom rested often and constantly lost her breath. They didn't do anything strenuous. I mean, Madison is six months pregnant, so you know they took it easy." I try to control my anger and fear. "I just wonder how long she's been like this, and what could be going on."

"Fuck!" Amy shouts, throwing her arms in the air. She fists her fingers in her hair in frustration.

Now, she seems to be on the same page with me. Welcome to my world. Fear sucks. "We need a plan," I inform her.

She stares at the barn for several long moments before suggesting, "I need to spend at least one of my days off each week with her. I usually come on a workday with the twins, and, of course, all of my attention is on them."

"Okay. So, one day a week, it will be just you and Mom," I repeat. "What else?"

"Well, all I can do is pay more attention to her when I'm with her," Amy states. "I'm not a nurse, so I can't diagnose or anything."

Madison joins us on the porch. She wraps her arms around my waist, resting her head on my chest. Immediately, my body and mind calms. She's a soothing balm.

"So, what's your little pow-wow about?" she pries.

Amy promptly fills her in.

Then, my amazing wife suggests, "We could ask Latham to bring Salem over once in a while, maybe on her day off while he works. They could invite her to dinner, too. Salem's a nurse; she could help us keep an eye out for any symptoms to be concerned about."

Amy smiles. "Do you think Salem would mind helping us?"

Madison pulls out her phone to call. Moments later, when she hangs up, she simply states, "It's done. Salem works tomorrow, but said she'd ride over with Latham the next day. She'll play it cool, so Memphis won't suspect a thing."

"Thank you, babe." I smile before placing a long, wet kiss upon her lips. I love this woman more every single day.

The ride to Chicago seems longer than the drive down to Athens. We strategically planned it for Liberty's nap time, so she quickly falls asleep. Madison struggles to find a comfortable position. I'm sure it will only get worse during the last three months of her pregnancy. I make the decision that this should be her last trip to Athens. It can't be good for her or the baby to sit so long in the car. I'm sure she'll fight me on it, but it's really what's best for her and the baby.

My mind replays our entire visit as mile after mile passes. I love that we shared our memories of the cemetery and other places around Athens during the treasure hunt with Liberty. I loved my childhood and want the same for my daughter. While I loved my time at the two baseball scouting events, analyzing talent and learning about the business side of baseball, I wish I could have been on the treasure hunt with my girls. Madison sent me several photos, and, while I appreciate them, I would have rather been there, sharing stories with our daughter.

With Foster's expertise, the paperwork to purchase the golf course with Winston is currently processing. I smile, remembering Madison's excitement when I shared Winston's proposal about the course. Although she doesn't enjoy learning every step or detail, she does like weighing in on investments and hearing how I plan to diversify our portfolio. Sometimes, she fakes interest, but I could tell she really liked the idea of owning the golf course.

I still haven't shared my dream of building a house on the farm with my wife. Mom and I talked about it for over an hour, and I asked her to keep it close to the vest until Madison has the baby. With her pregnancy hormones, I'm not sure how she will react to my idea. I set a few things in motion, but after the scare with Mom's health, I think I might consider starting construction sooner rather than later. In order to start construction, I'll have to talk to Madison. I make a mental note to chat with Mom about the best way to bring it up with her.

172

MADISON

As I walk back toward my office after my mid-afternoon writing break, or, as Hamilton likes to call it, my pregnant potty break, Hamilton's cell phone vibrates on the kitchen counter. He's putting Liberty down for her nap, so I approach to find Athens General Hospital on the caller ID. My heart sinks, and all the air evaporates from the room. My hands shake as I answer and begin walking toward Liberty's room.

"Hello," I greet with a quaking voice.

"Madison?" the female voice says.

"Amy?" Why is she calling from the hospital and not her cell phone?

"Yes. I left my cell in the car," Amy explains.

At the bedroom door, I whisper for Hamilton to come quickly while I place the call on speaker phone.

"Amy, you're on speaker phone. Ham's here now," I state as fear continues to tighten in my throat.

"I just brought Mom to the ER. She's having heart issues," Amy says. We can hear the tears in her voice. "She's alert, which they say is a good sign. They're running tests now and claim we will know more within the hour. Mom's fine; in fact, she forbids me to call you." Her words are quick, short gulps of breath between them.

"They're running tests now. Salem is working and says it's probably a mild heart attack. We will know something in an hour."

She's repeating herself, and I feel sad that she's there by herself.

"I'm pitching tomorrow," Hamilton reminds her. "I need to call Coach..."

Amy interrupts her brother. "There's no need for you to come here. I talked with Salem and two doctors before I called you. They know you play for the Cubs. They all stated it's not that serious. Like I said, we will know more in an hour."

Hamilton releases a groan while he fists his hands in his hair. He feels helpless, too far away, and scared for Memphis.

"So, they think we should wait for the test results before we make plans to come to Athens?" I seek clarification from Amy.

"Yes," she confirms. "They're wheeling Mom back now. I'll call you as soon as we get the test results; I promise."

"Amy, I want to be there." Hamilton's voice breaks.

"There's nothing you can do. She's okay at the moment, and the staff seems to think there's no need for you to drive here. Please wait for my update before you call your coach or hit the road." Amy ends the call without another word.

I know he feels as helpless as I do. Hamilton sits on the sectional, slumped forward, his head in his hands. I position myself on the cushion beside him, tucking a pillow to my chest. I wish I had the words he needs at this moment, but nothing comes to me. We sit in silence for several long minutes.

"I knew something was wrong. That's why I talked to Amy before we left," Hamilton mumbles. His palms are pressed to his eyes. "We should have stayed one more day. I should have asked her to go to her doctor."

"Honey, we both know your mom would not have gone," I remind him. She's stubborn and strong. "Amy's in the same boat we are. She's second-guessing herself and hating every minute she has to wait for the test results. There's nothing any of us can do."

"But, she's there. She's with Mom," he argues. "She's there, and I'm six hours away. I can't lose--" A sob escapes before he can finish his statement.

He can't lose her. We can't lose her. Please, Lord, I can't lose anyone else. I still need Memphis' knowledge, guidance, and support. I don't want to think of our world without her. I fetch a bottle of water from the kitchen and a box of tissues. I place both on the coffee table in front of Hamilton. I don't say a word. Instead, I hug him from the side and wait for Amy's update.

It feels like a year passes by the time his cell phone rings again. The caller ID shows Amy's name and number. Hamilton quickly answers and switches to speakerphone.

"Hello?" His deep voice cracks with fear. I place my hand on his forearm in support.

"Hi, honey," Memphis greets.

"Mom?" He's clearly excited to hear her voice.

"Honey, I'm okay. In fact, we're in Amy's car right now, headed home." Memphis sounds good. She actually sounds just like she does any other time we've been on the phone.

"So, that's it?" Hamilton looks towards me in shock. "I think we need to get a second opinion."

"Hamilton, let mom finish before you wig out," Amy orders.

"We are headed home to pack a bag," Memphis explains. "Amy reserved us a hotel room near St. Luke's Hospital, so we don't need to get up early in the morning and drive down. I have an outpatient appointment tomorrow. They'll place one stent in my heart, observe me for a couple of hours, and I'll be home tomorrow night."

"An outpatient heart surgery..." Hamilton repeats, not believing it.

Amy tries to calm her brother. "Mom suffered a minor heart attack. She has 85 percent blockage of one artery in her heart. They will place the stent in that artery tomorrow to increase blood flow. Evidently, they perform this surgery with even three or four stints as an outpatient procedure now. Mom's cardiologist is the head of the cardio department at St. Luke's, so she is seeing the very best doctor possible. She'll be in good hands."

"I know you would like to be here," Memphis adds. "But, I'm okay. I was scared, but now that I know what caused the pain, I'm not. They said this procedure is as common as a tonsillectomy nowadays, so there's no reason for you miss any games to be here. We can talk before and after the procedure. I promise."

"Mom, I could talk to Coach..." Hamilton explains, but gets interrupted.

"Hamilton," Memphis' tone is stern. "I don't need you here. I love you, and I know you want to be here for me. There's nothing you can do, though. Amy will be bored sitting in the waiting room during the procedure. Then, she'll be by my bed, waiting for them to observe me for hours before they discharge me. There is no reason for you to mess with the pitching rotation."

The sadness in his eyes breaks my heart. Unlike me, he grew closer to his mom after his dad's death. Although I never had that relationship with my mother, I understand why this upsets him. I'm close to Memphis—closer than I was to my own mother. Her heart attack and upcoming procedure worries me. I'm scared and really want to be there by her side. Even though both Amy and Memphis state it's an outpatient procedure so there is minimal risk, the worst possible outcome scares me.

"Hamilton?" Amy calls. "Are you still there?"

"I'm just struggling to process all of this," he confesses. "Mom, will you call me after dinner tonight?"

"Sure," Memphis answers immediately.

When they end the call, I slide into Hamilton's lap. With my hands on his, I wrap them around my back. "I love you," I remind him, gazing into his eyes.

Hamilton fists his hands in my hair, pulling my mouth tight to his. His kiss is urgent. He wastes no time, his tongue seeking mine. Our tongues wrestle; our mouths dual. His fear causes his aggressiveness. As quickly as it began, he pulls his mouth away, resting his forehead to mine. His eyes close tight as he gasps for breath. His eyelids raise, and, in his eyes, I see his war. He's struggling to gain control of his fear.

"I love you," he whispers.

A smile slides upon my face.

When his mouth finds mine again, there is no urgency. He's soft, slow, and gentle. As we kiss, he slips his hands in the waistband on my leggings, tugging down. Taking the hint, I lift myself from his lap, slide them down, and toss them to the hardwood below. Before I crawl back onto his lap, his hands on my hips halt me. His lust-filled eyes glide over my bare legs and up my exposed core while his thumbs caress my hips. Grabbing the hem of my shirt, he slowly tickles my skin as he glides it up, up, up and over my head. With one quick snap, my bra loosens, and he tugs then tosses it behind me.

I fidget under his gaze while my body heats. Unable to wait anymore, I climb on him, grinding myself against this lap. As needy as me, he releases his cock. Immediately, I impale myself upon him. This is the perfect way to release our fears.

173

HAMILTON

I'm not in the right headspace for the game today. I barely slept last night; Mom, her procedure, and the possible outcomes haunted my every thought. I've just gone through the motions this morning. The cell phone in my back pocket feels like a scalding, hot anvil. Mom's surgery is heavy on my mind as I wait for the call to tell me how the procedure went. My coach and teammates all stare at me from a distance. They worry about my ability to pitch today while all I worry about is my mom.

When the vibrations signal the call, I close my eyes, pulling in a calming breath before I answer. She has to be okay.

"Ya," I greet, anxious to get answers.

"Hi, honey." Mom's voice is a salve to my soul.

"I needed to hear your voice." My own cracks.

"I'm in a room, ordering lunch, and Amy is pulling the game up on the internet for us to watch," she states.

"How do you feel?" I'm finally able to pull in deep breaths for the first time today. The tightness in my chest releases, and the weight of the world seems to lift.

"I'm tired and have a little discomfort," she admits. "The doctor says everything went according to plan, though, and I should be home around supper tonight."

"Is Amy there?" I inquire, needing more assurance.

"Don't you believe me?" Mom asks, pretending to be mad.

"I'm here," Amy states into the speaker.

"How does she look?" I ask, signaling thumbs up to those staring at me in the locker room.

Amy laughs before answering, "She's tired, but she's sitting up and talking to the nurses. Ham, she's good. I promise."

"Okay. Thanks for being there and for putting up with all my phone calls." It's killing me not to be with them, and I fear my constant phone calls annoy them.

"Get your head in the game so we can watch you send all the Cardinals hitters back to their dugout with their heads down," Mom laughs. "You need to focus on your game now, okay?"

"Yes, ma'am," I answer. "I love you, and I'll call you after the game."

"Love you, too. Bye," Mom responds and disconnects.

I send a prayer of thanks to heaven and ask God to continue to look out for her. Then, I take deep breaths as I strike yoga poses I've learned from attending Madison's classes in the off-season. They help my focus on the approaching game. No one speaks to me. They understand that I'm attempting to channel my energy in an hour instead of the entire morning as I'm used to.

I'm a little more nervous than usual and shaky for the first two batters. My catcher calls time out and approaches me on the mound.

"Are you gonna let Madison's team get the best of you?" he pokes, knowing it will spark more life into me.

"Hell no!" I reply.

"Then, throw strikes," he orders and jogs back to the plate.

His motivation allows me to strike out the next seven batters I face. My mind is on my work, my head fully on each batter and the game.

During the next two weeks, I'm in constant contact with Mom. We FaceTime every day instead of once or twice a week. Amy also checks in with me every couple of days.

While Salem and Mom's doctors agree that Mom's heart is healing and there are no other concerns at the moment, I still worry. I reach out to Troy and Latham. They will help out more at the farm until we hire someone permanently. Of course, Mom fights me on this, but when I mention she can visit Liberty more often, she subsides.

The guys tell me Mom is now letting them work alone and only rides the Gator out to check on them once in a while. Mom reports she's joined a ladies' walking group three days a week in the church gymnasium. It seems she's following the cardiologist's orders for relaxing and exercising. For the most part, her diet met his heart-healthy guidelines already. I'm happy to find she's taking her heart attack seriously.

Amy and I are discussing two different dates that she might be able to bring Mom to Chicago for a visit. I'm not ready for her to drive the six hours on her own.

Since she's a doctor, Taylor helps ease my concerns and talk me off the ledge when my worries spiral out of control. Madison texts or calls her when she feels my anxiety growing. As much as I hate when she does it, I do feel better after speaking to Taylor.

I struggle with the distance between Chicago and the farm. My mind wars with my career with the Cubs and my need to help Mom with the family farm. With each passing week, the pull towards Athens grows stronger.

174

HAMILTON

Baseball in early August is hot and messy. The thermometer claims it's 110 degrees on the turf today. I sweated through my shirt long ago, and I struggle to keep my fingertips dry enough to grip the ball. I've warmed up and currently wait for the arrival of the first batter in the bottom of the fourth inning. I'm pitching to the top of their lineup and anxious to place a couple more strikeouts on my stats.

With the batter in the box, I step on the white rubber, looking to my catcher for the sign. He signals for my fastball, but I shake him off. It's too predictable—he'll be looking for it. Next, he signals slider; I nod. I come set, take a deep breath, wind up, and pitch. The ball sails, floating low and outside. The umpire signals strike. I fully expected the batter to swing at that pitch. He's usually a sucker for my junk pitches.

Next, the catcher signals for my curveball, and I deliver a beautiful pitch barely crossing the outside corner of the plate. The umpire signals ball. I turn my back before mumbling a few choice words. That was a perfect placement across the corner—definitely a strike. I school my features while bouncing the rosin bag in my hand. I'm calm and unaffected when I face the plate again.

Fastball. Yes, now I'll give him the fastball he's expecting. Get ready, batter. I'm going to burn it past you. The official yells strike in a long, drawn out tone. My catcher signals, and I nod. Let's do it again. This time, the batter catches a bit of my fastball, sending it foul into the stands behind him. When my catcher signals for the third fastball in a row, I smile devilishly. Time to send this batter back to his dugout. I send the ball flying across the center of the plate.

As I bend at the front of the mound, watching my pitch, in the blink of an eye, the ball soars back to me. One second I'm in front of the mound, the next I'm lying on my back atop the mound. It takes every ounce of my energy to will my eyes open as my sluggish brain attempts to process the situation. I see my coach and several players standing like pillars above me. With their help, I rise to a sitting position. I raise my glove, realizing there is something inside it. I pull the ball out with my left hand and raise it for all to see.

I vaguely hear my teammate yelling, "He caught the freaking ball!"

It doesn't register—I can't process the meaning of his words. The world spins around me, and I feel drunk. I inspect my left hand. Wasn't there a baseball in it a moment ago? I remove my glove, still looking for the ball. Frustrated, I place my hand on the right side of my face. It's wet. When I pull my hand away, I find my fingertips red. I pinch them together, watching the red liquid coating them. My vision blurs, and my stomach roils.

Beside me, my coach and trainer's mouths move, but I don't hear anything. Slater extends his hand to me, and I take it. Stan and our short stop assist me in walking to the dugout. I faintly recognize the crowd cheering. They pass me off to the players in the dugout who assist me to the locker room. I groan loudly as the entire right side of my face throbs in pain.

Next thing I know, I'm on an exam table with a much-too-bright penlight shining in my eyes. Then, a jackhammer assaults my jaw.

"Easy," I yell, pulling my face away from the doctor's fingertips.

I nearly barf as my world spins out of control with my movements. Several sets of hands assist me in laying down on the table. It seems like everyone speaks at once, and I can't understand any of it. A commotion swings my eyes to the door.

Madison

"Get up. Hamilton, get up," I beg with one hand on my heart and one on my baby bump. I watch, frozen in horror, as he lies on the mound, nearly motionless. Moments pass as if they're centuries. When he finally sits up, I release the breath I didn't know I held in.

"He's moving. He's okay," Delta soothes, standing at my side and slipping her arm around my back.

"I need to go to him," I say, covering my mouth. I glance over my shoulder at Liberty playing with Aurora on the floor near the back of the suite. She's oblivious to the events on the field.

"Go. I'll keep Liberty with me until I hear from you," Delta offers. "They'll take him to the training room by the locker room."

I dart out the door, jogging through the hallway. Crap! The training room is on the third base side; I'm going the wrong direction. I stop to gather my wits. Elevator. I need to take the elevator down. It doesn't go fast enough. This has to be the slowest elevator in the world. When the doors open, I scan the packed concourse in search of an usher. I spot a woman in a gold, "Event Staff" shirt and rush over.

"My husband..." I struggle to speak through my ragged breathing.

"Are you in labor?" She panics.

I shake my head. "My husband's a player. He just got hurt on the field. I need to get down to the locker room. Can you help me?"

She places me back in the elevator, swipes a keycard, then presses a button, and I'm lowered below the stadium. When the metal doors open, a body-builder type in the same "Event Staff" shirt blocks my exit from the elevator.

I place my hands on his arm, attempting to push through as I speak. "My husband is Hamilton Armstrong. He's hurt, and I'm on my way to be with him."

His arm doesn't budge. I suddenly have the urge to pee, so I place my hands on the bottom of my belly.

"You don't have a security pass," he grunts.

"I'm Madison Armstrong," I state. "My husband is Hamilton Armstrong." I lift my suite pass on its lanyard as if it might prove my statement. My temper, as well as my desperation, skyrocket. I point, my index finger millimeters from his nose. "Don't think that because I'm pregnant, I won't knee you in the balls and poke out both your eyes," I spit.

"Madison," a male voice calls from a few feet away.

I leave my finger near his nose as I turn to find a man in an expensive suit with a name badge signifying him as the Assistant GM standing nearby.

"Let her through," he orders the guard.

Immediately, the beefy arms lower, and the security guy backs away. He resembles a dog after its nose has been rubbed in pee. I throw my shoulders back as far as a pregnant woman can as I pass him. The suit signals for me to follow as he guides me through the maze to the training room. I quickly waddle over to Hamilton's side.

"Hey," he greets as he attempts to sit up but hands hold him down.

"He needs to lie down," the team doctor informs me.

"Honey, listen to the doctor. I'll be right here beside you." I caress his arm as I speak.

"I'm going to inject a numbing agent so I can stitch you up. Then, we'll transport you to the hospital," the doctor states with the syringe in hand poised near Hamilton's jaw.

I lean over my husband to get a better look at the doctor's work. Hamilton raises one hand to my tummy, and he murmurs to the baby in its close proximity. Next thing I know, his hand slides to my backside, and he squeezes my butt.

"I can't wait to tap this," he states, loud enough for the entire room to overhear.

My back stiffens, and my face flames. I'm sure he didn't mean for all to hear him. I keep my eyes downcast, not wanting to see their reactions.

"All done," the doctor states, helping Hamilton to a sitting position. "Now, let's get you to the hospital for a CT Scan."

I can't help myself; I need more information now instead of later. "What will that tell us?" I ask the doctor.

"I apologize." The doctor looks directly at me. "Hamilton has a concussion. He lost consciousness for a while from the impact he experienced on the field. The CT will look for any fractures to his face or the back of his head. It will also reveal any swelling or bleeding on the brain."

My eyes widen. I didn't even think it might be that severe. My heart races, and tears well in my eyes.

The doctor moves to my side. "I don't anticipate either of those outcomes. During my assessment, I didn't find anything that led me to believe we should stress."

Is he trying to calm the pregnant lady by telling me what I want to hear, or is he telling me the truth? I guess I will find out soon enough at the hospital.

"How are the two of you holding up?" the doctor asks at my side, indicating my bump.

"We're good," I inform him.

"May I check your pulse?" When I nod, his hand quickly finds my pulse point. Pleased with my numbers, he nods.

The Assistant GM informs us an SUV waits to drive us to the hospital. As the team doctor and Slater, our friend and team trainer, follow him to the door, Hamilton announces, "We'll be out in a couple of minutes. I need some alone time with my sexy wife." He tries to wink at me.

His hands begin groping me as his mouth latches on to my neck. I push him away, not believing his behavior. Hamilton sways as if he's drunk. Slater quickly moves to his side, as does the team doctor. They lift him under his shoulders as they help him to his feet and escort him through the door. I follow behind.

On the way to the hospital, Hamilton continues with his attempts to flirt suggestively and fondle my body. In the close confines of the vehicle, all the men hear and see it all. I bat away his hands while I beg him to stop. He's acting like a horny 16-year-old.

As if feeling my embarrassment, the team doctor further explains Hamilton's condition. "A concussion affects how the brain works. It may affect memory, speech, balance, and coordination." He turns toward us in the backseat. "Symptoms include headache, nausea, vomiting, dizziness, balance issues, blurred vision, ringing ears, confusion, poor concentration, sensitivity to light or noise, and personality changes."

With his final words, his eyes lock on mine. Is he trying to tell me Hamilton's horniness is a symptom of his injury? Could it be permanent?

"Some become aggressive," he continues. "Some yell or become angry. It's temporary and further proof of his concussion."

Looking to my husband, I notice he stares off into space, not aware of our conversation. His head and shoulders swirl a bit. Unable to control his movements, he reminds me of a bobble head. The severity of his concussion slowly settles in, and I worry about the length of his recovery.

175

MADISON

When the driver delivers us at the hospital, Slater and the doctor promptly swoop in as Hamilton staggers from the SUV. They glue themselves to his sides, assisting him into the hospital where the Cubs staff ensures we are whisked up to a VIP room. I'm surprised to find a couple of security guys arriving to protect our privacy. Oh, the perks of being a pro-athlete.

Hamilton continues his horny ways, much to my humiliation. The others do their best to ignore his behaviors, but there is no way they will forget his actions. He mentions at least three times that the hospital bed is big enough for me to climb on and straddle him before they wheel him out for his CT.

"Knock, knock," Taylor says, walking into the room seconds after he leaves.

"I'm sorry, Taylor, but my patient doesn't need a cardiology consult," Hamilton's doctor states on his way out of the room.

"I'm here to see my sister and brother-in-law," Taylor informs him.

I miss the remainder of their conversation as my call connects with Memphis. I deliver her an update and promise I will call her again when we get the CT results. Taylor remains quietly at my side as I shoot a text to Salem to see if she can make a visit to check on Memphis today. I worry that the stress of Hamilton's injury might be bad for her heart.

When I put my phone away, Taylor wraps me in a hug. "How are you?" She places her palm on my belly as she waits for my answer.

"I'm fine," I reply.

"Fine? Fine is not good," Taylor states, smiling.

"Okay, I'm scared, but we're good," I promise as I rub my belly.

Taylor wraps her fingers around my wrist, taking my pulse. Why won't anyone believe me when I state we're okay today? When she pulls her hand away, now believing my response, I smirk at her.

"So, how's the patient?" she asks.

"Why weren't you at the game today?" I counter.

"I'm on call and had an emergency surgery," she whines. "I told my husband I can't miss any more games since this happened while I wasn't there."

I shake my head at her. "Ham's fine." I laugh.

"W-h-a-t?" She draws out the word, knowing there's more to my answer.

"He's behaving like a horny high school boy," I state.

Her eyes widen and eyebrows rise.

"And he's not the least bit sly about it," I complain. "He flirts incessantly, and it's like fighting off an octopus." I'm sure my face flames red just speaking of it.

"Oh, this is good," she celebrates, clapping her hands and bouncing a little on her toes. "I can't wait to witness this. I'm going to record it. He will die of embarrassment when he's better and learns what he did."

I roll my eyes at her reaction. "You can't…"

"I won't post or share it," she promises, crossing her heart. "I just need to show it to him, because it will embarrass him. You have to let me do this. I need to pay him back for all of his teasing about my boy-crazy daughters."

Slater reenters the room. "What?" He smiles at our blushes and giggles.

"Madison was just telling me about Hamilton's personality swing," Taylor blurts.

"Oh, it's bad," he agrees. "But, it's hilarious. I plan to tease him about it, but it's so uncomfortable."

"Right?" I agree. "I mean, guys from the head office are in here."

Taylor bends over, laughing.

"If you're just going to add to my embarrassment, you can leave now," I inform her, pointing toward the door.

"I'll behave," she promises when her laughter is under control. "Cameron's flying up to help you for a week or so."

Wait. What?

"You have your hands full on a good day," Taylor explains. "She claims she can work a little while she's here. You'll need help with Liberty and Hamilton. It's a lot for you to take on while you're pregnant, and you don't need the added stress. She'll deal with Hamilton so you can rest or write during the day. Then, she'll play with Liberty after Fallon leaves at night."

Apparently, Taylor and Cameron have it all figured out.

Hours later, back at home, I sneak down the hall to see what Liberty and Hamilton are up to in her room. Liberty rises from her spot on the carpet with her little finger over her lips. As she pulls me into the hallway, I smile at my sleeping husband on her twin bed, an open book resting on his chest.

"Daddy sweepy," Liberty whispers as I follow her.

Last I knew, she was reading to him. It's so adorable that she read him to sleep; it's the opposite of what he does for her each night. I hate that he's hurt, but I love that she can help me take care of him. I set a timer on my phone to wake him up in a half hour as I'm following the doctor's instructions.

Liberty's eyes dart to me when there's a knock at our door. I open it, allowing Cameron and her luggage entry.

"Aunt Cam-Cam!" Liberty shouts, running into her open arms.

"Liberty Bell," Cameron greets her back. It's a nickname that is slowly growing on me.

While the two chatter like schoolgirls, Slater and Fallon say their good-byes. It was so kind of them to stay to assist with Hamilton until backup arrived. Slater makes me promise to call or text him if I need help. He reminds me, loud enough for Cameron to hear, with Hamilton's dizziness, I have no business trying to help him walk since I am pregnant.

Hamilton

The first six days of my ten days on the injured list suck. At the start of day seven, I begin to worry that I'll be on the injured list for another ten. I'm still a little dizzy and struggle to focus. Slater's allowing me to add a leg workout to my arm bands today. Of course, he watches me like a hawk, ready to swoop in and end the workout if I appear to be having any trouble. I'm ready for my independence back; I want to work out by myself and be cleared to drive. I'm ready to get back in the rotation. Plus, I need to get out of the house before Madison throws me out.

Her shut office door signals she's not to be interrupted. She sent Cameron home yesterday, stating I've improved enough. She complains she's had writer's block for several days, so I hope the closed door signifies words are flowing for her once again.

The calendar tells me Fallon and Liberty are at swimming lessons for the next hour. I've thought a lot about the farmhouse during all of my free time. I decide to use this opportunity to make a few private phone calls. I slip back to our bedroom, closing the door to ensure I'm not overheard. I pull up Troy's contact information and tap to connect.

"Hamilton, what's up?" Troy answers after the second ring.

"I'm going stir crazy," I admit. "Can you talk?"

"Jami's asleep in my lap, so I'm your captive audience," he states.

I love when Liberty sleeps on me, and now, I feel a little guilty for admitting my extra time at home is driving me crazy.

"I'm ready to get started on the construction we visited about in July," I inform him. "Are you ready for the project to begin?"

I'm asking him to back out of a couple of his part time projects to devote the time he's not in his squad car to our construction. I fully intend to pay him handsomely for this, and I believe he will be a great general contractor for us.

"Man, you are going to make several people in Athens very happy," Troy announces. "With the lull in construction, your project will be very well received. I have two crews able to begin within a week and another that is booked two or three weeks out."

I hear the sounds of Jami waking up in the background and shuffling noises before Troy tells me to hold on for a minute.

"I'm back," Troy states before continuing. "We'll need the floor plans and land survey before we start."

"I guess I'm giving you permission to order the survey, and I'll mail the blueprints to you in a couple of days." I can't help the excitement in my voice. "I'll talk to Madison tonight and call you with an update tomorrow."

"Wait," Troy hedges. "You haven't talked to her about this yet? Dude, that's not cool."

"Chill! I've talked to Mom about it, and we thought it best not to stress her out until I was ready to start construction," I inform my friend. "You know how it is with the pregnancy hormones."

"Yes, I do," Troy chuckles. "And when she finds out how long you've been planning this without mentioning it to her, she may lose it."

"No, she's not like that," I argue.

"Normally no, but she's very pregnant. She's tired, stressed, and hormonal. You're screwed, dude," he laughs.

"I'll take the risk," I tell him. "My finance guy, Foster, has your contract ready. I'll ask him to email it to you along with the forms to fill out, so we can send you your first paycheck and add you to the account for the project."

"I'm asking as your friend and not your employee," Troy begins. "What will be the function of this house?"

Ah, that's the big question. "It'll be our future home," I explain. "We'll use it on our trips to visit Mom, so we have more room to spread out. And, maybe I can talk Madison into living there during the off-season."

"Cool. I'll get things moving on this end," Troy states.

"Thanks! I'll call you tomorrow and let you know how Madison reacts," I vow before hanging up.

Next, I need to text Stan for his help.

ME

is the fam free Saturday night

STAN

depends…

ME

dinner with my fam

STAN

just need a time and place

ME

thanks, I'll be in touch

I'm sure Madison will gladly utilize Delta's expertise in the design aspect of our new place. Delta claims it's a hobby, but we've seen her designs and ideas. She's awesome. Maybe this project will help take the baby-fever pressure off of Stan.

Now, I need to text Madison.

ME

we're putting Liberty to bed early tonight

She'll think I plan on sex—boy, will she be surprised.

My nerves grow as Liberty drifts off to dreamland. When Madison peeks into the bedroom, I slide away from my girl's side.

"I'll meet you in the bedroom." She winks and waves.

"Kitchen first," I direct.

She raises an eyebrow then heads that way. Butterflies flutter in my stomach, and my pulse quickens. My wife sips from a water bottle, leaning against the end of the kitchen island, eyeing me as I approach.

"I need to share something with you," I blurt.

Her face morphs from lust to horror. I didn't think this out enough. She probably thinks I've kept something about my health from her. I need to fix this. Fast.

"It's not about me—I'm fine. I promise." I raise my hand to the back of her neck, pulling her in for a kiss. I gently place my lips on hers then brush my tongue between them. Instantly, she opens to me. She trusts me. I pull away before her body distracts me from my task.

"I want to build a house," I state instantly. I search her eyes for a reaction.

"A house?" she asks as a smile fills her face.

"It's always been my dream to build a house on the land between the cemetery and your parents' place," I confess.

Tears fill her eyes, and she wraps her arms tight around my waist. With her head against my chest, I continue explaining, "I want it to be a place for us to stay when we visit Athens. We'll be able to spread out; Mom and Amy could even stay with us. We can host our friends instead of always going to their houses. It will be our vacation home and maybe even our off-season home." I pull her from my chest, needing to witness her reaction.

She's a hodgepodge of emotion. She wears a smile as tears flow down her cheeks, and she fans her face. Try as I might, I'm not sure I can read her.

"What do you think?" I ask, dying to know. A part of my brain thinks that I've messed up.

"I..." she stutters through her sobs. "I'm..." She clears her throat. "When can we start construction?"

176

MADISON

I thought my worries about Hamilton would cease when he began unrestricted practice last week, but that isn't the case. His mood didn't improve. I worry that while he's focused on physical workouts, he hasn't healed mentally.

A couple of times each week, he's restless for several minutes as he sleeps before he bolts upright, waking from his dream. His body is coated from head to toe in sweat from his flailing.

Although I attempt to learn the subject of his dreams, he refuses to share. When I suggest he see someone to work through his fears and issues, he walks away from me, ending the conversation.

He doubles his workouts and the amount of time he studies opposing batters while pulling away from Liberty and me. I'm sure he's depressed on some level, but he's unwilling to hear my concerns.

I don't doubt he loves us. He's withdrawn into his own head instead of enjoying our moments together. He's irritable and has little patience with Liberty. He calls Memphis daily to check on her and her health but refuses to allow me to inquire about his.

I worry that he will regret his actions once our baby arrives. He was so excited to experience every part of the pregnancy with me in the beginning. Now, I almost force him to place his hand on my belly to feel our baby move.

Hamilton

My head is all over the place. It's been four weeks since my concussion, and I still can't focus. Everything works during practice and while throwing in the bullpen. When it's game time and a batter stands at the plate, though, my mind won't focus, and my arm refuses to perform. While in the bullpen, my pitches remain constant; on the mound, I lose several miles per hour.

Coach tells me not to fret; my speed is average for a lefty. Average. I've never been average. I've prided myself on throwing harder and faster than other southpaws. I won't allow myself to be average.

I find I throw more pitches in each game that I start as my lack of focus causes my accuracy to slip. Now, I worry more about injuries than before the accident.

As a pitcher, I was aware of the risk of injury to my hand, elbow, or shoulder and took precautions to prevent them. Now, along with line drives, I worry I might be hit by a pitch, pull a muscle, or twist an ankle running the bases. I see danger everywhere, at home and at work.

My lack of sleep starts to weigh heavy on me The line drive haunts my dreams, and I often wake up covered in sweat. I don't sleep any better on the nights I don't have a nightmare. I worry I'll hurt my pregnant wife during a bad dream, so my fear keeps me awake.

Of course, in the dark silence, my mind strays to everything I need to plan. I must get my ducks in a row in case my career ends suddenly. I need to make sure Mom, Liberty, and Madison will be taken care of.

More and more often, I run through scenarios where I retire instead of moving to the free agency portion of my rookie contract. As construction continues on our farmhouse in Athens, I'm eager to move my family there.

I imagine working on our three farms full time with Latham. Sometimes, I envision coaching a local baseball team and working as an MLB scout. Other times, I start my own training business, complete with a large facility near the house. With every scenario, Madison easily continues to write from home and play with our kids.

Tonight, I plan to open up to her. I've arranged for Liberty to spend the night with Taylor and her teenage daughters. Miss Alba's preparing a special dinner, and I will confide in the woman I love.

I'm not worried about her reaction. I've seen the concern she wears on her face every day. She's ready for me to share. She loves me and will support me, no matter what. I'm ready to unburden myself. Tonight, Madison and I will hash out a plan for our future.

177

HAMILTON

My cell vibrates in my gym bag as I stretch on the mat.

MADISON

where are you?

FALLON

call me ASAP

My cell rings in my hand before I can reply.

"Hello…?"

"Hey! Are you ready?" Delta asks.

I want to answer her. I want to act cool, but I'm scared shitless. The reason for the two texts and phone call registers, but I still can't move, let alone react. In my head, I hear my mom's voice yell at me, "Get it together! Madison needs you!"

"Madison's in labor," I state and ask at the same time.

"Her water broke," Delta shares. "Fallon will stay with Liberty. I'm gonna drive Madison to the hospital. You can meet us there."

"It's really happening," I say, sprinting to my truck.

"Yep, Dad, so you better freak out, get under control, and meet us at the hospital," Delta teases.

"I'm on my way," I inform her. "How's my girl?"

"Liberty…" Delta begins to answer.

"No, is Madison in pain?" I spit, frustration clear in my tone.

"Her water broke, but contractions haven't started so she's calm," Delta promises.

"Drive careful," I implore. "I'll meet you there."

My eyebrows feel like they're on top of my head. My wife lies in her hospital bed beside me, face tight, but not reflecting her pain as the monitor registers the biggest contraction yet.

"That was a big one," I state as the monitor signals its end.

"Wanna trade me places?" she asks, straight-faced.

"Don't answer that," Taylor instructs from the other side of Madison's bed. "It's a trap."

I mime zipping my lips shut.

"Madison," Dr. Humphreys' voice interrupts our teasing, "let's see how you are progressing."

She doesn't wait for permission, lifts the sheet covering Madison's lower half, places Madison's feet in the scary-as-shit metal stirrups, and disappears beneath the blanket.

I kiss my wife's cheek then anxiously wait for the doctor's assessment. Her head emerges, her latex gloves are removed, and the doctor rises to murmur instructions to the nurse.

"Madison, you're not dilating as your contractions have progressed to less than a minute apart," Dr. Humphreys states. She tilts her head. "We're going to prep you for a repeat C-section."

C-section? My mind sprints through everything I've heard about them. It stops on the memory of Madison's video journal entry just before Liberty's birth. She was smiling. She seemed happy to head to surgery. I shake away the memory, peering into my wife's eyes. If she didn't seem scared for Liberty's C-section, surely I don't need to be scared for this one.

"I can't wait to meet our son," I confess, a humongous smile decorating my face.

"Our daughter," Madison squeezes my hand. "Can you bring Liberty in for a second?"

I nod then look to the doctor for her approval. Permission granted, I scurry to the obstetrics waiting room. At Madison's insistence, I texted Fallon to bring our daughter to the hospital a half hour ago as Taylor anticipated the baby would arrive soon.

Liberty hugs her mommy's neck, lying beside her in the hospital bed.

"Mommy's going to surgery. In a few minutes, you'll see your baby sister or brother in the nursery. You keep an eye on the baby until Mommy and Daddy come back. Okay?" As Madison speaks, I play with Liberty's chocolate curls.

Liberty nods. Fallon carries her from the room, and I try to process Madison's words. Apparently, the baby returns before Madison. I definitely needed to ask more questions during our expecting parents' classes.

Madison squeezes my hand; I look to her. "Things happen fast now, so get ready," she tells me.

My wife is headed to surgery, and she's worried about me. I constantly marvel at her strength. As if on cue, a nurse tells Madison she's going to prep her for surgery. Since she's waxed, they move right to the catheter insertion. I wince and look away while Madison laughs at me. Another nurse whisks me away to dress in scrubs, complete with blue booties. I'm antsy; I don't like being away from my wife. I wait at the nurses' station as directed until I see her. I walk by Madison's side as she's rolled to the surgery center on a gurney.

I can't speak; I'm scared. Suddenly, a line drive toward my face, ending my career, seems trivial. Two-thirds of my world rest in the hands of a surgeon. Madison's experienced this before. The first time, she was alone, scared, and faced all of this without me. I need to channel her strength to get me through the procedure.

My head spins, and my world tilts as my son emerges from Madison's open abdomen. I can't pull my eyes from his face as the medical staff secure the umbilical cord before detaching him from his mother. I plead with God to help him take his first breath, for Madison to recover in her room, and for my daughter to love her little brother.

When a baby's wails cut through the surgical suite, I release the breath I didn't realize I held. Peeling my eyes from my son, I look to Madison. Her eyes are already studying me.

"I love you," I whisper.

Her smile widens. I place my hand in hers. She doesn't squeeze or lace her fingers in mine. I look to our hands questioningly.

"It's numb," she informs me.

I'm such an idiot. I remember the anesthesiologist pinching around her neck and shoulders to ensure the spinal tap had taken effect.

"Want to hold your son?" A nurse's voice breaks the moment.

I look to Madison, worried how she'll react if I hold him first.

"I can't," Madison reminds me. "Do it."

I marvel at the tiny human in my arms. His chubby face remains red from the trauma of the birth process. His eyes are closed, and his little fist rests upon his lips.

"Talk to him," my wife prompts.

What should my first words to my son be? I search for a prolific quote. "Hi." I clear the frog from my clogged throat. "I'm your daddy." There you go; I'm nothing if not eloquent. "This is your mommy." I maneuver my arms toward Madison's face on the surgery table. "In a little bit, you'll meet your big sister, Libby," I murmur so as not to disturb his slumber.

In my large hands, he looks so small. Even watching the videos Madison created of Liberty, she never seemed this tiny, this vulnerable.

EPILOGUE

Madison
12 Years later

From my lounge chair, my heart swells as I witness our children reunite, swimming in our pool with Stan and Delta's family. It took a lot of work, but we kept in touch in the years since Hamilton left the Chicago Cubs. Technology helps, but it's the in-person visits that kept our friendships intact.

"I can't be this old," Delta states from the lounge chair next to mine. "How can I be the mother-of-the-groom?"

I rest my sunglasses on top of my head. "I'm so happy they chose our farm to hold the wedding."

"Webb's still infatuated with your books and all things Hamilton." Delta shrugs it off. "He's loved our yearly visits here. You may not be so excited to host when the entire wedding party and mother-of-the-bride arrive tomorrow," she teases.

Judging from the bride-to-be's phone calls, she'll fit right in with our friends and family. We've talked a lot in planning the wedding over the past two months.

Hamilton's voice clearing above me catches my attention.

"Hey, babe," I greet, squinting up at him in the afternoon sun.

"I thought the two of you were chaperoning," he barks gruffly.

I glance towards the kids in the pool before looking back to him.

He points at the lounge chairs where Liberty and her best friend lay, sunning themselves. I shake my head, unsure of what his problem is.

He grasps my wrist, gently tugging me from the lounger to follow him into our house. While I quietly protest, he paces our kitchen.

"They… he…" Hamilton fights to control his anger.

"Ham, just breathe," I urge.

"If you don't put an end to it, I'm going to jail for murdering Webb's Best Man and groomsmen," he confesses through gritted teeth, his jaw ticking.

My hand upon my mouth, I attempt to hide my amusement. This isn't the first time Hamilton has overreacted to his daughter growing up. She's now and taking after her father's family, tall and developed early for her age.

I thought he'd have a stroke when Memphis, Amy, and I drove her to KC for a girls' day of shopping and to buy her first bra. The day I texted him that our 13-year-old daughter started her period, he got so drunk at Salem and Latham's that I had to drive across the gravel road to pick him up. He's in complete denial that our daughter is a young lady.

"I want to take a hot fire poker to their lecherous eyes," he spits pointing toward our backyard pool.

Lecherous? Really? If I didn't know better, I'd think he's been reading the steamy romance novels I enjoy. I can't contain the giggles that escape.

"You laugh now," he scoffs. "You'll get tired of the commute to Leavenworth to visit me in the Federal Penitentiary."

"Federal… a federal pen?" I laugh. "Do you plan to kidnap the boys and transport them across state lines…?"

"Boys?" Hamilton interrupts. "Boys? They are not boys. Those are 20-something men lusting after our 15-year-old daughter."

"Ham," I attempt to soothe, "those guys are not interested in Liberty." I feel deep-belly laughter building inside me.

"Please, I'm a guy. I know exactly what they're thinking," Hamilton argues.

"Their girlfriends and his fiancé arrive any minute," I remind him. "I think you need to seek therapy before you have an aneurism."

"I told you not to let her wear that bikini in public," he growls.

"She doesn't wear it in public," I state, smirking. "She's at home."

"She's wearing it in front of guests," he protests. "Dirty, pervy guests."

At the sound of the sliding glass door, our eyes watch Liberty and her friend enter.

"What?" Liberty whines in the way only a teenage girl can.

In sync, we shake our heads. She huffs off to her room, mumbling under her breath.

"They're going to a movie with three other girls," I inform him as the vein in the center of his forehead continues to visibly pulse. "Delta and I were going to drive, but since you're done, you can."

"She better not…"

"Ham, she knows your rules. 'Bend over. Touch your toes. If anything shows, go change your clothes,'" I mock.

He shakes his head at me, mumbling, "Thank God we have four boys."

Yes, four boys. Hamilton and I tried for another daughter until I waved the white flag to surrender after fourth son. Upon the sonogram confirming our fifth child was a boy, Ham reluctantly visited the urologist for a successful vasectomy. He fought the idea until I purchased him a box of condoms. At the thought of donning a latex raincoat until I hit menopause, he quickly completed the procedure.

At age 15, our oldest child, our only daughter, is five-feet, nine-inches tall and very curvy. She's not the rail-thin teenager many of her friends are. She resembles an 18-year-old more than a 15-year-old.

The two facets of her personality contrast drastically. Liberty loves shadowing her father on the farm and doesn't shy away from pulling calves or castrating hogs. The apple of Hamilton's eye, she excels at tennis, basketball, track, and softball.

Her other side butts heads with Hamilton at every opportunity. She's "friends" with several boys from school. She enjoys hanging out, working out, and competing with them. Of course, her father only sees them as raging hormones and walking erections. Sometimes, she attempts to dress like her friends, and Hamilton blows a gasket. He detests her experimentation with makeup and slightly more mature clothing choices.

Of course, Adrian and Savannah love taunting Hamilton at every opportunity. Their daughters, although younger, dress too provocatively for his tastes. Our friends have even stooped so low as texting him headless pics of other girls, claiming they are Liberty out and about in Athens.

I pity the poor boy that invites her to her first high school dance. She'll be a sophomore this fall, so it's going to be here before we know it.

After Liberty, Hamilton tells me parenting is all downhill. While raising the boys is easier for him, I find it frustrating. Our four boys only span seven years. In my book, they're too close in age. Their constant dares stress me out as they often end with trips to Salem or the emergency room. Ranging in age from six to thirteen, we've already experienced five broken bones, twenty stitches, two concussions, and multiple black eyes and bloody lips with our boys. They are all boy in every way possible.

I've stopped asking Hamilton to explain why they do the things they do; they seem alien to me. One day, the two oldest ran from the house toward me in the pasture, screaming, "We peed in an 'X'! We peed in an 'X'!" Upon my interrogation, I learned they crossed streams while peeing. All I could imagine was urine covering the walls, from the ceiling to the tile floor, and every other surface. That night, Hamilton vowed to find a cleaning lady to help me out each week.

Another time, as I walked through the family room on my way to the laundry room, our third son slept on a blanket in the middle of the floor. I paused upon noticing a dark smudge on his cheek. After further examination, I found his ear full of black dirt from my nearby potted palm. Two hours and a hundred dollars later, my little ones' ear was flushed clean by our doctor, and his two older brothers confessed that they did it on a dare.

Our second son adamantly refused to brush his teeth suddenly for over a week. After a mom to son chat, I learned that he couldn't brush his teeth because of his attempt to urinate into the tip of the toothpaste pump.

After years of asking Hamilton to explain why boys do the things they do, how they think of those things, and his answering, "I don't know; they just do," I stopped asking. I've resigned myself to the fact that I'm a mom of four boys. I can't control or understand them.

I'm blissfully happy with our life in Athens. Hamilton's foresight to build the large farmhouse proved a blessing as he retired during the off-season after its completion. His recovery and fear of a future head trauma caused him to change his focus to our family and his mother.

We've enjoyed filling each bedroom in the years since he left the Majors. While I work in my office, the children attend school and Hamilton works in our large metal building with hot, new baseball talent. During the summers, our friends bring their children over to enjoy the pool and watch my brood while I write.

The boys enjoy working out with Hamilton and the ballplayers. They would sleep in the batting cages if we would let them. They've definitely inherited Hamilton's love of all things baseball.

Hamilton's baseball instruction business has grown each year as he trains players from across the United States, Mexico, Puerto Rico, and The Dominican Republic. Occasionally, entire teams come to sleep in the barracks we constructed and use the facilities. Hamilton's instruction is sought from young tournament teams all the way to college teams. He loves what he does and the flexibility to work near his family.

My books continue to top the charts as Cameron works closely with me. Now, we live closer to each other, and she brings her kids to visit while we work. Berkeley's still my personal assistant. We video conference weekly as she remains in Chicago.

Latham and Salem have transformed my parents' house into a loving home. I no longer avoid entering the house or fear the ghosts that once haunted me there. With Latham's help, Hamilton has combined my grandparents', my parents', and his mom's farm into one large operation. With a hardworking staff, Latham runs it with ease. He claims he never regrets leaving his brothers and his family's farm to come work with us. We are blessed that he loves the work he does.

As the men work the farm, Memphis is now free to relax more and stress less. Her heart has benefited, too. She enjoys visiting with the grandchildren, attending school and sporting events, and being active in the church and community.

I love our life on the farm and in the small town of Athens. Our children continue to blossom in the proximity to Hamilton's family and our friends. I still shake my head at 18-year-old me for wanting to leave and never return to this town. I was blind to many of the aspects that make the small community the perfect place to raise a family. It took me 15 years to realize that small-town life is the life for me.

The End

Help other readers find this book and give me a giant author hug—
please consider leaving a review on <u>Amazon</u>, <u>Goodreads</u>, and <u>BookBub</u>—
a few words mean so much.

Check out my <u>Pinterest Boards</u> for my inspirations
for characters, settings, and recipes.
(Link on following pages.)

ALSO BY HALEY RHOADES

Ladies of the Links Series-

Ladies of Links #1 -- Gibson, Ladies of the Links #2 -- Christy, Ladies of the Links #3 – Brooks, Ladies of the Links #4 – Kirby, Ladies of the Links #5 -- Morgan

Boxers or Briefs

The 7 Deadly Sins Series-

Unbreakable, Unraveled, Unleashed,

Unexpected, Uncaged, Unmasked, Unhinged

Third Wheel(The Complete Surrogate Series)

The Surrogate Series-

The Proposal, The Deed, The Confession

TRIVIA:

1. Athens, Missouri is a fictitious town. There was once a township of Athens, but I could find no town.

1. The first and last names of *ALL* characters in this book are the names of towns in Missouri. (Except McGee & Indiana/Indie the dog.)

1. Haley Rhoades is my pen name. I created it using the maiden names of two of my great-great grandmothers on my father's side of our family.

ABOUT THE AUTHOR

Haley Rhoades's writing is another bucket-list item coming to fruition, just like meeting Stephen Tyler, Ozzie Smith, and skydiving. As she continues to write contemporary romance, she also writes sweet romance and young adult books under the name Brooklyn Bailey, as well as children's books under the name Gretchen Stephens. She plans to complete her remaining bucket-list items, including ghost-hunting, storm-chasing, and bungee jumping. She is a Netflix-binging, Converse-wearing, avidly-reading, traveling geek.

A team player, Haley thrived as her spouse's career moved the family of four, fifteen times to three states. One move occurred eleven days after a C-section. Now living the retirement life, with two adult sons, Haley copes with her empty nest by writing and spoiling Nala, her Pomsky. A fly on the wall might laugh as she talks aloud to her fur-baby all day long.

Haley's under five-foot, fun-size stature houses a full-size attitude. Her uber-competitiveness in all things entertains, frustrates, and challenges family and friends. Not one to shy away from a dare, she faces the consequences of a lost bet no matter the humiliation. Her fierce loyalty extends from family, to friends, to sports teams.

Haley's guilty pleasures are Lifetime and Hallmark movies. Her other loves include all things peanut butter, *Star Wars*, mathematics, and travel. Past day jobs vary tremendously from a radio-station DJ, to an elementary special-education para-professional, to a YMCA sports director, to a retail store accounting department, and finally a high school mathematics teacher.

Haley resides with her husband and fur-baby in the Des Moines area. This Missouri-born girl enjoys the diversity the Midwest offers.

Reach out on Facebook, Twitter, Instagram, or her website…she would love to connect with her readers.

amazon.com/author/haleyrhoades

goodreads.com/haleyrhoadesauthor

bookbub.com/authors/haley-rhoades

instagram.com/haleyrhoadesauthor

tiktok.com/@haleyrhoadesauthor

facebook.com/AuthorHaleyRhoades

twitter.com/HaleyRhoadesBks

pinterest.com/haleyrhoadesaut

linkedin.com/in/haleyrhoadesauthor

youtube.com/@haleyrhoadesbrooklynbaileyauth

patreon.com/ginghamfrog